EAGLES &
RED POPPIES

Eagles and Red Poppies

Copyright © Lawrence Bell 2019 All Rights Reserved
The rights of Lawrence Bell to be identified as the author of this work have been asserted in accordance with the Copyright, Designs and Patents Act 1988
All rights reserved. No part may be reproduced, adapted, stored in a retrieval system or transmitted by any means, electronic, mechanical, photocopying, or otherwise without the prior written permission of the author or publisher.

Spiderwize
Remus House
Coltsfoot Drive
Woodston
Peterborough
PE2 9BF

www.spiderwize.com

A CIP catalogue record for this book is available from the British Library.

The views expressed in this work are solely those of the author and do not necessarily reflect the views of the publisher, and the publisher hereby disclaims any responsibility for them.

ISBN: 978-1-912694-82-2

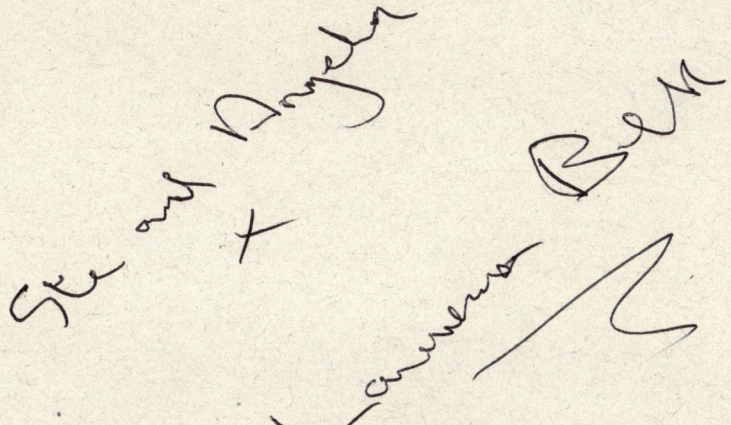

EAGLES & RED POPPIES

LAWRENCE BELL

This book is dedicated to the brave people of Poland

With special thanks to Colin McMorris
for his patience and advice

Photography by Ania Pankiewicz
www.aniapankiewicz.co.uk

CHAPTER 1

It was an almost perfect day.

And in theory, all he had to do was point the rifle in the right direction, pull the trigger and shoot...and he could change the world.

In the late morning on a bright summer's day, Pieter Szabo made his way silently through the dense pine forest and onwards to the summit of the hill that he had spent the last three hours climbing. Steadily onwards and ever upwards, he continued. And with the help of his old walking stick, he picked his way noiselessly through the tall and seemingly ageless trees. Szabo was just twenty-three years old, and he was young and he was fit, very fit. In fact, he didn't need the old wooden walking stick that he carried. Well, certainly not for walking.

An hour later, and he arrived at the designated spot on the high crest of the hill, halfway up the side of an imposing and most majestic of mountains. He stood there for a moment, and he looked out at the magnificence and the timeless beauty of the Bavarian Alps, and the stunning hills and valleys that lay below, stretching for miles into the distance.

It was by then early afternoon, and Szabo took off the heavy rucksack that he carried on his back, and along with the walking stick, he propped them both against a sheltering tree. He squatted down, opened the rucksack and took out a pair of binoculars. Szabo then knelt on one knee as he looked through the high powered binoculars, down towards the valley below.

And there it was. His target.

A beautiful villa, with a large outdoor terrace, it was perched on the hillside more than a mile below. The villa overlooked the pretty Bavarian town of 'Berchtesgaden', but it was nestled high enough on the hillside to provide the most spectacular and commanding views across the Alps. It was magnificent, such a wonderful sight. But that was why the owner lived there, although only on specific occasions, and certainly not all of the time.

Because the owner was an exceptionally busy man.

Szabo took a deep breath. He was perspiring from the heat of the warm midday sun and he wiped his forehead with the cuff of his sleeve.

He looked down at the villa. He'd made it, he'd finally got there.

And now it was time for him to go to work, Szabo would have to prepare himself.

He reached over for his old wooden walking stick. Taking the stick firmly in his hands he twisted the 'crook' end which surprisingly easily unscrewed. Then he did the same with the bottom of the stick and released the capped section which was about half an inch long. His old wooden walking stick was now reduced to a single pole. But the stick wasn't wooden and it certainly wasn't a pole. It was the barrel of a gun.

Szabo looked down the inside of the barrel to inspect the gun's unique rifling. The craftsmanship was remarkable. He then laid the barrel carefully on the ground. Reaching into his rucksack he then rather bizarrely took out an old wooden clock. The oblong shaped clock was worn with age and quite plain. In appearance, it looked to be made from a single block of seasoned walnut, mounted on a darker wooden pedestal with a similar capped top. It had an off-white coloured dial which was encased in a faded and scratched glass cover. On the back of the clock was a small brass winder. In theory that handle was there to wind up the clock's mechanism, but when the winder was turned nothing happened. The clock was obviously broken. And it would have been, if it had been a clock.

Szabo twisted the dial, and it popped out of the front of the clock. He then unscrewed the pedestal and the capped top of the clock, which easily came away. Then, quite astonishingly, the clock split into three sections. The larger middle section was long and triangular shaped. It was in fact, a rifle stock.

Szabo then picked up one of the clock's outer sections. It contained four bullets, each one slotted into individually drilled holes. He took out one of the bullets and examined it. It was perfect, it was always perfect.

The smooth lead bullet had a dozen small but faultless spiral grooves cut into it. The grooves swirled along the body of the bullet, flawless and aerodynamic. It was the perfect bullet for the perfect gun. Designed and built by a genius.

Szabo put the bullet into his breast pocket and then slotted the gun barrel onto the rifle stock. They connected with an efficient click. It was an ingenious design, the stock contained the breech along with trigger. He looked at the dark brown rifle in his hand. From a distance it would almost look like a piece of old wood. And if it was ever left in some scant foliage or in some random bushes somewhere, it would be almost invisible. Yet it was one of the most remarkable weapons of its time. In the right hands, and with the right bullets, the rifle could shoot with amazing accuracy for distances up to one and a half miles.

And Pieter Szabo had the right hands. And he had the talent, he had a wonderful talent.

He took the 'third' section of the clock and tapped it lightly. Out of another drilled aperture slid a slim telescopic sight. Similar in colour to the rifle, it was the length and shape of a 'good' cigar. It had been designed by a man of outstanding ability and knowledge in the production of specialized optics. Pieter Szabo slid the telescopic sight into place along an almost invisible groove set into the rifle's barrel, and then he sat back.

He was still perspiring, but now it wasn't through exertion, and Szabo suddenly began to realize that fact. He also felt his stomach begin to knot and ache, and that wasn't good. He had a job to do.

Szabo knew that he had the best part of an hour to wait. The people down at the villa would only step onto the terrace after two o' clock. It was always the same, it would be just after two o' clock. And they would all step outside into the bright sunshine and drink and laugh and talk.

Yes, it was always the same, because the owner of the villa was a creature of habit and that was the accepted protocol.

Szabo lay back against a large pine tree and he tried to sleep. Everything had to be perfect. But it wasn't. Because there was something seriously wrong within his stomach.

Szabo had spent the best part of two weeks, cautiously making his way to Berchtesgaden. The previous day he'd caught a rabbit and cooked it over the low flame of his small campfire. He'd only allowed himself a small fire because he didn't want to draw attention to himself in the dark forest. And in that same darkness, he'd hadn't noticed that the rabbit wasn't cooked properly and that some of the meat was still quite raw. The repercussions of that meal were suddenly beginning to take their effect, and Szabo was beginning to feel nauseous. He lay there sweating for the best part of the hour, his stomach continually churning.

At two o' clock he checked his watch. It was time to prepare.

Szabo once more wiped the sweat from his brow. This was not good, not good at all. But he was there for a reason. He couldn't allow himself to fail.

He picked up the rifle and went back over to the open ground. He knelt there for a moment, and after taking up his binoculars, Szabo once again peered down at the villa. The owner's guests were beginning to come out onto the terrace. Some wore suits and others were in uniforms and everyone was talking and smiling, and waiting. Waiting for their host to make an appearance.

Two or three waiters were busily making sure that everything was running efficiently. Drinks were being served and there was a buffet in the corner on a large table, it was brimming with food. But nobody could go near it, not yet. Not until their host had arrived.

Suddenly, a strikingly beautiful blonde woman walked out onto the terrace. All heads turned as she strode out into the sunlight. At her side was a large dog, it was a beautiful German Shepherd dog with the most remarkable colouring. The dog was almost blonde, almost as blonde as its owner. It had the long flowing fur that was typical of the breed, but unlike the usual pattern of black and dark brown, this particular animal's colouring was a lighter shade of tawny blonde. It was a beautiful animal, and the dog never left the woman's side as she met up with the other guests.

Finally came the moment. Everyone turned as he walked out onto the terrace. Nobody would speak until he spoke, because that was the sign of respect.

For once, he was out of uniform, he wore a simple brown suit and matching tie. And why not, wasn't he amongst friends? Or it could be said that he was with the only people that he could possibly consider as being 'friends'.

But whatever, on that afternoon there were no dignitaries present, and no politicians or official visitors. No, he was amongst personal friends and acquaintances, and he could relax in their company. The blonde woman went over to him straightaway, and she kissed him on the cheek. He smiled as he spoke to her and then he leant down to stroke the dog. The dog wagged its tail enthusiastically. It was happy to see its master, almost as happy as its mistress.

Everyone stood there, ready to meet their host. For them, he was the most important man in the world. He was without doubt, the most important man in their world.

Szabo put down his binoculars and he picked up the rifle. He lay down on the ground and made himself comfortable. It was a practised routine, because he was a professional. He looked through the telescopic sights and down onto the terrace. It was unbelievable, because as he looked through those extraordinary lenses, his target seemed to be less than ten feet away. Pieter Szabo almost felt that he was standing there on the terrace with the other guests. And now he would watch and wait. Wait for exactly the right moment. Because there was no doubt about it, he had to kill this man. He had to, for everyone's sake.

Because the year was 1941. And the man was Adolph Hitler.

Down on the terrace the guests were all enjoying themselves. In turn, they spoke to Herr Hitler, always with a smile and always with the right amount of reverence. The blonde woman was Eva Braun, Adolph Hitler's long-term mistress, and everyone made a fuss of her too, along with 'Blondie', her beautiful German Shepherd dog

Amongst the guests was Heinrich Himmler, Hitler's right-hand man and confidant. Himmler was as always, wearing his menacingly black SS Officers uniform. It made him feel important, and feared, and he liked that. A uniform was always an excellent piece of clothing to hide behind.

The guests mingled and the food was served and everyone was happy to eat and drink, now that their master had arrived. The afternoon continued in the warm sunshine and the guests enjoyed the views from the terrace of the villa known as 'The Berghof'. It was after all, Hitler's favourite residence. From that terrace, he could look across the Bavarian Alps, and from there he could see for miles and survey everything around him. It made him feel like a god.

And at that moment and at that time, Germany wanted a god.

The rich, the powerful and the famous had all lined up in their turn to visit Adolph Hitler at his Villa 'Berghof'. They'd all bowed and stooped to him in blind denial. Those guests included Mussolini, and the Aga Khan, and the misguided British prime minister of the time, Mr Neville Chamberlain, who had arrived, and then left again with the promise of 'peace in our time'. A promise almost laughable, had it not cost millions of people their lives.

And of course there was the biggest disappointment of the British realm, the Duke and Duchess of Windsor. Duke Edward and his shrew of a wife arrived at the Berghof to pay a simpering homage to Hitler, whilst the British people back home stared on in horror and disbelief.

The 'would be' king, Edward, was a weak, misguided imbecile, and a fop of a man who disgraced himself by his actions. England was without doubt the better for his spineless and cowardly abdication, when he stepped down and handed the Royal throne to his brother George, the stronger and finer man.

The Duke of Windsor's only legacy was that he would be associated with a certain design of chequered fabric, named after him when he was the Prince of Wales. He was nothing more than an arrogant peacock, who thought more of his dress sense than he did of his people.

Thankfully, he never managed to produce an heir.

Hitler sat on a stout wooden chair, where he held a plate of sausages, with mustard pickle and a small slice of wheat bread. And as he ate, he spoke casually to the head of Germany's Deutsche Bank, a boring little man whose name was 'Schieseler'.

Several feet away, Heinrich Himmler was slowly stroking 'Blondie' the German Shepherd dog, as he sat talking to the beautiful Eva Braun. And as they chatted away it struck Himmler that he would much rather be petting Miss Braun, instead of her dog. Himmler had always had a thing about her, in his darkest dreams.

Back up on the mountain, Pieter Szabo observed it all. And now was the time.

Hitler was stationary, he had a plate of food in his hand and he was sitting and he was talking.

It was perfect, almost perfect.

During the last half an hour, Szabo's stomach had continued to churn and on two occasions he'd almost vomited. He felt hot and he was still perspiring profusely. He was out in the open and there was no shade and the sun continued to shine down on him through the cloudless sky. From a sniper's point of view, it was a faultless day. Visibility was perfect and there was little or no breeze. To take a shot at a target more than a mile away took great precision and concentration. The wind would always be the enemy. There was always the opportunity of being able the gauge the effect of a slight and steady breeze, but a sudden gust of wind could send a bullet dramatically off course, even Pieter Szabo's specialist bullets. And Szabo's bullets were without doubt special. Designed by an aeronautical engineer of outstanding ability, the bullets weren't simply shot out of the rifle, they actually 'cut' through the air, and that fact alone made their accuracy incredible.

Szabo took the grooved bullet out of his breast pocket and he loaded it into the breach of his rifle. The gun only fired one bullet at a time. From a sniper's point of view, that was all you would ever need. After the first shot, a second attempt would always fail. The target would have been alerted to the threat.

If the first shot missed it was over. A second shot could give away your position, a second shot could be a disaster. The art of the game was to take out your target and then disappear immediately.

Szabo once again settled himself down on the ground and he got himself into his tried and tested and most comfortable position. But as he stared once again through the telescopic sight his stomach suddenly rumbled and knotted and he wretched. Pieter Szabo was in trouble and he knew it. But he had to concentrate, he had to take the shot. It was a Sunday, and sitting on that terrace, along with his friends, was Adolph Hitler's favourite and most precious event. It was almost a tradition. The next day was Monday and it would be 'back to business' and probably a return to Berlin.

For Szabo there was no other option. He took aim.

He stared down at his target through the telescopic sight. Adolph Hitler was looking totally disinterested as he sat there listening to the banker. He was nodding at the man, and as he did, he picked up another sausage from his plate and took a bite of it.

Szabo watched that action through the cross-hairs of his sight, the rifle was aimed exactly at Hitler's temple. Szabo was motionless. Now was the moment, the exact moment. He was in complete control, and without taking a single breath he simply squeezed the trigger and the gun fired its shot.

And at the moment he pulled the trigger, Pieter Szabo's bowels suddenly burst forth and he flooded with diarrhoea. The bullet was already in motion, exploding down the barrel of the rifle and on its way to its target in a matter of a second. But the tremor that went through Szabo's unfortunate body was enough. That minuscule fraction, that quiver of movement as the bullet screamed out of the end of the barrel was enough to change everything. As the bullet travelled down the hillside at immense speed it veered ever so slightly. And in that one second, before it slammed into its proposed target, the bullet had moved sideways by a couple of inches. And it would make a world of difference.

The bullet scorched across Adolph Hitler's top lip, taking with it a certain amount of flesh. The turn in trajectory then sent the bullet straight through Heinrich Himmler's right hand, and from there it unfortunately hit the dog in the head. The top of the dog's head suddenly exploded and was blown off completely.

Hitler, Himmler and Eva Braun all screamed out at exactly the same moment. Eva Braun was covered in the dog's blood and bits of raw flesh, as Himmler held his right hand and howled in agony. However, they were both ignored in the rush, as the rest of the guests hurtled themselves towards the main door and into the shelter of the villa. It was up to three of the waiters to drag Hitler back inside and into safety. Then and only then did two of them go back out to attend to Miss Braun and Herr Himmler. The dog was past saving.

Up in the hills, Szabo cursed and swore at himself. He'd missed. He'd missed his shot by a fraction and even though he'd seen Hitler fall over, Szabo knew that it was Adolph Hitler's head that should have exploded everywhere and not the dog's. His mission was a failure. And now he was lying there, up on a mountainside, with his pants full of shit.

It was a complete and utter disaster.

Down at the Berghof, the villa was in panic.

Hitler was immediately carried to his car and carefully lifted onto the back seat. Along with Eva Braun, the black Mercedes Benz sedan then set off at high speed to the doctor's surgery down in Berchtesgaden. The staff had already rung the doctor there and instructed him as to what had happened. Secrecy was of the uppermost.

Another car and driver was eventually found for the very distressed Heinrich Himmler. It was an interesting observation, but the man who would cause death and suffering to millions of people, was himself not very good at handling pain.

Szabo lay there for another five minutes as he collected his thoughts. There was nothing he could do. It was time for him to move. Eventually someone would figure out what had happened and then the troops would be sent up to scour the mountain.

He had to go.

He stood up, and was immediately disgusted with himself as he felt the discomfort of the diarrhoea. But he couldn't stay there. Three hours of walking back down the hillside would bring him to a stream where he could wash and clean himself, providing he had the time. Szabo disassembled his rifle and repacked his rucksack. Once again the amazing weapon was reduced to nothing more than an old clock and a walking stick. He left the binoculars behind. They would look too suspicious, and they were the only evidence that could incriminate him.

As he made the long and arduous hike back down to the valley, the tall pine trees seemed to surround him, ever hampering his way. It was almost as if they were judging his failure.

The outcome of that attempted assassination would have many repercussions.

During the afternoon the doctor managed to stitch back the remaining part of Adolph Hitler's top lip and a team of surgeons were immediately dispatched from Berlin. Back at the Berghof and for the next several weeks, Hitler would undergo a number of facial operations that would rebuild his face. The operations were fairly successful, but it was a true fact that Hitler would sport a moustache for the rest of his despicable life, so as to hide the scarring and a slight deformity.

Himmler, his right-hand man, suddenly had a hole in his own right hand. But that too would unfortunately heal.

The dog was soon replaced. The original breeder was contacted and another young pup with very similar colouring was found, it was then trained and renamed.

Yet another 'Blondie'.

Security however, was another matter. Someone had tried to kill the 'Fuehrer'. But since the assassination attempt had taken place in Bavaria itself, there could be no reprisals. It couldn't possibly be a German citizen?

However, after that event, the Fuehrer's security would be doubled and more frequently scrutinized.

Never again, would it be allowed to happen.

Szabo finally made his way back down the mountain and he found the stream. He washed and cleaned himself and rinsed out his trousers, but things were not ideal. He was now faced with spending the night wearing wet clothes. He set off once more.

He was angry. He was angry with himself. He'd failed to carry out the most important mission of his life. All the time and the training, and all the effort, and it had been all for nothing.

Pieter Szabo was Polish. He'd fled from Poland after the Nazis had murdered his family and everyone he'd ever loved. He'd fled to England, where the British had trained him and armed him. But now he was back in Europe. He was back and under instruction to complete his mission. But that mission had failed. And in theory, after completing his assignment and no matter the outcome, Szabo had been ordered to return to England. But Pieter Szabo had no intention of returning, not yet anyway. He had one more task, and it was almost an obligation, a duty to the people that he had loved and lost. Pieter Szabo was going back to Poland. There was another mission. There was still something that he needed to do.

After walking for another three miles he came across a smallholding, a decent timber-built house with a couple of outbuildings. Daylight was quickly fading and Szabo could see that the downstairs lights of the house were all switched on. He walked down the path towards the house. It was a pretty and well-kept place, almost too well kept. The borders of the garden were immaculately tended, and at the front of the house there was a rockery with little alpine plants, all perfectly placed. The whole house looked as though it should have been on the front of a box of Swiss

Chocolates. Szabo quietly walked over to the front window, he could hear music. He looked through some net curtains and into the front room of the house. A man with a shaved head was sitting in a large lounge chair, Szabo could see the back of the man's head. The man was sitting there in front of an open fire listening to a record which was being played on an old gramophone. The music was quite loud. Above the fireplace there was a large painting of a man with dark hair and a dark moustache. The man in the painting wore a brown uniform with a red armband which sported the Swastika, a broken black cross on a white circle. The man in the painting was Adolph Hitler.

The music from the gramophone seemed to be getting louder. It was a recording of something by Wagner, supposedly Hitler's favourite composer. The man in the chair nodded his head along to the music, blissfully unaware that he was being watched. A moment later a woman entered the room carrying a mug containing some sort of hot drink. She was about sixty years old and had short brown hair, cut into a stark shaped bob. She spoke to the man, who presumably was her husband, and she handed him the mug and then turned around and left the room, presumably to go back into the kitchen.

Szabo stared through the window at the back of the man's shaven head. Szabo had already made up his mind. They were both Nazis. There would be no mercy.

Szabo turned and walked back over to the perfect rockery. There he found himself a jagged rock that sat well enough in his hand. Szabo then walked back to the house and quietly opened the front door and walked straight into the living room. The man sitting there in the lounge chair was still listening to the record as Wagner's loud and prevailing music flooded the house. Szabo walked straight across the room and stood right behind the chair as the man's shaven head continued to nod in time to the music. Szabo never even saw the man's face, but that didn't matter, the man was a Nazi. Szabo raised the rock high in his hand and smashed it down onto the man's shaven head, and then once again, a second devastating blow. His victim never even uttered a sound as his skull and his brain were instantly crushed under the force. Szabo then quickly turned, and he walked straight through the house and into the kitchen. The man's wife was at the sink, preparing and washing some vegetables for their evening meal. The last thing she would ever see was Szabo's reflection in the kitchen window as the rock smashed down on the back of her head. She too died instantly.

Szabo walked back into the living room to turn off the infernal music. In disgust he kicked the gramophone over and stamped on it, smashing it and the record to pieces.

Then he went back into the kitchen. Something smelled rather good. When he opened the oven door he found a casserole cooking in a cast iron pot. Szabo went through the kitchen cupboards and found an assortment of pots and various sized pans. He filled two of the largest of the pans full of water and put them on top of the oven to heat. He would be able to wash himself properly. He also took the vegetables out of the sink and put them into a smaller pan, which he then filled with water and placed on the oven to boil.

Upstairs he found a bathroom, which was quite adequate. He then went into the bedroom and rummaged through the drawers until he found some decent fresh clothes that would fit him well enough.

Later, after he'd washed and shaved, Szabo put on the fresh clothes. He was feeling quite well. The diarrhoea had obviously flushed out whatever illness was in his stomach and he was suddenly hungry again. He went back downstairs and stepped over the dead woman's body as he went over to the oven and took out the casserole. The vegetables were also cooked and he drained them and then tossed them straight into the pot along with the casserole. Szabo sat himself down at the kitchen table and ate until he was full. Finally, and after belching loudly, he went to prepare some coffee.

He had no concern at all for the body of the woman that he had to continually step over. She was a Nazi. And for Szabo it was a simple enough choice, the Nazis had murdered his family. So why should he care? His major annoyance however, was that he'd missed his one chance to kill Hitler. The killing of Adolph Hitler would have wounded every single Nazi loving bastard in Germany.

But he'd failed, and failed miserably.

Szabo drank his coffee and deliberated. There was a door in the hallway that led down to a cellar.

In the end, he dragged both of the bodies and threw them down the cellar stairs, and then he closed and locked the cellar door and put the key in his pocket. He locked the kitchen door from the inside and then went into the living room and drew back the net curtains. After gathering up his kit and putting on his jacket he turned off all the lights. The house was in total darkness. As he left he locked the front door and put that key in his pocket too.

Szabo knew that the soldiers would eventually arrive. They would comb the whole area looking for him. But when the soldiers came to the house there would be no sign of anyone. There would be the possibility of them checking the outhouses, but not the house. They wouldn't want to break down the door and cause any damage to the house. After all, there was a huge picture of Adolph Hitler hanging in the living room, and the people who lived there, they were Nazis too.

Szabo set off down the road. He kept close to the trees, just in case. If anyone came around any corner he could immediately dash into the forest and hide. It was a full moon and the visibility that night was excellent. After a couple of miles he reached into his pocket and took out the two keys, and as he continued to walk, he simply threw them into the passing trees.

To have killed Hitler would have changed the world. But he hadn't killed Hitler. And all the planning and all the hard work had been a waste of time. It would be up to others now, if there were others. But he'd failed, and he'd failed badly. There were other men in the world that Pieter Szabo wanted to kill, but he had missed his chance to assassinate Adolph Hitler.

Pieter Szabo had a long way to go, but he wasn't going back to England, not yet. Instead he would head east, and then northwards and make his way back to Poland, back to his homeland.

There were other men that he needed to find. Because Pieter Szabo had a debt to settle.

CHAPTER 2

Poland 1939

Two years before, it had been a different story. It had been a different life.

Pieter Szabo was at that time just twenty one years old. He was a happy young man because he had a happy family, he had a mother and father who loved him and an older and a younger sister, both of whom he adored. The Szabo family lived in Lodz, the third largest city in Poland. His father, Franz Szabo, was a well-respected doctor, and his mother Leah was a part-time teacher at the local infant's school. Pieter's eldest sister Ilsa, was twenty five years old at the time and was employed as a teller at the local bank. Pieter was employed as a trainee draughtsman in an architect's office where he was slowly dying of boredom, and his younger sister Elise, worked at the local post office as an assistant. Elder sister Ilsa had just become engaged to Adam Breslav, a young man who also worked for the bank, he was a trainee manager at the same branch.

But the most wonderful person in Pieter Szabo's life was without doubt, a young lady by the name of Miss Francine Korczak.

Pieter had been courting Miss Korczak for nearly a year. He'd first met her when he walked into the Lodz Central Library where she worked. Pieter had initially gone there to find some literature on guns.

Guns and shooting were Pieter's consuming hobbies, and he and his father were both enthusiastic members of the prestigious Lodz District Rifle Club. From an early age, Pieter had been noted as a rising talent and there had been discussions about the possibility of him representing his country in the next Olympics. He was considered to be good enough, and he was certainly one of the best marksmen in the club, along with his father.

On that particular day, Pieter had gone into the library and he'd wandered up and down the rows of shelves that contained thousands of books, but in truth, he hadn't a clue where to look. Finally he'd gone in search of a librarian, someone who could possibly assist him. He couldn't find one.

And so, being an impetuous youth, he marched up to an office door that was marked private, and he knocked on the door and walked straight in. At that particular moment, Miss Francine Korczak was adjusting her stockings and had her leg on a chair as she pulled her stockings up and past her knee. Pieter burst through the door just as Francine was openly showing most of her naked thigh. He just stood there staring at her as she screamed and in panic toppled over. Pieter immediately went to her to help her up off the floor, but by then her skirt had run up to her waist. Miss Korczak was totally embarrassed by the whole affair but Pieter found it all very hilarious and couldn't help but laugh. Luckily, and luckily for him, Francine Korczak also had a good sense of humour and she too started to giggle, if for no more reason than to cover her blushes. In the end, she brushed herself down and Pieter apologized profusely. Then he stood there and looked at her. She was really very pretty.

Francine Korczak lived in the Gadka district of Lodz with her elderly mother. Francine was the same age as Pieter, she was quite petite and had the straightest dark blonde hair which she twisted and pinned up into a smart chignon. Prim and proper was the effect that she'd always tried to promote, however since Pieter Szabo had just seen most of her naked thighs, any thought in that direction had suddenly become a lost cause. And suddenly, she quite liked this young man. He had a sense of humour, and the thought of him seeing her legs made Francine feel rather giddy and slightly flushed.

Ever the gentleman, and after his accepted apology, Pieter asked Francine for her assistance in finding him the books on firearms. As she took him to the appropriate section Francine asked him about his interest in guns.

'I'm in the Lodz District Rifle Club,' he told her.

'Oh really,' she'd replied, though in truth she knew little about it.

'Yes,' Pieter continued, 'I'm trying to get into the next Olympic team.'

Francine new about the Olympic Games of course and she was suitably impressed.

'Oh really,' she said again, but this time with a little bit more enthusiasm.

Pieter smiled at her and Francine smiled back at him, and for a moment neither of them spoke. It was the timeless 'chemistry', and it was the obvious attraction when boy meets girl and all the emotion that goes with it, begins to happen.

And then they both realized that they were just staring at one another and that neither of them was speaking, and they both started to blush slightly.

Francine turned to the shelf full of books.

'So what are you actually interested in?' she asked hurriedly.

At that moment, Pieter Szabo could have given her a couple of completely different answers really, and neither was to do with guns. He smiled at her.

'Let's look,' he replied, as he too started to search through the different titles.

They were both standing close to one another. Each was aware of the other's presence and suddenly the library seemed a little bit warmer.

Pieter finally found a couple of books that he really wanted to read.

'I'll take these,' he said to her, and then he had a quick thought, and he turned around and put one of the books back on the shelf.

'No, I'll just take this one,' he said.

'Don't you want them both? You can take out several books at a time if you wish,' Francine told him.

But no, Pieter suddenly only needed the one. He knew exactly what he was doing.

'I'll just take this one,' he said to her, smiling, 'and as soon as I've read it I'll come back and pick another.'

She looked at Pieter. 'Well, we're always here,' she replied. And it was the biggest hint she could possibly give him. Not that he needed one.

They went over to the main desk where Francine stamped the book for him. She wrote his name down in a ledger...'Pieter Szabo' she said to herself.

'Okay then,' he said, 'I'll see you soon.'

Francine smiled at him.

'I hope so,' she replied.
Pieter looked at her.
'Oh, I'll be back. I'm a very quick reader,' he said, 'Very quick.'
'I hope you are,' she said.
And they suddenly both burst out laughing at the boldness of it all.
'What's your name?' he asked her.
'I'm Francine Korczak.'
And at that moment they shook hands, and it was almost as if a deal had been done.
They both knew it. It was the beginning of something.

Four days later Pieter returned. There was no one at the main desk at the front of the library, and so Pieter strolled around the library looking for Francine. He finally spotted her down one of the aisles carrying a pile of books. She had her back towards him and at that moment was returning a couple of books into the cookery section. Pieter walked silently up to her and said 'Hi', out loud as he put his hand on her shoulder. Francine squealed and dropped the books all over the floor. She spun around, only to see Pieter Szabo once again laughing at her.
'You..!' she said loudly. Luckily the library was empty.
Pieter just shook his head and continued to laugh. Francine started to smile and then giggled. She launched a punch at him which landed harmlessly on his chest.
'I'm sorry,' said Pieter, 'I couldn't help it.'
Francine started to pick up the books and he went to help her.
'I've come for another book on firearms,' he said to her.
'I'm going to buy a gun and shoot you myself,' she laughed.
Pieter suddenly looked at Francine.
'Have you ever done any shooting?' he asked her.
'What me? Oh no,' and she shook her head.
'You should try it. You should come to the gun club with me sometime.'
It was a clumsy and poor attempt at romance, but he had to try something.
Francine smiled back at him, she understood the gist of what he meant. It was a start.
They talked, and Pieter helped her to replace the books to their

appropriate shelves. Then they went over to the firearms section where Pieter picked out another book relating to guns.

They finally went back to the main desk where Francine stamped his book and once again he left, smiling.

Two days later he returned. He'd not read the book, but that didn't matter. Not to him anyway.

Pieter found Francine and they talked as he picked out another book from the firearms section. They stood at the main desk chatting and laughing and enjoying each other's company, and this time when Francine stamped his book, Pieter asked her if she would like to go for a coffee whenever she was free. Francine took up his offer, in truth she'd wondered why he hadn't asked her before. She'd certainly tried hard enough to send out the right signals. But then to her amazement, he simply bid her goodbye. He just smiled at her as she stared back at him, waiting for him to set a time or a date. But he just turned and walked away.

Francine Korczak bit her lip in frustration. This young man was driving her crazy. There was a passion inside her and every time they stood close together in the library she had a physical urge that made her slightly flustered and agitated. It was quite simple really, she wanted young Pieter Szabo to take hold of her and kiss her passionately.

As Pieter walked out of the library he turned and waved back to Francine. She stood there with her hands on her hips. He was grinning at her, and she suddenly realized his little game.

Pieter Szabo liked to tease her.

'Right then, Mr Pieter Szabo,' she thought to herself...'two can play at that game'.

At that same moment, the office door behind her quietly opened. A tall slim man then walked out of the office. He'd been watching their conversation through the glazed door.

'Who was that?' he said, so abruptly that it made Miss Francine Korczak instantly spin around.

'Oh, you startled me,' Francine exclaimed.

The man stared back at her. He'd seen her laughing and talking with that young man and he'd seen how she was behaving, he'd been watching them both for some time. What 'on earth' did she think she was doing? She was acting like a whore.

And at that moment he could have physically hit her.
That man was Wilfred Staszic.

As Principal Librarian of the local Library, Wilfred Staszic considered himself a man of position. He was thirty eight years old and lived locally, and on his own. He was a confirmed bachelor and a particularly dour one at that. Mr Wilfred Staszic's problem was that he was not a good communicator. He found it difficult to talk to people and he had spent most of his life hiding in or behind books. Hence, he'd decided to become a librarian, his line of thought being that since he spent most of his life in the library, he may as well work there too.

Wilfred Staszic had worked there as chief librarian for fifteen years and was only offered the position when the previous head of the library had passed away. Since there weren't many people lining up to do the job, Staszic had been handed the position on the 'proverbial' plate. And that had suited him fine. He was the master of his own little domain, his own personal dynasty, and a dynasty which he ran with absolute preciseness.

Staszic demanded order, that was his world, and every single book within the library had to have its correct alphabetical location. Every book had its own place in its own section, be it fiction or nonfiction. Every section in the library had to be categorized correctly, making sure that those were also in alphabetical order. And then there were the authors, each had to be in the exact place on the library shelf. All hell would break loose if the likes of either 'Keller or Kieller' were on the wrong side of each other.

Wilfred Staszic had only one friend. He was Henryk Kober, and he and Staszic had been friends from their schooldays. Henryk Kober was a small-minded man who worked as a personal secretary to one of the councillors in the finance department of Lodz City Hall.

Kober had always dreamt of becoming a councillor himself some day, a wish that he'd always considered he was capable of but had little chance of ever fulfilling, until just lately. And now it seemed that times could be about to change.

It had been Henryk Kober that had suggested to his boss that Wilfred Staszic would be the ideal man for the position of chief librarian. The councillor had passively agreed, it was just a job in the library, what harm could the man do?

Staszic had been ever grateful. He and Kober would meet once a week on a Friday evening at The Cafe Pineska coffee house, which was a short walk from the library. They would both sit there with a coffee and a small pastry and bemoan just about everything. They felt that the whole system of government in Poland was wrong and unjust, and if they were given the chance, how they could both do so much better. They were small men with small minds. However, and though they didn't realize it at the time, their moment was fast approaching.

Staszic ran the library with an iron fist, and because of this and his unrelenting attitude, the junior librarians who worked there under his stern direction never stayed there for long.

It was another topic that he and Henryk Kober would discuss in the Cafe Pineska on those Friday evenings. Staszic couldn't understand why his staff kept leaving. He regarded it as a lack of moral fortitude. The library was a wonderful place to work. He himself was proof of that, he'd worked there for years and he was perfectly happy.

And then his life had suddenly changed. Because Miss Francine Korczak had been employed as the new junior librarian, and the day that she walked into Staszic's office and nervously introduced herself, was a day that Wilfred Staszic would never forget.

Miss Francine Korczak was stunningly pretty. She was young, and in Staszic's eyes she was an innocent, and he liked that. And for the first time ever he relented somewhat and he took a more conciliatory attitude with his new junior recruit. As time went on, the two other women who worked there as librarians saw his change of attitude to the 'new girl' and both raised an eyebrow. As they got to know her better, one of them gave young Francine an appropriate warning and some friendly advice.

'I think Mr Staszic has a bit of a thing for you, my dear,' the librarian had told her.

Francine was slightly taken aback. She had no idea.

'He's always been a gentleman, he's always seemed so nice,' she'd replied.

'Exactly,' the librarian said to her, 'but believe me, dear, he's a complete bastard.'

Francine had taken the advice on board. However, she needed the job.

She had her elderly mother to support. So she decided to keep her wits about her, and she also made the decision that she would do her very best at her job.

That decision impressed Wilfred Staszic even more. He'd noticed that Francine was ever enthusiastic and very efficient. She'd straightaway understood his system of filing, she was keen to work and was totally dedicated to the ethics of 'the book being in the right place'.

On their Friday nights at the Cafe Pineska, Staszic would ever extol her virtues to his long-standing friend Henryk Kober. It seemed to Staszic that Francine Korczak could do no wrong. However, it had been the other librarians who had tutored Francine on Staszic's almost obsessive demand for alphabetical order in his library, and Francine had been intelligent enough and bright enough to understand how the system worked.

At one point, and over their coffee, Kober had told Staszic that he should ask the young lady out. Staszic was horrified. Rather naively, he'd never even considered it and neither would he. Even though he was really quite smitten with Francine Korczak, because of his lack of communication skills he just couldn't bring himself to ask her. In fact, other than on the subject of books, whenever he spoke to her he became rather tongue-tied and the thought of asking her out and then being rejected would put him in a very awkward position. After all, he was her boss, He was the principal librarian and he was in charge of the library. If things were to go wrong, their relationship at work would definitely suffer. No, it was better to leave things as they were.

Staszic also made a mental note that in future he would never again mention Miss Francine Korczak to his friend Henryk Kober.

And so, on that evening when Wilfred Staszic had first caught Francine laughing and talking to young Pieter Szabo, he was angry. And Francine saw it in him, and she knew exactly what it was. It was jealousy.

Her excuse had been that the young man was 'a bit of a joker'. And she certainly didn't mention that Pieter had been into the library on previous occasions.

'The library is no place for such tomfoolery, Miss Korczak.' he'd told her quite sternly. Francine realized the seriousness of her 'offence' when he'd used her last name.

Staszic had taken to calling her 'Francine', especially when they were on their own, and on one occasion he'd asked her to call him 'Wilfred'. But quite cleverly, she'd told him that it may be seen as 'improper' by the other librarians and that she respected his position.

That comment had only served to raise Staszic's esteem for Francine Korczak. He applauded her honesty and her correctness of attitude. She had standards, and in Wilfred Staszic's eyes that made her just about perfect.

But Francine suddenly realized that she would have to keep her wits about her. She knew from the past how it could end. Predatory males at the workplace could be a problem, she knew this, and she'd suffered the same predicament before and had lost her job over it. Francine saw the look in Staszic's eyes and his attitude towards her, and on the numerous occasions she'd caught him staring at her from a distance. She'd also seen how he treated the other librarians and was aware of how differently he acted when he was with her.

She was his 'favourite', and she knew it. So she made the decision that whenever possible, she would never be on her own with Wilfred Staszic. Never to give him the chance to take their relationship that one step further. Francine was no fool, she knew that any refusal in any way would be taken as an insult, and then there would be the embarrassment, and ultimately it would lose her the job. The job that she really needed.

And now she had another problem. It was Pieter Szabo.

Pieter Szabo, who she really liked and wanted to see again, but not there in the library, definitely not there in the library. Wilfred Staszic would be watching her from now on. The next time Pieter arrived, and he undoubtedly would, she would have to take him to one side and explain things to him. She was sure that he would understand her dilemma.

The next evening at six o'clock, Francine turned off all the library lights after making sure the building was empty. It was her turn to work late. Each of the librarians, including Mr Staszic, would normally finish at five o' clock, leaving one of them to work the extra hour in their turn and then close up the library at six. It was a system that worked quite well.

However, Mr Staszic always stayed the later hour on Friday nights, so that he could leave the library and then go straight to the Cafe Pineska to meet up with his friend Henryk Kober. But tonight was a Wednesday, and it was Francine's turn. Not that she was really bothered. The library was warm and quite peaceful, and in truth, she had nothing to go home for.

Her elderly mother had started to go to bed early, and that left Francine on her own most of the time, and she was lonely.

On her 'late' evenings at the library, and once all the other staff had left, she would find a good novel and sit at one of the tables and then read to her heart's content. The library would sometimes have one or two other people in there too, but that was never a problem. She would keep her eye on the main desk and would always be available should she be needed. Sometimes Francine would stay an extra hour, especially if she was enjoying her reading. The library was timeless, and it was a peaceful haven for her from the difficult world outside.

But on that particular Wednesday evening, she'd decided to leave on time. At six o' clock she'd checked that the library was empty and she'd switched off the lights, and as she left she closed and then locked the two large library doors. Francine was hungry, and that was one of the reasons she'd not stayed late. As she turned the key in the locks she thought about the meal she would prepare for herself once she'd arrived home, and her mind was elsewhere, when suddenly she felt a firm hand on her shoulder. Francine screamed and threw the library keys into the air. She instantly spun around, only to find Pieter Szabo bent over double and laughing at her.

'You..again!' she said. It seemed to be her only greeting to him. 'You...again!'

Pieter Szabo was in hysterics.

'You're such an easy target,' he said through the laughter, 'and you always scream.'

Francine launched yet another punch at him, and as she came forward he grabbed hold of her and put his arms around her.

'Now I've got you,' he said to her.

She looked up at him, and then all of a sudden she giggled.

She liked his arms around her, and she liked the physicality of it. He picked her up and spun her around and they both laughed at the silliness of it all. But more than that, it was bodily contact for the first time. He held her in his arms and she looked up at him and genuinely smiled. They were there, they'd taken the first step. They'd finally made it.

'I've come to take you for the coffee that I promised you,' he said.

'How did you know I would be working late?' Francine asked him.

'I didn't,' he replied, 'I've been standing here for over an hour. I've been waiting for you to come out.'

She looked at him and shook her head.

'Why didn't you come in for me?'

He looked at her and smiled

'I just wanted to see your face,' he said. And in his heart he truly meant it.

They walked across the square that faced the library and went into a small coffee shop known as the 'Cafe Florentine'. It was a warm and intimate sort of place, there were two or three other customers in there but at that hour it was fairly quiet. Pieter led Francine to a corner table and they ordered some coffee and some pastries from a young waitress. It was very comfortable, and they sat and talked for over an hour. It was effortless conversation, there were no breaks, no awkward silences. They just spoke openly to each other. Francine found out about Pieter and his family, about his father the doctor and Pieter's mother and his sisters. She was intrigued. He told her about his job as a trainee draughtsman and how much he hated it. And he explained to her about his passion for shooting.

She in turn, told him that she lived over in the Gadka District with her elderly mother, and how her father had died when she was very young and that she'd never really known him. Money had always been a problem for her. Her mother suffered from ill health and living in the Gadka District was hardly ideal. The 'Gadka' was one of the poorer parts of the city, and the area was well known for its unemployment and bad housing.

Pieter listened intently. And then suddenly, and on nothing more than an impulse, he reached forwards and kissed her on her cheek. And as he looked at her, she took hold of his hand and drew him back to her, and then she too leant forwards, but this time she kissed him on his lips. Pieter responded and for several moments they held one another until a passing waitress tactfully coughed. What they were doing was not really acceptable in the Cafe Florentine.

They stopped immediately, almost with embarrassment, and then they looked at one another and suddenly burst out laughing. But the deed and the deal was done. And without more ado, they were an item.

Pieter ordered some more coffee and their conversation carried on for another hour.

'Our office isn't that far away, I could call in during the day and see you at the library,' said Pieter confidently.

And at that moment, Francine's expression suddenly changed.

'Whatever's wrong?' he asked.

'That's actually not a good idea,' Francine replied.

Pieter was quizzical.

'It's my boss,' she said to him, 'I have a slight problem.'

'And what is that?' Pieter asked.

'I think...well no, I know, that my boss has a bit of a thing about me. It's not a problem really, but the other day when he saw me talking to you he was really angry.'

'Who is he?' Pieter asked.

'He's called Wilfred Staszic. In truth, he's a bit odd, but he's also very strict. He runs the library as though he owns it, and he treats the librarians as though he owns them too. Mr Staszic is not a very nice man. He's very disrespectful to the staff and can be quite offensive. He's also fanatical about every book being in its right place. It's an obsession with him. If ever any of the books are in the wrong section he goes mad.'

Pieter frowned.

'So you say he has 'a bit of a thing' for you.'

Francine raised her eyebrows.

'Yes, it's all a bit pathetic really, but he's always watching me. And though he's often really quite rude to the other librarians, he's always gone out of his way to be exceptionally polite to me. The other girls at the library can see it. It was them who warned me about him.'

Pieter looked at her.

'What do you mean 'warned you'?' he asked.

'They let me know what he was really like. They'd seen how nice he was being towards me. It was all a bit obvious really. I try to keep out of his way as much as possible and I try never to be alone with him. But he always seems to be hovering around and he's always staring at me. And one time he asked me to call him by his first name...'Wilfred'. But I managed to get out of that one, I told him it would be 'improper' in front of the other librarians and that a man in his position needed to be respected. Luckily he agreed with me. But I don't trust him. And the problem is that if anything happens, it could cost me my job.

'What could happen? I don't understand,' said Pieter.
'I worry that he will ask to take me out...or worse.'
'And what do you mean, 'worse'?'
Francine looked at him.
'If he ever puts his hands on me, Pieter, that's what I mean. That's why I try never to be alone with him. I know the type of man he is. If I say 'no' to anything at all he'll take it as an insult and he'll be embarrassed. We'll no longer be able to work together and from there he'll get rid of me. The thing is, I need this job. Its steady work and I need the money.'
Pieter shook his head and sighed. He wasn't very happy at what he'd just been told.
'So I won't be coming to the library to see you?' he said.
Francine looked at him. It was time to change the subject, all this talk about Wilfred Staszic was spoiling their night.
'Of course you can come to the library. I always have to stay there late at least one night in the week, usually on Wednesdays. Staszic always goes home before five o' clock and I'm in there until six. Sometimes I stay longer. It's always warm in the library, and there's usually nobody else in there. After six o' clock I'm normally on my own.'
Pieter grinned at her when he heard that piece of information. She saw the expression on his face and her stomach fluttered when she realized just what she'd told him, and of course, the possibilities.

Another half an hour passed by, and then Francine suddenly realized the time.
'I've got to go home, I've got to catch the tram, My mother will be wondering where I've been.'
They both stood up from the table and Pieter helped her on with her coat and then he went to pay the bill. They stepped out of the Cafe Florentine and walked over to the tram station. As they stood there talking, Francine wondered when she would see him again. But Pieter just kept talking to her, not making any arrangements at all. The tram finally arrived and she turned to get on it.
'Well goodbye,' she said to him.
'Yes, goodbye,' he said in return. It was as simple as that. Not a kiss, not even a peck on the cheek, and Francine suddenly felt quite annoyed with him. She didn't understand what was happening, and so she turned and

got onto the tram. She sat herself down and wasn't even going to bother to wave to him through the window.

And then somebody sat down at the side of her. She quickly looked around, and it was Pieter, and once again he was laughing at her.

'You really do fall for it every time,' he said to her.

Francine bit her lip, and then she thumped him once again. But all he did was laugh.

'What are you doing?' she said to him. But he just smiled at her.

'I taking you home Miss Korczak, that what I'm doing,' and he kissed her cheek.

'Oh,' she replied, and she gave him a slightly surprised look.

He looked directly at her.

'Francine Korczak, I don't know whether or not you know this, but you are now 'my' girl. And I am here to look after you, and I will not let you go home on your own at this hour. I will see you home and take you to your front door.'

Francine took a deep breath. Nobody had ever looked after her. She was quite taken.

She slid her arm through his and then smiled happily.

'You're my knight in shining armour, Pieter Szabo.'

He turned to her.

'Yes I am. And I will always look after you,' he promised. And this time he kissed her.

Half an hour later, they arrived at Francine's home, it was one of a small row of cottages that had seen better days.

They stood outside the door and kissed again. She looked at him.

'Would you like to come in?' she asked.

'No, it's too late now. You go in and speak to your mother and let her know you're alright.'

She nodded.

Pieter continued, 'And then tell her all about me, and tell her that I will be calling on Sunday afternoon to take her daughter out.'

Francine laughed, 'you really are crazy, Pieter Szabo.'

'And you are truly beautiful, Miss Francine Korczak.'

They kissed again, and then he left to catch the tram back to the city centre, and from there he would make his way home.

As he sat on the slow moving tram, heading back to the centre of Lodz, Pieter Szabo realized that he had a problem. And it was more than just a nuisance, it was something that would eventually lead to trouble. Because it always did.

And that problem was Mr Wilfred Staszic.

Pieter had listened to what Francine had told him. And deep inside he'd felt the warning signs. He knew what would happen. He knew what always happened. It was always the same. Eventually, this man would try his luck. He would grow bolder, and he would persist and pursue, and then he would harass. Yes, it was always the same.

In the past, Pieter's two sisters had been put in similar positions. Pieter had solved their problems. He'd always known that he would have to look after them both.

There was an unknown side to Pieter Szabo. A darker side to his personality, a dark, violent part of him that not even his parents knew about or even suspected.

Only Pieter Szabo himself knew what he was capable of.

His eldest sister, Ilsa, had been the first.

It had been four years ago. Ilsa worked in the bank where she'd worked for several years as a bank teller. She'd started working there straight after leaving school and had always seemed quite happy. There was no reason not to be. They were a happy family.

Pieter was sixteen at the time and was in his last year at school. He planned to leave at the end of the year and had been promised a job to train as an architect. One of the members of the Lodz District Rifle Club was a Mr Bruno Huelle, he was a friend of Pieter's father and he ran a successful architect's office on Piotrkowska Street, right in the centre of Lodz. Franz Szabo had spoken to Bruno Huelle and Pieter had been promised the job. It wouldn't be a problem. Bruno Huelle respected Franz Szabo, and Pieter too. Father and son, they were both excellent shots, probably the best in the club.

So all was well, or so it seemed.

It was on one evening as the family sat down for dinner. There was the customary hustle and bustle and everybody, as usual, seemed to be talking at the same time. But on that evening, something was different. There was a change in Ilsa, and something was wrong. Nobody noticed at first, but

Pieter did. Their evening's dining habits were always the same, his mother and father would talk to one another as his mother doled out the dishes of hot food. It was then left to Ilsa, Pieter and his youngest sister Elise to fight over who got what. There would be the constant bickering and their mother would chastise them all and their father would shake his head in mock derision. That was how it was, and that was how it had always been. But not on that night.

Their mother had served up a delicious casserole, and there were potatoes and a side dish of beetroot. But Ilsa just served herself a potato and the tiniest piece of meat and that was all. Pieter saw this and he wondered. So did his mother.

'Is that all you're going to have Ilsa?' asked her mother.

'Yes mamma,' she replied.

Pieter watched.

Everyone started to eat and young Elise chattered away to everyone in her usual precocious way.

But Ilsa just pushed her food around the plate, she hardly spoke a word. And in the end, her mother spoke to her again.

'What's wrong Ilsa?'

Ilsa looked up.

'Nothing Mama. There's nothing wrong. I'm just not hungry, that's all.'

Mrs Szabo just shrugged, and the family continued with their meal. But Pieter watched his sister, and he knew that there was something, just something.

Ilsa hardly spoke. And in the end, and with enough nodding and prompting from his wife, Franz Szabo put down his knife and fork and turned to his eldest daughter.

'What on earth is wrong with you, Ilsa?' he asked, 'Your mother has cooked this beautiful food and you won't eat it. Why?'

It was all a bit heavy handed and not in the way his wife wanted him to go about it, but fathers will be fathers. And Ilsa started to sob.

'What's wrong Ilsa?' asked her mother in a slightly softer tone.

But Ilsa just stood up.

'I don't feel well Mamma,' she said through her tears, and then she turned and almost dashed out of the room.

There was a moment's silence, as Mrs Szabo watched her daughter hurry from the room and then run upstairs.

Franz Szabo shrugged his shoulders.

'Women's problem,' he said to his wife. It was his answer to all things peculiar in women. But Mrs Szabo obviously knew that it was not.

Franz Szabo turned to Pieter, the only other male in the house.

'She's in love, she'll have had a row with her boyfriend,' he said to Pieter, and to anyone else who cared to listen.

But Pieter wasn't listening, he was thinking.

His mother stood up and she went upstairs to talk to her daughter. But she returned ten minutes later none the wiser.

Franz Szabo looked at his wife for a possible answer. But Mrs Szabo just shook her head.

'I don't know what it is. She won't talk to me.'

Franz shook his head.

'Young women, they're all the same,' and he looked down the table at his youngest daughter.

Elise just shrugged and giggled. She'd always found her father's chastising rather funny.

Later that evening, Pieter had been in his bedroom reading. He was suddenly thirsty and he went downstairs for a glass of water. As he came out of his bedroom he heard his sisters talking in the next bedroom. Their bedroom door was slightly open, and Pieter stopped because he could hear Ilsa sobbing as she spoke. Elise was talking to her, and though his youngest sister was only fourteen years old at the time, she was nobody's fool.

Pieter caught the gist of the conversation. There was a man involved, and it seemed that Ilsa was frightened of him.

'What are you going to do?' asked Elise.

'There's nothing I can do,' Ilsa replied, 'No one would believe me anyway, he's very clever. He always makes sure there's no one around.'

'Can't you tell Papa?' said Elise, trying her best to be helpful to her sister.

'No I can't,' replied Ilsa, 'it would only cause upset and it would still be the same. He's a respected man and nobody would believe me. He would lie, and then I'd be in trouble.'

Elise suddenly stood up, she needed to go to the toilet. As she came out of the bedroom she stopped dead in her tracks. Pieter was standing there. He'd been listening.

Pieter put his finger to his lips and shook his head. Neither of them spoke, but Elise understood. Pieter then turned around and went back to his bedroom.

The next morning Pieter sat at the kitchen table with his mother and Elise. They were having their breakfast. Franz Szabo and elder sister Ilsa had already eaten and had gone off to work. And as Pieter and Elise were finishing their food, Mrs Szabo was already busying herself around the kitchen, when suddenly she sighed out loud.

Pieter looked up.

'What's wrong Mamma?' he asked.

'It's Ilsa, she's forgotten her lunch. It's here wrapped up for her and she's gone without it. She's hardly touched her breakfast, I don't know what's wrong with that girl at the moment, I really don't.'

Pieter and Elise looked at one another. But nothing at all was said.

'Don't worry Mamma,' said Pieter, 'I can take it with me to school. At lunchtime, I'll go to the bank and drop it off there for her.'

His mother smiled, it was another problem solved and she went over and mussed his hair.

'You're a good boy Pieter. You must get it from my side of the family,' and she laughed.

Lunchtime arrived. And as promised, Pieter made his way to the bank. It wasn't actually that far, a twenty minute walk at the most. When he got to the bank it was virtually empty, just one of the clerks, an older man, who was sitting at his desk in a far corner behind the counter. He was typing, but there were no customers in there at all. Pieter called out to him but the man didn't hear, he was busy with his work. However, Pieter was in a bit of a hurry too, he had to get back to school and he'd yet to eat his own lunch. He turned to the office door on his right, it was the office where Ilsa worked. Pieter had been there before, several times. He knew that she would most probably be in there, so he walked towards the door. There was no need to knock, he never had done before, and so he turned the door handle and walked straight in.

And then he stopped, he stopped dead in his tracks.

There were only two people in there. One was his sister. The other was a dark-haired, robust man, probably in his early fifties.

Ilsa was pressed up against a tall cupboard, her blouse was undone and the man was pushing his face into her open breasts. She was trying to push him away but the man was far too strong, he was immensely strong. He was Mr Karl Brenner, the head teller at the bank. Pieter recognized him immediately. Ilsa was struggling, and Pieter saw her face. She was terrified.

She kept saying 'No...Please no...Stop, please stop.'

But Karl Brenner wasn't listening.

Pieter just stood there. And then he realized why his sister had been so upset. And everything suddenly dropped into place. It was all because of this bastard.

Pieter immediately screamed out at Brenner.

'Get off her...Leave her alone!'

Ilsa's head suddenly shot around, and then she called out...'Pieter'.

Brenner realized straightaway that they were no longer alone. But he was still full of lust. He'd finally managed to get his hands on the Ilsa Szabo's firm young body, at last he'd managed it. For months he'd pursued her, dreamt about her, and now was his moment of triumph. He would make love to her there in the office. That was Karl Brenner's fantasy, to make love to young Ilsa Szabo in the office where they worked together each and every day.

His plan was to drag her to the floor and make love to her there and then and damn the consequences. Because in his mind he was sure that 'afterwards', she would be grateful. And afterwards she'd want him again and again, surely?

But now his plan had gone astray, and Brenner cursed himself for not locking the door. He'd meant to, it had been all part of his plan. But in his eagerness, he'd forgotten.

He'd always had a thing for young Ilsa Szabo. She was young and firm and very bright. Not like his plain faced wife back at home. He'd married a woman who had forgotten how to smile. She'd even forgotten how to be pleasant. Their lovemaking had stopped years ago and not unsurprisingly, they were childless. But suddenly, there was Ilsa. And during the last few months, Brenner had become more and more confident and even more infatuated with her. He'd started to grab her by the waist when there was no one around and he'd begun to touch her inappropriately. He seemed to consider it as his right. On two other occasions he'd manoeuvred her into a corner and once he'd trapped her there he'd squeezed her bottom and cupped her breasts. Ilsa had pushed him away, but on the second occasion it had been his intention to catch hold of her and drag her back, but he was interrupted when he'd heard two of the other bank tellers approaching.

And now this. He'd planned everything. He knew that Ilsa would be alone in the office, simply because he'd sent the rest of the staff off for an early lunch. And that included her rather tiresome and somewhat naive boyfriend, the young mister Adam Breslav.

Brenner was stunned when he heard Pieter shout out at him, and now he was angry.

He turned to Pieter

'Get out, get out of here you little bastard,' he snarled.

But Pieter was having none of it. This man, this animal, was attacking his sister. Pieter flew at Brenner and grabbed hold of his arm, but Benner just cuffed him out of the way and Pieter fell to the floor. But that one movement had momentarily freed Ilsa and she squirmed out of his grasp. Brenner cursed as Ilsa ran to the office door.

She quickly buttoned up her blouse and then she shouted to her brother.

'Come on Pieter, run!'

Pieter got up from the floor, but he didn't run. He stood his ground. Pieter just stood there and stared at Brenner

'Go home Ilsa,' he called back to her. And then he faced Brenner, who was now livid with anger.

'Get out, the pair of you,' Brenner shouted, 'and you Miss 'bloody' Szabo are finished here, I'll see to that. Get out and don't come back.'

Brenner came forward but Pieter blocked his path. Brenner's hand shot out and he hit Pieter hard on the side of his face causing Pieter to fall to the floor again. It was only when Ilsa started to scream that Brenner had to control himself. The game was up and if anyone heard her screaming it would draw attention and things could get out of his control. He certainly didn't want any witnesses. After all, he was the head teller. And one day he was determined to be the bank's manager. He'd already waited too long for that promotion.

Mr Karl Brenner straightened himself. He had to regain his dignity.

'Both of you,' he said, now more reservedly, 'leave the bank immediately. And Miss Szabo, don't come back. Your services are no longer required.'

Pieter stood up and rubbed the side of his face, it hurt and it throbbed somewhat. He went over to Ilsa and they quickly left the office and went out through the bank's main hall. It was still empty, the clerk was still typing over in the corner. He'd never heard a thing. The whole episode had been over in less than a few minutes.

When they got outside Ilsa was shaking. Pieter walked with her, and they kept walking so that she could calm herself down.

'How are you?' he finally said to her. Ilsa just shook her head. Pieter took her over to a nearby bench and they both sat down there. And then Ilsa started to cry.

Pieter tried his best to comfort her.

'It's alright, it's over now,' he said to her.

'Oh Pieter,' she sobbed, 'It's been terrible. I thought he was going to rape me.'

Pieter had already considered that. He already knew that Karl Brenner intended to rape her. There was no doubt about it.

'How long has all this been going on?' he asked her.

'A few months really,' she replied, 'at first I thought he was just being friendly. I know it sounds stupid now but he was really nice, and quite funny. We used to laugh a lot and get on, and I used to really enjoy my work. But then he started getting more serious and I decided to try and stay out of his way, but he was always there and he was always making suggestions. Then he started to touch me, and once he'd started that he wouldn't leave me alone. It was then when the problems started. I just didn't know what to do. He's in charge, he was my boss and even if I complained to someone, nobody would believe me. Mr Brenner's a very well respected man. He would just say that I was lying. Nobody would ever believe me Pieter, nobody.'

And with that Ilsa started to sob again.

Pieter put his arm around his sister. He tried to comfort her, but deep down inside there was a cold anger, an anger that he'd never felt before.

'It's a good job I turned up,' he said to her.

She looked at him. 'Why did you come to the bank?'

'You'd forgotten your lunch. I was bringing it to you.'

They were both silent for a moment.

'I've lost my job, Pieter. I've lost my job at the bank. I loved working there, but now I can't go back because of him. What am I going to tell mamma and papa, Pieter? I'm so ashamed.'

They both just sat there. Ilsa was almost struck dumb with worry. Pieter however, was not. For the first time in his life, Pieter Szabo was filled with hatred. A cold hatred, and there was something inside him, some deep emotion that he'd never known. But it would be an emotion that he would carry with him for the rest of his life.

He turned to her.

'Go home Ilsa,' he said, 'Go home. Tell mother that you've finished early. Don't say anything about what has happened, don't say a single word.'

'But I'll have to tell them Pieter. What about tomorrow? What about tomorrow when I don't go into work?'

'Don't worry Ilsa. I'll sort it out,' he said to her. He stood up and took hold of her hand and helped her up from the bench. He looked at her, she was his sister and he loved her so much.

'I will always look after you, Ilsa,' he promised her.

It was a statement that would guide his life.

'Go home Isla,' he said to her, 'You can go to work again tomorrow, I'll see to that.'

He reached over and hugged her, and then he kissed her on the cheek.

'Go home, and don't worry,' he said again.

And with that, he turned and walked away.

It took him twenty minutes to get back to the bank.

Once he was there, he crossed the road and stood a short distance away, watching the entrance. After a while, and after giving it some thought, he wandered off and found a cheap clothing shop. He went into the shop and bought himself a brown woollen cap. When he got outside he pulled the cap down tightly onto his head. It was ideal.

He went back and stood across the road from the bank, and he waited. He waited all afternoon.

At five o' clock the city of Lodz came alive as the people finished their day's work and began to make their way home. The light was beginning to fade as the hustle and bustle continued and people began queuing for the trams and the buses, it was almost organised mayhem.

But Pieter just stood there, and he watched, and he continued to wait.

And finally it happened. He knew it would, of course. Karl Brenner walked out of the bank.

Brenner was wearing a long dark woollen coat and a scarf and he was carrying a black briefcase. He actually looked very smart. He stood outside the bank for a moment and then looked up at the sky. He ran his hand over his head and then turned to make his way home.

He crossed the road to where Pieter was standing, but Pieter just turned sideways as he approached and Brenner walked straight past him, not more than ten feet away. Brenner never even noticed him. Pieter knew he wouldn't. The light was fading and Pieter was wearing his woollen cap. Pieter then slowly turned and began to follow Mr Karl Brenner. In his mind he had a specific plan, it was so simple. If it worked.

He followed Karl Brenner for quite a way. And as he walked behind him, Pieter wondered what Brenner was thinking about. Did Brenner realize what he'd done? Or was he thinking about how he'd had hold of Ilsa Szabo's beautiful half-naked body? Pieter suddenly felt the anger rise in him again, the almost uncontrollable anger, and he remembered how Brenner had hit him in the face and how much it had hurt.

They crossed over to a second square where there were a mass of people, all waiting at a dozen different tram stops. The trams were all busy and full and everyone was standing at the stops, waiting for their own particular tram. As the different trams sped by the people would stand back as they passed. Brenner joined a queue and he stood there staring into space as the trams travelled past him. And Pieter stood there too, just fifteen feet away, staring at the back of Karl Brenner's arrogant head. The man was a bully, nothing more.

The next tram, all lit up and full of people, came swiftly along the track. It wasn't stopping.

Pieter watched it, and he made his decision.

The tram was less than twenty yards away when Pieter set off running. He sprinted towards Karl Brenner as fast as he could run. He was at full pace when he ran straight at Brenner and shoulder charged him in the back. Brenner was a stout man, but Pieter's onslaught hit him with such a force that he instantly fell forwards, straight in front of the oncoming tram. The tram ran straight over him, its steel wheels cut Karl Brenner's body in two.

Pieter immediately screamed, he had to get everyone's attention.

He shouted out, 'A man's just fallen under the tram,' and he pointed towards where Brenner's body lay. People immediately saw the guts and the gore and some of the women began to scream too. The tram had stopped immediately as the driver had felt his vehicle hit something. He feared the worst. It wasn't the first time that someone had been run over by a tram. But it was usually a drunk or an idiot, and certainly not someone who worked at a bank.

Pieter stepped back and let the crowds come forwards. There was always a morbid curiosity. Everything was in chaos and Pieter was just about to turn and leave, but even he couldn't help himself. He leant down to look through the crowd of gathering people. He just wanted one last look. And then he saw it.

Lying on its side near the edge of the track was Karl Brenner's black briefcase. It just lay there, nobody else had even spotted the briefcase. And for some strange reason, Pieter couldn't resist it. It was almost a trophy. And without any fuss, he quietly pushed his way forwards and leant down to pick up the case. He stood there for a moment with the case under his arm. He didn't move, because he didn't want to draw any attention to himself. But nobody had seen him, no one at all. Nobody had seen him knock Brenner over and no one had seen him pick up the briefcase. Everyone was more interested in the blood and the mangled body that was lying under the tram.

Pieter slowly turned and walked away. Nobody even gave him a second look.

On his way home he stopped near the local park. The park was closed and the wrought iron gates to the entrance had been locked for the day He sat down on a bench that was sparsely illuminated by one of the old gas lamps and he opened the briefcase. He opened it and he looked inside. There was a canvas bag in there and also a quantity of paperwork. Pieter dismissed the paperwork and he peered inside the bag. For a moment he was absolutely astounded, because inside the canvas bag was a sizeable amount of money. He immediately looked around, but there was no one there of course. He took a deep breath and looked around again as he made another quick decision. He took the bag of money and he stuffed it into his jacket. Then he stood up and made his way home. As he walked along he emptied the briefcase. Every couple of hundred yards he would randomly throw away the contents of the case. They were mainly papers and various bank statements, envelopes and letters. Pieter watched as the different papers scattered away in the breeze. All to be lost.

If Pieter had actually stopped and read those papers and examined those bank statements, he would have realized that Karl Brenner was in fact, embezzling money from the bank.

Brenner had been regularly stealing money from the accounts of the elderly, those people who rarely ever came to the bank. They were people who had money, and they trusted the bank to do their best with it. It was money that was now suddenly wasted on Brenner.

Karl Brenner was dead.

Half a mile from home Pieter threw the then empty briefcase into some bushes. If anyone found it, the case couldn't be traced to anyone. Then he made his way home. When he arrived there he immediately went around to the back of the house and to an old wooden shed that held all their gardening implements and other useful rubbish. Pieter hid the bag in a stack of old terracotta plant pots. He then went around to the front of the house to the front door. Pieter stopped as he suddenly had to gather himself. He took a couple of deep breaths and then burst in through the front door. He slammed the door loudly behind him so as to be heard, and then he went through to the dining room where his family were already having their evening meal. They were all sitting there, and they turned to look at him. Ilsa again had hardly any food on her plate. Her face was ashen with worry.

His mother was just about to ask him where he'd been, both she and Franz had been concerned. It wasn't like Pieter to be missing at mealtimes. He was always so dependable. Always.

But Pieter burst forth with the news before anyone could speak.

'I'm sorry I'm late, mamma,' he said breathlessly, 'but there's been a terrible accident. I'm sorry but I had to stop. Somebody from Ilsa's bank has been killed in a terrible accident. I was trying to find out who it was.'

Without waiting for anyone to speak Pieter turned to Ilsa.

'It was a man called Karl Brenner. Do you know him, Ilsa?'

Everyone turned to look at Ilsa, her lip trembled. It was the effect Pieter wanted.

'Did you know him Ilsa?' asked Franz Szabo.

She looked at her father. She was stunned, and she was visibly upset.

'Yes papa, I know him well. He works in my office.'

Her mother stood up from the table and went to hug her daughter. She could see the distress in her eyes.'

'What happened to him, Pieter?' Franz Szabo asked his son.

'He was hit by a tram father. He must have tripped up and fallen in front of it. That's all I know.'

'Oh dear god,' said his mother, 'How terrible!'

'Yes mother,' said Pieter, 'It was terrible, it was absolutely awful.' And again he looked across at Ilsa.

And with tears streaming down her face, Ilsa just stared back at him.

Later that evening, as he passed his sister's room on his way to his own bedroom, Ilsa suddenly opened her door. She'd been waiting for him. They both stood there and looked at one another. Isla was going to ask for an explanation. But in the silence, Pieter put his finger to his lips and shook his head. Don't ask.

He leant forward and he kissed her cheek.

'I told you. I'll always look after you,' he whispered.

And now it was happening again.

After taking Miss Francine Korczak home, Pieter sat on the tram heading back to Lodz.

He thought about Francine, and he thought about Wilfred Staszic. And he knew what would eventually happen.

Was it arrogance or was it stupidity? Why were there men out there who thought that they could have anything they wanted? Men who would reach out and grab hold of anyone or anything. And all for their own ends.

If only Pieter Szabo had known what the future held.

As he sat there on the tram he thought about Elise. Little Elise, his ever precocious younger sister. It had been almost three years ago.

It had been the same obsession, and the same problem really. But this time the perpetrator had been 'Uncle Freddy'.

Frederick 'Freddy' Wasser had been a family friend for longer than any of Franz Szabo's children could ever remember.

Frederick Wasser was a very well respected dentist, one of Lodz's finest, and he had been a good friend to the Szabo family for so long that he'd naturally enough inherited the position of 'uncle'. He was one of Franz Szabo's longest standing friends, and he would repeatedly retell the story of how he was the 'best man' at Franz and Leah's wedding, and how it was one of the most memorable days of his life.

Freddy Wasser had never married. He'd always joked quite openly that no woman would ever take him on, it was a point well taken. Freddy was a large rotund man. Put quite simply, he was grossly overweight. But he didn't care, Freddy loved his food and he recognised his weight problem and just laughed about it. He was a good dentist and he was quite wealthy, and he also had the Szabo family, where he could call in and be fed whenever he liked.

Uncle Freddy Wasser had quite a good life really. But for some reason, it wasn't enough.

Elise had just turned sixteen, she was a blossoming young girl who shared her sister's beauty. The Szabo's held a birthday party for her at the house and all of Elise's friends and her cousins had turned up. The party started mid-afternoon and the rest of her relations arrived later in the evening when all the commotion had died down.

Uncle Freddy was there of course, and why not? He was always there.

Freddy arrived early. He actually helped Leah Szabo with the food whilst he helped himself to the cake and the wine. Everything was going well, Elise's friends had arrived and were out in the garden, chattering away and enjoying the food. The Szabo family were happily ensconced in the dining room. Ilsa was there with her boyfriend, Adam, who worked with her at the bank. There were various uncles and aunties there too, along with Pieter and his parents. And of course, there was Freddy.

Everyone was busily talking to one another when Elise suddenly skipped into the room. All heads turned and everyone greeted her and wished her a happy birthday. Elise beamed with excitement, she was at an age when it felt wonderful to be the centre of attention.

Pieter watched his little sister, she was so lovely. And he thought about her growing up. Always precocious, she had somehow grown into a young lady right before his eyes. The promise of womanhood was evident. She would be beautiful.

At that moment, Freddy came forward and made an announcement.

'A happy birthday to my favourite girl,' he said to her, 'and now I have your birthday present.'

Elise's expression suddenly changed, and she looked at Uncle Freddy rather nervously.

And Pieter noticed it.

'Here you are my darling,' he said to her. And from his inside pocket, he produced a white leather case. Everybody in the room looked on as he handed Elise the case. But she just stared at it, and then looked back at Freddy.

'Well come on Elise,' he prompted her, 'Open it and see what your uncle Freddy has bought you.'

Elise slowly opened the case, and inside there was the most beautiful pearl necklace. It was absolutely stunning. Everyone in the room gasped. But Elise just stood there, speechless.

At that moment, her mother tactfully intervened.

'Oh Freddy, it's absolutely beautiful. You shouldn't have.'

Everyone still looked on in amazement.

Freddy laughed, 'She's my favourite little girl, and she deserves only the best.'

Elise's mother turned to her

'Say thank you to Uncle Freddy, Elise.' It was more than a hint.

'Thank you, Uncle Freddy. It's really beautiful.' Elise replied.

Freddy leant forward, 'Give your uncle Freddy a kiss then,' he said to her, and he turned his cheek expectantly.

Everybody was still watching.

Elise hesitated for a moment, and then she kissed him on the cheek.

Pieter was watching his sister's rather awkward expression. Something wasn't right.

'Let me put it on for you, darling,' said Freddy.

And Elise handed him back the leather case.

Freddy took out the necklace and put the case on the table at the side of him.

'Turn around darling,' he said to her as he undid the clasp.

Elise dutifully turned around as Freddy carefully put the pearl necklace around her slim neck. He then placed his hands on her shoulders to show everyone the necklace.

Everybody made a fuss, and Elise just smiled at them nervously, somewhat ill at ease.

Eventually, everyone returned to their conversations. But Freddy just stood there, still with his hands on Elise's shoulders, and his thumbs were massaging the back of her bare neck, and he persisted. He was almost caressing her. And as he stood behind her, Freddy suddenly leant forward and began to whisper something into her ear. Elise never moved, she just stared out in front of her. And he continued to whisper in her ear and he continued to caress her neck, but Elise still didn't move, and her face was totally expressionless.

Beads of sweat began to form on Freddy's forehead as he stood there smiling to all and everyone in the room, but his hands were still on Elise's neck, softly stroking her pale skin.

But even more strangely, nobody seemed to see it. No one even noticed what was happening right in front of them. No one even gave it a thought.

But Pieter did.

He stood there. And he was completely astounded at what was happening there in front of him and in front of everyone else. He blinked. Was he mistaken? No, he couldn't be. It was all too sexual, and the perspiration on Freddy's forehead told another story. The man was in complete ecstasy.

Then Freddy suddenly stopped what he was doing and he stepped back. The sweat was beginning to run down his face and he immediately took out a handkerchief and wiped himself. Not wanting to become too conspicuous, he turned and quietly walked out of the room leaving Elise standing there, almost rigid with fright.

Pieter stood there too, and he watched her.

Almost immediately Elise took a deep breath, it was a release. She stood there for a few seconds and then started to look around. She was looking to see if anyone had noticed anything, but no one had. And then she turned, and there was suddenly a look of complete horror on her face as she saw Pieter looking straight at her. They both stood there, staring at one another, and Elise's eyes widened in disbelief. In an instant, she quickly turned around and almost ran out of the room.

But Pieter had seen it all.

The afternoon party progressed into the evening. The adults stayed in the dining room and continued to talk and eat and drink. Elise and her friends had left the garden and had moved into the living room where they chattered away noisily. One by one they left, and in the end Elise disappeared too. Pieter stayed with the adults and tried to enjoy the rest of the evening. But what he had seen had worried him. There was something wrong, he was sure of it. He'd seen that look of dread on his sister's face.

Pieter had been watching Freddy. As 'Uncle Freddy', he knew everybody, and he spoke to all and everyone. He joked and laughed, and he ate and he drank. At one point he had his arm over Franz Szabo's shoulder. They were old friends, the best. Franz Szabo thought the world of Freddy Wasser. Pieter could see that, it was written all over his father's face. The alcohol flowed and at one point Freddy stood in between Franz and Leah and he hugged them both. Leah Szabo slapped Freddy's huge stomach and made some comment and everybody laughed. After that Freddy excused himself to go to the toilet and the conversation and the drinking continued into the evening.

Pieter watched Freddy stroll out of the room. His large frame almost waddled through the open door.

One of Pieter's uncles suddenly started to talk to Pieter about his shooting. And he caught Pieter's attention. They spoke for quite a while about the club and his uncle quizzed him about the possibility of his own son joining the club too. Pieter discussed his young cousin with his uncle and he gave him some advice. He also recommended that his uncle have a word with his father, Franz. Pieter knew that his father was well connected at the shooting club, and it shouldn't really be a problem. His uncle then wandered off to speak to Franz.

Pieter stood there for a moment. He was on his own again and he looked around the room. Ilsa and her boyfriend, Adam, were leaning against the far wall. She was looking up at him and tousling his hair, and he was talking to her and laughing. They made a nice couple, one day they would marry. Pieter had already realized that, and then it would be up to Adam to look after Ilsa. His promise fulfilled, Pieter would then be left to look after Elise.

Suddenly he frowned. Where was Elise? The birthday girl should be here enjoying herself and being made a fuss of. It wasn't like her.

And then Pieter suddenly had the strangest of feelings. Where was Freddy? He'd excused himself for what was more than twenty minutes ago and he'd never returned. Pieter took a deep breath. He felt something dig in the pit of his stomach. It was his natural instinct, it was fear for a loved one. He'd already experienced the same thing once before.

Pieter walked out of the dining room and he went out through the kitchen and into the garden.

Sometimes the men went out there to smoke a cigar, but there was no one there. He went around to the front of the house, but there was no one there either. He went back into the house and back through the dining room. Freddy still hadn't returned and so Pieter went to check the living room, but it was completely empty.

He stood there in the hallway, and he looked at the stairs. Up those stairs was the only place left. It was the only place that either of them could be. Pieter began to breathe deeply, and then with a terrible feeling of trepidation, he took the first step.

When he got to the top of the stairs, Pieter looked down the landing. On the left, there were three doors. His sisters now had their own rooms. The first was Ilsa's bedroom, the second was Elise's and the third was his own room. On the right was his parent's bedroom and then the bathroom. All the doors were closed. Pieter went over to Elise's room, he grabbed hold of the door handle and marched straight in. There was no one there, the room was empty.

Pieter stood there for a moment wondering where Elise could be, and of course Freddy. Then suddenly he heard a noise and he turned around. The door to Elise's room had closed somewhat, but Pieter saw somebody walk straight past. He opened the door and went back onto the landing, and watched as Freddy quickly went back downstairs. He seemed to be in a hurry, he'd never even noticed Pieter.

Pieter just stared as the huge man struggled with the stairs and had to hold on to the bannister for support. And at that moment Pieter heard a sound. He turned around. The bathroom door was now open and the noise was coming from in there. Pieter went over to the bathroom and walked in, and he instantly stopped, appalled at the sight in front of him.

Elise was bent over the bathroom sink, she was retching violently. Pieter stared at her.

'Elise,' he said. It was all he said.

Elise spun around in complete horror. Her face and blouse were covered with semen.

Pieter almost staggered backwards. Elise panicked and tried to wipe her face, then she turned the tap and tried furiously to splash some water over herself. But it was all too late. She was embarrassed and upset and started to cry in panic.

Something snapped in Pieter Szabo's brain. He was blind with rage. He stormed out of the bathroom and the last thing he heard was Elise shouting to him, begging him not to say anything. Pieter dashed down the stairs and went straight into the kitchen. He went over to the cupboard and opened a drawer that held the family's cutlery. He grabbed hold of the carving knife which was always in there, and then he spun around and headed directly for the dining room. He looked around, but Freddy wasn't there. In Pieter's mind, he held one certainty, that he was going to stab and slit Freddy Wasser's throat there and then in the middle of the room. Of that he was absolutely sure. But Freddy wasn't there. Pieter turned to the uncle that he'd been speaking to earlier. The uncle didn't notice the carving knife in Pieter's hand that he was holding by his side.

'Where's Freddy?' Pieter asked him. He tried to keep the emotion out of his voice. The uncle smiled back at him, he'd had several glasses of wine and was by then a little vague.

He didn't notice the desperate tone in Pieter's voice.

'Oh Freddy,' the uncle replied, still smiling, 'Oh he's left, he's gone home, he waved everybody goodbye a couple of minutes ago.'

Pieter almost dashed out of the room as he headed for the front door. He stepped out and on to the road. But there was no Freddy Wasser. He'd disappeared into thin air. Pieter looked up and down the road but there was no one there, no one at all. The road was completely deserted.

Pieter stood there breathing deeply, he knew he had to control himself. He had to. He had to do something. But what?

Suddenly he thought about Elise. He turned around and went back into the house. Everybody was still laughing and drinking and enjoying themselves. Nobody noticed.

Pieter put the knife on the table and then walked out of the room and back upstairs to Elise's bedroom.

Freddy Wasser stood there in the back garden, urinating on one of the flower beds. He'd very quickly said his goodbyes to everyone at the party and had immediately left. He'd had his fun.

Better to let those drunken fools carry on without him. They were all fools, and Freddy had put up with them for years. Those perfect families with their perfect children. Freddy smiled to himself when he thought about that. Yes, their perfect children. Little did they know how many times Freddy had abused those children, when they'd been sat in his dentist's chair, and after Freddy had administered the gas. He'd tampered with them and molested them for years. And he'd got away with it. He would assure the parents that he always administered gas to children so as to allay their fears. He didn't want their children to be frightened. If he put them under with the gas, the dental work was painless. And over the years, many of those children had their teeth extracted and had been given fillings that they never needed. The children were always queasy afterwards, of course they were. It was understandable.

Freddy stood back and fastened up his trousers. He was in the Szabo's back garden.

He stood there and looked up at the clear night sky, and then he glanced back up at one of the windows of the house. He smiled. Elise would be up there, she would still be up there. Pretty little Elise, with her pretty little mouth. And as he thought about her, his body began to stir.

It was so good, so perfect. He was absolutely captivated by Elise's pretty little mouth.

It had all started when Elise was just ten years old. That was when it all began. Freddy had always been captivated by her elder sister Ilsa. And he'd played with Ilsa's body too, as she'd lain unconscious in his dentist's chair. But it wasn't enough. Freddy had become bored with unconscious children, he'd wanted something more. And suddenly there was Elise, yes little Elise. And as 'Uncle Freddy' he had access to her. Access whenever he wanted.

When she was just ten years old, Uncle Freddy had started to go into her bedroom to read his 'favourite niece' a bedtime story. It was all so innocent. Freddy would arrive once or twice a week, and he would always bring a 'special' book with him. The family were always so appreciative, especially when Freddy told them that he considered little Elise 'so gifted'.

'She understands every story I read to her,' he'd often said, 'and some of them are really quite complex.'

In fact, the stories that he read to her were nothing more than nursery rhymes. He would read them to her quickly and then they would play 'games'. Those games involved him showing little Elise how to 'stroke him'. And it was always 'their' little secret. A couple of years on, and Freddy had tired of that pleasure too, and wanted something more adventurous. So he taught Elise how to kiss him in that 'special place'. By the end of the year, he'd tutored her in how to perform oral sex on him on a regular basis, and it had gone on for years.

Freddy Wasser was a pariah.

But on that evening as Freddy stood in the Szabo's back garden fastening up his trousers, fate had dealt him a helping hand.

At the same time that he was urinating onto the Szabo's flower bed, Pieter Szabo was standing on the main road at the front of the house with a carving knife in his hand, looking to rip Freddy's throat out. Pieter would have murdered him there and then.

Pieter was so upset and shocked at what he had just witnessed, that in his rage he never considered looking around the back of the house. It was understandable. Had Pieter known he was there, Freddy Wasser would have been a dead man, and Pieter would have then had to suffer the life changing consequences of his actions.

As it was, Pieter went back into the house, and Freddy walked out of the side entrance to the garden and onto the main road. He strolled home, happily contented. It had been a wonderful night for him. The exhilaration that he'd felt, knowing that all those people were just seconds away, as young Elise had performed her duty. Standing there in the bathroom with his pants around his ankles with the lovely Elise on her knees, doing exactly what he'd trained her to do was a delight. At one point he'd held her head onto him and was in ecstasy when he heard her gag. He pulled back and ejaculated, and he stood there breathing heavily. It was over, and for Freddy Wasser, it had been heaven.

Freddy Wasser was an absolute malevolent. He was a depraved and wicked man.

Pieter Szabo walked into his sister's bedroom. He didn't knock, he just walked straight in. Elise was sitting on the edge of the bed. She was crying and she was upset. She'd been caught, and now her secret fear would be open to all.

Pieter just stared at her. She was his little sister. She would forever be his little sister, but he had to talk to her.

'Elise, please talk to me. Please tell me what's been going on,' he asked her softly. He realized straightaway that if he took an aggressive tone or a harder approach, it would be a mistake. She was being abused, badly abused. She would need love and support and care. It was the only way, if he wanted to get some honest answers.

Elise looked up at him.

Pieter went over to her and he got down on his knees and took hold of her hands.

'Elise, I'm here to look after. I'll sort this out, I promise I will, just leave it to me. But please, please, just tell me what's been going on.'

Elise just stared at him, and then she burst into tears again.

'It's all my fault,' she began to say, 'I know it is.'

Pieter didn't understand.

'What do you mean Elise, What do you mean it's 'your' fault?'

'I never said 'No'. I know I should have done, but I couldn't. You see, Uncle Freddy would have told Mamma and Papa.'

Pieter was amazed that Elise couldn't stop herself from calling her abuser 'Uncle'.

'So how could it have been your fault?'

'Because Uncle Freddy told me it was.'

But Pieter still didn't understand her.

'Why was it your fault, Elise?'

'Because when I was young, it was me who started the game.'

Pieter couldn't comprehend what she was trying to tell him.

'When you say you were 'young', how long has this been going on for Elise?'

Elise just looked at him.

'It's been going on for years, Pieter, since I was a little girl, and as long as I can ever remember.'

Pieter felt his stomach churn. That bastard Freddy Wasser had been coming to their home for years under the guise of being a family friend, but it had all been a lie. He'd been there for one reason and one reason alone. To prey on Pieter's little sister.

'I don't understand,' Pieter continued, 'what was the 'game' that you supposedly started?'

'Uncle Freddy told me, he said that when I was little, I always wanted to stroke him 'down there'. And he just let me because it made me happy. And things just went on from there. I did it for years. And then he made me start kissing it. And then from there, from there...' and at that moment Elise started to flush and then she looked down in shame. She couldn't bear to look at her brother anymore as she spoke to him.

'From there he started to put it in my mouth, Pieter. I didn't want too, I hate it. It makes me sick. But I had to.'

At that moment Pieter thought that his brain would burst. He had to take a deep breath, he had control himself. He had to try to remain calm.

'What did Freddy say to you Elise, what exactly did he say when he said that he was going tell Mamma and Papa?'

'He told me that I'd been a bad girl and that we should never have done any of this. But now he couldn't stop himself and it was all my fault. The only way he could stop was by going to Mamma and Papa and telling them everything, and what I had been doing. And how upset they would be when they found out. He told me that they'd be disgusted with me. He said it would be better if we kept it a secret. Nobody needed to know, nobody ever needed to know.'

Peter looked at his sister. He saw the desperation and he saw the fear. She'd been totally controlled by Freddy Wasser. She was still being controlled by him.

'Look at me Elise,' he said to her, 'Look at me.'

Elise lifted her head and stared back at him.

'Listen to me Elise, because I'm going to tell you the truth. You have done nothing wrong. You have been used by this man, and he's used you and he's lied to you for years, ever since you were a little girl. And you are not 'bad'. It's Freddy Wasser who is bad. He's an evil man and a liar and he's put all these ideas into your head and he's made you go along with it. You were only a child. You didn't know any better.'

Elise stared at him, she was trying to understand.

'But I'm not a child anymore, am I Pieter? But I've kept on doing it.'

'Yes, but only because he's made you. And because he's threatened to tell Mamma and Papa.'

'But what if he tells them, Pieter? I couldn't bear it. I couldn't live with the shame. I think I'd kill myself.'

Pieter grasped her hands tightly.

'He would never tell them, Elise, never. Don't you see? He's the guilty one. He took you as a child and he's used you for all these years. Nobody ever knew and no one would ever know. It's his secret, not yours. He would never tell anyone, he couldn't. He's the liar. He's the one who's the bad person.'

Elise sat there, listening to what her brother was trying to tell her.

'Elise,' Pieter said to her, 'listen to me. I'm going to sort everything out.'

For a moment she panicked.

'You're not going to tell Mamma and Papa?'

'No darling,' he said to her, 'I'm not going to tell anyone. No one will ever know, only us. And that will be our secret.'

She just looked at him, she still didn't fully understand. She never would.

Pieter stood up.

'There's just one thing. If Freddy comes anywhere near the house again, you must get out of here. I want you to get out of the house and get away from him. Don't let him see you and don't go anywhere near him. Okay?'

Elise nodded as she wiped her eyes.

Pieter put his arms around her and kissed her cheek.

'Trust me Elise' he said to her, 'I promise you, I'll always look after you.'

The next morning when the family got up for breakfast, Pieter complained about a toothache.

His mother checked the inside of his mouth for him.

'I can't see anything Pieter,' she said.

But Pieter still complained.

'I'll get in touch with Uncle Freddy,' said his mother, 'I'll make you an appointment at the dentists. He can have a look at it for you.'

The family were all sitting around the table, and at the mention of

Freddy's name, Elise glanced uneasily at Pieter. She'd been almost silent all morning. But Pieter just turned to her.

'Could you pass me the butter please, Elise?' he said casually, as he reached across the table.

The following day, a sunny Monday morning, and Pieter made his way to the surgery.

'F. Wasser. Dental Surgeon' was in Lodz centre and was on the way to the office where Pieter worked. Pieter walked in through the front door and went over to the receptionist's desk. The receptionist, a rather middle-aged lady with greying hair recognized him and wrote down Pieter's name in the book.

She seemed to have always worked there, Pieter could never remember there being anybody else. Oddly, he couldn't think of her name, even after all those years. Though in truth, Pieter rarely went to the dentists. He had exceptionally good teeth.

Pieter sat down in the reception area and waited.

Ten minutes later, the door across from him opened and out walked a man who was holding a handkerchief to his mouth. Closely behind him was Freddy Wasser.

'Don't worry Mr Koplik,' Freddy was saying to the man, 'the bleeding will stop shortly and the pain will ease.'

The man moaned something as a reply, and then left through the front door.

Freddy clapped his hands as he looked around and immediately saw Pieter sitting there.

'Ah Pieter,' he exclaimed, 'Your mother told me that you'd be coming. Come through, come through.'

For an instant, Pieter just stared at him. And at that moment he wanted to beat the man to a pulp, right there and then. But he had to control himself. He had to calm down and control himself. If he wanted his plan to work.

Pieter stood up and followed Freddy Wasser into his surgery. As he walked in behind him, Pieter stared at Freddy's fat neck and his waddling body. He was without doubt, a most repulsive man.

'Sit yourself down in the chair,' said Freddy, 'and we'll have a look at what's troubling you.'

It was time for Pieter to put his plan together.

'Actually, I think I could be wasting your time Uncle Freddy,' he said. He chose the word 'uncle' carefully. He needed to put Freddy at ease.

'Ah...and why is that?' Freddy then asked.

'Well I had a toothache and it was really sore. But this morning when I woke up, I had a small piece of rabbit bone in my mouth and the pain had gone. I think the bone must have got jammed between my teeth somehow. We had rabbit for dinner the other night. Mamma made us her rabbit casserole.'

'Ah,' said Freddy, licking his fat lips, 'you're mother's rabbit casserole is to die for.'

Strangely, that was just what Pieter had planned.

'If I'd have known, I would have called around,' Freddy continued, as he started to look into Pieter's open mouth.

The thought of Freddy Wasser coming around to the house again and sitting at the same table as Elise or being anywhere near her, made Pieter grip the sides of the chair.

He had to control himself.

Freddy was only inches away from his face as he examined Pieter's teeth. And Pieter could smell the man, and his stomach churned. Just inches away from him was the man who had abused and mistreated his sister since she was a girl. And now he was using her like a whore.

Pieter closed his eyes.

'There doesn't seem to be any problems,' said Freddy, as he stepped back.

Pieter blinked. It was over.

'It must have been that bone,' he continued, 'there's nothing at all wrong with your teeth.'

Freddy turned to wash his hands. And now was Pieter's chance.

'Do you still go fishing Uncle Freddy?' Pieter enquired.

'Yes, all the time. In fact, I go most weekends, I love it.'

'Can I come with you, Uncle Freddy?' Pieter suddenly asked.

Freddy was quite taken aback, Pieter had never asked him before.

'I thought that shooting was your game, Pieter?'

'Yes it is,' Pieter replied, 'but I'm getting a bit stale with doing nothing but target practice all the time. I thought I might tag along with you and do a bit of hunting. I could even try my hand at fishing too,' and he laughed.

Freddy looked at him.

'Well, I've found a lovely spot along the River Ner. It's backed by forest. I've no doubt that there will be some sort of hunting up there.'

Pieter smiled 'When will you be going?'

'Ah, well, I was thinking of going on Saturday actually,' Freddy replied.

'That would be great Uncle Freddy. I'll tell Papa that you're taking me. He'll be really pleased. He's always telling me that I should get more fresh air,' and Pieter laughed again.

As he left the surgery, Pieter smiled at the simplicity of it all. Of course he knew that Freddy went fishing every Saturday. Every week when Freddy came around to the house he would tell everyone all about his fishing exploits and what he'd caught.

Yes, thought Pieter, every single week, when he came to the house.

On the following Saturday morning, Pieter met up with Freddy at the surgery. Freddy was loaded with an assortment of bags, containing his fishing tackle. Pieter just brought his rifle in its canvas cover.

They boarded a tram to the outskirts of the city, and then they used Freddy's regular driver to take them the River Ner, to the place where Freddy routinely fished. It was a truly beautiful spot, a quiet riverbank which overlooked the whole expanse of the river and was surrounded by forest. It was perfect.

The driver left them with the agreement that he would return at around five o'clock, and then they would start their journey back home. It was a beautiful summer's day and Freddy was keen to set up his pitch and start the day's fishing. After twenty minutes conversation, during which time Pieter did his best to look vaguely interested, Freddy then hinted that he wanted to get on with his fishing and that Pieter should go off and shoot something.

If Freddy had only known, he may not have been so keen.

Pieter took his rifle out of its canvas carrier and walked into the forest. He had enough ammunition with him to shoot quite a few things, though he only had one particular animal in mind.

The forest led up a hillside and Pieter walked up there and then climbed the rest of the way until he came to a clearing which looked down onto the river below. Two hundred yards below him Uncle Freddy sat there idly fishing. He was wearing a pair of very long waterproofed rubber waders that came up past his thighs. Freddy was sitting on the side of the riverbank with his legs in the water, his baited line was casually bobbing along in the river.

Pieter looked down at his rifle, he'd brought along his trusted old Karabinek. He was in no hurry, and he took a used oiled rag from his pocket and wiped his gun. It was a practised habit. A rifle always deserved to be kept in pristine condition.

Pieter had two rifles. This one was his trusty Karabinek wz.29. It was the rifle that his father had given him when Pieter had first joined the Lodz District Rifle Club. Pieter had only been fifteen years old at the time and the Polish-built rifle had seemed rather large for a boy so young. But Pieter had mastered the gun, and he had mastered the art of shooting, and noticeably so.

The previous year, Pieter's father had bought him his second rifle. It was a Mauser Karabiner 98. The Mauser 98 was a German made rifle and was without doubt, quite superb. Franz Szabo had bought two of them, one for himself and one for Pieter. The Mauser Karabiner 98 was the most efficient rifle of its time, so much so, that it had become the latest weapon of choice for the German army. It was a mystery to all at the Lodz District Rifle Club as to how Franz Szabo had managed to get hold of two of these rifles, and it was also generally considered that they must have cost him a small fortune. For Franz Szabo however, the cost had been immaterial. He had in his son a possible Olympic contender, and for Franz Szabo, that achievement would have been priceless.

Pieter stopped polishing his trusted old Karabinek. He loved the old gun. It was tried and tested, and it would do the job.

Pieter slid five shells into the breach and then he lifted the rifle and peered down the sights. It was a practised move. He'd done the same thing hundreds, if not thousands of times.

The gun, as always, felt so comfortable against his shoulder.

Yes, it was perfect

Two hundred yards below, Freddy Wasser stared into the flowing waters of the River Ner. However, his mind was on other things, he was thinking about Elise. For Freddy, this was the beauty of fishing. It wasn't just about the fish, it was about being left alone to think. Away from that damn surgery and the same complaining people who couldn't be bothered to look after their own teeth properly. He was sick of it, sick of it all. But Freddy had plans, he had plans to retire. Freddy Wasser had made a lot of money through dentistry, in fact, he'd amassed a small fortune. In his heart, he wanted to leave Lodz. He wanted to buy a house near a river, similar to where he was at that particular moment. And then all he would have to do was go fishing every day. He would be so happy. So why not?

Freddy sighed to himself. There was only one thing keeping him in Lodz. Well, two things really. The first was Elise. At that moment he had her in his power, and she would do anything that he told her to do, and there was still so much more. The other thought was of course, the other young girls that came to him at his surgery. One or two of them were quite delicious, and Freddy was sure that with time and with his usual ingenuity, he could eventually train those young ladies to perform the same kind of 'tricks'.

The thought of that, and thinking about Elise made Freddy's body begin to stir. And there was another thought that had been wandering around in Freddy's mind. It was ever since Pieter had asked him to come along on this fishing trip. Freddy fantasized, and he began to wonder if it would be possible to get Elise to come here with him, and on their own. He'd always practised sex on her in her room or in the bathroom, or even at his surgery. Always stolen moments, intimate and desperate moments that were over all too quickly. It had to be that way so as not to cause any suspicion. But the thought of having her here all to himself on the riverbank enthralled him. He would have her naked, they could both be naked and he could lie back on the grass while she performed on him. And even more than that, if he could get her here, he would finally find a way to impregnate her.

The thought of her little body writhing on top of him began to make Freddy Wasser breathe more deeply, and he started to rub his hand up and down his fat crotch.

Pieter knelt there, and he stared down the gun's sights. And as he slowly aimed the rifle at Freddy's head, his finger felt for the trigger. It was an easy shot, easy for Pieter. At two hundred yards, he could blow a hole the size of an apple in the back of Freddy Wasser's fat head. Pieter considered it. And then he wondered if he couldn't do more. A straight killing shot seemed too easy, too easy for Freddy Wasser, the man who had abused little Elise for all those years. Maybe he should shoot Freddy in the lower back and watch him writhe in agony. And then he could shoot him in the leg, and then the arm, before he finished him off with one final shot to the head. Or maybe not.

As he stared down the sights of his rifle Pieter came to a sudden conclusion. It wasn't enough. It wasn't going to be enough for him to just shoot Freddy Wasser in any part of his body. And then put him out of his misery, just like the dog he was.

No, Freddy needed to know 'why' he was going to die. He needed to know and understand the same fear that he'd put Elise through. And Freddy needed to know, what it was like to be tormented and terrified. It was the only way.

Pieter lowered his rifle and he stood up. He took a deep breath and began to make his way back down to the river. As he came out from the trees, another thought suddenly struck him. Something that he hadn't considered at all. What about the body?

Pieter stopped dead in his tracks. It was something that he hadn't really considered. He'd originally concocted the idea that this could all be put down to an unfortunate hunting accident. But a body with several bullet holes in it could hardly be construed as an 'accident'. And in reality, a single shot straight through the back of the head would definitely be looked upon with suspicion.

No, there had to be a better way.

Pieter stayed there in the shadow of the trees for several minutes, he had to think.

And then finally, he understood what he had to do.

Pieter strode out of the forest and walked over to the river bank. When Freddy heard him approach he glanced around for a moment, then he turned back to his fishing.

'Did you shoot anything Pieter?' he asked loudly.

Pieter didn't reply.

'I didn't hear any shots,' again Freddy called out.

But Pieter still didn't reply. He just walked over to where Freddy was sitting and he raised his rifle and smashed the butt into the side of Freddy Wasser's face. Freddy howled as he keeled over. Then Pieter kicked Freddy in his fat round face as hard as he could. Freddy's nose split open and broke as Pieter kicked him again and again. Eventually, Freddy rolled over and fell into the shallows of the river. He turned around in the water and he screamed back at Pieter.

'What are you doing? What the hell are you playing at?'

As he shouted, the blood from his smashed nose ran down his face.

Pieter watched Freddy as he floundered around in the water, the man's bulk made him quite defenceless. Pieter then walked over to the edge of the riverbank. He raised his rifle to his waist and then he pointed it directly at Freddy.

Freddy Wasser lay on his back in the water. He couldn't believe what was happening to him.

He just didn't understand.

'Pieter, Pieter. Have you lost your mind?' he called out.

But Pieter just stood there. He looked down at the man that he despised and loathed, and he said one word. Just the one word.

'Elise' he said. That was all.

Freddy stared back at him, and his twisted fat mouth fell open. And he suddenly realized his predicament. His secret was out. His little secret, his little fat lie. It was all over.

Freddy struggled to speak. He had to think of an answer, he had to think of an excuse. Anything at all that would stop Pieter Szabo from shooting him. Because Freddy Wasser realized that he was in great danger. He knew that Pieter Szabo had every intention of killing him. Of that, there was no doubt.

'Pieter, I can explain,' he shouted.

Pieter just stared at him.

'Go on then, you pig. Yes, go on then Freddy. Before I kill you, you'll have to explain to me why you've been abusing my little sister for years. Tell me Freddy, tell me why?'

On hearing those words, Freddy began to panic. He tried to stand up, and Pieter put a shot into the water, straight in front of him. The water erupted and Freddy screamed.

'Please Pieter, Please.'
'No Freddy, No,' Pieter replied.
'Think of your parents Pieter,' Freddy shouted, 'Think of how this will affect them. We've been friends for years, your mother and your father.'
At the mention of his parents, Pieter's temper began to rise.
'You bastard.' he shouted back at Freddy, 'You've been coming to our house for years and my parents have always looked after you. And all this time you only came to get your filthy hands on Elise. I know what you've been doing with her you depraved bastard. She's told me everything. Do you hear me? She's told me everything.'
Freddy was speechless. He had no more excuses. There were none, none at all.
'What...What are you going to do?' he rather stupidly asked.
'I'm going to kill you, Freddy,' Pieter replied. There was almost no anger in his voice anymore, he'd almost run out of emotion, he'd had enough. It was time for Freddy Wasser to die.
Pieter raised his beloved rifle to his shoulder and aimed. Freddy screamed out for mercy.
'Stand up,' Pieter ordered.
Freddy stopped for a moment. He didn't understand.
'Stand up,' Pieter said again.
For a moment, Freddy almost saw a glimmer of hope. If Pieter had changed his mind, he could possibly get himself out of this mess.
Freddy caught his balance and he slowly stood up. He was waist deep in the water.
'Pieter,' he said out loud, 'I have money, lots of money. You can have it, I'll pay you. We can sort this out. We can come to an agreement.'
Pieter just stared at him. He couldn't believe what he was hearing. Freddy Wasser actually thought that he could buy him off with an offer of money. He actually thought that Pieter would put money above his sister's wellbeing?
Pieter shot at Freddy again. The bullet missed him by inches.
'What are you doing?' Freddy screamed. He totally misunderstood what was about to happen.
'Move back.' Pieter told him.
'What?'

'Move back into the river you bastard. Or I swear I'll shoot you in the face and you'll die in agony.'

Freddy just stared at him.

Pieter raised the rifle once more.

'Okay, okay,' said Freddy, and he stepped backwards. Then he stopped.

'Keep going,' said Pieter loudly.

'But I can't swim,' Freddy howled.

Pieter shot at him again. This time Freddy actually felt the bullet as it whistled under his armpit. Another inch to the left and he would have been badly injured.

'Alright, alright' Freddy screamed. The water was now up to his chest. And Freddy had moved into the main part of the river where the current was stronger.

'Further,' Pieter ordered, 'keep going.'

'I can't,' shouted Freddy. He was terrified.

Pieter watched him. He knew Freddy Wasser couldn't swim. He'd always known.

In the summer months when they were little, Pieter and his sisters would go to the city's open-air swimming pool with their parents, and Uncle Freddy would always tag along. The children were there to learn how to swim. Freddy was there, simply to gaze at all the other children. Freddy would always sit on the side of the pool and dangle his feet in the water. But he would never actually get into the water. And Pieter had always remembered the day that his mother had jokingly pushed Freddy into the pool. Freddy had started to scream as he panicked and he floundered about. Pieter's father had to jump in and help Freddy out of the pool and Freddy had been extremely annoyed and began to shout at Pieter's mother. She in turn, had to apologize profusely and for a few awkward moments the whole incident became rather embarrassing. That was until Freddy realized what he was doing, and he calmed down, gave Pieter's mother a hug and a kiss and laughed it off. His mother however, would never attempt that same prank again.

Pieter shot at Freddy again. The bullet hit the suddenly faster flowing river right in front of him and showered Freddy with water. He fell backwards. And then he went under. A couple of seconds later he reappeared. But now he was out of his depth and his feet no longer touched the bottom of the river. His rubber waders were waterlogged, now full of water, they were dragging him down.

He went under again, and Pieter watched his flailing arms as he disappeared. He surfaced once more and let out a gurgling scream. Then the current got hold of him and swept him under.

Pieter walked along the bank for at least twenty minutes, but Freddy had gone. He'd drowned, and Pieter was glad of it. His sister, and in all probability, many more young children would never again be abused by their favourite dentist, Uncle Freddy.

Pieter sat there for the rest of the afternoon. At one point he fell asleep in the sun. When he awoke he felt refreshed. He felt good.

When the driver arrived, Pieter went into action. He put on a suppressed act of worry and explained to the driver that he'd been looking everywhere for his uncle. The driver went down to the riverbank with Pieter and he too expressed his worry. It was well known to the locals that the current in the River Ner could be highly dangerous. In the past, it had claimed many unsuspecting victims.

When they got back to the town where Pieter and Freddy had earlier arrived by tram. The driver immediately took Pieter to the local constabulary where the officials there were alerted as to what may have happened. Pieter was directed to a telephone and he contacted his father with the terrible news. The officials informed Pieter that it was too late to do anything and that a search would be organized the very next morning. Pieter was to be installed in a room at a local tavern for the night and his father would drive over the next morning to pick him up.

The following day a dozen men made their way down both sides of the River Ner. Freddy's body was finally found jammed above a weir, two miles down from where he'd been fishing. It was generally concluded that Freddy must have been swept away by the river's unfathomable current. His voluminous waders were deemed to be his downfall.

Pieter and his father returned home. As they drove back, Pieter explained to his father that he'd gone hunting up in the forest and he'd left Freddy happily fishing on the river's bank. When he'd returned, Freddy wasn't there. He'd simply disappeared.

The family were distraught. Pieter's mother and sister Ilsa were in constant tears. Elise too seemed to be in shock, and her parents found that understandable. They knew that she loved her uncle Freddy. They were almost inseparable.

That evening, there was a quiet tapping on Pieter's bedroom door. He knew who it would be. He opened the door, and there in front of him stood Elise. He ushered her in and straightaway closed the door behind her.

Elise turned and looked at him.

'So he's dead then,' she said.

Pieter looked at her.

'Yes, he's dead,' Pieter replied, 'He's dead and he's gone. And he's never coming back and you'll be safe from now on.'

A single tear ran down her cheek, but she didn't move. And if truth be known, she was in some form of shock. Pieter went to her and he hugged her and he didn't let go.

She suddenly started to shake, and then the tears burst forth. It was the final release.

Pieter held her as she sobbed.

'Don't worry. It's over,' he kept saying to her.

But Elise needed to cry. She'd suffered years of abuse at the hands of a man who had crushed her resistance, and from whom she'd not had a chance of defending herself.

In the end, Pieter dabbed her tears with his handkerchief.

As she looked up at him she asked the question.

'What really happened to him, Pieter?'

He looked down at her. She was so lovely, so pretty.

'He drowned Elise, that's all you need to know. It's all that anybody needs to know. He's gone now and that's it,' and he wiped her eyes again. 'And no one will ever know what he did to you, no one. It will be our secret, and I will never tell anyone. Okay?'

She nodded.

'And we will never speak of this, ever again,' he said to her.

And she nodded once again.

There was a moment's silence between them.

'Thank you for looking after me Pieter,' she said softly, 'You said you would.'

'Yes, and I always will.'

She just stared at him.
'Elise,' he said to her.
'Yes, Pieter?'
He smiled at her.
'Go to bed. It's over,' he replied.

So, by the age of twenty, Pieter Szabo had already killed two men.

They were justifiable killings, justifiable to Pieter anyway. Both those men had been harming his sisters, and Pieter was there to defend them. He would have done the same for any of the other members of his family. He would always protect the ones he loved.

And now he loved Francine Korczak. Of that, there was no doubt in Pieter's mind. She was the one and only, and he knew that there would never be another woman. His mind was set, he only loved this one woman and he considered that a man only needed one wife.

Miss Francine Korczak was that one special person, and on that same evening as he sat on the tram heading back to the centre of Lodz, he continued to think about her. She was perfect.

However, there was still that one problem. It was Wilfred Staszic. The man was the principal librarian and he was also Francine's immediate boss.

Pieter's past experiences had taught him a lot about human nature. It seemed that Wilfred Staszic had taken more than a liking to Francine, and Pieter knew that it would be in the man's nature to pursue her, come what may. And that behaviour would eventually lead to trouble, because it always did.

Pieter finally arrived home and he went to bed. But he lay there, still thinking. It was time to make plans. He needed to know a little more about Mr Wilfred Staszic.

CHAPTER 3

The next morning, Pieter got up early and left the house a good hour earlier than usual. He had something to do before he went into work. He then made his way back to the library. Once there, Pieter stood back just across the road so that he wouldn't be seen by Francine when she too came into work. He didn't want her to know what he was doing and he didn't want her to worry.

Half an hour before the library was due to open, a man appeared. He was quite tall and slim, with a thin dour looking face. He took a key from his pocket and unlocked the library doors, and then he walked quickly into the building. From across the road, Pieter stared intently at the man's thin face. It was Wilfred Staszic, it had to be. Pieter looked at the man and he felt the cold anger rise within him. Yes, it was Staszic. And Pieter would remember his face.

At that point, Pieter should have made his way to work. But he didn't. He waited, and fifteen minutes later Francine walked around the corner as she made her way to the library. Pieter just stood there and watched her. And he smiled to himself. He just couldn't resist seeing Miss Francine Korczak again.

That same afternoon, Pieter managed to leave his office earlier than usual. He gave some excuse about going to the doctors, and after a few bouts of false coughing and sneezing his boss let him go home early.

Pieter then made his way back to the library. It was half past four. At a quarter to five, Wilfred Staszic strolled out through the front doors of the library. Briefcase in hand and wearing a long dark coat, Staszic began to make his way home. Pieter followed him, all the way to Staszic's apartment, which was situated in a quieter part of the city's Narutowicza District.

The next evening, a Friday, Pieter stood outside the library again. This time Pieter didn't have to leave his work early. Fridays were Staszic's evenings to stay late, Francine had told him that. And at just after six o'clock Wilfred Staszic came out of the library, he then locked the doors and walked away. This time he went in a different direction. And Pieter again followed him. He strolled along behind Staszic, all the way to the Cafe Pineska. Pieter watched him go in, and then through the cafe window, he saw Staszic go over to a table where he met up with another man. The two men then sat there talking as they were served coffee and pastries. Pieter continued to watch them both for several minutes, and then he suddenly recognized Staszic's companion. He'd seen him somewhere before, but he couldn't think from where?

After another half an hour Pieter left. He'd seen enough. He now knew where Staszic lived and he'd seen enough of the man to recognize him anywhere.

But it was as he made his way home that Pieter suddenly remembered something. It was the man who Staszic had been talking to at the Cafe Pineska. Pieter remembered him. The man had at one time caused an incident at the Lodz District Rifle Club. Pieter tried to remember his name and what had actually happened. It had been the previous year, the man had been given an introduction to the club by one of the other members and it had caused some sort of an issue.

Then it came to him...'Kober', that was the man's name, 'Henryk Kober'.

Pieter remembered his father talking about Henryk Kober to some of the other club members. They were complaining about Kober's attitude. Apparently, after being introduced into the long established rifle club for only a couple of months, Henryk Kober had taken it upon himself to instruct the other members on what they could or couldn't do. Kober had read the club's extensive rule book from page to page, and he intended to personally see that those rules should be followed 'ad verbatim'...to the letter.

However, of those rules, countless were totally outdated and had become obsolete. And certain rules, such as what apparel could or could not be worn by members in the Rifle Club's popular bar area, were just one example. After being a member for only several weeks, Henryk Kober began to tell some of the other longtime members that they would have to go back to the changing rooms and dress appropriately, failing that, they would have to leave the bar. Kober tried to impose his own interpretation of the rules onto the other members too. And noses were quickly being put 'out of joint'. Some of those members were quick to tell Henryk Kober to 'bugger off'. But Kober had always been a stickler for the correct procedure, and he would immediately produce his copy of the club rules and straightway notify the 'offender' as to what they were doing wrong. Any objector would be taken to task by Kober at the club's weekly meeting, when Kober would stand up and take on the role as almost a legal prosecutor, as he berated any wrongdoer who wouldn't toe the line.

Things came to a head when Kober discovered a historic clause that gave a 'time limit' to shooting on Sundays. There was also a sub-clause which dictated that along with the limited shooting, the bar would also have to close early. That announcement caused pandemonium. The members were infuriated with him. In short, Henryk Kober was driving everybody mad.

However, things were about to change.

Fairly or unfairly, two of the members got together and gathered some information on Henryk Kober. They discovered that Kober was just some personal secretary for one of the city councillors. In effect, he was a nobody. Just some 'jumped up official' who wanted to give himself some authority and have power over others.

And rightly or wrongly, they devised a plan.

One of the 'better' guns that belonged to a prominent club member suddenly disappeared. And those two members stated categorically that they had seen Kober leave the Rifle Club with that very same rifle tucked under his arm. It was looked upon as theft.

Kober was brought before the Club Captain and several other senior members where he was brusquely interrogated and then with no more ado, was asked to immediately leave the club. Had he not, it was hinted to him that the Lodz City Council would be informed, and that bit of scandal would have probably cost Henryk Kober his job.

Kober left the club an angry man. He was enraged by the decision. He was after all, innocent. But no one would believe him and he was shunned by all.

He stormed out of the Lodz District Rifle Club vowing retribution. The other members there just shook their heads in disbelief at his empty, but very threatening words.

Maybe they should have listened, because Henryk Kober would in time take his revenge.

The one positive result of Henryk Kober's exclusion from the Rifle Club was that the rest of the club members then wholeheartedly voted to rip up the club's rule book and start again.

One could say that it was possibly too little, and too late. The damage had already been done.

Staszic and Kober themselves were rather complicated associates. They were both small-minded men who considered themselves above most other folk. And they were both frustrated and lonely men who had spent most of their lives at the bottom of the social ladder. They craved respect, and they longed for the power and the dignity that came with it.

However, Staszic and Kober needn't have worried. All they would have to do was wait.

Their time would come.

As Pieter made his way home that evening he considered himself a wiser man. He was also quite excited. The weekend was approaching and with it he would have the opportunity to call on Francine and take her out. Life was good, he suddenly had a girlfriend and she was beautiful and clever and funny. Yes, life was good. But in the background, there would always be the threat from Wilfred Staszic. Pieter would have to deal with him at some point. He knew he would. He had to protect Francine.

After all, that was what he'd promised her.

At just after twelve o' clock on the Sunday afternoon, Pieter Szabo knocked on the front door of Francine Korczak's home for the very first time.

Francine opened the door, she was quite flustered.

'Oh, you're early,' she said to him straight away.

Pieter laughed.

'Well I said Sunday afternoon,' and he glanced at his watch, 'And it is after midday.'

She pulled a funny face at him.

'I didn't know that you were such a stickler for time 'Mr Szabo', she replied mischievously.

'The earlier I am, the more time I spend with you,' he said to her.

Francine conceded with a giggle.

'In that case, you had better come in.'

And then she leant forward and whispered, 'My mother's downstairs, you'll have to talk to her while I finish getting ready, sorry.'

'Why, what's wrong with what you're wearing?' he asked her.

'Pieter, I'm in my dressing gown.'

He just shrugged. 'Looks alright to me,' he said, and he winked at her.

They both knew that she was wearing very little under her gown.

Francine giggled again.

'Come in Pieter,' she said in a slightly louder voice as she almost dragged him through the door.

Francine's mother was sitting in the living room in front of the fire.

'Mother, this is Pieter,' she said, again in a loud voice.

The old woman just looked up and smiled and kept nodding.

'Is it Tuesday?' she asked

'No mother, it's Sunday. I keep telling you, it's Sunday.'

The old woman gazed down at the floor, and then she looked up again and smiled.

'Is it Tuesday?' she asked again.

Francine turned to Pieter.

'Good luck,' she said to him, 'I'm going to go and get changed', and with that, she skipped up the stairs.

After Pieter had discussed 'Tuesday' with the old lady for another twenty minutes, Francine came back downstairs.

Pieter looked at her. She was wearing a navy blue skirt and matching jacket, along with a white blouse with a frilled front. She wore a small navy blue hat which matched her suit.

Pieter took a deep breath. She looked absolutely stunning.

'Francine,' he said as he stared up at her, 'You're beautiful.'

Francine smiled back at him, because she knew that he meant it, and more. She also knew that here was a man she could depend on. And he made her laugh.

They got ready to leave.

'Right mother,' said Francine, 'we'll be back later.'
The old woman looked up at them both.
'Is it Tuesday?' she asked once more.
'Yes Mrs Korczak, it's definitely Tuesday,' Pieter told her.
Mrs Korczak sat there, and then she smiled. She liked Tuesdays.

Pieter and Francine had their first day out together. They walked and talked and had lunch and laughed, they laughed a lot. They strolled along arm in arm, so comfortable in each other's company and it all seemed so natural. And at that moment in time, Pieter Szabo thought that his god, and the sun and the moon were smiling down on him. He was as happy as he'd ever been in his life because he'd found this girl, this wonderful, wonderful girl.

And he was never going to let her go.

They spent the day together, and they did what young couples do. As they walked through a secluded part of the park, Pieter took hold of her and he held her against an ageless oak tree as he kissed her passionately. They both kissed, and they smiled at each other, both knowing the promise that was drawing ever closer. And with it there was a feeling of contentment, there would be no rush, they would just let nature take its course. As ever, there would be a time and there would be a place.

They began to meet up at the library.

Pieter and Francine started to have the 'late' nights together, generally a Wednesday or a Thursday, when Francine worked overtime at the library. Pieter would leave his work and then arrive at the library at around half past five when Wilfred Staszic and the rest of the staff had all left.

If there was anyone else there when Pieter arrived, he would simply give Francine a peck on the cheek and then go and pick a book from the firearms section. From there he would find a table in a quiet corner and read. The library had always been a place of designated silence, and for many it was a place of solitude. Francine knew that if it became anything different, there was the chance that Wilfred Staszic might receive complaints, and that in turn would cause problems.

However, after six o'clock when the library officially closed and everyone had left, it was a different story. Francine would close and lock the large library doors and she and Pieter could finally sigh with relief, and then fall into each other's arms. Within the last few months they'd become lovers in the true sense of the word. And it had happened in the library, of all places. It had been a Wednesday evening and Pieter had been helping Francine to replace some of the returned books to the library shelves. Pieter was playful, they both were, and he suddenly tickled her, and that caused Francine to drop all the books that she'd been carrying. She turned to thump him and he grabbed hold of her arms. Suddenly they were in a clinch and Francine realized she couldn't win. But she didn't want to win. She just stared back at him and smiled. Pieter responded, he saw the look on her face and he leant forward to kiss her. She too realized what was happening, and she pressed herself into him as he slid his arms around her. He ran his hands down her back and over her buttocks and he squeezed her firmly, and she gasped at the feel of it and the excitement. She was his, and he could do anything he wanted with her. She would let him do anything, she loved him. Pieter began to breathe deeply and Francine unbuttoned her skirt for him and as it dropped to the floor she stepped out of it. He ran his hand down her stomach and she struggled for breath. Then he reached for her and she felt the absolute pleasure of the human touch. There would be no turning back. Francine quickly unbuckled his trousers and slid them down his legs, and then she took hold of him and felt his first uncontrollable thrust. He moaned as he felt her fingers on him, and he ran his hands inside her blouse to feel for her breasts.

It was all too much and neither of them could stop. They didn't want to stop. They finally slid to the floor and made love between the piles of books. It was ecstasy and it was pure and honest joy. Afterwards, they lay on the floor looking at one another, both breathlessly happy. Pieter rolled over and looked down at her. She was so beautiful

'I love you, Francine,' he said to her.

She reached up and kissed him.

'And I love you too, Pieter Szabo,' she replied.

And that was the start. And those late nights became 'their ' nights. Pieter would go around to the library on those evenings and he would sit in a corner and quietly read his book. But as soon as it turned six o' clock and the library emptied and the doors were closed and securely locked, he and Francine would make love, there in between the bookshelves. It was reckless and it was irresponsible, but they didn't care. To be on their own in that warm building, along with the exuberance of both being naked in the glaring library lights made them more than eager. And there was a feeling of eroticism too. Making love in a public place where moments before there had been people sitting and reading, gave them a sense of mischievousness, they both felt like naughty children. The pair of them giggled enthusiastically as they made love on the reading chairs or on the floor between the rows of books, and even on the main desk in the reception. Anywhere and everywhere, and for both of them, it felt like a wonderful commotion. Reckless and breathtaking.

Eventually they would put their clothes back on, and then they would leave the library and make their way to the Cafe Florentine where they would eat and then drink some good coffee. Finally, Pieter would take Francine home where they would chat for an hour and then afterwards he would take the late tram home.

It was during this time that Pieter spoke to Francine about his dislike for his present job. Pieter was bored at his work, more than bored, he was weary with the whole repetition of it all. Being a trainee draughtsman seemed to him to entail doing nothing more than drawing straight lines all day long. And it wasn't enough. Not for Pieter Szabo. Pieter's ambition was to represent his club and his country at the Olympic Games. And Pieter's dream, his ultimate dream was to win an Olympic medal. He was good enough, he knew he was. But he needed to get even better, and he couldn't get better whilst he was wasting his every day in an architect's office. His boss, Mr Bruno Huelle, was a good friend of Pieter's father and that was the reason Pieter got the job. And Pieter, to a point, felt guilty, and he also felt that he was letting his father down and also Mr Huelle. Something would have to be done, and he and Francine had discussed his dilemma and it was decided that Pieter should speak to his father and ask his advice. Hopefully, his father would see the sense in it and he would speak to Mr Huelle on Pieter's behalf. In that way, there would be no embarrassment or awkwardness.

It was a good decision, but there was no immediate hurry. Pieter Szabo had other things to think about.

But all the while, the dark clouds and the problems were never far away.
   And the instigator of those problems was Wilfred Staszic.
   Staszic was becoming increasingly infatuated with Francine Korczak.

In fact, he was so besotted with her that his feelings had begun to develop into an obsession. In the past, Staszic had spent most of his time watching Francine, and always from a distance. But his misguided intentions were turning into a desire that even he didn't fully understand. He'd taken to following her around the library, and then he would 'accidentally' collide into her and then always reach out to steady her, so that he could place his hands on her arms, or shoulders or her waist. And if Francine was sitting at the main reception desk, cataloguing the books, he would lean over her and he'd started to put his hands on her shoulders. Francine was aware of this and she certainly didn't like it. But what could she do, other than try to avoid Staszic all day long, which was rather difficult given the restrictions of the library building? Neither did she want to mention it to Pieter, because she didn't want to upset him. And Staszic was very clever. He never approached Francine when any of the other librarians were around.

In truth, he was acting like a lovesick juvenile.

And then, Wilfred Staszic came up with a plan. It was a foolish plan and it was ill-advised, but Wilfred Staszic was totally besotted and in love. Or what he thought was love.

He decided that he would return to the library late on the Wednesday evening when he knew that Francine would be there, and that she would be on her own. He was going to wait outside for her, and as she closed the library doors, he would be 'accidentally' just passing by. He was then going to offer to take her for a coffee. He was going to take her to the Cafe Pineska, and in his dreams they would have coffee and pastries and hold hands and fall in love.

How lovely...in his dreams.

So the following Wednesday arrived, and so did Wilfred Staszic. He stood across the road from the library for half an hour and watched as the last people visiting the library finally left. Then at six o'clock, he saw Francine come outside to close the doors, and he briskly set off across the road towards her. But to his amazement, she didn't leave the library. She just closed the doors behind her as she went back inside. Staszic stood on the pavement, slightly bewildered. This wasn't at all going to plan. So he went back across the road and waited there for another half an hour. But still the doors were closed. Staszic presumed that Francine must have decided to work a little later, and he admired her dedication. But after another half an hour he began to wonder. Then he had a thought. He could go into the library and talk to her there, and then he would ask her out. So he walked back across the road. But when he tried the library doors, they were locked. He stood back and stared, he didn't understand.

This was all very strange.

At the rear of the library was a forgotten door, a secondary entrance. It was actually the door to the cellar, but from it, there was access up to the main library through a series of steps. And Wilfred Staszic was the only person with a key.

So Staszic turned and walked around to the back of the building and down the cellar steps.

He unlocked the door and quietly entered, and then he switched on the downstairs lights. From there he walked along a short corridor and then up another series of steps which brought him to another door which led directly into the library. He unlocked that door too, and he walked inside.

The lights were still on, and everything was well lit and warm.

His mind was still set on taking Francine for a coffee at the Cafe Pineska. And he stood there for a moment in the silence, listening, as he wondered where she could be.

And as he thought about Miss Francine Korczak, he considered how nice it would be to be here alone in the library with her. Here on their own. And then suddenly, his mind conjured up a different line of thought. She was on her own. And the doors were locked. And Wilfred Staszic thought about all the times that he'd managed to subtly touch Miss Francine Korczak, and how he'd leant over her and then felt her arms and held her shoulders.

For him, it had almost been an embrace. And he remembered those few incidents when he'd 'accidentally' bumped into her and he'd grabbed her slim waist and felt the firmness and the curve of her buttocks. And Wilfred Staszic suddenly felt the thrill of desire. He was in his favourite place, in his own little empire. And he was alone with the woman he yearned for. The library was his private domain, and he was king. He owned everyone in there, every one of them worked under him. And suddenly Wilfred Staszic realized his power. Francine Korczak was his too, of course she was, and he could do whatever he wanted with her. And the thought of it made his mouth water.

And then he heard a noise.

Staszic had been standing there in some sort of sexual trance. But suddenly the spell was broken. He heard somebody squeal, it was a woman's voice. And then he heard laughter, but the laughter came from a man.

The squeal came from Francine Korczak, he realized that at once. He would recognize her voice anywhere, after all, he knew her so well. She was his one and only love.

But there was also the man's voice and the laughter. Who could it be? And what was a man doing in Wilfred Staszic's library at this time at night? And why was he laughing, and why on earth was she squealing?

And suddenly, Wilfred Staszic went sick to the pit of his stomach, and suddenly he was livid with anger.

His little empire had been invaded by some stranger. And all his evening's plans began to fall apart as he realized that Miss Francine Korczak was in 'his' library with another man.

Staszic just stood there for a moment, and then he clenched his fists as he heard the sound of laughter again. This time the voices were intertwined. There were distinct giggling noises and laughter from two people. And then suddenly, there was silence.

Wilfred Staszic was infuriated. He realized the reason why Francine had locked the library doors. She'd wanted privacy, and she wanted privacy so that she could be with this man. Staszic seethed with the jealousy of betrayal. He stood there shaking with emotion. What could she be thinking of? Surely she must have realized by now that he loved her and her alone. And deep inside, he felt an anger that could have killed.

But now there was the silence, there was no more laughing, nothing at all. And Staszic just stood there, and he wondered what was happening. He still didn't understand. And then he heard something, he heard a sound, and it was something that brought all of his hopes and his dreams to an abrupt end.

He heard Miss Francine Korczak moan in ecstasy.

Staszic was shocked and appalled. He couldn't believe what he was hearing. And for a moment he didn't know what to do. He was upset, and once again he felt utterly betrayed. And then he became livid with anger.

He silently stepped forwards and he looked down the aisle of books, but there was no one there. And then he stepped forward again to the next aisle, and still there was no one. Then he heard a noise again, it was the sound of intimacy, and Staszic quietly moved along to the third row and he slowly looked down the aisle. He stood there for a moment, just watching. He couldn't move. He couldn't believe his eyes.

Halfway down the aisle, there in between the shelves full of his precious books were a young couple, they were both naked. A man was lying on top of a woman, and his hips and buttocks were pumping into her open legs as she gasped loudly. The man began to grunt as the woman continued to moan in ecstasy. She raised her legs and wrapped them around the small of the man's back, and the man continued his thrusts forwards, on and on as the woman started to squeal again.

Staszic stared down at the couple, and some desolate urge made him keep watching. He was disgusted and yet he was totally fascinated at the same time. Staszic had never seen a woman's naked body before, and this was the closest that he had ever been to any sexual act.

He was spellbound by the rhythm of their lovemaking, the dominance of the male over the open submission by the woman. Staszic felt hot as his own body stirred. He was fixated.

But then the spell was broken, as the woman writhed, she started to shout 'Pieter...Pieter'.

The voice belonged to Francine Korczak, to the woman who Wilfred Staszic thought he loved. And at that moment, all of Wilfred Staszic's hopes and dreams collapsed, and his mood suddenly changed into seething anguish.

'Stop it!' Staszic screamed at the top of his voice. The sound resounded all around the library.

The naked couple stopped instantly. They too were in shock, their precious intimacy suddenly shattered. They thought that they were alone. So astonished was the young man that he rolled off the woman, leaving her lying there, naked and with her legs open and splayed.

Staszic looked down at Francine Korczak, he saw everything. He stared at her open pubic hair and her lolling breasts and nipples. And Francine just lay there, helpless and vulnerable and in complete shock.

Staszic seemed to tower over them both, and for a brief moment they were in total disbelief.

'You dirty, little bitch,' Staszic shouted at Francine, his voice full of shock and loathing.

'You dirty fucking whore,' he screamed at her again.

Staszic was so consumed by her treachery that he never even bothered to look at Pieter Szabo.

'Get up and get your clothes on you filthy bitch,' Staszic yelled at her. 'You're finished here you filthy little whore. Do you hear me? You're finished.'

Staszic was so preoccupied with Francine Korczak's wholly naked body, and he was so angry, that he didn't take any notice when Pieter stood up. Staszic considered the young man's nakedness as a weakness too. And Staszic felt that he could berate the pair of them in any which way he wanted. After all, they were the intruders. They were the wrongdoers. This was his library, his and his alone.

But Pieter Szabo wasn't bothered about being naked. Not one bit. However, he was incensed that another man was staring down at Francine's naked body, and he was infuriated at what Staszic had just said to her. And Pieter was more than upset at what this 'bastard' had just called her. This was Wilfred Staszic, the ever present problem, the predator that was always in attendance, just waiting for his moment. He'd recognized Staszic immediately. And Staszic had just insulted and threatened the one woman who Pieter loved.

Pieter Szabo had made Francine a promise. That he would always look after her.

Pieter stretched out his right arm and he straightened his fingers until they were absolutely rigid. He took one step forward and coughed, and with his left hand, he then pointed to a row of books. Staszic turned to look in that direction, and at that moment Pieter rammed his rigid fingers into Staszic's open neck. Staszic howled in pain and twisted his head as Pieter then grabbed hold of his ear. He spun Staszic around and he punched him in the face and then he spun him around again, and with great force, he smashed Staszic's face into the wooden shelving. The shelf broke Staszic's nose and the blood then sprayed all over his beloved books.

Staszic moaned and fell to the floor, but Pieter then proceeded to kick him in the face. Then he began to stamp on Staszic's chest with the heel of his foot until he felt the man's ribs crunch and break. Pieter was in the blind fury that he had twice felt before. And he was going to kill this man, nothing would stop him. Staszic was just like the others, and he had to die. Pieter had promised. He'd made a promise to Francine.

And then he heard the screaming, and he felt the arms around him, pulling at him. And he heard a voice, a voice shouting at him to stop. A voice he knew so well.

And suddenly it was over.

Pieter turned to her. Francine was screaming at him and he had to blink and focus before he realized what had truly happened. She was crying and she was terrified, and Pieter grabbed hold of her and he hugged her tightly.

'It's alright,' he said to her, 'It's over. It's all over.'

Francine stared up at him.

'What are we going to do, Pieter?' and now she was in a state of panic.

Pieter took hold of her shoulders, she was shaking.

'Pick up your clothes,' he told her, 'and go to the other side of the library and get dressed.'

'What are you going to do Pieter?' she asked him.

'I'm going to have a word with Mr Staszic here.'

Francine's eyes widened.

'Don't worry,' said Pieter, 'it's only a nosebleed,' he lied. 'Now off you go and wait for me.'

Francine picked up her clothes and hurried away as Pieter too dressed himself.

As Pieter finally slipped on his shoes, Staszic began to moan as he regained his senses.

Lying there on the floor he opened his eyes and stared up at Pieter Szabo. Pieter turned and kicked him violently in the stomach. Wilfred Staszic retched and again he moaned in agony.

Pieter then squatted down at the side of him and began to slap Staszic's face. He needed to get his full attention.

'Can you hear me Staszic?' he said. 'Can you hear me?'

Staszic looked up. There was no fire in him, not anymore. He was beaten and hurt, and he was crushed. All that he could do was nod his head.

Pieter looked down at him.

'Francine doesn't want me to hurt you anymore. Okay?'

Again, Staszic nodded slowly.

'Right then my friend,' said Pieter in a low voice. 'And now I need to have a word with you.'

Staszic just lay there and looked up at him.

'I already know that you have a 'thing' about Francine.'

Pieter stared at him and Staszic momentarily looked away. His secret was a secret no longer.

'Yes,' Pieter continued, 'I know all about it Staszic, and I know all about men like you. So this is what's going to happen. Francine won't be coming back here, it's over. And I know that might not be a problem for you, and that it would probably be for the better. However, once you've recovered, you might take it into your head to inform the authorities about what's just happened in here tonight. You may want revenge Staszic, and you could probably have me arrested. I do know that. I am well aware of what you could do once we've left, especially with your present injuries. And I would probably end up in prison for a while, there's no doubt about it. But what you need to know Staszic, is that once I got out of prison, I would be coming for you. I've killed men before Staszic. And the next time, I'll kill you, and I'll kill you badly. You need to know that, Staszic. You really do need to know that.'

And with that, Pieter slapped him hard across the face.

Staszic whimpered in pain.

Pieter looked down at him.

'Now do you now understand me, Staszic?'

Wilfred Staszic stared up at Pieter and nodded. He was utterly terrified.

With that, Pieter stood up and walked away. He collected Francine and they both left the library. They didn't even bother to lock or close the doors behind them.

Pieter then took Francine home. But she was worried. She knew that she could never go back to the library, ever. And with the loss of her job she would have no money, and she had her elderly mother to look after and she had rent to pay. But Pieter wasn't worried, he knew what to do.

He would speak to his sister, Ilsa. And Ilsa, in turn would have a word with her fiancé, Adam Breslav, who was now the head teller at the bank. Between them, they would find Francine a job there. Ilsa would make sure of that.

And as for Francine needing any extra money, Pieter still had money hidden away in the garden shed, the money that he'd collected from the previous head teller at the bank, the ill-fated Karl Brenner, who'd unfortunately fallen under a tram.

CHAPTER 4

After Pieter and Francine had left, Wilfred Staszic continued to lie on the library floor for the best part of an hour. He was in agony and he could hardly breathe. He had three broken ribs and he'd suffered a broken nose and cheekbone. His chest hurt and his face was swelling rapidly. Staszic just lay there. He knew he had to get home, somehow he would have to try to stand up. And as he lay there he wondered what was going to happen next, and what he was going to do. He would not report any of what had happened to him to the authorities, of that there was no doubt. Pieter Szabo had terrified him. Staszic had never in his life known physical violence. The only person who had ever hit him was his mother when he was a young boy, but apart from that, nothing. And Staszic remembered Pieter's threat, that whatever happened, he would return. Staszic believed that, just as he had believed Pieter when he'd said 'I've killed men before'. Staszic had seen the raw violence in Pieter Szabo's eyes.

Yes, Pieter Szabo would kill him. Wilfred Staszic was sure of it.

Finally, Staszic managed to stand up. With a great effort, he made his way unsteadily to his office. Staszic knew what he had to do. He took a sheet of paper from the drawer of his desk and on it he wrote to one of the members of his staff, informing them that his aunt had died suddenly and that he would be away from work for at least two or three weeks. He had to sort out the funeral arrangements and any other possible legalities. He also informed them that Miss Korczak had resigned. She had apparently found employment elsewhere.

He managed to sign the letter and place it in an envelope, and then he wrote the name of the appropriate member of staff' on the front of it. He took the letter and placed it in a prominent position on the main reception desk in the library entrance. He stumbled as he went to switch off all the lights, and then he closed down the library and locked the doors behind him. The journey home to his apartment took Staszic almost two hours, he was in agony. Once home, he went straight to bed.

He wouldn't leave his apartment for a month.

On the Friday evening, Henryk Kober sat alone at the Cafe Pineska. He couldn't understand why his old friend Wilfred Staszic hadn't turned up. The next day Henryk Kober visited the library to speak to Staszic, but was informed by the staff there that Mr Staszic's aunt had died and that he was away arranging the funeral. Kober was quite surprised. Wilfred Staszic had never mentioned any aunt. In fact, Kober was quite sure that Staszic had once told him that he had no relations at all. The following Friday, Henryk Kober was even more disconcerted when once again Staszic failed to show up. The next morning he went round to Staszic's apartment, he was quite perturbed. He wondered if he'd upset his old friend in any way, but when he considered his own question, he knew that he hadn't.

He climbed the stairs to the first floor and walked down the hallway to Staszic's apartment and knocked on the door. There was no answer. Kober waited for a couple of minutes and then he knocked again, this time a little harder. Suddenly there was a reply.

'Who...who is it?'

There was a voice from within, slightly strained, but it was Staszic.

Kober then replied.

'It's me, Wilfred. It's Henryk. Are you alright?'

There was again a silence, but Kober waited. He was about to knock again when he heard a shuffling noise behind the door. Then the lock turned and the door slowly opened. Standing there in a pair of old pyjamas was Wilfred Staszic. But Wilfred Staszic was a broken man.

Kober stood back in horror. He couldn't believe what he was seeing. Staszic's face was a mass of black and purple. His broken nose was twisted and swollen out of shape. Staszic was in agony as he crouched over holding his chest.

'My god,' Kober almost whispered. 'What on earth has happened to you, Wilfred?'

Staszic just stared back at his old friend, and then he began to cough.

He bent over double with the pain and then he screamed in agony. Then finally, he collapsed to the floor.

Two days later he awoke. He opened his eyes and stared across his own bedroom, only to see Henryk Kober sitting there. Kober was comfortably reading a small leather-bound book.

Staszic coughed, and when Kober heard him stir, he looked up from his book.

'Ah, you are finally awake Wilfred. Thank god for that.'

Staszic just lay there for a moment. Then he raised his hand to his face and felt the bandages.

'How do you feel?' Kober asked.

Staszic just nodded.

'I had to have the doctor come and attend to you,' Kober continued, 'He's reset your nose. It was broken, along with your cheekbone and three of your ribs. He's bandaged you up as best he could.'

Staszic instinctively felt his chest, and then he winced.

'You're going to be out of action for the rest of the month,' said Kober.

Staszic again nodded.

Kober looked down at him.

'What's happened to you Wilfred?' he asked sternly.

But Staszic shook his head. 'Not now,' he groaned.

Henryk Kober took a deep sigh. There was certainly more to this than someone just tripping up or falling down the stairs. Something wasn't right.

Staszic coughed. 'My work. They'll need to know,' he said slowly.

'Don't worry,' replied Kober, 'I'll go in and tell them that you've had an accident.'

For a moment Staszic looked alarmed.

'I'll take care of everything,' Kober continued, 'I'll tell them you fell down the stairs.'

Staszic again nodded, and then he closed his eyes and tried to go back to sleep.

Henryk Kober glanced at him and shook his head, and then with no more ado, he returned to his small leather-bound book.

What he was reading enthralled him.

After another week, Staszic was somewhat improved. His nose was still sore and his ribs continued to ache, but he was physically better. His psyche however, was not. The whole incident had affected him emotionally. Staszic had not only been beaten, but he'd also been physically frightened.

Kober had visited him twice a day and he'd noticed the change in Staszic's mental state. He would bring hot soup and bread, and as Staszic ate, Kober would brew them both two mugs of hot fresh coffee. He would sit in the chair at the side of Staszic's bed and make mostly singular conversation. His old friend had little to say in reply.

However, every day saw a slight improvement and by the end of the following week Staszic, though still very quiet, was actually responding to Kober's constant attempt at some form of dialogue. And later, when the time felt right, Kober finally asked him the question.

Kober spoke to him quite seriously.

'Wilfred, you have to tell me what happened to you. You need to tell me, and I need you to share your problem with me. Otherwise I can't help you.'

Wilfred Staszic lay there in his bed. He just stared down at the blankets. And then inexplicably, he started to weep.

Kober was quite surprised at his friend's sudden show of emotion.

'What is it Wilfred?' he asked

Staszic turned to him, tearful.

'It was that bitch, Henryk...that dirty, rotten, bitch. It was my librarian, Miss Francine Korczak and her damn boyfriend.'

Staszic relived the whole story. He told Kober everything. And in truth, he felt better for it. But Kober was absolutely stunned by the brazenness of the events, and the course of the brutality.

Both men sat there for a moment in disturbed silence. And then Kober spoke.

'She's nothing more than a whore, Wilfred.'

Staszic looked uncomfortable and slightly perturbed. But then he nodded.

'You're quite right Henryk,' he agreed, 'I realize that now. But I would have looked after her. I could have made her happy.'

Kober scowled.

'Happy? You could never make a woman like that happy. Women like that just 'use' good men like us, Staszic, and that's the problem. You would have never been able to trust her, ever, and she would have led you a dog's life. Truth be known Staszic, all women are whores. They live off the backs of good and honest men like us, and that's a fact of life.'

Staszic nodded in agreement. His friend Kober, was of course telling the truth as he saw it. And in Wilfred Staszic's eyes, Kober was the wiser man.

'And what about the bastard who beat you?' said Kober.

Staszic's eyes widened.

'I don't know who he is,' he blurted out.

'Yes,' replied Kober. 'But someone must know him.'

'No!' said Staszic, his voice was suddenly raised, 'I don't want anything to do with him.'

'And why not?' Kober asked? 'Surely we could have him arrested for what he's done to you. I do have certain connections with the authorities you know.'

'You don't understand Kober...'that man', it was the look in his eyes. If it hadn't been for Miss Korczak he would have killed me. She had to pull him off me. She was screaming at him to stop. That man then threatened me. He said that if I reported him, no matter what happened, he would come back for me and he would kill me. He'd do it, Kober, I know he would. He told me that he'd killed before. That man is capable of anything, Kober, anything.'

And with that, Staszic slumped back onto his pillow.

'I couldn't live with it, Kober. I couldn't spend every day just watching and waiting.'

Henryk Kober looked down at his old friend, and he saw the fear, the absolute fear.

'Alright Wilfred, don't you worry. If that's the case we'll have to let it go,' he replied.

Wilfred Staszic took a sigh of relief.

'I'll get myself better and then I'll return to work. And that will be the end of it.'

Henryk Kober took a deep breath and he looked at his old friend. And he thought about the injustice of it all. Kober was sick and tired of his world and the way that his life was being run by people, who in his eyes, were not worthy of the job. He was sick of autocracy and favour, and being looked down upon and despised. He was sick of bullies and being bullied.

Kober worked for a council that was deeply corrupt, he saw it every day. He himself had been pushed to the bottom of the pile, while the well connected were rewarded and profited. All of his life, he'd felt that he had always been held back by others. And he remembered the divisive and unfair treatment that had been dealt out to him at that 'damn' shooting club. It had been his one chance to 'step up' socially and mix with a better class of people. Or so he thought.

But no, those bastards had colluded in a lie, and he'd been humiliated and castigated as a thief and a cheat. But things were going to change. Oh yes, things were going to change, and when the time was right, Henryk Kober was going to seize his chance.

'Staszic,' he said suddenly, 'I am going to give you a book to read. I want you to read it, read it and think about it. It is a book of aspiration and great ambition. The author is a genius, a wonderful man whose ideals are honest and truthful and far reaching.'

Kober reached into his inside pocket and took out his small leather-bound book. He passed the book to Staszic.

'What is it?' Staszic asked.

Kober gazed down at his old friend.

'The book is called 'Mein Kampf'. It's written by Adolph Hitler.'

Two days later, Henryk Kober returned to Staszic's apartment. As usual, he knocked on the door and let himself straight in. To his surprise, and his delight, Wilfred Staszic was up and out of his bed and was sitting in front of the open fire. He was reading. And the book that he was reading was Kober's leather-bound copy of 'Mien Kampf'. Staszic looked up as he heard his friend enter the apartment. Both men nodded enthusiastically to each other and Kober smiled.

'Ah Wilfred,' he said, 'you're finally up and out of bed.'

'Yes,' replied Staszic. 'Actually, I've been up all night.'

Kober was quizzical.

'Yes, ' Staszic continued, 'When you left I started to read your book. I found it totally enthralling, and in the end I got myself out of bed and stoked up the fire and made some coffee. I've done nothing but read and sleep for the last two days. This book is a work of genius, Kober. This man, this 'Adolph Hitler', he has all the answers. He understands everything.'

Kober smiled.

'Yes my friend,' he replied, 'Adolph Hitler is a visionary. He has recognized our problems and he has all the answers, without doubt.'

Staszic nodded in agreement.

'I'll make us some fresh coffee,' Kober continued, 'because I need to talk to you Staszic. Now that you've read the book, and now that you too understand. I need to talk to you about something of great importance.'

Staszic just sat there. He'd always admired and respected Henryk Kober, and if Kober had something important to say, Staszic would listen to him.

Kober made the coffee, and then he pulled up a chair and sat down at the side of his friend.

There were a few moments of silence and contemplation as Kober stared into the flames of the open fire. The room was warm and comfortable. It was ideal.

'It's time for a change, Wilfred,' said Kober. 'And believe me, there's going to be a change. There's going to be a change across Europe. Adolph Hitler will see to that. You have read his wisdom, Staszic. He is leading the German people to a glorious future, and that could be our future too.'

Staszic sat there, spellbound.

Kober continued. 'Under Adolph Hitler and the glorious Nazi Party, we will be entering a new era. The face of Europe is about to change. Hitler has just annexed Czechoslovakia, Poland will be next.'

Staszic stared at Kober.

'Do you really think so?' he asked.

'Definitely,' Kober replied. 'It's all there in the book, the future is written in 'Mien Kampf'. Adolph Hitler will reunite Europe under the German flag, there's no doubt about it. The remaining countries will fall like dominoes to Germany's iron will. What else can they do, they're all powerless against Germany's military might. It will be wonderful, Staszic. And if we have our wits about us, true talent and true followers such as you and I will be able to rise to the top.'

But Staszic still didn't fully understand.

'And how would we manage that Kober? Who would take any notice of us?'

'Ah,' Kober replied, and he smiled, 'I have something to tell you Staszic. I have met someone, someone who has a plan. He too is a visionary and he too can see the future, and he wants to do something about it. He's formed an association. It's called the 'PNP', it stands for the 'Polish National Party', it's an underground society. At the moment there are over a dozen of us and we hold secret meetings, usually every week.'

Staszic was amazed at what Kober was telling him.

'I had no idea Kober, you never said anything.'

'Yes I know Staszic,' he replied, 'and I'm sorry about that, but everything has had to be done in secrecy, I'm sworn to silence. I had to get you 'onboard' first. I needed you to read the book and I needed to know how you would respond to it. To be in the Polish National Party you have to be a true believer. I have already joined the 'PNP' and I would like you to join too.'

'What would we do?' Staszic asked.

Kober looked at him.

'It is our job to prepare the way,' he said. 'We must gather information, any information at all, and then we pass it on to our group leader. He in turn passes everything on to a higher authority within the party, and eventually everything is sent to the Nazi Party in Germany. They in turn will use that information once they invade Poland. I am personally writing dossiers on all the corrupt people who work for the city council. Those people will be taken out of office once the 'New Reich' takes control and they will be replaced by a proper, honest workforce. The people who deserve to be in charge will be given control because of their own merit. People like you and I, Staszic, honest and upright people like you and I. We will rise to the top because of our loyalty to the party. We will be rewarded for all our hard work. Our group leader will see to that. We will all be rewarded under the Third Reich and we will be given positions of power and authority. It will be our turn to run things Staszic. It will be our turn!'

Kober stood up, he was becoming quite fervent. And his passion had begun to ignite a flame in Wilfred Staszic's mind. Staszic too had spent his life at the bottom of the proverbial pile. And for most of that life, he'd felt awkward and bullied. He'd aspired to become the chief librarian. But to his own dismay, even then some young thug had walked into his library, into his own personal territory, and beaten him half to death and then taken away the only girl he'd ever loved. And suddenly Wilfred Staszic wanted revenge, and he wanted the power and the dignity. He wanted all those things, and now his friend Kober was offering to help him to achieve that ambition.

Yes, he would follow Kober. Of course he would.

'I'm with you Kober,' he suddenly replied, 'I'll join the 'PNP' too.'

Kober smiled with satisfaction, and he leant forward to shake Staszic's hand.

'Thank you, my friend,' he said, 'I'll contact our team leader, he'll be very pleased. I've mentioned you on more than one occasion. He'd like to meet you.'

Staszic smiled. He felt the elation. It was recognition at last.

'Can I ask who he is?' Staszic enquired.

'Yes of course,' Kober replied, 'the man is a born leader and a genius in his own right.

His name is Igor Sym.'

For Pieter Szabo and Francine Korczak, life took a subtle twist.

After the incident at the library, Francine never returned. However, her worries were shortlived when Pieter's eldest sister, Ilsa, quickly arranged for Francine to have an interview at the bank where she herself worked. After the interview, Francine was immediately given the job. It was never really going to be a problem, Pieter knew that.

But then, three months later another crisis arose. Francine's elderly mother passed away suddenly. The old lady died in her sleep as she sat in her chair in front of the open fire. It was a peaceful ending.

The funeral was a small affair. The Szabo family all attended, but there were hardly any others. One week after the funeral, Pieter went around to Francine's house. They were supposed to be going out for the evening, but Pieter had a change of mind. It was of course all planned. He went down on one knee and he proposed to Miss Francine Korczak.

After all, she was the love of his life.

Two events then happened.

Pieter and Francine were married within a couple months. They made the decision that they wanted to be married as soon as possible, and not be an 'engaged' couple and have to wait for a year or two.

The other event was triggered by Pieter's father, Franz Szabo. A month before their wedding, Franz Szabo took the young couple into his study and sat them both down. He then suggested that once Pieter and Francine were married, they should both move into the Szabo family home. To Franz Szabo it made more sense. The house was quite large and there was more than enough room for all of them. He also considered that for them to pay rent to some landlord was a waste of money. Pieter and Francine could live with the family and save all their hard earned money, and if need be, and when the time was right, they could eventually buy a house of their own.

Privately, Franz Szabo didn't want his son and young bride to continue their married lives in the Gadka district. The landlord was a shark, and the 'Gadka' was a well known poorer area of Lodz, in a rougher part of the city. There were some bad and undesirable people living there, people that you certainly didn't want as neighbours. And not surprisingly, Franz Szabo wanted a better start for his son and his new daughter in law.

Pieter and Francine willingly agreed. Francine was delighted. The Szabo family had readily taken her under their wing and had already made her feel like she was one of the family. The family obviously loved Pieter, and it was only natural that they would love his wife too.

All was well, for a while.

Once Wilfred Staszic had regained his health, he immediately returned to work. After a month's respite, his poor library staff were once again subjected to Staszic's tyrannical regime. Within the week he'd replaced Miss Francine Korzak, this time by an older and far dowdier woman: Wilfred Staszic had undeniably learned from his mistakes.

On the second Friday, Staszic as usual met up with his friend, Henryk Kober at the Cafe Pineska. But this time their visit was short lived. After a cup of the cafe's delicious coffee and a single pastry, both men left.

Half an hour later they arrived at a bleak warehouse in the Pozama District, an industrial area of Lodz. By then it was dark, and both men walked across a deserted yard to the seemingly closed building that had at one time been a warehouse. All around there were broken fences held together by rusty barbed wire. The whole place looked desolate. At the front of the warehouse there were two large industrial doors which were locked together by a thick steel chain, but to the side there was a small doorway that could be used as a more practical entrance. The building itself had seen better days. It was now a faded structure with several different coats of paint showing through on its once red brick walls. A large painted signboard lay propped against the wall. In worn lettering, it proclaimed that the warehouse was once the business premises of 'Lebowitcz Textiles'. Although, how long ago that actually was, would be debatable.

Both men walked along in silence, and at that point Staszic was feeling rather nervous. He was slightly reticent with what he was getting himself into. He knew he was there to meet some people, Kober's people. And that was the problem. Staszic had never been good at meeting anyone. He was a poor communicator, and he was also well aware of his own shortcomings.

Moreover, he'd had to put his complete faith in his old friend, Henryk Kober. It was Kober who'd first given him his copy of 'Mein Kampf' to read. And Staszic had read the book in its entirety and then openly proclaimed Adolph Hitler as a genius. The book had stirred him. And as both men walked across the empty yard, Staszic once again reflected on Hitler's words. And yes, Hitler was right, he was absolutely right. And his preaching's were the only way forward for a new, glorious future. With that in mind, Staszic suddenly felt more confident, more self-assured. He'd spoken at length to Kober, who had explained to him that the people they were going to meet tonight were all of similar minds. And in truth, they were all very similar people most of whom were in the same situation, they all held positions as minor officials, just as Staszic and Kober did. They were people who craved power. They were people who wanted control and influence and authority, and they wanted to be 'important'. They wanted to be soldiers but they didn't want to fight. Let someone else do the fighting, and after the hostilities they would be the people who would reap the benefits. Power over others was the reward they sought.

It was like a drug.

Both men approached the warehouse and it was Kober who knocked on the small door that led into the main building. There was a silence, and Staszic turned to Kober.

'Are you sure there's anyone here?' he asked.

'Just wait a minute,' Kober replied.

A few seconds later there was the sound of footsteps, someone was coming down the stairs. Then a dull light appeared under the door and a voice called out.

'Who is it?'

Henryk Kober almost stood to attention.

'It's Herr Kober,' he replied.

Staszic glanced sideways at his friend. He'd never heard Henryk Kober call himself 'Herr' anything before.

Two steel door bolts slid back and a key turned in the lock before the door finally opened. Standing there was a middle-aged man who was dressed totally in black. He wore a black shirt with matching black trousers and he was also wearing black shiny boots. His hair was cut extremely short around the sides and back, and the top was slicked over. The man wore a red armband. Embroidered onto it was the black swastika on a white circle. It was the symbol of the German Nazi Party.

The man quickly glanced over Kober's shoulder. They were alone.

'Come in Herr Kober,' he said. 'Come in and go straight upstairs.'

The man stood back as Kober and Staszic entered. He gave Staszic a curt 'nod' as he led them both up the wooden stairs, apparently to a room above the warehouse. At the top of the stairs he opened another door and he then ushered Kober and Staszic into a large well lit hall. As he entered the hall, Staszic blinked. He couldn't believe his eyes. The hall was opulently decked out with large red hanging curtains. All of the windows had been blacked out for secrecy and privacy of course, and the large thick curtains would mask anything that could have been missed. They also deadened any possible noise. There were several desks and typewriters, and in one corner a there were a couple of rows of chairs which were facing a small stage. Hung on the walls there were different depictions of the Swastika, everything from flags to murals. And hanging on the wall behind the stage, and in pride of place, was a large picture of Adolph Hitler, dressed in a black SS uniform. Underneath it was a wide banner, on which was written,

  Adolph Hitler

'The Polish National Party honours you'

Standing across the room were a dozen men, all aged between thirty and fifty and all dressed in the same black attire and wearing the 'Swastika' armband.

They immediately greeted 'Herr Kober'. And Staszic watched with some amazement when Kober took off his old brown woollen coat. Underneath,

Kober too was wearing the same black shirt, trousers and boots. Staszic had never even noticed. Kober then reached into his coat pocket and pulled out a swastika armband which he immediately slid up his shirt sleeve. He then faced the others and raised his arm.

'Heil Comrades,' he said loudly.

The other men immediately returned his salute...'Heil'.

Kober took hold of Staszic's arm and then he again turned to the men.

'This is my friend, Wilfred Staszic. I have spoken to you about him.'

One of the men stepped forward. He was a tall, suave looking man, in his early forties and with dark hair, cut and slicked back. He reached out to shake Staszic's hand.

'This is Herr Igor Sym,' said Kober immediately, 'Herr Sym is the leader of our group.'

Igor Sym smiled as he shook Wilfred Staszic's hand.

'Ah, Herr Staszic,' he said, 'I am very pleased to meet you. Herr Kober has told me all about you of course. I believe that you wish to join our group, the Polish National Party.'

Staszic nodded.

'Yes...yes I do,' he replied. Wilfred Staszic had just been addressed as 'Herr Staszic' and for the first time in his life he'd been given a title. He was suddenly somewhat enthralled.

'That's good, Herr Staszic,' replied Igor Sym, 'Very good. I take it that Herr Kober has told you all about us. Who we are and what we do, and what we stand for.'

Staszic once again nodded

'Yes, Herr Sym. Herr Kober has explained everything to me.'

Igor Sym turned and gave Henryk Kober a curt nod of approval.

'We support Adolf Hitler and his Nazi Party.' Sym continued, 'We are preparing for the future, when Poland will join Germany and we will all be incorporated into the glory of the Third Reich. We have a job to do, we must pave the way. There will be difficult times ahead for all of us, and we will have to face adversity. But we 'will' succeed. And then all our efforts will be rewarded.'

Staszic was overwhelmed by Igor Sym's self-belief.

'I have fully read Mein Kampf, Herr Sym,' said Staszic. 'It is a work of genius.'

'Yes it is, without doubt. Adolph Hitler is a true genius. We are honoured to serve him.'

And at that moment Igor Sym raised his arm in the Nazi salute.

'Heil Hitler' he commanded.

All the other men followed suit and they raised their right arms in salute.

'Heil Hitler,' they all shouted in unison.

Staszic couldn't help himself, and he immediately followed their example. For 'Herr Staszic' it was a moment of great emotion.

Igor Sym once again turned to Wilfred Staszic.

'You must now take the oath of allegiance, and display your loyalty and your solemn duty to the Polish National Party, to Adolph Hitler, and to the German Nazi Party.'

Staszic almost stood to attention.

'It would be an honour, Herr Sym,' he replied.

An hour later it was all done. Staszic had stood in front of everyone as he read out the 'Oath of Allegiance' which had been written in thick black lettering on a sheet of stark white paper. He was then ceremoniously handed the swastika armband and it was Kober who was given the honour of placing it on his friend's arm. Staszic then saluted the rest of the men. There was then a certain amount of enthusiastic applause.

And although he was the only person wearing a white shirt, it didn't seem to matter. Staszic would visit an outfitter's shop the very next day and purchase the blackest shirt he could find.

After the swearing-in ceremony, Igor Sym spoke to the whole group about their future plans. Information was of the uppermost importance. Any information at all that could be dispatched back to Germany to the heads of the Nazi party, and from there to the dark and secret offices of the Gestapo. Information was knowledge, and knowledge was power.

Also discussed, was the role that Herr Staszic could play. The Polish people needed to be educated, they needed to know and understand the principles of the Polish National Party and they needed to read and also learn how to appreciate the new Nazi doctrine.

Igor Sym had produced a political pamphlet which outlined the ideology of the PNP. The group as a whole had already distributed the pamphlet in and around Lodz. But it would be Staszic's task to make sure that it was widely available in the main library and the rest of Lodz's smaller local libraries.

However, there was a greater and a more important assignment for Staszic. Igor Sym wanted to introduce Hitler's 'Mein Kampf' into every library in Lodz. And he wanted a dozen copies of Hitler's book in each of those libraries, not just one or two. Sym wanted the Polish people to take notice of the book. In essence, he wanted 'Mein Kampf' to be widely read, it was the only way to make the Polish people really understand.

Igor Sym's plan was that the book should be made available, either officially or unofficially. The official route would obviously be the more preferable, but failing that, 'Mein Kampf' would have to be 'unofficially' distributed by Staszic, who could use his position as leverage.

Staszic was slightly nervous over Igor Sym's request. This was all very new to him. Then there was a short discussion about how the library actually acquired its books. Apparently Staszic, as chief librarian, would put in a request to the City Hall for any new books. That request was then forwarded to the Procurements Section and it was then passed on to the Finance Department where it would be finally approved and accepted. It would be a difficult process to alter or change. But it was Kober who came up with the answer. One of the men in their group, Herr Geller, already worked in the Procurement Section at the City Hall and Kober worked in The Finance Department. Kober then put it to the group that all Herr Geller had to do was sign the request and send it directly through to him. Kober would then make sure that it was passed straight through the Finance Department. Kober would simply forge his own boss's signature and then have the order finalized. Kober's boss was an idle and an arrogant man and Kober regularly forged his signature, if only to save time.

The plan was agreed. Staszic was thankful, and Kober got the glory.

As they left the meeting that night, it was Staszic who personally thanked Kober for his support.

'Thank you Henryk,' he'd said, 'your idea was brilliant. For a moment there I was put in a rather awkward situation. I would have looked ridiculous if I couldn't have fulfilled Herr Sym's very first request.'

'It was not a problem,' Kober replied, 'we must all work together for the good of the Party. We have a long way to go and we have much work to do.'

But it was actually Kober who was the happier man. Once more he'd solved a problem for Igor Sym. On several other occasions, Kober had advised and guided Herr Sym and had managed to come up with a positive answer to some dilemma or other. Igor Sym had been appreciative, and he'd begun to trust and rely on Kober's judgement. And that was exactly what Henryk Kober wanted. It was Kober's intention to become Igor Sym's right-hand man. He would become second in command and he too would then have power over the others.

And power was the drug that drove Henryk Kober. It was something he'd never tasted, and its promise was like an addiction to him. And there were all the possibilities of so much more.

Once the Third Reich took over in Poland, everything would change, Because of the Party's loyalty and hard work, Igor Sym would be given a command. And Kober intended to be right there beside him. If all went well, Kober too could rise to a position of influence and authority.

And as he and Staszic walked home that night, Kober smiled to himself. Being a Nazi was going to be wonderful.

Back at the old warehouse in the Pozama district, Igor Sym sat down at his desk and lit a cigarette. He'd just seen the last of his men leave, all with their usual 'Heil Hitler' salute and the same fired up enthusiasm. And that was just what Igor Sym wanted. He'd lit their fire, and he'd awakened the passion within. Everything was moving in the right direction.

Sym took another draw on his cigarette and he smiled to himself. All was going to plan.

Igor Sym had been leading a double life. He was in fact, a professional actor, and it was something that he was not entirely happy to disclose to his devout and somewhat reverent band of followers. Sym was an actor, and not a very successful one at that. He'd originally informed 'his men' that he was a writer and a director, and that on occasion he had actually performed on the stage, usually when one of the others in the cast had been taken ill, or whatever.

In the past, Igor Sym had acted on the stage and he'd also at one time managed to get himself a small part in a film. However, Poland wasn't America and Lodz was never going to be Hollywood.

He'd had a variety of reviews in some of his past stage plays, some good, some not so good. At times there had been accolades and admiration, and on other occasions there'd been insults and even eggs thrown. Igor Sym soon came to realize that it was all about the quality of the play, and not just about him. And he felt surplus and he'd become quite discontented.

And then he'd travelled to Berlin. He'd initially gone there to try and get a part in a forthcoming film, but he'd unfortunately failed to get any part at all. However, while he was there he attended one of Hitler's rallies. And he was absolutely enthralled. That same day he procured a copy of 'Mein Kampf' and he went back to his hotel room and began to read. In the early hours of the following morning, Sym stood in front of the mirror in his room and mimicked Adolph Hitler's performance. And he discovered that he was quite adept at it. And the more he read 'Mein Kampf', the more he saw the possibilities.

Sym returned to Lodz, but two months later he returned to Berlin to attend another of Hitler's rallies. But this time he took with him a plan. He attended the rally, which once again utterly stirred him. Hitler really was a genius, the way he handled his audience and manipulated the crowd to his own ends, was for Sym, an act of brilliance. Sym realized that Adolph Hitler was a man of outstanding ability. Hitler's foresight, and the promise of a glorious and a better future left Igor Sym totally spellbound. The following day Sym made his way to the Nazi party's propaganda department which was in the New Reich Chancellery building on the Voss Strasse.

Rather naively, he just walked in there and approached the reception, and then simply asked to see someone about the future of Poland. The receptionist, a rather bemused young man with a smile on his face, disappeared into one of the rear offices. Five minutes later he reappeared, but he was no longer smiling.

'Come this way, Sir,' he said to Sym, and this time there was a note of respect in his voice.

Igor Sym was rather surprised.

He was then taken through to the office of Wilhelm Kruger.

Major Wilhelm Kruger was a tall athletic man, aged around fifty. Slimly built, Kruger had dark blonde hair and an aristocratic face, and was gifted with the pure arrogance of a true Nazi. He sat behind his desk and he stayed there as Igor Sym was led into his office.

'Sit down please,' said Major Kruger, as he nodded at a chair. It was more of a command.

Igor Sym did as he was told.

Kruger then took a deep breath, it was almost a sigh.
'And who are you?' he then asked.
Igor Sym gave a determined look.
'I'm a man who wants to serve Adolph Hitler. And I'm the man who wants Poland to become part of the Third Reich. My name is Igor Sym.'
Major Wilhelm Kruger smiled.
'Well then Igor Sym,' he replied, 'you may just be the person that I'm looking for.'

Both men then spoke for over an hour.
Sym told Wilhelm Kruger about his plan to form an underground party. It would be called the PNP...'The Polish National Party', which could obviously soon be renamed 'The Polish Nazi Party', and it would still be spelt the same, the PNP. They went on to discuss the main issue, the gathering of information, the strategic information that the Nazis would need if they were to invade Poland. Kruger informed Igor Sym that he was already in the initial stages of setting up structured groups of similar informants in both Warsaw and Krakow. But suddenly, Sym had come up with the idea of forming an underground party, a party that would recruit new members. It was simple genius. There were enough disgruntled and dissatisfied Polish Nationals who would be eager to snatch power if given the chance, just as the Nazis had done so successfully in Germany.

Kruger and Sym discussed the future, and a possible future that would reap rich rewards for all those who worked with the Nazis. It would be the job of the PNP to form an efficient infrastructure which would gather up important information, and that information would then be sent directly to Kruger and his department, there at the Chancellery in Berlin.

At the end of their meeting, both men stood up and shook hands.
'Come back here to my office tomorrow,' said Kruger, 'and I will have the money here to fund our plan.'
Igor Sym held back the urge to smile as he then saluted Wilhelm Kruger.
'Thank you, Herr Kruger,' he said.
Kruger however, did smile, as he replied
'And thank you, 'Herr Sym'. And welcome to the Nazi Party.'

CHAPTER 5

On September 1st, 1939, Germany invaded Poland.

Within a matter of weeks, the German forces had completely crushed the outnumbered and overwhelmed troops of the defending Polish army. Poland had no other choice, and almost immediately capitulated. The whole incursion took just one month and five days, and by the 6th of October 1939, the once free people of Poland were completely trampled under the brutal heel of German rule.

In the City of Lodz, Igor Sym and the members of the Polish National Party were ecstatic.

The invading German troops were instructed to liaise and work with the supporting members of the PNP, in particular with their leader, 'Herr Sym'. By that time there were nearly fifty members in Sym's PNP party. Once the country was firmly under German rule, it was Sym who would immediately instruct his followers to openly wear their black Nazi-style uniforms and to don their swastika armbands. Within weeks, they were supplied with the official German SS uniforms and were then fully integrated into the Nazi Party. The Polish National Party in its then present form disappeared almost overnight. It had served its purpose.

A week after the invasion, Major Wilhelm Kruger left Berlin and rolled into Lodz to take over the control of the city from the German military commander. Most of the German troops would of course, remain there, but they would be under direct orders from Kruger and his SS troops.

On meeting up with Sym, and after a jubilant reunion, Major Kruger promoted Igor Sym to 'Commander', and the members of the former

PNP were all given elevated positions within the SS. Sym's hard work had been more than appreciated. His information had been first class and had provided Kruger and the Gestapo, with a full and up to date working knowledge of the city.

Igor Sym's right-hand man, Henryk Kober, had written a damning account, describing the total mismanagement that was taking place at Lodz City Hall. He gave a personal and candid report in which he accused the City Council of inexcusably poor administration, coupled with appalling corruption.

Kober's frank and outspoken report had been sent, word for word, directly to Major Wilhelm Kruger in Berlin, and when Kruger did finally arrive in Lodz, he immediately dismissed the whole of the Council and put Igor Sym in charge. That left Sym somewhat dumbstruck. Sym was an actor, a very good actor, but he was totally clueless as to the management and the administration involved in the running of a city council. Luckily for him, he had a man who did. His now right-hand man, Henryk Kober, was ready, willing and able to step up and take on the responsibility. It was the moment that Kober had been waiting for, it was what he'd planned and prepared for, and now it was his time. And in his new position of responsibility, Kober too, would also need his own 'right-hand man'. And the person he chose, and the only person he could trust, would, of course be his old friend and ally, Herr Wilfred Staszic.

It had always been Adolph Hitler's plan, to get rid of or exterminate every living Jew in Europe, and in Poland that plan would continue.

The Jewish community in Lodz was around 230,000 people and they accounted for around one third of the city's total population. Major Wilhelm Kruger was under direct instruction from Hitler himself, to rid the country of every Jewish citizen. Similar orders were given to Kruger's corresponding SS counterparts serving in the other major Polish cities of Warsaw and Krakow.

And so Kruger, together with Igor Sym, began to organize a system of annexation. It was quite simple really. Jewish homes and property were seized and then re-appropriated. Those 'displaced' Jewish residents were then moved to a designated 'Jewish Ghetto', which in the city of Lodz, was in the rundown Gadka District.

It was hardly a surprise when the residents living in the 'Gadka' were more than happy to give up their shabby and extremely dilapidated dwellings, in exchange for the much finer and capacious Jewish owned homes. In fact, there was almost a stampede.

Man's greed, as ever, was immeasurable.

German troops, led by the SS, combed the city searching for innocent Jewish families. Some families fled, and some just sat there and waited for the ever expectant knock on the door. Others locked up their houses and hid in the cellars, hoping against hope that they wouldn't be discovered.

Many would rely on their friends and neighbours in not telling the Germans the truth as to their whereabouts. They were the friends and neighbours who would then put themselves and their own families in jeopardy. For many it was an impossible choice, the risks being far too much to contemplate. Anyone found shielding the Jews would also be arrested, and that included their wives and the children. Some were never seen again, it was a high price to pay. And it was a brave man who would risk the lives of his family, when it was much easier to look the other way.

A new regime quickly formed, and Major Kruger and Herr Sym eagerly rounded up the Jewish community and herded them into the ghetto. It was the first step to the final solution.

Concentration camps were being hurriedly constructed. All were conveniently built close to the lines of the railway tracks, ready for the trains to deliver their doomed cargoes of innocent men, women and children, to an appalling and inexcusable end.

Kruger, freed from the confines of his Berlin office, was more than enthusiastic with his new posting. For years he'd wanted more responsibility and promotion. Sitting forevermore in his office in Berlin was not quite what he'd envisaged. Kruger wanted to get out into the field and see some action and he was quite happy to be posted to Lodz, once the actual fighting was over.

He and Sym were enthusiastically scouring each and every district, dissecting each area almost street by street in their quest to find any of the Jewish families who could still be hiding there. Kruger found it all very invigorating. He enjoyed being a man of action.

He was also very happy with Henryk Kober. 'Herr Kober' had taken on the administration and the running of Lodz City Council and was doing a splendid job. And it was a job that Kruger didn't actually want. He'd certainly had enough of all the paperwork and the repetition that came with it whilst he was in Berlin, and now he was looking for something a little more stimulating. Herr Wilhelm Kruger was a clever and cunning man, who was fully committed to one important principle. He intended to keep Adolph Hitler happy.

It was Igor Sym who had advised Kruger that Henryk Kober would be the right man to reorganize the City Council. And Sym's advice had been correct.

Kober had completely transformed Lodz City Council. For years he'd seen the inefficiencies and gross mismanagement. And he'd had to watch in disgust as those incompetent senior officials who ruled him, had turned a blind eye to everything that had been going on. But not now, Kober had swept in and made radical changes in almost every department. And in most cases for the better, but not necessarily for the people who worked there, who suddenly discovered that they had to actually work for a living. Yes, it was a new regime.

And in truth, Henryk Kober was a very clever and talented man. And he was a man who had been overlooked and had never been justly promoted, simply because he was not prepared to 'work' the system. His immediate bosses had always known that Kober would never take a backhander or a bribe, and that he would never be prepared to 'look the other way'. That had been the way of things, and in the past it had been Kober's downfall, but not now.

Reorganizing Lodz City Council had become almost an obsession for Kober. And working with him was his most ardent of followers and longtime friend, 'Herr Wilfred Staszic'. Kober and Staszic would sit in Kober's office until late at night, discussing the matters of the council and making plans for the future. Staszic had left his position in the library to work alongside Kober, and it was Staszic's job to run the council offices in the exact same manner as he had done when he was the chief librarian. He would rule the council offices with that same iron fist, and that was exactly what Henryk Kober wanted.

There were to be no complaints or questions from any of the staff. Blind obedience was required from all. And to reinforce that obedience, Kober and Staszic always wore their black SS uniforms. No one would ever dare question a member of the German SS.

Herr Kober was rising in stature and importance, as was Herr Staszic. Both men were now given respect. More than that, they now demanded respect. Suddenly they had power, and the power to dominate others. Kober realized that he could now pass any decision he deemed necessary, within reason of course.

And with that in mind, he'd commandeered his own small squad of soldiers who would accompany him whenever need be. It was another show of his power. Whenever he and Staszic stepped out of the City Hall they were accompanied by half a dozen troops. Kober always felt gratified when he saw people scurry out of their way. And there would always be a table ready and waiting for them when he and Staszic visited the Cafe Pineska, always.

On occasion, both Kober and Staszic had been invited by Major Kruger and Igor Sym to accompany them when visiting certain Jewish households. Kruger and Sym had decided that it would be advantageous to involve Kober in the 'Jewish process', and the handling of the Ghetto, and of course what was being planned for the future. And now both Kober and Staszic were becoming used to being out of the office and dealing with saluting soldiers and questioning all those nervous and frightened people. Power was something that they'd always craved for, the power to rule others.

However, there was also a method in Kruger's decision to involve Kober in the Jewish process. He wanted and needed Kober totally onboard, because Henryk Kober was a very intelligent man. He could use Kober, but he couldn't bribe him, Igor Sym had already warned Major Kruger against that. And even though Kruger knew that in reality he could get Kober to do anything he wanted, just by barking orders at him, barking orders didn't buy loyalty. And it was loyalty that Major Wilhelm Kruger required. Undivided loyalty.

For Igor Sym, Kober had never been a problem. In fact, handling Kober had always been quite easy. Sym had simply promised Henryk Kober a future. However, Kruger would need more than promises. He would have to use some form of leverage.

The Edelman's were a wealthy Jewish family who lived in a large and well-appointed house in the elegant Piotrkowska district. One afternoon

Kruger and Sym and a dozen troops turned up at the Edelman's house and evicted them, and then they shipped the whole family off to be re-housed in the ghetto at Gadka. The Edelman's house was beautifully furnished and was staffed by a host of servants and a good cook. Once the family had been driven off in a truck, Kruger turned to Sym and offered him the house, servants and all. The state would of course, pay their wages and any other overheads. Igor Sym was overjoyed. He was being offered the opportunity to be the 'king' of his own castle. And finally, he would become the owner of his very own property. He immediately accepted Herr Kruger's kind offer. Of course he did. His allegiance to the Reich was now complete. And Major Wilhelm Kruger would later repeat that same course of action with Henryk Kober, in return for his undying loyalty.

It was a strange fact, that even though Herr Kruger could have had any property he wanted in Lodz, he chose to install himself and his German SS Staff into the imposing and historic Grand Hotel. He took a full suite on the top floor and the rest of his staff were accommodated in the rooms below. Several other of the hotel's rooms were then turned into offices.

The Hotel was in a central location and it served Major Kruger's needs, all of them. Because one of Major Kruger's most overwhelming desires was his lust for women, and Major Wilhelm Kruger had one special penchant, and that was his fondness for Slavic women. He was fascinated by them, those Eastern European beauties with their hard Slavic looks and their prominent features and high cheekbones. These were determined and tough women, who were slim and tightly built and slender and taut. They were a far cry from the females in Berlin, who were devoted to the German diet of sausages and beer and carried the telltale bulk that was regrettably associated with it.

Of an evening, Kruger would dine in the hotel restaurant, usually with some of his SS colleagues, and then afterwards they would all return to the bar. The Hotel manager was a man called Yaslov Slowowski, and he too was in Major Kruger's pay. Slowowski was an astute man, and very resourceful. And on the evenings that suited Kruger, Slowowski, the ever dutiful manager, would arrange for one or even two stunningly beautiful prostitutes to be waiting for Herr Kruger in Kruger's very private upstairs suite. They were there to pleasure Major Kruger, which they always did. And they would be insatiable, or so it seemed.

The time had come for Herr Kruger to gain Henryk Kober's friendship and true appreciation.

It had been arranged that he and Sym should take Kober to another previously owned Jewish home. It was an 'off the cuff' excuse, the excuse being that it was believed there were hidden valuables in the house which they needed to find. Herr Kruger, Sym and Kober turned up at the empty house in the middle of the afternoon, accompanied by half a dozen troops. The soldiers searched the property and obviously, nothing was found. Sym then took the troops out into the garden, leaving Herr Kruger and Kober alone. It had all been prearranged. For a while, both men discussed current council policy and some various planning details. And at that moment Major Kruger asked Kober the real question.

'What am I going to do with this property Herr Kober?' he asked.

Kober stood there for a moment, and then he shrugged.

'Well, I suppose the residents from the Gadka will eventually invade the place, once they get to know that it's become empty.'

Kruger sighed. 'Yes, I know that. But just look at this place. It's a beautiful house, it's much too good for that rabble. And it's in a much better area. It's far too good for those people and I don't really want to upset the other residents. We've had complaints in other areas after the Jews have been moved out and relocated.'

And indeed they had. Vacant Jewish homes were usually in the better areas of Lodz and there had been a public outcry when the mob from the Gadka had just marched in and taken over. The Gadka district had always been a poor area, and in truth, some of its residents were little more than gypsies.

'I know, and it 'is' becoming a problem Major,' Kober agreed.

Kruger again shrugged.

'I'm not having those people moving in here Kober. It's far too nice, just look at the place.'

Kober looked around the luxurious room that they were both standing in.

'Yes, you're right Major.' he said, 'this is a really beautiful house.'

'Actually, I've been talking to Herr Sym', Kruger then continued, 'he tells me that you live in an apartment, somewhere over in the Brzeziny district?'

Kober turned to him 'Yes I do,' he replied. He was actually quite surprised. He had always quite purposefully kept his private life to himself. Even his old friend Wilfred Staszic, had only been invited there a couple of times.

And that was the moment Kruger had been waiting for. He was about to offer Henryk Kober something that he couldn't refuse, and with it, the reward for his loyalty.

'Why don't 'you' move in here Herr Kober?' said Kruger suddenly.

Kober was speechless.

Wilhelm Kruger smiled at his own brilliance.

'Yes, and why not?' Kruger continued. 'You can have this house Kober, I'll sign all the papers and the state will hand this property over to you. The house will be yours.'

Kober couldn't believe what he was hearing. Major Kruger wanted to give him a house, this house. This big beautiful house.

Kruger shook his head assertively, and he continued.

'Herr Kober. Your work at the City Council has not gone unnoticed. You are doing a first class job there and you deserve a reward for your achievements. It is also a fact that you are now a person of some standing in this City, and it is only right and proper that you live in a more dignified property in a more affluent area. Living in some little apartment somewhere, it just won't do anymore Kober.'

Kober nodded, he was still stunned.

'You must move in here as soon as possible Herr Kober,' said Kruger. 'The house is now yours. And you'd better employ a cook and a cleaner, and probably a gardener too. Put all your expenses through the city council Herr Kober. You've certainly earned it and it's only right that the city should pay for your services.'

Henryk Kober was absolutely flabbergasted.

Herr Kruger smiled at him, and then he put his hand on Henryk Kober's shoulder.

'You are an important member of my SS team Herr Kober, and you are also a member of the Nazi Party. We look after our own Herr Kober, we always look after our own. And when you think about it, the past owners, the Jews who previously owned this property. They're never coming back are they?'

And that was it. In one stroke, Henryk Kober had been totally won over. For the first time in his life he was being rewarded and treated with kindness and respect. And at that moment he would have done anything for Major Wilhelm Kruger and the Nazi Party. And at some point, he was going to have too.

Herr Henryk Kober, a man who had been looked down on and sneered at for all of his life. A man who had been passed over but had always craved for something better. And finally his time had come. He now had power and he now owned his very own house, and it was a very good house. Yes, the Nazi Party had looked after him, and what Major Kruger had said was indeed true, they did look after their own. And for Henryk Kober, they were the only people who ever had.

The next day, Kober made a decision. He told Wilfred Staszic about the house, and then he asked Staszic if he would like to live there too. The house was huge, it wouldn't be a problem. Staszic immediately took up the offer. After all, Henryk Kober was his only friend.

It turned out to be a good move for both of them. In the evenings when Kober and Staszic had finished their dinner, both men would go into the living room to drink coffee and discuss the day. Staszic would give Kober an everyday account on how the council was running, he spent every day patrolling the different offices, always making sure that its employees were working hard and working correctly. Kober in turn, would discuss his proposed strategies with Staszic, along with his plans for future efficiencies.

Everything seemed to be going exceedingly well.

However, there was one little thing at the back of Henryk Kober's mind. It was the one thing that he'd never really forgotten, and something that he'd truly never gotten over. And as his command had grown and he'd become more confident and more powerful, he'd always known that it would just be a matter of time. And that time had finally come.

Revenge, oh sweet revenge.

The moment had become a reality and it was now time for SS Commander Herr Henryk Kober to revisit the Lodz District Rifle Club.

Kober had already spoken to Herr Kruger and Sym about the Rifle Club. At a meeting, he'd expressed his worry about the number of guns that were stored there. Were those guns to ever be stolen and then get into the wrong hands, there could be a problem. Another dilemma was the club itself. Kober described its members as aloof and arrogant. Those members would be the first to complain about the actions of the Lodz City Council, in fact, they probably already had. The club members were mainly well-off professionals who carried a certain amount of influence in Lodz. Influence that went hand in hand with their 'so-called' affluence.

Kober felt that it was 'unhealthy' for these people to have a totally private meeting place where they stored weapons and where they could actually be plotting and planning anything. These people had money, and many of them had wealthy Jewish friends. Herr Kober had described it as a complete conflict of interests.

Major Kruger was not happy when he heard about the possible Jewish connections that these people held. With money, they could help their Jewish friends to disappear, and in Kruger's eyes, that wasn't good.

Igor Sym held the same opinion as Herr Kober. The combination of guns and money was hardly acceptable to the new regime. These people could be a threat and could endanger the Nazi party's plans for Lodz and also for Poland. Any form of discontent could lead to a possible backlash. There could be a resistance. No, allowing those members to own and store weapons was not wise, definitely not. Major Kruger saw the sense in it all. He decided that the Lodz District Rifle Club must be closed down as soon as possible. The guns would have to be confiscated and the club itself would be shut down and the doors locked until further notice. In effect, indefinitely.

After the meeting, Kober spoke privately to Herr Sym. Both men shook hands.

'Didn't I tell you, Herr Kober,' said Sym, 'I told you your day would come.'
'Thank you Herr Sym,' replied Kober. 'Thank you, my friend'.

Even before the German invasion, Igor Sym knew all about the Lodz District Rifle Club. Back in the days of the PNP, Kober had sat with Igor Sym one evening and told him all about the disgraceful treatment that he had suffered at the hands of the Rifle Club members. Those 'arrogant bastards' who had dishonestly accused him of theft, and had then thrown him out of the club.

Igor Sym had listened to Kober, and he'd seen the anger. It was an anger that he would use.

'You will have your revenge Herr Kober,' he'd said, 'I promise you. Work with me, and you will have your day.'

And now that day had arrived.

Kober chose a Saturday afternoon, which was when the club would be at its busiest.

Kober knew that, because of his past but very brief association there. Kober and Staszic had discussed their strategy, Staszic being very well aware of his friend's feelings in the matter.

Kober and Staszic were driven to the Rifle Club in a staff car, accompanied by three other SS guards, one of which was the driver. Along with them were twenty German soldiers, who followed behind in two canvas-covered trucks. Everyone was armed.

The club itself was a large and ageing, single storey stone building that had at one time been used as council offices. Long ago it had been had been taken over by the Lodz District Rifle Club, so long in fact, that nobody really knew what its previous use had been. The club had been split into a shooting range, a gymnasium, some changing rooms and of course the bar area. There were also several other rooms and offices that were used for administration and secure storage. The building was actually deceptively large.

Once they'd arrived, Kober and Staszic took charge and marched in through the front doors, along with their SS Guards and the soldiers.

They strode through the club and straight into the crowded bar. The stunned and amazed members there just stared on in disbelief.

'Silence!' Kober shouted at the top of his voice.

Everyone in the room froze.

'You will all stay silent while I give you your instructions. Nobody will speak.'

Nobody even moved.

Kober continued, 'I am under instruction from the highest authority to shut this club down immediately, until further notice.'

There were immediate mumblings from the shocked and rather confused members.

'You will be silent,' Kober again shouted. 'You people will obey my orders.'

Once again the room froze.

'Firstly, you will all collect your rifles and any other guns and ammunition, and you will take them outside and hand them over to my troops,' Kober ordered. 'You will then stand in line while we take your details.'

At that moment some of the members suddenly began to recognize Herr Kober, and the mumbling started again as word was passed around.

Kober heard his name being mentioned. It was the moment he'd been waiting for.

'Ah, so some of you remember me,' he said out loud. 'That's good, that is very good. And now you will have the chance to remember me even more. You arrogant fools will have to learn some new lessons. To you all, I am now 'Herr Kober' of the German SS. You will follow my orders or you will be punished, and severely punished. Go and get your rifles and bring them outside please gentlemen, or I may let my soldiers shoot some of you.'

And he let those last words dwell for a moment.

'Now go immediately!' Kober ordered.

There was some slight disarray as the members put down their drinks and as ordered, went to collect their rifles. Several of the soldiers went to accompany them.

Kober and Staszic then went outside, followed by the rest of their troops. A desk was commandeered and was also brought outside, along with the club's membership books. The books contained each and every one of the member's names and addresses and their personal details. All of this had been carefully planned by Kober and Staszic, and having these people stand in a line and awaiting orders was an excellent form of humiliation. It had a humbling effect. But more was to come.

The club members came outside carrying their prized rifles and ammunition. The ammunition was loaded onto the back of the trucks, but the rifles were stacked up in a large pile on the ground. The members were then made to form an orderly queue at the desk, and as they all stood there, one of the soldiers poured a can of petrol over the rifles and then set fire to them.

It was a bonfire. Handcrafted rifles that were worth fortunes went up in flames. Their seasoned stocks burned fiercely, only to leave blackened and warped barrels that had once been used to shoot so accurate and true.

Staszic stood at the desk, taking people's names and checking them with the entries in the members books. Their names and addresses were all then written down. The three SS guards stood at the side of him as a menacing presence.

But for Herr Henryk Kober it wasn't over. The best was yet to come.

He folded his arms and began to slowly stroll down the line of unhappy, dejected members. And as he moved along the line he looked into the faces of the people who had once despised him, and he saw it in their eyes. They still despised him, but now there was nothing they could do, because he had the power, and it was he who was now in control.

And then he stopped. He stopped dead in his tracks, because there they were. Standing in front of him, trying their best not to be noticed were the two men who had accused him of the theft. The two men who had lied and had falsely accused him of stealing an expensive rifle, the two men who had caused him to be humiliated and thrown out of their prestigious 'Lodz District Rifle Club'. And now he'd caught the bastards.

'Guards,' Herr Kober immediately called out.

The three SS guards, dressed in their black uniforms, moved forward.

'Arrest these two men,' Herr Kober commanded. 'Put them in the back of the truck.'

The guards dragged both men out of the line and pushed them in the direction of the two trucks.

As the two men were being led away a voice spoke out. A man called out after them.

'Stop,' he shouted. The man who had spoken out loud was Isaac Milosv.

Isaac Milosv was around sixty years old, slightly built and with thinning grey hair. He was a long standing and well known member of the Lodz District Rifle Club. He was also a defence lawyer who had worked ceaselessly over the years at the Lodz District Central Courts.

Isaac Milosv was a dedicated liberal who had stood up and defended the rights of the individual for most of his life. He saw the invasion of his country by the Germans as a disgrace, and he looked upon Adolph Hitler as the madman who was going to plunge Europe into flames. And now this gang of Nazis had burst into a private club, his private club, and they'd burned and destroyed everyone's precious rifles and they were now dragging away two of the club members to god only knew where?

It was all too much. And it was certainly too much for Isaac Milosv.

Milosv left the queue where he's been standing and he strode over to Henryk Kober.

He took a deep breath and stared Kober straight in the face.

'This is outrageous,' said Milosv in a loud voice. 'What the hell do you think you're doing? You've come here and you've destroyed valuable property. You are illegally trying to close a private club, and now you think that you can arrest its members without a warrant or a charge. This is ridiculous. You simply cannot do this.'

For a brief moment, Kober just stared back at Isaac Milosv. Then he turned to his SS Guards and nodded to one of them. The guard came forward. And as he did he lifted his rifle and in one quick movement he swung it around and smashed the rifle's wooden butt straight into Isaac Milosv's open face. There was an awful crunch as Milosv's nose and face was broken and crushed. Milosv gave a slight groan as he collapsed to the floor. The guard then kicked and stamped on Milosv's head with the heel of his jackboot, leaving the poor man severely damaged and unconscious. There were copious amounts of bright red blood pouring from Milsov's mouth, his nose and ears, and his teeth had been smashed out of all recognition.

The assault on Isaac Milosv had an immediate consequence. Some of the members turned away in disgust. Others just stood there, shocked at the realization of what was happening, along with the possibility of what could happen to them. Suddenly, all were fearful. Some were terrified.

Herr Kober then spoke to his SS Guard.

'Put him in the back of the truck with those other two,' Kober ordered.

Isaac Milosv had to be carried to one of the trucks. For him, life would never be the same.

Isaac Milosv had been one of Lodz's leading defence lawyers, but now it was all over. And as he was carried away, most of his friends and his acquaintances from the club couldn't even contemplate whether Milosv was actually dead or alive.

Kober's voice suddenly caught everyone's attention.

'You will all be processed and then you can go home. Do not bother to return. Your days at this club are over.'

This time there was no outcry.

Kober looked at the rest of the line of members. There was no one of any interest. He walked over to Herr Staszic to have a few words with him and then he went back into the club.

He wanted a few moments on his own to gloat privately.

Kober walked into the empty bar. He stood there with his hands on his hips and looked around, and then he smiled. He went behind the bar and found a glass and poured himself a very large brandy. Standing there alone, he revelled in his success. He drank to celebrate everything he'd manage to achieve. Then he took another drink, simply because he was proud of himself. Kober picked up the bottle of brandy and then he went for a stroll around the club.

It was his club now. And he could do whatever he liked.

Outside, Herr Staszic continued to process the remaining member's names and addresses as the line of men continued to move slowly forward.

Near the back of the line stood Doctor Franz Szabo, with him was his son Pieter.

And unknowingly, Pieter Szabo was standing in a queue that was going to bring him face to face with Herr Wilfred Staszic, the man who he had once severely beaten and then threatened with his life. Strangely, both Pieter Szabo and Herr Wilfred Staszic were completely unaware of each other's presence. After the incident in the library, Pieter had never seen or sought out Wilfred Staszic ever again. The same could be said of Staszic, who without doubt never wanted to meet up with Pieter ever again. Staszic had never forgotten the beating. And the memories of it, and the threats from Pieter Szabo of further violence and murder, still haunted him.

Slowly, the line of members continued to move forward.

The SS guards loaded Kober's two accusers and the still unconscious lawyer, Isaac Milosv, into the back of the truck. The unhappy accusers were handcuffed and the SS guards left two of the other regular soldiers to keep an eye on them. The SS guards then went back to find Herr Kober, and after speaking to Herr Staszic they walked over to the club and went inside.

They eventually found Herr Kober, who took his guards back to the bar and shared his bottle of brandy with them. The operation had been a complete success and they could now all celebrate. Kober was in high spirits, he was elated. In his eyes, justice had finally been served.

Pieter Szabo had just entered the bar when Herr Kober had marched into the club and had started issuing his orders. Pieter had recognized and remembered Henryk Kober, and he also remembered Kober being barred from the club because of the theft of one of the rifles. It had been a bit of a scandal, the talk of the club. But now Herr Kober was a member of the SS and things had changed. Kober was now in charge. And Pieter realized that Kober now wanted retribution, and that was what this was all about, Kober wanted his revenge.

But unfortunately, Pieter had completely forgotten about Kober's association with Wilfred Staszic. And why would he remember? He'd only ever seen Kober together with Staszic on that one evening when both men had sat together at the Cafe Pineska. And at that time Pieter had never realized that Kober and Staszic were such good friends.

He'd had other things on his mind.

Outside, Herr Staszic took down another man's name and address.

Standing further down the line, Doctor Franz Szabo was trying his best to pacify his son.

Pieter and his father had waited and queued with the rest of the Rifle Club members as they'd been ushered out of the club and been made to stand in the line outside as the ridiculous charade continued. But then the incident with the two members and then the vicious beating of poor Isaac Milosv had taken place and Pieter had almost erupted with anger. His father had to physically restrain him before Pieter did something regrettable and stupid. Pieter eventually calmed himself down, but he stood in the line, morose and angry and deep in thought.

Pieter had a secret, a secret that was his alone. He had already killed two men, two men who deserved to die. And Pieter was capable of more, so very much more. And though his parents knew nothing about their son' past dealings, both of his sisters certainly did. But nothing had ever been said. And at that moment, Pieter Szabo was already making plans. If Isaac Milosv died, Pieter would find Kober and he would kill him, of that he had no doubt in his mind. As a young man, Pieter had been introduced to Mr Milosv at the rifle club and had respected him for the good and upstanding man that he'd always been.

Pieter made a decision. There would be no place for Henryk Kober to hide.

By a strange twist of fate, only one of Pieter's guns had been destroyed in the fire, and he was still in possession of his second rifle. It was Pieter' habit to store his guns at home. Unlike most of the other members, including his father, Pieter was quite prepared to carry his rifles to and from the Rifle Club. It was a long-standing habit that he'd gotten used to. Pieter would spend hours and hours at the club, honing his skills. It was his ambition to be the best. He would usually take both of his rifles with him, his faithful old Karabinek and also his superb Mauser 98. He'd used his old Karibinek from being a boy, but when his father had realized Pieter's talent he'd purchased the Mauser 98 for his son. The Mauser was one of the finest rifles that money could buy. Pieter treasured both of his guns, and at home he would constantly disassemble the rifles to lubricate and polish the parts and then reassemble them with care. Pieter knew each and every individual moving part belonging to either of his guns, and his other reason for taking the rifles home with him was to practice his shooting and his stance. He and his father had set up a small shooting range at the rear of their large garden and would use it at the times when it didn't affect the neighbours. An important part of that practice was to improve his stance. Pieter had spent hours standing and holding the rifle in the shooting position. It took strength to hold a rifle for long periods. Over the years Pieter had built up an impressive amount of strength in his upper arms and shoulders, and once a rifle could be held effortlessly, the shooter could concentrate on his aim and his target, and finally, the shot.

But on the day that Herr Kober and his soldiers had marched into the Lodz District Rifle Club, Pieter had only brought one of his rifles with him, his trusted old Karibinek. On that particular afternoon he'd set off late to the club, his father had driven over there earlier and Pieter had made his own way there and arrived late, and because of that and because he would only have around an hour's shooting, he'd only taken the one rifle with him To take both would have been a complete waste of time and effort. So he'd picked up his old Karibinek, which was already in its usual canvas holder, and he'd slung it over his shoulder and set off for the club where his father would be waiting for him.

Pieter had watched, seething in anger, as one of the German soldiers had thrown his trusty old rifle into the flames. It had been Pieter's first proper rifle, the rifle that had served him so well. Over the years he'd honed his skills with that gun. He knew every inch of the weapon and it was like an old friend to him. And as he'd watched his rifle blacken and burn, the beginnings of an idea had formed in Pieter Szabo's mind. This was all wrong. The Polish people had done nothing to deserve all of this. The Germans had no right to invade Poland and treat innocent people this way. Something had to be done. And it struck Pieter that surely there must be someone thinking the same as him, and that somewhere there must be a resistance or people out there forming some kind of resistance, there had to be. And a thought came into his mind. Whoever and wherever those people were, he would search them out. They were the people who were willing to fight against the German occupation, and he would join them. Pieter knew that back at his home he had another rifle, a superb rifle that he could use with great efficiency. Pieter Szabo had the skills, and at that moment he made a decision. He would become a sniper, an assassin.

The line of men continued to move forwards as Wilfred Staszic stood at his desk and took their particulars. And then the inevitable, Franz and Pieter Szabo stepped forward.

At first, Herr Staszic never even looked up.

'You're name?' Herr Stazic asked.

'Franz and Pieter Szabo, we're father and son,' Franz Szabo replied politely.

'And you're address?' Herr Staszic then asked as he scribbled their names into his book.

'We live at number 95 on the Poznanska Road. It's in the Dabrowski District.'

'And your work?' asked Herr Staszic

'I'm a Doctor,' Franz Szabo replied. Staszic gave a small nod, a slight show of respect.

'And you, your work?' he said to Pieter Szabo, though at that moment Herr Staszic had still not bothered to look up from his writing. There was a short pause, and then Franz Szabo once again spoke for his son.

'He's training to be a draughtsman,' he said.

Something caught in Herr Staszic's mind. It was almost an annoyance. Could the young man not speak up for himself?

And at that moment Herr Staszic looked up from his book.

Staszic was about to chastise the boy for his silence and his ignorance, and he was already speaking the words as he looked across at the young man standing in front of him.

'Your father says you're a trainee draughtsman. Is that correct?'

Pieter had been staring down at the ground. He'd been thinking about his own plans and not really been listening to the jack booted thug standing in front of him. But suddenly he'd been prompted, and he glanced up.

'Yes,' Pieter replied rather resentfully. 'Yes, I'm a trainee draughtsman.'

Pieter glanced up at Herr Staszic for only a moment, but what he took in was a uniformed man dressed all in black. The man of course, was wearing an SS commander's hat and uniform, and with it all the usual Nazi regalia. But Pieter was still angry over everything that had happened and he didn't wish to speak to the SS officer for any longer than he had to. So he looked down at the ground once more as his father, Franz Szabo, held his breath.

But if Pieter Szabo had looked properly, and he'd taken notice, he would have been astounded.

However, Herr Staszic just stood there in shock.

He couldn't believe it. He couldn't believe who he was looking at. Standing there in front of him was his most feared nemesis. Standing there was the man who had beaten him so badly that it had nearly destroyed him. Here was the man who had almost traumatized Wilfred Staszic beyond belief.

Staszic stood there, and in that instant he was once again terrified. He couldn't control his fear, he couldn't speak, and he couldn't continue to write. He just stared back at Pieter Szabo. Staszic's right hand suddenly began to shake and his breathing became erratic and for a brief moment he wondered if he was going to pass out or that his brain was going to explode.

Herr Wilfred Staszic just stood there, paralyzed with fear, and stunned and helpless.

Franz Szabo held his breath.

He could see that there was something very wrong. But Franz Szabo's worries were for all the wrong reasons. Franz Szabo stared at Herr Staszic, and he thought he saw anger and amazement in the SS Officer's eyes, amazement at his son's attitude with a Nazi officer. Pieter's somewhat 'remote aloofness' was going to get the boy into trouble, Franz was sure of it. Pieter's curt reply and his manner in addressing Herr Staszic were quite discourteous and could be perceived as impolite.

Franz Szabo swallowed and he readied himself to speak on his son's behalf. He was going to apologize for his son's rudeness and he was readying himself to verbally chastise his son in front of the officer, by way of an excuse, hoping that Pieter would come to his senses and apologize.

And in a sudden moment of panic, Franz Szabo was even prepared to physically slap Pieter as a pretext of his own annoyance. Better that he beat his son, rather than his son being arrested and then being beaten by others. Franz Szabo stood there, waiting.

But nothing happened.

Herr Staszic just stared at Pieter Szabo for what seemed a full minute, but still nothing happened.

Wilfred Staszic had started to sweat. It was the middle of the afternoon and it was cool, but still he started to sweat, and for all the wrong reasons.

And at that moment, Staszic was lost. He just stood there feeling helpless and distressed. He didn't know what to do. He had to think, but in his head his thoughts were spinning.

'Think damn you...think!'

He quickly stared back at Pieter Szabo, he was almost too frightened to look at him for fear of that promised retribution. But Pieter Szabo just continued to look down at the ground, his mind elsewhere. And then Wilfred Staszic realized something. He suddenly understood why Pieter Szabo didn't recognize him. And Staszic suddenly saw a ray of hope and a chance to escape his awful predicament. Staszic had suddenly grasped the situation, and he realized that Pieter Szabo didn't recognize him because he was wearing his full SS uniform. And why would he remember? They'd only met that one time in the library. Staszic unconsciously shuddered as he remembered that awful night. And now standing here in front of him was the perpetrator of that terrible beating, and with it the threat of being murdered.

Suddenly Staszic had to get away, he knew he had to. If their conversation carried on there was the chance that Pieter Szabo would look up and this time he would recognize him.

Staszic had to get away.

Trying his best to appear somewhat nonchalant, Herr Staszic casually turned to the other SS officer who was standing nearby.

'Take over here will you,' he said to the officer, 'I have to speak to Herr Kober.'

The officer dutifully obeyed, and Herr Staszic turned and walked towards the clubhouse.

It was over. And though he felt like running, Herr Staszic slowly walked away.

Meeting Pieter Szabo for the second time in his life had actually taken less than four minutes. But in that short time, Wilfred Staszic had relived every second of that terrible night in the library.

The SS officer looked at Franz Szabo and his son and he checked their details in Herr Staszic's book. There were the names, the address and their occupations. It was enough.

The officer looked over their shoulder.

'Next!' he ordered.

Franz and Pieter Szabo walked away in complete silence. After twenty yards Franz Szabo turned to his son.

'You bloody fool! What the hell were you thinking?'

Pieter looked at his father with some surprise.

'You idiot' Franz continued. 'Are you completely stupid?'

Pieter Szabo was slightly shocked at his father's outburst.

'What do you mean?' he said.

Franz Szabo took a deep breath.

'You're attitude to that SS officer, you were rude to him, and you completely ignored him.'

Pieter turned to his father.

'I don't care,' he replied. 'You saw how they beat up poor Mr Milosv, they may have killed him. And look how they arrested those other two members for absolutely nothing. These Nazis are bastards. They can't treat people this way.'

Franz Szabo stopped and he suddenly gripped his son's arm.

'Listen Pieter, these people can do whatever they want to do. They're rounding up all of our Jewish friends and putting them into the ghetto. And now they've started to clear the ghetto too, they're sending everyone to the Concentration camps. We have friends that are going to be locked up there indefinitely and then god only knows what. We may never see those people again. They will never be allowed to return to their homes in Lodz, never. And it's not just the Jews either, any political activists, the dissenters, they're getting sent there too. And there are the rumours that they're turning those camps into 'Death' camps. Anyone who doesn't follow the rules will get themselves into serious trouble.'

'I don't care,' said Pieter loudly, too loudly, 'I'm not bowing down to those pigs.'

Franz grabbed hold of his son's shoulder.

'Shut up Pieter, do you want to get us arrested?'

Pieter shrugged, 'I don't care.'

Franz Szabo was incensed at his son's careless attitude.

'And what about your mother and your sisters? And what about your wife, Pieter? What about Francine, do you not care about her either?'

Pieter stood there breathing heavily, he was so angry.

'And what about me?' Franz Szabo continued, 'Do I want to see my only son disappear? What are you thinking of Pieter?'

At that point, Pieter Szabo suddenly capitulated to his father's words. He understood his father's warning and then he sighed and nodded in respect as he relented.

'I'm sorry Father,' Pieter replied, 'I wasn't thinking. I was just so angry over what's happened. And now the club's to be closed. It's over, it's finished.'

Franz Szabo shook his head at the hopelessness of it all.

'Yes, and our beautiful rifles, all burned and destroyed.'

At that moment, Pieter was going to tell his father that he still had his Mauser Karabiner, and that his superbly crafted rifle was still back at their home. But something stopped him. Something in his mind told him not to tell his father. And the more Pieter thought about it, the less that his father knew, the better.

Franz Szabo took a deep breath.

'Pieter, we're all going to have to learn to keep quiet and try to get on with our lives. It's the only way. The Germans have now overrun us and they rule us. We can only hope that things will settle down and that eventually we can get back to some sort of normality, but at the moment we're going to have to learn to keep our mouths shut or we could get into trouble, all of us.'

Franz Szabo was trying to give his son a warning and Pieter recognized that.

'Yes father, Pieter replied dutifully, 'I realize that. The Germans are now running things and there's nothing we can do about it.'

And with that, they walked back to their car and quietly made their way home.

But Pieter Szabo was lying to his father.

Pieter had no intention at all of cowering to those 'Nazi bastards', and he had no intention of just standing by while these invaders destroyed people's lives. Not one bit.

Yes, he'd agreed with his father, just to keep the peace. But he had no intention of honouring that promise.

No one knew what Pieter was capable of, nobody. But Pieter did, and he had no problem whatsoever in killing people, none at all. He'd already murdered without any doubts or any misgivings. In fact, killing a person who deserved to die gave him an immense sense of satisfaction.

So with that in mind, once they returned home, Pieter pulled up one of the floorboards in their old garden shed and he then wrapped his Mauser rifle in its canvas carrier, along with some boxes of ammunition, and he hid them under there. He also put the remainder of the money that he'd salvaged from the 'ill-fated' bank manager, Karl Brenner, and he hid that there too.

Pieter Szabo had plans. Plans for revenge.

However, the events of his past were about to overtake him.

Herr Wilfred Staszic made his way directly to the clubhouse. He had to get away. He had to get away from Pieter Szabo before he was recognized. Staszic almost ran into the club. Once inside there, he would be safe.

As he entered through the main doors of the building he heard the noise. It was the sound of men talking and laughing, and that gave Staszic a degree of comfort. It was more a question of safety in numbers. He straightaway walked into the bar area where all the noise was coming from. Leaning on the bar and drinking brandy was Herr Kober, along with the two other SS guards. Surrounding them were most of the other German soldiers, who all seemed to be drinking beer. Herr Kober was busily talking to the SS guards and when he saw Staszic enter the room he immediately hailed him over. He shook Staszic's hand with a certain amount of glee.

'We've done it Herr Staszic,' said Kober out loud, 'we have accomplished our mission. This club is finished, it's now closed down and all those weapons have been disposed of and are no longer a danger or a threat.'

Staszic smiled weakly, as Herr Kober poured him a glass of brandy. Kober then raised his own glass and gave a toast to everyone for the success of their mission. Glasses clinked and the men cheered.

Kober then took Staszic to one side. He was overjoyed

'We've done it, Wilfred,' he said and he grinned, 'I've finally had my revenge. I've finally given those bastards a slap in the face. Did you see them Wilfred, all lined up like frightened children? And did you see their pathetic faces when I burned their precious bloody rifles, and then the 'icing on the cake', when I caught those two lying swines, standing in line trying their best not to be seen. Did you see the look on their faces when I had them arrested?'

Staszic looked at Kober.

'I'm really happy for you Henryk,' he replied, 'you've fought hard and long for this, and now you've finally got your justice.'

Herr Kober smiled at his friend. Yes, it had taken a long time. All the effort and the planning and the waiting, but it had been worth it, because now at last, he was running things. There was even more work to do. This was just the beginning.

Herr Kober raised his glass to his friend.

'To the future Wilfred, and to our glorious future.'

Staszic raised his glass too, and at that moment Henryk Kober noticed something.

Wilfred Staszic's hand was trembling. And as Kober watched him, Staszic's hand began to shake. So much so that Staszic had to put his glass back down on the bar again.

Kober stared at his friend, but Staszic looked away in embarrassment.

'What on earth is wrong Wilfred?' Kober asked him.

Staszic just shook his head, but he couldn't face his friend.

Kober put his hand on Staszic's arm. He could see that Staszic was upset, but why? This was supposed to be their moment of triumph. This was something that they'd discussed and talked about at length and something that they'd both planned. This should have been their own personal celebration, but here was his friend Staszic, falling apart in front of him.

'Wilfred,' said Kober again, quietly. 'Talk to me. Tell me what's wrong.'

Staszic slowly turned to face him, and to Kober's utter dismay, his friend had tears in his eyes.

'My god, Wilfred,' said Kober, 'what on earth is wrong?'

Staszic took a deep breath and he stared back at Henryk Kober.

'Not here,' he replied, 'I can't talk to you here.'

Kober looked around the bar, by that time most of the German soldiers were in there and were enjoying themselves. He commandeered the nearest soldier and told him to find half a dozen bottles of brandy and put them into the back of the staff car. The soldier was then given instructions that he would be driving Herr Kober and Herr Staszic home immediately, and then he should return to the Rifle Club to pick up the other SS guards.

Herr Kober then turned around to address to the rest of the troops.

'Attention everybody... Attention!' he called out in a loud voice.

There was an immediate lull in the general conversation.

'Gentlemen,' he spoke out loud. 'Gentlemen, you have done well this afternoon, the operation has been a complete success. And now I will give you your final orders. As a reward, you will now drink every bit of alcohol that remains in this club, every last drop.'

There was suddenly great laughter, glasses were banged on the bar top and a cheer started up from the men. Kober had to wave his hands in an effort to maintain the silence.

Then he spoke again.

'And then gentlemen, once you have finished drinking, I want you to smash this club to pieces.' Kober stopped for a moment as he looked around at his troops.

'But now listen to me, all of you,' he continued, 'I want you to destroy this club, but there must be no burning and there must be no fires, none at all. I want this club closing down permanently, but I do not want the building destroyed. Do I make myself clear?'

There was a certain amount of agreement and a nodding of heads

'Smash everything,' he said loudly, 'starting with this bar and then demolish the rest of the club. I don't want to see one piece of furniture left standing here, not one single chair. Do you understand?'

Again there was agreement.

Kober then stood to attention and raised his arm in salute.

You have all done exceedingly well...'Heil Hitler!'

The German soldiers stood together as one and returned his salute, 'Heil Hitler'.

Staszic collected the club membership books and then he and Kober returned home in relative silence. It was impossible for them to speak openly while the driver was still present. Once home, Kober had the driver carry the case of brandy into the living room. Kober and Staszic followed him and then the driver was dismissed with the usual salute.

'Sit down by the fire Wilfred,' said Kober, 'I'll pour us two brandies and then we'll talk.'

Staszic put down the books and walked over to his regular chair, a large comfortable leather Chesterfield. He sat there for a moment, looking into the large open fire, watching the flames dance along the evenly burning logs. There was the clink from the glasses as Kober sat down opposite him. Kober leant forwards and passed Staszic a full glass of brandy.

'Cheers my friend,' he said to Staszic. Staszic raised his glass to toast his friend and then he took a large gulp of his brandy. It tasted good and he could feel its heat as he drank. Both men then sat there, silently sipping their drinks. The room was warm and comfortable and was subtly illuminated by the flames from the fire and from a large lamp that stood in a corner. Kober and Staszic had spent many hours there, discussing their plans and their futures. It was so comfortable. It was their place of solace. And it was Kober who finally spoke.

'Do you want to talk about it, Wilfred?' Kober finally asked.

Staszic said nothing. He just continued to stare silently into the flames.

Kober sipped his brandy and he waited.

'What is wrong Wilfred, tell me please?' he then asked.

Finally, Staszic turned to his friend.

'I've had a bit of a shock, that's all,' he replied.

'Well something's obviously troubled you,' said Kober, 'I've never seen you so upset.'

Staszic just nodded, but he remained silent.

'Can't you tell me what's happened, Wilfred?' Kober asked again, 'Surely I can help you.'

Staszic suddenly took a deep breath. He would tell Kober everything.

'It was this afternoon Henryk,' said Staszic, 'At the club, when we were dealing with all the members, when we were taking their names and their details.'

Kober nodded, yes he remembered.

'Yes Wilfred,' he said, 'what about it'?

Wilfred Staszic took a drink from his glass of brandy and he stared at Kober.

'He was there Henryk,' said Staszic suddenly, 'He was there at the club.'

Kober frowned.

'Who was?' he asked.

Just as he was about to reply, Wilfred Staszic's hands began to shake again, and Kober again witnessed it.

Staszic suddenly blurted it out.

'It was him Henryk, I know it was. I would recognize him anywhere.'

Staszic suddenly grasped his glass with both hands to stop himself from spilling the brandy.

'It was him,' he continued. 'It was the man who beat me, Henryk, the man who attacked me that night in the library and beat me half to death.'

At that point, Staszic took another gulp of brandy from his shaking glass.

'What!' said Henryk Kober out loud.

Staszic took another drink, and for a moment he couldn't speak. But Henryk Kober did.

'You mean to tell me that 'bastard' was there at the club? And that he is one of the members?'

'Yes,' Staszic replied. 'Yes, he is.'

'Why on earth didn't you tell me, Wilfred, why didn't you come and find me? And why didn't you have him detained? We could have arrested him there and then.'

Staszic just sat there staring at Kober, he was becoming emotional.

'I just couldn't,' Staszic replied nervously, 'I just couldn't Henryk. You see, I was so shocked to see him there. I never expected it. I never expected to see him again. I've never wanted to ever see him again.'

And at that moment the tears began to well up in Wilfred Staszic's eyes.

'You see Henryk, I've never told you this, but I'm frightened of that man. On the night that he beat me and he threatened to kill me, he absolutely terrified me. I was shattered by the experience. At one point I thought that I was going to have some sort of nervous breakdown over what happened, I can't tell you just how much it upset me. And in truth, it still does. I've never forgotten that night Henryk. I don't think that I ever will.'

Kober watched his friend suffer. And yes, he remembered how badly Staszic had been beaten, cruelly beaten. And he remembered having to look after Staszic, and in what a terrible state he'd been in. And as Kober looked across at his friend he started to become angry. Staszic had nearly died that night, and whoever this bastard was who'd attacked him, had nearly killed Kober's one and only true friend. Kober was angry. But he would have to handle everything correctly, and he had to look after his friend. He could see that Staszic was in turmoil, and he needed Wilfred Staszic, he and Staszic had formed a working partnership. Staszic patrolled the council offices and saw everything. Staszic was incredibly efficient in his manner and always had been. And Kober had plans, bigger plans for both himself and Staszic, but not with Staszic in the condition he was in at that moment. Kober realized exactly what he had to do. He had to once more instil in Wilfred Staszic a sense of pride and confidence, and also leadership. He had to help his friend, Wilfred Staszic, to destroy his personal demon.

Kober reached over and put his arm on Staszic's shoulder, so as to reassure him.

'Wilfred' he said.

Staszic looked up.

'Let's talk about what happened on that evening, Wilfred,' he said, 'I know we've spoken before about that particular night, but I just need to talk to you again.'

Staszic sat there in silence, but Kober continued.

'On the evening you walked into the library to find your librarian, what was her name again?'

'Francine...Miss Francine Korczac,' said Staszic. And Kober noticed that Staszic had still used her Christian name first and then her full name. And that in itself told a story.

'Yes,' said Kober, 'Miss Korczak. Well Wilfred, on that evening when you walked into the library and found Miss Korczak and her boyfriend openly copulating on the floor, and you were quite rightfully horrified. Am I right?'

Staszic nodded as he remembered the disgusting memory of it all.

'What if she was being raped, Wilfred?' asked Kober

'What do you mean?' Staszic replied.

'What would you have done if Miss Korczak was being raped by this man?' Kober again asked.

Staszic thought about it for a moment, and then he gave an honest answer. 'I would have had to intervene of course.'

'Of course,' said Kober, 'and then presumably there would have been some sort of tussle and that man would have probably still beaten you.'

Staszic nodded. 'I suppose so,' he said.

'And after that, you would have informed the authorities and had the man arrested.'

'Yes, I would,' said Staszic.

'And that was because he was acting illegally, because rape is an illegal act,' said Kober.

'Yes,' replied Stazic.

'But it wasn't rape was it?' said Kober. 'It was consensual sex, because they were both fucking each other on the library floor. They were both having consensual sex in a public library, a public place. And not only that, they were in 'your' library Wilfred. They were both having consensual sex in a public building, and that Wilfred, is illegal, totally illegal. And when you tried, quite rightly, to remonstrate with them you were beaten and you were beaten severely.'

Staszic could only agree.

'So' Kober continued. 'You caught two people committing a crime, an illegal act in a public place and you were beaten for it. So why didn't you inform the authorities? That is the question? Kober continued to look directly at his friend....'I'll tell you why you didn't, I'll tell you why you didn't have that thug arrested. Because of lost loyalties Wilfred, that's why. Young Miss Korczak had wheedled her way into your affections and she'd led you on. She had become your 'little star' librarian because she was chasing her career. She knew damn well that you would have given her a promotion and a first-class reference if need be.'

Kober stopped for a moment to let it all sink in.

'Wilfred, let me say something to you, and I don't want you to feel embarrassed. I know that you had 'feelings' for this young woman, and I realize that you were looking for more than just a friendship, maybe even the possibility of making her your wife. And that's a natural enough assumption, and there's nothing at all wrong with that at all. But some women are very clever, and you won't be the first man to be duped by some deceitful young lady who blinks her eyelashes and smiles all the time. She led you on Wilfred. All the time that she was smiling at you, she was seeing this other man, and she was having sex with him. She didn't care about you Wilfred, and in fact, she was laughing at you. And ask yourself the question? She would see you leave the library, knowing damn well that her boyfriend would arrive later. And then they would end up having sex on your library floor. It was an insult to you Wilfred, you'd been good to that girl. You'd looked after her.'

Staszic sat there listening to his friend, and it was all the truth. Yes, he'd had feelings for Francine Korczak, and more than that, he'd fallen in love with her. And the memory of her being naked on the library floor and her screaming in ecstasy with that man on top of her was more than he could bear to think about. But now all those memories came flooding back to him. And yes, he had looked after Francine Korczak, it was true, and she in turn, had made a fool out of him. And she'd just stood there and watched as he'd been beaten by her lover. She'd never loved him, never. Kober was right, of course he was right.

And suddenly Wilfred Staszic became angry, and suddenly and after all that had happened, he hated Francine Korczak for what she'd done to him, and he despised her.

Staszic took a deep breath.

'You're absolutely right Henryk,' he said to Kober, 'and yes, you were right all along. I did have feelings for her. That bitch of a woman cheated on me.'

'Yes,' said Kober quickly, 'Miss Korczak knew exactly what she was doing. She used you Wilfred. They should have both been arrested. Their lewd 'goings on' in your library were bad enough, and it was illegal of course. But the physical beating that you sustained was totally unacceptable. I'll always remember how I had to nurse you back to health, Wilfred, only I know how much you suffered.'

Staszic looked across at his friend.

'Yes I know Henryk, and I am eternally grateful. I think you truly saved my life.'

Kober in turn. nodded to Staszic. Yes, his plan was finally working.

'But now Wilfred,' Kober continued, 'now we are at another time and these are different days. And now Wilfred, we are in charge. Your assailant got away with it Wilfred, or at least he thought he did. That man nearly killed you, and he was guilty of an assault on you, and in my mind, he still is. And now we know who that bastard is and we know where he lives. It's time for you to have your revenge my friend. You must never forget how much he hurt you. We in the Nazi party have long memories too. We have both fought long and hard to get where we are Wilfred, and we will no longer be bullied and we will no longer let people laugh at us behind our backs, not anymore. Always remember Wilfred, we in the Nazi party look after our own.'

Wilfred Staszic quickly nodded at his friend. Kober's words were working. Staszic could see the truth in it all now and he was becoming angrier as Kober's words fuelled his memory. However, there was a problem.

'How would we prove that he assaulted me?' asked Staszic. 'After all, there were no other witnesses.'

'We are at a point where 'we' don't need witnesses, we don't have to prove anything,' Kober replied. And then he gave the matter a little consideration.

'However Wilfred, you may be right. The members of the rifle club are well connected and there may be one or two smart lawyers there who would defend him in court, and that could be a lengthy process. No, there may be a better way. Who is this man anyway?'

'I have his name and address in the membership books,' said Staszic. 'He apparently lives with his family, his father was with him. I have the address.'

Staszic stood up went to retrieve the club's membership books.

When he returned and sat down again with Kober and turned the pages of his files.

'Ah, here it is,' said Staszic, 'Number 95, on the Poznanska Road, in the Dabrowski District.'

'I know it,' said Kober. 'It's quite a good area.'

'His name is Pieter Szabo,' said Staszic. 'His father is Franz Szabo, a doctor apparently.'

Kober suddenly smiled, he had a plan. It was perfect.

'Write their names and their address on a separate sheet of paper for me will you please, and then we'll dine. I think the cook's prepared us some of her special goulash.'

Kober and Staszic ate heartily that night, the goulash was accompanied with a good bottle of strong Hungarian wine and they then drank some more of the brandy that had been taken from the rifle club.

Kober lay in bed that night, full of good food and drink and ideas. The Poznanska Road in the Dabrowski District was a wealthy area.

There would be a reward for him there, unquestionably so. Because where there was wealth, there would also be Jews.

CHAPTER 6

The next day Kober commandeered two of his SS guards. He gave them explicit instructions. They were to go with another two regular German soldiers and make their way to the Dabrowski District. Once there they were to call at every house on the Poznanska Road, including the Szabo residence. They were there to determine whether any Jewish families were still living in that district. Some of the houses were closed up, but there was always the suspicion that someone may still be living there. The neighbours would, of course, know any of the Jewish families who were in hiding. It was so obvious.

The SS guards and the soldiers went about their work. At each and every house they threatened the family with retribution if they were found to be lying. The threat of the whole family being carted off to one of the Concentration camps was too much for one man. He had a wife and two young children. So after being promised anonymity, he admitted to the SS guards that the Spiegleman family at number 88 Poznanska Road were hiding in the cellar and that some of the neighbours were supplying them with food and other essentials. When pressed, the man informed the guards that Doctor Franz Szabo and his family were also involved.

The SS guards then went to call on the Szabo family at number 95 Poznanska Road. Their interview with the Szabo's was a fairly casual affair. They spoke to Franz Szabo and asked him if he knew if there were any Jewish families in the area, their excuse being that they were ordered to transport any remaining Jews to the Ghetto. Franz Szabo told them that there were no Jews living locally, none that he knew of anyway. The SS guards happened to mention the Spiegleman family, who lived just down the road. Franz Szabo informed the guards that the Spieglemans had left some time ago and that nobody really knew their whereabouts.

However, the SS guards already knew more. The Spieglemans were a wealthy Jewish family who owned a textile factory which had been taken over by the Germans. The Jews had been prohibited from owning businesses. The Spiegleman family were thought to have fled, but now, apparently not. The SS guards knew better, and they also knew that Franz Szabo had been lying to them.

Nothing further was done. The SS guards went back to report their findings to Herr Kober, and the following week, Herr Kober put his plan into action.

Kober had already spoken to Herr Kruger and Herr Sym about his plans to root out any Jewish families who were in hiding, and who were also possibly concealing their wealth. An enthusiastic Kruger had immediately given Herr Kober the go ahead.

At six o'clock on the Wednesday evening, Kober, Staszic and three other SS guards were driven in an official black staff car to the home of Doctor Franz Szabo. Accompanying them were two trucks, carrying a dozen German soldiers. One of the trucks stayed with Kober and the SS guards. The other made its way down the Poznanska Road to number 88 where the soldiers would break down the Spiegleman's front door and eventually find the family hiding in the cellar.

Kober and Staszic got out of the car, along with the guards. Kober glanced across at Staszic. Herr Staszic had been nervous, but Kober had spoken to him earlier and had once more encouraged him to see sense. Staszic would have to remain strong. Kober had then convinced him that Pieter Szabo had senselessly and brutally attacked him. Herr Staszic had been an innocent victim. It was time for justice to prevail. Better still, it was time for revenge.

Everything had been planned. It was to be a show of force.

Kober walked straight into the house through the front door and Staszic and two of the SS guards followed him. The rest of the German soldiers had climbed out of the truck and remained outside the house with the remaining SS guard who was awaiting further orders.

At that moment, the Szabo family were all sitting around the large table in their dining room and were in the middle of eating their dinner when

Kober and his men suddenly burst into the room from the hallway. The family sat there in shock as Herr Kober informed them that they were all under arrest. Franz Szabo immediately stood up. He'd instantly recognised Herr Kober, especially after the fiasco at the Rifle Club, and he realized straightaway that Kober was a dangerous man.

'What on earth is going on?' Franz Szabo demanded.

'You are all under arrest,' Herr Kober repeated himself.

'What the hell for?' Franz Szabo asked angrily.

'You have been harbouring enemies of the state,' said Kober.

'What on earth are you talking about?' said Franz Szabo. 'You have no right bursting into my home like this, no right at all.'

Kober stared at Franz Szabo for a brief moment, as the rest of the Szabo family sat there, shocked and confused

'Ah well, that's where you may be wrong Doctor Szabo,' said Kober, 'We actually do have very reliable information that you have been assisting and also harbouring the enemies of the state.'

'What enemies of the state?' Franz Szabo asked.

'The Jews of course, Doctor Szabo...the Jews,' Kober replied.

Franz Szabo stared back at Herr Kober.

'I don't understand,' he said, 'we've not been harbouring anybody.'

'It seems that you have Doctor Szabo, and we know that you have. You do realize that Adolph Hitler has decreed that the Jews are the enemies of the state, and he has authorised us to arrest all the Jews and their families and arrange for their relocation.'

'You mean the Concentration Camps?' Pieter Szabo suddenly interrupted.

There was an immediate silence.

Franz Szabo turned to his son and almost hissed the words, 'Pieter, be quiet.'

Herr Kober turned to Pieter. Yes, everything was going to plan.

'Shut you're stupid mouth, 'boy', Kober ordered.

Pieter's mother suddenly reached out and took hold of her son's arm, and Pieter turned away in disgust. And Kober saw that too.

'I think there's been a mistake,' Franz Szabo tried to explain, 'we're not harbouring anybody. There are no Jewish families in this house.'

'I never said there was,' Kober continued, 'what I did say was that you were assisting them.'

Franz Szabo didn't understand.

Kober stared at him.

'The Spieglemans, Doctor Szabo,' said Kober, 'You've been helping the Spieglemans.'

Leah Szabo glanced up at her husband. And Kober saw that too, it almost made him smile.

Franz Szabo tried his best to remain calm.

'The Spieglemans left Lodz a while ago,' he replied, 'It was after their factory was closed down. I've not seen anything of them since.'

Herr Kober laughed. 'And now you are telling me lies, Doctor Szabo. You know as well as I that the Spieglemans are still living down the road at number 88, and that they are hiding in their cellar. And the only reason that they are surviving there is because you and your family are supplying them with food and other essential supplies. That is what's been happening Doctor Szabo, and that's the simple truth of it.'

Franz Szabo was dumbfounded. And he wondered how Kober had found out about the whereabouts of the Spiegleman family. Nobody was supposed to know.

'It's not true,' he argued, 'your information's totally wrong.'

Kober replied with a lie.

'Doctor Szabo, we have already arrested the Spieglemans. We've interrogated them and they've admitted everything. We've also spoken to some of your neighbours, who told us just where the Spieglemans were hiding and also how they were managing to survive. So your lies will not work Doctor Szabo, we have all the evidence we need.

Franz Szabo, and his family, were all left speechless. And that suited Herr Kober exactly.

He continued.

'You must understand Doctor Szabo, that anyone who assists an enemy of the state must also himself be considered an enemy of the state.'

Herr Kober then turned to his SS guards.

'Bring in the rest of the troops immediately, and arrest everyone.'

Wilfred Staszic had followed Herr Kober into the Szabo's dining room and then he'd stood back with the two other SS guards as Herr Kober had taken charge of the situation.

And as Herr Kober had deliberated and then questioned Franz Szabo, Staszic had looked around the room. Everyone was sitting at the dining table The Szabo family had been eating their dinner, and as they sat there Staszic looked at their faces. He saw the two Szabo sisters and another man, Adam Breslav, who was either engaged or married to the eldest sister. And then he looked at Franz Szabo's wife, and he saw the fear in her eyes. Mrs Leah Szabo was a very frightened woman.

And then he looked to her side and at her son. And for a brief moment, Herr Wilfred Staszic felt physically sick. Seeing Pieter Szabo again brought on a feeling of shock, and once again those dreadful memories of that evening in the library flooded back into his mind. He stared at Pieter Szabo and he fought back the urge to look away. Because Kober had been right. He needed to conquer his fear, he had to.

Pieter Szabo didn't take any notice of Herr Wilfred Staszic, he still hadn't recognised him. Pieter was staring down at the tablecloth and he was listening to Herr Kober's little speech and accusations. Pieter was angry, more than angry, he was incensed. How dare these people barge into their home and threaten his family. Directly in front of Pieter was a large silver serving platter, and on the platter were the remains of the loin of pork that they'd eaten for their dinner. And also on that platter was the carving knife that they'd used to slice up the joint of meat. The knife was razor sharp, Pieter knew it was. He continued to stare at the knife, it would be so very easy. Pieter knew that in an instant he could snatch up the knife and launch it into Herr Kober's throat. He would kill Kober immediately and then set upon the other three SS guards. He could take out another two men with certainty, but the third man would be the obvious problem. The other two he could kill easily but then the element of surprise would be lost. And then he suddenly decided on another option. In the first instance he would knock the third guard to the floor, and by the time the man had managed to get to his feet, Pieter would have killed the other two SS guards and then be on him. Pieter sat there and he began to breathe deeply, he had to get the oxygen into his lungs and into his blood system and he needed to get the adrenalin levels built up in his body. And then when the moment was right, he would spring out of the chair and attack these men with the knife. And he would kill them, he would kill them all. Pieter sat there breathing slowly and deeply. No one else in the room even knew what he was thinking, no one. But Pieter Szabo did. He could kill at ease. Killing someone wasn't a problem, not one bit.

Herr Wilfred Staszic shifted his gaze.

He'd no need to worry. He was safe. With him were Herr Kober and the other two SS guards. And outside the house there were another half a dozen German troops. Yes, he was safe, and now he was in a position of command. But more than that, he'd suddenly realized something more significant. To his amazement, he realized that Pieter Szabo still didn't recognize him. Staszic stood there for a moment and almost gave a sigh of relief. Pieter Szabo still had no idea.

When they'd been standing in the queue at the rifle club, Pieter Szabo hadn't realized that he was being questioned by Wilfred Staszic. And now here, in the Szabo's dining room, Pieter still didn't see that it was Staszic who was standing there right in front of him.

It was of course, the uniform. Standing there in his SS regalia and dressed all in black, Herr Wilfred Staszic was a long and distant memory from Wilfred Staszic, the chief librarian at Lodz Central Library.

And then Staszic glanced at the woman on Pieter Szabo's right. And he almost went rigid with shock. Because sitting there, and staring back at him, was Francine Korczak.

Stazic looked at her, she was still lovely and she was still beautiful, and in that split second his heart jumped a beat. Staszic had never once seen her after the incident at the library, and now here she was, sitting right in front of him and looking more striking than ever. And for a moment he was completely dumbfounded. But then he suddenly realized that Francine was staring directly at him too. And for one stupid moment he thought that she would smile at him in recognition, just like the Francine of the past would have, the Francine that he'd once loved, and still loved. But she just continued to stare at him strangely. Because Francine realized that she knew the SS officer standing there in front of her, but couldn't place him, also because of his uniform and also because of the stressful events that were taking place at that particular moment. And then her eyes suddenly widened and her mouth fell open as she finally recognized the man who was staring at her. The man standing there in front of her, the man wearing the SS uniform, was Wilfred Staszic.

Francine gasped in horror. And she spoke out without realizing the consequences of her actions.

'You!' she said out loud. 'Oh god no...It's you.'

Everyone suddenly looked at her, as Francine in shock, suddenly put her hand to her mouth.

Pieter immediately turned to her.

'What?' he asked. It was one single question, just one.

'It's Staszic...It's Wilfred Staszic,' she replied.

And that one reply would determine the events that would affect them for the rest of their lives.

Pieter Szabo shot around to look at the Nazi who was standing there, staring at them.

And then for the first time, he suddenly realized who the SS guard was. It was Staszic, the bastard who had wanted Francine all to himself. Wilfred Staszic, the man who'd pursued Francine and who had started to grope her and who would have eventually cornered and abused her. Staszic the bully and the abuser, and now here he was again, bullying and abusing Pieter's family.

In an instant, Pieter grabbed the carving knife and shot out of his chair, but at the same time Francine stood up too. That action stopped Pieter moving to his right, with the knife in his hand Francine could have been injured in the struggle. So he launched himself to his left, but he had to get past his mother and his sisters. His actions were reckless, a decision which had been driven by anger. It was however, the wrong decision.

Wilfred Staszic just stood there, paralyzed with fear. He was stunned at what was happening. He couldn't believe the speed and the force of Pieter Szabo' attack. In a fraction of a second Pieter had snatched up the knife and was heading around the table and coming straight for him. For Staszic, it was all happening again. This man, this Pieter Szabo was going to hurt him again. And this time Pieter Szabo intended to murder him.

Staszic tried to move away, but he was so shocked that he found he couldn't do anything. All he could do was stand there in disbelief and await his dreadful fate.

Pieter Szabo was moving towards him, it would only be a matter of seconds.

And then suddenly, someone began to shout.

'Stop where you are right now Szabo. Or your mother will die.'

It was Henryk Kober. And in his hand was a dark grey Luger pistol, which was pointed directly at Leah Szabo's head.

'One more step Szabo, and I will shoot your mother in the face. I will kill her and then I will shoot the rest of your family, one by one. It's up to you.'

Pieter Szabo knew that he had to stop. He had no other choice. He stood there with the knife in his hand, shaking with rage. But he was beaten, and he knew it. It was over.

Pieter had to put the knife back down on the table.

His family sat there, rigid with fear around the table, they were speechless.

Kober broke the silence. He immediately ordered one of the SS guards to call in the troops and within a minute the Szabo's dining room was full of German soldiers. The Szabo family were then taken outside and loaded onto the truck, but not Pieter and Francine.

Pieter Szabo was handcuffed to one of the dining chairs, he sat there with his hands firmly cuffed behind his back. Francine Szabo stood silently by the dining table, pale and frightened.

Kober had ordered everyone out of the house except for himself and Staszic. And that left the four of them alone. And now it was time for Pieter Szabo to understand the consequences of his past actions.

For a brief moment Kober stared at Pieter Szabo, and then he looked across at Francine. He didn't understand Staszic's fascination with her, and he certainly didn't see her beauty. But in Kober's case, he didn't see the beauty in any woman. They were of no interest to him at all. Kober's one and only love had always been the acquisition of power and with it, respect. It was the only thing that he was truly devoted to. There had been times in Henryk Kober's life when he'd needed the physicality of a woman. But for Kober, that urge had been easily remedied by a visit to one of the local brothels, where the services there were rendered to him by cheap prostitutes, and for as little money as possible.

Kober suddenly turned and walked out of the dining room and back into the hallway, leaving the three of them in an almost awkward silence. A moment later he returned, carrying with him a stout wooden walking stick that he'd picked out of the family's coat stand. He walked back into the dining room swinging the stick in his hand and feeling its measure.

He then went over to Pieter Szabo and stood in front of him, repeatedly tapping the walking stick on the wooden floor.

'So Mr Szabo, we all meet again,' said Kober.

Pieter looked up at him.

'Actually Kober, we've never met. During your short time as a member of the Rifle Club, I never spoke to you, not once.'

Kober smiled. This was really very good. Young Pieter Szabo had just thrown in a little insult, and that was just what Kober needed, an excuse. And now Kober was a little bit angrier, because he'd just been insulted.

He stared down at Pieter Szabo.

'You will address me as 'Herr' Kober,' he said to Pieter.

Pieter gave Henryk Kober a look of complete loathing, and then he shook his head in disgust and turned away. It was the moment that Kober had been waiting for.

He raised the walking stick high and then smashed it down the side of Pieter Szabo's face with all his might. Pieter howled in pain and Francine started to scream.

Kober immediately turned to her.

'Shut up you bitch,' he shouted, and he then raised the stick to her and she stumbled backwards against the table. Kober suddenly swung the stick again and he once more slammed it into the side of Pieter Szabo's face. Pieter groaned in agony as two bright red wheals swelled up on the side of his face. Francine began to cry as her husband sat there, handcuffed and helpless.

'Please, please stop' she implored Kober.

'Ah,' said Kober, 'And now it's a different story, isn't it? When your boyfriend here brutally beat my comrade, 'Herr Staszic', in the library that evening, there was no mercy for him, was there now?'

Francine suddenly blurted out the words that would change their future, and bring her no mercy at all.

'But he's my husband,' she sobbed.

It was the final stroke. It was almost an act of genius.

Kober, enthralled by that piece of information, turned around to look at Wilfred Staszic.

Staszic stood there staring at Francine. She was the love of his life, or had been. And in truth, he'd never really stopped thinking about her. And in the farthest corners of his mind he'd always wished and dreamed that at some point she would come to her senses and come back to him and beg for his forgiveness. And he of course would forgive her and they would put all that past nonsense behind them and finally marry. But that was only in his dreams, and now, suddenly no. That possibility was never going to happen.

The last few moments had been quite extraordinary for Wilfred Staszic. It had all the started with his fear of being attacked once again by Pieter Szabo. His past memories had never left him. And then suddenly, and amidst all the confusion, the soldiers had been called in and Pieter Szabo had been handcuffed to the chair. And suddenly here was Pieter Szabo, helpless and weak and powerless. He was no longer the bully and no longer was he Wilfred Staszic's nemesis. But still the memories remained. And then Kober had hit Pieter Szabo across the face with the walking stick, and Pieter Szabo had howled in agony, just like Staszic had, on that evening in the library. And as Staszic watched Henryk Kober, he'd been both horrified and fascinated. More than that, he was spellbound, even joyous. Because this was pure revenge, a sweet revenge for the physical and the mental abuse that he'd had to endure. And when Herr Kober had hit Pieter Szabo the second time, Staszic was glad of it. For Staszic, it was almost as though he was wielding the walking stick himself, and it was he who was now mercilessly beating Mister Pieter Szabo. And Wilfred Staszic suddenly felt rather hot and flushed as his pulse quickened and his blood began to run a little bit faster. And there was something else there too. Finally, there was anger.

And now this, the most dreadful revelation of all, because now Francine had told them that she was married, Francine had married Pieter Szabo. She was now married, and all the dreams that Wilfred Staszic had secretly hoped for had suddenly come crashing down.

And it was Pieter Szabo who had stolen her. And now Staszic could never have her because it was all too, too late.

And suddenly, Herr Wilfred Staszic was more than just angry. He was about to go into a frenzy. He turned to Kober

'Henryk...Give me the stick.'

Kober, fascinated by this, did as he was asked.

Staszic took the stout wooden walking stick in both hands and he raised it up and slammed it down on the top of Pieter Szabo's head. Pieter Szabo again cried out in agony, and hearing that hopeless cry only made Staszic want to hit him again

Francine Szabo screamed.

'No...Please no...Please don't, she began to shout.

But Kober grabbed hold of her and he spun her around and as he did he took hold of the back of her dress and ripped it off her shoulders. Underneath she was almost naked. She tried to struggle but Kober was too strong for her and he cruelly twisted her arm up behind her back and she screamed out in pain. Kober turned her to face Staszic, the front of her dress was ripped wide open and her breasts were exposed. She couldn't move, she couldn't do anything.

Kober had seen the look in Wilfred Staszic's eyes. He'd finally got Staszic to do something physical and something completely out of character, because now was the moment, now Kober had Wilfred Staszic angrier than he had ever seen him before.

'Look at her, Staszic.' said Kober in disgust, 'Look at this dirty little whore. She took you for a fool, Wilfred. She never loved you, she never did. She was always fucking 'young Szabo' here, and they were doing it in 'your' library, Wilfred, and they were both laughing at you behind your back. And then that bastard beat you Wilfred, beat you and injured you so badly. Well now it's your turn...it's your turn 'Herr Staszic'.

Wilfred Staszic stared at Francine Szabo's open nakedness. But now he looked at her with loathing. She was a bitch and she'd lied to him and she'd laughed at him. And as he stood there he stared at her pale open breasts, almost in revulsion. No longer was she beautiful, no, far from it. Now she was suddenly dirty and ugly, because she was used. And strangely, as he looked at her he was both repulsed, but also somehow mesmerized.

For Staszic, it was akin to pornography. And as he stared at her he suddenly became hot and flushed as his loathing for her took on a strange sexual hatred.

And as he stared at her naked body, he raised the walking stick once more.

Through the pain and the agony, Pieter Sazbo heard his wife scream, and that sound alone made him regain his consciousness. He shook his head as he stared groggily around the room, and then he saw her. And with a sudden jolt of anguish, he again realized what was happening. Standing there in front of him was his wife, and her dress had been ripped open and she was partially naked. She was struggling and she was in pain because Kober had her arm twisted up behind her back. And as he looked directly at Francine, he saw the distress and the fear in her eyes.

Pieter Szabo's heart nearly burst. He had to save her. That was the one thing he'd always promised her. That he would look after her. He glanced at Kober and then across at Staszic. He tried to do something, tried anything at all, but it was useless. He was handcuffed to the chair and as helpless as a child, and Pieter seethed with frustration as he tried to break free, but it was useless.

'Let her go or I'll kill you,' he screamed.

And then Pieter heard a whir, and then he felt the agony.

The walking stick once again slammed into the side of his face and Pieter cried out in pain.

For a moment his vision was blurred and he had to shake his head to bring himself to his senses. He could hear Kober's voice. He didn't really understand what was being said, but he could hear Kober's voice.

'Mr Szabo, wake up. Wake up Mr Szabo, we need to talk to you.'

Pieter opened his eyes.

'Ah, you're back with us,' said Kober, smiling. He still had hold of Francine, but now Francine had the look of dread etched across her face.

'Ah Mr Szabo,' Kober laughed. 'Your threats to kill us now seem rather pathetic. You see, Herr Staszic and I are now in charge. And you are a 'nobody' Mr Szabo. And your so-called 'wife' and the rest of your family are also nobodies. It's all over for you people.'

Pieter looked up at Kober with hatred in his eyes.

Kober smiled.

'Let me tell you your future Mr Szabo,' said Kober. 'You and your family will be taken to the transit camp and then separated. The men will be imprisoned, and your wife and your mother and sisters will be placed somewhere else.'

Kober again smiled.

'You know Mr Szabo, the women in your family are really quite pretty. They will make exceedingly good sport for the guards at the camp.'

Pieter grimaced and he clenched his fists.

Kober saw the anger in Pieter Szabo, again that same frenzied anger. But Kober hadn't finished.

He leant forward and whispered quietly into Francine's ear.

'My dear, if you make one movement, if you even flinch, I will shoot your husband in the head, right here and now. I'll kill him where he sits. Do you understand me?'

Francine Szabo nodded her head.

'Mr Szabo,' Kober then continued, 'we have you, and there's not a thing you can do about it.'

And with that, Kober let go of Francine's arms and then he ran his hands around to her waist and onto her stomach, and then he reached up and slowly took hold of her breasts.

Pieter looked on, horrified.

Kober then began to caress and squeeze Francine Szabo's open breasts.

But she didn't move, not one inch, she daren't. Kober began to squeeze her nipples and Francine involuntarily gasped. But she still didn't move. Tears of hurt and humiliation and fear began to form in the corner of her eyes. She was terrified.

Pieter looked at her, and he knew. He knew everything, and he loved her.

'I'll kill you for this,' Pieter grunted. But he was powerless, and there was nothing he could do to stop Kober from molesting his wife. And as he sat there handcuffed to the chair, he suddenly wondered if there was worse to come. Where would all this end? Were these two men going to rape Francine, right there and now in front of him?

Pieter became incensed.

'I'll kill you,' he said again. 'I'll kill you both,' and with that Pieter looked up at Staszic, hoping that the threat of violence might work.

But Herr Wilfred Staszic wasn't looking at Pieter Szabo. No, Herr Staszic was staring at Pieter's wife. He was looking at Francine's half-naked body, and he watched almost transfixed, as Herr Kober continued to caress her breasts. And then when Kober had squeezed her nipples and Francine Szabo had gasped out loud, Staszic had misguidedly considered it an expression of erotic pleasure. For Wilfred Staszic, this was more than simple pornography, this was ecstasy.

And then he'd suddenly been distracted by Pieter Szabo's threat. He turned to face Szabo. How dare this bastard threaten him. Not after everything that had happened.

Kober turned to Staszic. Kober had seen Staszic watching him, almost hypnotically as he'd continued to fondle Francine Szabo. Kober knew that his friend was still obsessed by this woman, but now there was Pieter Szabo's outburst and the threat. Something would have to be done. A lesson had to be learned.

'Herr Staszic,' shouted Kober, 'this cheeky bastard needs to know that he and his damn wife are nobodies. He now needs to be taught that lesson.'

Kober then reached forward, and with both hands he tore off Francine's dress. She was almost naked underneath. Kober then grabbed hold of her cotton panties and brutally ripped them off her. Francine screamed as Kober he put his arm tightly around her neck so that he could hold her still.

'Look at this whore,' Kober shouted, and he then plunged his free hand in between Francine's legs. She screamed out, but Kober wouldn't stop and her legs began to flail as he took hold of her.

Pieter began to shout, but Kober wasn't going to stop. Because Kober was a sadist, he had no regard for any woman at all.

'Herr Staszic, hit the bastard,' Kober ordered. 'Beat him...beat him now.'

And with that Kober thrust his fingers between Francine's legs and into her body, and he pulled her head backwards and then leant forward and sank his teeth into her pale neck. Francine screamed in shock, and Kober once again grabbed at her breasts. He was hurting her and she tried to break free, but he was far too strong. Kober lifted his head and snarled into her ear and then he laughed. His teeth were stained with blood.

Pieter began to shake with rage, as Staszic began to smash the walking stick over Pieter's head, but he wasn't looking at Pieter Szabo, he was still watching Kober. Staszic was fixated by Kober's actions and he suddenly found that the pure joy of someone else's physical abuse was absolutely enthralling. Staszic was still fanatically clubbing Pieter Szabo with the stick as Kober continued to abuse Francine. He'd watched with glee as Kober's fingers entered her, but when Kober bit into her neck and had then drawn away, Staszic had seen the blood run down her chest and her breasts, and at that moment Wilfred Staszic went into a frenzied ecstasy. He screamed with high pitched laughter and he continued to beat Pieter Szabo about the face and head, over and over again.

Pieter Szabo was knocked unconscious, but Wilfred Staszic didn't stop, he couldn't.

Pieter collapsed sideways and the chair fell over with Pieter still handcuffed to it. But Staszic continued to club him until the walking stick finally snapped in two. Staszic then began to kick Pieter in the stomach and the chest, and then he started to stamp on his face. And as Francine Szabo continued to scream, Kober looked on with a sense of satisfaction. He'd finally pushed his friend into jubilant violence. There would be no turning back now for Wilfred Staszic. 'Herr Staszic' had just become a true Nazi.

In the end, Kober slammed his fist into the side of Francine Szabo's face and he knocked her to the floor. She lay there in shock, she was dazed and hurt and bleeding.

Kober strode over to Staszic and grabbed hold of his arm and pulled him back.

'Enough Wilfred, enough, you've taught him a lesson that he'll never forget.'

Staszic just stood there, breathlessly staring down at the floor and at the man he would have gladly killed, and enjoyed doing so.

'You've done it,' said Kober. 'Finally Wilfred, you've beaten the bastard. You've crushed your demon.'

Staszic stood there breathing heavily. Something had just happened to him. It was the violence of it all, he was in awe of the violence. There was the feeling of tremendous power and the raw brutality, he felt phenomenal. And suddenly he realized that there was another life out there and another world too, for 'Herr Wilfred Staszic'.

Kober walked out of the dining room and down the hallway, he needed some of his troops to arrest Pieter and Francine Szabo and then take them away. And for a moment, that left Wilfred Staszic alone with Francine and her unconscious and injured husband. Staszic and Francine Szabo could only stare at one another, both were still breathless. Francine was still on the floor and still in shock.

Herr Staszic looked down at her in disgust. She meant nothing to him now, not any more. She was filth. And whatever he'd ever felt for her had just been beaten out of him too.

He looked down at her, and then he gave the thinnest of smiles.

'You should have let 'me' fuck you. You stupid bitch,' he said slowly.

And then he leant forward and spat in her face. Staszic then raised his hand to slap her, and Francine closed her eyes and raised her own hand to protect herself. She knew what was about to happen.

But there was nothing, nothing at all. And wWhen she opened her eyes, Wilfred Staszic had left.

The soldiers happily leered at Francine as she managed to pull her ripped dress back on, then they took her and her still unconscious husband, and loaded them onto the back of the truck with the rest of the family. Pieter's mother cried out when she saw the extent of her son's injuries. Pieter's whole face and head was swollen and bleeding.

The Szabo family were then driven to the army's refugee holding camp on the outskirts of Lodz. Pieter, his father and Ilsa's husband, Adam Breslav, would end up being put into one of the designated prisoner cells, and the women would be led off to one of the huts where a large number of Jewish women and their children were also being held.

Strangely, everyone seemed to arrive at the Lodz army camp at once.

First of all the truck carrying the Spiegleman family arrived. As the soldiers were ushering them off the back of the truck, Herr Kruger and Herr Sym came out of their office to check proceedings and the evening's events. The six members of the Speigleman family stood there in despair, Mother and father and two teenage boys, and two slightly younger sisters. Kruger and Sym observed them, but had nothing to say. Then the soldiers lifted two large brown suitcases from the back of the truck and carried them over to the two commanders. Herr Kruger sniffed, almost in disgust, but Herr Sym's eyes widened in anticipation. This was the part he enjoyed the most.

One of the soldiers, a corporal, stood to attention and saluted both Herr Kruger and Sym.

'We found these cases, sir, along with the prisoners.'

'Ah good,' said Herr Kruger. 'Open them will you please, corporal.'

The corporal turned and nodded to two of his men who immediately opened the cases.

The first case was crammed with money, there was a fortune in cash. The second case contained a large amount of jewellery, the family's trove of gold and diamonds that over the years, and in better times, had been adorned by the past members of the Spiegleman family, wives and daughters. Also in the case were a couple of smaller oil paintings that could have originated from the 'Dutch' School. They of course, would have to be examined by the experts in Berlin.

Herr Sym just stood there smirking. It was a result. Another Jewish family and another hoard of riches and cash, and Herr Sym was a happy man. As was usual, he would take charge of the 'assets', and he would count the money and have the jewellery catalogued. And if anything should go missing, or some of the cash was to disappear, who would know?

Herr Kruger however, was far from smirking. He stood there and eyed the Spieglemans with disdain. Then he walked over to them and spoke to the family as a whole.

'You people,' he began, 'you people are the filth that has been put upon this earth. And this is your downfall.'

Kruger then turned to the two suitcases and he pointed at them.

'This is your god,' he said out loud. 'This is your only god. And your religion is nothing more than Greed.'

The Spiegleman family just stared down at the ground. There was nothing that they could say or do.

'Take them away,' Herr Kruger commanded his corporal.

At that same moment, the black SS Staff car carrying Herr Kober and Herr Staszic arrived, followed closely by the second truck.

The car pulled up in front of Herr Kruger and Herr Sym and the truck pulled past them and then stopped.

Kober and Staszic got out of the car, almost smiling in anticipation

Herr Kober saluted as he strode over to Herr Kruger and he shook his hand.

'Good hunting, Herr Kober?' said the appreciative Herr Kruger. And he turned and nodded to the two suitcases.

Kober acknowledged the compliment.

'I knew it would be a success,' said Kober. 'If the Jews are in hiding, there will always be money hiding with them.'

That anecdote quite amused Herr Kruger, and for the first time that evening, he actually laughed.

'And you're other little problem?' Kruger enquired, and he then nodded to the second truck.

Kober acknowledged the question, he'd already told Igor Sym everything, and Herr Sym had of have course repeated the story to Herr Kruger.

'Ah,' said Kober, ' I see Herr Sym has spoken to you about our little problem, Dr Szabo and his family?'

'Yes,' replied Herr Kruger, 'and I believe it's the son who's prone to violence?'

'Yes he is,' said Kober, 'at one time he nearly killed my friend, Herr Staszic. He beat him mercilessly. Herr Staszic almost died and he nearly suffered a nervous breakdown, it was terrible.'

Kober then gave Herr Kruger scant details of what had happened that evening at the Szabo's house. Kober took a deep breath as he continued.

'Herr Staszic is a very good man, Herr Kruger. Part of my success is because of his success. And that is why I asked him to join the Nazi Party. As you already know, Herr Staszic has been an outstanding member, and his contribution has been immeasurable. He deserves his justice.'

'I agree,' said Herr Kruger. 'Apparently, what happened to him was completely unacceptable.

Herr Staszic is an SS Officer, and that is a position that demands respect. Herr Sym has often spoken to me about Herr Staszic. His commitment is unquestionable. And as I've told you before Herr Kober, we in the SS look after our own. Your work today has been commendable.'

Herr Kruger then turned to Staszic.

'Ah, Herr Staszic'

Wilfred Staszic came forward and Herr Kruger shook his hand.

'You have both done well today,' said Kruger.

Staszic had an overwhelming feeling of pride.

'And I am also aware of what's gone on in the past, Herr Staszic. But now you must put it all behind you and continue with your work for the party. Well done.'

'Thank you. Herr Kruger,' Staszic replied, and he saluted.

Herr Kruger then turned to the truck.

'Right then, let's see what you've brought me?'

As Herr Kruger and Kober and Staszic walked over to the truck, Igor Sym quickly ordered his guards to carry the Spieglman's cases into his office. That done, he followed on behind his three comrades.

Some of the soldiers were lifting Pieter Szabo out of the truck. He was bloody and bruised and still unconscious. Franz Szabo helped to lift his son and as Pieter lay on the ground he tried to attend to him. The soldiers then began to unload the others, another young man and then the four women.

Herr Kruger looked down at Pieter Szabo.

'So this is the young man who's been causing all the problems.'

Franz Szabo turned to him, 'Why is this happening, there was no need for any of this,' he said.

Unfortunately, Franz Szabo had never known that his son had at one time attacked and beaten Wilfred Staszic, a man who was now an SS Officer.

'Ah, Herr Doctor,' said Kruger. 'Well, events prove different Doctor Szabo, and let me tell you how things now stand. You are all collaborators, and by shielding and helping the Jews you have broken the law and now you and your family will have to suffer the consequences.'

Franz Szabo just stood there, he was helpless. He knew that to argue with these people could only make things worse.

'I'm sorry,' was all he could say, and he shook his head, 'we were unaware.'

Kruger smiled at him.

'Of course you were Dr Szabo,' Herr Kruger replied, 'Of course you were.'

Herr Kruger then turned to speak to Sym, Kober and Staszic. They were talking about Spieglemans and their hidden wealth, when suddenly there was a commotion. The rest of the Szabo family were standing behind the truck with the soldiers. But a young woman had started to cry and had tried to go over to Pieter, but the soldiers had stopped her and she was remonstrating and trying to reason with them.

Herr Kruger and his three officers turned to see what was happening, and then they turned back and continued with their conversation. But not Herr Kruger, he just stared at the woman. And though his three officers were still talking, Herr Wilhelm Kruger was not. And as he continued to look at the young woman, his thoughts were suddenly elsewhere. Kruger gazed at her, he was transfixed. She was so beautiful, so very beautiful. This striking young woman was a true Slavic beauty, She had the prominent features and the sculptured face that had always fascinated him. Yes, Francine Szabo was absolutely stunning.

And for Major Wilhelm Kruger, she was everything in a woman that he had ever wanted.

There was a sudden halt in the conversation, and Herr Kruger turned back to his three officers, only to find them looking at him. They'd lost his attention, or vice versa. But Kruger was astute, and he realized the situation and immediately took control.

'Right, I've seen enough gentlemen,' he said, 'Herr Sym and myself will sort these people out.'

And then he turned to Kober and Staszic. 'And you two must go and celebrate your success.' Herr Kruger put his hand on Wilfred Staszic's shoulder. 'Especially you Herr Staszic, today has been a personal triumph for you.'

Staszic could only nod in respect.

As Kober and Staszic drove away, Herr Kruger turned to Igor Sym and gave him his instructions. The family were to be split up. The men could go into the cells for the time being, the women would be housed with the Jews.

'We can use Dr Szabo,' said Herr Kruger, 'there are too many sick people in this camp.'

Igor Sym agreed.

'I will take care of everything, Herr Kruger, leave it to me,' he said.

Igor Sym was eager to get rid of Kruger, in fact, he was eager to get rid of everyone. He had the Spiegleman's money to count.

As he was being driven back to his suite at the Grand Hotel, sitting in the back of his SS staff car, Herr Kruger was in deep thought.

The Szabo men were in the army cells and the women were to be housed with the Jews. But not for long. And certainly not for Francine Szabo, Kruger had other plans for her.

He simply couldn't get her out of his mind.

The next morning, Pieter Szabo finally regained consciousness. It had been Franz Sabo's decision to let his son sleep. While Pieter was asleep he would feel no pain. However, when he awoke, he suffered in more ways than one. As Pieter blinked in the early morning light, his father went to attend to him. Pieter lay on a crude wooden bed in the corner of the cell, he was disoriented and sore. The first thing he felt was the physical pain, his head ached and his face was swollen and very bruised. His breathing was laboured and his stomach hurt because Wilfred Staszic had tried to kick him to death. Pieter lay there in silence as his father examined him and checked for broken bones, amazingly there were none. He tried to remember what had happened and he didn't quite understand where he was. He glanced to his side, only to see Adam Breslav looking down at him.

'How are you Pieter?' Adam asked quietly.

Pieter shook his head, he still didn't understand where he was. And why were his father and Adam with him, and why was he in so much pain?

'You don't remember?' Adam again asked.

And Pieter again shook his head.

Adam Breslav looked at Franz Szabo.

'We've got to tell him, Franz.'

Pieter turned to his father.

'What's wrong?' he asked.

Franz Szabo looked down at his son.

'I don't want you to get upset Pieter, you've been badly injured.'

But Pieter just lay there, and he wondered if he'd had he had some sort of accident?

'Do you remember Pieter, last night when the SS arrived? Those two bastards, Kober and Staszic?

At that moment Pieter's brain went into freefall. Like a flash of light, it all came flooding back to him, the soldiers and the SS with Kober and Staszic. And he remembered his family being arrested. And then he suddenly remembered the attack on Francine and being beaten, and his brain nearly exploded.

He immediately cried out, 'Francine!' And he immediately tried to get up, but fell back.

'It's alright,' said his father, 'she's alright Pieter.'

Franz Szabo had spoken to Francine in the back of the army truck on their way to the camp and he knew exactly what had happened.

'She's alright Pieter, everyone's alright'

'What about Mamma and the girls?' Pieter asked urgently.

'They're alright too, you need to keep calm Pieter.'

But Pieter looked across at Adam Breslav, and his face told a different story. Worry and panic were etched all over his brother in law's face.

With some effort, Pieter finally managed to sit up.

'Where are we father?' he asked.

'We're in the prison cells at the army camp.'

'And where are the girls?'

Franz Szabo glanced back at his son in law.

'We believe they've been housed in one of the huts with the Jewish families.'

Pieter's eyes widened.

'Oh god, no' he said.

There was a moment's silence, which was broken by Pieter.

'They'll send them to the camps.'

'What do you mean?' said Adam Breslav.

'They'll send them to the Concentration camps with the rest of the Jews.'

Adam Breslav shook his head.

'No, they can't. We're not Jewish' he insisted.

Franz Szabo tried to dismiss his son's outburst.

'We don't know that Pieter,' said his father quickly.

'They are going to send them to the Concentration camps, father. We're never going to see them again. You know the rumours, they're killing everyone who gets sent there.'

'Oh my god,' Adam Breslav started to panic. 'Don't say that. They can't do that to my Ilsa.'

Franz Szabo looked across at his son in law.

'Calm down Adam,' he said, 'we don't know anything yet.'

But Adam Breslav wasn't about to calm down. He began to pace around the cell, and then finally he went to sit on one of the other wooden beds and he put his head in his hands.

Franz Szabo looked down at Pieter and he shook his head silently.

Later that morning, two armed soldiers took Franz Szabo out of the cell and escorted him to Herr Igor Sym's office.

As Dr Szabo entered the office he found Herr Sym sitting behind his desk busily writing. Sym was scripting a fabricated appraisal of the money and the jewellery that had been found in the Spiegleman's two suitcases.

'Ah, Dr Szabo,' said Herr Sym, as he put down his pen. 'Sit down, do please sit down,' he continued as he pointed to the chair placed in front of his desk.

Franz Szabo sat down.

'How are you?' Sym enquired.

'As well as could be expected, under the circumstances.' Franz Szabo replied curtly.

'And your son, Dr Szabo, how is he?'

Franz almost flinched.

'He will need continual medical attention, the attack on my son could have killed him.'

Igor Sym looked directly at Franz Szabo

'It was not an attack, Dr Szabo. We have reliable information that your son picked up a carving knife and was himself about to attack one of our officers, SS Officer Staszic. And we are also informed that he would have readily killed Herr Staszic. Your son is lucky that he wasn't shot, Dr Szabo, very lucky.'

Franz Szabo sat there in silence. He knew he had no answers. There was nothing he could say. And at the back of his mind he knew that Igor Sym was telling the truth. What on earth had Pieter been thinking of?

Herr Sym continued.

'Our commandant, Herr Kruger, and I have discussed matters. It has been decided, doctor, that you will work at the camp. We have a large number of soldiers here in Lodz, plus the transient Jews that we have housed here who are awaiting further transport. We do of course have our own German army doctor to mainly attend to our own men. He has a couple of local women who are assisting him as nurses. However, his workload is becoming rather overwhelming.'

Franz Szabo sat there in silence, in his mind he was trying to think everything out.

Herr Igor Sym continued.

'You will be housed separately Dr Szabo and you will attend to the Jews, that seems to be where your sympathies lie. We will call it your 'surgery'. And by assisting us in this matter, we will also allow you to attend to your son's needs every day.'

And there it was, the offer that couldn't be refused.

'And what about my wife and my family?' Franz Szabo asked.

'What about them?' Herr Sym replied.

'I want to see them.'

'We'll see what can be arranged,' replied Herr Sym. 'However, things are quite difficult at the moment.'

And with that Herr Sym leant forwards in his chair.

'The only thing that I 'can' tell you Dr Szabo, is that as long as you cooperate with us, your family will be safe.'

Igor Sym, was of course telling a lie.

But Franz Szabo just sat there. What else could he do but agree, there were no other options, none at all.

Franz Szabo was led away to his new lodgings. It was one of the original smaller wooden huts that had accommodated the Jewish men when the idea of a holding camp was first conceived.

Igor Sym sat in his office. The Jews now had their own doctor, and it would be up to Franz Szabo to look after them. 'Split the family up', were Herr Kruger's orders. Well, thought Sym, 'it was a start.'

Events however, were going to proceed more quickly than was expected.

At twelve o' clock on the same day, a black staff car arrived at the camp. Two SS officer got out of the car and made their way to Herr Sym's office. There was the usual saluting and the compulsory 'Heil Hitler', and then the officers told Sym their orders. They were there to pick up Mrs Francine Szabo and take her to the Grand Hotel for interrogation by Herr Kruger. Igor Sym considered this request quite strange. What possible information could Francine Szabo have? However, Herr Sym was certainly not going to question Herr Kruger's orders. He sent two of his guards to fetch Francine

Szabo and they put her into the back of the SS staff car. As the SS officers were about to leave, Herr Sym asked them when they would be returning Mrs Szabo?

The two officers glanced at one another.

'Oh no, Herr Sym,' replied one of them, 'Mrs Szabo isn't coming back.'

Francine Szabo was driven to the Grand Hotel in complete silence. She sat in the back of the car looking out of the window. She didn't know where she was going, and she was frightened. The last twenty four hours had terrified her, and she'd also suddenly realized that these men could do whatever they wanted. She was powerless.

The two guards had just walked straight into the hut where the women were being housed. One of the guards had called out her name, and she'd come forward. She rather naively wondered if they were going to give her some information about Pieter's wellbeing. But no, she was simply being instructed to go with them. When Pieter's mother, Leah Szabo, had asked the guards where they were taking Francine, one of the guards had turned to her menacingly.

'Shut your mouth you Jewish bitch,' he cursed. And then he spat at her.

Leah Szabo turned her head and stepped back, there was nothing that she could do. Even though she wasn't Jewish, to try and argue with these men would only cause more trouble. She also had her two daughters there with her who she would have to try to protect.

Francine glanced back at her mother in law as she was led away.

It would be the last time that they ever saw one another.

Herr Wilhelm Kruger had everything planned.

Francine Szabo was taken to the Grand Hotel. The two SS officers took her into the hotel where they were met by the manager, Yaslov Slowowski. He directed them to the hotel's lift, and the four of them then went up to the top floor. Once there, Francine Szabo was taken down a well lit landing to one of the rooms. The manager, Slowowski, unlocked the door and escorted them into one of the hotel's better rooms.

Francine stood there and looked around. She couldn't understand what was happening.

'You will be residing here for the time being,' said one of the officers.

And with that, the two SS officers, along with the manager, turned and left the room.

The door quietly closed behind them, but then Francine heard the key turn as the door was locked. She was still a prisoner, and she went over and sat on the edge of the bed. This was all so very strange. Why was she there?

What Francine Szabo was unaware of, was that Herr Wilhelm Kruger had ordered Slowowski the manager to make that specific room available. And she was also unaware that Herr Kruger's private suite was on the same floor, just a short way down the same landing.

Franz Szabo was immediately appointed as the camp's new doctor. He was allocated an assistant, again a local woman who had some knowledge of medicines. At one time she'd apparently worked in a chemist's shop in Lodz.

Anyone in the camp who was ill had to speak to one of the guards, and eventually a guard would take them to Dr Szabo's makeshift surgery. Apart from being able to visit his son, Dr Szabo was forbidden to leave his surgery. That was the rule.

It was all very basic and there were very few medicines on hand. Igor Sym's view was that it was all a waste of time and money. The Jews wouldn't need medical attention, not for long. Not where they were going.

Pieter Szabo and Adam Breslav lingered in their cell. Pieter was still recovering and he slept for long periods. But Adam Breslav was becoming more and more agitated. He had no idea what was happening or even worse, what was going to happen. His wife and the other women had been taken away, and now Franz Szabo had disappeared too. Adam Breslav had taken to pacing up and down the cell, he was troubled and disturbed, and the distress of it all was beginning to get the better of him.

Whether it was circumstance, or just Herr Igor Sym's cold callousness, it would be hard to tell. But two days later, in the very early hours of the morning, a line of trucks pulled up at the camp. In the darkness, the Jewish women and their children from two of the huts were herded onto the back of the trucks. From there they were taken to a railway siding and packed into closed cattle wagons with no food, water or sanitation. Their destination would be the Auschwitz concentration camp. Along with those women and their children were Leah Szabo and her two daughters, Ilsa and Elise.

It was their end. There would be no coming back.

When the Germans first invaded Poland there were 230,000 Jews living in the city of Lodz.

By the time the war was over, only 10,000 had survived.

CHAPTER 7

Four long hours had passed by and Francine Szabo still sat there, waiting.

And during those hours, Francine had spent most of her time gazing out of the window of her room at the Grand Hotel. The two SS officers had brought her there from the camp and had then immediately left. She'd looked down from the window and had watched the people below going about their business. Only twenty four hours before, she had been one of those people, but not now. Their arrest by Wilfred Staszic and his friend, Herr Kober, had put an end to it all. Her life had been shattered. And as she sat on the edge of the bed, she wondered once more, why she was there.

She was surrounded by splendour. The hotel room was beautiful, the colour theme was deep blue, and the satin curtains matched the dark blue satin bedding along with the sumptuous deep blue carpet. The Grand Hotel had never lost its standards, not even in those miserable and austere times in hard struck Poland

At precisely six o'clock, there was a knock on the door and the key turned in the lock. Francine stood up immediately. Who would it be? In her heart she prayed that it would be her family. And that this had all been a big mistake and that Franz Szabo had somehow managed to sort everything out.

What she didn't expect, was Major Wilhelm Kruger, the head of the SS.

Francine just stood there terrified, as Herr Kruger walked into the room. Dressed in his black SS uniform, he was an imposing figure and that alone made Francine take a step backwards. But Herr Kruger simply removed his hat and smiled at her.

'How are you, Mrs Szabo?' he asked her.

Francine just stood there. She didn't know what she was supposed to say or do.

Kruger continued to speak to her.

'I believe that your first name is Francine, I shall call you that. It seems so much more informal. And so Francine, may I introduce myself, my name is Major Wilhelm Kruger.'

Francine stared at him. She recognized him from the camp. He'd been there talking to Wilfred Staszic and Kober and another man, they were all SS officers.

Herr Kruger looked at her, he was still smiling.

Suddenly, Francine had to ask the question.

'Could...could you please tell me what has happened to my husband... and my family?'

Kruger almost let his smile slip, almost. The mention of her husband slightly irritated him.

Her husband was no longer of any consequence. But she wasn't to know that yet.

'Ah, yes my dear,' he responded, 'It's been quite a mix up hasn't it? Well, there is a problem of course. Your husband did pull a knife on an SS officer, and that is quite a serious offence. However, your father in law, Doctor Szabo, is a man of some standing. And until everything can be sorted out, he has insisted on helping us by becoming the doctor at the camp. Unfortunately, there is a slight dilemma, and this whole thing cannot just be dismissed. You see, you have all been found guilty of helping the Jews and that in itself is also a serious accusation. We can't just send you all home and forget about it, it would be an insult to the officers involved, and to the Reich. However, we will try to see what we can do.'

'But why am I here? Francine asked, 'and why are the rest of my family still in that camp?'

'Oh, the women aren't in the camp anymore,' Kruger lied, 'we've had them moved into different accommodation too. It's just that under the circumstances we can't just let you wander off home. The SS officers would be humiliated. They're looking at more serious charges I'm afraid.'

'You mean Wilfred Staszic and that other man, Kober.'

'Yes,' replied Herr Kruger, still smiling.

'But he attacked me,' Francine tried to explain. 'That man Kober ripped my dress and then he bit me, he bit my neck.' And Francine turned to show him the inflamed wound on the side of her neck. 'My dress is ripped, my mother in law had to give me her cardigan to cover me up.'

'Oh dear god, that's terrible,' Herr Kruger lied again, 'I will have a serious word with Herr Kober. That type of conduct is absolutely unacceptable.'

Herr Kruger's act of credibility was beginning to work.

Francine actually gave a sigh of relief. She felt that she could better explain the events and everything that had happened to this man. He was listening to her. And she was even more relieved when she'd heard that Mrs Szabo and Ilsa and Elise had all been moved out of the camp too. At least it was a start.

'You've had a very long day, Francine,' said Kruger, 'I'm going to have some food sent up to you. And I'll have a word with the manager, we'll have to get you some fresh clothes to wear.'

Francine smiled weakly, 'thank you, Major Kruger'.

'It's alright Francine,' he replied. And with that he turned and left the room, not forgetting to carefully lock the door behind him.

As Herr Kruger walked down the hotel landing he smiled to himself. Francine Szabo was without doubt, a ravishingly beautiful woman.

Yes, it was a start.

The next morning, Francine had breakfast in her room, and at midday when her lunch arrived, so did her new clothes. A young lady who was the hotel receptionist had called in on her earlier to see Francine and ask for her sizes. There were several cardboard boxes, which contained skirts and blouses, underwear and two pairs of shoes. In one of the smaller flatter boxes there was a beautiful rich green evening dress. It was absolutely stunning, and as Francine looked at it she was quite taken aback. The receptionist later called Francine to check that everything fitted, and Francine asked her if the hotel had any books or reading material. She'd been there all day with nothing to do but worry about Pieter, constantly wondering if Wilhelm Kruger really could help them. Within the hour a porter returned with half a dozen books. Francine thanked him, but she noticed that as he left, the door was once again locked. She was still a prisoner, but in a pretty gilded cell.

She sat there all alone. Everything had all gone so terribly wrong.

The evening that they'd all been arrested should have been such a happy one. Francine had waited until she was sure that the time was right. And after their evening meal, Francine was going to turn to the family and announce to everyone that she was pregnant. But it never happened, and now, nobody knew. Not even her husband.

After her lunch, Francine washed and then changed into her new clothes, and she felt better. She then spent the afternoon reading, it was a welcome respite which took her mind off her present predicament. At one point she stopped reading and wondered once again how Pieter was, and when would she be able to see him again. Perhaps she should talk to Major Kruger about it. Maybe he could help.

At six o' clock there was a knock on the door, the key turned and Wilhelm Kruger walked into the room. As he saw Francine he again smiled.

"How are you my dear?' he asked.

Francine stood up to return the compliment.

'I'm very well thank you,' she replied, 'and thank you very much for the clothes.'

'Well we couldn't leave you in a ripped dress, could we? And how is your neck?'

'It's a lot better thank you, I've washed today and it's started to heal.'

'Very good,' said Kruger. 'And I believe that you have started to read?'

Francine turned to the array of books littered on her bed.

'Yes, I have. The hotel brought me some books. It passes the time.'

'Yes I can understand that,' replied Kruger sympathetically, 'it must be a long day.' And then his expression changed slightly.

'I have an idea Francine. You must dine with me tonight, I could do with some company. Dealing with soldiers all day long is quite tiresome and I too miss my family back in Berlin. It will be a welcome change. I'll come back for you in an hour or so.'

Francine didn't know what to say. She'd been coerced. It had been both an invitation and a command, but under the circumstances she could hardly refuse.

As Herr Kruger was about to leave, she again had to ask him the question.

'Is there any news Major Kruger? Do you know how my husband is?'

For a split second, Kruger struggled to maintain his pleasant smile. He turned to her.

'I am informed that he is doing quite well and is back on his feet.'

Francine gave a visible sigh of relief, which irritated Herr Kruger somewhat. And then he had an afterthought.

'However, I'm afraid that the other problem isn't looking very promising at the moment. The assault with the knife is being taken very seriously. But don't worry my dear, I'm sure that I will be able to do something about it. Unfortunately, it's going to take longer than we thought.'

Francine looked justifiably anxious.

'Try not to worry, Francine,' Kruger continued, 'you must leave things to me.'

'Thank you, Major Kruger,' she replied quietly.

And Kruger kept smiling.

'Francine,' he said to her, 'I think that when we're on our own, you could call me 'Wilhelm'.

It would be much more agreeable. Alright then, I'll call back in an hour.'

And with that Wilhelm Kruger turned and walked out of the room, once again carefully locking the door.

And as Francine watched that door close behind him, she realized that Wilhelm Kruger was the only answer to her prayers. She would have to work with him, be clever, and bide her time.

As Herr Kruger walked along the landing he took a deep intake of breath. It had taken all of his willpower to control himself. He'd been alone in that room with the beautiful young Francine Szabo. And she had been standing there at the side of the bed, the bed with those deep blue satin sheets, and it had taken all of his self-control not to take hold of her and ravish her there and then. But no, he knew that wasn't the answer. Trying to rape her wasn't going to be enough. It would destroy the relationship that he was trying to build, because Wilhelm Kruger wanted so much more. But he too would also have to bide his time, and wait.

Just over an hour later, he returned.

There was the usual tap on the door as he turned the key in the lock, and then he walked straight in. Francine was sitting on the edge of the bed, waiting. She had an open book in her hand but that was just a pretence.

She'd spent most of the last hour wondering what the outcome of this night would be. She didn't even know where they were going.

'I hope you're hungry?' Kruger asked pleasantly, and the smile returned.

Francine stood up at once, and then she flattened down her skirt and pushed her hair into place. It was as though she had to make herself presentable. Kruger saw this, and he was pleased. She was at least trying, surely that was a good sign.

'Err, yes, I am quite hungry,' she replied nervously.

'Good,' said Kruger, 'very good.'

And then he turned to the door and bid her to follow him. It was only a short walk. About thirty paces in all.

He took her down the hotel landing to his private suite, and then he opened the door and invited her in.

As Francine entered Herr Kruger's suite, she was immediately taken by the opulence that surrounded her. The suite was magnificent. In total it consisted of four rooms. A huge living area, a palatial bathroom and two large bedrooms, one of which Herr Kruger had cleared and turned into a sizeable, functional office. The suite was highlighted in colours of deep yellow and gold, even the rugs, the carpets and the curtains were all tastefully matched. Any metalwork, including all the light fittings, were made from gleaming polished brass or had been fastidiously painted in gold leaf. The accompanying furniture was constructed from flawlessly varnished dark oak, which complemented the suite. The whole effect was one of grandeur.

Francine was somewhat taken aback by it all.

'It's beautiful,' she said to Herr Kruger.

Francine looked around the room. The living room was comfortably fitted out. Two large satin covered settees faced each other in front of an open cream and white, tall marble fireplace. A highly polished oak coffee table sat between them and the flames from the fire reflected against it and gave the suite a feeling of relaxed warmth.

Kruger watched, as Francine gazed at her surroundings. She was impressed, and that was good, and he smiled.

In the centre of the room, a large table had been set out for two people to dine.

Interestingly, even the crockery was matched to the suite. Every cup, plate and saucer were made from pure white bone china and each piece had a painted yellow and gold patterned border. The whole set was immaculate, and curiously, had been specifically ordered from the famous Spode pottery factory in England, back in better times and better days.

Herr Kruger walked over to the table and pulled back one of the chairs.

'Take a seat, my dear. Make yourself comfortable.'

Francine did as she was told.

A multitude of thoughts were running through her mind at that moment, worry and fear, and a certain amount of reticence. Her husband was still locked up in that camp and here she was living in utter luxury. But what could she do? She had to work with this man, she had to keep him happy and on her side because she was powerless to do anything else. He was the only person, her one chance to somehow obtain her husband's freedom.

Herr Kruger walked around the other side of the table and comfortably took a seat. There was a chilled bottle of German Hock waiting in a silver ice bucket and Kruger took the bottle and poured them both a glass of wine. He never considered to ask.

'Cheers,' he said to Francine as he raised his glass. Francine responded rather meekly.

'Yes, thank you,' she replied.

'I have this specially brought in from Germany,' Kruger continued. It's a beautiful wine, a much prized Riesling.'

Kruger took a drink from his glass, and he laughed.

'You know my dear, the French may have the edge when it comes to red wine. But the white wine that we Germans produce in the Rhine is incomparable to anything else in the world. Try it, Francine,' he urged.

Francine took a sip, and her eyes brightened. The wine was actually very good.

'It is lovely, Major Kruger,' she replied.

'Wilhelm, Francine. You can call me Wilhelm when we are in private.'

'Oh sorry,' she replied again...'Wilhelm'.

Herr Kruger was just about to speak, when there was a knock on the door.

'Yes, come,' he said loudly, and the door opened.

In came a waitress, pushing a brass metal serving trolley, on it were two covered silver platters.

'Ah,' said Kruger, 'At last, our food.'

The waitress came over to the table, and then carefully placed the platters in front of them. When she lifted the lids, there were two bowls of steaming hot 'Rosol', the famous Polish chicken broth. It smelled delicious. The waitress then reached under the serving trolley to a lower shelf and produced a woven wicker basket, it was full of thick chunks of dark rye bread.

Kruger thanked the waitress as she left the room. And then he turned to Francine.

'I love Polish food,' he said, as he offered her the basket of rye bread. 'It's such a refreshing change from the fare back home. I've had a lifetime of German cooking, and it's nice to try something new.'

Francine agreed with him, of course she did.

Herr Kruger continued to carry the conversation and Francine continued to nod in agreement.

The soup was actually very good, and as Francine ate, Herr Kruger poured more wine.

When they'd finished, Herr Kruger sat back and took another drink of his favourite Riesling.

'Are you comfortable here?' he asked.

'Oh yes,' Francine replied, 'my room is quite beautiful.'

'Ah, good' said Kruger.

Suddenly, Francine decided to ask a question.

'Where are Mrs Szabo and her two daughters now staying?' she asked, almost innocently.

But Herr Kruger was ready for this and he had all the answers. He'd already prepared himself for any awkward questions, the difficult questions that he could easily and effortlessly reply to. All lies, but good lies.

'Oh, they're in some other accommodation,' Kruger replied casually, 'I think they're in another hotel somewhere. But then again it could be a private house or an apartment; I'm not really quite sure, but I would think a hotel.'

'Are they alright?' Francine again asked.

'I would think so,' Kruger replied vaguely. 'They're probably dining on good Polish food like you and I, however I don't think the food will be to the same standards as here at the 'Grand'. The chef here is really very good.' And with that Kruger laughed at his own comment.

'So they're being looked after?' said Francine, carefully.

Kruger looked at her, and then he put his glass down. He placed both of his hands on the table and then he began to tap a finger. His face was both concerned and yet sympathetic. It was a practised move.

'Francine, of course they're being looked after,' Kruger used her first name and he spoke to her with familiarity. He wanted to bring a certain closeness into their conversation, he needed to build her confidence and gain her trust and her friendship, and with it, so much more.

He continued, 'But there is a slight problem. Your family, the Szabo family, have been publically accused of assisting the Jews, in this case the Spieglemans. And it is a very serious charge. So you see, you will all have to be confined, but you will be confined in the least inhospitable way. The laws dictate that we can't just let you walk away from the charges, that would be impracticable. And at some point you will be interviewed by a higher authority, however, that is where my plan comes into play. Because you were all separated immediately after your arrests, there could be no coercion between you. Put simply, there would be no time to fabricate a story. I've no doubt that you will all be interviewed individually, and then you will of course, all be seen to be innocents. Dr Szabo himself may get his 'wrists slapped', and will probably receive a strict reprimand for his mistaken actions. But in the end, I'm hoping that it will all come down to paperwork and nothing more.'

Francine smiled at him in earnest.

'I can't thank you enough, Wilhelm,' she said.

Kruger reached over and gently took hold of her hand.

'You're not to worry Francine. I'll take care of everything. Trust me.'

Just three days later, at the Auschwitz Concentration camp, Leah Szabo and her daughters, Ilsa and Elise, would be innocently led into one of the gas chambers and executed.

'You're not to worry. I'll take care of everything. Trust me.'...Herr Kruger had said as he held Francine's slim and delicate hand. But everything was a lie.

Francine had smiled at him pleasantly, her mind was suddenly more at rest.

However, for Herr Wilfred Kruger, there were different emotions. At last, he'd finally managed to physically touch her. Just holding her hand was an intimacy that left him quite breathless and his imagination began to run wild. His body too began to stir with excitement, and as he held her hand, he couldn't help but glance across at his ever awaiting bedroom.

Maybe his plans could change.

But then there was a knock on the door. And suddenly the spell was broken.

Kruger held his breath for a moment, and then he silently sighed. And after taking a deep breath, he turned around.

'Enter,' he ordered sharply.

The door opened, and once again the same waitress pushed another serving trolley into Herr Kruger's opulent suite. It felt like an invasion of privacy, but a timely one. The waitress's intervention, be it good fortune or luck, coincidence or fate, it was certainly good timing.

Herr Kruger would have raped Francine Szabo, he knew he would. He couldn't have controlled himself, and then all of his plans would have come to an end. Kruger knew he had to take more care. Because he had plans for Francine Szabo, long term plans.

Kruger made his choice. It would be wiser to gorge himself on the mouth watering food that had just arrived, rather than tasting Francine Szabo's soft white skin.

He glanced back at Francine. She was still smiling. She had no idea.

The waitress pushed the trolley over to the table. And once again it was filled with an array of silver platters.

'Just put them on the table in front of us,' Kruger ordered.

The waitress did as she was bid, and then from under the trolley she produced another bottle of Kruger's favourite Riesling. It had been uncorked and the cork had been loosely replaced.

'Your wine sir,' the waitress muttered.

'Is it chilled correctly?' Kruger asked.

'Of course sir,' she dutifully replied.

"Very good,' said Kruger, 'you can leave us now.'

And with a near sigh of relief, the dismissed waitress quickly left the room.

As the door closed behind her, Kruger pulled the cork from the bottle and refilled their wine glasses. Francine sat there. She would wait for Herr Kruger to take the lead, and Kruger took notice. He liked that.

Domination and subservience were two of his most favourite things.

'Now, let's see what we have here,' he said to Francine, even though he already knew.

He had after all, specifically ordered all of the food.

He lifted the silver lids to reveal dishes full of steaming hot 'Pierogi', the Polish national dish of hot dumplings, stuffed with an array of different fillings.

'Beautiful,' he said as he looked at the food, and then at Francine. He could have been speaking about either, and was.

'Oh, it's Pierogi,' Francine remarked, 'so you really do like our food.'

Kruger had to blink for a moment before he spoke. He was still staring at Francine. She really was a truly beautiful woman.

'Yes,' Kruger replied hastily. 'Yes, I thought you would like these.'

Francine grinned, 'I'm Polish, and we all love Pierogi, Wilhelm. We are brought up eating Pierogi from an early age.'

'Well let's see what we have here,' said Kruger, as he inspected the food. 'These are filled with cheese and onion and potatoes. I think that these are the mushroom and cabbage. The rest are beef and onion and pork and sauerkraut, but I don't know which is which,' and he laughed.

'This is quite a feast,' Francine remarked. 'Will we be able to eat it all? They're very filling you know.'

'We'll try them all,' Kruger replied, 'and then we'll decide which we prefer,' and he laughed again.

And so their meal began, and it was all very pleasant. Good manners and pleasant conversation, as Wilhelm Kruger casually advanced his devious act of friendship.

They finished their meal with apple pie, served with thick warm custard, and then they had a pot of good coffee. Kruger was in the mood for brandy, but then thought better of it. He was becoming infatuated with this woman, and he recognised his own weakness. And who knew where too much brandy could lead? No, it was time to end the evening and be the perfect gentleman. He had already drunk enough wine and his eyes were beginning to roam over to Francine Szabo's ample breasts. He'd continued to glance at the movement of her body as she slowly breathed, and he realized that there would be a slight embarrassment if she'd caught him staring at her. But he found her so intoxicatingly physical, so much so that he felt hot and roused and slightly flustered. So Kruger inadvertently looked at his watch and made some comment about the time. Francine took his lead, and they both commented on how the evening had passed so quickly. Kruger stood up, as did Francine, and he escorted her back to her room. Kruger opened the door to Francine's room, and there was a moment of indecision. Francine turned to him. She was about to bid him goodnight, for her the evening was over. But then there was a split second of uncertainty, surely he wouldn't expect to enter her room?

But Kruger was ready, he'd planned well and he was sticking to that plan.

'Thank you for a lovely evening, Francine,' he said to her. 'We will do this again when I have more time. I've really enjoyed your company, you are an intelligent woman.' Praise indeed.

And with that, he leant forward and gave her a peck on the cheek, just as you would to a sister or a friend's wife. There was no passion, it was a casual act of friendship, to seal a friendship.

Kruger held the door open and waved her in.

'Thank you, Wilfred,' she said, smiling innocently.

Herr Kruger closed the door behind her, and then quietly locked the door.

Francine stood there, as she heard the key turn. She took a sigh of relief. For a moment she'd wondered just which way the evening was going to end. But no, Wilhelm Kruger had been a perfect gentleman. And then she sat down on the edge of the bed, and as she thought about the wonderful food that she'd just eaten, she wondered what Pieter would have had for his evening meal. And she suddenly felt guilty, she instinctively put her hand onto her stomach. Somewhere deep inside her was a baby, and poor Pieter, he knew nothing about it. Nobody did.

Herr Kruger walked back down the hotel landing, back to his own suite. He was breathing heavily and he had only one thing on his mind.

That one simple act had inflamed him. As he'd briefly leant forward and kissed Francine Szabo on her cheek, he'd felt the sudden flush of intimacy. He'd finally kissed her skin, and in that briefest of moments he'd smelt her perfume and he'd smelt her body, it had almost overwhelmed him and it had left him breathless and wanting.

He walked into his room and went straight over to a small black telephone that was placed on a corner table. He picked up the receiver and dialled a number. It was the private line to the hotel manager, Yaslov Slowowski.

At the other end Slowowski picked up the phone.

'Hello, Yaslov Slowowski here,' he answered indifferently.

Slowowski...It's Herr Kruger.

Yaslov Slowowski went rigid.

'Yes, yes Herr Kruger. How can I help you? Is there a problem?'

'Slowowski,' Kruger quickly replied. 'Get me a woman, get me a good whore. And get her up here right away.'

'Err yes, yes Herr Kruger. 'Straightaway, I'll do that straight away.'

Yaslov Slowowski took a deep breath.

'Is there anything else I can do for you, Herr Kruger?' he asked nervously.

'Yes,' replied Kruger. 'Send me up a good bottle of brandy, send it up immediately!'

The next evening, Kruger had a different plan. He left Francine on her own the whole of the evening, and then at ten o' clock he tapped on her door and invited her for a nightcap.

Francine was almost relieved to see him. She'd sat alone all day in her room, only to have her meals brought to her, and then she'd eaten alone and in silence. She'd read of course, but her thoughts had been interrupted. She sat and wondered about Pieter and the rest of the family. And those thoughts had made her feel uneasy.

Wilhelm Kruger's friendly smile was a welcome relief. They went down the corridor to his comfortable suite, where the fire was burning brightly in the hearth. It compensated for the softer lighting which had been subtly turned down, though Francine didn't seem to notice. And then instead of sitting at the table as before, Kruger led her over to the fireplace and to one of the silk covered settees.

'Make yourself comfortable,' he said to her, as he sat down on the settee opposite. Then he stretched back on the settee and yawned easily.

'I'm sorry Francine' he said to her, but it's been a long day, I'm quite exhausted.'

And For Herr Kruger, it 'had' been a long day. He'd spent most of the previous night drinking brandy and ravishing a dark-haired Polish prostitute. In his drunken state, he'd fantasized that the girl was Francine, and that fact alone had made him all the more ardent.

On the coffee table in front of them, a decanter of brandy and a couple of crystal glasses had been strategically placed on a silver tray.

'Would you pour us both a decent brandy please, Francine,' Kruger asked, as he feigned another yawn and stretched again. 'I've ordered us something. It should be here in a minute.'

Francine was about to ask Herr Kruger about Pieter, but for some reason decided against it. Major Kruger was obviously very tired, and she felt that this just wouldn't be the right time.

So she began to ask him about his day, and Kruger began to tell her some tale and an added bit of cheap gossip and rumour, just to add some spice to his story. It was all lies of course, but Francine seemed to enjoy the conversation, simply because she needed some conversation. And they were actually both laughing, and as Kruger told her some other made up story about the antics of an inept corporal, there was suddenly a quiet tap on the door.

Kruger turned and called out, 'Enter.'

A waitress appeared, pushing a serving trolley. She brought the trolley over to them by the fire and served them with a plate of warm honeyed toast and another of rich buttered fruitcake. There was also a pot of hot coffee and some cups and saucers and small plates, along with the milk and sugar.

Kruger simply nodded at the waitress, and she immediately left.

Francine took it upon herself to pour the coffee and then she put some of the toast and the fruitcake on each of their plates. Kruger watched her. She was talking to him as she served out their food and the coffee, and Kruger was fascinated. It all felt so comfortably correct.

They sat and they talked easily. And they ate the food and drank the coffee and sipped their brandy. An hour slipped by, and then once again Kruger looked down at his watch and made a comment about the time, and Francine realized that the evening was over.

Kruger walked her back to her room. As he opened her door, she wondered if she should ask about Pieter, but decided that it would be better not to.

'Goodnight Francine,' Kruger said to her, and he leant forward and once again kissed her cheek. This time Francine turned to accept it. It all seemed so normal, from a friend.

The next evening, Kruger never turned up at all. And Francine sat there all day and then all night by herself.

She'd tried to make conversation with the different staff that had brought her meals to her room. But for some strange reason, they hardly spoke a word in return. What Francine didn't know was that the staff had been given strict instruction not to communicate with her at all. Francine and her family had been found to be collaborators against the Germans, and anyone who was found to be fraternising with her in any way at all could easily find themselves in a lot of trouble. And that was a risk that no one was willing to take.

It was of course, all part of Kruger's plan. If Francine was left on her own she would be lonely, and if she was lonely she would be more appreciative of his company. Kruger wanted Francine Szabo to become dependent on him, and he in return would look after her.

And eventually there would hopefully be a balance, hopefully.

However, there was another reason for him not to visit her. Herr Wilhelm Kruger's day had been more than eventful. It had turned out to be a day of disaster and decisions.

Early that same morning, Kruger had turned up at the camp for a meeting with Igor Sym.

Herr Sym was running the camp quite successfully, and the meeting was somewhat of a formality. The ever-resourceful Sym had by then set up an effective method of human disposal. Herr Sym's initiative was to have the Jews systematically removed from the Lodz Ghetto and into the camp. After a week or two of internment, they were then led onto the train for their final journey to Auschwitz. The whole process left people disorientated and confused, and rather ingeniously, it also broke down any line of communication. Auschwitz was simply looked upon as another, larger prison camp.

However, on that particular morning Herr Kruger had something else on his mind, something that he needed to discuss with Igor Sym.

Both men were sitting in Sym's office and were comfortably drinking some freshly brewed coffee, when Herr Kruger finally broached the subject.

'How are the Szabo family?' Kruger enquired.

Igor Sym just shrugged.

'Nothing's changed really,' Sym replied. 'In fact, I was going to speak to you about them. We are still using Dr Szabo's services as the camp's doctor,' and with that, Igor Sym chuckled. 'He's been rather busy. The Jews seem to do nothing but constantly moan about their ailments, and so the good Doctor is kept permanently on his toes.'

'Does he have any suspicions about his wife and family?' Kruger asked.

'Oh no,' Sym replied. 'He thinks that his wife and his daughters are still somewhere in the camp. I do know that he constantly queries the Jewish women that he attends to, but everyone on the camp is so isolated, and none of them really know anything.'

'Good,' replied Kruger, 'and what about young Pieter Szabo, and that son in law of theirs? I can't remember his name?'

'His name's Breslav,' Igor Sym answered. 'He is, or 'was', married to the eldest daughter.'

There was an emphasis on the word 'was'. Ilsa Breslav was probably already dead, her body burned in the ovens and turned into ashes.

Herr Kruger thought for a moment before he spoke again.

And then, 'I want you to get rid of Pieter Szabo, and the brother in law.'

Igor Sym nodded in agreement. 'Yes, that won't be a problem. We're shipping another trainload of Jewish men to the Auschwitz camp tomorrow. I'll simply have them put on the train along with the others.'

'Well done Herr Sym, you are as efficient as ever,' Kruger concluded

Igor Sym nodded to Herr Kruger. Once more he would serve his master and be recognised for his efforts. How his life had changed, now that he had authority and command, now that he was respected.

'And what will you tell Dr Szabo?' Kruger asked.

Again Igor Sym shrugged.

'When he asks, I'll inform him that his son and son in law have been moved to another prison cell in the 'German section' of the camp and that the cells that they were in are needed for Jewish prisoners. I'll tell him that his son is now under the care of our own German doctor. Whether he believes it or not doesn't really matter. What can he do? If he causes any problems, I'll send him to Auschwitz along with the rest of his Jewish friends.'

Herr Kruger once again took notice of Igor Sym's efficient methods.

Nothing was a problem for Herr Sym. Herr Igor Sym was a very resourceful officer.

'Just one thing,' Kruger continued, 'let's keep this conversation between ourselves.'

'Of course, Herr Kruger,' Sym replied.

It wouldn't be a problem. Igor Sym kept everything to himself.

Kruger then stood up to leave.

'There's no need for me to inspect the camp, you're doing an excellent job here, Herr Sym.'

Sym followed Herr Kruger out of the office and they walked over to Kruger's ever waiting staff car. They both saluted, 'Heil Hitler.' And then Kruger got into the back of the car and was driven away.

As the car left through the camp's gates, Igor Sym began to wonder. The Szabo family were being systematically exterminated, and it would only be a matter of time before Dr Szabo himself ended up on a train and was on his way to Auschwitz. But what was happening to Francine Szabo? Igor Sym had of course made discreet enquiries, and he knew that Mrs Szabo was being kept in a luxurious room at the Grand Hotel, and that her room was just along the landing, down from Herr Kruger's own private suite. Sym had also heard the stories about Herr Kruger's proclivity for Slavic women and his taste for Polish prostitutes. Herr Sym didn't fully understand what was happening, but he had his suspicions. He remembered Francine Szabo, and yes, she really was a very beautiful woman.

Igor Sym stood there, and he smiled as Herr Kruger's car disappeared from view.

Unfortunately for Sym, within the next two or three hours, Herr Kruger would have to return.

Igor Sym went back to his office to falsify some more paperwork. An hour later, one of his corporals tapped on his office door. Herr Sym bid him enter.

'What is it corporal,' Sym asked, hardly bothering to look up from his creative accounting.

'We're having problems with one of the prisoner's sir.'

'Really,' Sym replied, still uninterested.

"Yes sir, we went in with their food and one of them started screaming and shouting. We think he may be having some sort of mental fit sir. If he'd been Jewish, we would of course just have beaten him senseless.'

Igor Sym suddenly took notice. 'Who are we talking about, Corporal?'

'It's one of the Polish prisoners, sir. It's Breslav. He's out of control.'

Igor Sym immediately stood up.

'Let's go and see what this is all about,' he quickly replied.

As they approached the cells, Sym and his corporal could hear the commotion. Two other soldiers were standing outside the building and when they saw Herr Sym approach they just shook their heads as they saluted.

Adam Breslav could be heard screaming and shouting loudly threatening abuse. Everyone in the surrounding area of the camp could hear him and Sym, quite rightly, decided that something would have to be done.

He took a deep breath. 'Leave it to me,' he said to his soldiers. And with that, he went into the cells to confront Breslav.

Adam Breslav was standing there with both his hands clenched firmly on the bars of the cell.

Behind him, sitting on a bed was Pieter Szabo. Pieter glanced up at Herr Sym as he entered, but that was all. Pieter sat there, almost indifferent, he'd tried for days to calm his brother-in-law down, but the inevitable was about to happen. Pieter had seen it coming. Adam Breslav was on the verge of having a nervous breakdown.

'You fucking bastards, where is my wife? Where is my Ilsa?' Adam Breslav screamed when he saw Igor Sym.

Herr Igor Sym was somewhat taken aback by the barrage of insults. He certainly wasn't going to be spoken to in that way, he wasn't used to being shouted at. And besides, his men were standing outside and they would all hear all that was going on.

'Silence,' Herr Sym commanded, 'you will not speak to a senior officer in that manner.'

'Where is my wife?' Adam Breslav continued, as though Sym had hardly uttered a word,

'I want to see her, do you hear me? I want to speak to her.'

'Silence,' Sym again ordered. 'Do you hear me? I said 'Silence'.

But Adam Breslav continued to shake the bars of his cell and again shouted, 'I want to see my wife.'

'That is not possible,' Sym replied curtly.
'Why not?' Adam Breslav howled at him. 'Why can't I see her? Why?'
'Because I've told you, it's not possible,' Sym repeated himself.
But Adam Breslav was having none of it.
'You're a fucking bastard,' he shouted back at Sym, 'You're a fucking coward.'
That outburst angered Herr Sym and it hurt his pride. And now it was Herr Igor Sym's turn to shout. Suddenly, Herr Igor Sym lost his temper.
'You will not speak to me in that tone. And you will not address a German officer in that way. Do you hear me?' he bawled.
And in a moment of clarity, Adam Breslav looked directly at Igor Sym.
'A fucking German officer? You're not a German officer. You're Polish. You're just the same as everyone who's being held in this camp. You're a Pole, not a fucking German, you bastard.'
For a second, Igor Sym was dumbfounded. He was left speechless.

But Adam Breslav wasn't, not one bit.
'You're fucking Polish, you bastard. You're not a German, you're a Pole dressed up like a fucking Nazi. You've swapped sides, you piece of shit. You've deserted your own people and joined with the enemy. And now you're killing your own people. Look at you in that uniform, you look fucking ridiculous. You're not a man, you're not even a soldier. You're a fucking coward hiding behind a uniform. You're a disgrace.'
And with that, Adam Breslav spat straight into Herr Igor Sym's face.
Igor Sym stood for a moment in shock, and then he went berserk. He was an officer and he demanded respect. He'd worked for years to become a member of the Nazi Party, and to finally attain the glorious position as an SS Officer in the Third Reich.
But somewhere, somewhere in Adam Breslav's ranting, there had been an affirmation of the truth. And Herr Igor Sym recognized it, and he needed that thought or any rumour of that thought to be buried. Nobody must ever know that all he'd ever been was an actor. And with it the real truth, that he was still acting.
Herr Sym wiped the spittle off his face in disgust, and then he reached down to his side and unclipped his leather holster and took out his highly polished Luger pistol. The gun was loaded, but had never been shot in anger. Herr Sym pointed his gun at Adam Breslav.

'Step back from the bars, you bastard,' he ordered.

But Adam Breslav didn't move.

'Step back I said, and I'll tell you where your wife is,' said Sym slowly.

At the mention of his wife, Adam Breslav blinked. Suddenly there was a hope, suddenly he could find out where Ilsa was. Maybe there was a chance after all. And he lowered his hands from the bars and stepped back. Finally, he'd obeyed.

And Igor Sym saw it, but it wasn't enough. This man's abuse was unforgivable, and now Herr Igor Sym wanted his revenge too, no matter what the cost.

Adam Breslav just stood there and stared at his tormentor.

'Where is she?' he asked. 'Where is my Ilsa?'

In an act of sheer cruelty, Herr Sym decided to take on an 'official' tone of voice. He could do that. He was an actor.

He stared at Adam Breslav with contempt. And then he spoke.

'I'll tell you exactly where she is. Three days ago, I arranged for all of the Szabo women, including your wife Ilsa, to be put on a train with the Jewish women and their children. They were then sent to the Auschwitz Concentration camp to await execution.'

For some strange reason, Herr Sym then looked at his watch before he continued.

'That was three days ago. Our people at Auschwitz are very efficient, and by now I can only assume that all of your women will have been exterminated, and their bodies will have been burned in the ovens.'

Sym had spoken about this in such an informal way, that for a moment, Adam Breslav didn't take it all in. He was confused. And then all of a sudden, the words hit their mark. And Adam Breslav gasped as he realized what had just been said. He started to scream out loud, and in an act of blind fury, he launched himself at the bars of the cell. His hands reached out through the bars and he grabbed hold of Igor Sym's outstretched arm as Sym stood there, still holding the pistol. There was a tussle as Sym tried to pull away, but Adam Breslav was the stronger man and he was frantically trying to drag Sym towards him. Breslav was in a complete frenzy and would have ripped Sym to pieces. At that moment Igor Sym panicked, he was terrified, he'd never been involved in any kind of physical violence before and his first instinct was to try and free himself. But he couldn't.

Adam Breslav was pulling Sym's arm into the cell, at any moment he could grab the pistol. Sym was caught, and he knew it. And so in sheer panic, Igor Sym started to pull the trigger.

He shot Adam Breslav four times in the chest. Breslav dropped to the floor as one of the bullets found his heart. It was all over in seconds.

Herr Sym just stood there with the smoking Luger still in his outstretched hand as the three soldiers ran in. For a moment they all stood there in silence, the soldiers looking down at Breslav's fallen body.

Sym looked across at Pieter Szabo, and what he saw astonished him. Pieter Szabo had not moved one inch. He was still sitting on the bed, and he was staring straight at Igor Sym. Pieter's face was completely expressionless. There was no anger, no shock, and no fear, in fact, no alarm whatsoever. Pieter Szabo had seen death before. He just stared at Igor Sym, as you would a goldfish in a bowl.

But Pieter had heard the words...'and by now, all of your women will have been exterminated and their bodies will have been burned in the ovens...'

It was over, it was all over. The love of his life was dead, they were all dead. His beautiful wife, and his beloved mother and sisters. All of them had perished, and all because of him and his own stupidity. He had promised them that he would look after them all. But he'd failed. His promises were now no more than empty words.

Pieter just sat there and he stared at Herr Sym. And in that one moment he realized that his life was over. Whether he lived or died, it was of no consequence anymore. He'd lost Francine. He'd lost his only true love. She was gone, she'd been taken away from him. And his life was suddenly worthless. He sat there for a moment. And then he closed his eyes.

The soldiers dragged Adam Breslav's bloodied body out of the cell and then outside, and one of the soldiers found some canvas sheeting and covered him up. Herr Sym was in a state of panic, and he dashed back to his office to contact Herr Kruger. He picked up the phone and immediately got through to Kruger. Sym hurriedly told Herr Kruger what had happened.

'I'll come over straightaway' Herr Kruger had replied. And that left Igor Sym sitting in his office, alone and in shock. He'd never killed anyone, never shot anyone, and never thought that he would ever have to. He was an actor. And at the back of his mind, Adam Breslav's stinging words kept playing in his ears.

'You're not a man. You're not even a soldier. You're just a coward hiding in a uniform.'

Within half an hour, Herr Kruger had returned. And after a brief conversation with Igor Sym in his office, Herr Kruger took full control of the situation.

A truck was found and Adam Breslav's body was unceremoniously thrown into the back of it, along with a couple of shovels. The two soldiers that had carried the body also climbed into the back of the truck, which then drove off into the distance. Several kilometres away from the city, a deserted spot was found and a grave was dug. There would be no ceremony or service. No words were even spoken.

Adam Breslav's body was thrown into the grave and then covered over. Another life, ended.

Herr Kruger sat with Herr Sym in his office. They were talking as they drank coffee. Almost an hour had passed, but Kruger noticed that Igor Sym was still quite upset over what had taken place.

Kruger leant forward and put his hand on Sym's shoulder.

'It was your first time Herr Sym, and that's always the hardest. If there ever is a next time, you will without doubt find it a lot easier.'

Igor Sym simply nodded in reply.

Herr Kruger continued. 'And what you told me about young Szabo. You say he just sat there, staring at you?'

'Yes,' Sym replied. 'He never moved a muscle. He never stood up, never moved, not even when the gun was being fired. His face was totally expressionless.'

Kruger shook his head, 'he's certainly a cold fish.'

Igor Sym said nothing.

But Kruger continued. 'You should have shot that bastard too. It would have saved us a job.'

Sym just sat there. He'd never for one moment considered shooting Pieter Szabo. It had all been too much.

'Send that bastard to Auschwitz straight away.' Kruger instructed him, and then he stood up to leave.

'I'll do it as soon as possible, sir' Sym replied.

'See that you do,' replied Herr Kruger, and he turned and they made their way to his waiting staff car.

As Herr Kruger was being driven back to the Grand Hotel, he considered the events.

If only Igor Sym had shot Pieter Szabo, it would have been a problem solved. He could have turned the incident into an accident, surely he could have. And then he could have become Francine Szabo's shoulder to cry on. She would have nobody else.

'Damn it,' he said to himself, 'Damn it.'

Pieter Szabo sat alone in his cell.

His mind was overflowing, filled with countless thoughts. And he thought about the past, his wonderful past. And then the present, and what had happened, it was more than just a terrible tragedy. And now the future, or whatever the future was going to lay at his feet. Pieter thought about his life. It was over. And everything that he had ever known and ever loved had been snatched away from him. He would never see Francine again, and he felt the pain and the aching loss. Whatever happened now was of no consequence. Had he been a weaker man, he would have given up and died, one way or another. But there was an unrelenting determination that would not let him simply give up. And his mind wrestled with the guilt and the rage, and a remorseless loathing for the people who had been responsible for his family's death. Despair, no. Not Pieter Szabo. Despair would instead turn into hatred.

It already had.

He sat there. His life was over, and he didn't care what happened to him now. But given the chance, and given any chance at all, he would slaughter Igor Sym for what he'd done to Pieter's family. And then he would find and slaughter Henryk Kober and Wilfred Staszic. And he would do it in a most terrible way.

And so, on that same evening, Herr Kruger hadn't called on Francine Szabo, he'd left her alone in her room, obviously unaware of the day's events.

It would be late the next evening before he finally knocked on her door again. Francine had once more been locked in her room all day and for most of the evening, but at nine o'clock Wilhelm Kruger knocked on her door discreetly, as he turned the key and let himself in.

He stood there, smiling at her. Like a long lost friend, and like a knight in shining armour, he'd come to save his damsel in distress. And Francine's reaction was just as he'd expected, because she seemed pleased to see him.

It was what he'd hoped for, and what he'd planned for. But he was misguided, because her response to him was for all the wrong reasons.

As he entered, Francine stood up immediately. She saw that it was indeed Herr Kruger and that he was smiling. And for the briefest of moments she thought that he was bringing her good news. The long awaited news that her ordeal was over, and over for all of them, and that the Szabo family could finally be freed and that everything could return to normal.

But sadly, no.

And with that in mind, Francine too greeted Kruger with an expectant smile. And that alone made Wilhelm Kruger's foolish heart skip a beat.

'Good evening, my dear,' he said to her warmly, almost expectantly.

'Oh Wilhelm,' she replied, 'You're here.'

Unfortunately, her reply was a mistake. First of all, it gave Wilhelm Kruger hope, and secondly, she was going to be disappointed. They both were.

'Yes my dear,' he replied, 'and I'm so sorry that I've not been able to see you, but things have been a little hectic.'

'Oh really,' she replied, again hopefully.

'Yes,' said Kruger, 'But I'm here now, and I've organized some supper for us.'

And with that, he took hold of her arm and led her down the landing to his suite.

The food arrived as usual, followed by coffee and good brandy. And Kruger laughed as he and Francine ate and drank and spoke effortlessly. Kruger was relaxed and comfortable, he was enjoying himself. He felt good, and Francine Szabo looked good. More than that, she looked perfect.

But Francine had other thoughts on her mind. She'd already realized that Kruger had no news for her, but in her mind there was still the nagging question and the doubt. And finally, and mistakenly, she had to ask.

'Is there any news yet, of Pieter, and my family?'

And with that, the spell was suddenly broken.

Wilhelm Kruger's expression changed from that of contentment to annoyance. More than annoyance, it was anger. And it was the realization that behind all the niceties and all the comfortable conversations, Francine was still thinking about her 'damn' husband. And that she was still Pieter Szabo's wife.

And suddenly, his temper finally got the better of him.

'Why do you keep asking me the same stupid questions?' he snapped.

Francine stared back at him, she was speechless.

"Over and over again, the same damn stupid questions' he complained furiously.

Francine just sat there. She had said too much and she knew it. And she suddenly started to blink, as her eyes began to fill with tears.

'I'm so sorry Wilhelm...I didn't realize.'

It was all she could say.

Wilhelm Kruger stared back at her fiercely. He'd just suffered the worst of human emotions.

It was jealously, pure and simple. Worse than anger and more terrible than greed, it was a condition that could turn men into murderers.

He heard her apology, and he looked at her. He gazed across the table at her beautiful face. And then he saw the tears form in her eyes, and he suddenly realized what he'd done. And for once in his life, Wilhelm Kruger felt regret. It was an emotion that was hard for him to understand. But he was wrong, he knew he was wrong. And his expression suddenly changed, it had too.

'Oh god, Francine,' he said to her, 'I am so very, very sorry.' And with that he immediately stood and went over to her. He took hold of her arm and lifted her from where she sat, and he hugged her.

'Iâ€™m so sorry, I don't know what came over me.' and he hugged her tightly.

'It's okay,' Francine replied, 'it's alright Wilhelm,' she said again.

'I'm...I'm under so much pressure at the moment,' he said to her.' No one understands. Every day I get new instructions from Berlin. Everything lands on my desk. You see, my position is constantly under threat, and if there was ever any suspicion of ineptness, then the axe would fall upon 'my' head. My career would be over, I would be finished.'

For a moment, Francine actually felt sorry for him, or possibly pity.

'I'm so sorry Wilhelm,' she said to him, ' I didn't know. I just didn't understand.'

Kruger still held her. But he knew it was time to let her go. His ploy had worked, hopefully.

As he finally stood back, he looked down at her.

'Are we still friends?' he asked, almost bashfully. And he feigned embarrassment.

Francine smiled back at him. 'Of course we are. Don't be silly.'

And with that, there was nothing more to say. But they both knew that the evening had come to an end.

As usual, Kruger glanced at his watch and Francine continued to smile and commented on how good the food had been.

'I'll walk you to your room,' he said.

'Yes, I'm tired too,' she dutifully replied. And the evening was over.

Kruger walked Francine back to her room and he opened the door for her.

'Again, I'm sorry for the outburst,' he apologized. 'It was inexcusable behaviour and very ill-mannered of me. I really am sorry Francine.'

'It's forgotten Wilhelm, really. Think no more of it ' she replied, and then smiled back at him as she received her customary goodnight kiss on the cheek.

The door was then closed behind her and locked.

Francine walked into her room and sat on the edge of her bed. She took a deep breath. Tonight had almost been a disaster, and she realized that she must take more care in what she said and did. There was another side to Wilhelm Kruger, she realized that. But she was obligated to Kruger, he was her only ally. And above all, she really needed his friendship.

Kruger walked back down the landing to his suite. He took a sigh of relief, it had been close.

He'd almost lost her, and all through his own stupidity. And why? Kruger could have kicked himself over what he'd done. One stupid outburst and he'd shown his true colours. All of his hard work, and all of the planning and the deliberate and cleverly accepted answers. And then to spoil everything with a jealous tantrum. And yes, he'd realized exactly what it was.

He walked back into his suite, and he looked at the coffee cups and the empty glasses that were left on the table. And Wilhelm Kruger suddenly realized that his own life was empty too. Standing there in his suite and on his own once more, the room was more than empty, it had become lonely. Already he missed her. And he thought about earlier that evening, when he'd taken her in his arms and hugged her. And he'd felt her shape and the wonderful feminine smell of her body. Kruger slumped into a chair. He would have to do so much better, and he would have to try his best to regain her confidence. He stared down sullenly at the richly carpeted floor, and he considered his future. He simply could not lose this woman. He adored everything about her. For the first time in his life, Wilhelm Kruger had finally found a woman to really love.

He looked at the brandy bottle on the table, but he declined. And then he stood up and walked over to his bedroom. The evening was well and truly over. There would be no prostitutes tonight, his desperation would only turn into hopelessness.

No one could compare. No one.

But later as he lay in his bed, Herr Wilhelm Kruger did have one consoling thought. Everything had been arranged with Igor Sym. In the early hours of the following morning, Pieter Szabo, along with a truck full of Jewish men, would be loaded onto a train and transported to the Auschwitz Concentration camp. And within a day or so, Francine Szabo would be a widow. Then things would be different.

Then all he would have to do was wait, be plausible, and be patient.

Before the daylight even broke on the next morning, Pieter had been roughly awoken by two German soldiers. In the dull semi-darkness, he was led out of his cell and made to stand in line with another two hundred exhausted and bedraggled men. All were Jewish. Many of them shivered in the cold as they stood in line, waiting, and not knowing why. After the best part of an hour, several canvas-covered trucks trundled into the camp and stopped in front of the prisoners. Each truck was pale grey in colour and had the black cross of the German army emblazoned on the side. They stopped and parked in a line, and the prisoners were instructed to climb into the back of the vehicles. Some managed to sit down, others couldn't. Two armed guards climbed into the back of each truck with another guard sitting up in the front with the driver. Once loaded, the trucks set off as a convoy into the early morning light.

It took an hour for them to reach their destination. The trucks finally stopped and the guards immediately climbed out of the back, leaving the occupants in silent contemplation. The guards were talking to one another, but it was almost impossible to hear what was being said. Suddenly the canvas awnings were pulled back and everyone was ordered off the trucks. Men blinked as their eyes adjusted to the daylight and it took a few moments for them to realize their surroundings. They were at a railway siding, which the Germans had infamously renamed as the 'Radegast' Station. There was a waiting train there with half a dozen wooden cattle trucks in tow. The prisoners were lined up and ordered to get into the rough wooden carriages. Once they were all packed inside, the carriage doors were immediately slid shut and then locked. Inside each carriage was a single bucket. It was there to be used as a toilet. There were up to sixty men in each carriage, and the journey to Auschwitz would take at least three days.

The Nazi's plans for the extermination of the Jews were quite simple really. Feeder trains from specifically designated railway sidings were used to transport Jewish men, women and children to the various concentration camps. The death camps from which they would never return. And not only Auschwitz, there were other camps at Dachau, Buchenwald, Belsen and Treblinka, to name but a few, and all were at the end of a railway line.

Pieter Szabo sat alone in a dark corner of one of the packed carriages as the train slowly moved away from the Radegast Station. He'd already realized that the trip was going to be a living hell. No water, no food, nothing at all, and everyone was going to suffer badly. Pieter knew that the only way that he was going to be able to survive was to close his body down, both physically and mentally, just as he had in his cell at the camp. So he sat in the corner of the cramped carriage and he hardly moved. His breathing became slower and he relaxed as best he could. He had to use the least amount of energy possible and try to retain his bodily fluids. So Pieter sat there and he closed his eyes and thought about Francine. When he closed his eyes she was always there and he could talk to her. It passed his time and it helped him to settle. When he closed his eyes he could see his family, and when he closed his eyes he could imagine that he was back at home again, and in his mind he was in a better place.

The days passed by, and on the Thursday afternoon at the Grand Hotel in Lodz, Francine Szabo once again sat alone in her locked room. She was trying to read a book but her thoughts kept returning to Pieter, and the tiny baby inside her. Her thoughts were broken when there was suddenly quiet tapping on her door. Francine looked up. She expected the key to turn in the lock and somebody walk straight in. It would probably be one of the hotel staff.

She would have been somewhat surprised if it had been Wilhelm Kruger. Herr Kruger only came to her room in the evening, and had been doing the same on most evenings, when he would escort her to his suite where they would either dine or take a nightcap. Everything depended on the lateness of the hour.

However, nobody entered her room, and Francine just sat there looking at the door.

And then, someone tapped on the door again. She was locked in of course. Francine couldn't open the door to see who it was, so she called out.

'Yes, come in please.'

She heard a key turn in the lock, and the door slowly opened. A man stood there in the entrance and he was staring at her. It was Yaslov Slowowski, the hotel's manager.

Francine looked back at him, it was the first time she'd seen Slowowski since the day she'd been brought there from the camp.

'May I come in?' Slowowski asked in a low voice, it was almost a whisper. And then he quickly looked over his shoulder, as if to make sure he wasn't being seen by anyone.

Francine found this all this very strange, almost absurd. Because it seemed that almost anyone could walk into her room, unannounced, and at any time. But strangely, not Yaslov Slowowski.

'Yes, yes come in,' said Francine rather nervously, and she stood up, she felt that she had to.

With that formality out of the way, Slowowski immediately entered the room and quickly closed the door behind him. Then he turned to Francine.

'You don't know me,' he said to her, 'but I am the hotel manager, Yaslov Slowowski.'

'Yes,' Francine replied, 'I do remember you. You brought me here to my room on my first day here, along with those two soldiers.'

'Ah yes,' said Slowowski, 'you were quite upset at the time. I didn't know if you would remember me'.

There was a pause in the conversation. Slowowski had obviously come to her room for a reason, and he also looked quite nervous.

'I shouldn't be here,' he continued, 'I could get myself into a lot of trouble. But there's something that you need to know, and there's something I need to show you.'

'Yes' said Francine, rather cautiously. 'What is it Mr Slowowski?'

'First of all, I need you to promise me something.'

Francine looked at him, and she wondered just why she would have to promise this very worried looking man anything.

'What's the problem, Mr Slowowski?'

Yaslov Slowowski looked at her with amazement.

'The problem is that this hotel is full of Nazis, and that Poland has been invaded by the Germans. That's the problem. And there's also the problem that you could be in grave danger, and so could I, just by being here.

Francine swallowed, because she suddenly realized the significance of Slowowski's warning.

'And what do I need to promise you, Mr Slowowski?' she asked him.

He looked directly at her.

'That you won't run away, or even try to.'

Francine was mystified, but she agreed.

'Alright Mr Slowowski, I promise not to run away, though I doubt if I actually could.'

'No, you don't understand young lady. At some point, you may have to.'

Francine was totally confused, but Yaslov Slowowski simply turned around and carefully opened the door. He looked down the corridor, there was no one there.

He looked back at her and put his finger on his lip, a warning to keep quiet.

'Come with me,' he whispered.

Slowowski closed the door behind her but didn't lock it, and then they both walked down the empty landing in complete silence. Francine almost shuddered as she walked past Kruger's suite, part of her felt that she daren't go on any further. Slowowski glanced at Herr Kruger's door and then at Francine, but he said nothing. On they walked, right to the end of the landing, and then they stopped.

To their immediate right and almost hidden away in the corner, was a door. Because of the length of the landing it could hardly be seen. The door was flush with the wall, there was no door frame at all and it was painted and decorated to blend in with the same pattern as the walls. It was almost designed to be concealed.

'It's the fire exit,' said Slowowski.

Francine said nothing, she just listened.

Slowowski continued. 'It's a fire exit, and it is also used as a discreet entrance for any of the tradesmen who need to do any work here. We can't allow the painters and decorators to come tramping through the hotel, so they use this backstairs for access.'

'It's almost invisible,' said Francine.

'Yes I know,' Slowowski replied. And he turned a small handle which opened the door.

'Take a quick look,' he said.

Francine stepped forward and looked down to see a descending flight of stairs.

'It's like that all the way down to the ground floor,' Slowowski told her, 'at the bottom is a door with a large sliding bolt and that lets you out of the hotel in case of an emergency.'

Slowowski suddenly looked uncomfortable, and Francine wondered if the term 'an emergency' could mean something more.

Slowowski suddenly glanced back down the landing, and then he quickly closed the door. They walked back to Francine's room in silence, but once they were inside he spoke to her.

"No one must know that you are aware of that fire exit. That's why I couldn't just let you go. If you just disappeared, the staff would be blamed and there could be terrible repercussions. In the past, our guests were informed about the fire exits as a safety precaution, there are similar doors on each floor. But now the hotel is full of Nazis, I don't think that half of them know about the exits.' Slowowski shrugged his shoulders. 'We didn't bother to tell the bastards. If the place ever does catch fire they'll all die.'

For the first time, Francine smiled at him.

'But what you need to know Miss, is that you have an escape route'.

Francine looked at him. 'And why would I need one Mr Slowowski?'

'Because young lady, Herr Kruger is a very dangerous man,' he replied.

Slowowski felt he could say no more and that he'd already said and done enough. He too had to live his life carefully. He nodded to her, and then he turned and left the room.

Francine Szabo just stood there, alone once more, as she heard the key lock the door.

Late that evening, Kruger invited Francine to his suite for a nightcap. They had a pleasant hour's conversation, but no food. And Francine was mildly surprised. But Kruger was in jovial form and at the end of the evening he walked her back to her room and gave her the compulsory peck on the cheek and then he left. As he walked back to his suite, he smiled to himself.

The next evening he did the same thing. At nine o' clock he arrived at her door and escorted her to his suite, where once again they had their usual nightcap, but again no food, not even a snack. And this time, Francine was rather disappointed. For some reason, the meals that had been served to her in her room for the last couple of days had been quite bland and repetitive. And quite often, there had little more than some dark rye bread and a lump of cheese. She had always dined well, but for the last few nights for some reason, no.

It was Kruger's plan of course, it was he who'd made the changes to Francine's daily menu, but she wasn't to know that. And it was all part of Kruger's contemptibly misguided plan, pitiable as it was, to lure Francine Szabo into his bed.

After an hour's conversation, Kruger glanced at his watch and Francine readied herself to leave. But Kruger just sat there, still comfortable in his surroundings, and he smiled at her.

'My dear, I feel that I've been neglecting you,' he said.

Francine looked at him, but said nothing. And Wilhelm Kruger continued.

'I've had an enormous workload this week. New orders from Berlin, which has involved a lot of paperwork, and of course I've been trying my best to sort out your little problem too. And then there have been one or two problems with my staff, which I won't bore you with. However, I've managed to appease Berlin, which is a weight off my mind, and I can now relax and enjoy the weekend. So I've decided to treat you, well, both of us really. Tomorrow is a Saturday, and tomorrow night you and I are going to dine downstairs in the hotel restaurant. I've organized everything, the food will be quite delicious, I've spoken to the chef.'

And almost to her shame, Francine began to smile. And that was a mistake.

She smiled because at that moment she was actually quite hungry, very hungry in fact. And the thought of being somewhere else, other than in her own room or Kruger's room would be more than a welcome change.

But the bigger mistake, was that her smile gave Wilhelm Kruger hope.

At the end of their evening, Kruger, as usual, escorted Francine back to her room. He opened the door for her and wished her 'goodnight' and lent forwards to kiss her briefly on the cheek. And Francine accepted it, as usual. Herr Kruger was just about to close the door behind her, and then, almost as an afterthought he spoke to her.

'I'll come for you at seven o' clock.'

'Yes, alright then,' she replied pleasantly.

'Oh yes, and by the way,' he continued, 'wear that green dress. It's going to be a special night.'

And with that said, he closed the door and locked it.

The train finally pulled into the Station at Auschwitz.

After three days of nonstop travel, and with no food and water, the sixty men crushed into the one compartment had suffered appallingly. Several of the elderly had already passed away and they had to be laid in a corner and eventually stacked together at the end of the carriage. But in truth, it could have been a blessing. Rather than having to suffer the dreadful events planned for the rest of them.

The train shunted to a slow stop at their final destination. And in every carriage the men waited, exhausted and traumatized, as they lay or stood there, waiting for the guards to finally open the doors to each of the carriages, and release them from the stench of death and defecation. But there was no relent. The guards at the Auschwitz station were prepared for their visitors. They'd seen it all before. But this time the train was filled with nothing but men. Past trains had been full of women, some with children, and the guards had waited eagerly for their arrival and then they'd had their pick of the young and the beautiful. Some of the female prisoners endured the cruelty of being raped before meeting their inevitable end. And this had been the terrible finality for poor Elise Szabo, who had suffered terribly at the hands of men whose acts were something worse than indescribable.

The prisoners were ordered out of the carriages en masse, and the guards stood there pointing their rifles, as men were unloaded like cattle. Pieter was still sitting in the corner and he watched the tired and the fatigued as they climbed down onto the platform. Everyone was struggling and it was taking time and effort as the guards threatened and shouted orders at everyone. Pieter stared at the corpses that had been pushed into the opposite corner of the carriage. They would all have to be moved, eventually. And there must have been other corpses in the other carriages too, because everyone had suffered. And Pieter suddenly had an idea. The corpses, the dead bodies lying in the corner. He immediately got up, and he walked behind the men who were still waiting to get out of the carriage. He went over to the pile of corpses, and then he quickly looked behind him to see if anyone was watching. No one was, because everyone was trying to get out of that stinking carriage as soon as possible. Pieter took a deep breath, because he knew what he had to do. He climbed on top of the dead. He pushed a couple of the corpses to one side and squeezed himself in between the stiff and foul-smelling bodies, and then he stretched out like one of them. He was careful to turn his back to the carriage door so that he would look like 'just' another dead Jew. The stench was horrific, but Pieter didn't care. He considered that he was as good as dead anyway, they were all going to die, it was so dreadfully obvious. He lay there on top of those stiff and rigid corpses and he wondered what would happen next. He lay there, and he waited.

When the carriage had finally emptied, one of the guards looked in to check.

'Several more dead in here,' he shouted to someone, and then he moved along to the next carriage and virtually repeated himself. Another guard further down shouted out the number of dead in the carriages that he was checking, and at that point, Pieter stood up. He moved to the door and then very carefully peered out. Some of the guards were still checking the other carriages, but the rest of them were herding the prisoners onto the awaiting trucks that would carry them to the camp.

And that was the moment, it was now or it would be never. Pieter slid out of the carriage and then silently rolled back off the edge of the platform and fell onto the railway line below. He lay there under the carriage, no one had seen him. Then he crawled under the carriage and came out from the other side. There was nothing there more than an incline, and then some scrub bushes and some open land that led to a thin line of scattered trees. Pieter slid down the incline and then crawled through the bushes until he reached the open land, and still no one had noticed him. He turned back to look at the train, and then he realized the obvious. Nobody could see him because the train and the carriages were blocking the view. He then wondered about the driver, and he looked down towards the front of the train, but the driver's compartment seemed to be empty. This was his one and only chance. He made the decision, better to be shot trying to escape, at least it would be quick. Pieter stood up, and then he bolted for the trees. It was a distance of about thirty or forty yards, but for Pieter Szabo it felt more like half of a mile. At any moment he expected to hear shots ring out, and the old story about 'never hearing the shot that kills you', kept racing through his mind. As he ran he listened for men's voices, shouting after him. But no, all he could hear was the sound of his own laboured breath as he ran for his life. He reached the trees and threw himself to the ground and rolled over, he'd made it. He turned around and looked back at the train, but there was nothing. There was no alert, and there were no guards chasing after him. He'd got away completely unnoticed. He was free.

Behind Pieter was a steep forested hill, and he set off immediately. He needed to get some distance between him and the train, just in case he was finally missed. It was a wise decision.

He walked at a fast pace or ran for the next hour or so, and when he finally stopped and looked down at the train, it was now far below and distant. He could just make out the smoke that was belching out of the train's funnel, and as he looked down the train began to slowly pull away, leaving the railway siding empty. The human cargo had already been taken away in the trucks. Pieter stood there and watched the train disappear. All that was left was an empty railway line. Pieter stared down at the line, just two steel rails, all the way from Lodz to Auschwitz, and then it was all over.

Francine had travelled on that line, and so had his mother and his sisters. Just one train ride, and they were all gone.

Pieter Szabo could have cried, and maybe he should have cried. But no, all he felt was anger. And that anger had already turned into cold hatred. Somebody would have to pay the price for the loss of his family, and he knew exactly who those people were.

And then Pieter realized that everything wasn't over. He'd managed to escape and his father was still alive, and he knew that his father was still back there at the camp. He knew that the Nazis needed his father's skills as a doctor, at least for the time being. And suddenly, Pieter suddenly had a revelation. Those same railway lines would eventually guide him all the way back to Lodz. All he had to do was follow the lines from a safe distance. He'd make his way back there, and then he would find his father and somehow get him out of the camp before it was too late. It would take time for him to return, possibly a week, maybe more.

Suddenly, Pieter Szabo was desperate. He could not lose another member of his family. He had to try, but time was of the essence. Pieter set off once more, even more determined, now that he realized he couldn't waste a single day.

Saturday evening at the Grand Hotel.

And at exactly seven thirty, Herr Wilhelm Kruger tapped lightly on Francine Szabo's door. He'd tactfully unlocked the door, but didn't enter. He felt that on this occasion it would be good manners to wait outside until the lady answered the door. After all, she may still be getting herself ready, and he certainly didn't want to barge in there and upset things.

And the reason being, that tonight he wanted everything to be perfect.

In fact, Wilhelm Kruger was actually quite nervous. And though he'd managed breakfast, he'd not eaten anything all day as he tried to concentrate on the evening ahead, because tonight, deep in his heart, he wanted to cross a threshold. And tonight, if things went to plan, Francine Szabo could change his life.

Francine heard the tap on the door and then she heard the key turn, but nobody walked in. Francine stood there in panic, it was seven thirty and at any moment Herr Kruger was due to arrive. But the only person who'd ever knocked on the door without walking straight in was her confidant, Yaslov Slowowski, the manager. This could be a disaster.

Francine had taken over two hours to get herself ready. She'd washed and bathed and dressed her hair up into a beautiful chignon. And then she'd put on the green dress. And when Francine had looked at herself in the room's full length mirror she'd almost gasped. She looked stunning. The dress was stunning, and she couldn't help but stare at herself.

The dress, a beautiful shade of green, was not too dark and it shimmered under the light. Slightly off the shoulder, it was cut low enough at the front to be seen as decent, but lower at the back, to give the effect.

And as she stared at herself she thought about Pieter. It was Pieter who should see her in this dress, and it should be Pieter who was taking her out tonight. Francine thought about him, still locked in that camp while she was here, and about to dine at the restaurant in the Grand Hotel. And Pieter still didn't know about their baby, and at that moment Francine felt like crying. But suddenly, no. She had to stop herself. If she ruined her make up, then she would have to start all over again and that would take time and she mustn't keep Herr Kruger waiting, not tonight. And this was what it was all about. She needed Kruger, more now than ever. He was the only person who was capable of obtaining an official release for her family. She would have to play her part.

Unfortunately, she wasn't aware of the events that had already taken place.

She stared at the door.

If it was Slowowski she would have to get rid of him immediately. Surely he would understand. Yes, of course he would.

And then there was a second tap, and Francine took a deep breath.

'Yes, come in,' she said out loud.

The door slowly opened, and standing there in his full SS uniform was Herr Wilhelm Kruger, SS Commander, and head of the Nazi party. He was the man who was in charge of every German soldier in Lodz. Conceited and arrogant, he stood there, proudly wearing his full regalia, along with all the Nazi badges and all of his medals. He even wore his Luger pistol, which was clipped into a smart black leather holster. He exuded power. Power in excess.

Strangely, the only part of Kruger's uniform that was missing was his SS hat, which for obvious reasons, was deemed unnecessary.

Francine just stared at him, he was handsome and yet threatening, and she was at a total loss. But Kruger didn't notice any of that. He just stood there and looked at her. She was beautiful, and she took his breath away. She was the most beautiful woman that he'd ever seen.

'Francine,' he said to her, 'you look absolutely stunning my dear.'

'Thank you, Wilhelm,' she said carefully, 'it's the dress, it's this beautiful dress.'

He smiled at her, 'No my dear, I think it's you.'

And with that, he walked across the room to her, and he took hold of her hand and kissed it.

'And now,' he said pleasantly, 'let us go and have an evening to remember.'

They took the hotel lift down to the foyer, and as the lift's doors opened, all eyes turned. Kruger moved forwards and took Francine's arm, and as she stepped out of the lift everyone in the foyer went silent as they looked on in unabashed admiration. Other SS officers turned and nodded respectfully to their commander. There was no saluting or 'Heil Hitler' of an evening in the Hotel. Kruger liked a more informal atmosphere there, and once his day was over, and on many an occasion, he would spend time at the hotel bar with his SS officers, enjoying casual but respectful conversations.

Suddenly, Yaslov Slowowski arrived from seemingly nowhere. He too was dressed for the evening, wearing a slightly worn black Tuxedo, not to impress the guests, more to let them know of his presence. He was after all, the manager.

'Ah, Herr Kruger...How are you, sir?' he gushed.

'Good evening Slowowski,' Kruger replied casually. 'Our table, I take it that it's ready?'

'Of course sir, everything is as you instructed.'

Slowowski then turned to Francine. 'Good evening madam,' he said charmingly, 'what a beautiful dress.'

'Thank you' replied Francine, and for the briefest of moments they glanced at one another. Nobody noticed. It was a though they'd never met.

'This way sir, please,' he said to Kruger, almost as if Herr Kruger had never been to the hotel.

Slowowski escorted them both through the foyer and down a short flight of stairs and into the hotel's dining room. As they entered Slowowski clicked his fingers, and two waiters appeared immediately, both were immaculately dressed in starched white jackets. The dining room was quite full, and all heads turned. Slowowski then led Kruger and Francine to their table. The two waiters were already there, holding the chairs, ready to seat their guests.

It was all planned, obviously, Herr Kruger had seen to that.

The table had been strategically chosen. Placed against the wall, they were not surrounded, but they could be seen. And though they could be seen, they certainly couldn't be heard. The lighting was perfect, it was intimate, but not dark.. Kruger wanted to be seen, but he didn't want distracting. Tonight he wanted Francine Szabo all to himself.

A bottle of chilled champagne arrived immediately. The waiter took the bottle from a highly sculptured silver ice bucket and as some of the surrounding ice spilt to the floor, he popped the cork with such effect, that the other diners almost applauded.

The champagne was delicious, and Kruger toasted Francine's glass before they drank.

Kruger smiled at her. This was perfection.

'The champagne, it's beautiful,' he said to her.

Francine took a sip and blinked, and then she gasped.

'Oh, it's the bubbles, they tickle my nose' she said, and then she laughed. They both laughed. And so the night began.

'I've ordered some wonderful food,' Herr Kruger began, 'I've spoken to the chef.'

'What are we having?' Francine asked enthusiastically. She was still hungry, but Herr Kruger already knew that, he'd kept her meals to a minimum. Francine had been living on small plates of bread and cheese for the best part of a week.

'Ah well, tonight we dine on Poland's finest dishes,' Kruger replied. 'We shall start with Sour rye soup with sauerkraut and cabbage, and then an assortment of Pierogi dumplings. I've ordered potato and cheese, wild mushroom with egg, and beef with fried onion. What do you think?'

Francine was almost overwhelmed, and she laughed.

'You certainly have studied our cuisine,' she said to him.

'Yes, I find Polish food quite delicious, but there's more to come. For the main course, I have ordered you're famous 'Bigos' casserole, the Polish 'Hunters stew'. The chef has specially prepared it from venison and black pepper, with plums and spicy sausage. He guarantees me that it will be quite delicious. And for our sweet, we shall be having Cheesecake, flavoured with wild cherries, along with Rhubarb sorbet and thick cream.'

And Herr Kruger laughed as he saw the expression on Francine's face.

'I hope you have an appetite,' he said to her.

'I have now.' she replied. In fact, she was starving.

But Kruger knew that she was hungry. He'd already seen to that.

He turned and clicked his fingers, and almost immediately, the second bottle of champagne arrived.

They dined, and Herr Kruger drank, and Francine let him. She cleverly kept lifting her glass on his bidding, but only took the tiniest of sips. And somehow, Herr Kruger didn't seem to notice. After the soup and the champagne, Kruger ordered a bottle of German Hock, his favourite Riesling, and he'd already had a couple of glasses before the next course arrived.

Along with the alcohol, the conversation flowed. Wilhelm Kruger was a happy man. He was sitting opposite the most beautiful of women, and along with the food and the wine he was having an interesting and intelligent conversation. This was a whole new experience for him. In the past he'd only dealt with whores and the thought of ever dining with them never even crossed his mind, and why would it? But now, here was Francine, and as they spoke he couldn't help but glance at her and appreciate her shape and her beautiful pale skin. Here was a woman that he could talk to, and talk he did, because Herr Kruger had hardly eaten a thing all day either, and the champagne and the alcohol were readily coursing through his veins.

After the assorted Pierogi dumplings, they took a short break. And in anticipation of their forthcoming 'Hunters stew', Kruger ordered a good bottle of red Burgundy. They sat there and the mood mellowed, along with the Burgundy.

'How did you come to join the army, Wilhelm? Francine asked him. 'Did you always want to become a soldier?'

Kruger smiled whimsically and he shrugged his shoulders.

'Strangely, not really,' he replied. 'You see, I had a difficult childhood. There were two of us, I have an elder sister. When I was very young, my mother disappeared. For years I was under the illusion that she'd died, and I was terribly upset because my mother doted on me. My father however was a very difficult man, a bully really. And in truth, he never really cared for me, there was never any affection at all from him. It was my sister, Annette, who was always his favourite. I always felt as though I was in the way somehow. Annette is several years older than me and because of the age difference, she took charge of me. In fact, when I look back, I realize that she absolutely ruled me. And she somehow took over the house as though she was my mother, and my father was happy to let her, or so it seemed. My father and I never had anything in common, he was a council official and was always at work. I think he was trying to pursue a political career, but nothing ever came of it. Maybe that was the problem. Anyway, when I was around ten years old I discovered that my mother hadn't died. No, she'd run away, run away from my domineering father. And in a way I could understand that, because by that time I hated him too. But what I couldn't understand and never have, was that she left me, she'd left me behind. I always thought that she loved me but she deserted me too. And not only that, she never came back, she never came back to see me, ever. She never even visited me. And at ten years old when I found out that she hadn't died and that she'd run away and left me, well, it opened up a whole new set of wounds. At ten years old I became introvert and shy. I couldn't speak to anyone. All I had was my overpowering sister who felt that she could run my life, and I had a father who didn't care.

And then I was a failure at school, I was never academic, not like my sister. No one ever encouraged me you see. And then when I was about thirteen or fourteen my sister married a Lieutenant in the army. He was a very smart and aloof sort of man who wanted promotion, he wanted to get to the top. My sister Annette liked that. She was always arrogant, and she thought that they could eventually end up associating with the higher echelon of the German Army, they both did. Her lieutenant husband didn't like me either, I was always in the way I suppose. So they got married and moved away, and I was left alone in the house with my father. We hardly spoke, and when we did it was always some form of criticism from him, always. When I was sixteen my father must have discussed my future with my sister, and she in turn must have spoken to her husband. Because the next thing, I was stood in my father's study where he informed me that I was going to be enrolled as an army cadet. Annette's husband had apparently pulled a few strings and I was automatically enlisted. I had no say in the matter whatsoever. One week later, I was packed off to the academy. The first six months were the worst of my life, and at times I felt like running away. But where would I go? There was however, a Captain Ritter, he was one of the tutors there, and one day he took me to one side and told me that I would have to shape up. He seemed to understand my problems, and I suppose really, he'd seen it all before. We were all lonely young men, away from our homes and our families. Captain Ritter told me that I would have to do better, and that I would have to forget my home and forget my family. He told me that I had to look upon the army as my family, and that they would look after me. And so I did. The army became my life. And I too became determined and I too wanted to rise to the top. And I have.

I studied hard and I worked hard, and I eventually arrived in Berlin and made a name for myself. It's not been easy, nothing ever is. But now I have the rewards.'

Herr Kruger reached for his glass and almost toasted himself. He was breathing heavily with emotion and Francine suddenly realized what drove this man. His ambition had been a substitute for love, it was so obvious.

'Do you ever see them at all? Your family I mean?' Francine asked him.

Kruger just blinked, he was almost in a dream as he delved back into his own past. And then suddenly he looked back at her.

'I'm so sorry my dear, what was that you said?'

'Your family Wilhelm, do you ever see them?'

Kruger shook his head.

'My father died, three, maybe four years ago now. He'd retired by then. I had to go back home for his funeral of course. It was an absurd affair. My father was obviously not a liked man and most of the people who attended were associated with the council. I doubt if half of them even knew him.'

'And was your sister there?' Francine asked.

Kruger exhaled. 'Oh yes, she was there, along with that bloody husband of hers.'

And with that, he reached for his glass and took another drink, and then he smiled at Francine.

'Oh yes, they were there. But suddenly the tables were turned. You see, we'd never been in touch, because she'd never bothered to. I was obviously seen as the family embarrassment and she wanted nothing to do with me. She must have thought that I was a foot soldier in the infantry or something, I really don't know. However, on the day of my father's funeral, I arrived in one of our black Mercedes Benz staff cars, and I was by then, 'Major Wilhelm Kruger' of the SS. My sister was dumbfounded, both she and her husband. You see, her lieutenant husband had only ever managed to rise to the rank of a captain in the regular German Army. During the service she must have given it all great thought, because afterwards, outside the church, she came strutting over to me with her stupid husband in tow. I remember it all. And once more, she tried to take charge of everything. She began to speak to me as though I was an underling and as though we were still children. She began to give me instructions about what was going to be done with the house, and what was to be done with my father's money. I let her carry on for a while, and I just stared at her. And then I spoke.

'Annette, will you shut your mouth you stupid bitch,' I told her.

She just stood there wide-eyed, and speechless. Her husband had the sense to keep his mouth firmly shut. He knew that I completely outranked him. And that I was in the SS.

'Now you can listen to me,' I told her, 'because this is what is going to happen. Any money that my father had, will be immediately donated to the Nazi Party. It will go to the Third Reich and to our glorious leader, Adolph Hitler. Put like that, she couldn't do a thing.

And then I continued.

'And I will have the house locked up, until I decide what should be done with it.'

She uttered one word...'But'

And at that moment her husband grabbed her arm and pulled her back. Then he came forward to salute me.

'Thank you, Herr Major,' he said, 'we shall of course, follow your wishes, 'Heil Hitler.'

And with that, I got into my staff car and was driven back to Berlin. I've never been back.'

'And what happened to the house?' Francine asked.

'Oh, it's still locked up as far as I know.'

Kruger looked at Francine and he smiled warmly at her.

'Do you know Francine, I've never told that story to anyone. Nobody knows my history, only me. And now, so do you.'

He stretched in his chair and he grinned at her.

'It actually feels quite good to get all that off my chest, it's almost a release,' and then in a moment of openness he said to her. 'You may not know this, but you are so good to talk to, Francine. You are the only person who understands me.'

Francine was quite taken aback by his declaration, and she didn't know just what to say. But the moment was suddenly broken as a host of waiters arrived at their table. They brought fresh warm plates and baskets of dark rye bread along with bowls of buttered potatoes and assorted vegetables. In the centre of the table they placed a large earthenware pot. One of the waiters took away the lid as another ladled the delicious 'Hunters stew' onto their plates.

As the waiters moved away, Herr Kruger called after them.

'Bring me another bottle of Burgundy.'

And the evening continued.

They finally finished the rich stew, and then they both sat back in their chairs for good measure.

'That was damned good,' Kruger remarked.

'Yes Wilhelm, it was delicious,' Francine replied, 'but now I'm so full.'

Kruger laughed. 'Yes I know, we'd better have a break before our desserts.'

Francine just laughed at him and openly shook her head. But Herr Kruger was having none of it, Herr Kruger was enjoying himself, because Herr Kruger was becoming drunk.

He turned to a passing waiter.

'Bring us some coffee, and cognacs.'

The coffee and the brandy arrived, and Kruger ordered himself another brandy just before their desserts arrived. Then he asked for another bottle of champagne.

The dessert was mouth-watering. A rich cherry flavoured cheesecake accompanied by a rhubarb sorbet which was topped with thick cream.

It was the perfect end to a perfect meal, for Kruger.

Francine too was astonished by the food. In her life, she had never imagined that she would ever dine at the Grand Hotel.

It was a heady evening. By this time Kruger was half drunk and even Francine could feel the slight effect of the alcohol, even though she'd tried to drink carefully. The problem was that they had both been drinking on empty stomachs. Francine was happy to let Kruger drink as much as he wanted. At some point he would hopefully pass out. But Kruger had other intentions. He was after all, with the woman he loved.

Halfway through the bottle of champagne, Kruger made a decision. They were to go up to his suite and finish off the champagne in comfort. He ordered a pot of fresh coffee to be taken up there, along with a bottle of his favourite brandy.

As they both stood up to go, Kruger stumbled slightly and Francine took hold of him to stop him from falling. Kruger laughed, and so did Francine, and as she propped him up to help him, his arm naturally reached around her shoulders. For Kruger, it was more intimacy.

He looked down at her and he laughed again.

'You saved me, Francine,' he said to her.

'Yes,' she replied. 'It's a good job I'm here.'

They were all the wrong words, with all the wrong meanings.

They walked to the lift together, Kruger with the champagne bottle in one hand and Francine in the other. It was the perfect evening.

They caught the lift to the top floor and they both laughed as Francine helped him all the way to his suite. Kruger's arm had by then, slid further down and was now around Francine's slim waist. They went into the suite and Kruger took two glasses from a cabinet and filled them with the champagne.

'To us,' he toasted.

'To us' replied Francine, good heartedly.

And just as Herr Kruger was about to say something, there was a knock on the door. Kruger took a deep sigh of frustration, but Francine didn't notice it.

'Come in' he said loudly.

The door opened and one of the waiters stood there with one of the hotel serving trolleys. On it was a pot of fresh coffee and some cups and saucers, along with the bottle of brandy.

Herr Kruger blinked for a moment, he'd forgotten all about the coffee that he'd ordered, but he smiled when he saw the bottle of brandy.

'Ah yes, good,' he said to the waiter, 'come in, come in.'

The waiter pushed the trolley over to the coffee table near the fire, and then Kruger dismissed him.

'It's alright. We can sort ourselves out, thank you.'

The waiter nodded at Herr Kruger and tactfully left the room. And Kruger, ever smiling, then turned to Francine.

'Would you sort out the coffee, Francine?' he said, and he went over to a chair where he took off his SS Jacket and the belt that held his holster and the Luger pistol

'At last I can relax,' he said as he loosened his tie. Then he went back to the cabinet and picked out two brandy glasses. He went to sit on one of the settees in front of the coffee table. Francine carried the tray of coffee and the brandy over to the table and she was about to sit opposite him, but no.

'Sit here at the side of me Francine,' he said to her, 'I want to talk to you about something.'

For a moment, Francine had hope. She actually thought that Kruger had some good news for her. Information that he didn't want to talk about while they were dining.

And she smiled at him, another mistake.

'Okay Wilhelm,' she said as she put down the tray down. And as she sat down beside him, Kruger uncorked the brandy and generously filled both glasses. He then reached for his own glass and took a drink. He sighed as he tasted it, and he sat back on the couch and took in the shape of Francine's beautiful body and her exquisite face. She was absolutely beautiful.

'We've had a wonderful night,' he said to her, and he took another large drink from his glass.

He was by now, quite intoxicated.

'It's been lovely,' she replied as she continued to pour out their coffee.

'And so has the conversation,' he quipped, as Francine slid his cup of coffee in front of him.

'Yes, it's been really nice' she replied.
'You know, you're a good friend to me, and more than just a friend.'
'Yes Wilhelm;' she said to him, 'we've become good friends over the last few weeks, haven't we?' And then she took her chance.
'Didn't you say that you wanted to talk to me?' she asked.
Kruger smiled at her, and he finished off his glass of brandy and the then leant forwards to put the empty glass back on the coffee table. It was time for him to tell her how he felt.
'Come here Francine,' he said to her and he reached out for her to give her a hug.
And still Francine thought that he was just being friendly.
'You mean more to me than anything in this world,' he then told her, 'and I want us to be together Francine. I love you, and I know you feel the same way.'
She was about to say something, and as she turned to face him he took hold of her and kissed her passionately on the lips. For a moment she was in shock, and she didn't know how to respond, and she just sat there. But Kruger took this as an acceptance. And as she sat there, Kruger slipped his hand across her waist and he reached up to her and cupped her breast. And when he began to fondle her, Francine suddenly realized what was happening and she realized that somehow she would have to stop him.
She shook her head, to stop him kissing her.
'No Wilhelm, please, please stop.' And then she tried to push his hand away from her. But Wilhelm Kruger was more than aroused. He was now fairly drunk and he was finally with Francine Szabo and he was kissing her and he had hold of her wonderful body. He wasn't even listening to her. Francine began to squirm, and that made him even more aroused and he reached up and quickly slid her dress off her shoulder. She was semi-naked and he stared down at her open breasts, and then he leant forward and nuzzled her and then tried to suck her nipples.
It all happened so quickly. Kruger was a powerful man and Francine's arms were caught up in her dress and she couldn't shake him free. And suddenly Kruger's hand began to reach for her thigh and Francine realized what was about to happen. She started to shout in his ear and then she finally freed her arm and started to hit him over the head.

Kruger suddenly stopped, something was wrong. And in a drunken haze he stopped what he was doing and he looked up at her.

'Stop it. Stop it,' she shouted at him. What are you doing?'

'What's wrong?' Kruger replied, rather stupidly.

'I can't let you do this Wilhelm, I can't.'

He stared at her, 'But why do you think we're here, Francine?'

'I thought you had news about my family, and about Pieter.'

Again he stared at her, through his drunken haze.

'Forget about them, Francine, and forget about that husband of yours. They're all gone. Everyone's gone, but I'll look after you now. I love you.'

And with that, he lurched forwards again and he started to kiss her once more and again he reached for her breasts.

She screamed angrily at him 'Get off me now, get off me.' And once more she pushed him away and she tried to cover herself.

Kruger stopped, he still didn't understand.

'I'm a married woman, you can't do this,' she shouted at him.

'Well now you can marry me,' he said drunkenly, 'I'm the better man. I'll propose to you right now. Will you marry me, Francine, will you?'

Francine stared back at him. And she suddenly realized that it was all a lie. He'd tricked her. He'd put her in this hotel and wined and dined her for one reason only. It had all been a lie. He'd never had any intention of trying to help her family.

And suddenly she was angry. She'd been misled and betrayed. What did he mean that everyone 'was gone?' What had he done with them?

She was seething with anger. And that was about to be her downfall.

Kruger smiled drunkenly at her and he reached out for her again.

'Will you Francine, will you be my wife?'

Francine Szabo exploded with hatred.

'Your wife...never,' she said with loathing, 'I've listened to you whine all evening about yourself and your poor little life. Let me tell you something. You don't want a wife. You want a mother.'

He stared back at her in complete shock. She was suddenly someone else, someone that he didn't know. He'd just admitted to her that he loved her and that he would marry her, and now she was screaming at him.

'What?' he said to her, and he shook his head to try and make sense of it all, and then, 'how dare you speak to me in that way.'

'You've lied to me,' Francine continued to shout, 'and now you're trying to rape me. I'm a married woman, you know that. You were supposed to be helping us. I love my husband, not you. I would never marry a man like you.' She almost spat the last words.

Kruger suddenly looked at her with rage and disgust. In his eyes, it was he who'd been tricked. She'd been so nice, and so very willing and accommodating. But now he realized that it had been an act, just to get her own way. And he'd been used and he'd been manipulated, and suddenly he was angry.

'A married woman? Is that what you think you are?' he sneered, and the alcohol in him started to make his blood boil.

Francine just stared up at him, she didn't understand.

'No, you're not a married woman any more Francine Szabo. You're a widow.'

Francine blinked as she tried to take in just what he was telling her. Was this another threat?

But Kruger was now angry and upset, and he was embarrassed because he'd told her everything that was important to him, and he'd told her just how much he loved her. But now, suddenly, she'd rejected him, and she'd done it with a vengeance.

And now, he wanted to hurt her. And he would.

'Your husband...and your family, all of them, they're all dead, Francine. I had them all shipped out last week. They were put onto the train and sent to the Concentration Camp at Auschwitz. They all died over a week ago,' and then he sneered at her, 'So you see, you have no one. No family, and certainly no husband. All you have is me, Francine'.

Francine just stared at him as she realized what he'd just told her

Kruger looked down at her, and even though she'd tried to cover herself, he could still see the beautiful curve of her breasts as she lay there, so very helpless. And love suddenly turned to lust as he realized that she was no different from the other whores that he used. He'd made a mistake, all women were whores, it had always been the same. They were bitches, just like his mother.

He pushed her back on the couch and grabbed her hands as he began to kiss her mouth. She could smell the brandy on his breath and she shook her head to try and shake him off. But he was incensed and he lowered his head to her breasts and he took her nipple in his mouth and sucked it roughly. He was on top of her and he was heavy and strong and overpowering, and her mind was still in shock over what he had just told her. He was hurting her, and then as he sucked her other breast his hands went under her dress and he began to feel his way up her legs. Her dress was suddenly up to her waist as he felt for her underwear.

She had to stop him, she had to think, she had too.

'Wilhelm,' she suddenly gasped, and she leant over and whispered into his ear. 'Wilhelm,' she panted, 'Wilhelm, it doesn't have to be like this. Wilhelm, you don't have to hurt me. If you want to make love to me, let's do it properly and without all this struggling. Let me take off my underwear and get comfortable. It will be so much better, I promise you.'

Kruger heard her voice, her soft voice, and in his drunken state he thought that she'd reconsidered. In truth, he was drunk and he didn't really care, but the thought of her taking off her underwear and then openly spreading her legs for him aroused him even more. He would make love to her there on the settee, and then he would strip her completely naked and carry her into his bedroom and ravish her until the early hours. It would be interesting to see if she was prepared to do the same things that the other whores were willing to do.

He pulled himself up and off her and he smiled drunkenly.

'That's better,' he slurred. And he watched her as she put her hands under her dress and then wriggled out of her underwear.

She smiled up at him. 'I'm so sorry I shouted at you,' she said submissively, 'it was silly of me.'

Kruger looked down and grinned at her. He was drunk and he didn't care. He climbed on top of her again and she opened her legs as he pawed her with one hand and tried to unbutton his pants with the other. For an instant, Francine felt sick. Not only was this man about to rape her, he had also murdered her beloved husband and her family.

And with that thought in her mind, Francine reached over to the coffee table for the brandy bottle, and she hit Kruger's over the head with it. The bottle didn't smash, but Kruger moaned and slumped forwards and with that, Francine pushed him off her and he rolled onto the floor. She jumped up and managed to get her arms back into her dress. But Kruger was beginning to stir and he suddenly looked up at her.

'You bloody bitch.' he shouted and he began to get to his feet.

Francine picked up the bottle again and this time hit him in the side of his face. Kruger fell back, but he was still conscious. Francine strode over to him and lifted the bottle again. This time she hit him in the face with all of her strength and the bottle smashed and lacerated the side of his temple and his eye. Kruger keeled over and collapsed, there was blood spurting all over his face.

Francine turned around. She had to get away, she had to run. She went quickly to the door and quietly opened it. The hotel landing was empty. Down the corridor to her left was her room, but Francine turned right. She ran to the end of the landing, trying not to panic, and there she found the hidden door to the fire exit. She opened the door and looked inside. It looked pitch black down there, but she knew she had no other option. Slowly, she began to make her way down the several flights of stairs, but the further she went, the darker it became. And the reason why? Because in her panic she'd left the fire door open so that she could see where she was going. And that was her mistake.

Kruger moaned, and he slowly rolled over. He felt the warm blood still running down the side of his face and for a moment he was disorientated. And then he remembered. It was Francine. And though still in a drunken haze, he wiped his face with his sleeve and looked to see that it was stained red. He looked around the room and then he realized that she'd fled. And with that, his temper returned and he staggered awkwardly to his feet. He shook his head and he looked around the room, and then in his drunken state, he made an immediate decision.

He was going to kill her.

He went over to the chair and struggled slightly as he took the Luger out of its holster. The blood was still running down his face and his vision was blurred and hazy, but he made his way out of the door and lurched down the landing towards Francine's room. Once there, he launched himself through the door, but the room was empty. Kruger then turned around and made his way back down the landing. He had to think. If Francine had gone down in the lift, she would arrive in the hotel foyer and somebody would have seen her, surely. And if she'd used the main stairs she would have still arrived in the hotel foyer. Would she take that chance, maybe she would, perhaps she'd walked straight out of the hotel. Or there was the possibility that she could have gone down to a different floor and be hiding in another room somewhere. The chances were slim, but if that were the case, she would be easy to find.

But somehow it didn't make sense.

Kruger looked back down the landing and back to his own room. The blood kept running into his eye and the side of his head throbbed uncontrollably. For a moment he passed out and he slid down the wall to the floor. After a moment he opened his eyes and once more struggled to his feet. He felt dizzy and he had to steady himself. He looked down at the floor, the carpet was stained with the blood from the gash down the side of his face. He looked back towards his own suite, and it was then that something caught his attention. Though his vision was blurred, he could see something at the end of the corridor. Once again he lurched forward and he slowly made his way past his own door and down to the end of the landing. Suddenly he saw it. The door to the fire escape was open, Francine had fled down the back stairs and would exit through the rear of the hotel. Slowly, Kruger made his way down the stairs, he had to find her.

Francine was halfway down the stairs when she tripped and fell. She tumbled down several steps and she lay there winded and sore. Her ribs hurt her and her breathing was heavy, and her leg and her ankle ached. She lay there for a while as she hoped and prayed that nothing had broken or was sprained. Finally she got to her feet. She had to get away, she had to. And she felt her way, rather unsteadily to the bottom of the stairs. It was still pitch black but Francine could just make out the dull light coming through the bottom of the door frame. She reached the door and felt for the bolt and somehow managed to open it, and then she stepped outside. She was at the back of the hotel. She'd made it. She hobbled away slowly. Now she had to escape.

But Francine should have closed the door behind her, and that was another mistake.

As Kruger made his way down the stairs he heard a noise. And when he looked over the balcony he saw down below him the dull light coming through the exit. He'd been right. Francine had come this way and she wasn't too far in front of him. He tried to hurry down the stairs but the alcohol and the damage to his head slowed him, and then he fell too.

Kruger tripped and went headlong down the darkened stairs and he again smashed the side of his face, this time onto one of the lower steps. He was in agony, and he felt his eye begin to swell and close as it continued to bleed. Somehow he managed to get himself down the rest of the stairs and he slowly made it to the exit as best he could, and then he too stepped outside and into the dull evening light. He staggered onto the road at the rear of the hotel, which was only lit by the occasional gas lamp. But he thought he saw something, a movement. He wiped his bloodied eye with his sleeve and then rubbed both of his eyes with the palms of his hands.

Something in the distance was moving. He reeled for a moment, but then he regained his balance and lurched forwards. After no more than a dozen steps he saw her. Through his one good eye he saw her green dress in the distance. She was no more than fifty yards away. It was Francine and she was limping and she too was struggling to walk. Kruger felt a wave of nausea run through him. He felt ill, he couldn't go any further, and he hadn't even got the energy to shout after her. He lifted his Luger and aimed, and then he pulled the trigger.

Fifty yards away, Francine limped away from the hotel as best she could. She was crying. After all the shock and the evening's events, she now fully understood Kruger's words. Her darling husband, Pieter, was dead. And so were the rest of her loving family. They were all gone, and all she had left in their memory was the baby inside her, and she sobbed in desolation as she slowly limped away. She would have to find somewhere and hide. If she could just keep going, maybe she could knock on someone's door and they would let her in and she could stay there for the night. Surely somebody would help her, and then she could get rid of this damn dress.

But suddenly from nowhere, there was the sound of a shot being fired, and a bullet whisked by her foot and buried itself in the ground in front of her. Francine stopped, for a moment she was paralysed with fear. Then she turned, and there, fifty yards away was Herr Wilhelm Kruger, and he was pointing a gun at her.

He'd just tried to kill her.

Francine turned, and she tried her best to escape, but it was no good. She struggled. She couldn't run.

Kruger began to sway, he was exhausted, and he suddenly staggered, but somehow he managed to stay on his feet. Blood loss, concussion and the alcohol, were all finally taking their toll. And as his head began to spin he realized that he was about to collapse. He stood there for a moment, knowing he had to concentrate. He slowly raised the Luger and he closed his damaged eye completely. He looked directly down the barrel of his gun, and he aimed at the centre of Francine Szabo's beautifully slender back. And for a split second he remembered her, and he remembered their wonderful evening together. It had all started with so much hope and so much promise. He would have done anything for her, anything at all.

But still he took aim. And then his own legs began to buckle and he felt faint, but in his last seconds of concentration he fired off three shots.

The darkness then closed in on him, but before he finally collapsed he saw the woman in the green dress fall over and slump to the ground. She was the only woman that he'd ever loved.

And now he'd killed her. It was over.

CHAPTER 8

It took Pieter Szabo over a week to return to Lodz.

The way back was a long and arduous trek as Pieter followed the railway lines all the way from Auschwitz, using the track as his unwavering guide. Occasionally he'd come across the odd farm or smallholding, and the good and loyal Polish people who lived there had helped him as best they could. Hot food and sustenance, and a change into warmer clothes and possibly a bed for the night were the best they could offer. Some had even offered transport. But Pieter, even though he was tempted, felt that he had to decline. If those poor farmers were caught helping him in any way, they would undoubtedly suffer the same consequences as his own family. The Nazis would use any excuse to beat the Polish people into submission, anything at all. The food and the shelter were enough, and when he told them his story, those same farmers wished him well when he left, always very early on the following morning.

But on other nights he'd had to shelter in the forest under some low lying branches or random bushes and try to find refuge and sleep. He couldn't light a fire that could possibly attract attention. So Pieter would lie there in the dark and once again remember Francine, totally unaware of the events that had taken place.

It was the fourth day, as he made his way through some dense forest that he heard the commotion. He heard a shot and then a man's voice shouting something in German, and then suddenly a woman began to scream. Pieter was immediately alert. He moved quickly forward through the trees until he came to a clearing. Less than fifty yards in front of him was a small farmhouse. It was a traditional Polish farm building, with a comfortable veranda and a thin plume of grey smoke rising out from the chimney. It was no more than a smallholding really, with a stone barn and a couple of other outbuildings.

Parked in front of the farmhouse was a grey car with the black and white German cross emblazoned on the door. Pieter looked on in disbelief, and for a moment he couldn't believe what he saw. Lying on the farmyard cobbles in front of the car was a dead horse, it had been shot through the head and it lay there in a pool of its own blood. There were two German soldiers, one who had his arm around a woman's neck. He was holding her tightly to stop her from struggling. Pieter noticed that in the soldier's free hand there was an opened bottle of vodka. The second soldier was violently kicking a man who was lying on the ground, the man had rolled up into a ball and was trying to protect himself, but the soldier was repeatedly attempting to kick the man in the head.

Pieter was shocked by what he saw, it was obvious that the soldier was trying to kick the man unconscious, or even kill him. And Pieter immediately read the situation, the man must be the farmer, and once he was taken care of and out of the way, the soldiers would be free to do whatever they wanted with the woman. She was aged about forty, and was still young enough to suffer the inevitable, the bottle of vodka would fuel the events.

Pieter moved to his right to where the trees thinned out at the side of the farmhouse. He moved quickly and was unseen, the soldier's attentions were on other things. He came out of the trees at the back of the farmhouse, and he sprinted silently to the back of the house. He stood there for a moment, trying to catch his breath as he wondered what he was going to do. He had no weapon. He had no gun, nothing at all, but he had to do something. He crept around the side of the building, still with no plan in his mind, and then he saw the answer to his prayers. Stacked at the side of the wall was a small pile of old red house bricks. There were about a dozen of them and they could have been there for years, and probably had. Age and frost had cracked some of them and several had broken in half. Pieter leant down and picked up one of the broken half bricks, it easily fitted into his hand and Pieter felt its weight. Now, suddenly he had something. He had a weapon.

He moved towards the corner of the house and slowly peered around the wall. No more than ten feet in front of him the soldier still had hold of the woman and he laughed and as he urged his comrade to finish the job. The woman screamed again but the sound was short lived as the soldier tightened his grip around her neck. The soldier again laughed and then he took another drink from the vodka bottle. The other soldier was now trying to stamp on the farmer's head, but he'd rolled into a tight ball, covering his head with his arms and now the soldier was having difficulty in reaching his attempted target. The soldier had a pistol in his holster and things were about to get worse.

Pieter walked straight out from behind the farmhouse. He strode over to the soldier and smashed the brick onto the top of his head. There was a slight crunching sound as the sharp corner of the brick crushed the man's skull. The soldier did no more than groan as he instantly died and dropped to the floor. That action should have given Pieter time to reach the second soldier, but unfortunately the dead soldier dropped the bottle of vodka, and as it hit the cobbled farmyard floor, the glass bottle smashed loudly.

At that point, the second soldier stopped kicking the farmer, who instinctively rolled away. The soldier turned around, and for a moment he didn't understand why his comrade was lying dead on the floor with blood gushing from a broken skull. The second soldier had been drinking too, and he had to shake his head before he realized what had happened. He looked across at the woman, and then he saw Pieter, who was standing there with the brick in his hand. The soldier swore loudly and then stepped back, and for a moment he and Pieter just stared at one another. And then Pieter moved towards him, but the soldier immediately grabbed for the pistol in his holster. Pieter was less than twenty feet away, but that distance gave the soldier enough time. He raised his pistol, ready to aim and fire, and as he did he cursed out loud. Death was seconds away.

But the last thing the soldier would ever remember was the intense pain as a knife plunged into the side of his throat, ripping and tearing at his arteries. The soldier dropped his pistol in shock, as a large hand covered his face and pulled his head back, and then the same knife cut across his throat and almost sliced his head off. The soldier did no more than cough, and then he died as he slid to the ground. Standing behind him was the farmer, and in his hand was a knife with the sharpest of blades.

The farmer wiped the bloodied blade on his pants and then folded the knife and returned it to his pocket. He stepped over the dead soldier and then walked over to his wife and hugged her as she burst into tears. Pieter just stood there and watched them. The farmer looked down at his wife and asked about 'the boy' and the woman nodded her head and wiped away her tears.

It was only then that the farmer turned to Pieter.

'Thank you, my friend,' he said.

Pieter just nodded.

There was the farmer, and of course his wife. And the 'boy' that they spoke about turned out to be their eleven year old son. His name was Alex.

The farmer sent his wife into the house and then he and Pieter carried the bodies of the two dead soldiers over to the car and heaved them onto the back seat. Some sheeting was found and the bodies were then covered up. The farmer went to get some rope and they tied the dead horse to the back of the car and then dragged it over to the barn and covered it with loose straw. After filling some buckets with water, they then swilled away all of the blood.

The farmer invited Pieter into the house where they washed and then sat around the kitchen table and quietly ate. Their young son sat with them, and because of that, the conversation was slightly stilted, the boy was quiet and still quite shocked.

After the meal, the farmer's wife took their son off to his room to read to him and to settle him down. And that gave Pieter and the farmer the chance to sit and speak openly.

'How did it happen?' Pieter asked, as he sat back in his chair and drank from a mug of black tea.

The farmer shook his head.

'Those bastards, they came from nowhere. The first thing we heard was their car coming down the track. They rolled into the farmyard and strutted around as though they owned the place. I tried to be friendly but they just walked into the house and demanded vodka. My wife gave them the bottle and made them some coffee. But they soon drank that and then demanded more. My wife put another couple of bottles on the table, but they got louder as they drank more of the vodka. And one of them kept looking at my wife, and I knew that we were in trouble. They asked for more vodka but I told them we had none. Maybe that was my mistake, I should have let them drink themselves stupid and when they collapsed we could have made a run for it. But that soldier kept looking at my wife and I knew what was going to happen.'

At that moment, the farmer's wife came back into the kitchen. She refilled the mugs with more tea and then sat down at the table with them.

'He wants to sleep' she told her husband. 'I've turned out the lights and drawn the curtains. He'll be alright.'

The farmer simply nodded to his wife. Then he turned back to Pieter.

'One of the soldiers walked outside with me, as though to distract me, the drunken fool. I knew what was happening. The next thing there was a scream from inside the house, and as I turned to go back he pulled out his gun out and aimed it at me. I could do nothing.'

The farmer's wife then spoke.

'The soldier grabbed hold of me around my waist and tried to push me against the kitchen sink. When I started to scream, our son Alex ran out of his room and tried to pull the soldier off me. The soldier grabbed him by the ear and smashed his head into the cupboard and knocked him senseless. Then he picked up the bottle of vodka and dragged me outside.'

'They were both drunk,' the farmer continued, 'the one with the gun told me to stand there with my hands in the air. And then he went over to the horse, it was tied to the fence. He then pointed the gun at the horse's head and said that 'he could do anything he wanted with us'. I pleaded with him. I need the horse on the farm, it pulls the cart and I need it to plough the fields. But he just laughed and pulled the trigger and he shot the horse in the head. In temper I called him a 'bastard', and with that he walked over to me shouting and cursing something, and then he hit me in the face with his pistol. I fell over, and the other soldier told him to 'thrash me', and that's when he started kicking me. Thankfully, he'd put the gun back in his holster before he started to kick me in the stomach and stamp on my head. That was when my wife screamed, but then the other soldier grabbed her around her neck to keep her quiet. I thought we were all going to die.'

'And that's when you arrived,' said the farmer's wife as she looked at Pieter. 'Thank god for that.'

Pieter looked at them both, 'I was in the forest. I heard the shot and somebody shouting, then the scream.'

'What were you doing in the forest?' the farmer asked.

Pieter looked at them both,

'I'm on the run from Auschwitz. I managed to escape from the train and now I'm trying to get back to Lodz.'

The farmer and his wife just stared at Pieter.

'Are you being followed?' asked the farmer, 'are they chasing you?'

'Don't worry,' said Pieter, 'they don't even know I'm missing.'

And with that, he gave them a brief account of his story. He told them about the murder of his wife and his mother and sisters. And he told them about his father back in Lodz, and how he was going to try and save him from the camp.

The farmer and his wife listened intently.

'Are you sure you should go back there?' said the farmer finally.

Pieter just shrugged. 'I have no other option. He's my father, I have no one else.'

The farmer's wife then took hold of his hand and she looked at him.

'We understand,' she replied, 'it's your family. You must do whatever you have to do.'

And with that, she glanced at her husband.

'I'll make up a bed. You can stay the night,' she said to Pieter. 'I'll make some food and you can set off again in the morning. You'll feel better.'

As the farmer nodded in agreement, Pieter intervened.

'No, you can't do that. It's not safe. When the soldiers don't return to their camp someone will come looking for them. And if they find the car you'll all be killed. Once it gets dark, I'll take the car and drive for about an hour, then I'll get rid of it along with the bodies.'

The farmer looked at his wife. 'He's right, and what he says makes sense. We don't want the soldiers back here.'

His wife sighed, but she understood.

'I'll get the food together for you.'

The farmer then turned back to Pieter. 'Will you come and help me butcher the horse?'

Both men walked out of the farmhouse and over to the barn. They uncovered the horse and the farmer once again took out his knife and once again unfolded the blade. He then lifted the poor animal's head and expertly sliced through its lower neck, removing the head completely.

'We'll bury the head.' said the farmer, 'if the Germans find that it was shot with a bullet it would look suspicious. I don't have a gun.'

Pieter agreed, and they took a couple of shovels and buried the head near the trees and covered it well. They went back to the barn and the farmer once again took out his knife and began to cut the back haunches away from the horse's body.

'We can eat these' he said, 'I'll hang them in the barn, its cold enough now, they'll keep.

'What about the rest of it?' Pieter asked.

"We'll drag it over to the tip and then I'll cut its stomach open. It'll rot, but it won't stink as much. If the soldiers do turn up, I'll tell them that the horse went lame and that it was almost useless and we needed it for food.'

Pieter stood there and he watched the farmer cut through the horse's flesh, almost effortlessly. His knife was exceptionally sharp and very easily sliced through the animal's muscle tissue and sinew. As the blade cut, Pieter remembered how easily the farmer had sliced open the soldier's throat, and he wondered.

'Your knife,' he said, 'I've never seen such a sharp blade.'

The farmer laughed and he held up his bloodied hand to show Pieter the blade.

'Yes, my friend...this is a 'Laguiole'.

Pieter looked at the knife, the blade was long and slim and delicately curved, but its point was like a stiletto.

'What's a Laguiole?' Pieter asked him.

The farmer smiled. 'It's the best, the best there is.'

As Pieter stared at the blade, the farmer continued.

'The Laguiole is a French knife. My uncle gave it to me on my wedding day. We have family in France and my uncle had travelled over there to see them. While he was there he bought me this. It's never left my side.'

The farmer continued, as he once more began to cut away at the horse's carcass.

'My uncle once told me a story about Laguiole knives. Many years ago, French workers used to go down to Catalonia in Spain to find work once the harvest season was over. They would bring back knives with this same shaped blade and carved handles and for the French workers, to own one became a symbol of pride. A blacksmith in the village of Laguiole took the shape of the blade and improved the design. He used the finest and hardest tempered steel and designed a spring that would close the blade into the handle. It was good, all the local herdsmen and farmers had one, farmers just like me. The blades are phenomenal.'

The farmer stood up and folded the knife, and then showed it to Pieter. The handle of the knife was slightly curved and compact.

The farmer smiled, 'the handle has the same shape as the horn of a young goat. It gives it a good grip. The French herdsmen used to boast that the blade had the same shape as a woman's leg,' and he laughed.

He unclasped the knife once more to show it to Pieter, who laughed when he realized that the handle did resemble a woman's leg. The farmer quickly finished off his work and then they hung the haunches of meat from the rafters in the barn. They dragged the remainder of the horse's carcass over to the farm's manure tip, it was a difficult task, and then the farmer slit open the horse's stomach. Both men stood there in the cold night air as the animal's entrails spilt onto the open ground.

'It was a good horse,' said the farmer as he shook his head, 'those bastards had no right to do what they did.'

'What will you do now?' Pieter asked him.

'We'll have to buy another, one of the other farmers will have something. We all stick together around here.'

Pieter simply nodded.

As they walked away, the farmer glanced back.

'The foxes will get at it, and then the crows. We get foxes at night, but at least it'll keep them away from the chickens.'

Both men walked back into the house and washed, then the farmer's wife produced two bowls of hot soup and they sat at the table to eat.

'I'll set off in an hour,' Pieter said, 'it will be dark by then.'

'I have some food for you,' said the farmer's wife, 'it will keep you going for a day or two.'

Pieter thanked her.

'And I have something for you,' said the farmer. And with that he put his hand into his pocket and then produced the Laguiole knife. He placed it on the table in front of Pieter.

Pieter stared at him. 'But this is your knife. It was a wedding present from your uncle.'

The farmer looked back at him. 'Yes, it was. But without you my friend, we would all be dead. Those Nazi bastards would have killed us all, and then burned the house down with our bodies inside. It's happened before, to others. You must take the knife, you may need it. You have no other weapon.'

Pieter realized the truth of it.

'You saved our lives, my wife and child,' said the farmer, 'there's nothing more to be said.'

An hour later, and it was time to leave. The farmer shook his hand and the farmer's wife hugged him tightly.

'God be with you,' were her final words.

Pieter drove off into the night, but he knew that he would have to take care. In the back of the car were two dead German soldiers and if he was stopped, it would all be over.

He took with him the Laguiole knife and a parcel of food that the farmer's wife had packed into a hessian sack. Also in the car was a case of empty vodka bottles. Pieter had also asked the farmer for a box of matches. At some point, he would have to set fire to the car.

Pieter drove for over an hour and he made good distance on the empty moonlit country roads before finally stopping. He was in what seemed open countryside and in the moonlight he could see down into a valley on his left. Pieter stopped the car and then he dragged the body of one of the dead soldiers from of the back of the car and onto the front seats. He then littered the empty vodka bottles in the front and back, and then with the engine still running he pushed the car off the side of the road and watched as it tumbled down the valley where it finally hit a tree. He stood there for a while and realized that he was going to have to make his way down there to set fire to the now wrecked vehicle. But at that moment he heard a crackle and a hiss and suddenly there were flames coming from the front of the car. Minutes later it was ablaze, and then there was an explosion and a large plume of flame as the car's petrol tank finally caught fire. The car burned fiercely, and with it the bodies.

Hopefully, when it was finally found, the assumption would be that the soldiers had crashed the car because they'd been drunk from the vodka, hopefully.

Pieter put the matches back in his pocket. He wouldn't need them, not tonight.

It took another three days of hard trekking before he finally reached the outskirts of Lodz. Once he reached the city, he easily blended into streets that were full of people who were going about their everyday business. In Lodz he became invisible and he became just one of the many. There were German soldiers everywhere, but none of them even gave him a second glance.

Pieter had to find somewhere, a place of safety. At first he considered going to the architect's offices where he'd once worked. He could speak to his employer, Mr Bruno Huelle. Mr Huelle would surely help him. Mr Huelle was after all, a member of the Lodz District Rifle Club. But after a brief consideration he decided, no. If things went wrong, to involve and implicate Mr Huelle could end up in sending another good man to the concentration camp. Pieter knew what he had to do, but he also realized that he had to get his priorities in order. First and foremost he had to try and find a way to save his father. That was his main concern. He had to somehow get his father out of the camp before the Germans replaced him with another doctor, and then put him on the train to Auschwitz. But for Pieter Szabo, there was also the need for revenge. He had the list drawn up in his mind. Herr Igor Sym had sent Francine and his mother and sisters to Auschwitz and he would have to die, and then there were those other two bastards, Henryk Kober and Wilfred Staszic. Pieter would never forget the night when the SS troops had invaded his home and Kober and Staszic had assaulted Francine and then beaten him. They were at the root of this tragedy, they were the instigators, and they too would have to suffer the price for their plotting.

But along the way and whenever possible, he would kill every Nazi that crossed his path.

All that however would have to wait. His father was his concern. And at that particular moment, Pieter Szabo had no other option, he needed somewhere to stay. He would have to make his way home.

It was in the evening and it had become dark when Pieter finally walked down the Poznanska Road towards his once family home. Pieter didn't know what to expect. In the last three or four weeks, his home as he'd known had it seemed a lifetime away. And he wondered if the house would still be empty. Everyone knew the stories of people moving into the splendid houses that were previously owned by the Jews, and Pieter wondered if some disgusting rabble had already moved in there. The thought of someone else living in his home made Pieter flush with anger. If there was anyone in there, he would threaten them and throw them out, or even worse. However, when he got there the house was in darkness. Pieter went quietly around to the back of the house and to the back door. He slowly turned the door handle and was surprised to find that it was unlocked. He carefully opened the door and stepped inside, closing the door behind him. Then he went through the kitchen. Even in the darkness, Pieter knew exactly where everything was. He'd lived in that same house for the whole of his life and he could almost walk around blindfolded. He stopped for a moment, and he took the Laguiole knife out of his pocket and unclasped it, then he made his way silently into the dining room. Everything was as it had been left, even the upturned chairs. There was no one in the house, he was safe. Pieter went through all the downstairs rooms and closed every curtain before then going upstairs to the bedrooms. The house was completely empty. He finally went into his own bedroom and he stood there in the doorway and looked around the room. It was full of Francine's trinkets. He looked at the bed that they had both shared, and he remembered all those happy and intimate moments. Pieter went over to the bed and sat down, and then he picked up Francine's pillow and he held it to his face. He inhaled, and he could still smell her beautiful perfume, and it was a though she was still alive within the pillow. He closed his eyes and he imagined that she was still there and that he was still holding her. And as he sat there he truly realized his loss, and for the first time and the last, Pieter Szabo began to cry.

He lay back on the bed and he hugged the pillow close to him, and he wept inconsolably

The physical exertion of making the trip back to Lodz and the mental fatigue of the last few weeks had finally taken its toll, and Pieter slept there in his own bed for over twelve hours. When he awoke, it was late afternoon the following day. The sun was already starting to turn, and Pieter went downstairs and made himself a mug of strong black coffee. He found some eggs in a cupboard and made himself a large omelette. And as he sat there alone at the once bustling family table, he began to make a plan. It would take stealth and patience, but Pieter Szabo had both.

As the last rays of sunshine disappeared, Pieter went down into the garden to their old garden shed. He moved some of the plant pots and various implements and then he prised up the floorboard to find his Mauser rifle, the ammunition and the money. He went back into the kitchen and took the rifle out of its canvas carrier and inspected it, and then he cleaned it. The rifle was in perfect condition. He then went into his father's study, to his father's old bureau. The bureau was stuffed with papers and old medical books, but Pieter knew that in the bureau's central drawer were his father's car keys.

He found the keys and then once more walked down through the garden to the side entrance of the house. The family car was still parked there as usual, on the side street. It was an ageing Polish built Polski Fiat, and even though it was over ten years old, it had always given the Szabo family excellent service. As a doctor, Franz Sabo had used it almost every day to visit his more housebound patients, and the car was almost as reliable as its owner. Pieter started the engine and he let it run for a few minutes to warm up. The car always had a full tank of petrol, Dr Szabo was a creature of habit, and he always preferred it that way. Pieter then turned off the engine and then went back into the house.

Within a couple of hours, Pieter had loaded up the car. His rifle, the ammunition and the money, a canvas sheet and also some blankets and an assortment of clothing, plus whatever useable food that was left in the house. He found a couple of flasks, which he filled with drinking water. He even managed to locate a pair of his father's old binoculars, and then curiously, he went back to the garden shed where he found an old wooden bucket. He picked up the bucket and stuffed that into the back of the car too.

Finally, he had to leave, but before he left Pieter couldn't help but lock all the doors. He somehow felt that it was his duty to the house, the home that had looked after his family so well over the years. Pieter doubted if he would ever return, it could never be the same. As he locked the back door, he turned and ran his hand over some of the brickwork on the side wall, and then he looked up at the house.

'Goodbye old friend,' he said quietly, 'and thank you.'

And with that, he walked out of the garden and got into the car, and then he drove off into the night. He didn't look back.

Pieter drove carefully back to Lodz city centre. He was wary, and because of that he took the quieter back roads wherever possible. He would have to somehow get himself across the city and beyond before he could finally make his way to the camp. He drove cautiously, and on the quieter roads whenever he saw a distant pair of headlights coming towards him, he would immediately turn off his own lights and stop the car by the side of the road and then duck down in the seat. Nobody took any notice of a parked car. Once the passing car had disappeared, he would set off again. Whether or not the other car had been driven by a German soldier he would never know, but he couldn't take the chance. He made his way through the city and headed on towards the camp. It took another fifteen minutes for him to finally get there and as he approached the well lit main gate, a guard came out of his sentry box to see if someone was arriving at the camp. The sound of a car could have meant the arrival of an SS officer and the guard would need to be seen to be alert at all times. But Pieter was ready for that, and he drove on past the camp entrance and past the guard, who stared at the car as it drove by. Pieter lifted one hand to acknowledge the guard but he kept looking forward, there was always the vague chance that he could still be recognized. He drove on up the road for another half a mile to the hill which overlooked the camp. Then he parked the car by the side of the road and walked through the bushes and into the dense forest. He had to walk back a fair distance, but he eventually came to the edge of the tree line and stopped as he looked down towards the camp. It was an eerie, almost unnatural sight for Pieter. At that time of night the camp was lit up by glaring yellow lights and Pieter could see and remember everything. The wire fences and the soldier's barracks, and the offices and the distant rows of huts surrounded by a high barbed wire fence, and he wondered which one of those huts held his father. And then he wondered which of those huts had held Francine, and his poor mother and sisters. He stood there for a moment, and his sorrow began to turn into a slow smouldering anger. Someone would have to suffer for this. The SS, the Nazis, the Germans, it was all their fault, and someone was going to pay dearly for what had happened.

Yes, those bastards, they were all going to have to suffer.

Pieter gathered his thoughts and then he went back to the car. He reversed it off the road and back into the trees. His line of thought being that if he was being pursued by anyone and he could make it back to the car, he could drive off straight away. Those few precious seconds, along with a quick getaway might possibly save his life. Once he'd parked the car, Pieter took his knife and began to cut some of the lower branches from the surrounding trees and some longer lengths of shrubbery, and he used these to camouflage the car so that it couldn't be seen from the road. Pieter then began to unload. He just took what he needed and from there he began to make his way back to the tree line, He once again walked slowly through the forest and down towards the camp and he stopped where the line of trees ended. He was about a hundred yards away from the camp's barbed wire fence. He was in a good position, in a raised area with the whole of the camp in front of him, and to his far left was the sentry box and with it the entrance to the camp. In the bright yellow lights, Pieter could see the guard, he was still sitting there in the sentry box and still trying to stay alert.

Pieter had brought with him some food and water, the canvas sheet and the binoculars. He found an adequate space just behind the tree line, and he laid the canvas sheet on the ground. Then he walked back into the forest and cut several small branches from the closest trees. With these in hand, Pieter lay down on the canvas sheet and pulled part of it over him for shelter. Then he covered himself with the cut branches, using them as camouflage. When daylight came, he would be invisible.

Now all he had to do was watch and wait and plan. He would observe, and he would learn how the camp ran. Everything ran to a timetable, he knew that. And everything would be done repetitively and efficiently. And he knew that too, because that was how the Nazi mind worked.

As Pieter lay there, comfortably warm and dry under the canvas sheet, he began to think about the beautiful countryside that he'd seen in Poland.

And as he considered it he smiled to himself. Luckily, Poland was a country full of forests.

As the evening grew late, Pieter watched as the camp closed down. It had been an industrial unit of some sort and at some time. But the German army had then commandeered the buildings for their own use. From there, they'd added makeshift barracks to house the troops, and long, basic wooden huts to house the Jews. The original central building was a red brick affair, very basic and stoic looking. The Germans had installed more efficient lighting and were using it primarily as offices.

The camp became relatively silent as the soldiers finally bedded down for the night. Only four sentries were left on guard. There was the guard in the sentry box, and another on the roof of the office building who was supposed to operate a floodlight there. Two others patrolled the wire fences around the long wooden huts that housed the Jews. It was all done at a very lacklustre pace. In fact, the whole setup seemed to be run in a very casual manner. And that suited Peter Szabo. Complacency was a niche that he would use.

It was after ten o'clock in the evening when Pieter noticed that one of the last lights in the office building had suddenly been turned off. Someone was leaving. He lay there and he watched.

A moment later an SS officer appeared from the building. He stood there for a moment as he straightened his hat and put on a pair of leather gloves. Then he made his way to the sentry box and spoke to the guard there. Pieter grabbed hold of his binoculars and focused on the sentry box. Under the light, the officer continued to speak to the guard as he offered him a cigarette. The officer then turned sideways for a moment, and that was when Pieter caught sight of him. The SS officer was Herr Igor Sym.

At the sight of Sym, Pieter Szabo snarled in anger and he cursed himself for not bringing his rifle with him. In that one uncontrollable moment of rage, Pieter would have taken aim and shot Sym. Here was the man who had sent his family to the death camps. Here was the man who was responsible for what had happened to Francine, one of the men.

Pieter had to breathe deeply, he had to calm himself down. This was not the plan, not yet.

Pieter had yet to find his father, somewhere in that camp, somewhere, was Dr Franz Szabo. He had to find his father and he would have to get him out of there.

Herr Sym was still talking to the sentry as a black sedan car slowly pulled out from behind the office building. The car drove slowly over to the sentry box and stopped. The driver got out and opened the rear door as Herr Sym bid the guard 'good night' and got into the back of the vehicle.

Igor Sym was going to the Grand Hotel in Lodz to meet up with Herr Wilhelm Kruger, but Pieter Szabo wasn't to know that. In fact, he knew nothing at all about Herr Wilhelm Kruger, nothing at all. At that moment, Pieter's first instinct was to run back to his own car and follow Igor Sym. Maybe he should kill Sym straightaway, maybe he should run Sym's car off the road and kill both Sym and the driver and then set fire to the car. He could make it look like an accident.

But suddenly, no, Pieter had to think again. And he stopped. There would be another way.

The car slowly drove away, and Pieter looked at his watch. It was after ten o'clock, and Pieter took note of the time. He stayed there under his canvas hideout for another two hours, and he watched the guards patrol the camp. The guard in the sentry box was reading a book, so he was obviously warm and comfortable enough. The sentry on the roof disappeared from time to time, and Pieter considered that he was sleeping, either on the roof or probably more likely that he'd sneaked back into the warmth of the offices below.

The other two guards spent most of their time smoking as they sat on some makeshift wooden boxes that were being used as a bench. In between their cigarettes, they would occasionally wander around the camp in a somewhat leisurely fashion. They had a casual attitude and were at ease, and why not? What had they got to worry about? Certainly not the poor Jews, locked away inside those cold wooden huts.

But the guards were all accessible, especially now that their Commanding officer had left the camp. Pieter saw it, he saw it all. And their complacency made Pieter think that Herr Sym may not be returning that evening, and he was right.

Eventually, Pieter slid out from under the canvas sheet and he made his way back to the car. He climbed onto the back seat and covered himself with the blankets and finally slept.

At five o' clock he awoke again. He took more food and a flask of water and he made his way back to his hide at the edge of the forest. After once more climbing under the canvas sheet and covering himself up with the foliage, Pieter reached for his binoculars and he lay there and watched as in the early morning mist the camp slowly came to life. Smoke and steam began to emit from some of the buildings as the kitchens began to prepare breakfast for the troops. Soldiers began to gather, and Pieter watched as they started to file into the main building. It obviously contained some sort of canteen. At approximately eight o'clock, a black staff car turned in through the main exit. The sentry came out of his box and saluted as the car drove straight past him and stopped outside the main building. The driver got out of the car and went to open the rear door. Out stepped Herr Igor Sym, once again immaculately dressed in his black SS uniform and shiny leather boots. And as he stood there he straightened his jacket and his tie, so full of his own arrogance and self-importance. Herr Sym turned to dismiss the driver and then he walked into the office building. A couple of minutes later a light appeared to have been switched on in one of the offices on the first floor. On the previous evening, Pieter had seen the light turned off in that very same office, just before Igor Sym had left the camp. And now Pieter Szabo knew exactly where he could find Igor Sym.

An hour later, and the camp had become a busier place. Breakfast was over and there seemed to be plenty of soldiers milling about, but everything was still quite relaxed and sociable. The men would stop to talk to one another and smoke as they went about their duties. Pieter noticed that the wooden huts that contained the Jewish refugees were silent. There was no smoke because there was no heating, and there was no cooking. There would be no breakfasts because those poor people were being systematically starved.

At nine o' clock, several canvas-covered trucks arrived at the camp and parked by the wire fence. Pieter stared down at the trucks, he knew exactly what they were for because he'd already travelled in one of them. They would be used to transport the Jewish refugees to the railway siding at 'Radegast' Station, and from there they would be shipped to the Auschwitz Concentration Camp to be imprisoned and then gassed.

A group of a dozen soldiers formed in two lines, they were headed by a sergeant who was giving them their orders. They then marched over to the Jewish compound, which was to the right of camp. One of the soldiers then unlocked the barbed wire gates. Once the gates were pushed open, the soldiers marched in. The sergeant was holding a sheet of paper, and he led his troops to the 'designated' huts as he reread his orders. Under his commands, a couple of the soldiers unlocked the doors to five of the huts and the inmates were then ordered to line up outside.

Pieter stared down at the poor and wretched people, bedraggled and hungry. They were women and children, all were about to be sent to their deaths. Pieter grimaced, and he clenched his fist in anger. Because there was not a single thing he could do. And then he remembered his only family once more. They must have suffered the same treatment, herded like cattle by those same Nazis.

Pieter watched through his binoculars as they were led over to the trucks, and he watched as those poor women climbed up into the back of the trucks with their children and were then driven away. Pieter shook his head at the brutality of it all. Why would a human being treat a fellow human in this way? The hatred of the Jews, led by Adolph Hitler and organized and controlled by the Nazis was callous and cruel and merciless.

And in that moment, Pieter Szabo promised himself that something would have to be done.

Later that afternoon, the trucks returned. In the back of the trucks were the new refugees, Jewish refugees, brought in from the Lodz ghetto. Fresh meat.

The new detainees were marched into the compound and to the huts that had been vacated only hours before. Their fates already sealed.

There seemed to be some sort of discussion going between the soldiers and a sergeant, and then a small group of the refugees were told to stand in a line. Two of them were men, both with bloodied heads and faces. Another, a woman, stood there with a toddler in her arms. The woman was crying and the toddler seemed to be hardly moving. At her side of was a young boy, her son, he was probably seven or eight years old and he was hobbling badly. The boy wore no shoes and his feet were wrapped in old rags as some form of protection. The sergeant gave two of the soldiers their instructions and they then led the small group of refugees away from the others. Pieter watched as the group walked behind the soldiers, and he followed their path through the camp and finally to one of the huts that was situated high and to the far left, by the side of the barbed wire fence. Pieter had noticed the hut before, there was a guard sat permanently outside on a wooden chair. During the day he'd observed a fairly regular flow of refugees entering and then leaving that same hut. And it gave him hope. When the group arrived there with the soldiers, the guard knocked on the door of the hut and immediately opened it, then he ordered the men and the woman with the children inside. The door was closed behind them and the other two soldiers simply walked away.

Pieter continued to watch. Almost half an hour later the door suddenly opened again. The two men walked outside, their heads freshly bandaged. They were followed by the woman, who was still carrying the toddler in her arms. Behind her was her young son. Pieter looked closely through his binoculars at the young boy and then at the boy's feet. The young lad was now wearing loosely fitting shoes that were somewhat large for him. But even from that distance, Pieter could see that someone had bandaged his ankles.

Pieter Szabo watched as the refugees slowly walked away.

And Pieter gave a sigh of relief, because now he understood. Now he knew exactly where his father was. Doctor Franz Szabo was locked inside that hut. The hut was his surgery.

Pieter stood up slowly, ever wary and always careful. He knew there was always the possibility of being spotted by some unsuspecting soldier, who could be casually gazing out into the forest. There was always that one chance, always.

Pieter turned around and made his way steadily through the forest and back to the car. He knew what he had to do. He'd planned it all.

He went to the car and began to sort out his equipment, knowing exactly what he would need. But strangely, the first thing he looked for in the back of the car was the old wooden bucket.

He picked up the bucket and then began to walk around the car. He was looking for something. And it was only as he began to move nearer the road that he found what he was searching for. There on the ground was a sizeable, dark grey rock. The rock was the right size and the right shape, because it would easily fit into Pieter Szabo's hand and it had a sharp edge on one side.

Pieter placed the wooden bucket on the ground, face down. He examined the base of the bucket, which had been made using three pieces of cut timber, they were no more than wooden slats really and were worn thin with time and use. The middle panel was as wide as a man's hand, it was just right for what he needed.

Pieter took the stone, and with great care he began to strike the base of the bucket. Within a couple of minutes, the middle panel began to crack and it eventually splintered and broke. Pieter carefully removed the broken panel and then he examined his handiwork. He now had a bucket with a hole in the bottom. Yes, it was perfect.

Pieter then loaded his Mauser rifle with five shells and slung it over his shoulder. He stuffed more ammunition into his pocket and then he took another of the blankets from out the back of the car. Finally, he picked up the bucket and then made his way back through the forest to his hide.

Once there he put all of his equipment on the ground, and then he took the blanket, shook it open and then very loosely rolled it up again. It took on the shape of a thick elongated pillow.

He pressed this into the bucket, pushing it to the sides so that the gap in the bottom of the bucket was clear and visible. Pieter looked down through the gap and he could see his own feet and the forest floor. Perfect.

Pieter took hold of his rifle and then climbed back under his canvas camouflage. Once comfortable, he reached over for the bucket and placed it on its side, just a couple of feet in front of where he lay. Then he looked through the gap in the bottom of the bucket, and he could see everything, the sentry box, the camp and the offices, and enough of those huts that held the refugees. Pieter relaxed, all was good.

Later and when the time was right, he would lie there with the Mauser rifle aimed at the camp. The end of the rifle's barrel would be inside the bucket and Pieter would take aim through the gap he'd made in the bottom. And when he eventually pulled the trigger and a shot was fired, the noise of the gunfire would not resound loudly around the forest, and neither would it be heard in the camp, just a hundred yards away. There would be no alert, and there would be no panic. Nobody would hear the shot, because all of the noise would be contained within that one padded bucket. Pieter Szabo had just created a basic, but highly efficient form of silencer. And it would work.

Pieter lay there for the next few hours, planning and re-planning. Everything would have to be done right, it would be all about the timing. The afternoon light began to wane as the welcoming darkness of evening slowly approached. Pieter watched, undisturbed. He was calm and composed. He saw the day come to an end, down there in the camp. The refugees were all locked away in their huts for the night and the gates to their barbed wire compound were locked too. Pieter saw the soldiers lock the door to the hut where his father was, and he took note of that. Another lock, and another key. He saw the rest of the soldiers head for the canteen to eat their evening meal, and then he saw them leave again. It was a comfortable regime, but not one that was afforded to the Jews. The soldiers finally headed for their quarters as the camp closed down. The pale yellow lighting around the whole compound was switched on along with the lights to the entrance of the camp and with it the sentry box.

Once again the guard appeared on the roof of the office building and once again he went through the motions of shining the spotlight around the camp for all of five minutes before stopping to light a cigarette. Ten minutes later, and he'd disappeared back downstairs into the warmth and comfort of the offices below. Predictable, complacent, and the careless attitude that would make Pieter Szabo's plan work. Down by the compound, the two guards who were supposed to be patrolling the camp were performing their duties with the same casual attitude. Through his binoculars, Pieter was almost amused when he saw the two guards not only sitting there smoking cigarettes, but also drinking a couple of bottles of beer.

Over in his sentry box, the guard had opened his book and was reading once more. Everything seemed peaceful.

Pieter waited until just after nine o' clock. He realized that if he left it too late, there was always the possibility that Herr Igor Sym would call for his staff car and leave the camp earlier than on the previous day. But Pieter had a contingency plan. If that were to happen, then he would run back to the car and then chase after Herr Sym and run him off the road, and this time he would kill Sym, and the driver and set fire to the car. However, that was not to be.

Pieter lay there and waited. And finally the guard on the rooftop reappeared. Pieter looked through his binoculars, the other two guards had wandered off to patrol the camp. He put down the binoculars and reached for his rifle. The Mauser slid under his arm in a practised move, comfortable and secure. Pieter took his time, there was no rush.

He took aim. One hundred yards away on top of the office building the guard lit another cigarette, it was almost a beacon. Pieter squeezed the trigger. The bullet went in just under the guard's left ear and blew his brains out. Pieter saw the guard spin and jerk and fall backwards. One down.

No one came running, no lights came on and no guards appeared, and the sentry in his box once again turned another page of his book. The padded bucket had contained the noise. It had worked. And up in his office and totally unaware of what had just taken place, Igor Sym was checking more of his falsified accounting, happy in the knowledge that he was becoming quite a rich man.

Pieter waited. He put down his rifle and once more picked up the binoculars. Eventually the two guards also reappeared. They ambled back and put down their rifles and took off their helmets, and as one of them sat down on the boxes that they used as makeshift chairs, the other reached down and produced another couple of bottles of beer. They must have had some sort of stash there, it was probably some beer that had been pilfered from the canteen.

And that was good.

Pieter watched the two guards, one was sitting down and the other remained standing as he passed his comrade the bottle of beer. Both men chatted and seemed quite jovial.

Pieter reached for his rifle. He lay there and made himself comfortable, and then he took aim.

The guard sitting on the box pulled out a packet of cigarettes and he took two out of the packet. The other guard said something to him and then turned and walked over to the wall, he needed to urinate, the beer had done its work.

The first guard lit the cigarettes, and Pieter squeezed the trigger. He shot the guard through the head, who then dropped the cigarettes, then slumped forwards and fell off the box. The second guard turned around, and it took him a couple of seconds to realize what had happened. His comrade was lying there in a pool of blood with a hole through his head.

And it's a fact of life, a man cannot instantly stop urinating. Another fact is that a man can't do anything while his penis is still hanging out of his pants, other than have sex of course.

And in that moment of panic, as the second guard just stood there fumbling with himself, Pieter squeezed the trigger again. He shot the man squarely in the chest and blew him off his feet. The guard fell backwards and died almost immediately.

Two more down. And still no one heard a thing.

Igor Sym looked up at the clock in his office. It was almost half past nine. He had another half an hour and then he would ring down for his staff car and make his way back to Lodz.

He would of course call into the Grand Hotel and meet up with Herr Kruger for a couple of drinks.

Sym would always call in at the same late hour and for good reason. It showed Herr Kruger just how committed he was. Long hours and total dedication to the cause were the order of the day. And Herr Kruger had always been impressed and had always shown his appreciation.

But another reason why he always arrived at that late hour was that he didn't want to spend the whole of the evening with Herr Kruger and his gang of subordinates. Kruger, he could stand, he would spend time with Kruger. But there was a certain amount of animosity from Kruger's underlings, his captains and his lieutenants and the other 'hangers on'. They were German, and Sym was not. And despite his rank, Sym was treated by them in rather an offhand way. They were the aloof and the pretentious, who thought of themselves as the German 'elite'.

This attitude offended Herr Sym, he had worked hard to earn his place and he too demanded respect. So he showed deference and he turned a blind eye to it all. But that didn't mean that he had to like it. The one positive, and the restorer of balance, was that Herr Kruger did actually like Igor Sym. He and Sym went back a long way, and Kruger admired Sym's tenacity and he appreciated Sym's help. Without Sym, it could have all been a different story. Kruger valued Herr Igor Sym, and the 'underlings' saw this and hence it had been the cause for the petty jealousness. Nevertheless, rank was rank. And if Herr Igor Sym gave an order, he expected it to be followed. And those under him would have to follow those orders, if only for fear of upsetting their senior officer and commander in chief, Major Wilhelm Kruger.

Igor Sym lived a singular life. He had no friends, and other than Herr Kober and Staszic, his closest friend was possibly Wilhelm Kruger. In his present position, he couldn't associate himself with the people from his past. He was now an SS Officer and he could hardly mix with a gang of failed actors, and neither would he want to. And Herr Kober and Herr Staszic were really more like associates than friends, no matter how well he treated them. He needed Henryk Kober and he needed Wilfred Staszic for obvious reasons. They were highly efficient, and they in turn made Herr Sym look efficient. But Igor Sym had always kept them at a distance. He would never consider inviting them to the Grand Hotel, it was out of their league. Kober and Staszic knew nothing of the happenings at the 'Grand', and neither should they. They certainly didn't need to know about Herr Kruger's little infidelities with the prostitutes, and then of the course there had been that strange affair with Francine Szabo, and even Igor Sym didn't know how that had ended, and he'd decided never to ask. But since Kober and Staszic had been personally involved with her arrest, Herr Sym had decided that the less that they knew, the better.

In his office, Herr Igor Sym was still looking at the clock, Yes, another half an hour and he would be finished.

Pieter Szabo reloaded his rifle and then he turned to his left, to the sentry box.

Pieter had given this some thought. The sentry box itself was constructed from timber and was fitted with large glass panel windows. Pieter could see the guard inside, still comfortably reading his book. It would be an easy shot.

But Pieter had a predicament, a slight problem. And that was going to be the glass, or more to the point, the breaking glass. Pieter already knew that his muffled shots couldn't be heard in the camp. However, the noise emitted from the smashed and broken glass was another problem altogether. It was a risk. And anyone in close proximity who heard the sound of breaking glass would be slightly more than inquisitive, and if discovered, all hell would break loose. The sound of breaking glass was something that naturally drew attention. Heads always turn when some unfortunate drops a glass in a bar. It's a natural reaction.

Pieter took aim. He lined up his sights and then shot twice.

The bullets ripped through the bottom of the wooden sentry hut and hit the guard in both legs. The shocked guard was knocked straight off his seat and he tumbled onto the floor.

Pieter took aim again, and he took two more shots. The bullets once again ripped through the sentry box, and the guard who was lying there on the floor was hit in the head and the chest. He died in a pool of his own blood.

Another one down, and now it was time to move.

Pieter stood up and he slung the rifle over his shoulder. He wouldn't need the rest of his equipment. He had to move. Time was suddenly of the essence. He set off to his the left, he had around a hundred and fifty yards of open ground to cover before he could reach the entrance to the camp. He didn't run, he walked, but he walked as quickly as possible. There was a difference between running and walking. Walk, and you can hear what's going on around you. Run, and you basically lose that ability. Run, and all you can hear is your own strained breath.

Pieter made it to the camp entrance without any problems.

No one had heard a sound, no one at all. As he walked past the sentry box he glanced inside. As was expected, the guard was dead, but he had to make sure. Any mistake could be costly. Pieter headed for the main office doors. It wasn't a problem, he knew where everything was and there was nobody around to stop him. Once inside he went up the metal stairways to the first floor. Then he walked down the corridor to the only office that was still lit. Pieter stood outside the door to catch his breath for a moment. Inside that office was the man who had sent his beautiful wife to her death, along with his dear mother and two sisters. And behind that door was the man who had shot Pieter's brother in law, poor, innocent Adam Breslav.

Pieter could feel his blood rise. His first instinct was to kick down the door and march in there and slaughter the man. He would rip him to pieces, literally.

But that couldn't happen. Because Pieter's main concern at that moment was in finding his father. That was the objective, and that was the plan. He knew what he had to do.

He calmed himself and he controlled his breathing, and then when he was ready, he tapped lightly on the office door. And he waited.

'Come', said a voice from inside. And Pieter stood there for a moment as he listened to that command, and the arrogance within it. There was no 'come in' or even 'yes'. It was just 'come'. It was almost as though Sym was giving a command to a dog.

Pieter slowly opened the door and stepped inside.

Herr Igor Sym was busy scribbling some figures onto a sheet of paper.

He was trying to concentrate and this interruption was somewhat of a nuisance. He had to balance his accounts because there could be no room for errors. If at some later date someone checked these figures, he had to make sure that they were correct. Numbers never lied. One and one always made two, two and two always made four. No, the numbers never lied. And if the figures added up, then no one could challenge you.

Igor Sym finally finished his additions. And as he wrote down another fictional number at the bottom of a column he managed to utter, 'What is it?'

There was no immediate reply, and Igor Sym began to check his figures again. And it was only when he'd got halfway down the column of numbers that he realized that there hadn't been a reply. He found that strange. And so he looked up.

Standing there in front of him was the last person on earth he ever expected to see.

Standing there was Pieter Szabo, and under his arm was a rifle, and the rifle was pointing directly at Sym's face.

Igor Sym just sat there. His mind wouldn't work for a moment. Standing in front of him was a dead man, a man from the past. But this man wasn't dead, he was standing right in front of him with a gun, a gun that was pointing directly at his head. And in that one moment a multitude of questions ran through Igor Sym's mind, some of which he unfortunately already had the answers to.

But at that moment all that Sym could say was...'You'!

Pieter Szabo was still alive, obviously. How could that be? Sym realized that Pieter Szabo must have escaped somehow, but how? And why hadn't he been informed? Sym was astounded and almost angry at the inefficiency of it all. Again, why hadn't he been informed? And suddenly, in that brief moment, Sym realized that he was going to die. Pieter Szabo was here to kill him. Sym had sent the Szabo family to Auschwitz and they were now all dead. And Sym had shot Adam Breslav and he was dead too. He'd stolen their lives, and now he too was about to die. Igor Sym began to tremble and shudder as he sat there. There would be no excuses and Sym knew it. And then strangely, a question formed in his mind, it was something that he needed to ask.

'How did you manage to get in here?' he asked.

Pieter Szabo, who hadn't spoken a word up till that point, just stared back at Igor Sym.

'I killed everybody,' he replied. It was as simple as that.

Igor Sym just sat there, and he began to feel nauseous.

'The guards?' Sym asked.

'All of them,' Pieter replied.

Igor Sym took a deep intake of breath. His first instinct was to put his hands over his eyes, he was beginning to panic. He tried desperately to think of some way out of the situation, but his mind wouldn't work. He was going to die. Unbelievably, somehow Pieter Szabo was here in his office and he had a gun. And the certainty of it all made Igor Sym feel sick to the pit of his stomach.

And then, suddenly, Pieter Szabo spoke.

'You are going to take me to my father,' he said.

Igor Sym looked up.

'What?'

Pieter repeated himself, 'You are going to take me to my father. I know he's here somewhere.'

Igor Sym suddenly grasped what had just been said to him. And he realized that he wasn't going to die, not at that moment anyway. There was a possibility. There was a chance.

'I know that he's somewhere in the compound,' said Pieter.

'Yes, he is,' Sym replied immediately. 'Do you want me to take you to him?'

Sym instantly assessed the situation, and he realized that in getting Szabo out of the office, he could 'buy' himself more time. Pieter Szabo would undoubtedly want to kill him, yes he would. But if he took Pieter Szabo down into the camp, Sym could possibly cause some sort of commotion and at least have a chance of escaping. If Pieter Szabo started shooting his rifle, then that would set off some sort of alarm. Sym had to think. Pieter Szabo was here for his father, his father was his priority. And then they would both have to flee, so shooting off a rifle would be out of the question, the camp would be alerted and they would never escape. Surely Szabo must realize that? And Igor Sym saw his opportunity.

'I take it you have the keys to the compound?' said Pieter, 'otherwise I will have to find another way.'

'Yes, yes,' Sym responded quickly, 'I have them here in my desk.'

Igor Sym needed to think quickly. Pieter Szabo had just shot four of his guards and had then walked calmly into Sym's office. This man was resourceful, and Sym realized that he would have to keep his wits about him. Pieter Szabo was without doubt, a very capable man.

'What about all the keys to the different huts?' Pieter then asked him.

'Oh, we only need the one key,' Sym replied, 'all the locks on the huts are the same. I have that key here too.' And with that, Herr Sym reached over to the top drawer of his desk.

Pieter raised his rifle.

'Steady Sym, and be very careful.' he said in a low voice.

Igor Sym immediately raised his arms in submission.

'No, no...I was just getting the keys, that's all.'

Pieter stared at him for a moment, and then nodded.

Sym once again reached for the drawer and slowly opened it. He took out a set of polished brass keys and placed them on the top of his desk.

'Now close the drawer again.' said Pieter.

Herr Igor Sym did as he was told. So far, so good.

'Now stand up, and turn around,' Pieter ordered.

Igor Sym was startled. He'd not considered this possibility. Pieter Szabo was obviously going to tie Sym's hands behind his back, and that would make things more difficult for Sym when he tried to escape. Difficult, but not impossible, it would all be a matter of timing.

Igor Sym sighed, and he slowly stood up and turned around. He actually placed his hands behind his back.

At that same moment, Pieter Szabo spun the rifle in his hands and smashed the wooden butt into the back of Igor Sym's head. Sym instantly fell forwards and then collapsed onto the floor.

Pieter stepped over him and picked up the keys. He glanced at them for a moment and then put them into his jacket pocket. Then he went over to Sym. He stared down at him. Here was the bastard who had murdered his family, everyone Pieter had ever loved. He rolled Sym onto his back and as he looked down at him he thought about Francine, and his mother and his sisters. And he felt the anger and he felt the heat rise inside him, and then the rage.

Pieter Szabo reached slowly into his pocket and he took out his Laguiole knife. And then he unclasped the blade.

He knelt on top of Igor Sym and started to slap Sym's face. After moaning somewhat, Sym eventually opened his eyes and began to blink. He finally came to his senses and then he looked up at the man who had him pinned to the floor.

'What, what are you doing?' Sym asked feebly, 'I thought that you wanted me to help you to find your father?'

Pieter looked down at him.

'No Sym, I know exactly where my father is. I just needed to find the keys.'

Igor Sym's eyes suddenly widened. He'd been fooled. And now all of his hopes were dashed. What was going to happen now? And then as his eyes focused he saw something reflect in the light, and he blinked again. And then he saw the blade in Pieter Szabo's hand.

Igor Sym turned pale and felt sick to the pit of his stomach. A feeling of despair and panic ran through him and his body was suddenly paralyzed with fear. He couldn't move, he just couldn't move, he just lay there and stared up at the knife and at Pieter Szabo.

But now Pieter Szabo was angry, the blood began to boil in his veins and all the emotion that he'd held back and all the rage was about to erupt.

He stared down at Igor Sym with hatred and loathing.

'You murdered my family you bastardurdered my family.'

Igor Sym was terrified. He tried to speak, but his mouth wouldn't move. He almost gagged. And then he finally managed to say something. It was a pathetic attempt, Sym tried to give an explanation, a feeble excuse in which he tried to justify his actions

'I was only obeying orders,' he said.

And that was it. It was all he could say. But that one sentence turned Pieter Szabo's rage to blind fury. He grabbed hold of Igor Sym's head and pressed Sym's face flat against the floor. Pieter was now breathing heavily as he clamped his hand over Sym's mouth. Then he leant forward and he whispered into Igor Sym's ear.

'Can you hear me Sym?'

Sym just lay there, trapped and utterly terrified.

And then in one swift movement, Pieter put the point of his knife into Igor Sym's open ear, and then he leant on the knife and pushed it with all his might. The stiletto blade went inside Igor Sym's ear and Pieter could feel the knife as it was forced down into Sym's head. The razor sharp blade sliced through the cartilage and the flesh of Sym's inner eardrum and there was a crunch as the blade pushed through the roof of Sym's mouth and sliced into his tongue.

Igor Sym tried to scream out in utter agony, but he couldn't. It was a though a red-hot iron had been thrust into his brain and his vision suddenly blurred when the blade burst through the roof of his mouth and sliced into his tongue, the pain was indescribable. He tried to violently shake his head, but he couldn't, and then he started to go into a spasm. He felt the burning and tearing inside his head, it was as though his whole being was on fire.

But the rage in Pieter Szabo hadn't diminished, and it wasn't over. He wanted to hurt this man and he wanted to damage him. Pieter wanted to inflict all the pain and the suffering on Sym that he and his family had endured. He pulled the knife out of the side of Sym's head and Igor Sym's body began to shake uncontrollably. Pieter turned the knife in his hand and then he thrust it into Igor Sym's left eye, then once more he pushed the blade all the way home. The knife travelled through Sym's skull and pierced his brain. The agony and pain was too much for Sym's body and at that moment he went into a seizure and passed out.

Pieter Szabo's rage turned to frenzy. He wanted more, he wanted this man to be awake and suffer, and continue to feel the pain.

But Sym was unconscious, he couldn't feel anything anymore.

Igor Sym was dying, and when Pieter Szabo realized what was happening he grunted in anger and frustration. He stood up, he was seething. He looked down at Sym in disgust, and then he started to stamp on Igor Sym's face with the heel of his boot, and he began to swear and shout, over and over again, 'you bastard, bastard, bastard.'

Eventually, he had to stop. His anger and his temper finally subsided and Pieter looked down at the bloody mass that was once Igor Sym's head. He had to breathe deeply and try to control himself. It was over, it was done. And now he had to gather his thoughts and he had to calm down and think. He had to control his actions. His night was far from over.

Pieter wiped the blade of his knife on what was once Igor Sym's pristine black SS shirt.

It only seemed fitting.

He closed the blade and put the knife back in his pocket. Then he picked up his rifle and headed for the office door. There was a key in the lock. Igor Sym left it there for when he needed moments of privacy when he was dealing with other people's money and jewellery. Pieter took the key out of the lock and he turned to switch off the light and lock the door. He took one last look at Sym's lifeless body, and then he locked the office door behind him.

As he walked away down the corridor he still felt the bitterness. The anger was still there, but in his mind there was a strange disappointment at what had just happened. It was revenge, but it had all been too quick and it had all been too easy.

It wasn't enough, Pieter Szabo had wanted more.

Pieter walked down the corridor and down the metal stairway and he made his way out of the office building and into the cold night air. He took a deep breath. It was cold and it was clean and it made him feel invigorated. He immediately strode off in the direction of the compound gates. Once there he found the key for the lock and after opening it, he quietly squeezed through the gates, carefully closing them behind him. He made his way through the silent rows of wooden huts and then headed to his left and up the embankment to where hopefully, he would find his father. Once he'd arrived at the hut he once more found the right key and carefully inserted it into the lock. He slowly opened the door and peered inside. In the darkness, he could see a bed in the corner and the shape of someone sleeping. Pieter crept over and then very cautiously put his hand on a man's shoulder and gently shook him. The man woke up and slowly turned over. In the pale yellow light emitted from the camp, Pieter Szabo looked down at his father.

Dr Franz Szabo was just about to speak, but Pieter put his hand over his father's mouth.

'Pappa, it's me. It's Pieter,' he whispered.

Franz Szabo eyes widened, and he looked up to see his son. There was a moment of recognition, and then Franz Szabo quietly nodded. He understood.

'We've got to escape Pappa, we've got to get out of here, now,' Pieter said hurriedly.

Franz Szabo got out of bed. He was fully clothed. There were no pyjamas for refugees.

Pieter watched as his father pulled on his shoes. Franz Szabo had lost weight, Pieter could see that and he saw the dishevelled look and the strain in his father's face.

Franz Szabo stood up and immediately grabbed hold of Pieter's arm.

'Where are your mother and the girls?' he asked desperately.

Pieter knew this would happen, and he'd readied himself. But he had to lie, because to tell the truth would have been a disaster. He had to keep his father alert and focused, it was the only way if they were going to escape.

'It's alright Pappa, they've been freed.'

'Oh thank god,' Franz Szabo gasped, ' I've asked everyone here in the camp, but nobody knew anything about them.'

'Come on Pappa, we've got to go.'

Pieter took hold of his father's arm and led him out through the door. They both ducked down as they made their way back through the rows of huts and then they squeezed through the compound's wire gates. Pieter locked the gates behind him. Franz Szabo couldn't understand how Pieter had a key, but there was no time to ask. It could all be explained later, hopefully.

They walked away from the compound and past the camp's offices. They walked quickly and very quietly. There were no guards at all, Franz Szabo couldn't believe it. Then they got to the main gates and walked straight out of the camp. The sentry box was all lit up, but it seemed to be empty.

Then they went left and set off down the road. Franz Szabo still didn't understand.

'Where are all the guards?' he asked.

'There are none,' Pieter replied.

'Where are we going Pieter?' his father then asked.

'To the car.' Pieter replied.

'To the car? Are we going home?' his father persisted.

'We haven't got time for this Pappa, I need to be able to hear and to listen. I need to know if the alarm has been raised,'

Franz Szabo suddenly understood his son's reasoning, and so they walked on quickly and in silence. But in his mind Pieter Szabo knew what was coming. The dreadful admission of the truth. It took another fifteen minutes for them to get to the car.

Once there, Pieter tore away the camouflage and then started up the car. His father sat next to him in the passenger seat. It was almost an exchange of authority.

Pieter drove back onto the main road and then he turned left and away from the camp. He would have to keep his wits about him. He drove steadily and he kept his eyes on the distant road. If there were any headlights coming towards them he would have to quickly pull off the road and turn off his own lights. Had there been any headlights following them, and at speed, it would mean that they were being chased. And at that point, Pieter would have halted the car and reached for his rifle and stood back. And if the car stopped, he would have shot the occupants. But it was late, very late, and the roads were deserted. They drove on in silence, the only noise being the steady hum from the car's engine.

After twenty minutes or so, Franz Szabo finally asked the question.

'Where is your mother Pieter, where are the girls?'

Pieter swallowed, he'd already made a decision. His father had to be told. There was no other way. He continued to stare straight ahead.

'They're dead Pappa, they're all dead. The Nazis sent them to the concentration camp at Auschwitz. They didn't survive. No one's left.'

Not another word was spoken. Franz Szabo put his head in his hands and he slumped forward in his seat. As Pieter drove onwards into the night, and over the noise of the engine, all he could hear was the sound of his poor father as he wept.

CHAPTER 9

Pieter Szabo drove into the night, along the dark country roads and twisting lanes.

There would be no more conversation. His father had taken the news badly, very badly.

As Pieter Szabo drove, he'd already made his plans. He'd realized the future and what was taking place, his beloved Poland had only been one slice of the cake. The Germans were going to invade the whole of Europe, along with Russia. Pieter couldn't go north or east or west, they would have to go south. He had to get his father to safety. There was only one place left for them to go to. He would have to try and get them both to England. And once his father was safe there, Pieter would return to Poland. He was somehow going to go back to Poland and murder Wilfred Staszic and Henryk Kober, and then he was going to try and kill every Nazi that he could possibly get his hands on.

As he drove, Pieter formed a map in his mind of the countries that they were going to have to cross in an attempt to finally get to England. He knew that he was going in the wrong direction. England was to the west and across the English Channel, not to the south. And his proposed route would take him hundreds, if not thousands, of miles out of his way. But what choice did he have? If they were caught, Pieter's fate was already sealed. But Pieter Szabo had a plan. They would have to head south.

Pieter had thought long and hard, and in his mind was a list of the countries that they were going to have to cross. But first of all, they would continue to drive south, through Poland and then into Slovakia. Slovakia too had already been invaded by German forces, but it was a wild, rough and rugged county. It was filled with mountains, with plenty of high lonely roads. It was a risk, but if they could get through Slovakia and then into Hungary they would be safe. The Germans hadn't yet invaded Hungary. But they would, eventually. It would be a long drive through Hungary, but from there they would make their way to Slovenia and then across into Italy.

Pieter's plan was to then head west, across northern Italy and down to the south of France.

From there they would continue south and into Spain, and then continue the long drive down the Spanish coast, all the way past Granada and then he would turn south again. To get to the one place that was forever England, the one place that would offer them shelter and their one and only chance of escape. It was Gibraltar.

If they could do that, if Pieter Szabo could get them to Gibraltar, then somehow he would get himself and his father onto a ship. And then they could sail to England.

Pieter's route would take them the best part of a month.

As they set off that night, Pieter wondered if their little car would manage the trip. He would have to drive sensibly, and somehow have to procure oil, petrol and water to keep the car going. There was going to be the problem of food too. Pieter had some money, but it was Polish money, their currency was the Zloty. And though Pieter knew that his money could still be spent in neighbouring Slovakia, if and once they reached Hungary it would be a different story.

Along the trip, Pieter began to buy petrol wherever possible. He purchased some steel Jerry cans along with some rubber hosepipe. Buying petrol was always going to be a problem, but Pieter would sometimes offer double the price and let it be known that he and his father were on the run from the Nazis. That fact alone would normally receive a sympathetic ear. The Poles were compassionate people.

But it was Franz Szabo who was becoming the increasingly greater worry. Pieter's father had turned to silence as an answer to his grief. As they drove, Pieter would try to talk to him, but he never received a reply. Franz Szabo would sit in silence for hours at a time, with his head down and his hands resting on his chest and his eyes firmly closed. In that way, he could remember his beloved family. With his eyes closed, he could see them again, happy and alive. Dr Franz Szabo wanted to shut out the world. His own world had come to an end.

They finally crossed into Slovakia and skirted the Tatra mountain range, always aware of the possibility of German patrols and military. It was always safer to drive at night, at night any vehicles at all who were also travelling the roads were visible by their lights. Pieter and his father had to get through Slovakia, once they were in Hungary they would be safe. Once they were in Hungary Pieter could drive all day and most of the night.

They drove south and slightly east, it was the quickest way to cross Slovakia, a long but reasonably narrow shaped country. They finally reached Roznava, a small town which was situated approximately fifty kilometres from the Hungarian border. Pieter drove slowly through the town centre, it was a small but busy place with enough shops and the occasional restaurant and bar, all of which had seen better times in better days. As he got to the end of town, further down the road on the left was a German patrol car and an army truck, they were parked by the side of one of the bars. The patrol car seemed to be empty, but there were some soldiers standing at the side of the truck, talking and smoking cigarettes. Very casually, Pieter immediately turned right, and drove off down a side street where he eventually stopped in a shaded, quieter area. He got out of the car and told his father that he wouldn't be away for long. There was no reply.

Pieter locked the car doors to make sure that his father would be safe, and then he walked back into the town centre. He retraced his route and came back onto the main road, lower down from where the soldiers were still standing by their truck. The patrol car was still empty, and Pieter surmised that the officers, or whoever, must be in the bar and that their driver was probably one of the soldiers. Pieter walked off in the opposite direction, back into the town centre. For a while he strolled around the small town, taking notice of the different shops. It was a pretty enough place and Pieter watched as the local townsfolk went about their business. Eventually, he found somewhere that he considered might be safe. It was a grocer's shop, which seemed to sell something of everything. The sign above the shop read 'Jesensky', and outside the shop on a veranda, there seemed to be almost everything conceivable for sale. There were sacks of potatoes and cases of eggs, along with metal buckets and brushes and mops and tied stacks of firewood. The owner, who Pieter presumed was 'Mr Jesensky' himself, seemed to be a busy and pleasant enough man. Aged around sixty, stout and silver-haired, Mr Jesensky was continually in and out of his shop, checking his stock and talking to his customers. Everyone seemed to like him and Mr Jesensky in return seemed to be an affable sort of man. Through the shop's window, Pieter could see two women behind the counter, an older and a younger woman. Pieter concluded that they were probably family, a mother and daughter no doubt.

After about twenty minutes, Pieter crossed the road and approached Mr Jesensky. At that particular moment, the grocer was for once on his own and was busily straightening up his sacks of potatoes.

'Excuse me,' Pieter said to him.

The grocer turned around.

'Could I possibly speak to you in private, sir?'

Pieter tactfully used the word 'sir'. It was polite, and it was a sign of respect.

Mr Jesensky looked at Pieter. He said nothing for a moment, and then slowly asked.

'Yes, son. What can I do for you?'

Pieter decided to tell the truth. It would be easier, and Mr Jesensky looked like the sort of man who could probably spot a lie immediately.

'I'm Polish, sir.'

'Yes I know you are,' said Mr Jesensky, 'I can tell by your accent.'

Pieter took a deep breath.

'I'm with my father, sir. He's not well, I've left him in the car. We have a car parked down a side street at the back of the town.'

Mr Jesensky said nothing. And Pieter quickly glanced around to make sure that there was no one else there before he continued.

'We've escaped from Poland, sir,' he said. 'We're on the run, from the Germans.'

Mr Jesensky still said nothing, and then he blinked. And for a moment Pieter wondered if he should make a run for it. He'd already said too much.

Mr Jesensky too looked from side to side, and then back to Pieter.

'You'd better follow me,' he said quietly, 'this way.'

And with that, he led Pieter into his shop.

Once inside, Jesensky spoke to his wife as he took Pieter past the counter and through into their living quarters.

'I need to speak to this man,' he said to her, 'about some business.'

The wife nodded briefly and gave Pieter a quick glance, but nothing was said.

Inside the back room, there was a table and some chairs and an open fire, and both men then sat down.

Mr Jesensky looked directly at Pieter.

'What exactly do you want?' he asked.

Pieter took a deep breath.

'We're trying to get to Hungary sir. I have an amount of money, but it's all in Polish Zlotys.

All I need is some food and some petrol, and some Hungarian currency if you have any. I'll take anything you can let me have. The money's yours.'

Jesensky stared at Pieter for a moment.

'Why are you on the run, what have you done?' he asked.

Pieter paused.

'I've killed several German soldiers.'

Jesensky's eyes widened. And Pieter realized that he would have to give a fuller explanation. So Pieter introduced himself, and then he briefly told Mr Jesensky what had happened to his family, and about his escape from Auschwitz and the subsequent escape from the camp at Lodz.

Mr Jesensky just sat there and listened.

When Pieter finally finished his story, Jesensky shook his head.

'I'm very sorry for your loss,' he said.

Pieter nodded.

'It's a troubled world,' said Jesensky. 'And in my eyes, all the troubles are being caused by the damn Nazis.'

He then sat back in his chair. 'We have problems too. You see, Slovakia wasn't invaded by the Germans. Our stupid politicians have basically handed this country over to them freely.'

Pieter sat and listened.

Jesensky continued. 'We used to be part of Czechoslovakia, but our 'high and mighty' politicians decided that we needed to break away from the 'old Czechoslovakia', and that Slovakia itself should become an independent state. They sided with Hitler and when the Germans invaded

Czechoslovakia, Slovakia was annexed separately and we were given our 'so-called' independence.' Jesensky shook his head. 'Independence', what a lie. We just took on a different set of masters, that's all. Eventually, the Germans will invade Hungary too and then we'll be trampled underfoot. There won't be a Slovakia or a Hungary, or even a Czechoslovakia. It will all become Germany. The whole of Europe will become Germany if Hitler gets his way.'

Pieter looked at him.

'That's the way I see it too,' he replied.

'Here in Roznava we are closer to Hungary than we are to Czechoslovakia,' Jesensky continued, 'I know the Hungarian people, I deal with them all the time. They're worried, they know what's coming. We have a German presence here in Roznava, there's a small camp just outside the town. They're an arrogant bunch, they strut around the town as though they own the place, ordering people about. They seem to spend a lot of time at one of the bars at the other end of town.'

'I've seen them there,' said Pieter.

'We're close to the border,' said Jesensky. 'I think that they've been sent here to keep their eyes on things and report back to Berlin or whoever. Something's going on and it's not good.'

Pieter sighed as he listened.

'I will help you,' Jesensky said suddenly, 'but it's got to be done quickly and it's got to be done right away.'

Pieter sat bolt upright in his chair. He'd not expected such a sudden decision.

'How much money have you actually got,' Jesensky asked him.

From each of his inside pockets, Pieter pulled out two thick wads of notes, and he placed them on the table in front of the grocer. After all, business was business.

'You'll have to count it,' said Pieter. Jesensky did as he was bid.

'Right,' said Jesensky when he'd finished counting, and he put the money back on the table.

'I have a supplier who sometimes calls with pork and bacon. He's from Poland, and I think I could pay him with this money. I also do have some Hungarian money, we're near the border and it comes in useful. You need to go and get your car and bring it to the back of my shop. We'll load your stuff out through the back door. I don't want anyone to see us.'

Pieter nodded in agreement.

'Just one more thing Mr Jesensky,' Pieter asked him, 'could you give me some safe directions to the border. I need to stay well away from that camp.'

Jesensky took a deep breath.

'Go and get your car,' he said, 'and then we'll sort something out.'

Pieter went back to his car, when he got there he peered through the window to check on his father. Franz Szabo was still in the exact same position as Pieter had left him. He was sitting in the front seat, arms folded with his head down and with his eyes firmly closed. Pieter got into the car and spoke to his father. There was no answer, there was never an answer.

He started the car and then drove around to the back of Jesensky's shop. Mr Jesensky was already waiting for him. The back door of the shop was open. Pieter got out of the car and followed Mr Jesensky. Inside, on the table was a stack of groceries and a can of petrol.

'That's all the petrol I can give you' he said, 'it's getting quite difficult to get hold of.' And then he shook his head. 'It seems that our German friends want it all.'

They quickly loaded everything into the back of the car and then went back into the house. Jesensky reached into his inside pocket and took out a roll of notes.

'Here's some Hungarian currency' he said, and he passed the money over to Pieter.

'Thank you very much,' Pieter replied. And he slipped the money into his own pocket without even bothering to count it.

Jesensky nodded. He appreciated the trust, and the respect. Then he pointed to the oven.

'My wife has made you a pot of goulash stew. It's in a tin pan, all you'll have to do is put it on the top of a fire and it will soon warm up.'

Again Pieter thanked him, and then asked, 'could you give me safe directions to the border, Mr Jesensky?'

'Actually, I'm going show you a road,' said Jesensky. 'It's a back road and in parts it's no more than a trail. But it'll get you into Hungary and there won't be any German soldiers on it.' Pieter was slightly taken aback by Jesensky's offer, it was an act of humanity, and it could also be dangerous.

Jesensky continued. 'But this is how we are going to have to do it. I will drive my own little van. And you will follow me, but at a distance. No one must think that we are together, especially if we get stopped by the Germans. I will eventually stop and you will carry on past me and take the first right turn approximately one thousand meters further on. That's the road that will take you into Hungary. You'll have to stop somewhere once it gets dark, the roads are too dangerous to drive at night. But you should make it by tomorrow.'

'From there we will be heading for Slovenia,' said Pieter, 'we need to get into Italy.'

'In that case, find a main road and head west, always west.' Jesensky advised. 'Your Hungarian money will spend in Slovenia, but try and get hold of some Italian lire. You'll need it.'

He then looked at Pieter.

'You're father, he's not well.'

"I know. He's in some form of shock. It's not good,' Pieter replied.

Mr Jesensky said nothing.

Both men shook hands and Jesensky walked across the yard and got into his own small grey grocery van. Both vehicles then set off. They took the back road out of town and then drove for almost half an hour before Jesensky finally pulled over. As planned, Pieter just drove straight past him and took the right turn further down the road. They were on their way.

They drove for a few hours, and as the sun began to wane, Pieter pulled off the road behind some trees. He needn't have worried, there was no one else around for miles. He gathered up some wood and made a small fire, and then he placed the tin of Mrs Jesensky's stew on top of the fire to warm it. Pieter got some blankets from the car and laid them on the ground. And then he got his father out of the car and sat him down in front of the fire. Mr Szabo uttered a few words, and then he folded his arms and closed his eyes again. On route, Pieter had bought his father a long woollen coat, along with a grey woollen hat and some gloves, they would keep Franz Szabo warm as he slept, and as the nights turned cold and chilled. Franz Szabo seemed to appreciate the comfort and the warmth. When the food was finally ready, Pieter fed his father and made him drink a little water. Then he wrapped another blanket around him. Mr Szabo just sat there in silence, then he laid back and rolled himself into a ball. Whether he was asleep or not, Pieter didn't know.

The next morning they slipped quietly into Hungary. There were no borders, the road they were travelling along simply joined on to another small road. From there they drove steadily for another two days, along and past the beautiful shores of Lake Balaton before finally reaching Slovenia. They seemed to have plenty of food, due mainly to Mr Jesensky's generosity. And in truth, Franz Szabo was hardly eating at all. So Pieter decided to use the spare money to buy petrol, wherever possible. It made more sense.

The language too was becoming a problem. The Polish language was not international. Pieter could manage a bit of German and he could speak English. It was Franz Szabo who had made the decision that all of his children must learn to speak English. He called it 'the language of the world'. And in his wisdom, he'd employed a private tutor to make sure that they could all speak the 'English language'. Pieter could only hope that his ability to speak English would possibly help them on there way.

They finally reached Slovenia and once again entered the country by means of a small disused country road. Pieter continued to buy petrol and also managed to exchange most of his currency. Then they travelled onwards, and through Slovenia to Ljubljana and to the border at Trieste, and then finally into Italy.

However, Italy was going to be a different undertaking altogether. Italy was going to be difficult.

The Italian Nation was still in love with Benito Mussolini, and they were also still in love with fascism. Mussolini, who had taken to calling himself 'Il Duce', in some godlike manner, was fast becoming Adolph Hitler's closest friend. Nazi Germany and Italy were embraced in Fascism and the Italians thought that they too could rule the world. They were arm in arm with a bully, and they thought that they were safe, and they thought they were untouchable.

Pieter drove onwards, he headed towards the coast and skirted past Venice, ever westwards and onto Verona. Then they would have to make their way over the arduous Apennine mountain range, Pieter's plan was to then head south and back to the coast to Genoa. From there they could follow the coast road and slip into France. That was the plan. However, it wasn't going to be that simple. As they continued to travel through Italy they were unknowingly heading for disaster. Up high, as they crossed the Apennine Mountains, all seemed so peaceful. They were heading towards 'Casalino', a small village of no particular importance, which lay halfway up the side of a mountain.

Halfway and half-forgotten, the village was no more than the central location for most of the outlying sheep farmers. The people in the area were poor, and some were poorer than others, and not all of them were farmers.

As Pieter drove through one of the most beautiful regions of Italy, the world seemed to be a lovelier place. It was so peaceful up there, peaceful and quiet.

But before Pieter and his father would even reach the village of Casalino, they were going to stumble across two cold-hearted and very dangerous characters. Pieter and his father were about to cross paths with Casalino's own inherited problem. The Calvino brothers.

Umberto Calvino and his younger brother, Antonio, were twenty eight and twenty two years old respectively. Both were quite well built and muscular, though the elder brother, Umberto, was the heavier of the two. They lived up in the hills in a broken down stone house that had at one time been the family farm, but no longer. At one time their father had reared sheep, but once he'd passed away, followed shortly by the death of their mother, the two sons had quickly sold off the family flock to the neighbouring farmers. The Calvino brothers had no interest at all in farming, and they promptly turned to hunting as a quicker and easier way to make a living. They wandered around the countryside, both armed with a couple of high powered hunting rifles, and they would shoot anything that moved, ran or flew. From there they would go down to the village and take their merchandise to the local butcher where they would demand too much money for their overpriced goods. The butcher had little option but to pay up and then try and pass on the costs to his poor but loyal customers.

Once their bit of business was concluded, the Calvino brothers would then make their way to Manzoni's cafe, where they would eat and then drink copious amounts of wine and beer, all to their heart's content. Afterwards, and as they staggered away, they would leave behind a pitiable amount of money on their table without ever asking the owner, Mr Manzoni, for the bill. Mr Manzoni could do nothing, the Calvino brothers were a couple of bullies who were well known for their violent tendencies. Others in the village had found that out to their cost, and their good health.

Mr Manzoni's only recompense was that for years, he'd spat into the Calvino's food.

It didn't pay the bills, but it made him feel better.

So the Calvino brothers would wander around the village, taking whatever they wanted, and there was no one there to stop them. And with time they grew bolder, and along with that boldness, Umberto Calvino began to make plans. And those plans were going to make the good people in the village suffer even more.

Pieter and his father were roughly four kilometres from Casalino, and Pieter had pulled the car off the winding road and parked it in the shade under some tall beech trees. It was midday and Pieter had driven all morning and he was tired and hungry. They were making slow progress over the mountains and driving along the ever-twisting roads had become more than arduous. He got his father out of the car and sat him in the shade under the trees. Then he lit a small fire and put a tin of stew over it to warm. Pieter went back to the car and took out his rifle. He had to replenish their food at all times, and this was the easiest way. If he could shoot a rabbit or a hare, or even some decent sized bird, it could all go into the pot. He looked across at his father. Franz Szabo had rolled himself into a ball and had seemingly gone to sleep, Pieter just didn't know what to do anymore. He stared at his father for a brief moment. Franz Szabo lay there in his thick coat with his woollen hat pulled down, almost covering his face. At least he was warm and comfortable.

So Pieter set off up into the hills. His father would be alright, Pieter knew that he would simply remain there, asleep under the trees.

On that same day and in that same area, the Calvino brothers were both out hunting too, but at a slightly more leisurely pace. They were strolling along in the sunshine and were discussing the future and with it, the possibilities.

'I've been thinking about something,' said Umberto to his younger brother, Antonio.

Antonio sniffed as he wiped his nose on his sleeve.

'And what's that brother?' Antonio asked.

'I think it's time that Casalino had a Mayor.' Umberto replied.

Antonio looked at his brother for a moment, and then he laughed.

'A Mayor...in Casalino? Are you sure? It's a village, Umberto. I thought that only towns had mayors.'

'Who's to say,' Umberto replied casually, and then he shrugged his shoulders. 'Or more to the point, who's 'not' to say?' And with that, he glanced at his brother and he laughed.

Antonio, who was always slower to follow, suddenly realized that Umberto was onto something.

'And how would that work Umberto?' he asked.

'Ah well, I would call for a meeting. We need to get all the villagers together. Everybody needs to be involved.'

'And all the farmers too?' Antonio asked.

Umberto thought about that for a moment.

'No,' he said, 'I don't think we need to invite the farmers. You see, the farmers need the village. And so they'll have to do as we say.'

Antonio smiled at his brother.

'And who is actually going to the Mayor?'

Umberto laughed. 'Why, me of course little brother, who else?'

Antonio laughed out loud.

Umberto continued. 'Yes, I'm going to organize a meeting with the villagers and let them know my proposal. I'm going to tell them that we need to turn Casalino into a thriving town and not just this poor little village. We need to grow and we need some investment. Under Mussolini's new government, there will be money made available. There will be grants and the money to build better roads.'

'Will there?' Antonio asked.

'I don't know,' Umberto laughed, 'and who gives a damn. But hey, you never know?'

'So why become Mayor, and what's in it for us?' Antonio again asked.

Umberto tapped his nose and smiled at his brother.

'Money,' he replied. 'We could set up some sort of office in the village, and we could live there too, instead of living in that damn house up in the mountains. It would be a much easier life for us in the village.'

'And who's going to pay for it all?'

Umberto grinned. 'Why, the villagers of course, and the farmers. They'll need to start paying rates, just like they do in the towns. They've all had it too easy and for far too long. And as Mayor of Casalino, and you as my assistant, we will have to be paid some sort of expenses and some wages for sorting out the village's affairs.'

Then Umberto suddenly had another thought.

'You know, we could go to Rome, and see if there actually is any money available for us.'

Antonio laughed again, 'I've always wanted to go to Rome, Umberto.'

Both brothers were suddenly very enthusiastic, it was all beyond their wildest dreams. But it was Antonio who broke the spell.

'But what if the villagers don't agree? What if they don't want a Mayor?'

Umberto turned to him. 'In that case little brother, you and I will have to knock a few heads together and persuade them.'

They walked on in silence. And after a few minutes, Antonio decided to tell his brother about his own little plan.

'I've got something to tell you, Umberto,' he said suddenly.

Umberto looked at his brother, but didn't reply.

'I've been thinking about this for a while now,' Antonio continued.

'About what?' Umberto finally asked.

'I'm going to get married, Umberto.'

As Antonio blurted out this little piece of information, Umberto stopped dead in his tracks.

'Married...you?'

'Yes...' said Antonio, rather nervously.

'But you're not even courting with anyone. How on earth can you be getting married?'

'Yes, I know that,' Antonio replied, 'but there's this girl who I want to marry.'

'And who is this girl?' Umberto asked. He was quite amazed by this, his brother's sudden declaration of love.

'It's Isabella Gambari.'

Umberto Calvino stared at his brother.

'What! You've been seeing Isabella Gambari?'

'No Umberto,' Antonio replied, '...but I want to.'

Isabella Gambari was the daughter of Giovanni Gambari, a sheep farmer who lived high in the hills above Casalino. The Gambari family owned a decent sized farm and along with it they also reared a decent sized flock of sheep. Isabella Gambari was just eighteen years old and was stunningly beautiful. Shapely and with waist length wavy dark hair, Isabella had spent most of her young life helping her father on the farm. She was the eldest child, with a younger sister, Natalia, who was just twelve years old. Isabella loved the farm, and she loved to be out on the high ground tending to the sheep. Little sister Natalia however, was her mother's girl and preferred to stay nearer the house and would help her mother with the cooking and the cleaning.

With time and knowledge, Isabella had become a good shepherdess and her father had let her continue to look after the sheep. Giovanni Gambari was a proud man, whose name stood well amongst the community, and he too knew the love of being out in those hills, breathing in the fresh air and surrounded by the beauty of nature.

Life was good for the Gambari family. They weren't rich by any stretch of the imagination, but they earned a living and there was always food on the table, and they'd always enjoyed the simple pleasures of life. Little were they to know, that the darkest of clouds were forming on their horizon. The Calvino brothers were making plans that would spoil everything.

Umberto Calvino continued to stare at his brother.

'What do you mean, you want to marry Isabella Gambari?' he asked.

'I've got to have her Umberto. I can't get her out of my mind,' Antonio quickly stuttered.

Umberto was puzzled for a moment.

'And when have you seen her?'

'All the time,' said Antonio, again quickly.

'All the time? And how?'

When I go out hunting, I make my way up the mountain to where they pasture their sheep.

I hide and I watch her. She's so beautiful Umberto, and she's so bloody sexy. Her body is unbelievable. I've watched her for hours.'

Umberto growled. 'Oh, so that's why you've not been bringing anything back with you these last few weeks. I thought your aim was out, but no, it's this bloody girl you've been watching.'

Antonio looked down at the ground. He was embarrassed.
'I know, but I just couldn't help it, Umberto.'
Umberto Calvino scratched his head.
'Well, I don't know what you're going to do about it. Because I'm telling you, Antonio, Giovanni Gambari is not going to let you marry his daughter. Not a chance. He's a stuck up bastard, and he doesn't like us anyway.'
'Yes, I've been thinking about that,' Antonio replied.

Antonio Calvino had been thinking about a lot of things just lately. But most of his thoughts were centred on Isabella Gambari's vivacious body. He'd also lied to his brother, Antonio had been spying on Isabella Gambari for months now and not just weeks. He couldn't think of anything else. And he'd been following her, and he knew exactly where Isabella would be taking the sheep on any particular day. He also knew where to hide and where not be seen. And he would watch her and gaze at her supple body as she moved the sheep along, and then he would suddenly become hot and restless. Isabella Gambari was a creature of habit, and every day her mother would pack her some lunch, always wrapped in a small sheet of knotted linen. And out in the hills, and after she'd eaten her lunch, Isabella would lie back in the grass and fall asleep for a while. And Antonio Calvino would watch breathlessly as Isabella's legs fell apart and her skirt would slide up those slender thighs. And in his deluded mind, he was on top of her, ravishing her, and she would be squealing with passion and delight and be urging him on and on. Yes, all in his deluded mind. And from his hiding place behind some rocks or some trees, he would reach into his pants to finally relieve himself of his own ardour.

Antonio Calvino was infatuated with young Isabella Gambari, and now that infatuation was fast becoming a most dangerous obsession.

'You've been thinking about what?' Umberto suddenly asked, trying to get hold of Antonio's attention once more.
Antonio blinked, his thoughts had been elsewhere.
'Yes, I know all about her father, Umberto. I know the old bastard's never liked us. But that won't matter.'
'And why's that?'
Antonio smiled. 'Because I'm going to fucking rape her, that's why.'
For a moment, even Umberto was taken aback.

'You're what?'

'Yes, I've thought it all out. Old man Gambari's never going to let me court his daughter. And let's face it. She's not going to want to go courting with me either, I know those Gambari's, they think they're above us.'

Umberto took a deep breath, he didn't like the Gambari's either. In Umberto's eyes, anyone else's success was an arrogance. Umberto Calvino was a jealous man, jealous of anyone at all who had done better than him.

'Yes, you're right there,' he said, 'but raping her. Are you sure?'

'Oh yes,' said Antonio. 'It's the only way really. I've planned it all. I'm going to sneak up on her when she's up in the hills with the sheep. After she's had her lunch and she's lying on her back I'm going to jump on top of her and fuck her rigid.'

Umberto shrugged and nodded his head. He saw the possibilities.

'And then what?' he asked.

'Once she's had my cock inside her, she'll want for nothing else.' And with that Antonio grabbed hold of his own crotch as a show of his own sexual capabilities.

'And then?' Umberto asked again.

'Well, then I'll take her back to their farm and tell her father what's happened.'

'He'll fucking shoot you, Antonio.'

'Ah well, I'll take my gun with me, just in case. Anyway, I'll tell him what's happened and that I'm prepared to marry her. If he doesn't agree to it, I'll threaten to tell the whole of the village what's been going on and that we've been together for months. And that maybe she's pregnant? He'll have to let us marry then because he just won't be able to face the shame.'

Antonio then started to laugh, 'And let's face it, once everybody knows that I've had her, no one else will want to ever go near her again.'

Umberto smiled, his brother was right. The Gambari family would be ridiculed.

'I have another plan, a safer one,' he said.

'And what's that?' Antonio asked.

Umberto grinned at his brother.

'We'll kidnap the bitch and take her home with us. Once we get her home you can lock her in the bedroom and fuck her morning, noon and night. After a week or so, I'll go and visit old man Gambari and tell him that his precious daughter has eloped with you and that now she wants to get married. He'll have to do the right thing by her. We might even be able to get some money off him.'

Antonio Calvino laughed. His brother's idea was cleverer than his own. Not that Antonio was really bothered about the money. His mind was on other things.

The Calvino brothers continued along their trail. Their minds were no longer really thinking about hunting. Umberto Calvino was still talking about his plans to become Mayor, Antonio however, had stopped listening to his brother, because he was busily dreaming about Isabella Gambari's breasts.

They were just walking over the bluff of a hill, when Umberto suddenly put his arm across his brother's chest. It was their personal sign to stop immediately, and remain silent.

There below them, parked by the side of some beech trees, was a car. There was a small campfire burning and there was the smell of cooking food. Near the fire and under one of the trees, a man lay asleep. The Calvino brothers stared down at the scene in front of them. The man lay there, he was wearing a long woollen coat and a grey hat pulled down over his ears and face.

It was of course, Franz Szabo.

Umberto and Antonio immediately knelt down on the ground, it was a hunter's first instinct.

Umberto turned to his brother.

'A car,' he whispered. 'It's a bloody car.'

Antonio nodded.

They'd both driven a car in the past, but had never owned one. And now, here in their wildest dreams was their chance, their chance to steal one. And why not? Here was one man and he was on his own. What could he possibly do? They looked around, and there were no signs of anyone else.

'Come on,' said Umberto and they slowly stood up and then stealthily made their way down the hill towards the almost deserted camp. It couldn't have been easier.

Once there, they approached the still sleeping Franz Szabo. Umberto rolled him over and then grabbed hold of his ear. Franz Szabo woke up with a start and he immediately howled in pain. And with that, Umberto Calvino punched him in the face.

'Shut up,' he said sharply.

Franz Szabo just stared up at him, he didn't understand.

Umberto shook him roughly.

'Who are you with, are you on your own?' he asked.

But Franz Sabo still didn't understand and he started to shout.

'Where's my son, where's Pieter?'

And with that, Umberto then smashed his fist into Franz Szabo's unguarded face and knocked him unconscious.

Umberto stood up and he turned to his brother.

'He's with his son, someone called Pieter, whoever that is.' And then he looked down at Franz Szabo's bloodied face. 'This one's going nowhere for a while. Come on, let's grab the car and get out of here. They threw their rifles into the back of the car and Antonio started the engine and then they began to slowly drive back towards the road. Sitting in the passenger seat, Umberto started to laugh.

'And now we have our own car. Things are definitely on the way up. Nice one brother.'

And then he turned to Antonio and punched his brother's arm.

Antonio laughed too. A wife, and a car. Yes, life was on the up.

Pieter was making his way back to their camp when he suddenly heard the car's engine start up. His first thought was that it must be his father and he immediately panicked. Surely his father wouldn't drive the car, and even if he did, where would he drive it too? A then it struck Pieter. It would be Poland, his father would try to go back to Poland. Pieter set off running back to the camp, and as he came over the crest of the hill he saw the car trundling towards the road. And then he glanced back towards the camp and there was his father, flat on his back, still wearing his hat and coat but his face was covered in blood.

Pieter ran to his father and gently shook him. Franz Szabo opened his eyes and looked up at his son.

'Pieter, Pieter,' he mumbled, and then he spat out some blood.

His father was alive. He'd been attacked but he was alive.

Pieter spun around, only to see the car disappearing back onto the road. Without the car it was over. They had to have a car.

Pieter set off running, his rifle was still slung over his shoulder. If there was any chance at all, he knew what he had to do. He ran to the road, only to see the car driving off into the distance. He stood there for a moment in despair, and then he looked down and at the direction of the road. Once the car had reached the bottom of the hill, the road curved to the right and it came back on itself as it the zigzagged down the mountain. So Pieter began to run to his right, and as he did, he unslung his rifle and ripped it from its canvas sleeve. He ran for about fifty or sixty metres and then threw himself to the ground. The car would pass directly below him and he had to get his breath back and be able to steady his aim. He watched the car as it slowly drove back towards him. Pieter then took aim, the Mauser ever comfortable in his hands. He stared down the gun's sights and at the driver. It was a warm afternoon and the driver's window was open. Pieter could see the driver's arm leaning on the window, just his arm and his elbow. Pieter steadied himself and controlled his breathing. He was calm, and he was ready.

The car was approaching him now, he had to wait for just the right moment, and as the car drove slowly past him he would have to shoot the driver through the open side window.

He looked down at his target. It was a long shot, but he could see the driver's arm, and he calculated exactly where the man's neck and head would be. And then he pulled the trigger.

Umberto and Antonio Calvino sat comfortably in their new acquisition. The sun was shining and now they had a car at their disposal.

Antonio turned to Umberto and he smiled.

'I'll tell you something brother,' and he laughed out loud. 'You can have the car, it's all yours. All I want to do is to get Isabella Gambari naked and in my bed, and you won't see me for a week, I promise you.'

And at that exact moment, the side of Antonio Calvino's face was completely blown away. Pieter Szabo's exacting shot had hit the younger Calvino brother in the temple and had then blown a large hole out of the opposite side of his head. Flesh and blood and bone matter were showered over Umberto as Antonio slumped over the steering wheel and the car slowly careered into the grassy bank where it immediately came to a halt. The engine died almost as quickly as Antonio Calvino had.

Umberto Calvino immediately understood what had happened. His brother was dead. They were under attack. He was under attack. And there was somebody up there with a rifle. Umberto quickly thought about the man he'd left up at the camp. He'd called out for someone, someone called 'Pieter'. Yes, that was it, 'Pieter'. Umberto stared at his dead brother, Antonio. Always his baby brother, Umberto had always had to look after him because their parents had both been uncaring bastards. And now this. Umberto was torn between upset and anger and rage. There was nothing he could do for Antonio, there was only revenge. Umberto reached into the back of his car for his rifle, and then he slowly opened the passenger door and he rolled out onto the ground. Less than five metres away there was an outcrop of large stone boulders which led into the trees. It was only five metres, but it felt like half a kilometre to Umberto Calvino. Umberto had no choice and no other option. He was pinned down and the right shot could go straight through the car and kill him outright. The man up on the top of the hill was an excellent marksman, there was no doubt about it. He'd just killed Umberto's baby brother from a distance of about five hundred metres, and they'd been a moving target.

Umberto would have to run to the safety of the rocks, he'd have to move fast, and so he readied himself. It would take him less than five seconds to cover the distance. He squatted down and took a deep breath and then he set off running. Five metres were about six or seven fast paces for him. He ran for his life, and he straightaway realized that his rifle was an encumbrance. It slowed his pace and he was unbalanced, and after the sixth step, Umberto simply dived for the cover of the rocks as a bullet screamed towards him and hit the boulder just above his head. Umberto lay there gasping for breath. He'd managed it, he'd escaped. And now, suddenly, the tables would be turned. Umberto Calvino was a hunter, he'd always been a hunter. And these hills were his territory, he knew them like the back of his hand. He and his brother, his baby brother, had spent a lifetime up there.

Pieter had taken his first shot. And he saw the car roll into the embankment and he knew that the driver was dead. What he hadn't known, was that the driver wasn't acting alone and that he had an accomplice. He would watch and wait. If need be he would fire another couple of shots into the car and take the chance of possibly hitting someone, but he didn't really want to damage the car. Then he saw the passenger door slowly open. He took aim.

It was his intention to shoot through the car. And then suddenly, from the back of the car, a man had sprinted towards an outcrop of rocks. Pieter cursed himself for his own carelessness. He turned his rifle and almost took the shot at the same time. The bullet was on target, but unfortunately a very large rock stood in the way. Pieter cursed again. He'd seen the man, and the man was carrying a rifle, a hunting rifle. The man was a hunter, and suddenly everything dropped into place. That was why these two men were up in the hills. And now Pieter had a problem. This man would have skills, and Pieter was trapped up there, alone with his father. They were in trouble.

Umberto Calvino lay there for five minutes while he quickly got his breath back.

He was undercover and shielded. From behind those rocks he could easily move to the trees and into the forest. He now had to make a plan. In theory he should wait for darkness, but the late evening was hours away and the shooter and his father could have disappeared in any direction by then, and in the dark he wouldn't be able to follow their tracks.

No, he would have to take the risk and make his way back up to their camp. And if they'd left he could follow them. Umberto Calvino knew the terrain, and he could travel faster and lighter. All he needed to know was the direction in which they were heading, and then he would get in front of them and sit and wait, and then ambush them. And then he would torture both men so badly, that they would beg him to let them die.

It took the best part of an hour for Umberto to reach the camp. Before he set off, Umberto first checked his rifle. It was an Italian Carcano M91, a very useful rifle that had the same efficient bolt action as Pieter's German built Mauser. It was a very good gun. Umberto and his brother both owned one. They'd stolen the guns of course, but that was the way of things with the Calvino brothers.

Umberto made his way back up the hill in the bright afternoon sunshine. It was an extremely difficult climb because he had to make sure that he was undercover at all times. But eventually he made it to the rise of the hill and he crawled behind a rock. He expected to hear the ricochet from a bullet at any time, but there was nothing, nothing at all. He slowly peered from behind the safety of the rock, and he couldn't believe his eyes. The camp was there exactly as he'd left it. The fire was still burning, the flame was low but the pot of food was still there. Umberto could smell it, still cooking. And by the side of the fire, and still unconscious, lay the old man that Umberto had knocked unconscious. But where was the son? This so-called 'Pieter'? The old man still lay there in his coat and woollen hat, but where was the son? Obviously he was waiting in ambush somewhere. But he'd left his father. For a moment Umberto wondered if he'd actually killed the old man, but he was sure that he'd not hit him that hard. And then he wondered if maybe the son had run off and left his father? Umberto thought about that for a moment, because he would have certainly left his own father behind. Umberto's father had been a bastard. No, it was some sort of trick, it had to be. Pieter must be hiding in the trees opposite and he must be waiting for Umberto to come over the hill, just as he had. However, Umberto was a hunter and he'd managed not to be seen. And now he would move to his right and make his way around the camp and come up through the back of the trees, and there he would catch Pieter. Umberto could imagine him lying somewhere under the foliage, aiming his rifle into the camp, waiting for Umberto to raise his head above the ground. Umberto almost smiled, and then he thought about his brother and the anger welled up inside him. And he made a silent promise to his brother that he would make this man suffer.

He carefully skirted the camp and came to the trees, now he would have to be careful. One snap from a broken twig, or even the movement of the bushes could give him away. It was like coming up against a deer. One false move was all it took, and the element of surprise was lost. But Umberto Calvino was good at this because he'd been doing it all of his life. He moved silently through the trees, stopping every couple of seconds to look for his prey. This man had to be somewhere. Then he stopped dead in his tracks. Had he been fooled? And at that moment he looked up into the trees. Had his prey climbed a tree and at that very moment was he aiming his gun? Umberto leant back against one of the trees and stared upwards looking for any signs of movement, but there were none. He took a deep breath, he'd been careless. It could have cost him his life. He stood there for a moment and again looked around. This man was good, but he had to be somewhere. Umberto moved forwards again, silently checking every possible space. But there was no one there, no one at all. He came to the edge of the trees and the camp was still there just as he'd left it. Umberto suddenly became angry, maybe this Pieter had run off, or maybe he was cleverer than Umberto had given him credit for. There had to be a way to flush him out, and suddenly Umberto saw the answer. It was Pieter's father. If Umberto moved to his left, Pieter's father was only three or four metres away from the tree line. Umberto could dash out from behind the trees and grab the old man and then hold the rifle to his head. It was a risk, but it would hopefully make the son drop his weapon and show himself. Either that, or Umberto would drag the old man back into the trees and shoot him through the head, and then see what happened.

Umberto moved forwards, it was now or never, it was the element of surprise. He launched himself from behind the trees and within seconds he'd reached Franz Szabo. Umberto put the gun to Franz Szabo's head and then he kicked him in the back. Franz Szabo groaned in pain.

"Get up you old bastard, move.' Umberto then turned around and began to shout.

'Come out, show yourself, or I'll blow his head off right now.'

Umberto looked around for any signs of movement, but there were none. He pressed the gun even harder against Franz Szabo's head and once again kicked him heavily in the back. Franz Szabo again moaned in agony as he lay there.

Umberto shouted again, 'You killed my brother you bastard. Come out now or your father's a dead man.'

Still there was no reply.

Umberto Calvino was furious. There could only be one answer. This man's son, this 'Pieter', he must have run off. He'd run away. And now there was only one thing left to do. Umberto would kill the old man and then he would have to try to find Pieter's tracks. He could shoot the old man through the head as he lay there, but that wasn't going to be enough. Umberto had made a promise to his brother that both of these men would suffer before they died. And Umberto Calvino suddenly decided that he would tie this man to a tree and blow his arms off and then his legs. He knelt down and grabbed Franz Szabo by the ear, who again howled in pain. But Umberto had had enough.

'Get up you old bastard, you're going to die,' and with that he started to pull Franz Szabo up by his ear. But this time Franz Szabo didn't howl, he simply rolled over. And Umberto Calvino suddenly felt an agonizing pain in his chest. He looked down, only to see a hand pushing a Laguiole knife into his rib cage and then twisting the blade. And with that same twisting movement, the blade was then extracted and Umberto Calvino watched in horror as his own blood pumped out of his chest and covered his shirt. Umberto looked at the man who had just stabbed him. Pieter Szabo pulled off the grey woollen hat that had covered his face. Umberto just stared at him, he'd been tricked, he'd been fooled by this man. This very clever man.

'It's...it's you,' were Umberto Calvino's last words. And then he fell backwards and began to die.

Pieter didn't understand what the man was trying to say, because Pieter couldn't speak Italian. He leant over Umberto Calvino and slapped his face to get Umberto's attention.

Pieter pointed to himself, and then he said slowly, 'My name is Szabo.'

And with that knowledge firmly imparted to him, Umberto Calvino coughed up a mouthful of blood and then died where he lay.

Pieter stood up and he took off his father's coat. Then he turned and walked back the half kilometre up the hill to find his father. Franz Szabo was exactly were Pieter had left him, under some cut branches. His father had been asleep and that was good. But his face was badly bruised from where Umberto Calvino had hit him.

Pieter Szabo had made his plans earlier, he'd had to get his father out of the way and to safety. If the bullets had started flying, there was every chance of his father getting shot during the exchange. He'd had to move his father and hide him somewhere. And his plan had worked. Pieter had worn his father's long coat and his grey woollen hat and had lain exactly where the Calvino brothers had left him. And Umberto Calvino hadn't noticed, he'd just taken it for granted that the man who was lying there was the same man that he's earlier beaten.

Pieter walked his father back to the camp and he put his coat and his hat back on him. Franz Szabo then sat back on the ground and closed his eyes again. Pieter then cleared the camp. He dragged Umberto Calvino's body into the trees and left him there. Then he kicked out the fire and then he made his way back down the hill to the car. Antonio Calvino's stiffened body was still slumped over the wheel, but Pieter managed to drag him out and push the body down the embankment. He took a blanket out of the car's boot and cleaned up the congealed blood and gore. Then he went back to Antonio's body and covered it with rocks. Finally, he got back into the car, it started easily and he reversed away from the bank and drove it back up to the camp. He loaded up the car and he put Umberto Calvino's rifle in the boot along with his brother's rifle. Pieter now had two rifles that he could sell. That was good, they needed the money.

He got his father into the passenger seat and then they set off once more. Pieter was glad to get away, he'd already had enough of Italy.

The villagers of Casalino never looked for the Calvino brothers. They were glad to see the back of them. There were rumours of course, that they'd joined the army, or they'd joined the mafia, and there were stories that they'd robbed a bank and were hiding in Bologna. Whatever had happened, the people in the village certainly didn't want them back.

Up in the hills, high above Casalino, Giovanni Gambari made his way through the fields and up to his flock of sheep. It was getting late, and now the sun was beginning to dip and it was time to bring his sheep home. He looked up to see his daughter Isabella and he waved to her.

'Hi papa,' she called back to him.

He made his way to her and he hugged her and kissed her on the cheek. She giggled. She was so beautiful, just like her mother.

Giovanni called in his sheep, though he needn't have bothered really. They knew their own way back to the farm. Giovanni walked along as he listened to his daughter chattering away. She was so full of life. And he smiled to himself. One day, one of the boys from the village would come a calling. A nice boy, hopefully.

After the incident in the mountains, Pieter was forced to change his plans. They would still be heading in the same direction but they needed to get out of Italy. They were also out of money. Pieter could always find food, one way or another. But obtaining petrol was a more immediate problem. Pieter devised a plan, he would simply steal it. And so, whenever they drove through a town or a village, they would stop on the outskirts and wait for it to go dark. Then in the middle of the night, Pieter would drive back into the town and park up somewhere out of the way, and then he would take a jerry can and a length of hose and siphon some petrol out of another car or a truck. It was a risk he had to take, but it worked.

En route, he managed to get rid of the Calvino brother's two Italian rifles. The first one was to a farmer, Pieter swapped the rifle for a good quantity of food, along with some petrol and a few lire. The second occasion was to a garage owner. It was a curious event. Pieter was driving past the garage, it was only a small place, which seemed to do a few car repairs, but also sold gasoline from a single pump. It also looked deserted, and that prompted Pieter to stop. He took two empty jerry cans out of the back of the car, and along with the rifle he walked into the garage. He shouted, to try and get someone's attention, but there was no one there. Pieter left the jerry cans by the side of the pump and walked into the workshop. The owner had been under a car, trying to repair a broken gearbox, and when he heard Pieter's voice he assumed, actually quite rightly, that someone wanted petrol. The garage owner was a small rotund man and he had to struggle to get from under the car. But he'd managed it, and he was just wiping his hands on a cloth as Pieter walked into the workshop, holding a high powered hunting rifle in front of him. The garage owner immediately held up his hands and started to jabber away in Italian. He obviously thought that he was about to be robbed. The garage owner was becoming hysterical and Pieter had to lower the rifle and shake his head and hand to try to explain that there was no danger. The garage owner then stopped jabbering. Pieter then led the owner outside to the petrol pump. He pointed to his two jerry cans and then he pointed to the rifle. It took a second or so, but then the garage owner suddenly realized what Pieter meant. The man suddenly began to nod, and then he became quite jovial. They filled the two jerry cans full of petrol and the owner even helped Pieter carry them to the car. Then he said to Pieter, 'un Momento,' and he went back into his workshop, only to reappear minutes later with a jug of engine oil. He lifted the car's bonnet and poured the oil into the engine. Pieter thanked him and both men shook hands on the deal. As he drove away, Pieter reflected, maybe the Italians were not all bad. The farmer who'd had the first rifle seemed to be a decent man, as was the garage owner.

And as Pieter drove away, the garage owner also considered that he too had been very lucky. That young man could have stolen the petrol and robbed him. He could have even been shot.

He picked up the rifle and looked at it. It had been a good trade. Petrol was becoming scarce, and the next person who wandered into his garage might have a different approach altogether.

Pieter and his father drove down to Genoa and then continued to travel west, they followed the coast road and eventually made it into Southern France. They drove ever onwards, and after two steady days, they'd passed through Nice and Marseille and then down to Perpignan, and then finally arrived in Spain. From there they headed for Barcelona, once again following the coast road, ever southwards.

These were better days for Pieter. The idyllic warmth of Spain gave him time to contemplate. He and his father would sleep on beautifully deserted beaches and Pieter would lie there, looking up at the stars and listening to the sea. And he would wonder about Francine, and the loss of his family. It could never be over for Pieter Szabo.

In the early mornings, Pieter would take his father down to the water's edge. He would help his father to wash and Pieter would swim in the clearest blue sea. Sometimes Pieter would offer to help the local fishermen and they in return would usually give him some fish and some bread. On one evening, a family invited Pieter and his father to celebrate their daughter's sixteenth birthday. Their family and friends sat out in the warm night air, on long tables. and they all drank strong red wine and ate paella. Pieter loved the food, the mixed grilled fish served with saffron flavoured rice, simmered with lashings of thick delicious fish stock and the citrus flavour of lemon juice. After an hour or so, Pieter excused himself and he took his father back to their camp on the beach. The family shook Pieter's hand. They too realized that his father wasn't a well man.

So onwards they travelled, ever south, and once they'd passed through Barcelona and Valencia they arrived at Almeria, where the coastal road turned slowly west as it took them on the long trek all the way down to Gibraltar.

Gibraltar, England's enclave, was also England's jewel at the entrance to the Mediterranean Sea. And from there, the English Navy could hold the German Navy at bay. If Gibraltar was the door to the Mediterranean, then the British held the key. The relationship between Gibraltar and Spain had always been strained. And for what seemed an eternity, the Spanish had tried to claim Gibraltar as part of the Spanish mainland. The British however had other ideas, and so did the Gibraltarians who lived there. Staunchly British, they paid homage only to one King and one country, and that country was England.

Spain at that time was held under the iron rule of its Fascist leader and dictator, General Francisco Franco. Franco had been ably assisted to that position by his somewhat anxious German ally, Adolph Hitler. Hitler had helped Franco to gain power in Spain by ordering the German Luftwaffe to carry out the infamous aerial bombing of the rebel town of Guernica, and that opened the way to the defeat of Bilbao and Franco's victory over northern Spain. However, and much to Hitler's annoyance, Franco would not be drawn into the war. He was never going to be Hitler's puppy dog, not like Mussolini. If however, Spain had become Germany's ally and gone to war, Hitler could have forced Spain to invade Gibraltar and free the way for him to get to the Middle East and to the Arabs, and with it, the oil.

But no, thankfully, Gibraltar and Spain would remain two countries apart.

Pieter and his father finally arrived at the Straits of Gibraltar.

Gibraltar itself stood out of the sea like a shining monument, alone, but defiant against all odds. It was so close, but still unreachable from the Spanish mainland. And so, Pieter would have to think again. He drove onwards to Algeciras, a small fishing town directly facing Gibraltar. And even though Gibraltar lay there just across a slim stretch of water, it was still another country and another world.

Pieter drove into sleepy Algeciras and parked the car down a quiet side street close to the harbour. It was the middle of the afternoon and he and his father sat there in the midday heat and ate a little and drank some water. Finally, Pieter got out of the car and locked the doors. He peered back in at his father, who had already closed his eyes and was either asleep or was trying to remember better days.

Pieter took notice of the street and his bearings, and then he strode easily down to the small harbour at the seafront. The fishing boats had arrived back earlier and were tied up and empty. The fish had been sold and the day was done. It was quiet and peaceful, now that the business of the day had been concluded. Most of the fishermen had disappeared and gone home for their afternoon 'siesta'. Those same fishermen would drink a glass of wine with a meal of the freshest fish, and then they would sleep. Tomorrow, they would start all over again.

Pieter strolled past the boats, watching them slowly and almost imperceptibly rise and fall in the calm water. In the afternoon's heat, the silence was almost hypnotic.

As he casually sauntered along the front, he noticed that someone was still working on one of the boats. And as he got closer he saw a man sitting on the back of a small, dark blue fishing boat, the man was mending some of his nets. Pieter walked over to the boat and watched the fisherman weave a thick metal needle and cord through a split in the net. The fisherman glanced up for a moment and then carried on with his repair. Pieter watched him, the fisherman was a small grizzled, simple looking man, but his hands worked with trained dexterity.

'Your net, it's broken.' Pieter finally said to him in English, ever hopeful.

'Si,' replied the fisherman, without even looking up from his work.

The fisherman appeared to be totally disinterested. But that one simple reply told Pieter everything that he wanted to hear. The fisherman understood English.

It was a start. It was an introduction.

Pieter started a conversation, and the fisherman replied, at first with a nod, and then a few words and then a little more. The fisherman's name was Camilo...'Camilo Colderon'. And the boat, 'La Pajarito' or 'the little bird', belonged to him alone. Yes, he owned the boat, and yes, in his own way he was the captain, and the captain of his own destiny.

Camilo Colderon was a simple but astute man. Aged around sixty, he'd been a fisherman from being a boy. And god willing he would die a fisherman, and preferably on his little boat and out at sea. Married to a good wife, he had two children who had disappeared to Seville and Granada respectively, both to make a better life. The sea was not for them.

They then came to a point in their conversation, where Pieter had to ask Camilo Colderon the one important question.

'My friend,' said Pieter Szabo, 'I wonder if you could help me?'

Camilo Colderon had been waiting for this. The young man who'd been talking to him for the last twenty minutes wasn't simply passing the time of day. There was an agenda, and a reason. And the young man, even though he spoke English, wasn't from England either.

'What is it you want?' Camilo asked.

'I need to get to Gibraltar, me and my father,' Pieter replied.

Camilo stared at him for a brief moment, and then took a deep sigh.

'You can't just 'go' to Gibraltar,' he said, and he shook his head. 'Gibraltar isn't Spain, it's English. And we're not allowed to go there, it's illegal, there are strict penalties.'

There was a finality in Camilo Colderon's voice, and Pieter understood why. But Pieter Szabo also knew that every man on this earth had his price, and so he had to try.

'I can pay you,' said Pieter.

Camilo looked up at him. A chance of some easy money? Camilo could always use the extra cash. His two children had never really left home when it came down to a matter of finance. Living in a city was always going to be expensive, and every day when he was out at sea, Camilo wondered if his children would ever see sense and come back home to Algeciras.

'How much' Camilo asked?

For a moment, Pieter was stuck. He had no money. So he decided to tell Camilo the truth.

'I can't pay you in cash.'

Camilo sighed and shook his head. Another broken promise, his world was full of broken promises. There was nothing more to say.

Pieter suddenly realized his error, he would have to come up with something and quickly, or this man was going to turn him away.

'No listen to me, I can give you something,' said Pieter.

Camilo almost smiled. 'And what is it that you think 'you' can give me?' he said.

Pieter held his breath for a moment. It was now or never.

'I can give you a car,' he replied slowly. It was all he had, his one and only chance.

Camilo stared at Pieter for a moment. And he wondered to himself, 'my god...a car.' And then he looked at Pieter.

'My friend,' he asked. 'Tell me. What have you done, and who are you running from?'

So Pieter briefly told him what had happened to his family, not the entire story, but enough of that sad and miserable tale to hold Camilo's attention.

Camilo just listened, but said nothing. Finally, he finished his repair, and as he tied the last knot he looked around for his knife, so as to cut away the excess cord. Pieter realized what Camilo was looking for and he took his own Laguiole knife from his pocket and offered it to the fisherman. Camilo stared at the knife for a moment, he took it from Pieter and opened the blade and inspected it. Then he cut through the cord, effortlessly. He stopped and he examined the blade again.

'This is a Laguiole knife.'

'I know,' Pieter replied.

'Did you know that the design was originally Spanish, it comes from the sheepherders up in Catalonia?'

'Yes, I know.'

'And how did you come by it?' Camilo asked.

'I killed two German soldiers who were going to murder a farmer and his wife. The farmer gave me that knife. It was his prized possession.'

'It is a superb knife,' said Camilo, 'a truly exquisite blade.'

Pieter saw another possibility.

'I'll give you the knife too, if you can get us to Gibraltar.'

Camilo Colderon shook his head. 'I could not and would not take your knife. It was given to you for honour. To accept it would bring shame on me.'

Pieter's shoulders sank in disappointment. He had to get his father to England.

Camilo Colderon stared at Pieter for a moment.

'Go and get your car,' he said. 'Let me have a look at it. Maybe we can do a deal.'

Peter Szabo looked at the fisherman, and then he smiled.

Pieter brought the car down to the harbour and Camilo Colderon met him there. Camilo walked admiringly around the vehicle. He'd never owned a car before and never needed one, perhaps until now. With a car, he and his wife could drive to Seville and Granada to see their children. And that would make his wife happy. And with a car he could bring his children back home to visit Algeciras, and hopefully remind them of what they were missing.

The deal was struck. Both men shook hands.

It was agreed that Pieter should return at midnight. Camilo would take

Pieter and his father to Gibraltar. It would be their one and only chance to escape.

At twelve o' clock that same evening, Pieter once again drove down to the now dark and deserted harbour. He parked the car against the stone harbour wall, some hundred meters away from Camilo Calderon's little blue boat. The car was away from the rest of the boats and would not draw any attention, certainly not for the next few days. And after all, it was Camilo Calderon's car now, and he could drive it away whenever it suited him.

Pieter opened the boot of the car and there in its canvas cover was his Mauser rifle. He slung the rifle over his shoulder. He also picked up one of the jerry cans, it was still almost half full of what was their remaining petrol. These would be the only things he was going to take with him, they were the only things he needed. Pieter then helped his father out of the car and they both walked over to Camilo's boat, 'La Pajarito'. Pieter held his father's arm tightly. Franz Szabo said nothing and asked no questions, he just walked towards the boat to where Camilo Colderon was waiting for them. The boat was ready to go and Camilo helped Pieter to get Franz Szabo onboard.

'We leave immediately,' said Camilo, 'very soon the others will arrive to prepare their boats.'

And with that, he released 'La Pajarito' from its mooring and then he started the engine, and within a matter of seconds, the nimble little boat had turned around and was heading out of the harbour and into open water.

Less than half an hour later they approached Gibraltar. Dark and looming, Pieter could make out the island's colossal outline in the starry cloudless night. Camilo cut the engine to a bare minimum and the boat's momentum carried them onwards and almost silently through the water. In the end, he turned off the engine completely and let the current do its work. They wouldn't be seen because 'La Pajarito' was virtually invisible against the inky blue sea.

Camilo gave Pieter directions as they rolled up onto a small deserted beach, just south of Gibraltar's harbour. As the boat gently nudged the sand, Camilo helped Pieter and his father over the side and into the warm, knee-deep water. Within seconds they were on dry land and Camilo Colderon bid them a silent wave as La Pajarito's engine popped into life and he quickly turned the boat around and disappeared into the darkness.

With his rifle slung over his shoulder and the jerry can in one hand, Pieter led his father off the beach onto a narrow unlit road. They then began to walk towards the harbour.

It only took them half an hour, and as they came over a rise in the road, there before them stood Gibraltar's harbour in all its glory. Everywhere was lit by dull yellow lights, lights that were so faded they almost took on an orange hue. But that decision was prudent and wise. Brighter lights would have given the German Luftwaffe an excellent target, if ever they were to fly far. And there moored in the harbour, murky and grey against the dull lights, was the long sleek shape of a British battleship. Pieter took a deep breath when he saw it. This was their chance to escape.

It was half past two in the morning by the time they got nearer to the ship. Pieter and his father approached cautiously, and they hid behind the various warehouses for cover. From where it was moored, Pieter could make out the name on the bow of the ship. It was a destroyer, the HMS Stork, and it stood out against the harbour wall like a huge grey steel monument.

There were two wooden gangplanks which led from the concrete harbour wall onto the ship, one was fore and the other aft. An armed guard strolled casually up and down between the two gangplanks. For him, it was going to be another long night.

Directly opposite the ship was a long row of single story warehouses. Pieter and his father slipped behind the warehouses unseen, they were facing the gangplank near the front bow.

It was so close, but with the guard there it would be impossible to get onboard. The guard would have his orders, no one other than navy personnel would be allowed onboard without official papers. And those were something that neither of them had.

Pieter made his father sit down on the ground. Franz Szabo was compliant, he didn't really understand what was happening and he simply followed whatever his son asked him to do. Pieter picked up the jerry can and walked quickly and quietly around the rear of the building, at the end he turned left and he was then facing the ship's stern. He looked around. There had to be something that he could use. And then he saw the answer to his prayers. Behind him were several small fishing boats. They were all similar in size to the little 'La Pajarito' and they'd been pulled out of the water and onto the dry harbour for either storage or repairs. In between the boats there were stacks of tarpaulins and various bundles of used fishing nets. Pieter put the jerry can down on the ground and then he grabbed hold of some of the tarpaulins and nets and stacked them against the end wall of the building, it took him four short trips before he'd gathered enough. Then he found an old metal dustbin which he quietly emptied. He unscrewed the top off the jerry can and poured some of the petrol into the dustbin, then he placed it rather precariously on top of the tarpaulins. He poured the rest of the petrol over the pile of old nets and tarpaulins and then he stood back and checked everything. It would have to do.

Pieter reached into his jacket pocket for his box of matches. He took out one match, struck it, and threw it onto the pile. Everything immediately burst into flames. Pieter then turned and sprinted back to the other end of the building where he'd left his father. He got Franz Szabo to his feet, and then he peered around the corner of the warehouse and waited. The guard was just lighting a cigarette. He stood there enjoying his smoke as he stared up at the night sky. All was well. As usual.

But suddenly there was the clanging of metal, and a blazing dustbin rolled out from behind the far end of the warehouse. The rest of the petrol tipped out of it and suddenly the harbour wall was ablaze too. The guard just stood there in shock, and for a brief moment he couldn't understand what was happening. Then he spat out his cigarette out and quickly ran towards the flames.

At that same moment, Pieter grabbed hold of his father's arm and they ran as best they could towards the ship. As the guard got to the corner of the warehouse and saw the burning tarpaulins, Pieter was ushering his father up the forward gangplank and onto the ship.

They'd done it. They were onboard. And now Pieter Szabo knew exactly what he had to do.

At that early hour, the destroyer's decks were deserted. Pieter walked along the bare steel deck until he found a set of steps that led down into the bowels of the ship. He helped his father down the flight of steps which then led to a long corridor. Along the corridor there were doors to the different cabins, and some of them had designated names on them. Pieter was looking for the right one, and suddenly he found it.

The door read 'Lieutenant J. Bancroft'. That would be good enough.

Pieter stood there for a moment, and then he knocked on the cabin door. There was no reply.

He knocked again, this time with a little more force. And finally there was an answer.

'Yes, what is it?' someone asked, rather vaguely.

Pieter said nothing. He just knocked on the door again.

'What is it?' someone asked again, this time the voice was a little more distinct.

Again Pieter didn't answer. He just stood there.

From within the cabin somebody began to curse as they made their way towards the cabin door. A handle turned and the door opened and a man stood there in pyjamas, looking slightly dishevelled. He just stood there for a moment, slightly surprised. He'd expected to see someone in naval uniform, but standing there in front of him were two civilians.

'Who are you?' he asked.

Pieter then spoke. 'You are Lieutenant Bancroft?' he asked.

And then a whistle suddenly blew, and within seconds there was the sound of men's feet running along the deck above. And at that moment, a naval seaman bounded down the steps, but stopped immediately when he saw the Lieutenant, still in his pyjamas, and the two men.

'What on earth is going on, seaman?' asked Lieutenant Bancroft, amid all the confusion.

'Someone's lit a fire on the harbour wall, sir' the sailor replied, and he glanced at Pieter and his father. 'We don't know who's done it sir, but we're putting it out, sir.'

And now it was Lieutenant Bancroft's turn to glance at Pieter and Franz Szabo.

But Pieter said nothing.

'Who the hell are you?' Lieutenant Bancroft demanded.

Pieter took a deep breath.

'My name is Pieter Szabo, and this is my father, Dr Franz Szabo. We are Polish, and we have both escaped from Poland, Lieutenant.'

'And why have you escaped from Poland?' the Lieutenant asked, still rather confused.

'Because I've been killing the Nazis, sir,' Pieter replied, rather bluntly.

Lieutenant Bancroft took another fleeting glance at the waiting sailor, who just stood there, slightly amazed at what he'd just heard.

Bancroft shook his head.

'And what 'on earth' are you doing onboard this ship, and what do you actually want?' he asked.

'We want to go to England, sir,' Pieter replied. 'We have to get to England, and I need to talk to your Captain.'

Lieutenant Bancroft heard the note of desperation in Pieter's voice, and at that moment he also noticed that Pieter was carrying something that could be a weapon.

'Is that a gun you're carrying, in the canvas holder?' Bancroft asked.

'Yes sir, it's my rifle,' said Pieter.

'Give it to me, now please,' Bancroft ordered, as he reached out his hand.

Pieter took the rifle from his shoulder and he passed it to the Lieutenant.

Lieutenant Bancroft then turned to the waiting sailor.

'Arrest these men,' he said. 'Take them to a cabin and lock them up.'

Pieter and his father were escorted to an empty cabin and Lieutenant Bancroft followed them there. Once they were locked in, the lieutenant took a deep breath. What was he supposed to do? It was definitely the wrong time in the morning to go waking up the Captain, the lieutenant would have to think this over carefully. Captain F. J Willoughby was not a man to suffer fools lightly. And Lieutenant J. Bancroft certainly wasn't going to become a target for the Captain's wrath. He would sort it out later. And so he decided to go and get dressed, and then he would see about that fire.

Pieter and his father were alone in the cabin. There was a bed in there and Pieter helped his father onto it. Pieter sat himself down on a stout wooden chair. He had to think.

So far, he'd done the right thing. To get onto the ship and then try to hide would have been ridiculous. They needed food and water and the obvious ablutions. And if they'd been caught by the lower ranks, the sailors would have simply just thrown them off the ship. It would have been simpler, and no questions would have been asked.

But no, Pieter had approached an officer. And that officer would be duty bound to inform his Captain. And from there, it would all be in the Captain's hands.

By eight o' clock that same morning, Captain Francis John Willoughby was up, washed and changed and had finished his breakfast. He was sitting in his reasonably small cabin at an equally small desk and was attending to some minor paperwork when there was a knock at his door.

'Yes, enter,' the Captain called out. The door opened and Lieutenant Bancroft stood there.

'Ah, come in Bancroft,' said the Captain.

Lieutenant Bancroft respectfully removed his cap and then stepped into the cabin.

'Good morning, sir,' said the Lieutenant.

'Yes, good morning. What is it, Bancroft?' Captain Willoughby asked, as he strategically moved his paperwork.

'Err, a bit of an incident last night sir. Well no, actually it was in the early hours of this morning, sir.'

The lieutenant rightly corrected himself, before his Captain did, and would.

'Yes, and what incident was that?' the Captain asked.

'There was a fire, sir.'

Captain Willoughby looked up at once.

'Whereabouts?' he asked.

'On the harbour wall sir, at the far end of the warehouse.'

Captain Willoughby took a short breath. For a moment he thought the fire had been onboard.

'What's the damage?' he asked.

'Oh none sir,' the lieutenant replied, 'someone had set fire to some nets and some old tarpaulins. It was quite a blaze, but no actual damage was done, sir. The men and I quickly put it out. I saw to it, sir,' Bancroft added, trying to make merit from his own usefulness.

Captain Willoughby raised his eyebrows slightly. He'd heard it all before.

'And what time was that?' asked the Captain.

The Lieutenant had to think quickly. He'd never considered the actual time.

'It would be somewhere after three, sir,' he replied casually.

'Somewhere?' the Captain asked.

'Ah, about quarter past, sir,' the lieutenant tried again.

'Mmm,' said the Captain. 'And could you tell me Lieutenant, why at 'somewhere' or possibly around a quarter past three o'clock this morning, someone decided to light a bonfire on the harbour at Gibraltar within yards of one of his Royal Majesty's battleships?'

Suddenly, Lieutenant Bancroft began to see the bigger picture.

The Captain continued. 'And while the harbour was ablaze, Lieutenant, why did you not see fit to wake me?'

Lieutenant Bancroft coughed. 'I didn't want to wake you, sir,' he replied rather feebly.

'Oh, so the ship comes under possible attack and you took it upon yourself not to wake the Captain.'

'It was hardly an attack sir, just a fire.'

'And who started that fire?'

'I don't know sir.'

'Have you considered Lieutenant, that while your attention was drawn to putting out a fire down at one end of the ship, someone could have come on board with guns or even a bomb and caused havoc. We're at war, Lieutenant, and the Spanish are hovering somewhere in between, and they would love to get their hands on Gibraltar.

Lieutenant J. Bancroft took a deep breath.

'Actually Sir, someone did come aboard.'

Captain Willoughby suddenly couldn't believe what he was hearing.

'Were they armed?'

Lieutenant Bancroft almost closed his eyes.

'Well, yes actually, they were armed, sir.'

The Captain nearly threw a fit. But the Lieutenant continued.

'Only one of them was armed, sir. He had a rifle. There were two of them, they knocked on my door and I had to get out of bed. The one with the rifle wanted to speak to 'you', sir.'

At that point Captain Willoughby shook his head. He counted to five and then looked up at his Lieutenant again.

'So you're telling me that two men sneaked onboard this ship last night, and they were armed and that they were asking to see the Captain? Good god man, we could have all been bloody well shot.'

Lieutenant Bancroft realized that he was burying himself under a mass of confusion.

The Captain however, continued.

'And now we know who lit the bloody bonfire.'

'Do you think so, sir?' The lieutenant stupidly asked.

Captain F.J Willoughby, of the Battleship HMS Stork and of the Kings Royal Navy, looked up at his Lieutenant and again realized that he was dealing with a complete imbecile.

'Tell me Bancroft. How did they get on board?' he asked.

'Probably up the gangplank, at the fore, sir.'

'And where was the guard?'

'He was fighting the fire, sir.' And at that moment, Lieutenant Bancroft suddenly realized what had happened. They'd been duped.

'Where are these men, Bancroft?' the Captain suddenly asked.

'I have them locked up, sir.'

'And the gun?'

'I have it, sir,' the lieutenant replied, trying his best to sound reasonably competent.

'And do we know anything about these men and why they were onboard this ship?'

'Yes we do sir,' the lieutenant continued. Both men are Polish sir, actually they're father and son. Apparently the fathers a doctor, but he doesn't look well, he never spoke a word. The son said that they are on the run from the Nazis.'

'And why's that?' Captain Willoughby suddenly intervened.

'Apparently he's been killing some of them, sir.'

The Captain shrugged. Things were looking somewhat better, if they were telling the truth of course. On the other hand, it could all be a complete pack of lies.

'They want to get to England sir, seem quite desperate actually. That's why the son wanted to speak to you, sir.'

'Did you get his name?' asked the Captain.

Lieutenant Bancroft gave it a moment's thought.

'Szabo sir, his name's Pieter Szabo.'

Captain Willoughby considered the events. This Pieter Szabo had been quite clever. He'd managed to get himself onto a Royal Navy Destroyer and had then surrendered himself. And then he'd asked for safe passage. In effect, he'd asked for British help. And the British had declared war on Germany because they'd invaded Poland. Therefore, Britain supported Poland and the Polish, and Pieter Szabo and his father were both Polish. The question was already answered. The British Navy was honour bound to help these people. It was as simple as that. However, there were some questions that needed to be answered, and Captain Willoughby would need to find out the truth.

He looked up at Lieutenant Bancroft.

'I need to speak to these people. Organize something in around an hour's time.' Captain Willoughby then glanced at his watch. 'Set up something in the Briefing room, I'll talk to them in there.'

'Yes sir,' the lieutenant replied, and he saluted and turned to leave.

'Just one other thing, Bancroft.'

The lieutenant stopped and turned around.

'Yes sir?' he asked.

'Lieutenant, you mentioned that you put out the fire with the men?'

'Yes Sir.'

'Yet at that actual time, you were dealing with this Szabo chap and his father, and then you saw to it that they were both locked up. Am I right?'

'Err, yes sir,' the lieutenant replied.

And so you couldn't have been fighting the fire 'with the men'?

'I got there straightaway, as soon as I could, sir,' he replied.

Captain Willoughby smiled. 'Surely not in your pyjamas, Bancroft?'

The lieutenant's shoulders dropped, he'd been caught out, again.

'No sir,' he said quietly, 'of course not sir.'

It was an admission.

Willoughby looked at him.

'You know Bancroft, stories are like numbers. They always have to add up.'

'Yes sir, sorry sir' the lieutenant replied.

Captain F. J Willoughby suddenly straightened himself in his chair.

'Alright Lieutenant, carry on, and sort out that briefing for me will you. Oh, and bring along that rifle too, please. I want to have a look at it.'

'Yes, sir.' Lieutenant Bancroft saluted, and then he left.

Captain Willoughby smiled and he shook his head. It was back to business, he would let it go, this time.

An hour later, Captain Willoughby and Lieutenant Bancroft both walked into the Briefing room. It was one of the larger rooms on the ship and the Captain used it whenever he needed to consult his officers, or for meetings when he needed a little more space than his own cramped cabin provided. Lieutenant Bancroft was carrying the canvas holder which contained the rifle.

Pieter Szabo and his father were both sat facing a large wooden desk. The only other person present was a guard. As they entered the room the Captain dismissed the guard and asked him to wait outside. The Captain seated himself at the desk. In front of him was a determined looking young man, obviously Pieter Szabo, and with him, presumably, was the father.

Franz Szabo just sat there in his long coat with his eyes closed.

Captain Willoughby placed some papers on the desk in front of him and took out his pen. And then he looked up.

'Gentlemen' he said.

Only Pieter responded.

'Sir?'

Franz Szabo didn't speak or move. Not the best of starts.

'Right,' Captain Willoughby continued, and he glanced down at his papers, 'I take it that you are Pieter Szabo and that this is your father, who is apparently a 'Dr Franz Szabo'. Is that correct?'

'Yes it is, sir.' Pieter replied.

The Captain looked across at both men for a moment.

'And you both claim to be of Polish nationality?'

Pieter nodded.

The Captain looked at his papers again.

'And in the early hours of this morning, you both illegally boarded His Majesty's destroyer, HMS Stork. Is that correct?'

'Yes it is, sir,' Pieter replied again.

'And could you tell me, for what purpose?'

'We want to go to England sir.'

'So do a lot of people,' the Captain replied. 'Do you have any papers to substantiate that you are both of Polish Nationality?' he asked.

Pieter shook his head.

'No I'm sorry sir, we don't. But I speak Polish sir,' he said hopefully.

'So do a lot of people,' the Captain replied again. 'Actually, your English seems quite good, Mr Szabo.'

'I can speak Polish, English, and some German too sir,' said Pieter, trying to be helpful.

'Oh I see,' said the Captain, 'so you are a Pole who can speak English, or possibly a German who can speak Polish, along with some English too?'

Pieter realized that this was not going well.

'I'm not a German, sir. I am certainly not a German.' And for a brief moment he was annoyed. And the Captain saw it.

'I take it that it was you who started the fire on the harbour wall last night?'

Pieter looked at the Captain and decided that telling the truth was going be the best policy. The Captain was a clever man, and one lie would only lead to another. Pieter needed the Captain as an ally. Better to tell the truth.

'Yes sir, it was, sir,' he replied.

'And why did you set fire to the harbour wall?'

'It was a diversion, sir. We needed to get on board, and I knew that if I simply approached the guard I would be turned away.'

The Captain looked at his papers again.

'Tell me Mr Szabo. Why do you want to go to England?'

Pieter glanced at his father, and then he turned back to the Captain.

'For my father's safety, and for his health, sir. We've lost everything in Poland, everything.'

'And what would you do, if you ever got to England?'

'I would make sure that my father was safe and that he got medical treatment. And then I would return to Poland, sir.'

Pieter's reply surprised the Captain.

'You would want to return to Poland?' he asked.

'Yes, sir,'

'And why is that?'

'To kill more Nazis, sir.'

'Oh really,' the Captain replied, with a hint of scepticism.

And Pieter heard the questioning tone. And he leant forward in his chair and he looked directly at the Captain. Now, his emotions were getting the better of him.

'You don't understand me, Captain. You don't know what's happened to us, and you don't know me. So let me tell you something important, it's something that you need to understand. I am a trained marksman, Captain. I trained to be in the Olympic team to represent my country. I have killed Nazis and I will continue to kill Nazis. And when I get back to Poland I will join the Resistance as a sniper. And then I'll cause havoc.'

Captain Willoughby looked up at his Lieutenant. Lieutenant Bancroft was quite surprised by Pieter's outburst.

'Pass me that rifle would you please, Lieutenant,' said the Captain

Lieutenant Bancroft did as he was asked.

The Captain laid the rifle on the desk and removed it from its canvas holder, and as he looked at it he was somewhat astonished.

The rifle was immaculate, it was a phenomenal weapon. Highly polished, and cherished, the wooden stock gleamed like a prized piece of furniture. The barrel, also highly polished, hadn't a scratch or a mark on it. The rifle looked better than brand new.

And at that moment the Captain noticed something.

Dr Franz Szabo had just opened his eyes.

Pieter looked at his rifle. It had never let him down.

'Is this yours?' asked the Captain

'Yes, it's mine,' Pieter replied.

'Are you sure?'

Pieter didn't understand.

'It's a beautiful rifle,' said the Captain, 'phenomenal, in fact. But are you sure it's yours?'

For a moment, Pieter didn't realize what the Captain was trying to imply. But the Captain continued.

'Come on Mr Szabo, tell me the truth please. You stole this gun, and probably off some dead German soldier. You're no more of a marksman than I am. Please, tell me the truth Mr Szabo. This isn't really your gun, is it?'

And at that moment, Franz Szabo slammed his hand on the desk and he began to shout.

'My son...my son...is the finest marksman you will ever see. He's the best, the very best,'

And with that, Franz Szabo started to cry. It was all too much for him.

For an instant, nobody moved. And then Franz Szabo slumped back in the chair and continued to weep. He closed his eyes again, as the tears ran down his face. He didn't speak another word.

Pieter put his arms around his father and tried to console him.

And Captain Willoughby looked at them both. He'd heard enough because he'd just heard the truth.

'Can we do something for your father?' the Captain asked, now rather more sympathetically.

'My father's not well,' said Pieter. 'He's been through so much.'

'Can we get him a cup of tea or something?' the Captain asked.

'Could you take him back to our cabin, sir, and give him a cup of tea,' said Pieter, 'and then I'll tell you exactly what has happened to us. My father shouldn't listen. It's all too much for him.'

The Captain nodded at Lieutenant Bancroft. Pieter then helped his father out of the chair and the Lieutenant took Franz Szabo back to their cabin.

Pieter sat down again and then he told Captain Willoughby the whole miserable story.

He explained about their arrest and about his family, and then Auschwitz. And then his father's escape and their long trek across Europe.

The Captain listened intently as Pieter Szabo told him what had happened to them. It was a tale of despair.

'And now you know why I have to go back to Poland.' said Pieter finally.

Captain Willoughby nodded. Now, he understood.

'I see,' he said. 'Your story explains a lot of things.'

'Thank you, Captain,' Pieter replied.

'Right then Mr Szabo,' said the Captain, 'one way or another, we're going to get you and your father to England.'

Pieter looked up. Finally, there was a chance.

'But, it won't be on this ship,' said Captain Willoughby. 'We're going on convoy duties. We've had orders to escort commercial shipping across the Atlantic, the tankers sailing from America to England with valuable supplies. We have to get them safely past the German U-boats. And after that, there are rumours that we'll be sent across the Mediterranean to back up the British troops in North Africa. So we're going to be away for quite some while. However, there is a troop ship heading back from there. The RMS Narkunda should hopefully be docking here in Gibraltar tomorrow or possibly the day after. There are sick and injured troops onboard who are being taken back home. We will put you on that ship and get you safely to England.'

'It doesn't really matter which ship we go on,' said Pieter.

'Exactly,' said the Captain, 'and once the 'Narkunda' gets under sail you should be in England in three or four days at the most, give or take.'

Pieter sat back in his chair and he gave a sigh of relief. After all they had gone through, all the turmoil of travelling blindly across Europe, and now suddenly, they were finally going to go to England.

'Can I ask you something Mr Szabo?' said the Captain, almost casually.

'Yes, of course,' Pieter replied.

'Are you really serious about going back to Poland?'

'Yes, I am,' Pieter replied, 'I owe it to my family, and to my wife.'

The Captain nodded, 'Well, in that case, I do know someone who may be able to help you.'

Pieter looked at him. 'You do?'

'Yes I do. A friend of mine, his name's Ballantyne. He's a lieutenant in the British Army and he works with Special Operations. We both went to University together and we have still remained very good friends. He needs people with your 'particular' talent, and I think that he could help you, and vice versa of course. I'd really like you to meet him.'

Pieter was enthusiastic, 'Yes, of course I will. It sounds good.'

'Right then,' said Captain Willoughby, 'you go and see to your father and I'll make all the necessary arrangements.'

Both men stood up and they shook hands.

'Thank you again,' said Pieter. 'Without your help Captain, I don't know what we would have done.'

'Well it's a long way to swim,' said the Captain, light-heartedly.

Both men laughed, and then Pieter left to take care of his father.

Captain Willoughby sat back at his desk, and then he took a sheet of paper and began to write.

'For the attention of'.
Lieutenant Vernon Ballantyne
Special Operations
Ministry of Defence
D/1 FIRS
BUCKINGHAMSHIRE.
ENGLAND

'Dear Vernon...with reference to our past discussions...the RMS Troopship Narkunda will be docking at Portsmouth in approx five days time...please meet up there to receive a Pieter Szabo and his father...Szabo could be the man you are looking for...yours... Francis W.'

Once he'd finished writing, Captain F. J Willoughby left the Briefing Room and made his way to the ship's Radio Office. He spoke to one of the operators there.

'Could you send this telegram to the War Office in London, to be forwarded to the address in Buckinghamshire, and immediately please.'

'Straightaway, sir,' replied the operator.

CHAPTER 10

It took almost a week for Pieter and his father to finally reach the grey and drizzle laden coastline of England. The RMS Narkunda sailed slowly and quietly into Portsmouth Harbour in the early morning, almost unnoticed. Without any fuss, she was quickly moored against the stone harbour wall and the sick and the wounded began to be taken off the ship. Many were bandaged, some were on stretchers, some limped. For many, life had taken a different course.

Pieter and his father got in line with the wounded troops and eventually made their own way down one of the wooden gangplanks. There were trucks waiting there, ready to take the injured soldiers to the military hospitals, and for many, anywhere else that was available.

Pieter and his father stood there alone. All they had with them were two small bags that contained a change of clothes. Over his shoulder, Pieter carried the canvas holder that contained his Mauser rifle. Captain Willoughby had seen to that.

Once Captain Willoughby had received a reply to his telegram from his longtime friend,

Lieutenant Vernon Ballantyne, the Captain had seen fit to forward a little more information about Pieter Szabo.

He sent a telegram which read...

'Szabo is a Polish refugee...apparently, a top class marksman...speaks English and some German...his father needs hospitalizing...mental problems. Ask Szabo to tell you his story...fascinating...he is prepared to go back to Poland as a sniper...he is a highly trained...he is also a tenacious and very clever young man...this could be the opportunity you've been looking for...yours...Francis W.'

As Pieter and his father stood on the side of the harbour wall, feeling slightly at a loss, suddenly someone spoke out.

'Mr Szabo?'

Pieter turned around, only to see a tall, man in uniform heading in their direction. Even before he reached them, Lieutenant Vernon Ballantyne held out his hand as a greeting. He was a tall, dark-haired man who spoke with a professional attitude.

Pieter automatically shook the Lieutenant's hand in return. The Lieutenant then turned to Franz Szabo, who just stood there with his eyes firmly closed.

'My father isn't well,' said Pieter, as an explanation.

'I believe so,' Lieutenant Ballantyne replied.

Pieter looked at him for a moment.

'Mr Szabo, I've received a couple of telegrams from Captain Willoughby. He's put me in the picture.'

Pieter accepted the response and simply nodded in reply.

Lieutenant Ballantyne continued. 'And so with that in mind, I've been advised to pick you up and look after you both.' Vernon Ballantyne then looked directly at Pieter, 'I've also been told that your father needs medical help, and so I've organized that he be admitted to a Convalescence Home where he will be looked after and given the medical care he requires.'

'Will I be staying there with him?' Pieter asked.

'Let me explain,' said Lieutenant Ballantyne, 'I have a car waiting for you around the corner. It will take you both to the Bicester Hall, that's the Convalescence Home. Bicester is a small village in Oxfordshire. They are expecting you, and you will both spend the night there. You'll be able to see that your father is made comfortable. I have to go to London for a briefing, but I will pick you up at Bicester Hall tomorrow, Mr Szabo. From there we'll be going to Aylesbury. We'll be staying at 'The Firs', it's a large country house where we run some of our special operations. It's very comfortable and you'll only be a fairly short car ride away from your father. I think it will all work out rather well. I'll tell you more tomorrow when I pick you up, but now we really need to be on our way.'

Pieter looked at the Lieutenant for an instant. Vernon Ballantyne was a tall, well-built man, somewhat athletic and certainly intelligent. He had a commanding quality that came across as coldly efficient. That suited Pieter, it seemed that the Lieutenant was a straight talker.

Lieutenant Ballantyne walked them to the car, the driver was sitting there with the engine running and ready to go. Pieter and his father sat in the back.

'Till tomorrow then,' said Ballantyne, and with that he turned and walked away.

The driver never spoke, he simply put the car into gear and they sped off immediately.

The following morning, as Pieter was having breakfast, Lieutenant Ballantyne reappeared.

He sat himself down at Pieter's table and somebody brought him a cup of tea.

'Has your father settled in?' Ballantyne asked.

'Yes,' said Pieter. 'He seems very comfortable.'

'Ah good. This is an excellent place, he'll be well looked after here.'

'Yes, and again, thank you,' Pieter replied.

Vernon Ballantyne smiled. 'You and I will be going over to our place in Aylesbury. But before we go anywhere, I have to ask you a question, Mr Szabo. How do you feel about helping us to do something positive against the Nazis?'

Pieter looked at Vernon Ballantyne. 'You've no need to ask Lieutenant. I've lost everything because of those bastards. I've even lost my father, I don't know whether he'll ever recover fully. I do know that he'll never be the same man again.'

Vernon Ballantyne nodded at the obvious conclusion.

Pieter continued. 'And so, yes Lieutenant. I'll do anything that you want me to do.'

Vernon Ballantyne listened to those words. It was exactly what he needed to hear.

'Shall we go then, Mr Sazbo?' he said.

Pieter quickly finished his mug of tea, and then he went back to his room for his bag and his rifle. Vernon Ballantyne was waiting for him outside in a car. This time there was no driver, just Ballantyne. Pieter threw his kit onto the back seat and then climbed into the front next to the Lieutenant. They then set off down the road,

'Right Mr Szabo,' said Ballantyne, 'while we now have the chance and the time. I want you to tell me your whole story. Exactly as you told Captain Willoughby.'

Pieter took a deep breath, and for the next half an hour he told Vernon Ballantyne everything that had happened to his family, his father, and himself.

Ballantyne listened carefully. And by the time Pieter had finished, Ballantyne understood.

He understood the deep hatred that Pieter Szabo held for the Nazis in Poland, and he also realized that once this young man was armed, he wasn't going to stop. And it wasn't that Pieter Szabo was suicidal, no, certainly not. It was that Pieter Szabo just didn't care anymore. His life had been smashed. He'd lost everything, and he couldn't see a future. His personal safety didn't matter any longer. It was more a question of survival and the ability to kill the people he hated so very much.

Vernon Ballantyne realized that he had possibly found the person he'd been looking for, a very clever and adept killer.

They finally arrived at Aylesbury.

'The Firs' was a rather huge old country house, about three miles outside the village. Set within grounds of more than twenty five acres, it was large and it was quiet, and it was private.

Once they'd arrived, Pieter was introduced to Sergeant 'Bill' Fazackerly. Pieter was handed over to Sergeant Fazackerly, who then showed him around the house. There was a room already prepared for Pieter, who was quietly grateful for the privacy. The house was full of different offices and departments, and everybody seemed to be busy. There was a canteen and there was also a large lounge, filled with several leather suites and it was obviously used as a recreation room. It was only as he was being walked through the grounds that Pieter suddenly showed a spark of interest. He heard the sound of gunfire, and he turned to the Sergeant.

'What's that?' he asked.

'Let me show you,' said Sergeant Fazackerly.

They walked along a narrow path for another hundred yards and then came out into an open area. And there in front of Pieter, there was a shooting range. A man lay on the ground and he was shooting at a distant target.

'This is one of the two ranges that we have here.'

Pieter turned to Sergeant Fazackerly, 'this is good Sergeant,' he said.

'Yes,' said the Sergeant. 'You can use the range whenever you like. In fact, we generally insist that you do.'

Pieter looked at Sergeant Fazackerly, 'That won't be a problem Sergeant. This is what I do.'

The sergeant glanced at Pieter, he couldn't figure Pieter Szabo out. There was no humour, none at all, not even a smile. He considered that Pieter was somewhat of a 'cold fish'.

But then again, the sergeant didn't know Pieter Szabo's past history.

'Well that's good,' said the sergeant, 'because tomorrow I'll be putting you through your paces.'

Pieter just nodded, but he wasn't really listening. He was more intent on watching the man shooting at the target. It was almost a hunger, and Pieter warmed to the thought that tomorrow he would have his Mauser rifle back in his arms.

That evening after dinner, Pieter was taken to the recreation room where he was introduced to some of the personnel who worked there, along with several soldiers who were obviously there for training too. The only person missing was Vernon Ballantyne. After an hour's uncomplicated socializing, Pieter went back to his room. He took out his rifle and then he began to carefully clean and polish it.

The next morning after breakfast, Pieter and Sergeant Fazackerly once again returned to the shooting range. Pieter brought along his rifle. The sergeant brought the ammunition.

As the sergeant sorted out the cardboard targets, Pieter lay on the ground and made himself comfortable. Then he loaded his rifle with five shells.

As the Sergeant walked back to Pieter he called out.

'The range is one hundred yards,' he said. 'Whenever you feel ready.'

Pieter didn't know what a hundred yards meant, he'd always dealt in metres. But it didn't matter, he could easily judge the distance.

He took aim and fired, all five shots within seconds. Sergeant Fazackerly had only got halfway back down the range when he stopped. He shrugged, and then he turned back to go and inspect the target. As he walked back, the Sergeant shook his head. Just another 'trigger happy kid', and someone that he would have to train and give a lecture to. He'd also have to speak to Lieutenant Ballantyne. It was all part of the process. Assessing the personality of each and every trainee was imperative. Those mental processes were all elements of a shooters capability.

When the Sergeant reached the target he stopped. He looked, and for a moment he didn't understand. There should have been five bullet holes somewhere, but there wasn't. In the dead centre of the target a large hole had been blown away, it was the size of a tennis ball. The Sergeant looked again, and it was only then that he realized. Pieter Szabo had fired five bullets that were so closely grouped that they'd blown out the centre of the target completely. Sergeant 'Bill' Fazackerly was amazed. He'd never seen anything like it in his life.

He replaced the target and walked back to Pieter.

'Okay, shoot again please.'

Pieter reloaded his rifle and then took aim. As he did, the sergeant watched him. Pieter lay there comfortable and totally relaxed. There was no awkwardness at all, this was a natural position for him. Pieter fired again, once more in rapid succession. And once again the Sergeant walked back down the range to inspect the target. The same result, 'unbelievable'. He took the two targets and he walked back to Pieter.

'Where on earth did you learn to shoot, son?' he asked.

Pieter looked up, 'At the Lodz District Rifle Club, in Poland, sir.'

'You can get up,' said Sergeant Fazackerly. Pieter did as he was asked.

'Tell me more,' said the Sergeant.

'I've been shooting since I was a child,' said Pieter. 'I was training to represent the Polish National Team in the Olympics. I was considered to be one of the best, sir.'

Sergeant Fazackerly raised an eyebrow. 'Why, was there someone else as good as you?'

Pieter paused for a moment before he spoke.

'Yes sir, there was. My father.'

There was suddenly a look of emotion in Pieter Szabo's eyes. And it wasn't sorrow, and it wasn't anguish. It was anger.

Sergeant Fazackerly saw it too, and he took note.

'You can continue with your practice,' said the Sergeant. 'We'll try a different gun.'

He returned to the house, where he found another rifle and some ammunition. Then he went back to the shooting range. Pieter was sitting on the ground, waiting. He'd run out of ammunition.

'Here,' said Sergeant Fazackerly, as he handed Pieter the rifle. 'It's a Lee Enfield, standard British issue. It takes five rounds of .303 shells. He then handed Pieter a box of shells too.

Pieter held the rifle to his shoulder and he looked down the sights.

'It doesn't feel too bad,' he said, 'maybe a little lighter than the Mauser, and the stock feels slightly different too, but it's not uncomfortable. It would just take a bit of getting used to.'

'Like any new rifle,' the Sergeant agreed. 'Do you want to give it a try?'

Pieter nodded, and as Sergeant Fazackerly went to fit another target, Pieter tried to get the feel of the weapon. The Sergeant walked back a way, and out of the line of fire. Then he shouted to Pieter to continue.

Pieter lay on the ground once more and loaded the rifle. He took aim and fired, this time not as quickly. The Sergeant then went to inspect the target. He pulled it away from the board and replaced it. Then he walked back to where Pieter was sitting. Pieter was busily adjusting the rifle's sights.

'You're out on this one,' said the Sergeant.

'Yes, I know,' said Pieter, 'it's shooting to the right. The sights need adjusting.'

Sergeant Fazackerly checked the cardboard target once again. There were five bullet holes just right of centre.

The Sergeant frowned. 'How did you know?' he asked.

'I could see them,' Pieter replied.

'You could see them?' said the Sergeant, 'five bullet holes from a distance of one hundred yards....how?'

'I just can,' Pieter replied. 'My father once told me that we both suffered from long vision.'

At that moment, 'suffered' was not the word that Sergeant Fazackerly would have easily used.

'Well, it seems to be working,' said the Sergeant.

'There,' said Pieter, 'that's better. I'll have another go.'

He reloaded the rifle and then got back on the ground. He aimed and then fired.

Sergeant Fazackerly once again walked back to the target.

Five holes, dead centre. Each bullet hole was less than an inch apart. It was maybe not as close as his first shots, but it was nevertheless an outstanding display of marksmanship. Especially for a second attempt with a totally different rifle.

The Sergeant raised his thumb and walked back.

'Excellent,' he shouted, and then he made his way back down the range.

Pieter was still adjusting the sights. They need fine-tuning.' he said.

'Okay,' said the Sergeant, 'you carry on and I'll go and get some more ammunition.'

He returned ten minutes later with another box of shells. Pieter was merrily shooting the target to bits by then.

'Let's try something else,' said Sergeant Fazackerly. 'Come on, follow me.'

Pieter stood up, and then together they strode out another hundred yards away from the target.

'Right,' said Sergeant Fazackerly. 'That's as near as damn to two hundred yards. Let's see how you go on.'

The Sergeant walked all the way back down the range and replaced the target. Then he stood out of the firing line and waved. Pieter took his five shots. The Sergeant replaced the target and Pieter fired again. The Sergeant once again took down the cardboard target and looked at them both. Each target, five bullet holes, all grouped less than an inch apart. He'd never seen shooting like it before.

He walked back to Pieter. 'We're done here,' he said. 'We can pack up.'

As they walked back to the house, Sergeant Fazackerly asked Pieter a question.

'Have you ever used a telescopic sight?'

Pieter shook his head. 'No sir, we never used them at the club. The range there wasn't long enough really.'

'Well tomorrow we'll try something new. We have another, longer range. Tomorrow we'll try it out'.

The next morning, and after breakfast, Pieter once again met up with Sergeant Fazackerly. The Sergeant brought the Lee Enfield rifle and with it a telescopic sight.

'You won't need the Mauser today,' he said, 'we don't have a sight to fit it.'

Pieter examined the telescopic sight and he looked through the lens.

'This is interesting,' he said.

'Believe me, it is,' the Sergeant replied.

They walked past the shooting range and continued down a narrow path for another ten minutes. Eventually they arrived at a large narrow field which was surrounded by trees. At the far end of the field, Pieter could see half a dozen targets, similar to the ones that he'd used as target practice the previous day. Five steel poles had been placed down the centre of the field. They'd been painted white and had black figures written on them.

'200...500...1000...1500...and finally...2000'

'They're distances,' said Sergeant Fazackerly. 'Today we'll be using the sight. We'll start off at 200 yards.'

They walked down the field to the pole marked 200 yards. Sergeant Fazackerly showed Pieter how to fit the telescopic sight and then how to use the adjustments to focus the lens.

Pieter was fascinated. He aimed the gun at the targets and focused the sight and was amazed when the targets appeared to be only a few feet away.

'This is unbelievable,' he said out loud.

The Sergeant laughed.

'The telescopic sight allows the shooter a totally different method of shooting. Greater distances are involved and greater detail than the human eye could ever see, even with your eyes. However, there are other challenges. With distance there is a loss of momentum, and eventually the bullet's trajectory will alter. In other words, the bullet will begin to drop. You have to learn to adjust for that, it all comes down to experience. Another major factor is the wind. The wind is the biggest problem because it's a variable. Gusts of wind, the direction and the wind speed, will all affect your aim over a longer distance. It all comes down to knowledge and practice. You have to learn to adjust to the conditions.

Pieter was fascinated. He realized that the telescopic sight was a tool that he would have to learn to use, a very valuable tool.

'I'm going to go over to the target area,' said Sergeant Fazackerly. 'I want you to shoot left to right. Put five shots into the first target and then stop. I'll inspect your shots and then I'll hold up my hand to let you know how many were on centre. Then I'll move out of the line of fire and raise my thumb. Then you can go onto the next target, okay?'

Pieter nodded, he understood. The sergeant then made his way down the field to the target area.

Pieter lay on the ground and began to adjust the sights. As he looked through the lens he saw the cross or the 'hairs', as the Sergeant had called them. Pieter adjusted the cross to focus on the targets. It was incredible, the targets appeared to be so close that they were crystal clear.

Looking through the sights, Pieter watched the Sergeant as he got to the targets. He looked back at Pieter and then raised his thumb in the air.

Pieter loaded the rifle with five shells, then he made himself comfortable and took aim at the target on the left, just as the Sergeant had instructed. He took the shot, and when he looked he could see that it was slightly off centre. He took another shot, and that too was off centre. Pieter stopped for a moment and readjusted the sight. Then he took aim again and the bullet struck home, it hit the middle of the target. He fired two more shots, they both hit dead centre. Pieter smiled, suddenly he understood how it worked, and he laughed to himself. This was going to be fun.

At the bottom of the field, Sergeant Fazackerly went over to inspect the target, and then he held up three fingers. Pieter smiled again, he already knew his score. Pieter Szabo had phenomenal eyesight.

The Sergeant moved out of the way and then raised his thumb. Pieter reloaded the rifle and took aim and fired. This time he put all five shots into the centre of the target.

The Sergeant once more inspected the target, he raised his hand and this time he held up all five fingers. Pieter also noticed that the Sergeant was actually smiling.

Pieter then went on to shoot at the other three targets. His shooting was consistent, all the shots were dead centre. Sergeant Fazackerly replaced the targets and then made his way back to Pieter.

'You seem to have got your eye in,' he said, 'how do you feel?'

'Not bad, I'm okay' Pieter replied.

'We'll move back to 500 yards,' said the Sergeant, 'and we'll see how you go on.'

They moved back to the next pole.

Pieter lay on the ground once again and as he began to adjust the sights the Sergeant went back to the targets. Pieter fine-tuned the hairs of the lens and reloaded the gun. He looked through the sights, and once again the target looked to be only a few feet away. He took his first shot and again it was just off centre. Pieter cursed himself as he readjusted the sights. Then he took the second shot and hit the middle of the target. The next three shots also hit dead centre. He did the same thing with the next five targets. He was learning.

The Sergeant replaced the targets and then made his way back.

'You're doing okay,' he said to Pieter, 'those were good shots.'

'I think I'm beginning to understand it,' Pieter replied.

For Sergeant Fazackerly, that was a bit of an understatement.

'We're eventually going to need some more ammunition,' said the Sergeant, 'I'm going to go back to the house for some. You stay here and practice.' And then he grinned, 'and I'll get a pair of binoculars too, I'm bloody sick of doing all this walking.'

The Sergeant went back to the house and the first thing he did was go to the canteen for a cup of tea. After that he wandered down to the stores and picked up some more ammunition and the much needed binoculars. As he walked back down the corridor, Lieutenant Ballantyne was just leaving his office. The Lieutenant stopped when he saw his sergeant.

'Ah, Bill,' he said, 'and how's our new recruit coming along?'

Sergeant Fazackerly stopped as he gave a quick customary salute. It was all fairly casual at 'The Firs',

The Sergeant grinned at the Lieutenant.

'Where on earth did you find this one, sir?'

Vernon Ballantyne smiled, 'Actually Bill, he found us. How's he doing?'

'Unbelievable.' the Sergeant replied. 'He's a natural, sir. I've just got him onto the long range and using a telescopic sight. He's never used a telescopic before, but he's consistently hitting the target dead centre at 500 yards. This lad's something special, sir, a rare talent.'

'Very good,' said Lieutenant Ballantyne. 'When you've got him up to spec, Bill, come and see me will you, and we'll do an evaluation.'

'Yes, sir, I will sir,' replied the Sergeant and he saluted once again.

'Okay, carry on then Sergeant,' said Lieutenant Ballantyne, 'Oh, and Bill, thank you.'

All of this put Sergeant Fazackerly in quite a good mood. Praise from Lieutenant Ballantyne never went amiss. And so the Sergeant decided to go and have another cup of tea, this time with a few biscuits. After a bit of chit-chat, he made his way back to the range. When he got there, he had a surprise.

Pieter Szabo was no longer shooting. Well, not at 500 yards.

Pieter had moved himself to the 1000 yard mark and was firing repeatedly. Sergeant Fazackerly just stood there for a moment, and then he reached for his binoculars and focused them on the targets a thousand yards away. The middle of each target was blown away. There were no telltale bullet holes around the perimeters. Every single shot was dead centre.

When Pieter had finished his round, the Sergeant walked over to him. Pieter looked up.

'I'm sorry, sir...err, I moved back a bit.' he said, somewhat apologetically.

'So I see,' the Sergeant replied. 'And how are you doing?' although the Sergeant already knew.

'I had to see how it worked at a longer distance,' said Pieter, as an attempt at an explanation.

'Not a problem,' Sergeant Fazackerly replied. 'And do you feel confident?'

Pieter took a deep sigh when he realized that he wasn't about to be chastised, and he looked down at the rifle'

'These sights, they're incredible,' he said, 'I never realized.'

Once he'd repeatedly hit the targets at 500 yards, Pieter's curiosity had got the better of him. And it certainly wasn't arrogance. He decided to move himself to the 1000 yard marker. It had seemed an incredible distance, but once he'd looked through the sights he could once again see everything quite clearly. Pieter had remembered what Sergeant Fazackerly had told him about distance, and he reset the hairs on the telescopic sight a tiny bit higher to compensate. And it had worked. His shots hit the centre of the target. And for some strange reason, it gave Pieter a feeling of power and satisfaction. He could suddenly and accurately hit targets that in the past he could never have dreamed of. It was a whole new world to him and he was fascinated by it.

'So you're getting the feel of it then?' the Sergeant asked.

'Yes I think so,' said Pieter enthusiastically. 'Using the sights gives you an incredible distance. And I figured out what you said about compensating for distance and adjusting the sights.'

Sergeant Fazackerly looked through his binoculars once again.

'You seem to have got your eye in,' he said. 'Right, I've got some more ammunition. We'll go and change those targets and then you can carry on shooting to your heart's content.

They spent the next hour usefully. Pieter used up all the ammunition and Sergeant Fazackerly sat back and watched him blow holes out of the centre of each target.

They eventually packed up and made their way back to the house.

As they walked along, Pieter asked the question.

'What's next Sergeant?'

'What's next is two thousand yards,' said Sergeant Fazackerly. 'However, that's a different kettle of fish altogether. At two thousand yards, the sights aren't just as efficient. Obviously, the bullet will begin to curve downwards. It's also how you handle the recoil. The slightest movement in any direction, up or down, or left or right will send your shot completely off target.'

Pieter nodded.

The Sergeant continued. 'And I spoke to you about the wind. The wind is the big bad enemy. It's not been windy today and you've been able to hit your target. But on a windy day and at a thousand yards your shot can end up all over the place. It all comes down to practice and the experience that goes with it. At two thousand yards, even a slight breeze will throw you out. But it's the gusty days that will catch you. Gusts are unpredictable, they come from nowhere, but they'll grab your bullet and blow it all over the place.'

'Is there any way around that?' Pieter asked.

Sergeant Fazackerly smiled. 'Oh yes, there's a way around it. It's all down to the timing.'

'And how does that work?' Pieter asked. He was intrigued.

'Gusts of wind are like the waves in the sea,' the Sergeant explained. 'They continually roll in, in much the same manner. And a gust of wind will always blow in strong, and then there's a moment of stillness as it subsides, just like the ebb in the tide. And when that moment happens, you take your shot.'

They walked on in silence.

'From now on, I want you to practice every day. I want you to learn how to shoot in the wind and also in the rain. I want you out there in all weathers and all conditions. It's the only way you'll gain the experience.'

'Yes, I realize that.' said Pieter.

The Sergeant continued. 'And you keep this rifle with you from now on. Just go down to the stores and get as much ammunition as you need, okay?'

Pieter nodded.

'Right,' said Sergeant Fazackerly, 'now let's go and get some food.'

As he lay in bed that evening, Pieter Szabo had a host of questions running around in his mind.

There was no doubt about it, he was being trained, and he was being trained to be a sniper. Pieter didn't have a problem with that of course. He was learning valuable skills that he could use when he finally got back to Poland. But he had the feeling that it wasn't going to be that simple. The British, along with Lieutenant Vernon Ballantyne, would want something in return. Pieter had agreed to help them to fight the Nazis, but it wasn't going to be a matter of him simply joining the British troops in Europe. Something else was being planned. Pieter Szabo was nobody's fool, but he would do whatever was asked of him. After all, the British had helped him to get his father to safety. And a debt was a debt.

The next day Pieter had an early breakfast. He then went to the stores and picked up some ammunition and then made his way to the shooting range. He set up some fresh targets and then he walked back to the 1000 yard marker and began his new daily regime.

An hour or so later, Sergeant Fazackerly arrived. He brought some boxes of ammunition with him.

'I thought I'd find you here,' he said. 'How's it going?'

'I'm doing alright,' said Pieter.

'Good,' said the Sergeant, 'now pick up your kit and let's go to 2000 yards.'

Later that afternoon, Sergeant Fazackerly knocked on Vernon Ballantyne's office door.

'Come in,' said a voice.

The Sergeant opened the door and walked in, the Lieutenant was sitting at his desk.

'Ah Bill,' he said, 'come in and sit down.'

The Sergeant did as he was asked.

Lieutenant Ballantyne looked up expectantly, 'Yes Bill?' he said, 'what is it.'

'Well I know I only spoke to you yesterday, sir. But you did ask me to move this project on and I didn't want to waste any time, sir.'

'Yes Bill,' the Lieutenant replied, 'that's absolutely right.'

'This Pieter Szabo, sir. He's a phenomenal shot. One of the best I've ever seen. Today he's started shooting at two thousand yards, and though it's a bit new to him, he'll conquer it. He's a natural, he just understands how to shoot.'

Vernon Ballantyne nodded at his sergeant.

'That's good, Bill, very good.'

'I think it's time to show him the 'new' gun, sir, if you want to move things along. He'll have to get used to using it. He's got to 'perfect' his shooting by using that gun and by knowing its capabilities.'

'Yes, the gun. You're possibly right, Bill,' said the Lieutenant, 'I do understand what you mean, and we can't delay things.'

'Well sir, you did imply that.'

'Bill, tell him to come and see me this afternoon when he's finished on the range, Say about five o' clock.'

'Right sir,' said the Sergeant and he stood up.

'Just one other thing, sir,'

Ballantyne looked up, 'Yes?'

'It's just a little thing, sir. Szabo doesn't give a lot away, but we were talking the other day about his shooting and he mentioned his father. I don't know what's happened in the past. But there's an anger there, sir. Some sort of deep anger.'

'Yes Bill,' said Lieutenant Ballantyne, 'I've already realized that.'

At five o' clock that same afternoon, Pieter Szabo knocked on Vernon Ballantyne's office door.

'Come in,' Ballantyne called out.

Pieter walked straight in.

'Sit yourself down,' said the Lieutenant, pleasantly.

Vernon Ballantyne was just finishing off some paperwork and as he scribbled away Pieter looked around the office. The first thing he noticed was the worn old walking stick on top the Lieutenant's desk. He looked at it for a moment and he thought it strange. He'd never seen Vernon Ballantyne using a stick before. In fact, he'd never even seen the Lieutenant limp.

'I'll only be a moment,' said Ballantyne, 'I've got all this damn paperwork to get done.'

And indeed he had. The Lieutenant's desk was stacked high with papers. There was an old oblong shaped carriage clock on the desk too, and it seemed to be in the way. The hands on the clock told the wrong time and Pieter wondered if maybe it was broken, it certainly looked old and broken. Pieter wondered why the Lieutenant didn't put it on a shelf somewhere and out of the way. It looked worthless. And then he noticed the clock on the Lieutenant's wall, and that seemed to be running fine.

The Lieutenant finally finished whatever he was doing and then he looked up.

'Sorry about that,' he said, 'one of the perils of the job, unfortunately.'

Pieter just nodded.

'Right,' said Lieutenant Ballantyne, 'I believe you've settled in fairly well.'

Pieter nodded again.

'And I believe Sergeant Fazackerly has had you on the shooting range and that you've become quite adept at shooting with the telescopic sight.'

'Yes,' said Pieter. 'It's been a bit of a revelation for me. The telescopic sight is a phenomenal aid. I'd never used one before but I'm getting the hang of it. I just need more practice, that's all.'

'Well, Sergeant Fazackerly seems to be quite impressed with your progress so far.'

'Really,' said Pieter. 'Well that's good.'

Vernon Ballantyne looked at Pieter Szabo for a moment. There was a change in him. Suddenly, Pieter Szabo seemed more confident and somehow more relaxed. And it wasn't arrogance and neither was it conceit. It was just that Pieter Szabo seemed more positive and more self-assured. Vernon Ballantyne was used to talking 'to' his personnel, not with them.

The Lieutenant continued. 'Starting tomorrow, you will need to polish up on your German. I have a tutor coming who is going to put you on an intense course. I believe you already have a basic knowledge of the language, but it is our intention that you will be able to speak German fluently, and as soon as possible.'

'Good,' said Pieter. 'That will be another valuable tool to use.'

'And also, at some point next week, you will be travelling up to the north of England to Cheshire. We have a place up there at RAF Ringway, It's a Parachute Training School. You will spend several days learning how to jump out of an aeroplane.'

'That will be fun,' said Pieter. 'I never thought I'd ever be doing that. However, if I'm going to go to Germany, flying there will certainly make things a lot easier.' Pieter smiled at Vernon Ballantyne, 'I take it that's where you're planning to send me?'

The Lieutenant looked at him. 'Something like that Mr Szabo,' he said, 'something like that.'

And the Lieutenant suddenly realized the obvious. That Pieter Szabo wasn't fazed by any of this. Not one bit.

Lieutenant Ballantyne took a deep breath.

'One of the reasons that I've called you in here today is to show you our new piece of specialised weaponry. We have a new rifle for you. And I've also spoken to Sergeant Fazackerly today and he wants you to start training with it immediately. You'll need to get accustomed to using it.'

'Oh, right,' said Pieter, 'can you show it to me?'

Vernon Ballantyne then smiled. 'Actually Mr Szabo, it's right in front of you.'

Pieter looked at the Lieutenant. There was no rifle. He glanced around and then at the side of the Lieutenant's desk, but there was nothing.

Pieter frowned. 'Is this a joke? I don't understand.'

'See the walking stick,' said Ballantyne. 'Pick it up please.'

Pieter picked up the walking stick and he looked at it.

'What do you think it is?' the Lieutenant asked.

Pieter shrugged. 'It's a walking stick of course,' he replied.

'Are you sure?'

'Why?' Pieter then asked.

'Because it's actually the barrel of a gun,' said Lieutenant Ballantyne.

Pieter held the walking stick in his hand, he waved it around and then he ran his hand down the length of it to feel the rough grain of the wood.

Pieter again looked at the Lieutenant. 'Don't tell me that you've made a gun barrel out of a piece of wood? That's ludicrous. It's impossible.'

'It's not wood,' replied the Lieutenant. 'It's a special lightweight alloy made from steel and aluminium. It's every bit as strong as steel, but it's half the weight.'

Pieter examined the walking stick. 'It looks just like wood, it even feels like wood.'

'We had a sculptor model it and then make it from a bronze cast. That's where the grain comes from. And then Imperial Chemicals up in Manchester developed the coating. It's a dyed plastic, apparently the same texture and colour as aged oak.'

'And how does it work?' Pieter asked.

The Lieutenant pointed to the stick. 'Turn the crook at the end, it unscrews. The cap at the bottom unscrews too.'

Pieter twisted the crook, which easily unscrewed. Then he removed the cap at the bottom of the stick too. What he was left with appeared to be a wooden pole, it was the same width as a normal rifle barrel but slightly longer.

Pieter looked down the inside of the barrel.

'The rifling is different,' he remarked, 'it seems more pronounced.'

'There's a reason for that,' said Ballantyne. 'It's all to do with the bullets.'

'And where's the rest of the gun,' Pieter then asked.

Lieutenant Ballantyne leant forwards and tapped the carriage clock on the desk in front of him.

'What am I supposed to do with that?' said Pieter.

'Just pick it up for a moment,' said Ballantyne.

Pieter put the gun barrel back on the desk and picked up the clock. It was surprisingly light.

'Pass it to me and I'll show you,' said Ballantyne.

'It doesn't seem to weigh very much,' said Pieter, 'has the mechanism been removed?'

'Slightly more than that,' said Ballantyne.

The Lieutenant took the clock and unscrewed the bottom pedestal and then the capped top, both came away easily. And then amazingly, the clock split into three sections. The larger main middle section was almost triangular. It was a rifle stock.

'Everything is made from lightweight pine,' said Ballantyne. 'The clock has been covered with a thin veneer which gives it the appearance of being solid walnut. We've had a master cabinetmaker construct it for us.

The veneers are seamless, making the joints between the three sections virtually invisible. The stock has been stained and varnished to match the barrel.'

Lieutenant Ballantyne took the gun barrel and slotted it onto the stock. The two connected together with an efficient 'click'.

'The breech mechanism has been very cleverly housed within the stock, it's all very compact. It's a single shot mechanism, and once the barrels connected the trigger automatically springs out of the stock.'

He handed Pieter the rifle.

Pieter Szabo took hold of the rifle and immediately felt the difference in weight.

'It's so light. 'It feels to be about half the weight of my Mauser.'

'It probably is,' Ballantyne replied, 'it's because of the lightweight stock along with the alloy barrel.'

Pieter lifted the rifle to his shoulder, as though to take ain.

'The barrel feels slightly longer,' he said.

'It is,' replied the Lieutenant. 'It's longer for greater accuracy, but without any significant increase in weight.'

Pieter continued to look down the barrel.

'It feels extremely comfortable. The weight and the balance are perfect.'

'Good,' said Lieutenant Ballantyne, 'now look at this.'

He took one of the outer sections of the clock and showed it to Pieter.

'Here are the bullets.'

Four holes had been drilled into the inside wall of the clock and each one contained a bullet.

'The gun will shoot a standard .303 bullet. But these four are special.'

The Lieutenant took one of the bullets and passed it to Pieter.

'It's something our Ordnance people have come up with, a completely new design.'

Pieter examined the bullet closely. It was the same size and shape as a normal shell, but the bullet itself had a dozen small but flawless spiral grooves cut into it. The grooves swirled along the body of the bullet, each one perfectly aerodynamic.

Lieutenant Ballantyne continued. 'The 'pronounced' rifling in the barrel makes the bullet spin at an incredible speed. And instead of being pushed through the air, you now have a bullet which is almost self-propelling.

Apparently, the accuracy is phenomenal because the bullet maintains a straight line momentum for much longer. They're talking distances of somewhere around a mile and a half.'

'That's incredible,' Pieter replied, and he shook his head, almost in disbelief.

'What about the telescopic sight?' Pieter then asked.'

'Ah, that's the clever bit,' said Ballantyne.

He took the other outer section of the clock and gently tapped it on his desk. A slim tube, similar in shape and length of a 'good' cigar, slid out of a drilled aperture.

'And there's your telescopic sight,' he said.

He passed the sight to Pieter, who began to examine it. It was exactly the same colour and had the same wood grain as the rifle and was made from the same lightweight alloy as the barrel.

This time Pieter laughed. 'And what's this, some kind of toy?'

'Hardly,' Vernon Ballantyne replied.

'It's so slim,' said Pieter, 'and so small. How does it fit on the rifle?'

'Look again at the sight, there's a darker line in the grain that runs all the way down one side, it's almost black. Look at it closely and feel it. It's a raised narrow strip. It slides into a thin channel on the top of the barrel. The channel looks like a dark groove too, so that it's quite visible once you know what it is. Try it out.

Pieter found the dark line of grain that ran along the sight, he lined it up and then slid the telescopic sight into place in the almost invisible groove set into the barrel.

'That's very clever,' said Pieter. 'Now, how do I adjust it?'

'Just twist the end,' said Ballantyne. 'It can apparently focus on any visible target up to two miles away. Take the rifle and look out of the window.'

Pieter stood up and walked over to a window. He raised the rifle to his shoulder and looked through the sights. Everything was blurred for a moment. Then he turned the end of the lens and suddenly everything came into focus. The clarity was amazing. Pieter then pointed the rifle over the trees and into the hills beyond. He focused the lens again and he couldn't believe the results. The landscape of those far away hills now seemed to be only a matter of a few feet away.

Pieter turned to Vernon Ballantyne in amazement.

'This is incredible, I can hardly believe what I'm seeing. These sights are phenomenal.'

'Yes I know,' Ballantyne replied.

Pieter spent the next few minutes looking over the surrounding countryside, and then he went back to sit with the Lieutenant. He put the rifle on the top of Lieutenant Ballantyne's desk, and then he looked at it for a moment.

'How did you ever design such a weapon?' he asked.

Vernon Ballantyne smiled. 'Actually, we've had the help of two Germans. Both are Jewish and both of them fled from Germany, almost a year ago now.

The designer of those very special bullets used to work in the aeronautic industry over there, a man called Leon Hirsh. He designs propulsion systems. It seems that the Germans are looking for something a lot faster than their conventionally propeller-powered aircraft. And Leon Hirsh was part of the team that was working on it. When we discovered that he was very unhappy with the Nazi party's plans for the Jews, our contacts over there got him out of the country, with the agreement that he would come and work for us. Apparently, we too have plans for some sort of new aeroplane engine, something to do with turbines, or so I'm told.'

'He made a wise choice in leaving,' said Pieter.

Pieter Szabo was already well aware of the Nazi's plans for the Jews.

Lieutenant Ballantyne continued. 'The man who designed those telescopic sights is Konrad Haber. Mr Haber was one of the more prominent scientists in the Experimental Research Department at the Carl Zeiss Optical Factory at Jena in Germany. The company specializes in optical lenses and microscopes. Over the last few years they've been producing some of the finest binoculars for the German Army. Mr Haber had managed to hide the fact that he was Jewish, from the authorities. And because of his position within the company, he thought that he was safe. However, somebody managed to discover that his wife was Jewish and then some officials from the local Nazi party called around to see Mrs Haber at home and had questioned her. Suddenly, their identity was suspect. Someone obviously held a grudge. And so, Konrad Haber and his wife discussed their future, or if they even had a future. The Haber's had no children as such, and so they decided that if they stayed in Germany everything was going to end in disaster. They too had heard the stories. So instead of waiting for the inevitable knock on the door, they packed their bags, and just like you, they got in their car and fled. In their case they headed north and made their way to Denmark, Thankfully, the Danish resistance found them and got them onto a fishing boat, which in turn got them to England. When they landed here they straightaway contacted the authorities. And when it was discovered just who Konrad Haber was and what he did, he was immediately commandeered by the Ordnance Division. The man's a genius. In fact, they both are. Hirsh and Haber are both doing valuable research for us. Their work could help us change the outcome of the war.'

'I see,' said Pieter. 'They were lucky to have escaped.'

'We're very lucky to have them,' agreed Ballantyne.

'And you say the Danish have formed their own resistance too,' Pieter suddenly asked.

'I think every country's formed a resistance against the Nazis,' Vernon Ballantyne replied.

It was only a simple question, but Pieter took note.

Both men sat in silence for a moment. And then Pieter Szabo spoke.

'And so Lieutenant, tell me something. Who exactly is it that you want me to kill?'

'I beg your pardon?' said Ballantyne. He was caught completely off guard by Pieter's unexpected question.

'Come on Lieutenant. I think it's time that we spoke truthfully,' said Pieter.

Vernon Ballantyne was almost embarrassed. He'd been caught completely unawares.

'At this moment in time, I'm not really in a position to speak about it,' he replied, rather uneasily.

Pieter looked at Vernon Ballantyne.

'Lieutenant, I've been here almost a week. And I've spent every day learning to shoot long distances with a telescopic sight. Now you tell me that I'm going to be parachuting out of a plane and that I'm going to learn fluent German, and very quickly. We've already agreed that I'll be going to Germany, and now you're showing me your latest weaponry, a rifle that can shoot incredible distances and with amazing accuracy. You're training me to be a sniper because you know that I can shoot, and you want me to be somewhere Lieutenant, and soon.'

'It's not just as simple as that,' the Lieutenant started to explain.

'It's not a problem Lieutenant,' said Pieter quickly. 'I'll go wherever you want me to go. I just need to know the plan, because I need to focus and plan too. Whoever the target is, it must be somebody significant. We need to work as a team and we need to share information. So tell me please, Lieutenant. Who is it?

Vernon Ballantyne sat there for a moment, and he thought about the question he'd just been asked. The mission was top secret, obviously. But Pieter Szabo had made a valid point. And he was right, they did need to share information. Everything needed to be planned correctly. Absolutely everything.

Lieutenant Ballantyne made a decision. 'No one must know what I'm about to tell you.'

He took a deep breath before he spoke.

'We want you to kill Adolph Hitler.'

Pieter sat there for a moment. This was something he hadn't expected.

'We need to get rid of him,' said Ballantyne. 'We need to take him out, and permanently. Without Hitler, the Nazi ideal would falter and fail. Adolph Hitler is their leader, absolutely and completely, and he makes all the decisions and he sets out all of the policies. Get rid of Hitler and there's no leader. His Generals would suddenly find themselves fighting for power. His commanders, Goering and Himmler would no doubt fall out, and nobody likes that little shit, Goebbels, anyway. They'd squabble between themselves and argue, and Germany's war machine would grind to a halt. From there we could negotiate and try to stop this madness.'

Pieter just nodded. He could see the sense in it.

'And so, what is the plan,' he asked.

We have a month,' said Lieutenant Ballantyne, 'a month to train you up and get you ready. Hitler spends much of his summer months at his retreat in Berchtesgaden. It's in the Bavarian Alps. In a couple of months the weather will change and it will start to snow, and then Hitler can't easily get there from Berlin. We have sources in Berchtesgaden, and we have information, a dossier. Hitler holds parties there at the weekends for his friends and his VIP guests. He's a man of repetition. It's all in the dossier.'

'How would I get there?' Pieter asked.

We're preparing a De Havilland Mosquito to fly you there. At the moment it's having extra fuel tanks fitted. You'd be flying at night out of RAF Fowlmere in Cambridgeshire and the pilot will do his best to get you somewhere near Berchtesgaden. We'd parachute you in there and then you'd have to make your own way on foot. We have all the maps and the plans for you to look at. Hitler's retreat is a villa known as 'The Berghof". There's a mountain behind it and that's where you'd have to get to. From there you can look down at the Berghof and get a clear shot.'

'So I get the chance to kill Hitler,' said Pieter.

'Yes, you would ' said Ballantyne. 'That's the basic plan, at the moment. After that, you'd have to make your way up to Denmark and meet up with our contact there. Everything will need to be finalized of course.'

Of course,' said Pieter.

'And so Mr Szabo, I have to ask you one question. Will you do it?'

Pieter didn't have to give the question much thought.

'Yes,' he replied, 'I'll do it.'

Lieutenant Vernon Ballantyne almost sighed with relief, and then he stood up and shook Pieter Szabo's hand.

'You've got a very busy month in front of you,' he said.

And with that, the plan was put into action. And a month later and after a lot of hard work and a lot of practice with the new rifle, Pieter Szabo was put onto a modified De Havilland Mosquito late one night and then flown off to Bavaria. He'd learned how to parachute and he'd learned the German language. He already knew how to shoot.

That evening, as Vernon Ballantyne watched the plane hurtle down the runway and take off, he wondered if Pieter Szabo was aware of his responsibilities. Thousands, if not millions of lives would be affected by Pieter's mission.

It was all in God's hands. Or maybe not.

CHAPTER 11

Pieter Szabo had failed.

He'd had the one chance to kill Adolph Hitler, the one chance. He'd had Hitler in his sights, but he'd missed. And Adolph Hitler was still alive.

A combination of a bad stomach and bad luck. And the tiny amount of movement that had sent Pieter's bullet a fraction off target. At the 'The Berghof', high up in Bavarian Alps, Hitler had been slightly injured, but even so, he'd still lived. And his Nazi troops would continue to crush Europe underfoot, still hell-bent on conquering the whole of Europe and then even more. Already, Hitler was moving on to Russia, his next major objective.

Hitler would never stop, not until he held the whole of the world in the palms of his hands. That was his master plan.

Pieter Szabo had missed his target, and the course of history would not be changed.

Pieter Szabo had a long way to go, but he wasn't going back to England, not yet. Instead, he would head east, and then northwards and make his way back to Poland, back to his homeland. There were now other men that he needed to find, because Pieter Szabo had a debt to settle.

His orders from Lieutenant Ballantyne were that whatever the outcome, Pieter should get himself to their contact in Denmark, and the people there would have plans to get him safely back to England. There were other missions to embark on. But even as he gave Pieter Szabo those orders, Vernon Ballantyne had the feeling that his instructions might not be followed.

Pieter Szabo was no longer encumbered by his father and he was now free to go wherever he liked. He could travel through Germany, he was now able to speak German fairly fluently. Pieter had worked hard to get his German perfect and now he could speak the language quite competently. He'd also been given the correct papers, Pieter had been supplied with official documents, the German 'Kennkarten' which were the identity papers that every German citizen had and was expected to carry with them at all times. Pieter's papers were officially stamped and declared him to be 'Pieter Schiller', from the small and rather insignificant town of Freiberg, which lay somewhere south of Dresden. Freiberg was actually quite close to the Polish border, and even Pieter's accent would be deemed to be correct. If questioned or searched, Pieter's story would be that he was an itinerant farm worker, looking for employment of any kind. His excuse for not being in the army was that he was partially crippled, a childhood accident and a broken leg which was never attended to properly. Hence, the walking stick. And the dirty old clock that he carried in his rucksack, along with his clothes, was something that he'd found along the way. It needed fixing, but then he could sell it.

Would Pieter Szabo return to England? Lieutenant Vernon Ballantyne knew Pieter's past history.

Pieter Szabo was driven by a hatred for the men who were responsible for the deaths of his wife and of his family. And there was anger, and there was the need for revenge.

Two weeks after the date of the attempted assassination, Adolph Hitler was reportedly still alive. Sources had sent back information that Hitler had been injured, but certainly not fatally.

The mission to kill Hitler had been a failure. And within a couple of months, Hitler would be
back in Berlin, preaching to the converted and giving speeches to the wide-eyed masses.

So the mission had failed. But whatever the outcome, Pieter's orders were that he should head north to Denmark, where he would meet a contact who would get him onto a fishing boat and then get him across the channel and to the east coast of England.

After two more weeks, Pieter had still not returned, and Vernon Ballantyne had to make one of two assumptions. Either Pieter Szabo had

been caught and killed, or that his sniper had intentionally disappeared and was possibly on his way back to Poland.
The Lieutenant suspected the latter.

Pieter Szabo finally did reach Poland, and then he made his way back to Lodz.

Whilst travelling through Germany he'd been stopped on a couple of occasions, which was a regular occurrence in those difficult times. The authorities were permanently on the lookout for anyone who was Jewish and who was trying to escape the Nazi regime. Pieter's documents, his false 'Kennkarten', always stood up to scrutiny. And in those days, no one was really interested in an unemployed, wandering cripple.

Pieter finally arrived back in Lodz, the city he once knew so well.

It was late in the afternoon, and this time Pieter made his way directly to the building where he used to work, the offices of the architect, Mr Bruno Huelle.

Pieter stood away from the office building, and once it turned five o' clock he watched the people who worked there begin to leave. Pieter knew them all of course, but he stayed out of sight. He certainly didn't want them to be involved. Twenty minutes later everyone had left, with the exception of one person, Mr Bruno Huelle himself. Bruno Huelle was a creature of habit, Pieter knew that Mr Huelle had always been the last to leave. Pieter walked through the main door and then went up a flight of stairs to the offices on the first floor. He entered the architect's offices through a glazed door and looked around. Nothing had changed. There were the same four drawing boards there as always, each with some technical drawing of a building or part of a building, there was obviously some work still in progress. Pieter walked past the drawing boards to the far end of the office where there was another glazed door, it was the door to Mr Huell's office. Pieter went over and tapped on the glass. Through the marbled glaze, he could make out the shape of someone sitting at a desk.

'Come in,' a said a familiar voice.

Pieter opened the door and walked straight into the office to face Mr Bruno Huelle.

Mr Huelle was writing a letter. He looked up to see Pieter, and he stopped, and then he suddenly dropped his pen.

'My god...My god, Pieter. It's you!'

Bruno Huelle immediately got up from his desk and went over to Pieter and hugged him.

'Pieter, oh Pieter. We thought you were dead.'

For a moment Pieter couldn't speak. It was the first time he'd had any true emotional contact since he'd lost his family, and he suddenly felt exhausted.

'Where have you been, Pieter? Where on earth have you been? We thought you'd been sent to the camps.'

'It's a long story, Mr Huelle, a very long story.'

'Come, you must sit down, Pieter,' said Bruno Huelle. 'You look tired. I will make some coffee, and I have a sandwich somewhere, and there's some cake. It's been someone's birthday and I don't eat the stuff.'

Pieter sat down on a chair facing the desk as Bruno Huelle disappeared into one of the smaller offices that they used as a kitchen, and after five minutes he reappeared with two mugs of steaming hot coffee, along with a huge slice of fruit cake. He went over to his desk and took a sandwich out of one of the drawers.

'My wife makes them every day, she makes far too much and I never manage to eat them all. Today I think its Salami.'

Pieter was ravenous and he started to eat. The coffee too tasted delicious. Bruno Huelle just sat there and watched him.

'Eat, my boy,' he said to Pieter, 'eat something first, we can talk later.'

Pieter devoured the sandwich and the cake and then he drank the last of his coffee. Bruno Huelle sipped his own coffee from his mug and he waited.

Eventually Pieter sat back in his chair, and he took a deep sigh.

'That feels better Mr Huelle, I didn't realize just how hungry I was.'

Bruno Huelle nodded. And now they could talk. There were things that Bruno Huelle needed to know.

'Do you know where your father is, Pieter?' he asked.

'Yes,' Pieter replied. 'He's in England.'

Bruno Huelle eyes widened. He was suddenly quite shocked.

'I...I didn't know that. How on earth did he manage to get to England?'

'I took him there Mr Huelle.'

'You did?'

'Yes, Mr Huelle. I got him out of the camp and we escaped. We drove across Europe and down to Spain, eventually we got to Gibraltar where we managed to get onto a British ship which then took us to England.'

Bruno Huelle looked at Pieter.

'So it was you who got him out of the camp?'

'Yes, it was.' Pieter replied.

Bruno Huelle took a deep breath.

'That explains a lot,' he said. 'Word got around about the shootings at the camp. And then we heard that your father had escaped. No one knew what to make of it. You see, we thought that you were all dead, Pieter.'

And at that moment, Bruno Huelle lowered his eyes.

'We heard that you'd all been sent to Auschwitz, Pieter. Your father was spared, only because he was a doctor.'

'My wife, and the rest of my family, they're all dead Mr Huelle. They did send us to Auschwitz, but I managed to escape. I came back for my father. It was already too late for my wife and my mother and sisters. But I knew that my father was still alive and that it would only have been a matter of time before the Nazis got rid of him too.'

Bruno Huelle nodded in agreement.

'Your mother was a wonderful woman, Pieter. They all were. I'm so sorry for your loss.'

They were silent for a moment, and then Bruno Huelle asked Pieter a question.

'So it was you who killed that treacherous bastard, Igor Sym. Along with the other guards?'

'Yes,' said Pieter. 'Sym sent my wife, Francine, and my mother and my sisters to Auschwitz, and then he shot my brother in law, Adam Breslav. And then he sent me to Auschwitz too.'

'Igor Sym was a traitor,' said Huelle. 'Shooting was too good for that bastard.'

Pieter looked at Bruno Huelle.

'I didn't shoot him. Believe me, I made him suffer badly, Mr Huelle. Igor Sym certainly didn't die an easy death.'

Bruno Huelle glanced at Pieter. His 'young apprentice' was a changed man. It was to be expected of course.

What Bruno Huelle wasn't going to tell Pieter was that as a result of that attack, twenty civilians had been rounded up by the Nazis and had been shot as reprisals. But that was nothing new. Every time the Polish Resistance shot or murdered a German soldier there were reprisals. It was the price they had to pay, and the Resistance knew that and would continue. And the Polish people knew that too, and they readily accepted what the Resistance had to do.

'After the attack on the camp, Herr Kruger tightened up security,' said Bruno Huelle. 'He was absolutely furious. Igor Sym was his right-hand man.'

'Who's Kruger?' Pieter asked.

'Major Wilhelm Kruger. He's the commander here. He's in charge of everything in Lodz.'

Pieter thought about it for a moment. 'My father spoke about him. I think he was there on the night we were all arrested.'

'Yes, he could have been,' Bruno Huelle agreed.

And then Pieter asked him a question.

'Do you remember Henryk Kober and a man called Wilfred Staszic?'

'Yes Pieter, I do,' Bruno Huelle replied. 'Kober was the man who came to the Rifle Club and closed it down. He's another traitor. He runs the Lodz City Council offices for the Nazis.'

'Yes that's him, and Staszic was with him on that same day.'

'I vaguely remember,' said Bruno Huelle.

'I need to find them both,' said Pieter.

'Why's that, Pieter?'

'Because I'm going to kill them both, Mr Huelle.'

For a second, Bruno Huelle said nothing. And it was Pieter who spoke first.

'I'm going to tell you everything that's happened, Mr Huelle, and how Staszic and Kober were the cause of all of this. They're the real reason why my wife and my family are dead.'

Pieter spent the next half an hour telling Bruno Huelle everything that had happened to him. All about Wilfred Staszic's jealousy and Henryk Kober's collusion. And then the family's arrest and their time at the camp. Finally, his father's escape and their trip across Europe to Gibraltar and then to England.

Bruno Huelle sat there and listened, he was concerned over Franz Szabo. Pieter's father had been a very close friend.

'And how is Franz now?' he asked Pieter.

'He's not a well man, Mr Huelle. He's in a home now, I went to see him before I left. My father has had some sort of breakdown. I don't think he'll ever be the same again.'

'And you've managed to get him into some kind of sanatorium?' Pieter nodded.

'Yes, Mr Huelle. You see, when we got to England, things changed.'

Pieter then went on to tell Bruno Huelle about being taken to Aylesbury to be trained as a sniper and then being flown to Germany and his mission.

Bruno Huelle was amazed by it all.

'And they flew you all the way back to Germany?' he asked.

'Yes, they did.'

'And tell me Pieter, what was your mission?'

Pieter looked at him for a moment.

'To kill Adolph Hitler, Mr Huelle. 'I should have shot Hitler. But I failed.'

Bruno Huelle was absolutely astounded at what he was hearing.

'My god Pieter, they sent you to kill Adolph Hitler?'

'Yes, Mr Huelle. And I had him in my sights, and then everything went wrong.'

Bruno Huelle just sat and listened as Pieter told him what had happened and why. And how he had made his way back to Poland. And now he was back here in Lodz.

'Killing Hitler would have changed everything,' said Pieter.

Bruno Huelle thought about that statement for a moment.

'Yes, I think it would have, Pieter, and it would have certainly damaged the Nazi party. But ask yourself, would it have stopped them?'

'I don't know Mr Huelle.' Pieter replied. 'I really don't know.'

'Himmler and Goebbels are both lunatics,' Bruno Huelle continued, 'and Goering isn't much better. They've all had a taste of power. They'll not let go, Pieter, they'll follow Hitler's plan as though it was written in stone.'

Pieter shook his head. 'Whatever happens, I think it's going to be a long war, Mr Huelle. A very long war.'

Both men sat in silence for a moment.

'So you've come back here to kill Kober and Staszic?' Bruno Huelle finally asked.

'Yes I have, Mr Huelle,' Pieter replied.

'And then what?'

'I'll make my way back to England. My father's there and I have a debt of gratitude to honour. The British have looked after us and I don't think that my work for them is over yet.'

Bruno Huelle looked at Pieter.

'What's your plan? And what do you need?' he asked.

'Well, I need somewhere to stay. And I need a car and a gun, a pistol.'

Bruno Huelle thought for a moment.

'You can stay with us for the meantime. And I will find you a car, and I'll get you the gun.'

Pieter looked at his old boss, he appreciated that Mr Huelle had always been a friend of the family. He was a good man.

'Thank you, Mr Huelle,' said Pieter, 'I can't thank you enough,' and then, 'Mr Huelle, I do realize that you could find me a car. But how on earth do you intend to get hold of a pistol?'

Bruno Huelle didn't answer straight away. He looked at Pieter.

'I've something to tell you, Pieter. But it's important and it has to be kept secret. We've set up a group, we've formed something we're calling the 'Polish Resistance' here in Lodz. Some of us are from the Rifle Club, most of which are the older members, we do all the planning. The others, well the others are the brave younger men who are the true patriots and are willing to risk their lives. We've managed to kill several German soldiers and we've set fire to some of their buildings and their trucks. The reprisals, however, have been quite terrible. For every German soldier we've killed, the Germans have rounded up and shot twenty Poles. It's been the same all over Poland I'm afraid, Similar reprisals have taken place in Warsaw apparently, and Krakow too. But we have to fight these people. We will never give in, Pieter, never.'

Pieter's response to this information was possibly not what Bruno Huelle expected.

Instead of being shocked and surprised, Pieter sat back and sighed with relief.

'Thank god,' he then said, 'thank god you're doing something, and thank god you're fighting back. These people are evil, Mr Huelle. They're treating us like cattle and they're murdering thousands at the camps.'

'We know all about the camps, Pieter. We all have Jewish friends who have been rounded up and herded into the ghetto. From there they're taken to the transit camp and then on to the Concentration Camp at Auschwitz. There are a host of other camps too. What the Nazis are doing is inhuman. We're trying to fight back, but there have been terrible casualties. When any of our resistance fighters have been killed or captured, the Nazis have arrested all of their family and relatives and they've shot them all, the men, women and children, regardless of who they are.'

'Your resistance fighters are brave men,' Pieter replied, 'the bravest.'

Bruno Huelle nodded. 'And that's the reason I can get you a gun Pieter. We have guns hidden away. And we will assist you in any way to kill those two traitorous bastards, Kober and Staszic. We will find you a car and we'll get you a gun.'

Bruno Huelle and Pieter Szabo switched off the lights and left the office. Bruno Huelle's car was as ever, parked behind the building and from there they made their way to his home.

Mr Huelle lived in a good house in the 'Gospodarz' district of Lodz, a once prosperous neighbourhood in a country that was fast becoming worthless. When they entered the house, Mr Huelle's wife, Eliza, was overjoyed to see Pieter and a few tears were shed when they spoke about the tragic news of his family. A meal was prepared, and Mrs Huelle left the men alone in the dining room to talk.

'And what are your plans, Mr Huelle?' Pieter asked.

'Well Pieter, the business will carry on as best it can. There is some work, but obviously not enough. We will stay open if only to provide some sort of income for the staff. But how long for, I just don't know.'

'And the resistance?'

'Ah, the resistance, well that's another story.'

At that moment, Eliza Huelle walked into the room with a pot of fresh coffee and they subtly changed the topic of their conversation.

After his wife had left the room, Bruno Huelle again turned to Pieter.

'Our families are told as little as possible. We don't want them to be implicated in any way and we don't want them to be worried all the time.'

'That's quite understandable. It's a better way,' agreed Pieter.

Bruno Huelle continued.

'Even so, we do have something planned, a major assault. It will be the most significant attack on the Nazis to date and it will hopefully hit the German's hard.'

Bruno Huelle took a deep breath.

'We're going to shoot their commander. We're going to kill Major Wilhelm Kruger.'

Pieter leant forward in his seat.

'And when and how will this happen?' he asked.

'Well, we're still at the planning stage. But we do have some very reliable information, and from a very good source. It's common knowledge that Major Kruger and his cronies have taken up permanent residence at the Grand Hotel here in Lodz. Apparently, they're all having a wild old time of it. There's drinking and prostitutes and all kinds of parties. The security there has become very lax, in fact we're told that it's almost nonexistent. '

'And who's giving you all this information?' Pieter asked.

'One of our Resistance has a brother in law who works there. He's actually the manager, a man called Slowowski, Yaslov Slowowski. He knows everything that goes on in that hotel but he has to be very discreet, and of course, he has a family too. He's apparently very nervous about being involved in any way, and we can understand why. So whatever we do, we have to somehow keep him out of it. However, through him, we've found out that Kruger is living in a suite on the top floor of the hotel, we even know his room number. His suite is very elegant and also very private. So private in fact, that it has some sort of hidden fire escape that runs down through the back of the building. There's an exit door at the back of the hotel, it's all locked up because it's hardly ever been used, according to Slowowski anyway. But it would give us direct access into the hotel and up to Kruger's suite.'

'How are you going to get in?' Pieter asked. 'Will this man, this 'Slowowski' open the door for you?

Bruno Huelle sighed. 'Actually, that's one of our problems. Slowowski won't do it. He says that if the Germans find out that the door had been unlocked, it would implicate him and the rest of his staff. The Germans would shoot them all, and probably their families too. And in all truth, he's most likely correct.'

Pieter thought about that for a moment.

'So you plan to go up the back stairs to Kruger's suite, and then what, you shoot him?'

'Yes,' said Huelle, 'we have his room number. We intend to walk straight in and shoot him and then disappear back down the fire escape.'

'It's a good plan,' said Pieter, 'it's so simple that it might work. However, I think it would still incriminate the staff, Mr Huelle.'

'Why do you say that, Pieter?'

'Well first of all, the unlocking of the door. Slowowski's right on that one. You could break in of course, but there's the noise and with it the chance of someone hearing you. The other thing is Kruger's body. Kruger's suite is on the top floor of the hotel and if no one hears the shooting, his body won't be discovered until the morning. Everything will look suspicious. Whatever happens, the Germans will immediately suspect that the hotel staff were involved.'

Bruno Huelle shook his head and he sat back in his chair. Suddenly, all of his well-laid plans were falling to pieces.

'It's not going to work is it?' he said quietly. 'There are too many innocent lives at risk.'

'Who's actually going to do the shooting?' Pieter asked him.

Bruno Huelle sighed. 'We'd planned for a team of three. We're not short of volunteers Pieter, our Resistance fighters are very brave men. However, there's always the possibility of them being caught, and for that reason, we don't want to use the married men with children. We are going to use younger, single men.'

'And what experience have they had?'

'None really, none at all. But they all know how to fire a gun.'

Suddenly, Bruno Huelle realized the enormity of the task in hand. And it wasn't going to be as simple as he thought. He sat back in his chair, now suddenly feeling rather disheartened.

'I don't think our plan's going to work, is it, Pieter?' he said. 'Maybe we should think again.'

Both men sat there in silence.

'I do have an idea,' said Pieter slowly.

Bruno Huelle looked up.

'What is it?'

'I'll do it,' said Pieter.

Bruno Huelle stared back at Pieter Szabo.

'You?' he asked.

'Yes,' Pieter replied. 'It would be a lot easier and a lot simpler.'

'But I thought you were going to kill Kober and Staszic and then make your way back to England?'

'Yes I am,' Pieter replied. 'But before I go, I'll shoot Kruger too. I've no doubt that bastard was somehow involved in sending my family to Auschwitz, he must have been.'

Bruno Huelle thought about it for a moment.

'You're possibly right, Pieter. He is the commander, and he must know everything that's happening in the camp.'

'Yes, I think so too Mr Huelle.' But at the back of Pieter Szabo's mind there was more, the ever unrelenting need for revenge.

Pieter continued. 'We'll use your plan and I'll get to Kruger's suite by going up the fire escape. The only change in your plan is that I'll be there on my own. Nobody else is to be involved.'

Bruno Huelle frowned at him. 'I don't understand you, Pieter?'

'If I'm caught, or I've been shot, I'll be identified as Pieter Szabo. They think I'm dead, I should be because I was sent to Auschwitz, and finally they'll realize that somehow I must have escaped. But, Mr Huelle, I have no family. Those bastards made sure of that. And they know my father disappeared months ago, and to god knows where? And that keeps your Resistance, and their families out of it, Mr Huelle. There are no ties, no ties to anyone.'

Bruno Huelle just sat there. But he did understand Pieter's logic. However, he still had his misgivings.

'But it's much too dangerous, Pieter. You could be killed?'

There was a moment's silence, and then Pieter Szabo spoke.

'You need to understand something, Mr Huelle. I don't care anymore.'

Bruno Huelle just stared at him, but Pieter continued.

'When they killed Francine, I lost the love of my life. I truly loved her, Mr Huelle, and I loved her from the moment I first met her. And then they murdered my mother and my sisters. Mr Huelle, I once promised Francine and my sisters that I would always look after them. And I didn't, I failed them, I failed them all.'

Bruno Huelle tried to reason with him.

'Pieter, there was nothing that you could have done.'

Pieter shrugged. 'Maybe, or maybe not. But they're gone. And as for my father, you wouldn't recognize him anymore, Mr Huelle. I visited him the day before I left England. He's lost his mind, he'll never be the same again.'

There was nothing that Bruno Huelle could say. All the condolences in the world would not hide the truth.

'The Nazis are evil, Mr Huelle. And I want revenge, revenge for my family. And I'm never going to stop, ever. I'm going to kill every damn Nazi that gets in my way. It will probably get me killed, but a lot more people are going to get killed if we don't stop them. Too many already have.'

Bruno Huelle took a deep breath.

'You're right, Pieter. We all feel the same way. And I've no doubt that the rest of the free world feels exactly the same.'

'Yes,' said Pieter, 'we don't have a choice. We have to do our duty, for Poland.'

Bruno Huelle took hold of Pieter's arm. 'Yes, you're right Pieter. And thank you. You are a wise head on such young shoulders.'

'A lot has changed Mr Huelle. We're living in a different world.'

Bruno Huelle could only agree.

'So tell me, Pieter, what are your plans, and what do you need?'

Pieter Szabo thought for a moment.

'I need a car that's untraceable. I need a good pistol. And I need some explosives.'

Bruno Huelle's eyes widened.

'Explosives?' he asked.

'Yes,' said Pieter, 'explosives. And there's one other thing.'

'And what's that?' Huelle asked.

'We need to speak to Yaslov Slowowski.'

Within a few days a car had been found, an old black Renault. It had been sourced from Krakow in southern Poland. The Resistance there had the car and they brought it to Lodz. It was fitted with false plates and the engine's serial number had been filed off and removed. The car was suddenly untraceable and it could have belonged to anyone and come from anywhere.

While all this was happening, Pieter Szabo began his hunt to find Henryk Kober and Wilfred Staszic. He began by going back to the Central Library, the place where it all began. He stood outside the ever imposing stone building and he watched and he waited. But there didn't seem to be any sign of Wilfred Staszic at all. As he stood there, Pieter remembered happier times and how he used to meet Francine in there. It felt so very strange. The library building looked exactly the same. But for Pieter, everything else had changed.

After three days there had still been no sign of Wilfred Staszic. However, people are naturally creatures of habit, something that Pieter Szabo was well aware of.

And with that in mind, in the evenings Pieter began to stand across from the Cafe Pineska and observe the comings and goings there. The Cafe Pineska was the old haunt were Kober and Staszic used to always meet up. Old habits die hard, and on the Friday night, as Pieter once more stood unseen in the shadows, a large black Mercedes Benz German staff car slowly appeared around the corner and parked outside the Cafe. Pieter stood there, transfixed. This was what he had been waiting for. A uniformed driver got out of the car and went to open the rear passenger door. And from the back seat, and in all their glory, out of the car stepped Henryk Kober, accompanied by his best friend, Wilfred Staszic.

Pieter Szabo clenched his fists in shock, and partly due to the rising anger he felt inside him. There they were, Stazic and Kober. Both of them stood by their car for a moment, both were immaculately dressed in their black SS uniforms, and they lingered there, wanting to be seen, wanting to be looked at and noticed, and even more, to be respected and feared.

Pieter Szabo looked on, the sight of them was almost hypnotic to him. Through everything that had happened, this was the moment that he had been waiting for. Meeting up with these two men again had been forever in the back of his mind. And now here they were, Staszic and Kober, pompous and arrogant and strutting about in their stupid uniforms, pretending to be Germans. Pieter looked at them in disgust, they were Polish by birth, not German, and they were traitors, they were responsible for the deaths of his beloved family. Pieter stood there in the shadows and he cursed them both under his breath. And he felt the rage inside him, the same rage that had led him to murder Igor Sym. If he'd had a gun with him, Pieter would have crossed the road and shot them both in the face, he knew he would. And suddenly, he had to breathe deeply to calm himself down.

No, there would be a better way. He knew there was.

Pieter watched, as both men went into the Cafe. Their driver got back into the car and lit a cigarette, he was used to waiting.

From where Pieter stood he could see Staszic and Kober being shown to their table by an ever smiling waitress. Pieter watched as the other customers respectfully moved their chairs out of the way to let the two officers pass. On one of the opposite tables, a man and his wife, silently finished their coffee and then stood up and quietly left. Neither spoke a word, but the almost vacant expressions on their faces told another story. They obviously didn't want to be anywhere near the two SS Officers.

Pieter stood there and watched as the waitress returned to Staszic and Kober and took their order. And that was good, because it gave Pieter a certain amount of time. He turned and walked away, it was time to put his plan into action. He then went to find his car.

Ten minutes later, Pieter returned. He parked the black Renault thirty yards lower down from the Cafe Pineska, from where he could see the cafe entrance and the parked black Mercedes staff car.

The best part of an hour passed by before Staszic and Kober finally left the Cafe. And that was good too, because by then it was dark. Their driver got out of the car immediately and held the rear door open for his two passengers. Pieter started his own car and then he sat and waited. A few moments later, the black Mercedes drove away, and Pieter let it turn the corner before he put his car into gear and followed it.

It took around fifteen minutes to arrive at their rather grand house. Pieter was actually quite surprised by it. What he was unaware of, was that Herr Kruger and his Nazi thugs had stolen the house from some unfortunate Jewish family and had then given it to Henryk Kober as his 'reward'.

Pieter parked his car far enough down the road so as not to be noticed and he looked at his watch. It was nine o' clock.

Staszic and Kober went into the house and the staff car drove away. Pieter sat there for the next couple of hours and he watched as the downstairs lights were switched on and an hour or so later he saw them switched off again and then the upstairs lights were turned on.

Pieter almost smiled when he suddenly realized that Staszic and Kober now lived together, he was sure of it, and suddenly all of his plans were falling neatly into place. And now he would bet money that these two men would arrive at home at the same time on every Friday night.

Yes, this was perfect.

Pieter returned to the house again on the Monday and on Tuesday at five o' clock. He parked the Renault further down the road and again waited. On both nights at exactly six o'clock the same black Mercedes staff car brought Staszic and Kober home. And on both evenings, and within fifteen minutes of them arriving, a portly woman, in her sixties, left the house. Pieter surmised that she was either the cook or possibly the cleaner. In fact, she was both.

When Staszic and Kober arrived home, they liked to have their meal waiting for them so that they could eat immediately. Their cook, Mrs Dabrowska, always obliged. And their evening meal would always be hot and ready, there in the oven. Staszic and Kober preferred to serve out their own food, along with a glass of good wine. It was their way of relaxing.

And the accepted routine of the house was that when Staszic and Kober both arrived home, Mrs Dabrowska would leave as soon as possible. And that suited both parties.

The only change to their routine was on Friday nights. On Fridays of course, Staszic and Kober always went to the Cafe Pineska. For those late evenings, Mrs Dabrowska would prepare them a casserole which she left to cook slowly in the oven. And on Fridays, she didn't bother to stay there till six o' clock either. At two o' clock in the afternoon she would lock the house and leave, usually with two bags full of stolen groceries, and occasionally with a bottle of their precious wine. And on every Friday, as Mrs Dabrowska prepared their equally precious casserole, she would carefully season the food by spitting into the pot several times. She always considered that had she been a younger woman, there were other bodily fluids that she could have added.

On the Monday and Tuesday nights, Pieter watched Mrs Dabrowska leave at just after six, and he recognized the routine. Mrs Dabrowska wasn't there on Friday evenings.

The following Friday arrived, and by then, so had Pieter's gun. It was a German Luger, stolen from a dead soldier that the Resistance had shot.

On that same morning, Pieter had visited a local hardware store where he'd purchased a small torch, several rolls of washing line, and a five-litre can of paraffin, plus an assortment of tools which included a hammer, a couple of wood chisels and a screwdriver.

After lunch, he drove over to Staszic and Kober's house. He still didn't know who exactly owned the property, but neither did he care. He parked the car in the usual place and he waited. There was no hurry.

At exactly two o' clock, Mrs Dabrowska left the house. She locked the front door and then picked up two bags, which seemed to be rather full, and then she made her way down the road in the opposite direction. Pieter waited for the best part of an hour, just to make sure that Mrs Dabrowska wasn't coming back. She didn't.

He got out of the car and took his tools out of the boot and then he made his way to the house. Pieter went around to the rear of the property and opened a wooden gate which led into a neat and well-tendered garden. He walked to the back of the house and checked the different windows. Finally he found a small window that seemed to lead into some sort of pantry. There were vegetables stored in wicker baskets and they were filled with potatoes and carrots and onions. And after a bit of effort and ingenuity, he managed to prise open the window using the screwdriver and one of the chisels. Pieter then climbed inside.

He walked around the house and studied each and every room. And then he went upstairs and checked the bedrooms. By looking through the wardrobes in each bedroom he soon discovered who slept where. Staszic was tall and slim, Kober was a stouter man altogether. And the jackets and pants in each of the wardrobes easily identified their owner.

Pieter went back downstairs and into the opulent lounge. There were two leather armchairs placed either side of the fireplace, and a fire was burning nicely in the hearth. Pieter reached down and put another couple of logs on the fire.

It would be nice and warm when Staszic and Kober both arrived home.

Pieter walked through to the kitchen. It felt warm in there too, and he looked around to see that there was a casserole pot in the oven. Something was cooking. Very nice.

He went to the back door, which led outside. It was locked of course, and Pieter started to look through the kitchen drawers to try and find the key. He finally discovered it hanging on a shiny brass hook in one of the cupboards.

Pieter unlocked the kitchen door and went outside, and then he locked the door behind him. He put the key into his pocket and made his way through the garden and back to the car.

He then drove away. He would come back later.

At half past eight that evening Pieter Szabo returned to the house. And half an hour later, so did Wilfred Staszic and Henryk Kober in their staff car.

Pieter sat in the car and again watched the same sequence with the house lights. Downstairs, the lights came on and remained on for the next couple of hours, and then they were turned off as the upstairs lights came on. After another ten minutes they were turned off as well. Staszic and Kober had gone to bed. Pieter watched and he waited. He didn't have to rush, he just sat there and remembered the brutality that those two men had inflicted on his wife on the night of their arrest. And after another forty minutes he got out of the car, he was now in the right frame of mind. He pushed the Luger into his belt and then he opened the boot of the car and took out the rolls of washing line, the can of paraffin and the torch. Then once again he went to the rear of the house where he carefully opened the wooden gate and then made his way through the garden to the kitchen door. Pieter took the key out of his pocket and he switched on his torch. He unlocked the door, opened it and walked into the kitchen. It had all been so easy, and so very simple.

Once again, Pieter went through to the lounge. It was much as he had left it. The two leather armchairs were there and the fire in the hearth was still burning, but beginning to smoulder. Pieter left the rolls of washing line and the can of paraffin near the door and went over to the fireplace. He reached down and put two or three logs onto the fire, and then he stood back and watched them as they slowly caught fire and began to burn.

After a while, Pieter turned and made his way into the hallway and then he silently climbed the stairs. He walked along the short landing until he reached the first door on his right. It was Staszic's bedroom. Pieter pointed the torch down to the carpeted floor, it gave just enough illumination, and then he slowly opened the bedroom door.

The moment had finally arrived. Pieter Szabo would have his justice

Silently, he walked over to the bed where he could hear Wilfred Staszic breathing deeply as he slept. Pieter shone the torch directly into Staszic's face and then clamped his hand over Stazic's mouth. Wilfred Staszic woke with a jolt, and as soon as he opened his eyes he was blinded. He tried to squirm and shout, but Pieter's hand stopped him from doing anything. And then Pieter leant down and whispered to him.

'If you move or call out, or do anything at all, I will shoot you and I will kill you. I have a gun, so 'nod' if you understand me.'

For a moment, and in total fear, Staszic did nothing at all, and then he began to slowly nod his head.

'Good,' said Pieter. 'Now we understand one another.'

Staszic just lay there, terrified. He didn't understand what was happening.

Pieter again leant forward.

'Do you know who I am, Staszic?'

Wilfred Staszic didn't move.

Pieter turned the torch and shone it into his own face, the upturned light made his features look almost ghoulish.

'Do you remember me now, Staszic? Do you remember Pieter Szabo?'

Wilfred Staszic went rigid with fear. And he let out a pathetic muffled cry as he once again looked into the eyes of his long-forgotten nemesis. He started to tremble and shake, and he was helpless.

And at that moment Pieter Szabo smashed his fist into Wilfred Staszic's unguarded face.

Staszic bounced back against the bed, he was momentarily dazed. And then Pieter once again clamped his hand over Staszic's mouth. Staszic blinked a little and his face throbbed. Like every bully, he wasn't used to being on the receiving end of physical pain. He just lay there, fearful of what was going to happen to him.

'Don't move or say anything,' Pieter commanded, 'Do you understand me, Staszic?'

Wilfred Staszic nodded three times.

'You need to see something,' said Pieter. And with that, he released Staszic and then reached for the Luger in his belt. He shone the torch on the pistol so that Wilfred Staszic could see it.

'We are now going to go downstairs,' said Pieter, 'I need to talk to you. But you must understand one thing, if you make one wrong move, I will kill you. Do you understand?'

And with that, Pieter turned his torch back onto Wilfred Staszic's anxious face.

Staszic again nodded.

Pieter stood up from the bed. 'Get up, now,' he ordered.

Staszic got out of bed, and Pieter turned his torch to the door to guide him out of the bedroom and along the landing and then down the stairs. Staszic's nerves got the better of him at the top of the stairs and he began to whimper and almost stumbled, but Pieter grabbed him and they both stood there motionless for a few seconds while Staszic regained his balance.

A multitude of thoughts and questions were running through Wilfred Staszic's mind at that moment. What was going to happen to him? Was Pieter Szabo going to kill him? And why was Pieter Szabo still alive? How had he got there? And then once again, was Pieter Szabo going to kill him? Staszic was grasping for the right answers, and then he remembered what Pieter Szabo had said, 'I need to talk to you', so perhaps he would be spared?

Staszic experienced a few seconds of misguided relief, but then he remembered what he and Kober had done to Francine Szabo on the night of the Szabo's arrest, and suddenly, Wilfred Staszic began to panic.

They reached the bottom of the stairs and Pieter guided Staszic into the lounge. And once there, Staszic could suddenly see better, and then he realized that it was because of the light from the blazing fire. The fire was burning brightly, and he considered that strange. The fire shouldn't still be aflame. And as he stared at the fire, Staszic experienced an even brighter, burning white light, when Pieter Szabo smashed the butt of the Luger into the back of his head and Staszic collapsed to the floor, unconscious.

Pieter stared down at him for a few seconds, and then he slowly turned around. He would go to wake Henryk Kober.

Kober would be a different man to handle, Pieter knew that. Henryk Kober would resist because Henryk Kober was a different type of coward.

So with that in mind, Pieter walked straight into Kober's bedroom and turned on the light. And as Kober lay there in bed, blinking his eyes and not understanding his rude awakening, Pieter went over to him and smashed him in the face with the Luger. Kober groaned with the shock of the pain. But Pieter then grabbed hold of Kober's ear and proceeded to drag him out of his bed, Kober began to howl in agony. And as he fell to the floor, Pieter smashed him across the face once again with his gun. Kober fell back, and as he did, Pieter forced the Luger's barrel into Kober's open mouth.

Henryk Kober lay there. The shock of being beaten about the face was not only very painful, it was also something that had never happened to him before. He was another bully who only knew how to dole out pain to others, having never experienced it himself. This beating was somewhat of a revelation to him. He blinked in disbelief as his face began to throb, and then something hard and metallic was jammed into his mouth and that painful intrusion suddenly brought him to his senses. He looked up, and his eyes widened in disbelief.

It was Pieter Szabo.

'So, you do remember me, Kober?'

Henryk Kober just lay there, breathing deeply.

'Try biting the barrel of this gun, Kober. The way you bit into my wife's neck.'

Kober's eyes widened as he remembered, he remembered it all. And at the back of his mind ran the thought. 'How can this be happening?'

Pieter once more grabbed hold of Kober's ear.

'Stand up you bastard.'

With some difficulty, Kober managed to get to his feet. Pieter Szabo had hold of his ear, the gun barrel remained jammed into his mouth. And with that, they too went downstairs. Pieter took the gun out of Kober's mouth as they went into the lounge. Wilfred Staszic still lay there on the floor. And seeing him, Kober stopped, thinking that Staszic could be dead.

'Don't worry, he's still alive,' said Pieter.

And with that, he clubbed Kober over the back of his head with the butt of his gun.

Over an hour passed before Staszic and Kober regained consciousness. And during that time, Pieter Szabo had been quite busy.

He'd dragged Staszic and Kober together, so that they lay side by side and were facing one another. They were several feet away from the fire and their heads faced the flames. Pieter had unwound the rolls of washing line and he tied their hands tightly behind their backs. He then wrapped the line around Staszic's ankles and then around Kober's ankles so that they were tied together. He did the same around their knees. Then he took more lengths of the line and wrapped it around their waists and then their chests so that Staszic and Kober were tightly bound together and were lying face to face. Once that was done, he threw another couple of logs on the fire.

And then he sat in one of the leather armchairs and waited.

As he sat there, Pieter thought about Francine and what these two men did to her. He remembered his family, his wonderful loving mother and his two darling sisters. And his anger started to rise. He stared down at Staszic and Kober, bound together like two pigs awaiting slaughter. They were the cause of everything. And suddenly, Pieter Szabo began to feel the rage rising inside him.

Finally, he'd had enough. He stood up and went into the kitchen and quickly filled a jug with cold water. Then he went back into the lounge and poured the water over their heads.

Stazic woke and his head jerked, and then Kober too opened his eyes. Their skulls ached and both men groaned with the pain. And then they couldn't understand why their faces were pressed together, it was an unwelcomed intimacy. As they tried to turn, they were both startled when they rubbed against each other's face. And then there was the shocking realization that they were bound together and that their hands were tied behind their backs.

They then tried to shake themselves free, but it was an impossible task.

Staszic began to breathe quickly.

'Henryk...what's happening?' he almost pleaded to his friend.

Henry Kober managed to turn his head sideways, and as he looked up he saw Pieter Szabo sitting in one of their leather armchairs, staring down at them both.

'Bastard,' Kober seethed.

'Yes, I am,' Pieter replied. His face was expressionless,

'What are you going to do to us?' Kober asked.

'Why, I'm going to kill you both,' Pieter replied again.

At that moment, Wilfred Staszic began to whimper.

Kober ignored him, he was trying to think.

'Let us go,' he demanded. It was the only thing he could think to say.

Pieter looked at him. 'Try using the word, 'please'.

Kober took a deep breath. 'Please let us go,'

'Ah,' said Pieter, 'and now you realize what it's like to plead for your life. Just like my wife, Francine did.

Staszic began to breathe very quickly.

'We were under orders,' Kober stuttered.

'No, no you were not,' Pieter said to him. 'You were not under orders. You're lying. What you did to my wife and my family was all planned by you two and you two alone.'

And then Pieter stopped and he looked down at Wilfred Staszic. Staszic was always the weaker link in the chain.

'I'm right, aren't I, Mr Staszic?'

Staszic stopped whimpering for a moment. 'Yes, yes, you're right,' he quickly replied. 'We're sorry, don't kill us, please.'

And with that admittance finally off his chest, Wilfred Staszic began to weep.

Henryk Kober looked at his friend with incredulity and disgust.

'Shut up Staszic,' he hissed, 'just shut up will you.'

Pieter sat there and watched them perform like the weasels they both were.

'Mr Staszic,' Pieter continued, 'you professed to be in love with my wife, and yet you stood there and let this bastard attack and abuse her. Even when he bit into her neck.'

And even as he spoke, the memory of it made Pieter's stomach churn and he had to take a second breath.

Staszic continued to cry. There could be no excuses, Pieter Szabo told the truth. And at that point, even Kober remained silent.

'Listen to me,' said Pieter. 'I actually intended to torture you both. I planned to tie you both naked to these two leather chairs. And I was going to take my knife and cut you to bits. I was going to puncture your heads with my knife, just as I did to your friend, Igor Sym.'

At the mention of Igor Sym's name, both men froze. They had both seen what was left of Sym's mutilated body. It looked as though he'd been attacked by some madman. Never had they ever considered that it could have been Pieter Szabo. After all, Pieter Szabo was supposed to be dead.

At that moment, Kober panicked.

'Let us go, please let us go. We'll give you anything.'

'You've already taken everything,' said Pieter abruptly.

Kober had no answer to that.

Pieter waited a moment before speaking.

'As I was saying to you both, I was going to torture you, just like you tortured my wife. But to tell you the truth, you two pigs aren't worth the effort. So I'm just going to kill you, and very painfully.'

Staszic and Kober started to squirm, but it was no use, they couldn't move, they couldn't do a thing. Pieter stood up, and Staszic began to weep uncontrollably and Kober twitched and grunted. And at that moment, both men realized that they were about to die, and it was a terrible reality for them to know that their lives were at an end. It was all over, and everything that they'd achieved by greed and for their own self-importance had all been a waste of time, for the both of them.

A wise man once said, 'Death is inevitable. Its how you die that's important.'

And it was true, a man could die peacefully in bed, or in absolute writhing agony. Unfortunately for Staszic and Kober, it would be the latter.

Pieter Szabo went over to the lounge door and picked up the can of paraffin that he'd left there. He removed the metal stopper from the can and put it into his pocket. Then he went back to Staszic and Kober and started to pour the paraffin over them. As soon as Henryk Kober smelt the paraffin's fumes he began to scream. He'd suddenly realized how he was going to die.

'No...No, you can't do that. Not that...please, no.'

And as the paraffin started to run down Staszic's face, he too, straightaway understood Kober's panic. They were going to be burned to death. And Wilfred Staszic too began to howl and squirm. Pieter Szabo said nothing. He was past talking. Revenge was now the only thing on his mind.

The can of paraffin was almost empty, and he carefully poured the last dregs along the carpet towards the fire. He threw the remaining paraffin onto the burning logs and the flames caught hold immediately. Pieter watched, as the flames slowly jumped out from the fire and onto the carpet. And then they slowly danced along the thin trail of paraffin and headed towards Staszic and Kober.

Henryk Kober looked over, and he saw the tiny line of burning flames approaching him. He and Staszic were both doused in paraffin, and he was suddenly totally aware of the fact that he was going to burn to death. And that moment he went berserk, he began to shake and scream. Wilfred

Staszic too, became hysterical and through pure terror, he began to urinate onto the carpet.

And then the flames licked their faces, and the men began to scream and shake their heads violently as they felt the fierce heat and the incredible burning sensation on their skin.

Pieter watched as both men shook and screamed and banged their heads against one another, both trying to escape the appalling agony. And at one point Wilfred Staszic butted Kober in the face and broke his nose. Not that it would matter.

And then with a sudden 'whoosh', both Staszic and Kober burst into flames. The screaming turned to shrieking, as both men tried to buck and turn and kick, but they were bound together, just as they were in life. And eventually, even though the shrieking stopped, Staszic and Kober both continued to shake violently, and in the end that too became a shudder, and then both men were dead.

Pieter Szabo stood there and watched it all. The room was filled with the disturbing smell of burnt human flesh, but still he stood there, looking at the blackened burning bodies.

Had it been enough? No, it wasn't. Nothing would ever bring back his wife, nothing.

Staszic's and Kober's deaths were an appeasement, but that was all it could ever be.

It had been a terrible way to die, but they deserved it. Not only had they destroyed Pieter Szabo's life, they were also responsible for the deaths of thousands of others. And those people were Polish, irrespective of whether they were Jews or any other religion. Those people, all those poor families were Polish, and they were brethren. Staszic and Kober were Polish too, but they'd shown no concern whatsoever in sending their fellow countrymen to be murdered en masse at the concentration camp at Auschwitz.

Staszic and Kober were greedy and evil men. They were both traitors of the very worst kind.

The flames from the burning bodies began to spill onto the carpet, and they quickly began to spread. Then the leather armchairs began to smoulder and smoke, and they too burst into flames. Pieter took two bottles of brandy off a side cabinet and he poured the contents onto the carpet and then threw the empty bottles to where the bodies lay. He watched as the fire took hold, and very soon the lounge was ablaze, it was exactly as Pieter Szabo had planned. The cord that bound them both together would be burned away. There would be no suspicious circumstances. Pieter picked up the empty paraffin can and he walked to the door. He didn't bother to look back. He left the house through the kitchen, exactly the same way he'd entered. He locked the door behind him as he left, no one would ever think to look for the key. Pieter then walked back to his car and he sat there for twenty minutes, watching as the flames engulfed the house.

Nothing could be done, the house burned to the ground. By the times the fire services finally arrived it was all too late. The next morning, as the police and the fire officials sieved through the charred building, two SS officers arrived in a staff car. The police showed one of the SS officers the blackened remains of what was left of Herr Staszic and Herr Kober. The bodies lay close together and they seemed to be embracing one another. Lying there side by side, there was a look of intimacy between them. And next to them were the two blackened brandy bottles. The policeman, ever mindful of what he said, implied the obvious, and then he raised an eyebrow. Evidently, Staszic and Kober had been homosexuals, and last night they'd both been drunken homosexuals. The SS officer gave a sarcastic grin and he shook his head. Both officers got back into their staff car and went to report their findings to Herr Kruger.

That night in the bar at the Grand Hotel, the other SS officers discussed Staszic and Kober. Everyone had always had their suspicions about 'those two'. There was a certain hilarity about the whole event. After all, two men living together, and neither of them ever showing any interest in women. Not even a hint of a prostitute. Yes, it was all very obvious.

And did their death's matter? No, not really. After all, they were only Polish.

Back in England, Lieutenant Vernon Ballantyne was having his first cup of coffee before starting another busy day. It was eight thirty in the morning and Ballantyne's secretary, after bringing him that all important cup of coffee, had then quickly returned with an armful of paperwork. Ballantyne groaned, and then put forth his usual discerning smile. His secretary, Nancy, smiled back at him as she placed the papers on his desk.

'Have a nice day, sir,' she said to him, and she laughed as she almost skipped out of his office.

She was a pretty young thing, and in better days and in better times, Lieutenant Vernon Ballantyne would have had slightly different intentions. But these weren't better times and Vernon Ballantyne had more important things on his mind. But still, he did consider it for a moment, and then he looked at the stack of paperwork on his desk and dismissed the idea altogether.

At twenty past nine, his phone rang. Ballantyne sighed as he picked up the receiver. He shook his head, this would be another unwanted interruption.

'Hello, Ballantyne speaking.' he said into the mouthpiece.

Through the crackling line, a voice replied.

'Is that Lieutenant Vernon Ballantyne?'

'Yes it is.' he replied.

'Ah good, I've been given your number to ring. This is Dr Lewis, over at the Bicester Hall Convalescence Home. We have a problem, Lieutenant Ballantyne.'

Why, what is it? Vernon Ballantyne asked.

'We have a patient, a Franz Szabo, and yours is the only contact telephone number we have.'

'Yes, I do understand that. And what is the problem, Dr Lewis?'

'I'm afraid Franz Szabo killed himself this morning, Lieutenant Ballantyne. He threw himself off the roof of our building. He died instantly.'

Vernon Ballantyne looked at the pen still in his hand. He put the pen down.

'I'm on my way over,' he said into the phone.

Just over half an hour later, Vernon Ballantyne arrived outside Bicester Hall Convalescence Home. It was a fine old stone mansion, built around a hundred and fifty years ago by owners whose fortunes were made from slavery, cotton and spices, and who then went on to become respectable merchant bankers and politicians. He parked his car and went inside. He then spoke to a receptionist who immediately picked up the telephone and made a short phone call.

Within a few minutes, Dr Lewis arrived, he was a smallish man with an efficient attitude.

'Ah, you must be Lieutenant Ballantyne,' he said, and with that, both men shook hands.

'We've put Mr Szabo's body back in his room and cleaned him up a bit, I'll take you up there now,' Dr Lewis continued, and he led the Lieutenant to a flight of stairs.

'What on earth happened to him, Doctor?' Ballantyne asked.

'You do know that Mr Szabo suffered from acute depression?' Dr Lewis replied. It was almost an excuse.

'Yes, I am aware of that, Doctor.' Vernon Ballantyne replied sternly

Doctor Lewis glanced at Vernon Ballantyne, and he realized that he would have to give a fuller account.

'One of our nurses took him in his breakfast this morning. Mr Szabo hasn't spoken a single word since he came here, in fact he's hardly ever opened his eyes. He sits for hours with his eyes closed, other than that he's asleep. We even have to feed him. Anyway, the nurse had taken in his breakfast and had started to feed him, then she had to nip to the toilet or something. When she returned to his room, Mr Szabo had disappeared. It seems he'd wandered off somewhere.'

'How did he get onto the roof?' the Lieutenant asked.

Dr Lewis carefully considered his reply.

'The stairs take you up there. He must have found the staircase and made his way onto the roof. We have the ventilators up there and a small incinerator to burn the medical waste.

Anyway, he got himself up there and he either jumped or fell over the edge. Who knows?

It was the gardener who raised the alarm. He came around the corner of the building and Mr Szabo's body was there on the tarmac. There was quite a lot of blood I'm afraid. We put him onto a stretcher and took him back to his room and cleaned him up. The nurse is quite upset, I think she blames herself.'

Lieutenant Ballantyne said nothing;

A moment later they arrived at Franz Szabo's room and they went inside. Lying there on the stripped bed was Franz Szabo's broken body. The left side of his head was raw and split and horribly swollen. Vernon Ballantyne stared at the body for a moment.

'I don't think he fell off the roof accidentally,' he said.

'You don't?' Dr Lewis replied.

'No, I think it was a suicide. He's thrown himself headfirst. If he'd tripped and fallen he would have somersaulted and the chances of him hitting the ground head first would be most extraordinary.'

Dr Lewis almost sighed with relief. He and his staff would be deemed blameless, and thank god for that.

They left the room, after all, there was nothing that could be done for Franz Szabo anymore. Dr Lewis took Vernon Ballantyne up the stairs and onto the roof, and both men looked over the edge, it was quite a height.

As they made their way back to the stairs, Lieutenant Ballantyne turned to the doctor.

'Why wasn't this door locked, Dr Lewis?' he asked.

'I...err, I don't really know,' the doctor stammered. He hadn't expected this.

'You're running a convalescence home, surely you have other patients here with mental problems?'

'Well yes, of course.'

'And yet you let your patients wander about, with open access to the roof?'

'Well, it's usually locked.'

'Usually'...isn't fucking good enough, doctor,' Vernon Ballantyne swore.

Dr Lewis couldn't answer. There were no excuses, and the Lieutenant was right of course.

'I shall of course, have to put this in my report.' Ballantyne said to him.

'A report, why?' the doctor asked.

'Because Dr Franz Szabo was under the promised protection of the British Government, Dr Lewis. The same British Government that is paying you people here at Bicester Hall to look after him. That's why.'

As he walked down the remainder of the stairs with Lieutenant Ballantyne, Dr Lewis contemplated the implications of all of this. The British Government were indeed funding many of the other patients there too, mostly the shell-shocked and the war-weary.

As they reached reception, Vernon Ballantyne asked the doctor 'what arrangements' had been made.

The doctor was at a loss, his mind was now on other things.

'The funeral,' said Ballantyne, 'have you given any thoughts as to the funeral?'

'We've not even got a death certificate,' Dr Lewis replied hesitantly, 'and I don't think anybody's thought to phone the funeral people yet.'

'Well I suggest you do, and as soon as possible.'

The doctor nodded. 'Yes, of course.'

'I take it you have a church here in Bicester, Dr Lewis?'

'Yes we do, it's St Edburgs. It's a lovely old church, beautiful in fact.'

'I want Dr Szabo to be buried there, a decent funeral and a good headstone please.'

'Yes Lieutenant Ballantyne,' said the doctor sombrely, 'I'll see to it.'

They walked outside to the Lieutenant's parked car.

'Keep in touch,' said Vernon Ballantyne, 'I shall want to attend the funeral,'

Dr Lewis suddenly turned to him, 'Ah yes, about the funeral, Lieutenant.'

'Yes, what is it?' Ballantyne asked.

'Err...we will, of course, organize the funeral, and we will also be prepared to cover all the expenses.'

Vernon Ballantyne nodded to him.

'That would go some way to set things right Dr Lewis, some way indeed.'

Once the Lieutenant had driven away, Dr Lewis stormed back through the Hall's main doors. He was looking for the nurse and that 'bloody' caretaker. He was going to sack them both on the spot. The pair of them should have known better, they should have both remembered the 'golden rule'. Always lock the 'bloody' doors.

Driving back to his base at The Firs, Vernon Ballantyne smoked a second cigarette. He wound down the window for some fresh air as he considered the events.

The Szabo's...had he now lost them both? Somehow he thought not. True, Pieter Szabo had not returned. Or maybe it was just that he hadn't returned yet. Pieter Sabo had always had other things on his mind, the Lieutenant knew that. And if and when Pieter did return, Ballantyne would have to break the news to him. And that was what the funeral arrangements had been about. Lieutenant Ballantyne needed to be seen to have done the right thing. He required Peter Szabo's respect, and his gratitude. Because if his 'little bird ' ever did decide to fly back home, Vernon Ballantyne had further plans for him.

CHAPTER 12

Major Wilhelm Kruger had not long returned to Lodz. He'd been summoned back to Berlin by no less than Heinrich Himmler himself. And it had been wonderful news. Both men had met in the lofty heights of the New Reich Chancellery building on the Voss Strasse and Himmler had praised Herr Kruger for his outstanding work in Lodz. Herr Kruger's methods of extracting the Jews and then transporting them to Auschwitz had been exemplary. Adolph Hitler himself had been notified and he'd passed on his personal thanks in the form of a short letter. Praise indeed.

And now it was time for a promotion of sorts. Himmler had asked Herr Kruger to take control of Warsaw, Poland's capital city and Herr Kruger had been quite taken aback. Himmler then explained to him that thirty per cent of the population there were Jews, several hundred thousand people. Apparently the Polish resistance there were causing havoc, and of those who had been caught, the greater percentage had turned out to be the Jews themselves. Himmler wanted Herr Kruger to repeat what had been done in Lodz. Herd the whole of the Jewish population into the Warsaw Ghetto and then transport them to the Concentration Camps. Treblinka was the obvious choice, and a special line of railway track had already been laid for that particular purpose.

Herr Kruger had agreed and accepted the post. It was a great honour. He was given 'carte blanche' to pick his own replacement in Lodz, the line of thought being, 'better the devil you know'. And after a brief discussion, Herr Kruger informed Himmler that he would be ready to take over in Warsaw in a month's time. That would give him long enough to gather the necessary information and plan a schedule. There was little mention as to the future of the man who he was replacing. But, Herr Kruger was confident. More than that, he'd been jubilant, especially when Himmler had hinted to him that as a reward for his success in Warsaw, Herr Kruger had every chance of being made a General.

On the train back to Lodz, Wilhelm Kruger had celebrated with a bottle of champagne. He was on his way up the ladder and heading all the way to the top, at last, he would be admitted into the higher echelon of the SS. He would finally stand in line with Adolph Hitler himself. As he sipped his champagne, he looked out of the window and he smiled to himself. Yes, he was on the way up. What could possibly go wrong?

When he got back to Lodz, of course, Kruger was immediately informed about Herr Kober's and Herr Staszic's tragic deaths. Kruger was about to give the order that thirty innocent citizens should be rounded up and shot, when he was told about the circumstances of their demise and how they'd both been found. It had all been hushed up until Herr Kruger himself had returned from Berlin. Kruger had not been overly surprised. He too had always wondered about Staszic and Kober. When he'd given Herr Kober the house, the first thing Kober had done was to move his friend, Herr Staszic, in with him. Kruger had always turned a blind eye to it, he'd actually never socialized with Kober and Staszic. Herr Kober and Herr Staszic had been very efficient and their input would be missed. However, that would no longer be Herr Kruger's problem. He would be in Warsaw.

Pieter Szabo sat having his breakfast with Bruno Huelle. Over coffee and toast, they were discussing their plans. Over a week had passed since Pieter had murdered both Wilfred Staszic and Henryk Kober. And there had been no form of retribution from the Nazis. Bruno Huelle had held his breath, waiting for all hell to break loose. But nothing had happened. There were no reprisals. In fact, everything seemed to have been covered up and kept secret. It had certainly not been made common knowledge, and Pieter's plan had worked perfectly.

But the plan to assassinate Wilhelm Kruger would bring into play a different outcome, the consequences of which could be dire. Bruno Huelle knew that, and the resistance and the people of Lodz knew that. However, that was the price that they would have to pay.

Living under Nazi rule was unbearable and it was going to get a whole lot worse. And for many, it was a life hardly worth living. But it was a life worth fighting for.

The date of the assassination was set for the following Saturday night, apparently there was to be a dinner dance at the Grand Hotel.

The manager, Yaslov Slowowski, had finally been coerced. He'd been persuaded to help the resistance without actually being involved. He had two jobs to do. Firstly, was to unbolt the rear door to the fire escape, and secondly, to simply light a cigarette.

He'd been promised that he couldn't be implicated in any way. Nevertheless, Slowowski had made his wife and their two teenage children leave the house and go to the farm in the country where their cousins lived.

The explosives had also been found, The resistance had a connection, someone who had a far-off relative who worked in a quarry somewhere. Two sticks of dynamite had been acquired and no questions asked.

On the Friday morning a workman ambled around to the rear of the hotel. He was wearing overalls and a cap and was carrying a hammer. Nobody took any notice of him, not even the staff. He walked up to the fire exit and then took a stout nail out of his pocket. He placed the nail in the centre of the door and hammered it half way in. He only had to hit the nail three times, and then he turned and walked away.

By nine o'clock on Saturday night, the dinner dance at the Grand Hotel was in full swing.

The Hotel was busy, full of smartly dressed German officers, the elite of which were the SS. Immaculate in their sharp black uniforms, they crowded around the bar as though they owned it. Some of the more high ranking Polish officialdom, mainly those who worked in the Town Hall were there too. They arrived with their wives, though it was doubtful if any of them felt as though they had a choice. Not to accept the invitation wasn't really an option, not if you wanted to keep your position.

A five-piece band were playing on a small stage and the guests sat and dined at tables which surrounded the dance floor. Some of the earlier diners were already on the dance floor, couples cajoling with one another and looking forward to the night's entertainment.

Wilhelm Kruger sat at his usual table. He was on good form. He'd decided not to tell his subordinates about his move to Warsaw until the following week, and for good reason. Tonight he wanted to enjoy himself. He didn't want any undercurrent, and he didn't want to see his officers huddled around the bar, discussing army politics and the change of command. Any changes would affect morale, he knew that. Kruger had always run a very efficient team and his men respected him. And he knew that too. But tonight, well, he just didn't care. There was a promotion in sight and the world was his oyster.

Sitting with him at his table were his three most preferred officers. All SS lieutenants, they were Herr Brecht and Herr Hauptman, and his chosen favourite, the sharper and the more intelligent, Herr Gunter Wolff.

Wilhelm Kruger had chosen the food, and in deference, they had all agreed with his choices.

They'd already started with the champagne and had already consumed a couple of bottles even before the food arrived. And when it did, it was all an assortment of Herr Kruger's favourite dishes. There was a variety of different types of Pierogi dumplings, followed by the chef's speciality, the glorious 'Hunter's stew', specially prepared with tender venison, with plums and spicy sausage and laced with black pepper. Along with the laughter, the flow of champagne never stopped. Several bottles were consumed before Herr Kruger's favourite sweet finally arrived. The crowning glory, the special Cheesecake flavoured with wild cherries, topped with rhubarb sorbet and smothered in thick cream.

More champagne was ordered and a bottle of good brandy, all to be left at the table. The four men were merry, and Kruger laughed at the freedom and the pleasure of it all. He could do whatever he wanted, in less than four weeks he would be gone to pastures anew.

The evening progressed, and the dishes were finally cleared away by the attentive waiters.

The officer's heads were suddenly turned when a dozen very well dressed young ladies appeared from out of the hotel reception. They were immediately ushered to the main bar by Yaslov Slowowski.

Herr Hauptman laughed out loud.

'Where does Slowoski find these women?' he remarked. 'The man's a genius.'

The other three officers laughed in agreement.

Kruger sat back in his chair as he swirled the brandy around in his glass.

'You younger men had better go and take your pick before those army officers steal them away from you.' Hauptman and Brecht glanced at one another, and then back to Herr Kruger.

'Is that alright with you, Herr Major? Brecht asked eagerly.

'Of course it is, Lieutenant,' Herr Kruger replied. 'You are young, go and enjoy yourselves. When you've had enough of the dancing, bring your young ladies back here to the table. There's plenty of champagne for everybody.'

Hauptman and Brecht both got up from their chairs immediately, they saluted and then quickly made their way to the already busy bar. But Gunter Wolff stayed where he was.

He leant forward and refilled Herr Kruger's brandy glass and then his own. Then he produced two good cigars and offered one to his Major. The cigars were lit and both men sat there for a moment and appreciated the smell and the taste of fine tobacco.

'Good cigar,' said Herr Kruger.

'Good brandy,' replied Gunter Wolff as he lifted his glass and toasted his commander.

Both men laughed, their conversations had always been easy and comfortable.

'You'd better get over there with your friends,' said Herr Kruger, 'or those German Field Officers are going to steal all the women.'

But Gunter Wolff just sat back in his chair and smoked his cigar, and he laughed.

Gunther Wolff was thirty years old. He had black, swept-back dark hair and a chiselled face.

He was both handsome and intelligent and he knew it. And once he'd set his sights on a young lady, he'd always known that it was only a matter of time.

'Not to worry, sir,' he replied casually. 'These women are all the same. And I am an SS officer, and when I walk over there to the bar, it will be me that they'll be looking at.'

Wilhelm Kruger laughed out loud and he slapped Gunter Wolff on the shoulder. He liked the young man's confidence, and his arrogance. Gunter Wolff was a good officer who would make a good commander. Herr Kruger had already made the decision. He would leave his command to Gunter Wolff. Herr Wolff was highly efficient, and in doing so Herr Kruger would be leaving the running of Lodz in a safe pair of hands.

They ordered more champagne, and then drank it. And eventually the temptation got the better of Herr Gunter Wolff and he shrugged his shoulders, stood up and saluted, and then headed for the ladies at the bar.

Herr Kruger poured himself another brandy and he smiled as he watched Gunter Wolff escort a young lady onto the dance floor. Yes, he'd made the right choice. And tomorrow he would speak to Herr Wolff and inform him of his decision. And that would get the ball rolling.

It was a wonderful night, and Herr Kruger and his party continued to drink copious amounts of champagne. They were joined at their table by different groups of young women who sat on the men's laps and helped themselves to the drink. They were all pretty young things who giggled a lot and the three younger officers were enthralled. But they were not for Herr Kruger, they were not his type at all. He preferred the more mature Slavic women, with their hard features and high cheekbones, all slim and slender and taut.

And then he remembered Francine Szabo. And his mood suddenly changed, because she would be his one everlasting memory of Lodz. And the thought of her made him sombre as he reflected on what should have been. Herr Kruger stood up, and he laughed as he excused himself from the evening's entertainment. Everyone made a fuss of him, but he ordered them some more champagne as an excuse. Then he picked up the brandy bottle and made his way past the bar and into the hotel reception.

Yaslov Slowowski was waiting there, dressed as always in his slightly worn dinner suit and bow tie. And as ever, he always understood Herr Kruger's needs.

'Ah Slowowski, how are you?' Herr Kruger asked.

'I'm very well, sir,' Slowowski replied, 'And have you had a good evening, sir?'

Herr Kruger smiled, and his mood lightened slightly.

'Yes, I have,' he replied. 'The food was excellent and so was the company, it's been a good night.'

And then he looked at the brandy bottle in his hand and then at Slowowski.

'Get me a woman will you. Try and get hold of that dark-haired girl, the one from last Saturday. She was quite superb. Get hold of her, give her a bottle of brandy, and send her up to my suite.'

'Yes, straightaway sir,' Slowowski replied. 'I don't think that it will be a problem, sir.'

Wilhelm Kruger belched, and then he made his way to the lift.'

Yaslov Slowowski watched him go, and as the lift doors slowly closed, Slowowski turned and headed for the hotel entrance. He walked outside and stood on the steps under the hotel's lights. Then he slowly took out a packet of cigarettes. He took one of the cigarettes and put it in his mouth and lit it. Slowowski then stood there for all of thirty seconds, openly smoking the cigarette. Then he threw it onto the ground and stubbed it out before going back into the hotel. Once there, he walked over to the reception and picked up the telephone. He would need to contact Herr Wilhelm Kruger's favourite prostitute.

Pieter Szabo sat in the Renault across from the Hotel and waited for the signal. He'd been there for over two hours, but that hadn't been a problem. He'd made sure that the car was parked in the right place and that it was facing in the right direction. After the job was done, he wouldn't be returning to Bruno Huelle's house. That would be far too dangerous. His car was loaded and ready to go. He had some clothes and some food, and he had a couple of jerry cans filled with petrol. And he had his clock and his walking stick. If everything went okay he would drive straight out of the city and head west, hopefully.

But at that moment, Pieter Szabo was still sitting in his car, two hundred metres away from the front of the Grand Hotel. He'd been waiting for a signal, and now there it was. As he'd sat there, a slim dark-haired man wearing a dinner suit and a bow tie walked out onto the steps of the hotel. The man lit a cigarette and stood under the hotel lights. He smoked the cigarette for exactly thirty seconds and then he threw it to the floor and stubbed it out, before going back inside. And that was the signal, and that man was Yaslov Slowowski.

And if things were going to plan, Yaslov Slowowski would now be waiting for a prostitute to arrive for Herr Kruger. Herr Kruger was apparently a creature of habit, and he required the services of a prostitute every Saturday evening, especially after drinking champagne, and Yaslov Slowowski knew that. And that would be Slowowski's cover, that he'd been busy obtaining the prostitute. And when the girl arrived Slowowski would stick to her like glue. He would even lock her in his office if he had too.

Pieter got out of the car and quietly made his way to the rear of the hotel. It was deserted, it was always deserted. He went to the fire exit and inspected it. He could see the nail sticking out of the middle of the door. Pieter took hold of the door and slowly pulled it. The door opened slightly. Slowowski had done well, he'd unbolted the lock from the other side as promised. Pieter then reached into his inside pocket and he took out the two sticks of dynamite. They were jointly fused and were tied together with a length of string with a loop at the top. Pieter looped the dynamite onto the nail and made sure that they were secure. Then he opened the fire exit door and went inside. After turning on his torch, he made his way up the stairs until he finally reached the top floor. Pieter took a deep breath and then he slowly opened the door and stepped into the hotel landing. It was deserted and quiet. The only perceptible sound was from the band playing downstairs as the revellers continued to dance the night away.

Pieter took the Luger from his belt and then crept silently along the landing. He made his way to Kruger's suite, and then he stopped for a moment and listened. Pieter looked down the landing to make sure that there was no one around, and then he noticed that there was another door further down the landing on the opposite side that led into another room or suite. For a moment Pieter wondered if there was anybody in there. But he had no choice. Whatever happened, he was willing to take the chance.

What Pieter would never know was that his wife had once stayed in that room and that she'd ran down this very same landing, trying to escape with her life.

Pieter tapped on Kruger's door.

Inside his private suite, Herr Kruger had made himself comfortable. He'd taken off his black SS jacket and his tie, and he'd unbuttoned his collar. Kruger wandered around his suite, smiling in anticipation. And after he'd poured himself a large brandy, he sat down on one of his comfortable couches and lingered there as he sipped his drink.

The girl he was waiting for was incredible. She had beautiful long black hair, the straightest hair he'd ever seen. There wasn't a hint of a curl or even a wave in it, and it hung across her shoulders and down her back like a shiny black curtain. She was sharp-faced with the high cheekbones that he admired so much. Her olive skin and her Slavic looks made the girl look like a gypsy. And she behaved like one. When her head went down on him her black hair fell across his chest and stomach and he thought he would explode with ecstasy. Her body was slender and taut and when she climbed on top of him she'd screamed and thrashed and he'd taken hold of her mane of hair and pulled her to him. They'd laughed and they drank more brandy and then they'd had sex again. The girl would do anything for him, anything at all. She spent the whole night with him and had then slipped away at dawn, leaving Herr Kruger physically drained, and with the rest of the day to recover.

And now she was about to return, and that made Herr Kruger a very happy man. He knew what she was capable of, and he knew what he could do to her, and that she would let him.

And then there was the tap on the door.

'Ah,' Kruger called out, 'come in...come in.'

And he grinned, because tonight she would have to earn her money.

But then he stopped grinning, immediately. As the door swung open and Pieter Szabo walked in, arms stretched forward and pointing a Luger directly at Kruger's chest. Kruger just sat there, open-mouthed, he still had the glass of brandy in his hand. He couldn't understand where this man had come from and what he was doing. Kruger shook his head to clear his thoughts as he wondered 'what on earth' was happening.

'What the hell are you doing here?' he said out loud. Kruger was a man who was used to giving the orders and he therefore demanded an answer.

But Pieter Szabo wasn't about to give him an answer, and he wasn't going let this man try to take charge of the situation.

'Put the glass down and stand up,' said Pieter calmly, 'or I'll shoot you where you sit, right now.'

Kruger's eyes widened. He still didn't fully comprehend what was happening, but he was beginning to realize that he was in great danger.

'You'll never escape,' he said. 'They'll hear the shot. You'll never get out of the hotel alive.'

But Pieter Szabo took no notice.

'Stand up you bastard,' he ordered, 'or I'll shoot you right now.'

Herr Kruger put his glass down on the coffee table in front of him and then he stood up.

'You are Herr Wilhelm Kruger of the SS,' said Pieter, 'and you are the Nazi who runs the German forces here in Lodz. Am I right?'

'That is correct,' said Kruger, trying to retain some form of dignity. But in his mind, he was trying to think of how to escape his predicament. He stared at Pieter, and suddenly there was a moment of recollection. He'd seen this young man before, but where? And he cursed the alcohol that he'd drank for clouding his brain.

'Who are you?' he asked. 'I've seen you somewhere before.' And he continued to speak to Pieter with a tone of arrogance in his voice, it was an arrogance that began to make Pieter Szabo angry. This man should be begging for his life, not asking damn questions.

Pieter looked at him and he sneered.

'My name is Pieter Szabo,' he said quickly. 'And you, Kruger, sent my wife and my family to Auschwitz to be murdered. And then you sent me there too, but I escaped and I came back, 'Herr' Kruger. And it was me who broke into your camp and saved my father, and while I was there I also killed your' right hand 'man, Igor Sym.'

Kruger stared back at Pieter, and he remembered seeing Igor Sym's mutilated body. Sym's death had been horrendous. He'd suffered an inhuman act of violence. And suddenly, Herr Wilhelm Kruger was worried.

But Pieter continued. 'And once I'd got my father to safety, I came back again. And last week I killed two more of your SS officers. I tied Wilfred Staszic and Henryk Kober together and then I set fire to them and watched them both burn to death.'

Herr Kruger was horrified. He'd thought their deaths had been an accident, everyone did.

He looked at Pieter Szabo. This man was a lunatic. This man, this...'Szabo'...was a maniac.

And suddenly, in a moment of complete clarity, Wilhelm Kruger suddenly realized who Pieter Szabo was.

'Szabo'...it was the name, and Kruger suddenly recognized it. It was Francine's last name. And standing there in front of Kruger was her husband. But Pieter Szabo should be dead, but now he was here? And Kruger just stood there as the events of the past once again rushed through his brain. And he suddenly realized how Pieter Szabo had gotten into the hotel, and how he planned to escape. It was that damned fire escape. And as Kruger looked at Pieter, he remembered Francine Szabo. She was so beautiful, she was breathtaking, and she'd been the absolute love of his life.

He'd truly loved her, until their last wonderful night together, when it had all gone so terribly wrong.

And then, Kruger suddenly remembered something, something that Pieter Szabo had just said. And he realized that Pieter Szabo had been wrong. He'd just said that his wife had been sent to Auschwitz, but Francine Szabo hadn't been sent to Auschwitz, she'd been here at the Grand Hotel, with Kruger. And he tried to think of something to say, something or anything that would save his life. He needed an excuse or an explanation that he could use, anything at all. And then Kruger's brain began to work. If he told Pieter Szabo that Francine hadn't been sent to Auschwitz and that he knew where she was, it might just work. It was both a plea and a lie, but at that moment he had no other options. Words formed in his mouth and he was just starting to say her name...'Francine'.

But Pieter Szabo didn't hear it. He'd had enough of Wilhelm Kruger, he pulled the trigger and blew a hole straight through the Wilhelm Kruger's head.

Kruger's body jerked backwards and his life ended as he fell back onto the couch. Pieter stared down at him for a moment. It was done, it was over. He then turned around and walked out of the suite, carefully closing the door behind him.

And downstairs at the dinner dance, the music still played on.

Pieter walked back along the landing to the fire exit and then he went quickly down the stairs.

When he got to the bottom he went outside and closed the fire door. He tucked the Luger into his belt and then reached into his pocket for a box of matches. He struck a match, and then he lit the fuse to the dynamite. It was a two-minute fuse, and Pieter had to hurry back to his car. He started the engine and drove away immediately. He'd gone no more than five hundred metres before the dynamite exploded. Pieter heard the explosion as he turned a corner and headed onto the main road that would take him out of Lodz. He needed ten minutes, and then Lodz could become a faded memory, he never planned to return.

Back at the Grand Hotel, all hell broke loose.

The explosion shook the building and clouds of smoke and dust filled the hotel's reception area. In the dining room, women screamed and the band stopped playing as glasses and bottles rocked and smashed around the room. There was panic, and everybody suddenly wanted to get out of the hotel when they realized that some sort of bomb had exploded.

Gunter Wolff was one of the first, he was guiding a young lady to safety, but then he left her when he saw Yaslov Slowowsky. Slowowsky was dragging a whore through the reception area as he tried to calm everybody down and give instructions. Then he spotted Gunter Wolff.

'Herr Wolff, there's been some sort of explosion.'

Slowowski was intentionally vague.

Gunter Wolff looked around. 'Where's Major Kruger?' he asked.

'He's upstairs in his suite. I was just about to go up there with this young lady. She's his 'guest.'

Wolff looked at the girl and he immediately understood. Then he saw Hauptman and Brecht with some of the other officers, they were making their way to the hotel entrance with a crowd of people.

Wolff waved them over. 'Come with me,' he said to them, I want to make sure that Major Kruger is alright. There may be a risk of fire.'

And with that in mind, the three men quickly headed to the stairs.

Slowowski watched them go and he waited a moment. Then he dragged the girl with him into the lift and he pressed the button for the top floor.

As the lift doors closed he turned to her.

'When we get to Kruger's room, if anything's happened, start to scream the place down, do you understand?'

The girl's eyes widened.

'Listen to me,' he said, 'something's happened, and if we don't play it right, these Nazi bastards will line us all up against a wall and shoot us.'

He squeezed the girl's arm. 'Do you understand me?'

She did. The girl had lived a tough life and was certainly nobody's fool. She realized that she was being used by Slowowski. But if she fled she could be implicated, and anyway, in one way or another, she'd been used for most of her life.

Gunter Wolff was knocking on Herr Kruger's door as Slowowski and the girl appeared out of the lift. There was no answer. Hauptman and Brecht glanced at the girl and stared at her for a moment. Wolff knocked on the door again.

'Major Kruger, are you alright? There's been an explosion.'

There was still no answer.

He knocked again, 'Major Kruger, are you alright?' And still there was no reply.

Gunter Wolff looked at Hauptman and Brecht, and then he took a deep breath before cautiously opening the door. The three officers entered Kruger's suite, but Slowowski stood back with the girl. Only when he heard one of them shout, 'oh my god', did he push her through the door. Lying on the couch with his face covered in blood and a gaping hole in his forehead was Major Wilhelm Kruger. He'd been shot, of course.

The girl promptly began to scream and Slowowski began to play the part of a shocked and horrified hotel manager. The three officers began talking frantically in German, and then Gunter Wolff turned to Yaslov Slowowski.

'Slowowski, get rid of the whore, now!'

That command was obeyed straight away. Slowowski pushed the girl back out of the suite and he took her to the lift.

'Disappear,' he said to her. 'I'll get some money to you. Don't worry, you'll be safe now.'

When the lift doors closed, Yaslov Slowowski immediately made his way back to Herr Kruger's suite. Slowowski would have to stick very closely to his enemies, and he would obviously aid and assist Herr Gunter Wolff, and help him in every possible way.

It was soon discovered that the explosion had happened at the back of the hotel. Word got around and Slowowski and Gunter Wolff were quickly informed. At that point, no one else knew about the Major's death. Wolff had left Hauptman and Brecht in Herr Kruger's suite with the strict instructions that no one should enter until he'd discovered what had happened. Slowowski guided Herr Wolff around to the back of the hotel to where there'd once been the door to the fire exit. A dozen people crowded there, some of them were the other officers and some were the invited guests. They all stood back as Gunter Wolff arrived. Herr Wolff looked at the gaping hole that had once held the door, and then at Slowowski.

'What's this?' he asked.

'It was the fire exit.' Slowowski replied, as vague as ever.

'I wasn't aware that there 'was' a fire exit,' said Gunter Wolff.

'Oh, it's not been used for years. We keep it locked up,' said Slowowski.

Wolff re-examined the fire exit, and then he turned to Slowowski.

'And why would you lock a fire exit?' he asked.

Yaslov Slowowski had to think quickly.

'The hotel got broken into and robbed several years ago, they got in through the fire exit. Since then it's always been locked.'

Slowowski's quick reply put an idea into Wolff's head.

'Where do those stairs lead to?'

'To every floor,' Slowowski replied.

Gunter Wolff's mind suddenly began to work.

'Come with me,' he said.

Both men started to climb the stairs, and then Gunter Wolff stood back.

'You lead the way Slowowski, you know these stairs better than me. Take me up to the top floor.'

They proceeded to climb several flights of stairs and then through the 'hidden door' and onto the landing that led to Herr Kruger's suite. They then went back into the suite to find Hauptman and Brecht. Kruger's dead body still lay prostrate on the couch. His bloodied face had begun to go pallid and drawn.

'I know how the bastards got in,' Herr Wolff announced. 'They blew the door off its hinges and got in up the back stairs, there's a fire escape. They shot Herr Kruger and then must have escaped the same way. It was all very well planned.'

Hauptman and Brecht looked at him.

'How did they know which was Herr Kruger's suite?' Brecht asked.

All eyes suddenly turned to the hotel manager.

'Could it be something to do with your staff, Slowowski?' asked Herr Wolff immediately.

Slowowski thought about it seriously for a moment. It was a good act.

'I doubt it,' he said casually. 'Surely that would be a bit too obvious. And I know these people, they have families and children.'

Then he suddenly clicked his fingers and looked surprised.

'Two weeks ago, a smart couple booked into the room just further down the hallway. They booked it for a week, they said they were here on business. But two days later they disappeared without paying their bill.'

Slowowski said nothing more. He'd put forward an idea, and now he would let the others take the bait. And it worked.

'Would you recognize them again if you saw them?' asked Herr Wolff.

'Yes of course,' said Slowowski, 'it was me who booked them in. I even offered to take them up to their room, but they said it wasn't a problem. I didn't see them after that, but I would definitely recognize them both again.'

'Right,' said Herr Wolff, 'Maybe they were from out of town.'

'They could have been, I don't know. I've certainly never seen them before.' Slowowski replied.

Gunter Wolff turned to Brecht and instructed him to get some men and some transport. They would have to remove Herr Kruger's body. Then he spoke to Slowowski again.

'I need you to speak to your staff and find out if they know anything about that couple, and also if they've seen or heard anything.'

'Yes of course,' Slowowski replied, and then, 'Excuse me, Herr Wolff, would it be alright if I just went to check on what's happening downstairs?'

He was dismissed with a wave of the hand. Gunter Wolff had other things on his mind.

Yaslov Slowowski headed for the lift. Yes, he would definitely have a word with his staff, and he would tell them to keep their mouths firmly shut. They knew nothing. He would also have a private word with the cleaner, on the day that the 'mystery couple' disappeared, their beds hadn't been slept in.

Slowowski thought about the assassin. Whoever he was, he was a clever man. With the fire door blown off its hinges, no one would ever know that it had already been unlocked. Slowowski was safe.

Major Kruger's body was removed. Some soldiers eventually arrived in a truck and they covered Kruger's body with the blankets from his bed and then carried him out of the hotel. Herr Hauptman and Herr Brecht went with them.

That left Herr Gunter Wolff alone in Kruger's suite. He looked around the place, it was really quite nice. After a respectable amount of time, he would move in there himself. But at that moment he had bigger plans. He would now take charge, and it would be him who would report directly to Berlin. He knew how to run things in Lodz, even better than Wilhelm Kruger. And he had plans of his own. Wolff smiled at what would be his own success.

Little did he know that he was taking over a position that was already promised to him.

Within a month, Herr Gunter Wolff had been promoted to Captain, as he took control of Lodz.

Earlier, he'd been called back to Berlin, where he too had met Heinrich Himmler. Wolff had managed to give a good enough account of himself and was given the promotion and the position. Himmler had enough on his plate. Someone else would now have to be sent to Warsaw to sort out the problems there. Himmler had taken Gunter Wolff to one side.

'Have you any idea who was responsible for Herr Kruger's assassination?' he'd asked.

Herr Wolff had to admit that they'd had no success.

'It was probably the local resistance,' said Himmler, 'therefore an example must be made. We cannot allow this sort of thing to happen.'

Captain Wolff completely understood.

When he returned to Lodz he had his men round up forty civilians. All were men and all were innocent. They were lined up against a high stone wall and machine-gunned. The bodies were left there for the relatives to retrieve. Such was Nazi justice.

Pieter Szabo drove west.

He had to head west and then go north to try and make his way to Denmark. That had been the original plan, several months ago. But Pieter had no other option.

En route he was stopped twice. The first was as he approached Berlin. He was stopped at a roadblock behind a line of cars. The soldiers were checking everyone and asking to see their papers. An officer and two soldiers approached Pieter's car, and Pieter had wound down the window and had his identity papers, his 'Kennkarten', ready for inspection. The officer checked Pieter's papers and then looked back at him.

'And where are your documents for the car?'

'I don't have any,' said Pieter straight away.

The officer stared at him.

'You are required to carry the vehicle's documents. Why don't you have them?'

'Because I stole this car,' Pieter replied.

At that moment, the two accompanying soldiers became interested too. The officer looked at this somewhat impudent young man and ordered him out of the car.

Pieter climbed out of the car, with the help of his walking stick. Making sure that the officer and the soldiers took note that he hobbled somewhat.

'Right,' the officer said, 'explain to me why you are driving a stolen car?'

'I stole it off a filthy Jew.' said Pieter rather indignantly. 'I'm from Freiberg, near Dresden. When the SS arrived they arrested the Jew and his family and took them away. The car was in his garage and so I stole it.' Pieter then laughed. 'After all, he wouldn't be using it anymore, would he?'

Both of the soldiers smiled at that remark.

The officer checked Pieter's 'Kennkarten' once more.

'Yes, you're from Freiberg. You're a long way from home. Where are you going?'

Pieter raised his head proudly. 'I'm going to Berlin, sir.'

The officer once again stared at Pieter. 'And why are you going to Berlin?'

'It's my leg, sir. I've tried to join the army twice. But I can't get in because I'm a cripple. My mother died last year and that left me with my stepfather. He's a bastard. So I decided to get myself to Berlin and do something for the Reich. I want to do my bit too.'

The officer looked at Pieter, he'd noticed that Pieter had a stick and had struggled to get out of the car.

'I see,' he replied.

Pieter smiled. 'Well, Herr Goebbels is crippled like me and he's made a success of his life'.

The officer nodded his head. 'Yes,' he said, 'you are absolutely right.'

It was true, the Minister of Propaganda, Herr Joseph Goebbels was a cripple. Born with a congenital deformity, his right foot turned inwards and that had left him with one leg shorter than the other. Goebbels reputedly wore a special shoe and he always walked with a limp. He too had been turned down by the German Army. At the outbreak of the First World War, he was failed when trying to enlist, again due to his deformity. It was something that was well known by everyone, though hardly mentioned.

And so with that in mind, the officer let Pieter go on his way. He waved to the guards who were holding up the line of cars to let Pieter through.

As he drove away, one of the soldiers turned to the officer.

'He didn't seem a bad lad, sir. You've got to admire him.'

'Yes,' the officer replied. 'He seemed a decent enough fellow. Wouldn't do anyone any harm.'

The second time Pieter got stopped, it was a different story.

Pieter had skirted Berlin and was heading ever north. It was late afternoon and Pieter had just driven past Lubeck, a small town close to Germany's northern Baltic Coast. Another couple of days of steady driving and he would cross into Denmark.

He's safely bypassed the town by taking the usual quieter back roads. And he'd continued to drive for another ten minutes and was heading into the countryside once more, when he turned a bend in the road only to see two German Soldiers walking towards him. The soldiers were both carrying dark brown bottles, which turned out to be the local white wine. The soldiers saw Pieter approaching and immediately started to wave their arms for him to stop. Pieter considered driving past them at speed but when he showed no signs of slowing down, one of the soldiers pulled out a pistol and stood in the middle of the road to block Pieter's way. Pieter pulled up, but he left the car in gear. The soldier walked up to the front of the car and put the open bottle of wine on the car's bonnet as he continued to wave his pistol in Pieter's direction. The soldier was laughing stupidly, and at that moment Pieter realized that both soldiers were drunk. The second soldier walked up to the driver's door and Pieter wound down the window.

'We're taking your car.' slurred the soldier, 'either that or you're going to have to drive us back to Lubeck. One way or another, but we're not walking any further.'

Pieter smiled. 'No problem,' he said.

Pieter reached under his seat for his Luger pistol and then he turned to the soldier and shot him point blank in the chest. At the same moment that he'd pulled the trigger he also stamped on the accelerator, and the car shot forward and ran down the other soldier. Pieter felt the second bump as the back wheels also ran over him. The soldiers died instantly, as the bottle of wine fell off the car's bonnet and smashed all over the road.

Later, Pieter would consider himself lucky not to have had a puncture.

Another two days and Pieter slipped into Denmark, through the small and unassuming town of Tonder. Thankfully, there wasn't a German in sight, but Pieter didn't stop, he'd never intended to. Another day's drive westwards took him to the port of Esbjerg. He arrived there only to find it a rather bleak and colourless place.

Once again Pieter found a quiet, deserted backstreet to park his car, and then he made his way down to the busy port area. The harbour there contained an assortment of ageing and rusty commercial ships along with a small fleet of hardy local fishing boats. It was hectic and swarming with men. There were three German soldiers there too, they stood near the harbour wall, smoking cigarettes and keeping their eye on everything that passed by them. But everyone else seemed to be busily working, trying to make a living of sorts. Around the harbour were the usual warehouses and a number of old bars and taverns. Pieter Szabo however, was looking for one specific tavern in particular. He walked unassumingly around the harbour and then back again, this time looking down the smaller side streets. And then he finally saw it. Down a narrow side street, an old timber-framed building, constructed from dark wooden beams, and walls rendered with faded yellow plaster. There was a sign on the front of the tavern. In large black metal letters, it read, 'Jungersens Ale Hus'.

This was the tavern that he should have made his way to many months ago after he'd tried to assassinate Adolph Hitler. That had been the plan. But Pieter hadn't stuck to the plan. He'd never intended to.

And now here he was, several months later, like some 'waif and stray', trying to make his way back home. He remembered the code words, and he remembered the name of the man that he was supposed to have met and spoken to. Pieter's contact was the landlord of the tavern, his name was Anders Jungersen.

Jungersen was with the Danish Resistance and he was supposed to have helped to get Pieter Szabo back to England.

Pieter looked through the tavern window, there were about a dozen people inside. It was early afternoon and some of them were still eating. Pieter glanced towards the bar. There was a large man serving drinks to a customer, Pieter could only hope that he was Anders Jungersen, the landlord.

He stood outside and waited, and he counted the customers as they left. Finally he went back to the tavern window, there were only two or three men left in there and they were sat at a corner table next to the open fire. Pieter walked inside and went up to the bar. Anders Jungersen saw him walk in and nodded as he waited for Pieter to order a drink.

Pieter leant forward.

'Could I have a glass of beer, please,' he said very quietly, and in perfect English.

Anders Jungersen blinked. He stared at Pieter for a moment and then he glanced across at the three men who were sitting near the fire. They were still busily talking amongst themselves.

'You're English,' said Jungersen in a low voice.

'No, I'm Polish.' Pieter replied, 'are you Jungersen, the landlord?'

Anders Jungersen nodded slowly.

'Good,' said Pieter. 'I have a clock and a walking stick that needs fixing. Could you help me?'

That phrase was the code word.

Anders Jungersen looked at Pieter, and then he picked up a glass and filled it with beer.

'Sit at the table near the door,' he said, 'and drink it slowly.'

Pieter sat himself down at the far table next to the door and looked out of the window. He couldn't speak Danish, and he didn't want to be drawn into a conversation with anyone.

Anders Jungersen kept an eye on his other three customers, and like the good landlord he was, he judged when the men were on the last dregs of their beer. Then he went over to them.

'Okay boys,' he said out loud. 'We're closing now, it's time to go.' And he remained there, expectantly. As the men finished their drinks, he picked up their empty glasses. The three men stood up to leave, and one of them moaned that 'they had just got comfortable'.

'Come back tonight,' laughed Jungersen, 'I'll keep the fire warm and the beer cold.'

His humour fell on deaf ears, and as the men approached the door, Pieter lifted the glass to his mouth and drank as though he was finishing off his own beer. That way, he wouldn't have to acknowledge the men as they left.

Anders Jungersen closed the door behind them and then he locked it. He turned to Pieter.

'Where the hell have you been?' he asked. 'You should have been here months ago. We thought you'd been captured, or killed.'

'I've been busy,' Pieter replied.

'Doing what?'

'Killing Nazi's,' said Pieter.

Jungersen shrugged. 'That's good.' he said, and then, 'Come with me.'

He led Pieter behind the bar and through into a large kitchen, and then he called upstairs to his wife. Kirsten Jungersen came down the stairs immediately, she was a plump middle-aged woman with greying blonde hair and a pleasant smile.

'Take 'our friend' to one of the rooms upstairs and give him something to eat,' said Jungersen.

Kirsten Jungersen glanced at Pieter and then at her husband. She knew not to ask questions. Kirsten Jungersen knew her husband's business and she knew what he was involved with.

'Go with her, and stay in your room' said Jungersen. 'We will contact your people to let them know you're here and still alive. Then we'll sort out a boat to try and to get you home.'

Pieter thanked him, and then Anders Jungersen grabbed a coat and left through the kitchen door. As he walked away down the quiet back street, Jungersen considered the fact that though he was risking his life, he didn't even know his new 'friend's' name.

It was better that way.

An hour later he returned.

Jungersen went straight upstairs to Pieter's room and knocked on the door. Pieter had been trying to get some sleep, but woke up immediately and bid his host to enter. After closing the door behind him, Jungersen spoke to Pieter.

'We've been on the radio. You must be pretty important my friend. They want you back as soon as possible, they're going to send a plane to pick you up.'

Pieter swung his legs of the bed and listened intently.

'We've got to get you up to Lemvig' Anders Jungersen continued, 'you'll have to travel north, there's a small disused airfield there which we've used once or twice before. I've got a driver, now it's just a matter of getting you there.'

'I have a car,' Pieter volunteered, 'it's parked in a back street on the other side of the harbour.'

'Even better,' said Jungersen. 'It can't be traced back to us should anything go wrong. You'll be flying to RAF Fowlmere, apparently. You'll be met there by someone.'

For a brief moment, Pieter thought about returning to England again. After all, he'd failed his mission, Pieter would have to explain everything to Lieutenant Ballantyne, and suddenly he felt a pang of guilt. The Lieutenant had been good to both Pieter and his father and Pieter felt somewhat indebted to Lieutenant Vernon Ballantyne. It was a debt of gratitude, a debt that he'd not been able to fulfil.

In the late hours the next evening, Pieter and Anders Jungersen shook hands as Pieter left.

A driver had been found, a young man named Karl, who was roughly the same age as Pieter. Karl's English wasn't that good, but they had a passable conversation as the young man tried to improve his grasp of the English language. They finally arrived at the deserted airfield at Lemvig at around three o' clock in the morning. They turned the car's headlights off and sat there in the dark for another fifteen minutes, and then someone suddenly tapped on the car window. It startled both Pieter and the driver, Karl. They got out of the car and shook hands with four other men who were also members of the Danish Resistance.

'Sorry to keep you waiting like that,' said one of them, 'but we had to make sure that you weren't being followed.'

Pieter nodded, it was understandable.

'The plane will be here in about two hours,' said the man, 'we'll just have to wait.'

'How will they know where to land?' Pieter asked him. 'Do we have to light fires to mark the runway?'

'No, no,' the man replied, 'that could draw attention. The Germans might see the flames or the smoke. No, we have white linen bed sheets. In two hours time it will just be becoming daylight. The pilot will see the white sheets. We've done it this way before, it works.'

After waiting for an agonizing two and a half hours, they finally heard the faraway sound of a plane's engine. The men went into action immediately. Several sheets of white linen were laid on both sides of the runway, and none too soon. In a matter of minutes, the plane seemed to swoop in from nowhere to make a perfect landing. It was the same De Havilland Mosquito that had flown Pieter to Germany all those months ago. The side door slid open and Pieter grabbed his kit and his walking stick and he ran to the plane and climbed inside. He didn't even have time to wave goodbye to the resistance men who had helped him,. The door was closed straight away as the plane's engine revved up and the Mosquito hurtled down the makeshift runway and took off immediately.

The pilot acknowledged Pieter. Once again it was the same pilot who had flown him out to Germany. The man who had pulled Pieter into the plane was the navigator. He strapped Pieter in and then went back to sit with the pilot. Pieter took a deep breath, he put his walking stick to one side and then he checked his kit bag. There was only one thing in there. A clock that didn't work.

They landed at RAF Fowlmere in the early hours of the morning. Though it was still grey, there was a chance of sunshine, and it was England. There was a single car waiting on the runway. The De Havilland Mosquito finally rolled to a stop and Pieter climbed out onto the tarmac. He looked across as the car's door swung open and out stepped Lieutenant Vernon Ballantyne. On seeing the Lieutenant, Pieter ran over to him and both men shook hands.

'I'm sorry, sir, I failed the mission,' said Pieter straightaway. He had to get it off his chest. It was a matter of personal responsibility.

'Yes, we realized that some time ago,' replied the Lieutenant. 'Not to worry. Get into the car please.'

Pieter was quite surprised at Lieutenant Ballantyne's rather informal reply. But they both got into the car and then drove off immediately.

It was the Lieutenant who spoke first.

'Hitler has been seen publically, so we realized something had gone wrong. You can brief me tomorrow, but first of all, I have to tell you something.'

Pieter turned to Vernon Ballantyne.

'It's your father, Pieter,' said Ballantyne.

Pieter stared at the Lieutenant.

'I'm sorry Pieter, but unfortunately, your father has passed away.'

Pieter didn't say a word. He was staggered. And for a moment he couldn't believe what he was hearing. How could this be, how could his father be dead?

Pieter sat there in silence as he tried to take it all in. And then he thought about all their struggles and trying to get his father to England to safety. And now suddenly, it had all been worthless. His father was dead. And as they drove on, both men remained silent for several minutes.

'How did my father die, sir?' Pieter finally had to ask.

He died in his sleep,' said the Lieutenant, 'they think it was possibly some sort of heart attack.' It was a lie, of course. But telling Pieter Szabo the truth would not do any good. There'd been enough upset in Szabo's life and Vernon Ballantyne knew that. His 'white lie' was the better way. To tell Pieter Szabo that his father had tragically committed suicide would be of no help to anyone.

'He died peacefully, Pieter. He hadn't been well.'

Pieter took a moment to think about it all. This was something that he'd never expected.

'I know he hadn't been well, sir. But I just hoped that he would recover. He's had a terrible time of it since my family died...' and his voice trailed off, suddenly he could say no more.

Pieter turned and looked out of the window at the passing countryside, and he bit his lip to hold back the anguish. He stared out at the endless green fields, surrounded by ancient trees. It was timeless and it was beautiful. England was without doubt, a truly beautiful country.

It was something worth fighting for.

Pieter finally turned to Lieutenant Ballantyne.

'He died peacefully, sir. No one can ask for better than that.'

Vernon Ballantyne swallowed uneasily. But he didn't regret his actions. Not one bit.

'I took it upon myself to have your father buried at the local church. St Edburg's is a lovely place. We're going to go there straight away before we do anything else. I'd like you to see his grave.'

Pieter nodded. 'Thank you, for everything you've done, sir,' he replied.

Forty minutes later, they arrived at St Edburg's Church in Bicester. Both men got out of the car and Lieutenant Ballantyne led Pieter to the corner of the graveyard to where Franz Szabo's grave lay. The Lieutenant turned and then went back to the car.

Pieter stood there, staring down at his father's final resting place. There was a pale, square granite headstone. It read,

Doctor Franz Szabo
Passed away 3rd April 1942
Loved and Respected by all.

Pieter looked at the headstone. It was a testament to the truth. He almost found it impossible to believe what had happened. His father was a good and honest man who had always cared for his family and had looked after his many patients back in Lodz. And now he was dead. All of Pieter's family were dead. Finally, he'd lost everyone.

He turned around and walked away. It was over.

He and Lieutenant Ballantyne got back into the car and drove away.

'Let me tell you what happened in Germany.' said Pieter, almost straight away. He needed to talk.

'It'll do tomorrow, it doesn't matter right now,' replied the Lieutenant.

'Yes it does,' said Pieter. 'We can go over it again tomorrow at the briefing, sir. But I'd like you to know what happened and where I've been.'

Lieutenant Ballantyne thought about it for a moment.

'Okay then, tell me,' said Ballantyne. And he suddenly realized that Pieter Szabo didn't want to speak any more about his father.

Pieter repeated his story, and of how he'd had Adolph Hitler in his sights and at the last moment had missed his shot. He then went on to tell Lieutenant Ballantyne how he'd made his way back to Poland to kill Staszic and Kober. He gave no excuses and not many details, he just told the Lieutenant the facts. He explained to Lieutenant Ballantyne how he'd become involved with the resistance in Lodz and their plan to kill SS Commander Wilhelm Kruger. At that point the Lieutenant took a greater interest.

'Ah, Herr Wilhelm Kruger, Now there's a man on our list,' said Ballantyne. 'We've got reports that he's responsible for deaths of thousands. He's one of Himmler's rising stars.'

'I've killed him, sir.' said Pieter.

For a moment, Vernon Ballantyne lifted his foot off the car's accelerator and the car slowed.

'He's dead?' Ballantyne asked.
'Yes sir, I shot him through the head.'
'Good god,' replied Ballantyne. 'We didn't know that. Tell me more.'
Pieter briefly told him about his work with the resistance and how he'd gone to Wilhelm Kruger's private suite at the Grand Hotel and shot him in the head. It was as simple as that.
Vernon Ballantyne audibly exhaled.
'Well then, the mission wasn't a complete failure after all. You've actually saved us a job. We were planning to send someone out there to get rid of Kruger.'
Pieter shrugged.
'From there I made my way to Denmark as originally planned. And now here I am.'
Vernon Ballantyne turned to Pieter.
'Well Pieter Szabo, it's good to have you back,' he said. And he meant it.

The next morning they met again at the briefing. There was very little to say about the mission, Ballantyne had already written his report from what Pieter had told him. But Vernon Ballantyne had another agenda, there was something else that he needed to discuss with Pieter Szabo.
After the perfunctory cups of tea, Lieutenant Ballantyne finally got to the business in hand.
'We need you to go back,' he said to Pieter.'
Pieter Szabo said nothing, he just listened.
The Lieutenant continued. 'We have to try and take out their chain of command. We have to do something to stop these bastards.'
Pieter interrupted him.
'I'll go sir.' he said immediately. 'Get me back over there, give me the names and exactly where they are and I'll try my best.'
Vernon Ballantyne looked at him.
'I thought I may have had to persuade you,' he said.
Pieter Szabo thought about it for a moment.
'No Lieutenant. I'll go back. There's nothing for me here.'

Ten days later, Pieter Szabo was flown back into Denmark. He wouldn't return for four years. He travelled throughout Europe and as far as the Greek Islands via the resistance networks. Working as a lone sniper, he caused disorder and confusion. Even when the war ended in 1945 he still didn't return. Following a constant flow of information from Lieutenant Vernon Ballantyne, Pieter Szabo pursued those fleeing Nazis who would never be sent to court to face true justice, the ones who'd burnt their SS uniforms and had then tried to become normal citizens by moving elsewhere. During those years, Pieter Szabo would become a cold, calculated killer. It became a way of life, a profession. And even when the war was well and truly over, he would never stop. Vernon Ballantyne would see to that.

CHAPTER 13

The United States of America...1962

The Director of the Federal Bureau of Investigations stood in his office, scowling with anger as he watched the performance on his television.

J. Edgar Hoover, head of the FBI, stared at the TV and at the sultry figure of the actress, Miss Marilyn Monroe, as she sang her own personal rendition of 'Happy Birthday Mr President', to the President of the United States, the one and only, John Fitzgerald Kennedy.

Dressed in a skin-tight, flesh coloured dress which left very little to the imagination, the audience had gasped as Miss Monroe stepped onto the stage at the Madison Square Garden in New York. The event was a Democratic Party fundraising gala, which just happened to coincide with the President's birthday the following week.

And as the platinum blonde film star simpered and pouted promiscuously, she crooned her private little love message directly to the President, and no one else.

J. Edgar Hoover seethed. Not only was he shocked, he was completely disgusted by the act, which he considered to be unbelievably distasteful.

'Damn you, you blonde whore,' he swore out loud, and then, 'and damn you too Kennedy, you cheap bastard.'

It was no secret. In the long halls of government in Washington, there were many who already knew about John Kennedy's ongoing affair with Miss Marilyn Monroe. Tongues were wagging and the press were finally beginning to take notice.

J. Edgar Hoover knew that it would only be a matter of time. And when the story finally broke, it would undoubtedly bring down the American Presidency. And the humble citizens of that great nation would have to hang their head in shame and disgust as the rest of the civilised world looked on and sniggered with glee.

America would be disgraced.

Hoover went over to his cocktail cabinet and poured himself a large glass of his favourite bourbon. He almost drank it all in one go. And once he'd finished, he poured himself another. As the alcohol began to flow into his brain, he started to mull things over. There were problems with Kennedy in the White House, many problems. Hoover thought about the decisions and the choices that would have to be made. The country couldn't carry on like this. Something would have to be done. And on that memorable evening, as he drank his second glass of bourbon, J. Edgar Hoover prepared himself. He'd considered all the options and the actions that would need to be planned and organized. But he'd come to one conclusion.

America needed a different President.

On the next day in the very same office, Hoover sat down and spoke to Mr Clyde Tolson, his closest friend and longtime assistant director. During a very private and confidential meeting, both men discussed John F. Kennedy, along with everything else they considered was wrong with the Presidency.

Things were going from bad to worse. Both Hoover and Tolson had been appalled with Kennedy's plans for a new 'Civil Rights Act'. The Act would outlaw discrimination based on race, colour, and religion. And it proposed equal rights in employment and promote education for everyone, no matter who they were. For Hoover and Tolson and many more Americans like them, the act was an outrage.

However, times were changing. And so was America, but the intolerance was rife.

And then there'd been Cuba and the 'Bay of Pigs' incident.

Cuba had been a disaster for President John F. Kennedy from the very start. When Castro and his revolutionary forces had taken command of the island in 1959, they'd severed all links with America. Castro had then taken control of all the American assets there, including the banks and the oil refineries, along with the sugar, the coffee, and the tobacco plantations.

Interestingly, Castro had also closed down most of the Mafia-owned hotels there too, which was a major blow for that organization. Those hotels brought in millions of dollars by providing drugs, prostitution and gambling for the rich and the famous, and anybody else who could afford it. Cuba had then unfortunately turned to Communist Russia as an ally, an act which was totally unacceptable to the USA.

All of this led to the disastrous 'Bay of Pigs' incident, in which the USA secretly armed and trained a force of Cuban exiles who were determined to invade the island. They were planning to land at the 'Bay of Pigs' on the southern coast of Cuba and then overthrow Castro and take the island back. But the invasion was doomed from the start. Castro had found out about the forthcoming incursion from the Russians, and he had his forces already there at the Bay, ready and waiting.

The invading forces were surrounded and needed immediate assistance, but when it was discovered that the invasion was going badly, Kennedy hesitated. And in a moment of indecision, he refused to send in the American military to help the stranded and abandoned Cuban exiles. More than twelve hundred were captured and many were then executed. The Cuban community back in America would never forgive Kennedy for his betrayal, and neither would many other concerned Americans.

In particular, was one very angry young man. His name was Lee Harvey Oswald.

As Edgar J. Hoover and Clyde Tolson discussed the President's escalating problems, Hoover then mentioned the 'embarrassing' behaviour by Miss Marilyn Munroe, which had been televised nationwide the previous evening. Tolson totally agreed. Kennedy's affair with the actress was not only a disgrace, but it also placed the Presidency in a highly precarious position. Hoover then went on to speak about Kennedy's constant philandering. There was a long list of women in John F. Kennedy's life and the FBI knew all about the President's frequent affairs. J. Edgar Hoover had made sure of that.

'The man's a whore. He's a disgrace to the Presidency,' said Hoover angrily.

'It's his poor wife that I feel sorry for,' said Tolson, 'she's such a wonderful lady.'

Hoover sat in silence for a moment. He was deep in thought. The reason being, was that

J. Edgar Hoover had his own personal little secret, something which no one knew about or even suspected, not even Clyde Tolson.

Hoover had met Mrs Jacqueline Kennedy, wife of the President, on several occasions. She was stunningly beautiful, and she was also an educated and very clever woman. Hoover was enthralled by her. For Hoover, who was a confirmed bachelor, Jackie Kennedy was everything that he found perfect in a woman. She had brains and beauty, and she was articulate and quietly confident. Whenever Hoover had met her, he'd found that he was slightly nervous and somewhat tongue-tied. However, Jackie Kennedy had been gracious and gone out of her way to make friendly and interesting conversation with him. This was all something totally new to Hoover. He'd dealt with Lady Judges and the female staff at the FBI all the time and he had no problems with them. It was simply business as usual. But somehow, Jackie Kennedy had gotten under his skin. And if truth be known, J. Edgar Hoover, head of the FBI, suddenly found that he had something of a 'crush' on the American President's wife. More than that, he was absolutely captivated by her.

Not that there was anything he could do about it, of course. She was the First Lady, and he was small and stout and thirty four years her senior. And of course, she was married to President John F. Kennedy, a man who was too good looking for his 'own damn good', as Hoover once put it. And so Hoover had taken the decision to protect her, in an almost fatherly way. It was the best he could do. Hoover had the FBI gather an extensive list of Kennedy's affairs with women, and he'd found it all quite disturbing. It seemed that Kennedy even had one personal assistant who he regularly used as his 'procurer' of willing women.

Hoover had taken to phoning Jackie Kennedy at least once a week for their 'little chat', and he just couldn't understand why Kennedy should want any other woman rather than his beautiful and loyal wife. It was unbelievable. There were rumours of course that Mrs Kennedy was very well aware of her husband's private dalliances, but that she had the dignity and the common sense not to cause any upset in the White House.

However, if the 'Marilyn Monroe' affair hit the headlines, all hell would break loose. And Mrs Jackie Kennedy, the 'First Lady', would be publically shamed. And J. Edgar Hoover felt that he just couldn't let that happen.

These facts, along with a host of others, had fuelled J. Edgar Hoover's ever-growing hatred and mistrust of Kennedy and his Presidency.

Hoover and Clyde Tolson sat there, and Tolson awaited his boss's verdict. They had a long-standing system. Hoover made the decisions and Tolson made the plans, and he then put those plans into action, thus protecting his boss from any direct involvement. And it worked.

If Hoover knew nothing, he couldn't lie about it.

Hoover stood up and went over to his cocktail cabinet where he poured two glasses of bourbon. He handed one to Tolson.

'Monroe's too dangerous,' said Hoover. 'We've got to shut that bitch up. She's got to go.'

Clyde Tolson nodded in agreement.

Hoover then looked directly at Tolson

'And at some point, we've got to get rid of Kennedy too. He's another disaster, he's got to go.'

In whatever context it was taken, those words spoken by J. Edgar Hoover that day would change the course of history.

Less than two months later, the actress Marilyn Monroe would be found dead in her home.

It was the beginning.

After his meeting with Hoover, Clyde Tolson made his way back to his own office. He picked up the telephone and made a call. Somewhere, in another office in Washington, a man picked up the phone.

'Yes?'

'It's me, Clyde Tolson. We have some work for you.'

'Where do you want to meet?' the man asked.

'Make it the 'Rib Room', the restaurant in the Mayflower Hotel. We'll meet there the day after tomorrow at eleven o' clock.'

'Okay, I'll be there,' came the reply.

Clyde Tolson put down the phone. He had things to attend to. He was going to be a busy man, a very busy man.

On the other end of the line, Conrad Stiller also put down the phone, and he smiled to himself. 'More business from the 'good old' FBI.'

And more business meant more money, for 'Lieutenant' Conrad Stiller.

Clyde Tolson remained at his desk and he stared at the telephone. He was thinking about Conrad Stiller, and the corrupt and devious 'bastard' that Stiller was. But he needed Stiller, and he and Stiller also had a system that worked, and on numerous occasions.

Tolson however, was nobody's fool. He had a secret FBI file on Conrad Stiller and he knew all about Stiller's clever tricks and all his little hiding places. Conrad Stiller was dangerous and he was ruthless, but he was also highly efficient. Stiller not only had connections within the FBI and the CIA, he also had an association with the Mafia. Not only that, he had contacts with other government agencies all around the world. Truly well connected, Stiller could find anyone who needed to be found, and then he would sort out whatever the problem may be.

However, Conrad Stiller was no simple Mafia stooge, thank god. No, Stiller was hidden away in a separate government department altogether, and away from the FBI and even the CIA, both of which held no authority over him at all. And that too, all worked efficiently well.

'Lieutenant' Conrad Stiller was actually a high ranking agent in the much fabled United States Secret Service, the USSS. He was the 'mole in the hole', and he was virtually untouchable.

The USSS was a wholly separate law enforcement agency which was actually part of the Department of the Treasury. It was originally formed to combat the widespread counterfeiting of the dollar, but in later years was it tasked with two distinctly critical security missions.

Firstly, it was to safeguard the financial systems of the USA from major fraud or any other illicit financial operations.

And secondly, it was to ensure the safety of the President of the United States.

Not that Conrad Stiller was part of the intelligence unit that was charged with the President's security, though it did give him access to a certain amount of personal information on John F. Kennedy himself.

But no, Stiller's main work involved major fraud and illegal financial operations. However, he was also working very illegally, for the Mafia at the same time, and in that respect, he kept them financially secure and away from any investigation. It was something that kept the Mafia bosses very happy and made Lieutenant Conrad Stiller somewhat invaluable to them.

Clyde Tolson was aware of Stiller's connections with the Mafia and he'd discussed the subject with his boss. The Mafia however, were also an excellent source of information, and it was information that could be used very effectively, it was a sort of two-way deal. And for that reason alone, a critical decision had been made by J. Edgar Hoover.

That the Mafia were to be left to their own devices.

Two days later, Clyde Tolson and Conrad Stiller met in the 'Rib Room', the men-only bar restaurant within the Mayflower Hotel in downtown Washington. It was a good place for business meetings by men who needed a little privacy. It was also J. Edgar Hoover's favourite restaurant.

Tolson arrived early, it somehow gave him a feeling of authority. He waved away the waiter until Stiller turned up at exactly eleven o' clock. The waiter then returned.

The 'speciality' of the Rib Room was the legendary 'Cannibal Sandwich', which was made from raw beef, onion, egg yolk and Worcestershire sauce, and was personally prepared at the guest's table by the dining room captain. But not today, Clyde Tolson simply glanced up at the waiter and ordered two coffees.

Both men sat there as the waiter scribbled something onto his notepad and then left to get them their beverages.

Clive Tolson was a tall, suave looking man, he was always well dressed and always wore a white shirt, usually with a 'nice' tie. Conrad Stiller was not a suave man and neither did he dress to impress. Stiller was slightly shorter than Tolson, not that it mattered, and he had dark brown hair that was a little too greased. He seemed to always wear the same grey suit and was a man that you could pass in the street and never give a second glance.

'How are you, Mr Tolson?' Stiller asked. Not that he was actually bothered, but their conversation had to start somewhere.

'I'm okay.' Tolson replied, with about the same amount of interest.

'So, I take it that the FBI requires my services?' said Stiller.

'Possibly,' Tolson replied sharply. He didn't particularly like Stiller's smug attitude.

'Okay,' said Stiller, 'well let's cut the crap. What's the problem?'

At that moment the waiter reappeared with their coffee, and both men broke off their conversation. Tolson thanked the waiter but lingered until he'd once again left. Tolson then turned to Stiller.

'The problem is with the damn President, along with that blonde whore of his.'

'I take it you mean 'Miss Monroe'? Stiller smirked.

'Yes I do,' said Tolson. 'Did you see that performance on the TV the other night?'

Stiller nodded. 'I caught some of it.'

Tolson shook his head.

'Kennedy's a damn fool. If it gets out that he's been having an affair with her, it will topple the presidency.'

'And it will get out, at some point,' said Stiller. 'And if and when he does finish the affair, that woman's liable to blow the whistle.'

Tolson nodded. He already knew all about Marilyn Monroe. The actress was tempestuous and slightly out of control, she was currently drinking too much and she was taking drugs. The woman was a 'loose cannon' and he knew it.

'So what's the answer?' asked Stiller.

'She's got to go. And I mean permanently,' Tolson replied.

Stiller took a drink of his coffee.

'Yes, okay. I can do that. It won't be a problem. I'll probably need a couple of your men.'

'Alright, yes of course,' said Tolson. 'And we have a file on Miss Monroe, I'll send it to you.'

'Okay,' said Stiller, 'and is that it? You'll make payment to me in the usual manner?'

'We will,' Tolson again replied.

Stiller said nothing for a moment, and then he picked up his cup of coffee and drank the last dregs.

'I'll be in touch,' he said. And with that, he stood up and walked out of the restaurant.

Clyde Tolson watched Stiller go. The waiter, ever attentive, came over to the table immediately.

'Would you like to order some food now sir?' he asked.

'No,' replied Tolson, 'I'm waiting for Mr Hoover.'

'Ah,' said the waiter, 'I'll bring you some more coffee.'

At exactly twelve o'clock, J. Edgar Hoover walked into the restaurant.

He strode over to his usual corner table and in doing so he passed Clyde

Tolson, who had been sitting there waiting for the last twenty minutes. Hoover nodded to him and Tolson stood up and followed his boss to their regular table. Both men sat down and the waiter quickly took their order.

It was a fact, that J. Edgar Hoover lunched almost daily at that same restaurant in the Mayflower Hotel, and always at the same corner table facing the door. When it came to dining, Hoover was a man of repetition. He didn't like 'fussy' food, just plain and simple American fare. His favourite meal was chicken soup, and then corned beef hash, followed by coffee and jello. Tolson usually ordered the same.

Another waiter arrived with a jug of water, he filled their two glasses and then left.

Hoover glanced across at Tolson as he picked up his napkin.

'How did it go, Clyde?' he asked.

'We're going to proceed as planned,' Tolson replied quickly.

'Ah, good,' said Hoover, just as the chicken soup arrived.

Two days later, the FBI file on Marilyn Monroe arrived on Conrad Stiller's desk. It had been sent directly to him by Clyde Tolson, in a sealed official FBI document pouch labelled 'private and confidential'. Stiller read the file on Miss Monroe, it was quite in depth, but neither was Stiller surprised. Hoover's FBI was outstandingly efficient. The report not only gave Monroe's home address and her phone numbers, it listed the names of her friends and boyfriends, and even her housekeeper, doctor and psychiatrist. From there it listed her medications both from her doctor and her psychiatrist, and from other possible sources. It was recognized that Monroe had slowly become addicted to barbiturates.

Marilyn Monroe's favourite drink in public was always endorsed as being Dom Perignon Champagne. However, the FBI had somehow managed to acquire her grocery receipts and it seemed that Monroe was drinking seemingly large amounts of vodka and Coca Cola, along with the occasional bottle of 'Bacardi' white rum. Neither was her film career progressing very smoothly either. Her last film, 'The Misfits' had critical reviews and had failed at the box office. A planned TV network production had fallen through, but then suddenly she'd been offered a leading part by 20th Century Fox in the comedy film, 'Something's got to Give'. Days after filming started, Miss Monroe became 'ill' and hardly showed up at the studios for the next six weeks. 20th Century Fox had promptly sacked her and issued a writ for $750,000 in damages.

Things were certainly not going well for Marilyn Monroe.

As Conrad Stiller read the report, he smiled. Everything looked good.

One of the positive aspects of Stiller's profession was that he wasn't particularly answerable to anyone. He had position and rank, and his reputation was well regarded. At any one time he could be working on several different projects. So if Conrad Stiller's desk was empty and he couldn't be found, nobody was ever going to ask any questions. All of this worked for Stiller, because he could be anywhere, home or abroad. And he frequently was.

Four days later, and after tying up a few loose ends, Stiller flew out to Los Angeles. He hired a car for the week and then drove out to the Brentwood district. Once there he found a decent motel and rented a room there, once again for a week. The next day he drove to Helena Drive and parked the car. Then he went for a pleasant stroll. Finally, he found 12305 Fifth Helena Drive. It was a beautiful single story Hacienda-style house, situated at the end of a quiet cul de sac. A gated property with its own swimming pool, the house was set back from the main road, shaded by trees, it was very private. It was also the home of Miss Marilyn Monroe.

For the next five days and nights, Stiller continually returned to the house. During the day he kept his eye on the comings and goings at the Monroe household, not that there was much to see. Eunice Murray, the live-in housekeeper, regularly flitted in and out of the place. The gardener arrived and then left again, and there could be visits from Monroe's personal physician or her psychiatrist at any hour.

In the evenings and once it was dark, Stiller climbed over the fence and hid behind some citrus trees. From there he could study the layout of the house. It wasn't difficult. The hacienda was a single story property and was very well lit. He soon discovered which bedroom was Miss Monroe's, and he watched her as she continually tottered around the house with a glass in her hand. Eventually she would retire to her bedroom and Stiller could only surmise that it was there where the pill taking took place.

Another interesting observation was that of the housekeeper, Eunice Murray. Once Monroe had retired to her bedroom, Eunice Murray would take out the bottle of white rum that she hid in the cupboard under the kitchen sink. Armed with a couple of bottles of Coca Cola and a glass, Eunice too, would head for her own bedroom and drink until she virtually collapsed.

Stiller smiled as he recalled the grocery receipts that the FBI had managed to get hold of...'large amounts of vodka and Coca Cola, along with the occasional bottle of Bacardi rum'.

For Eunice, it must have been one of the perks of the job.

And then Marilyn disappeared.

Stiller only realized when he went back to the house one evening and Miss Monroe simply wasn't there and she didn't return the next day. And that left Eunice Murray to her own devices. As Stiller waited, he watched Eunice open a bottle of Miss Monroe's most expensive Dom Perignon Champagne, and then later, she staggered off to bed with the vodka.

The next day, Stiller flew back to Washington.

Once he got back to his office he rang Clyde Tolson immediately.

'I need two of your men to go over to Los Angeles,' he told Tolson.

'I'll get onto it,' Tolson replied.

'I want Sloan and Hughes. I've worked with them before, they're good enough. Get one of them to ring me straight away.'

'Okay, no problem.'

'Oh, and another thing,' said Stiller, 'I'm going to need some stuff from your Toxicology department.'

'Okay,' Tolson replied, 'Let me know what you need. I'll send it over.'

An hour later, Stiller's phone rang.

'Hi, it's Agent Sloan, Clyde Tolson has instructed me to ring you, Mr Stiller.'

'Do you know what this is all about?' Stiller asked him.

'Tolson's given us the brief. Yeah, we know what's happening.'

'Good. Get yourselves over to Los Angeles. I want one of you to watch the house in Brentwood, and then one of you go and find out where she is at the moment. Okay.'

'Okay, Mr Stiller,' Sloan replied.

Stiller gave the FBI agent the name of the Motel that he'd stayed at and the directions and the address of Miss Monroe's house, and the best place to climb over her fence.

Several days later, FBI agent Sloan made a phone call to Conrad Stiller.

'Okay Mr Stiller, we've got some information. She's away on holiday somewhere, but nobody's saying where. It's a strict secret apparently, but at some point she's going to have to come back here anyway.'

'Yes obviously, but I need to know when? Stiller replied.

FBI agent Sloan continued. 'Well, there's talk of her starting filming at the Fox studios again.'

'I thought they'd sacked her?' said Stiller.

'Nah, apparently they've kissed and made up, so she's going to be coming back here to Brentwood. I'll keep my eye on things, and I've got Agent Hughes watching Fox studios.'

'Okay, keep in touch,' Stiller replied. Then he took a deep breath and put the phone down.

Two weeks later, Miss Monroe returned to her home in Brentwood once more.

Agent Sloan then rang Conrad Stiller over in Washington.

'Hello Mr Stiller, she's back home.'

"Do you know where she's been?' Stiller asked.

'There have been rumours that she's been in some private hospital somewhere, apparently some ongoing problem with gallstones. Whether that's true or not we don't know, it could be an excuse.'

'Okay,' said Stiller, 'keep an eye on her and let me know her routine. Keep me informed.'

'Will do, Mr Stiller,' Sloan replied, and with that, he put the phone down.

Three days later, Agent Sloan once again rang Conrad Stiller.

'She's back on the booze and the pills again,' he informed Stiller. 'She's bombed out of her head every night. Gets up at about two in the afternoon and goes to sleep it off by the side of her pool. By five o' clock she's back on the vodka.'

Stiller thought about it for a moment.

'Right,' he replied, 'carry on as normal and I'll fly over there next week, we'll meet up.'

'Okay Mr Stiller, said Sloan, 'let us know when you're flying in and we'll pick you up at the airport.'

However, things weren't going to be that simple. The following afternoon Sloan rang Conrad Stiller again.

'Mr Stiller, she's gone.'

'What?' Stiller replied.

'A limousine picked her up this morning, it took her to the airport.'

'Do you know where's she gone? Stiller asked.

'New York.I got Agent Hughes to ring the studios at Fox. He told them he was the press, he's good at that sort of thing. Some receptionist there told him she'd flown to New York. She's doing some fashion shots for Vogue and then she's doing an interview with Time Magazine.'

'I'll ring you back,' said Stiller, and he slammed down the phone. A few seconds later, he rang Clyde Tolson.

'There could be a problem,' he said straightaway to Tolson.

'Why, what's wrong?'

'It's Monroe, She's back on the booze and the pills, and this morning she got on a plane to New York. She's doing an interview with 'Time Magazine'.

Clyde Tolson nearly stopped breathing.

'She's doing what?' he almost shouted down the phone.

'You heard me,' said Stiller. 'And let me tell you something, most of the time that lady's half bombed out of her brain.'

On the end of the telephone line, Clyde Tolson wiped his hand across his forehead. He was starting to panic.

'Do you think she'll talk?' Tolson asked.

After a moments silence, Stiller replied.

'I think she'll answer any question they throw at her.'

Tolson took a deep breath, and then he made a decision.

'We can't afford any repercussions. We can't let her do any more interviews. It could all blow up over Kennedy. When she gets back from New York, I need you to take her out of the equation, Stiller. We need to shut her up for good.'

Another three days passed by, and then Marilyn returned home.

The next evening, Stiller, Sloan and Hughes sat in their rented car and waited. It was midnight, the air was hot and still and it was quiet. But that was no surprise really. Brentwood was a nice, quiet sort of neighbourhood. Quiet and very private.

Agent Hughes got out of the car and wandered over to the fence at 12305 Fifth Helena Drive.

Through the trees, he could see that all the lights were still on at the Monroe house. He walked back to the car and reported to Stiller.

'We'll wait a while longer,' said Stiller. 'I doubt if she'll have any visitors after one o' clock.'

An hour later, the three of them got out of the car and walked around the property to where the fence gave easy access. Once they were in the garden they stayed behind the trees and watched. Things were going pretty much to a routine in Marilyn's house. The lights were all blazing away, and so was Marilyn really. There was music playing and Marilyn was swaying around the house with a glass in one hand and a bottle of vodka in the other. At the other end of the Hacienda, the housekeeper, Eunice Murray, lay on the top of her bed trying to read a magazine. But she was having difficulty. On her dressing table was a nearly empty bottle of white rum and quite a few discarded bottles of Coca Cola. They watched as Eunice finally got off the bed and tottered into the kitchen. Moments later she returned with a second bottle of Bacardi's finest.

They waited for almost another hour. By then the music had stopped and Marilyn had returned to her bedroom and had managed to close the curtains.

At a quarter to two, Stiller checked his watch.

'Okay, put on your gloves, let's go,' he said to Sloan and Hughes.

They crept silently from behind the citrus trees and made their way to the back of the house.

Sloan took out a key pick to gain entry, but when he checked the handle, the door wasn't even locked.

Stiller turned to the two agents.

'Sloan, you come with me. Hughes, you go and check on the housekeeper. If she wakes up, slug her. We'll slide her into the swimming pool later. Make it look like a drunken accident.'

Hughes nodded.

They entered the house and walked down the hallway. Stiller and Sloan went left into Marilyn's bedroom, and Hughes turned right, towards the housekeeper's room. As Stiller and Sloan entered her room, Marilyn was lying on her bed, she was asleep. On the dressing table were a couple of empty bottles of vodka. On her side table next to her phone were half a dozen bottles of pills. Stiller picked two up and examined them. The FBI report had been correct, a mixture of different barbiturates and tranquillizers.

Stiller then took off his jacket. Underneath he was wearing a simple white shirt and a brown tie, all very unassuming. He reached into his jacket pocket and took out a small cardboard box. Inside, there were two glass bottles and a syringe.

The FBI had always retained a small but highly efficient Toxicology department. Poisons and various toxins were always available, and in many different forms.

It seemed that in the real world, the courts couldn't deal with everyone fairly and justly, not when some very smart lawyer was there on hand and made available. Sometimes, there were other ways to bring a felon to justice.

Stiller had rung Tolson and told him what he needed. The next day the box arrived at Stiller's office, packed into an FBI pouch.

Stiller looked across at Sloan.

'Pass me one of those empty glasses off the dressing table,' he said quietly.

Agent Sloan obliged.

Stiller took one of the bottles out of the box. He unscrewed the top and poured a light brown liquid into the glass. Then he turned to Marilyn and gently shook her arm.

'Wake up,' he said in a low voice. 'It's time to wake up, Marilyn.'

He did this twice, and finally her eyes fluttered as she regained consciousness.

'Wake up Marilyn,' said Stiller softly, 'wake up please.'

Her eyes slowly opened, but she was disorientated and slightly confused. She stared up at Stiller but she didn't recognize him.

'Who...who are you...what's happening?' she asked through glazed eyes.

'It's alright Marilyn,' Stiller crooned. 'I'm a doctor, you've not been well. Your doctor, Dr Engelberg has sent me. He's on his way over here now. He's told me to give you this medicine.'

At the mention of her own doctor's name, Marilyn sighed and calmed down a little. But she didn't really understand.

'Listen to me Marilyn, you've got to drink this in one go. That's what Dr Engelberg said, 'All in one go.'

Marilyn listened, but she just lay there. So Stiller put his arm around her shoulders and slowly lifted her forwards. Then he put the glass to her lips.

'Come on Marilyn, all in one go. That's it, and then you can go back to sleep.'

He poured the liquid into her mouth and Marilyn swallowed. She would have swallowed anything. She lay back on the bed and the two men stood there and watched her. A couple of minutes later her eyes suddenly fluttered open, and she groaned and she arched her back, almost in convulsion. And then just as quickly she fell back, her eyes now wide open, but she was still breathing.

Sloan stared down at her.

'What the hell did you give her?' he asked Stiller.

'Liquid heroin,' Stiller replied. 'You could hit her with a baseball bat now and she wouldn't feel a thing. She's out of it, and she can't move and she can't speak.'

He then took the other bottle out of the box, along with the syringe. The bottle had a thin rubber seal. Stiller pressed the needle through the seal and filled the syringe. He then injected the whole of it into Marilyn's arm. She didn't move. She never even blinked.

Stiller stood up and he and Sloan stood there and waited. In less than a couple of minutes her breathing became irregular, and then she began to take very short sharp breaths. Her eyes were still wide open, but there was no reaction at all. And then suddenly, she stopped breathing altogether. She simply died. And for one of America's most iconic actresses, it was all over.

Sloan glanced at Conrad Stiller.

'That's it. She's dead,' said Stiller. And he leant over and closed her eyelids.

'What was in the syringe?' Sloan asked.

'Nembutal, in liquid form,' Stiller replied. 'I've used it before.'

'And what actually is it?' Agent Sloan was curious.

It's what's she been taking in those little bottles. It's what been prescribed to her by her doctor and her psychiatrist. I've just bumped up the dosage and sent it straight into her heart, plus the heroin, of course. It'll just look like suicide, a drug overdose.'

Stiller picked up the two bottles and the syringe and put them back inside the box.

'Come on, let's go,' he said to Sloan.

As they were leaving the room, Stiller stopped. He handed the box to Sloan and then went back to Marilyn's body. He took the phone off the side table and placed it on her bed, then he turned her on her side and pushed the receiver between her ear and the pillow. It was as though she'd died just as she was about to ring someone.

'Nice touch,' said Sloan.

They walked back into the hallway to see Hughes standing in the doorway of the housekeeper's room.

'What's happening?' asked Stiller.

'Agent Hughes just shrugged his shoulders and he grinned.

'No need to do anything,' he said. 'She's completely out of it.'

'That's good,' said Stiller. 'Let's keep it nice and simple.'

And although the housekeeper, Eunice Murray, would never realize it, on that particular evening, Bacardi had saved her life.

Stiller, Sloan and Hughes flew back to Washington the next day, just as the news was breaking about the tragic suicide of Miss Marilyn Monroe.

Apparently, drugs were involved.

Despite the speculation and the controversy, Kennedy's presidency continued. And whatever was said at Marilyn Monroe's final interview with Time Magazine, nothing derogatory about the President was ever printed. After all, Marilyn was now dead and she couldn't defend herself. But the Kennedy's could, and in court it could have cost the magazine millions of dollars in damages. A possibility that could have made Time Magazine rethink its editorial.

But then, two months later, all hell broke loose as the world was almost plunged into a nuclear war.

'The 'Cuban Missile Crisis' as it became known, was brought about when it was discovered that the Russians were placing nuclear missiles on Cuban soil. And Cuba of course, was only a stone's throw away from the

American mainland. From there, the Russians could have targeted any of the major cities in the United States of America, and in simple terms of distance alone, during the 'first strike' they could have destroyed the whole country in one single attack.

Then it was discovered that more Russian cargo ships carrying nuclear missiles were heading directly for Cuba. The USA set up a naval blockade of the island and for almost two weeks the world held its breath as Russia and America traded verbal threats.

Kennedy at one point began to dither once again, and who could have blamed him. No other President in America's history had faced such challenges. But his administration and his advisers got behind him. They couldn't afford another 'Bay of Pigs' fiasco. Not at this level. And from there, Kennedy was made to stand his ground and face up to his presidential responsibilities. Not that the American public realized what was actually going on at the White House at the time. The public relations people then got together and wrote Kennedy a brilliantly powerful speech, which was aired on national television and was then seen all over the world.

His words..."*It shall be the policy of this nation to regard any nuclear missile launched from Cuba against any nation in the Western Hemisphere as an attack by the Soviet Union on the United States, thus requiring a full retaliatory response upon the Soviet Union.*"

Kennedy was the consummate actor and showman. And he pulled it off. The Russian ships turned around and crept back home. And for the American public, John F. Kennedy became a hero.

Eventually, the whole affair died down and most people went back to work generally got on with their lives. However, in the dark halls of Washington there were mutterings, and in the higher echelon of the military, there was again complete bewilderment. This whole escapade should never have happened. It was Cuba once again. And the man behind it all was as ever, Fidel Castro.

The general consensus of the military and the government in opposition was that Cuba was a complete disaster, and would continue to be so.

There were many who still despaired over the 'Bay of Pigs' debacle. In their view, Kennedy should not have stood down. And now, because of what had just happened, there should be a full military invasion of the island and Cuba should be taken back under American control. The Russians had all left, they no longer had any standing there and Fidel Castro could have been overthrown and probably tied to a tree and shot. In the military's eyes, it was Kennedy who was at fault. His indecision had let the Russians get a foothold in Cuba and had led to Russian nuclear missiles being placed just a hundred miles away from the American coast.

And so the question was put to Kennedy again. Now was the perfect time to invade Cuba. The Russians had left and they certainly wouldn't return in a hurry. The time was right for America to invade Cuba and finally rid themselves of Castro for once and for all.

But Kennedy would hear none of it. He didn't want to become involved with Cuba again. And with that he refused the military option, and the opportunity was once again missed.

Suddenly, Kennedy's ability to lead the nation was being questioned, and in higher office, the opposition was growing.

None so much as over in FBI headquarters and at the office of J. Edgar Hoover. The initial reports that Hoover had received over Kennedy's floundering during the missile crisis had infuriated him. In a private meeting with Clyde Tolson, Hoover had ranted and raged over Kennedy's weaknesses and inadequacies. The problem was that the White House had skilfully stage-managed the President. And after Kennedy's 'clever little speech' to the nation, the general public now perceived him as their champion.

But for Hoover, the decision still stood, Kennedy would have to go, one way or another, and now more than ever. And once they got rid of Kennedy, Vice president Lyndon B. Johnson would have to step up take his place. Hoover considered that Johnson was the better man, and he could work with Johnson, at least for the time being.

However, Edgar J. Hoover had made a new friend, a future president in the making, and someone who was as sharp as he was honest. His name was Richard Nixon, a man whose credentials were almost unimpeachable.

At the end of their discussions that day, Hoover spoke to his assistant director, Clyde Tolson.

'Clyde, something's got to be done.' Hoover shook his head in despair. He'd had enough of Kennedy. It was time to put his plan into action

'Clyde, will you speak to 'our friend', please.'

Tolson nodded. He knew exactly what to do. Once again he would contact Conrad Stiller.

Two weeks later, Clyde Tolson and Conrad Stiller met again in the 'Rib Room' Restaurant at the Mayflower Hotel in Washington. It was just after three o'clock in the afternoon and the restaurant was reasonably empty. And that suited both of them.

Since Tolson wasn't dining with his boss, he insisted that they both ordered fillet steak, accompanied by a good bottle of Claret. Conrad Stiller would have been just as happy with a hamburger, but he wasn't complaining.

Eventually, their conversation turned to politics. Tolson expressed the gathering reservations as to Kennedy's ability to lead the nation, now that his competency was being questioned. There were many in Washington who were unhappy about the direction that the President was taking the country. And there were many in the military who were simply appalled and disgusted at Kennedy's apathy when under pressure. In their eyes, it was almost a dereliction of duty.

'At least the Monroe's things over,' said Stiller, as he pushed his steak around his plate.

'Well, yes, that's one less problem,' Tolson replied, as he quickly wiped his mouth with a napkin. 'The thing is with Kennedy, he can't keep it in his pants. And it won't be long before he's chasing some other woman's tail.'

Stiller grinned. 'Well let's hope it's someone a little less well known.'

'Actually, there's a lot more to this than just Kennedy's affairs.' Tolson continued. 'There are a lot of people who were unhappy in the way Kennedy dealt with the 'Bay of Pigs', and now of course, we've had the Cuban Missile Crisis. You know he nearly screwed up again. When it came to it, he hadn't got the balls to make a simple decision. The man's weak, Stiller. Thank god there were others there to hold his hand and advise him.'

'Yes, I heard about that,' Stiller replied, 'I believe that Kennedy got the jitters again. And yes 'thank Christ' that somebody wrote him that speech, it was brilliantly done. Anyway, I suppose it's all over now and that's the end of it. Just another pack of lies for the history books.'

Clyde Tolson looked across the table at Stiller, and he thought for a moment before he spoke.

What he was about to say would change the face of America, its politics and its future.

'No, actually, that's not the end of it,' said Tolson hesitantly. 'A decision has been made. We need a better President. And we've got to get rid of Kennedy.'

Conrad Stiller never even blinked.

For the next half an hour, both men discussed aspects of the presidency and the direction in which Kennedy had taken the country. Tolson made it sound more like a capitulation. And after his term in office as President, it would be a sure bet that Kennedy would want to promote his younger brother, Robert, as the next President-elect. And that would mean more years of mismanagement.

Stiller listened. Finally he leant forward, because no one had to hear what he was about to say.

'So Tolson, let's just get this clear. And this is between you and me only. You're asking me to rid the country of Kennedy, for good?'

Tolson stared back at him.

'Yes I am,' he replied.

Stiller took a deep breath.

'It's going to cost a lot of money.'

'We know that,' Tolson replied. 'Funds will be made available.'

'This can't happen overnight, it's not like Monroe,' said Stiller cautiously. 'It will take a huge amount of planning, and it will have to be done right. There have to be no repercussions, and we must make sure that nothing can ever lead back to us. Nothing at all'

'Of course. We understand that and we fully agree.' Tolson replied.

Stiller finished the last of his wine, and then rather uncharacteristically, he shook Clyde Tolson's hand.

'Okay, I'm done here,' he said to Tolson, and with that, he pushed his plate to one side. 'I've got to get back to my office. I've got a lot to do.'

Their meeting was over.

'I'll be in touch,' he said to Tolson, and then he stood up and walked out of the restaurant.

Clyde Tolson sat there and watched Stiller leave. And he wondered about the decision that he'd just set in motion. Stiller had been right. They would have to cover their tracks. He pondered over it for a moment as he too drank the last of his wine. Then he caught the waiter's attention. Clyde Tolson suddenly felt the need for something sweet.

Maybe some pie.

Conrad Stiller didn't go back to his office. Well, certainly not straight away. Instead, he made his way to Washington's Central Park. It was all part of his method. When he had a problem, Stiller liked to stroll around the park on his own. It somehow cleared his mind and helped him process his thoughts. He would sit on a bench near the Washington Monument, or he could walk to the other end of the park and look at the Capital or further to the Lincoln Memorial.

On that particular afternoon, Conrad Stiller had a lot on his mind. He realized that his earlier conversation with Clyde Tolson had just opened a lot of doors. Doors that could never be closed. For Conrad Stiller, the time had finally arrived. This was the big one. He'd always known that something like this would come along. But he'd always expected to be asked to arrange the assassination of another country's President. Certainly not his own.

Conrad Stiller had always lived a rather complex life. During the Second World War, he'd worked in Intelligence and had quickly risen to the rank of Lieutenant. In fact, he was one of the youngest lieutenants in the United States Army, where he was considered to be somewhat of a 'rising star'. But when the War finally ended, Stiller suddenly found himself at somewhat of a loose end. At some point, he realized that he would be conscripted out of the army and he had to consider his future. The possible options were to go into Law or maybe Journalism, and he hadn't much enthusiasm for either. Life for Conrad Stiller was about to become rather boring, and after the excitement of the War, this wasn't what he'd really envisaged.

And then suddenly, he was offered another option.

In 1945, President Truman worked with the United States Army to initiate a newer and more functional intelligence agency. From there, the 'Counter Intelligence Corp', or the CIC as it became known, was then formed. In future days the CIC would become the basis for the CIA.

And because Conrad Stiller had already been working for Army

Intelligence and he was young enough and bright enough, it was a natural progression for him to be asked to join the new agency, the 'CIC'. After a 'bedding in' period of several months, Stiller was given his own project and his own small department, which at first actually only consisted of one shared secretary. But that suited Conrad Stiller just fine. The project that he was given was somewhat sensitive.

At the end of the war, the high ranking Nazi leaders were all rounded up and were charged with 'crimes against humanity' at the infamous Nuremberg trials. However, there were many who escaped and fled, and then there were hundreds of lesser-known Nazi officials who had simply disappeared into thin air. Some changed their names, some moved away, and others simply ran off to another country. And in those towns and villages throughout Europe which were still sympathetic to the Nazi cause, those same people would become councillors and bank managers and business owners, all in an effort to disguise their past. Men who had tortured and murdered thousands of human beings in the camps were now vying to become respectable citizens. And it was beginning to work.

Conrad Stiller was charged with the job of finding those same Nazis. Many would never go to court. Those living abroad were usually in countries that had no extradition laws and were untouchable. Places in Latin America, such as Argentina, Bolivia, Paraguay and Chile. All were havens for the escaped Nazis.

However, victims do have long memories. And a steady influx of information began to stream into the offices of the CIC, and in particular onto the desk of Lieutenant Conrad Stiller.

Before long, Conrad Stiller had two full-time secretaries.

It was once said that 'Information is power'. And it was during that period that Stiller realized the mammoth task that was ahead of him. And though he had all the vast facilities of his own Counter Intelligence Corp at hand, it wasn't enough. He needed multinational cooperation. And to that end, he contacted his most obvious ally, the British Secret Service.

The British themselves had set up a new counter intelligence department. It would be known as MI6. And within that department, there was another lieutenant who had been similarly disenchanted at the thought of being eventually relegated back to civilian life. He too had jumped at the chance of a new position within the newly formed MI6.

And in the strangest twists of fate, that was how Conrad Stiller had first met the man who would be his longtime counterpart at British Intelligence.

The man in question was Lieutenant Vernon Ballantyne.

Stiller had managed to get himself onto an American Air Force carrier plane to London where he met up with Lieutenant Ballantyne. They came to an agreement immediately, both men were straight talkers and they were very efficient at what they did. It seemed that the British too were interested in the concept of bringing any former Nazis to justice. When the allied forces had discovered what had been happening in the Concentration Camps, they, along with the rest of the civilized world had been absolutely horrified at what they saw. And it had been deemed internationally that some sort of justice would be necessary.

Stiller and Ballantyne decided that the best way forward would be to share any information, totally. And already, a steady inflow of information was being accumulated via reports from both the English and American troops who were still serving throughout Europe and were dealing with the victims of Hitler's Nazi regime.

Stiller and Ballantyne formed their own alliance. Conrad Stiller flew back to the USA, armed with a list of names and the general whereabouts of several former Nazis. Once there, he sent back his own findings directly to Vernon Ballantyne in London.

However, their joint venture got off to a rather shaky start. In the first nine months they'd discovered the exact location of half a dozen different men, all living across Europe, and all who were wanted for crimes against humanity. But when it came to their arrest, each one had suddenly disappeared. They'd already been warned and had fled elsewhere.

Things finally came to a head with the capture of the French-born Nazi, Henri Rimbaud.

Rimbaud had been one of the senior Nazis in charge of the Natzweller-Struthof Concentration Camp in the Alsace region of France. The Struthof camp was the only true death camp to be created by the Nazis on French Territory. At least eighty six of the innocent Jewish prisoners who were imprisoned there were put to death in the gas chamber. Henri Rimbaud had been arrested and was being held at a local prison where he was awaiting trial. At this, their first success, Lieutenants Stiller and Ballantyne both flew out to Strasbourg, which was the nearest city with an airport. From there they were then driven to the town of Schirmeck, where Henri Rimbaud actually lived and where it had been decided that his trial would take place.

The trial itself was a complete farce. One by one, the Judge dismissed the witnesses, or at least those who were brave enough to turn up. And it turned out Henri Rimbaud was now a town councillor himself, and that half of the court and the jury were made up from the members of the Town Hall. In his final briefing, the Judge told the court that Henri Rimbaud had simply made a mistake. He'd made the wrong choice when he'd been coerced into helping the Nazis. As a cautionary lesson, Rimbaud was given a six months suspended sentence, and then he walked out of the court, a free man.

Conrad Stiller and Vernon Ballantyne immediately made their way back to Strasbourg. They were both incensed at what they'd seen. That evening they sat in a bar and drank several beers in an effort to contain their disappointment. Their enthusiasm was being slowly crushed and after the best part of a year, they'd not had one result. They both discussed that fact, and they both realized that at some point, the heads of their respective departments would be asking the same question. Why?

And at that moment, Lieutenant Stiller came up with a somewhat nondescript comment.

'We should just shoot the bastards,' he said to Vernon Ballantyne.

'Really,' said Ballantyne, in a casual 'English' sort of way.

'Yes, we should,' said Stiller. 'We're just wasting our time. If every time we find someone, and they know we're coming, they'll just disappear. And I'm not prepared to keep flying over to Europe if this is the way they're going to hand out justice. Christ, that bastard Rimbaud was responsible for the deaths of more than eighty innocent people, and then he walks away free. It's a damn disgrace.'

'Yes, it is,' Vernon Ballantyne agreed. 'And maybe you're right, maybe we should shoot them and just take them out of the equation, permanently.'

Stiller eyed Vernon Ballantyne for a moment.

'You serious, Ballantyne?'

'In truth, I don't really know,' Vernon Ballantyne replied, 'but I'll tell you something. I'm not prepared to carry on like this. It's just a complete waste of time.'

Stiller thought for a moment.

'You know Ballantyne, the way things are, what with the Nuremberg Trials and all. I do know that if I talked to some of my people back in the States, they would probably turn a blind eye to a few 'indiscretions'. As long as we came up with some results and that none of it was ever traceable.'

Vernon Ballantyne raised an eyebrow.

'Really...well that's quite interesting, Lieutenant Stiller.' And he smiled.

'How would it work your end?' Stiller then asked.

'Ah well,' said Ballantyne, 'You see, the British Intelligence and MI6 work slightly differently. Truth be known, I can do whatever I want. Nothing must be traceable of course. Well, certainly nothing that could cause any embarrassment to my government. But if I used a bit of discretion and gave a hint as to what was going on, everyone would generally look the other way and let us get on with it. And as you say, as long as we got some results instead of all this pussyfooting about.'

'So you're up for it?'

'Of course I am dear boy,' said Vernon Ballantyne, and then he laughed. 'The way I look at it, we've nothing to lose anyway.'

'And how would we go about it?' Stiller asked.

'It's quite simple really,' replied Ballantyne. 'We find out the exact whereabouts of our Nazi friends, and then we send somebody out there to shoot the bastards. And if we come across another of these 'smart buggers' who thinks he can bend the legal system, then we'll just shoot him before he ever gets to court.'

Stiller laughed at Vernon Ballantyne's seemingly casual attitude to everything.

'Okay,' said Stiller. 'When I get back to the States I'll put a plan into action. This puts a whole different aspect on things. And as well as that, I'll get onto our military. They can look through their records and find us a shooter, somebody who's pretty handy, maybe some sniper. We already have men stationed throughout Europe, there's bound to be somebody.'

Vernon Ballantyne looked back across the table at Conrad Stiller.

'You've no need to bother,' he said slowly.

'And why's that? Stiller asked.
'Because I already have someone.'
'Is he good?'
'Yes he is,' Vernon Ballantyne replied. 'He is without doubt, the very best.'

That had been almost eighteen years ago. And for Conrad Stiller, they had been very productive years. He and Vernon Ballantyne started to work together and were very successful in their never ending pursuit of those former Nazis who were in hiding all over the world. And to that end they'd used only one man for the job, Pieter Szabo.

In the latter years of the war, Vernon Ballantyne had sent Pieter Szabo to the Greek island of Crete to help the partisan forces there fight back the German troops. The inhabitants of the island were facing virtual starvation as the German invaders tried to bring them to their knees. But the Greek spirit would not submit and the partisans fought back as best they could. However, the reprisals taken against the Cretan population by the Germans were also appalling. In some cases the inhabitants of whole villages had been shot and their villages then burned to the ground. Pieter Szabo had been parachuted onto the island and had straightaway joined up with the partisans. From there he had taken a deadly toll on the German high command. He had one simple strategy, and that was to take out the officers, those who were in charge. Armed with his rifle, Pieter Szabo could shoot at a target from over a mile away. And it was always the same shot. He would put a bullet through the victim's head. It was the shot that would cause shock to others. To see the top of a man's head blown off was a stomach-wrenching sight, and it put the fear of God in the other commanders who realized that they too could be next. Being a mile away from his target meant that it didn't matter whether Pieter Szabo took the shot during the day or at night. And for the German officers there it soon became common practice, never to leave a light on in an open room at night.

At the end of the war the German forces in Crete surrendered. Pieter Szabo stayed on there for almost a year while the Allied troops took charge. But then he was once again recalled. Lieutenant Vernon Ballantyne required his services.

Pieter Szabo was immediately flown back to England. He finally landed at Croydon airport where he was met by a driver. This time however, he wasn't going back to his usual base of operations in Aylesbury. The driver took him directly into Central London to the offices of the newly formed MI6 at the Broadway Building in Westminster.

The Broadway Building, the actual address was 54 Broadway, was a large imposing stone affair with frosted glass windows. The driver pulled up outside and simply pointed to a door and told Pieter Szabo to go up to the fourth floor. Pieter picked up his pack and got out of the car. As he was about to enter the building through the front door, he noticed a brass plaque on the wall identifying it as the 'Minimax Fire Extinguisher Company', which he considered was a little strange. Inside, the building was quite old and dingy, and Pieter got into an ancient looking lift and pressed the appropriate button which took him up to the fourth floor. When the lift doors opened, Pieter was quite surprised to see that the place was bustling with people who seemed to be coming in and out of a host of different offices. A secretary noticed him immediately as he stepped out of the lift and was curious as to what he was doing there.

'Can I help you?' she asked, rather smartly.

Pieter Szabo blinked. 'I'm supposed to be meeting Lieutenant Ballantyne?'

The secretary stared at him for a moment.

'Come this way, please,' she said, in a somewhat different tone. And then, 'could you tell me your name, please.'

'My name is Pieter Szabo.' he replied.

'Alright then, Mr Szabo, just follow me, please.'

They walked down a well lit corridor of offices and at the end they stopped as the secretary tapped the glass on the door and opened it slightly.

Pieter heard her say, 'There's someone here called 'Pieter Szabo', to see you, Lieutenant.'

He heard the scrape of a chair and then Lieutenant Vernon Ballantyne's voice.

'Bring him in, straightaway,' said Ballantyne. And as Pieter entered the office, Vernon Ballantyne had already come around his desk and he met Pieter with a firm handshake.

'Mr Szabo,' he said heartily. 'It's good to see you.'

Then he turned to the secretary, 'Could you organize some coffee for us, my dear,' he asked pleasantly.

The secretary smiled and then obliged.

Vernon Ballantyne then turned back to Pieter.

'Have a seat,' he said, as he pointed at a chair. 'And tell me what you've been up to.'

An hour, and several cups of coffee later, Lieutenant Ballantyne was a more informed and wiser man. He was impressed by Pieter's work, some of which he already knew about from reports that had seeped back to England, all about the problems that the Germans had encountered on the island of Crete. And Vernon Ballantyne had always suspected that Pieter Szabo could have been the cause of many of those problems.

Vernon Ballantyne sat back in his chair as he contemplated the moment. It was all part of his plan, of course.

'And so Pieter,' he said eventually. 'What about the future? What now, now that the war is over?'

Pieter Szabo sat in his chair and shrugged.

'I don't know,' he replied, 'I've never given it much thought,' and then he laughed, 'I suppose I'll have to get a job somewhere. I once trained as a draughtsman, but I don't really know...' and his voice trailed away.

It was the perfect moment for Lieutenant Ballantyne to act.

'I may have something for you.'

Pieter looked up. 'You do?' he asked.

It was time for Vernon Ballantyne to tell Pieter Szabo all about his plans.

'We've formed a new agency here Pieter, it's known as MI6 and its part of British Intelligence. My job, our job is to hunt down all those missing Nazis who have escaped justice.'

Pieter stared at Vernon Ballantyne for a moment. This was a complete revelation to him.

Ballantyne continued.

'There are thousands out there that are still accountable for their actions. Many have gone to ground, others have managed to take positions of respectability and many have fled Europe entirely, and have travelled to places as far as South America.'

Pieter just sat there. He'd been totally unaware of everything that had been happening. With the end of the war, he'd naturally considered that all the Nazis would have been easily rounded up and hopefully hanged for their crimes. But apparently not.

Vernon Ballantyne waited for a moment before he spoke.

'Pieter, what I am about to tell you is of the utmost secrecy. Nobody must ever know what I am about to tell you.'

Pieter looked across at Vernon Ballantyne and he nodded.

'I have an associate in the United States. He works in counter intelligence there and we are both working together towards the same end. We are using joint intelligence to find these people, and up to a point it has been working fairly well. However, we have encountered major problems. Every time we go to arrest someone, they've already been alerted and they've simply disappeared. On the occasion we've managed to get anyone to court, the cases have been virtually dismissed. The judicial system in Europe is in a mess. I set up this department almost twelve months ago, Pieter, and it is with great disappointment I have to tell you that we and the Americans haven't made one significant arrest.

Pieter Szabo just sat there and listened.

Vernon Ballantyne continued.

'My counterpart in the States is a man called Stiller. We've met on several occasions. And the last time we met we came to a decision. We have to change our methods and things have got to be handled differently. So we have decided to take matters, slightly into our own hands. And our intentions in the future are that when we do discover some Nazi in hiding, we won't arrest them. No, what we intend to do is to send someone over there and just shoot them. 'Eliminate' is probably the better word.'

Pieter Szabo had been listening intently, and now he suddenly understood.

He looked across at Vernon Ballantyne.

'And I take it that you want me to do the 'elimination'.

'We do,' Ballantyne replied.

Pieter thought about it for a moment.

"I will need to be paid,' he said finally. 'The war is now over. And if this is going to be my new profession, I will need to be paid.'

'Funds will be made available,' Vernon Ballantyne replied. 'I have already spoken to Mr Stiller over in the States and he has confirmed that too. Don't worry Pieter, I will make certain that you're paid appropriately.'

It was now time for Vernon Ballantyne to lay out his plans.

'I have already sorted out your accommodation. You will be based in London, at least for the time being. We have secured you an apartment in Bermondsey. It's all furnished and taken care of. We will also open a couple of bank accounts for you and put some money in them. That should keep you going.'

Lieutenant Ballantyne took a key out of a drawer and slid it across his desk.

'That's the key to your apartment. I'll have a driver take you over there later.'

Pieter smiled. 'So you were pretty sure that I would take the job.'

Ballantyne grinned. 'Yes, reasonably sure,' he replied.

He then went on to explain the present position politically, and how everything was to be done undercover and had to be completely untraceable.

Pieter Szabo understood, he understood everything. He'd been a victim too. And he would gladly shoot any Nazi that he came across, be it for the British government or the Americans.

'There is just one more thing,' said Vernon Ballantyne finally. 'You will only ever work through me, Pieter. You will not work directly for any other agency, either the Americans or anyone else.'

Pieter nodded, but at that point he didn't really understand the Lieutenant's reasoning.

'Pieter, I don't trust anyone,' Ballantyne continued. 'Friends can very quickly become enemies, and times change and friends become foes. The Allies and the Russians are already at each other's throats and who knows where that will all end. If you only deal through me, nobody will ever know who you are. You yourself will become invisible and untraceable. And that will allow you to travel anywhere and go anywhere.'

Pieter again nodded. He could understand the sense in it.

'We will lose your name and you will work under a codename,' said Ballantyne. 'Your codename will be 'Eagle'. You must only ever work under that name. That way your identity will remain secure and protected. Do you understand me?'

'Yes, I understand,' Pieter replied, 'and I do realize the need for secrecy, Yes, that's okay.'

Everything was agreed, and fifteen minutes later both men shook hands and Pieter left the Broadway Building and was then met outside by a driver. From there he was taken across the River Thames to Bermondsey to his new home, and a new life.

It was a start.

All that had been eighteen years ago.

During those years, Pieter Szabo travelled the world. And he and Vernon Ballantyne and Conrad Stiller had been successful in their mission. And in the end, the Israelis assisted them too. They had been contacted by Mossad, the national intelligence agency of Israel, who readily bought into Conrad Stiller's slightly unethical but highly efficient method of ridding the world of those former Nazi perpetrators. And a method of funding was put into place. Funding that went directly to Conrad Stiller himself. And that had been the start of Stiller's business. And that business became very lucrative. Very much so for Mr Conrad Stiller.

Eighteen years later, and during those years, Conrad Stiller had moved from Counter Intelligence, and into the United States Secret Service. It had been a wise move, because it gave him the capacity and the freedom of movement that he needed.

And Conrad Stiller was running his nice little sideline, his own highly successful business.

It was a private company which he solely owned. There were no offices and there were no staff. Neither was there a business address or an open contact number. Conrad Stiller had set up a company known as 'System Securities Inc'. Stiller was the company's sole employee, in fact, he 'was' the company. And not only did System Securities Inc. work for the FBI, it also did work for several other different government agencies around the world. More than that, Stiller also had links with the Mafia and the criminal underworld too. Conrad Stiller was connected, and he was highly efficient and so was his company. And that was the reason why the FBI and the likes of Clyde Tolson used him when something extraordinary needed to be done.

And now he'd been asked to rid the country of its President. He'd always thought that something like this would come along. This was the one, and it would also be his last. After this he would close down the company and disappear. And he would have to. Stiller was well aware of how the

FBI worked. Once his work was done, he would be the one 'loose end', and that was something that the FBI wouldn't want. He knew that. And if Stiller was out of the way, any investigation would simply hit a brick wall. No, Conrad Stiller was nobody's fool, he knew what he would have to do. And to that end, he'd already acquired a second identity, passport and name. He would charge the FBI a million dollars prior to his services. And at the same time he would request an early retirement from the Secret Service. He'd done his time there. Then he'd move the remainder of his funds to his bank account in Switzerland where his money would be safer than anywhere else in the world. And then, after Kennedy was taken care of, he'd simply disappear. Preferably to somewhere warm, with a beach and where the sea was turquoise blue. The Caribbean was a possibility, or maybe even Australia.

But before any of that, Conrad Stiller would have to make a phone call to London, to the only man he could ever call a 'partner'. He had to speak to Vernon Ballantyne.

Conrad Stiller would need the services of the man whose codename was 'Eagle'.

CHAPTER 14

'Accept the things to which fate binds you, and love the people with whom fate brings you together...though into each life, some rain must fall...'

(mixed quotes)

New York City, 1963

It was late morning, on the Lower East Side District of New York. And in his apartment, Pieter Szabo sipped a cup of coffee as he sat reading the day's copy of the New York Times. The sun shone pleasantly through the apartment window and it was warm and comfortable and Pieter Szabo felt relaxed. He'd not worked for nearly a month, but that wasn't particularly unusual, and neither did it bother him. He didn't need the money. In fact, Pieter Szabo was quite a wealthy man, and at the back of his mind he always knew that at some point the phone would ring, because it always did. And it would always be the same person.

Pieter Szabo was now forty five years old and quickly approaching forty six. He was still fit, very fit in fact. But his face was beginning to give an indication of the life he'd lived and there was the odd fleck of grey in his once dark hair. Not that Pieter Szabo gave a damn.

And at times, he would quietly reflect on how different the first twenty years of his life had been, as opposed to the last twenty years. For the first twenty years, he'd lived quietly within the bosom of his loving family. The last twenty years however, had been rather more tumultuous. Pieter Szabo had travelled the world, working from the information that he'd received directly from the counter intelligence agencies of Britain, America and

Israel. And armed with that information, and along with his rifle, he'd crossed the continents in pursuit of those former Nazis who thought that they were safe. The ones who thought they'd got away with their crimes.

In later years though, Vernon Ballantyne and his American contact, only known to Pieter as 'Stiller', had together used Pieter Szabo's skills for slightly different purposes. Pieter had been employed to eliminate certain political undesirables who were promoting terrorism in countries friendly to the United States and Great Britain alike. And Lieutenant Ballantyne too had sent Pieter to Northern Ireland on several occasions, in a bid to halt the rise of the IRA. For Pieter Szabo it was merely a job. These people were just names to him. And he justified his actions simply on the understanding that they were very bad individuals. And if truth be known, he simply didn't care. He was getting paid handsomely to do something he was very good at. And in a cold and calculating way, it had become almost entertaining to him. Pieter Szabo held no fear anymore. He was a paid killer. He had no one to worry about but himself. And he'd always considered the obvious. That at some point his luck would run out. But a bullet to the head was quick. He knew that.

Pieter Szabo lived at three separate residences, where he lived at different times of the year, or whichever suited the contract that he was working on at the time. He still lived at his original apartment in London, just across the river in Bermondsey. It was in theory still government owned, but Vernon Ballantyne had made sure that the deeds to the apartment, the paperwork, and all of the expenses in running the property were buried so deep that the British government would never know that it actually still belonged to them. Vernon Ballantyne had also made sure that he was the only person who knew that Pieter Szabo lived there.

  Pieter however, owned two more properties which nobody else knew about. And one of those was his apartment on the Lower East Side District of New York City. Over the years Vernon Ballantyne and Conrad Stiller had supplied Pieter with the false passports that would enable him to travel around the world. Also included had been the residency papers and the birth certificates to back everything up. Pieter Szabo, under a long list of assumed names, was not only a resident of Poland, Germany and England, but also of America, Spain and even Argentina. It had been recommended that Pieter should be taught to speak Spanish fluently, a language that came in handy as he travelled the length and breadth of South America. When contracted there, Pieter had always flown directly to Argentina, and because of his citizenship there, it had never been a problem. From there he could take untraceable flights to Paraguay, Colombia and Brazil.

His comfortable apartment in New York was registered under his assumed American name as belonging to 'Mr Ernest Heller'. Pieter had the paperwork of course, and he also had an appropriate bank account in the New York branch of The Bank of America. Everything was, as always, correct and above suspicion.

Vernon Ballantyne knew that Pieter Szabo spent a certain amount of time in the United States and he also knew that Pieter had some sort of accommodation in New York City. But he didn't know just where, and he was certainly never going to inform Conrad Stiller.

However, Pieter Szabo had a 'third' property, and it was the nearest thing that he could ever think of as his true home. At one point, Pieter had returned to Spain, back to where he'd discovered some kind of peace and calm as he and his father had fled to Gibraltar before finally sailing to England. He'd gone back to Catalonia, and from Barcelona, he travelled south heading for Valencia. He drove along the winding coastal road with the warm breeze drifting across his face. En route he discovered the harbour town of Benicassim. He'd stopped, and he'd stayed.

Benicassim was a small fishing town with only a dozen or so ageing wooden boats there, all of which had seen better days On the tiny harbour front there were a couple of bars and a cafe, the 'Cafe Maximo'. The food there was good and the cafe owner, his name was Maximo Baroja, had a room to rent. Pieter stayed, and in the evenings he would sit with the fishermen and listen to their stories and the gossip. The locals seemed to accept him and Pieter felt at ease. He used the same name that was on his Spanish passport, which declared that he was 'Mr Pedro Rivas'. But nobody believed that for one moment, and nobody asked, or cared.

A month passed evenly by, during which time Pieter helped the fishermen with their boats and nets, and then later he would sit and eat their freshly caught fish at Maximo's Cafe. Sometimes he liked to walk up into the hills and take in the surrounding countryside. He would stand and look down at the azure blue sea below him and appreciate the pleasure in its beauty. And slowly, Pieter began to realize that he loved the country and its people.

One afternoon as he was walking, he came across a small and almost hidden road. It had been an entrance, possibly to a field. There was a broken gate there and the road itself had fallen foul to Mother Nature and was almost completely overgrown. Curiosity, for once, got the better of Pieter Szabo and he pushed the remains of the gate out of the way and made his way through the waist-high grass and along what he could see of the road. At one point he considered that he was wasting his time, but then again, he had all the time in the world and so he carried on, it would be a challenge. The road seemed to turn sharply to the right and was shaded by two large trees that almost formed an arch above him. Pieter made his way past them and then he stopped in his tracks. There in front of him, hidden and forgotten, stood a derelict farmhouse that at one time must have been quite a substantial building. Pieter was quite taken aback when he saw it, and he stood there for a while, just staring at the property. And then, for whatever reason, he decided to explore. He pushed his way through the long grass and up to the steps that led onto the remains of a large veranda that led into the house. Half the roof was missing and Pieter could hear the sound of birds rustling about in the upstairs rooms. The entrance to the house was through a set of faded green double doors that were held together by rusted locks. Pieter forced the doors open, and then felt a pang of guilt as he realized that he was breaking into somebody else's house, and for a brief moment he remembered his own house back in Poland, and he wondered who lived there now.

But as he looked around, he quickly recognized the fact that nobody had actually lived there for a very long time. He wandered around the place, everything was old and broken and he wondered about the people who must have lived here at one time, and once again he thought of Poland, and of the old house there that he would never return to. Finally, he went back onto the veranda and looked out in awe. There were clear views all the way down to the sea, a mile and a half below. It was staggeringly beautiful, and peaceful.

That evening, Pieter spoke to the cafe owner, Maximo Baroja, and he asked him about the old farmhouse up on the hill. Maximo, of course, knew the house and the family that owned it.

Maximo Baroja knew everything that happened in Benicassim and he knew everyone who lived there. He was a large man, typically Spanish, and with a head of prematurely silver grey hair. It would be hard to judge Maximo's age, but Pieter considered that he was possibly in his early fifties.

Pieter had made a decision. If there was the possibility of buying the house, he would be interested. Maximo promised to speak to the owners, who apparently also owned the adjoining farm. Two days later, Maximo told Pieter that he had arranged a meeting with the family at Maximo's Cafe, of course, and he advised Pieter that he should provide food and wine for the family. Pieter grinned at Maximo's resourcefulness, but he agreed to the meeting and so it was arranged.

The following evening Pieter met the farmer, Arturo Cercas, a small and unassuming man who had brought along with him his family, a wife, a son and a daughter.

Maximo introduced everyone and then served the food and then sat himself down at their table and ate too. It seemed to be the Spanish way of doing things. After Maximo's delicious food and a couple of bottles of wine, the conversation flowed. Pieter learnt that the farm actually belonged to Arturo Cercas's grandparents and that there were nearly twenty hectares of land surrounding the farm. When Arturo's grandparents had died, the house was just left empty and time and nature had taken its toll. The family still used the land, but not the house.

The negotiations began, and eventually, it came down to the price. At that point, Maximo decided to become the mediator.

A price was mentioned, it was an inflated figure, but Maximo had to explain to Pieter that the family would be losing a large piece of land and hence their income. They were not wealthy people. Arturo Cercas nodded, as his two children stared at their father and then back at Pieter. Mrs Cercas just sat there, nervously silent.

Pieter said nothing. He realized that this was the obvious time to barter, but he'd observed the family in front of him. They were poor. And living off the land in Spain was a very hard life. That he knew. And so he took a deep breath.

'I will pay you the full asking price,' he said to Arturo Cercas.

Arturo Cercas sat there as his eyes widened. His wife immediately looked at him, it was as though she didn't understand. In truth, Arturo

Cercas thought that the negotiations would take all night. He'd never thought that Pieter would ever agree to the first price put on the table.

In truth, Arturo would have accepted half the named amount, he needed the money, and he was staggered by the offer, but there was more to come.

Pieter looked at Maximo for a moment, and then back to Arturo Cercas. 'I will give you the full asking price,' he said, and then he smiled. 'And I will give you back the land.'

Arturo Cercas couldn't believe what he'd just heard, and he and his wife just sat there open-mouthed. It was Maximo who broke the moment. He laughed out loud and slapped Pieter across the back.

'Well done my friend, well done.' And then he shouted into the kitchen for someone to bring more wine.

Arturo and his family began to laugh too. This good fortune would change their life, considerably.

Pieter shrugged, 'I'm not a farmer,' he said, 'I wouldn't even know what to do with the land.' And then he laughed too. At that moment, Arturo Cercas's young daughter stood up and went over to Pieter and shook his hand and quickly kissed him on the cheek and smiled. She somehow reminded him of when his own little sister, Elise, had been the same age. And Pieter smiled back at her as he realized that he'd done the right thing by them. Benicassim was a small town, and he'd not only bought a property, he'd also bought into a community. And he also knew Maximo Baroja, by tomorrow everybody in the town would know about the house and the land that had been given back to the family. Pieter Szabo had not only bought a house, unknowingly, he'd also bought respect.

However, on that morning as he sat in his Lower East Side apartment in New York, Pieter Szabo's mind was on other things rather than Spain.

Later, he would go to his bank to check his balance and make sure that the money had gone into his account.

A month earlier, Conrad Stiller had requested the services of the 'Eagle'. There was another contract to fulfil. And once again he'd rung Vernon Ballantyne in London.

Pieter's phone had then rung in New York and Ballantyne's familiar voice had asked 'Eagle?'

Pieter was given a number on which to ring Conrad Stiller. Pieter would as always, call Stiller from a phone box somewhere and then receive his instructions.

And once Pieter's work had been accomplished, Stiller's company, 'System Securities Inc', would pay a specified sum of money into Vernon Ballantyne's personal account at his private bank, based in the Isle of Man. From there, Vernon Ballantyne would then pay Pieter Szabo a lesser specified amount into the bank account of Pieter's choice, be it in England or the United States.

The Isle of Man is a small island off the North West coast of Britain, which is still part of Britain, but by some historical quirk of fate, has its own separate banking and tax system. It is a smaller version of Switzerland, and just like Switzerland, it holds great wealth, usually for people who want to avoid the British tax system.

Vernon Ballantyne was one of those people.

Ballantyne was now married to a woman who he didn't particularly like, and he had two sons whom he adored. He'd used up a considerable amount of his government salary and savings because of buying his wife the 'right' house, and also by sending both of his sons to the 'right' universities. But it was only a matter of time. Vernon Ballantyne had siphoned away enough money to keep him in clover for the rest of his life. And when the time was right and his sons had become self-financing, Lieutenant Vernon Ballantyne would 'close the shop' and retire. And having to give his miserable wife half of the house would be the least of his worries.

So on that particular morning, and after reading the pages of the New York Times that interested him, Pieter finished off his cup of coffee and then headed for the shower. Half an hour later he was showered and dressed and heading for the door, newspaper in hand. It was by then early afternoon, and as usual, he took the three flights of stairs down to the ground floor. For some reason he rarely used the lift, and anyway, going up and down the stairs kept him fit. He stepped out of his apartment building and into the dazzling bright sunshine. It was going to be another beautiful day.

And that was when fate stepped in and decided to play Pieter Szabo its finest ace.

Whenever he travelled around New York City, Pieter liked to take the bus.

He'd always found the subway too manic, and Pieter Szabo was never in a hurry to go anywhere really. He would sit on the bus along with the regular New Yorkers and listen to the gossip as he continued to read his folded newspaper. It was a habit he enjoyed.

Pieter's branch of the 'Bank of America' was up in Manhattan, over on 8th Avenue. And with that in mind, he turned left out of his apartment building and headed down the street towards his usual bus stop. It would take him about ten minutes, a pleasant enough stroll on a sunny day. And as he walked, he started to think about his last contract.

He'd flown out to Las Vegas about a month ago. He'd been given a name and a general location. The rest had been up to him.

The target was a man called Salvatore 'Sonny' Cullotta, an obvious Italian, with a dubious past, no doubt. But Pieter Szabo was not employed to ask the reason why? Other heads had already made that decision. No, it was Pieter Szabo's job to implement that decision, and as efficiently as possible. However, over a period of time, Pieter had also realized that he was no longer just chasing Nazis. Over the last few years he'd been contacted to eliminate several similar targets in major cities all across America. All were Italian, and Pieter quickly realized that he was being employed to assassinate certain members of 'the mob'. And from there it was an easy assumption to figure out that Stiller had direct links to the mob and that he must be dealing with the Mafia.

It wasn't hard for Pieter to find 'Sonny' Cullotta.

Mr 'Sonny' Cullotta lived a very high profile lifestyle. In fact, anybody who was anybody in Las Vegas knew Sonny Cullotta, and most of them quite rightly feared him. Sonny Cullotta was the right-hand man and enforcer for the mobster who ran the whole of Las Vegas for the Chicago Mafia. He was Tony Spilotro. However, it now seemed that Sonny Cullotta had bigger and better plans, plans of his own. He'd decided that he wanted to run Las Vegas, and that he would get rid of Tony Spilotro.

Unfortunately for him, Tony Spilotro had already found out. Spilotro, in turn, took a flight to Chicago to meet up with the Mafia Godfather, the one and only Sam Giancana. Giancana had his own ideas on who should be running Las Vegas and it certainly wasn't going to be 'Sonny' Cullotta. Sam Giancana then gave Tony Spilotro his blessing and told him not to worry. Giancana then contacted Conrad Stiller at System Securities Inc, a company that he'd used very successfully in the past. He and Stiller had spoken, they were after all 'friends'.

And Stiller had promised Sam Giancana that everything would be taken care of.

It turned out that Sonny Cullotta was a creature of habit, like a lot of people really. And Sonny liked to take long lunches at 'Giuseppe's Family Trattoria', a well respected Italian Restaurant on the corner of Flamingo Road West. He would usually arrive there with his entourage at around one 'o clock in the afternoon, and then he would stay there for a couple of hours, along with his band of ardent followers, as they ate Giuseppe's authentic Italian meatballs and discussed Tony Spilotro's downfall. And come three o' clock, when the food was finally finished and the plotting was done, they would all leave.

So, for Pieter Szabo, it was all really quite simple. He booked himself into a nondescript hotel about a quarter of a mile down the road from Giuseppe's Italian Restaurant. He took a front facing room on the fourth floor that looked down towards the restaurant's entrance, and then with the help of a pair of binoculars, he just watched and waited.

Pieter had followed Sonny Cullotta for three days and he'd discovered Cullotta's regular dining routine. And then from his hotel window, Pieter had watched Cullotta as he arrived at Giuseppe's on the Thursday and Friday, again arriving at one and leaving at around three. Saturday and Sunday were a no-show. Obviously, like all good Italians. Sonny Cullotta would be at home, dining with his family.

But on the Monday, Cullotta returned, and then again on Tuesday. However, this time Pieter wasn't watching him through his binoculars. This time he was looking at Cullotta through the telescopic sights of his rifle. And at three o' clock on the Tuesday afternoon, Sonny Cullotta came out of the restaurant as usual. Ever the man of habit, Cullotta had the same routine whenever he left Giuseppe's restaurant. He would step out into the sunshine, and as his driver came to pick him up, Sonny Cullotta would stop and look up to the sky, and then give a loud belch in appreciation of the delicious food that he'd just eaten.

And on that Tuesday afternoon, as Sonny stood there, momentarily still, he proceeded to let out his usual belch. And at that same moment,

Pieter Szabo pulled the trigger and put a bullet straight through Sonny Cullotta's head.

Panic then ensued. Cullotta's body was dragged into the car and driven off at speed. Some of his men followed him. Others were looking upwards to try to find out where the shot had come from. No one even considered the possibility of it being somewhere down the block, a quarter of a mile away. But for Pieter Szabo, the shot was as simple as swatting a fly away from his face.

Several minutes later, Pieter had hidden the binoculars under the bed, and had left the hotel. He was wearing a worn hat and a long coat, and he walked with a slight stoop. No one would give a second glance to an old man with a walking stick, carrying a bag that contained an old broken clock.

That had been almost a month ago. And the usual protocol was that the money would now be placed in Pieter Szabo's New York bank account.

Pieter strolled up to the bus stop and stood in the short queue of people that were presumably also heading uptown. As he stood there, he again thought about his trip to the bank. The money would be there, it was always there, he knew that wouldn't be a problem. But once he got to the bank he would, as usual, relocate most of his money elsewhere.

Pieter had always had his contract money paid into his banks in either New York or London. But then he would transfer a sizeable amount of it into a private bank account in Switzerland. In Switzerland his money was safe, untraceable, and tax-free. And once the money was safely secured there, Pieter would ring his bank in Switzerland and provide them with a password, and then he would transfer another specified amount to Spain, to his private account there at the Bank of Bilbao.

Once there, the money in Spain had been used over the years to slowly transform his derelict property into a beautifully restored farmhouse. The whole house had been totally refurbished. There was now a stone paved road which led through imposing wrought iron gates, directly to the front of the property. At the entrance to the house was a large new veranda which took in the views down the hillside and all the way down to the sea. And below the veranda there were beautifully tended gardens. Pieter always smiled when he thought about the gardens. His part-time gardener was in fact, Arturo Cercas's teenage daughter, the daughter of the farmer who'd sold Pieter the farmhouse. Teresa, now nineteen, looked after the house and the gardens for Pieter whilst he was away. But it hadn't started well. After a lot of arguments with her parents, Pieter had demanded that Teresa had to be paid for her work. The family finally capitulated, and Pieter as ever, celebrated this minor success by taking them all to Maximo's for a meal.

Maximo Baroja had also worked hard, and his small cafe had become a popular, thriving restaurant. But there was always a welcome at Maximo's for the man who everyone liked to call 'Pedro'.

Life was good in Spain. And in Benicassim, Pieter had friends. Good friends.

The bus finally arrived, and Pieter followed the queue and paid his fare, and then sat down on an empty seat on the left-hand side on the third row. The bus set off and Pieter began to read his paper once more. It was that simple. Three or four stops later, the couple sitting in front of him stood up and got off the bus, leaving the seats empty. At the next stop, some people got on again, and a young lady suddenly sat herself down on the empty seat. She was accompanied by a large, seemingly older man. Pieter looked up. The man and the young lady were talking, it was a continued conversation, and Pieter presumed that they were father and daughter. Pieter was just about to return to his paper when he noticed the girl's hair. For some reason, it caught his attention, but he didn't know why. Then thinking no more about it, he began to read his newspaper again. Another ten or fifteen minutes passed, and a man sat down next to Pieter as the bus became quite full. It stopped once again to let more passengers on and off, and a woman got onto the bus, she was in her sixties, and as she looked down the length of the bus to find an empty seat, she noticed the man and the girl who were sitting in front of Pieter.

'Oh hello, Arthur. How are you?' she suddenly asked.

The man looked up, 'Oh, hello Mrs Bleecker. Nice to see you.'

The woman then turned to the girl.

'And how are you dear. And how's your mother.'

'She's coping thank you, Mrs Bleecker,' the girl replied. 'We're on our way to the hospital now to see her.'

'Well, give her my best wishes will you, Leah,' Mrs Bleeker replied, and then she moved down the bus to find herself a seat.

Pieter immediately looked up. The young woman in front of him had the same name as his mother. It was a name he rarely heard anymore. It felt quite strange, and for a moment he thought about his beautiful mother, his mother who had been murdered in a Concentration Camp all those years ago. And as Pieter returned to his newspaper he again glanced at the girl's hair, and for some reason he frowned, but he didn't understand why.

There were several more stops, and finally the man and the girl both stood up as they'd reached their destination. There were quite a few people getting off at the same stop and the man and the girl waited in turn until they could eventually step into the queue. At the last moment, the girl looked down the bus and she waved to someone.

'Goodbye Mrs Bleeker,' she called out.

Pieter looked up at her. And at that moment his world suddenly turned upside down.

For a split second he was completely astounded. He stared up at the girl, not believing what he was seeing. What he saw, just couldn't be.

The young woman standing there in front of him was the image of Pieter's long lost wife. The girl was an absolute reflection of Francine, it was unquestionable. She was without doubt, her exact double.

Pieter froze, and he stared at her in disbelief. He was shocked, not only shocked, he was astounded, and he felt that his head was about to explode. And then the one question came crashing through his brain.

'It's Francine...but it can't be?'

He tried to utter something but he couldn't speak. He just sat there, stunned and confused, and then the young woman turned around and began to make her way off the bus.

Pieter was in a daze, he was totally bewildered. This girl, she had the same face, and the exact same colour of hair. And that's what he'd noticed, it had been there in front of his face and he'd not recognized it. But why would he? And all of these thoughts were screaming at him as the young woman stepped off the bus. He watched her go, she was speaking to the older man and then she linked his arm and they walked away. Pieter actually watched them go, and then he suddenly realized what he was doing. He was just sitting there in a daze. And suddenly he had to find out, he had to know who this young woman was, and he needed to know why?

He immediately stood up and stepped over the man at the side of him.

The man grunted and made some remark, but Pieter didn't have the time and he just didn't care. He managed to get to the exit just before a new queue of passengers were about to get onto the bus. He almost leapt off the bus as he burst onto the pavement and looked quickly down the road. The young woman and the man were only about twenty yards in front of him. They were walking together, both comfortable and chatting amiably, a father and his daughter.

Pieter straightened himself up and began to concentrate, and then he followed them.

It took about ten minutes for them all to arrive at the entrance of St Vincent's Hospital in Lower Manhattan. Pieter stayed a respectable twenty yards behind them. Walking casually and still holding his folded newspaper, he would be totally inconspicuous. He knew that, he'd done it a hundred times before.

He followed them up some steps and then through the large main entrance and into the hospital. They walked across the open reception area and got into an empty elevator. As the doors closed, Pieter looked up at the illuminated numbers above the lift, and suddenly the number for the second floor lit up.

Pieter glanced around quickly, and to his right were the stairs. He quickly skipped up the steps to the second floor and when he got there the man and the young woman were already out of the elevator and had started to walk down the corridor. After turning a few corners, they came to the reception and stopped for a moment to speak to the receptionist, it was all very friendly and Pieter realized that they must be regular visitors. The receptionist smiled and the couple turned and made their way down another corridor to their right. Pieter followed. He strolled past the reception, half reading his newspaper, comfortably looking as though he knew exactly where he was going. The receptionist never even glanced up. Behind the reception, there was an annexe that was used as a waiting area. It was quite busy, and there were people sitting on the long rows of seats, waiting patiently to visit their loved ones. As he walked past, an intercom called out someone's name, and an elderly woman with a weary face stood up and made her way forwards.

Pieter turned a corner, just in time to see the man and his daughter stop and then go into one of the rooms. Pieter continued walking towards them, and as the door to the room closed he caught the hint of a conversation, but nothing more. He stopped for a moment and looked. It was Room 219. Then he turned around and walked back to the waiting area. He found an empty seat and made himself fairly inconspicuous at the back of the room, and then he began to read his newspaper, and he waited.

An hour later, the young woman and her father left. Pieter sat there and watched them as they walked past him. And again he stared at the girl, Leah. He was mesmerized. It was like seeing a ghost. She didn't just resemble Francine, she was Francine. Francine as she was all those years ago. She was the Francine who he'd met in the library, and the Francine who he'd loved and treasured and married. He was still astonished. How could this be? Was this girl somehow related to Francine's family? As far as he knew she was an only child. Maybe there was another story, a family secret. But neither had Francine ever mentioned any cousins or any other relatives at all for that matter. But who knew? The only possible answer was with the woman in Room 219, the young woman's mother.

Pieter sat there, deep in thought, and still he waited.

Within the hour, two of the nurses began their rounds. They were pushing a trolley that was full of everyone's prescribed medication and they were there to administer the different medicines to the patients there on the second floor. Pieter stood up and moved to a seat at the other end of the waiting room. To stay in one place for too long was to draw attention to himself. That he did know.

Two more hours passed, and by then Pieter had read almost every single article in the New York Times, but still he waited.

An hour later, two more nurses passed by, this time they were pushing a large metal catering trolley that contained everyone's evening meal. Pieter stood up and moved to another seat, he checked his watch, and then he propped his paper up in front of him so that he looked as though he was still reading. And then he closed his eyes and dozed off.

When he awoke, it was approaching seven thirty. He checked his watch and then went to find the men's bathrooms. From there he walked around a few of the corridors, the hospital was now noticeably quieter as many of the nurses and day staff had already left and the visiting time was coming to a close as the night shift approached. Pieter walked back to the waiting area, it now was empty, as was the reception. And so he kept on walking down the corridor until he once again reached Room 219. He glanced to either side of him, the corridor was still empty. And so he carefully turned the handle and opened the door and went inside.

He stood there for a moment, there was a woman lying in the hospital bed, she was asleep.

Pieter stared at her. And he blinked. He didn't understand. And he suddenly found it difficult to breathe properly. And as he looked down at her, he bit his lip. All he could do was stare. And then finally, he began to cry. It was all just too much for him to take in. He could not comprehend how this could be.

Lying there asleep in the bed was Francine. His Francine.

Pieter stood at the bottom of the bed looking at her. It was her. Francine was here and she was alive. She was alive, and still he didn't understand.

He looked down at her, the woman he'd lost forever, all those twenty years ago. And beautiful, she was still beautiful. Twenty years hadn't changed her. She was thinner and pale, and obviously unwell, but Pieter just stood there, feeling totally helpless. Part of him almost felt like turning around and leaving. To go somewhere and gather his thoughts, and then make some sort of plan. But he couldn't leave. Not now.

Francine suddenly took a deep breath, she moved her head for a moment but stayed asleep. And Pieter just stood there, absolutely dumbfounded.

Another ten minutes passed by. And Pieter took a handkerchief from his pocket and wiped a tear from his eye. He tried to calm himself. And still he stood there, and he waited.

Nearly an hour passed. And Pieter looked at her, remembering everything and everything about her. And then Francine coughed, and she suddenly opened her eyes.

She blinked and looked around as she realized where she was. Of course, she was in the hospital. And as she gathered her thoughts, she was suddenly aware that she was not alone. There was a man in her room. He was standing at the foot of her bed, staring down at her. And for a moment she didn't understand. He wasn't a doctor. She looked up at him, and at the face and the eyes that were gazing back at her. And then suddenly, the unbelievable.

Her eyes widened as she saw his face. She exhaled in shock and she shook her head.

Pieter remained at the bottom of her bed, and a tear in his eye. There was no doubt now, it was her.

Francine began to tremble. And she put her hand to her mouth.

'Please God. Please tell me I'm not dreaming. Please...this can't be.'

Pieter looked down at her.

'It's me Francine,' he said slowly. 'It's me.'

'Pieter...Pieter,' she gasped, and then she began to cry out loud.

Francine suddenly held out her arms to him. And she wept.

He went to her and leant down and embraced her. Francine put her arms around him and hugged him with all her strength.

He breathed in, and he could smell her natural perfume, and remembered the beautiful aroma that he never thought he'd experience again. He nuzzled her neck and he buried his face in her hair. Nothing had changed. Pieter turned his head to face her, and for a moment they both examined each other's face, and then he kissed her lips. And a thousand memories flooded back. She was here, and his heart had found its home.

For the next ten minutes they both kissed and held each other closely, not really understanding anything.

She whispered to him. 'I've never stopped loving you Pieter, never. Every day I've thought about you. Every single day.'

Pieter looked into her eyes, there had never been any other woman in his life. No one.

She put her hands on his face.

'I don't understand, Pieter...you're alive.'

He looked at her, 'Yes, and so are you.'

And with that, she leant forward and kissed him.

Pieter lay on the bed with her and they held one another. He stroked her face and they kissed and looked at one another and time floated by.

But then finally, he had to ask. 'Why are you in the hospital?'

She looked at him and smiled calmly, 'I've not been well. I'm having some tests that's all.'

But it wasn't the truth.

She kissed him and stroked his hair, 'How did you ever find me?' she then asked him.

Pieter explained.

'It was just the strangest coincidence. I saw your daughter, Leah, on the bus. She's your absolute double. I couldn't believe it when I saw her, it was unbelievable. And then I followed her here.'

Francine nodded quickly, 'I know, she looks like me.' And she stared back at him.

There were so many questions, and so many explanations.

And in Pieter's mind too, there came the inevitable rush of questions.

He wondered about what had happened all those years ago, and had Francine escaped from Auschwitz too? She must have, but how? And then suddenly, Pieter thought about the man, and who actually was the girl?'

The questions spiralled in his brain, but they would all have to wait, because Francine was here with him, and she was alive.

They lay together on the bed, almost clinging to one another, but eventually they had to talk. The past was too important for them both.

'They told me they'd sent you to Auschwitz, Pieter. They told me that you were dead.'

He looked at her.

'Yes, they did send me to Auschwitz. But I escaped. I made my way back to Lodz to find my father. I broke into the camp and we escaped, and then we drove across Europe to get to Gibraltar. Once we got there, we managed to get onto a boat and we sailed to England.

'You're father!' Francine exclaimed. 'Your father's still alive?'

Pieter shook his head. 'No, he died of a heart attack once we were in England. He never got over losing my mother and my sisters, Francine. It broke him'

Francine looked at him. 'I'm so sorry Pieter. He was a good man, and so were your mother and sisters. They were all wonderful.'

She gazed at him and sighed. 'We lost everyone. I thought I'd lost you too.'

Pieter took a deep breath, and he kissed her again and he stroked her face. 'When my father died, I thought everyone was gone, everyone.'

And then he asked her.

'How on earth did you manage to escape from Auschwitz?'

Francine sighed. She had to concentrate, because she had to tell him. She had to tell Pieter everything. Because now, Pieter Szabo was her husband.

'I was never there Pieter. I was never sent to Auschwitz.'

'But, I was told...'

He never finished his sentence.

'I know what you may have been told, Pieter. But it was all a lie, it was all nothing but lies.

I was taken to the Grand Hotel in Lodz. I was taken there to meet a man called 'Herr Wilhelm Kruger', he was a Major in the German Army. He installed me in a room there and he told me that he was trying to help us and that it had all been a big mistake.'

Pieter couldn't believe what he was hearing, 'The Grand Hotel', and the name, 'Herr Wilhelm Kruger'. Suddenly he wanted to tell her everything, but it would have to wait.

Francine then began to tell him her story.

'Kruger led me on and like a fool I trusted him. I had no other choice, he told me that he was helping us. And I just wanted us all to be safely back home and together again. But in the end he tricked me. In the end, it had all been a lie. All that he wanted was me, Pieter. On my last night there he got drunk and he actually proposed to me. I refused him of course. My excuse was that I already was married, married to you, Pieter. But then he laughed at me, and he told me that you were already all dead and that you and all the family had been sent to Auschwitz and had been executed there. And then he tried to rape me. But I smashed a brandy bottle in his face and managed to escape. There was a hidden fire escape at the end of the corridor which the manager had shown me. I managed to get down the stairs, but then I fell and hurt myself. Somehow I managed to get to the ground floor and out of the hotel. But Kruger followed me, I couldn't run, but he was injured too. Then he fired his gun at me, and the shot missed. He was going to shoot again, but at that moment I slipped and fell, and his shots missed me again. When I got to my knees, Kruger was on the floor. He was unconscious. I managed to get to my feet and then I got away as best I could. I managed to escape. A family took me in and I hid in their home for a week. They took a great risk. I thought that Kruger would have sent out his troops to find me. But strangely, he never did. I think he must have tried to cover up the whole incident. It could have been a huge embarrassment for him.'

Pieter just stared at her. This was unbelievable.

'Francine,' he said quietly, 'I killed Wilhelm Kruger.'

Francine looked at him. 'You killed him? You killed Major Kruger?'

'I was working with the Resistance. I went to the Grand Hotel and I went up through the same fire escape to Kruger's suite. I walked in there and put a bullet through his head.'

Francine shook her head in sheer amazement.

'I was kept in a room just lower down from his suite,' she tried to explain.

Pieter remembered the corridor and then he remembered the door to what had been her room. He'd never known or even suspected. But how could he?

Francine squeezed his hand.

'He was a horrible man, Pieter. He sent your mother and sisters to the camp at Auschwitz.'

'Yes,' said Pieter. 'And while I was there in Lodz, I also found out where Wilfred Staszic and Henryk Kober both lived.'

Francine visibly shuddered at the mention of their names. The memories were too awful.

'I killed them both, Francine. And I made them suffer for what they did to us.'

And Pieter was suddenly angry, but Francine put her arms around him and kissed him, she needed to calm him down. Then she looked directly at him.

'I'm glad, Pieter. I'm glad you killed them. They were evil men, they all were.'

They were both silent for a moment as they remembered the events of the past. But then Francine continued, because she needed to tell him everything.

'The family that hid me knew somebody with the resistance. I'd told them what had happened to me and they contacted someone. They knew that I needed to get out of Lodz. Not only that, I wanted to get out of the country and far away from the Nazis. I knew that Turkey was a neutral country that they hadn't been drawn into the war. The resistance got me out of Poland to the Ukraine and then took me south. They gave me money and put me onto a train that took me to Romania. Then I got onto a series of trains that took me through Romania and Bulgaria and then finally to Turkey where I reached Istanbul. I found work on a cargo ship that traded from the Black Sea and went through to the Mediterranean. I worked in the kitchen and cooked and cleaned with another two women It was hard work, but when we finally reached Cyprus, I jumped ship '.

Pieter was astounded at what he heard. But it wasn't the full story. Francine's route had not been that simple at all, in fact, it had been dangerous and hard and it had cost her dearly. She'd had to travel by road, rail and by sea. And she'd had to beg for help and for money in the only possible way. She'd given herself to men. She'd been used, and she'd had to share a dozen different beds with different men, and in return she'd been given food and money, and transport. But Francine had little choice, and it was better to give herself freely, rather than be raped. She'd had no other option. Totally alone and desperate, she was pregnant, and that was the only thing that gave her the will to carry on. Other than that, she couldn't have done any of it. She had no one, her husband was dead and so were her family.

But all of that was Francine's secret. And nobody else would ever know. Nobody would know what she'd had to do and what she'd had to put herself through to survive.

She'd had nothing and she had no one, no one but the baby inside her.

'It was while I was in Cyprus that I met Arthur.'

Pieter looked at her. 'Is he the large man who was with your daughter?'

Francine looked back at him, and suddenly her eyes faded, she was tired, very tired. And Pieter saw it too and he took hold of her arm.

'Are you alright Francine,' he asked?

She steadied herself. 'I'll be okay, I think it's the shock of everything, that's all.'

But that wasn't the truth either.

'I'll go,' said Pieter. 'I can call back tomorrow.'

'No Pieter,' she replied, and there was a certain desperation in her voice. She had to tell him everything, and she had to tell him now and get it over with.

'Arthur was a pilot with the American Forces. I was working as a cleaner at the Allied Airbase there. We became friends, Pieter.'

Pieter nodded, and he realized what was coming and what he would have to accept. Francine had been alone and she'd thought that Pieter was dead. And that was the end of it. He understood her dilemma, a woman on her own and in a country where she was a stranger, especially after what she'd been through.

'It's alright Francine,' he said to her, 'I understand, I really do.'

'He took care of me, Pieter. I was lost.'

Pieter again nodded and he took hold of her hand and smiled.

'His name is Arthur Morris. He was flying supplies to the island of Lesvos in Greece, to help out the Resistance there. I knew he could never be you Pieter, but he loved me and I was fond of him. When he had to fly back to the USA, he wouldn't leave me. So he hid me in the cargo plane that he was flying and we eventually reached the United States. Once we get there he immediately took me to the authorities and admitted what he'd done. But it was wartime and they weren't going to send me back. And by that time I was pregnant and so Arnold and I got married straightaway. I'm so sorry Pieter, but I thought that you'd been killed'

Pieter realized the obvious truth. It had been at the back of his mind, but he didn't want to acknowledge the reality of it all

'I'm glad Francine,' he said to her. 'Truthfully, I am. You deserved some happiness in your life and you deserved a family. Your daughter is truly beautiful.'

Francine looked into his eyes, and then she smiled at him.

'No, she's your daughter, Pieter Szabo. Leah, she yours and mine.'

Pieter stared at her, not believing what he was hearing. It was almost impossible for him to comprehend. He was speechless.

'I found out on the day we were all arrested Pieter, I was going to break the news to you and the family that evening, and then everything went so terribly wrong.

'I...I have a daughter? Pieter finally managed to say, and he blinked back the tears

And Francine looked at him, and then she smiled again.

'More than that Pieter, you also have a son. You see, I was carrying twins.'

Pieter was absolutely dumbfounded. He stared at her in disbelief. In one single day he'd found his wife again, and now he was being told that he had children, he had a family.

After all those years of loneliness and of not caring about anyone, he had a family.

And then suddenly, Francine fell forward. Pieter caught her as her eyes closed, and then she blinked and her eyes closed again.

'Francine, what's wrong?'

She took a deep breath and then she managed to look at him.

'It's my illness, Pieter. It makes me weary. I'm so tired.'

Pieter realized that the events of the day must have taken a toll on her. She needed to rest, and he laid her back on the pillow.

'Francine,' he said to her. 'You need to sleep. Don't worry, I'll come back tomorrow and we can talk then. You need to rest.'

And then he kissed her forehead.

'I love you, Francine.'

She looked up at him. She was exhausted, but she had to tell him.

'Pieter,' she whispered. 'Pieter, our son...his name is David.'

And then her exhaustion took over and she closed her eyes and finally slept.

Pieter returned home. But he didn't sleep well. In fact, he hardly slept at all. He spent most of the night pacing his apartment, trying to work everything out in his mind. He was in a daze. He'd found his wife, and she was ill. And she was also remarried. And then he'd found out that he had children, he had a family. But where did that leave everybody, and what was going to happen? And what about Francine's illness? Pieter thought about her lying there in the hospital. Her being ill now that he'd found her again was worrying and he wondered what exactly was wrong with her. There was nothing that he could do. And now he had a son too, a son called David, and Pieter wondered about him. And so tomorrow, he would see Francine again, and that thought alone made him happy. Tomorrow they would talk again. And with that in mind, he went back to his bed. But he just lay there, with those same thoughts running through his head, over and over again.

The next day, Pieter returned to St Vincent's Hospital. And once again he sat in the waiting area, reading his newspaper, and waiting. But now his reasoning was slightly different.

He wanted to see Francine, and they would talk. But he also wanted to see Leah again. She was his daughter, and that feeling alone made him feel different, he was overjoyed. So he sat there. And eventually the man that he'd learned was Arthur Morris, returned. And along with him was Leah.

As they walked past, arm in arm, Pieter stared at her. She was stunningly pretty, just like her mother. And as Pieter watched them walk by he felt a moment's loss, the loss for all of the years that he'd missed and that he'd never been there to see her grow up. And then his thoughts turned, and he wondered about the future, and for the years that he could still possibly miss. And once again, he worried about the outcome of everything that was happening.

It was nearly two hours later before they left, and once again Pieter watched as they walked past him. Arthur Morris had his arm around Leah's shoulders to comfort her. And Pieter then realized how close they were.

Pieter waited again, and he observed as the hospital's regular routine continued. First, there were the nurses with the medications and then later they returned with the meal trolleys.

Pieter sat there for another hour as the waiting area began to empty, and then once again made his way to Room 219. He tapped quietly on the door and went into the room. Francine was sitting up in bed and when she saw him her eyes lit up as she smiled and then laughed. He went to her and they hugged and kissed.

'I thought I'd dreamt everything,' she said, she was still smiling, 'this morning when I woke up I thought I'd been dreaming, and then I saw your newspaper at the side of the bed and I remembered everything. It wasn't a dream, you're alive Pieter, I can't believe it. I've been waiting all day to see you.'

Pieter kissed her again, and all of his emotions returned. He was never going to let her go. Whatever happened, he was never going to lose her again.

They sat and they talked.
'Tell me about the children,' he asked her. 'Tell me about Leah and David.'
Francine took a deep breath, and then she sighed.
'This is going to be quite difficult, Pieter.'
'Why, what's wrong?' he asked.
She looked at him.
'Arthur and I got married, I was pregnant and he went back to the War. Arthur was from New York and I moved into his apartment. Whilst he was away I gave birth. I named Leah after your mother. But I named David

after Arthur's father. I'm so sorry Pieter, but I felt I had too. I'd told Arthur everything, and if I'd named the baby after you it somehow wouldn't have felt right. For Arthur, I think it would have been a constant reminder. I sent him a telegram overseas and when he finally replied he was overjoyed. He's been good to me, Pieter, and the children too. He's brought them up as his own, Leah thinks the world of him.'

'Yes,' said Pieter, ' I realize that. I've watched them together, I can see that they're very close. And you were right about David's name. I can understand that Francine, of course I can.'

'Leah's a lovely girl, Pieter. She reminds me so much of your sister, Elise. She has a spark about her. She is without doubt a 'Szabo'. And then Francine laughed.

And David? Pieter asked.

Francine looked at him.

'Well, Leah looks like me, but David certainly takes after your side of the family.'

And then the smile suddenly left Francine's face.

'David...David's a different story I'm afraid, Pieter.' And she sighed, 'It's been complicated.

David's life has been difficult, for all of us. Everything was going okay, but when the children reached the age of twelve, we'd always decided that we would tell them the truth about you and me, and what happened to the family. It seemed the right thing to do at the time, but on reflection it was probably a mistake. Leah took it all very well and to her, her daddy was still her daddy, no matter what. But David took it differently somehow. He thought he'd been lied to, and the man who he'd always thought of as his father suddenly wasn't anymore. It troubled him, and we saw a change in his attitude. And suddenly the arguments started, and he would go out of his way to disobey Arthur. He became withdrawn, not with Leah, but with us. He and Leah have always been close. And whenever I was with him on his own he was okay. But as soon as Arthur walked into the room the problems would start again. By the time he was fourteen, he was running wild. And then he started getting into trouble with the police. He'd got involved with some gang and they were causing trouble. At sixteen he was put into a juvenile's detention centre. That was the start of it, we found out that he'd been dealing in drugs. When he came out of there he was a different person. If it hadn't been for Leah, I don't think we would have ever seen him anymore. He would disappear for days at a time. We never knew where he was or what he was up to. At eighteen, he was arrested again and he spent six months in a Federal Prison. Again for drugs.'

At that point, Francine became tearful. 'I don't know what we did wrong, Pieter. We always loved him, but he wouldn't listen. After that he moved away, to Chicago.'

Pieter put his arm around her as she wiped her eyes.

'Where is he now?' Pieter asked.

Francine looked up at him tearfully. 'He's in prison again. They caught him with a large amount of drugs. He was sentenced to seven years, Pieter. At first he refused to see us, but finally Leah and I went there because we needed to talk to him. He's in the Stateville Prison in Joliet City, it's a Correctional Facility over in Illinois. We went there on the Greyhound bus, it's about an hour out of Chicago. It was awful, Pieter. He told us that he was innocent and he'd been 'set up' by the police, but that nobody would believe him.'

Francine wiped her tears away. 'There's nothing we can do Pieter. Arthur's tried, but it's hopeless.'

They sat there, both silent for a moment. And then Pieter turned to her.

'I've got to see him, Francine.'

She looked at him and nodded.'

'My life has changed, Francine. 'Our' lives have changed and I can't waste any more time.'

'I do understand, Pieter,' she replied. 'But be aware, he's hostile and he's very angry. I still think that he blames us for everything that's happened to him."

Pieter listened. But he was determined. At some point he had to see his son and he certainly wasn't going to wait for seven years. And with that in mind, he suddenly had to ask Francine the most important question of all. He looked at her.

'I need to know something Francine. What are we going to do? And what's going to happen? Me and you...and the children? And of course, you're husband. You're married now.'

Francine stared at him, almost in disbelief.

'But Pieter, you're my husband. You've always been my husband, always.'

'I know, Francine. But what about you're...' and he stopped himself from saying that word, 'but what about Arthur...Arthur Morris?'

She took a deep breath and rubbed her eyes. And once again she began to look weary. And Pieter saw it as he sat and watched her

'At some point, Pieter,' she finally replied, 'we're going to have to tell everyone, I know we are. But not now, please not now. I just want us to be together and enjoy this. I know it's very complicated and that we're going to have to explain everything. But I can't face it at the moment, I really can't.

Pieter nodded, and then he hugged his wife.

'Whatever happens,' she said softly, 'We're never being parted again, Pieter, never.'

Pieter stayed until she finally fell asleep, and then he left.

And that became their routine. Pieter would sit in the waiting area with his newspaper in hand, and watch as Leah and Arthur Morris arrived, and then later he would watch them as they both left. Sometimes Pieter would go and sit on a bench in the hospital garden for an hour. It was quiet and peaceful, and he could gather his thoughts there as he looked down at the ever-bustling city below. He would sit there and think about Leah, he was fascinated by his daughter, and it was understandable. She was his flesh and blood, and at times he felt as though he should go over and hug her. But he couldn't.

On one late evening, a nurse had walked into their room as Francine and Pieter were lying on the bed together. She was quite shocked at the obvious intimacy between the couple. And knowing that Francine was married, the nurse muttered something about 'irregularities' and that 'visitors' weren't allowed at that late hour. The nurse was quite embarrassed and turned to leave. But Pieter stood up and followed her into the corridor. He explained to her that he was Francine's ex-husband, but that they still had feelings for one another, especially now, and that the only time that they could briefly see one another was in the evenings because they didn't want to upset anyone. The nurse, who was a true romantic, totally believed Pieter's story, even more so, when Pieter informed her that he and Francine had been childhood sweethearts. The nurse almost swooned, and then when Pieter pressed three hundred dollars into her hand for her secrecy and their privacy, she was almost swept away with emotion.

Another week passed by. And the visits continued.

They'd talked about each other's lives, and it turned out that Francine had worked as a secretary at a clothing factory. After the war, Arthur Morris had returned to selling insurance. Leah worked in a bank, and Pieter laughed at that. His sister, Ilsa had also worked in a bank and Pieter made some remark as to how it must be a family trait. When Francine asked Pieter what he did for a living, he had to make an excuse. He hated to lie to her, especially now. But he couldn't tell her the truth.

'I work for a security company as a consultant,' he said vaguely. It takes me around the world I suppose, but it's just a job. I just check up on different companies. There's a lot of paperwork involved, but they pay me well enough. I can't complain.'

'Yes,' Francine had replied, 'Arthur's the same. He's up till all hours, filling in forms and writing letters.'

Pieter nodded, and he changed the subject. But Francine looked at him. She knew Pieter Szabo and he hadn't changed. When he went blasé and a little distant, it meant that he didn't want to talk about something. She knew that he wasn't telling her the truth. But did it matter? No, not really. Not now.

However, Pieter did have one other problem. When he was back at his apartment on the Lower East Side, his phone had begun ring, and it would continue to ring. It could only ever be one person, it had to be Vernon Ballantyne. If Ballantyne was phoning him, it would mean one thing. There was a new contract. And at that moment in time, Pieter Szabo had other, more important things on his mind. There was nothing he could do, and so he purposely ignored the phone calls.

And somewhere back in England, Lieutenant Vernon Ballantyne wondered what had happened to his special assassin and where was he, where was codename 'Eagle'?

On the Sunday evening, Pieter announced to Francine that he was going to see David.

'What are you going to say to him?' Francine had said straight away, she had been quite shocked. Pieter sat and explained that he had already arranged for a visit to the Stateville prison over in Chicago.

'I told them that I was from some legal firm and that the family had hired me on some sort of 'pro bono' deal. The man on the end of the phone just huffed a bit and gave me a time and a date. I told him that I wanted to be there on Monday, but he wasn't having it. He told me that it would be Tuesday or nothing. So I let him win that one, and it kept him happy, He was one of those men who obviously likes to be in control. I suppose it goes with the job'

'What are you going to tell David about us, Pieter?'

'I don't know, I really don't know. I'm just going to see how it goes and I'll take it from there. If I do tell him, I don't know how he'll react. I don't even know David, do I?'

Francine was worried. 'He'll be angry, Pieter. He's always angry, you don't understand.'

Pieter shrugged.

'He may well be, but that doesn't change anything. He's my son and I need to see him. You've got to understand Francine, he's my flesh and blood, I've wasted all these years and he's still our son, no matter what he's done.'

Francine did understand. And she understood how all of this must have come as a shock for Pieter, probably even more than it had been for her. He'd spent most of his life not knowing anything at all about his family, but she'd had the joy of living with them almost every day.

She calmed herself.

'You're right, Pieter.' she said to him. 'Whatever happens, will be. Life's too short'.

On the Monday, Pieter flew out to Chicago.

He hired a car and drove to Joliet City where he booked into a small motel that was about a fifteen-minute drive from the Stateville Correctional Facility. He spent a restless night in his room as he lay on the bed, trying to watch anything of interest on the TV.

The next morning he was awake early. He went to a local diner for some breakfast and then went for a walk and finally in a roundabout fashion he returned to his motel. At quarter past ten he got into the car and drove to the prison. After a ten minute drive, he parked in the car park and then made his way to the main gates. There were two guards. One let him in and the other straightaway checked him for weapons. He was then directed across the yard to the visitor's reception. Pieter walked in through a side door. There were about twenty people already waiting there, and all eyes turned to glance at whoever walked through the door next. Pieter went over to the reception and told the guard behind the desk that he was 'Mr Ernest Heller'. Pieter used his American pseudonym and he produced the corresponding documentation. The guard checked his list and Pieter told him that he was there to see Mr David Morris. The appointment was at eleven o' clock. The guard then ticked the appropriate names on his list and everything was in order. Pieter was then told to sit and wait and that his name would be called. He sat there for another fifteen minutes as several other visitors arrived and booked themselves in at the reception. Strangely, hardly anyone spoke, and those that did, quietly whispered. Pieter felt uneasy, and it was understandable, he was about to meet a son who was a complete stranger to him.

    A buzzer sounded. And the guard at the reception stood up and called out the half-dozen names of the people who were to be the first batch of visitors. The name 'Heller' wasn't one of them. Another guard then led them through a door at the end of the room and everyone else sat back and sighed. Half an hour later, the buzzer sounded again. This time, 'Heller' was the second name called. Pieter stood up and followed the line of people through the same door.

    In the next room were a row of separated booths. There were four guards there to keep their eye on things, one of which held yet another list. He asked Pieter his name and then pointed along the row.

    'David Morris, end booth,' the guard confirmed.

    Pieter walked to the booth. There was a young man sitting on the other side of the booth with his arms folded. He didn't look up. Pieter took the corresponding chair and sat down.

    There was silence. For Pieter it was almost laughable, not the best of starts, so Pieter spoke first.

    'You're David Morris' he asked?

    After another brief silence, 'Yeah, right,' came the reply. And then the young man looked up at Pieter and was just about to say something. But he suddenly stopped. He looked at Pieter for a moment and frowned. For an instant he stared, it was almost as though he recognized Pieter, but then he dismissed the thought and shook his head.

    'So what tin pot firm of lawyers do you represent, Mr Heller? And are my family still living in hope, or are you just here to prove a point so that you can screw them over like all the others?'

Pieter just sat there, only half listening. Because sitting in front of him was a young man who had all of the features of his own father, Franz Szabo. Pieter continued to stare, he'd always known that he too looked like his own father, and Francine had said that David had the same family resemblance, and now Pieter saw it too. The one person who didn't was David Morris.

The awkward silence began to make David uncomfortable. He stared back at Pieter.

'So what's your problem, man? What the hell do you want? Lawyers, you're all the damn same. You're wasting your time, man, both yours and mine.'

'I'm not a lawyer, David,' said Pieter quietly.

David stopped talking, and his eyes suddenly narrowed.

'Who's sent you? Have they sent you? What do they want now?'

'Nobody's sent me David,' Pieter replied. 'And who are 'they'?

David suddenly looked worried. He stared at Pieter. He didn't understand just what was happening.

'So who's sent you then, the Feds?' he asked.

Pieter looked at his son for a moment, and he began to wonder just what it was that David had done, and who he'd got himself involved with?

'No David,' he replied, 'I'm not with the Feds either. I'm here for something entirely different. It involves your family.'

David slumped back in his chair.

'Awe, Christ man, what do they want now?' But there was also a sense of relief in his voice. 'Leave me alone, man. I've nothing to say to you,' and he moved his chair back, he just was about to stand up.

'Your last name, its Szabo,' said Pieter.

David stopped, he didn't move. And he looked at Pieter.

'Hey man, my last names 'Morris', okay. Didn't you read the list? And he glanced over at the guard.

'No it's not Morris,' Pieter replied. 'You're real name is David Szabo.'

David stared at him.

'Who the fuck are you, man? Have you been talking to my dim shit of a mother?

Pieter was suddenly annoyed. He didn't appreciate Francine being talked about in that manner. Not one bit.

'Do not speak about your mother like that,' he said in a low voice.

David just sat back in his chair. 'Yeah, right...okay. So what?'

Pieter took a deep breath. He would try again.

'Your real family name is David Szabo. You do know that, of course?'

'Yeah, yeah, I know all about that,' David replied

'What do you know about your family, the Szabo family?'

'Nothing, and that's about all I do know,' David replied. 'They were Polish and were all killed in some concentration camp somewhere, Christ only knows. I was brought up here in America as someone else's son. What a joke. So my name's not Szabo, it's Morris. Okay?'

'No, it's not okay. Not all of your family died in Poland, David.'

David turned to him, he was becoming annoyed.

'So fucking what? What am I supposed to do, jump up and down for joy? What's it got to do with you? And anyway, who the hell are you?'

Pieter stared at him.

My name isn't Heller, David. It's Szabo, Pieter Szabo. And I'm here because we didn't all die in that Concentration camp. I managed to survive. And I'm your father, David.'

David looked at Pieter Szabo. For a moment he said nothing, and then he sneered.

'What sort of scam is this? Is it something that my family's cooked up?'

'No David,' Pieter replied, 'it was all by pure accident, I saw your sister, Leah. And then from there I found your mother.'

'Yeah, of course you did,' David replied cynically, 'and I believe in the fairies. Fuck off, man, my father died years ago. And hey, and if you're my father, where the hell have you been all these years?'

Pieter tried to explain.

'I always thought that your mother had died in the camps too, along with the rest of our family.'

David stood up.

'It's over, man,' he said. 'Forget it. I'm not listening to your 'bullshit' anymore. You can go back to New York and tell them that it didn't work.'

Pieter stood up too, to face him.

'You do know that you're mother's ill in hospital?'

'Yeah, so what,' David replied.

That one answer infuriated Pieter. And he stared back at his son in disgust.

'David, you're an imbecile. And you're right, you're not a 'Szabo'. You're not fit to carry that name. Your mother loves you, and you're locked up here in some prison for dealing in drugs. You're a disgrace.'

David was about to say something, but Pieter interrupted him.

'Go back to your cell, David, and spend your miserable life in here. But remember my face and remember it well. And then take a good look in the mirror and see who's staring back at you.'

And with that, Pieter turned around and left.

Pieter managed to get on a late flight back to New York, and he arrived back at his apartment after midnight. He was tired and he was still angry. His meeting with David hadn't gone well at all. It had hardly been the reunion he'd envisaged with his long-lost son, but no matter. It was done. He'd met David and that was it. Whether or not David would ever believe him was another story, but David would have several long years in prison to think about it. And that fact too had infuriated Pieter. The boy was a fool, a disgrace. And then he thought about the relationship he'd had with his own father, and he remembered how close they'd been.

Pieter just shook his head. If only he'd known, if only he'd had the chance, and David could have led a normal life. If only.

The next evening, he went to visit Francine. He watched Arthur Morris and Leah come and go and he waited another hour or so as the nurses finished their usual rounds. Then he slipped into Room 219. Francine lay in her bed, she was awake but looked tired. And as he entered, she suddenly glanced up at him.

'Pieter, you're back,' she said excitedly, and she smiled at him.

He went over to her and kissed her.

'Tell me, tell me all about it, she asked urgently, 'how is he, is he alright?'

Pieter sat down at the side of her.

'Yes, he's alright, he seems to be anyway. But it didn't go well, Francine. I told him who I was, but don't think he believed me.'

Pieter then went on to tell her about his meeting with David, and how it ended. Francine sighed.

'That's typical of him,' she replied, 'always the hot head.'
'Well, I gave him something to think about,' said Pieter, 'maybe he'll figure it out. I don't know.'
They talked, and then Francine said something to him.
'Leah has always known something about your life, Pieter. At some point she'll need to know the rest of it.'
Pieter was silent for a moment. He couldn't tell any of them about his life.
He stayed until midnight, but Francine was tired, and worried. And when she fell asleep, Pieter went home. He needed to think things over too. When he got back to his apartment the phone began to ring. Once again he ignored it and went to bed.

Another week passed, and every day followed the same routine.
And then on the Tuesday, something changed. That evening, when Arthur Morris and Leah were leaving the hospital, they were both visibly upset and Leah was in tears. Pieter stared at them as they walked past him. Something was wrong, something was definitely wrong. And as soon as they'd left, Pieter went straight to Francine's room. He wasn't going to wait.
When he entered, Francine was sitting up in bed, her eyes were red with tears. She looked up to see Pieter, and then she started to cry. And Pieter felt the knot in his stomach suddenly tighten. It was something that he hadn't felt for twenty years, fear.
He went over to her and put his arms around her.'
'What's happened Francine, tell me.'
She sobbed for a moment.
'The doctor's been in to see us with my results, Pieter.'
'And what did he say?'
'I have an illness, Pieter.'
'Do they know what's wrong with you?' he asked her.
It was the moment of truth for Francine. In her heart, she'd always known that it was something serious but it had been simpler to avoid the reality of it all, especially now.
Francine nodded. She had to tell him.
'It's leukaemia. I've got leukaemia, Pieter.'
Pieter stared at her for a moment. He almost couldn't believe what he was hearing.
'How bad is it, Francine?'

'It's severe; I'm suffering from a chronic form of leukaemia. The doctor says that the outcome isn't good. It's terminal Pieter, there's nothing that they can do for me.'

She began to cry. And then they both cried.

'I'm so sorry, Pieter,' she said to him.

But he just hugged her.

'I don't want to lose you, Francine. Not now, and not ever.' And he held her tightly, he wouldn't let her go.

The prognosis wasn't good. Two or three months to try to hold onto her life. In Francine's case, the disease was particularly aggressive.

That night, Pieter never went home. He stayed in the hospital with her. They both lay together in bed, and they talked to each other, as they'd always done. Always.

Francine fell asleep in his arms. Pieter watched her, and he questioned how life could be so cruel. He'd found her, and that had been a miracle. And now she was going to be taken away from him again. A memory reopened, like a wound.

In the morning, Francine told Pieter that he needed to go home, he was exhausted.

As he sat on the bus on the way back to the Lower East Side, the thoughts that had been rolling through his head all night continued, 'What could he do?' And the answer was always the same, 'nothing', nothing at all. He was going to lose her again, and everything was about to be dashed and broken. Pieter had made plans, in his heart he'd made lots of plans. He'd always thought that Francine would get well again and that everything would be all right, one way or another. And he would take her to Spain and they would live there happily ever after, one way or another. But no, not now.

Pieter finally got back to his apartment and he went straight to bed. But an hour later he was still lying there, still wide awake, still thinking. Suddenly the phone began to ring. The phone, the damn phone, and he turned on his side and tried to ignore it. But it kept on ringing, as though trying to drag him back into a life that he no longer wanted or cared about.

Three more days passed. But their lives had taken a twist, and now Pieter's visits had taken on a slightly different role. They talked and they kissed as usual, but now there was almost a feeling of desperation between them as the clock and the calendar ticked by with every passing day. And at the back of Pieter's mind there was always the unanswerable question.

How long could he keep her?

On Saturday, Arthur Morris came to the hospital alone. Pieter didn't quite understand, maybe Leah wasn't well. And he missed seeing her.

When Arthur Morris finally left, Pieter went to Francine's room and he eventually asked her about Leah. Francine told him that Leah had been called into work at the bank and that there was nothing to worry about. That evening, Francine seemed somehow calmer and more relaxed, and they talked and laughed, and they giggled as they remembered their courting days. When Pieter left, Francine was asleep. And as he walked along the hospital corridor, a thought suddenly struck him. As far as he knew, the banks never opened on a Saturday.

The next day, a Sunday, and this time Leah was with Arthur Morris as they came to the hospital to visit Francine. Pieter watched as his daughter walked past him. She fascinated him. And as they both walked by, Pieter wondered about the future, and what would happen when Leah lost her mother.

Pieter sat there for a while, he was feeling restless. And so he got up and stretched, and then he went for a walk in the hospital's gardens.

It was another beautifully sunny day, the gardens were always quiet and peaceful, and Pieter sat on his usual bench and closed his eyes as he felt the sunshine warm his face. His thoughts were elsewhere and everywhere. And to a point, he was lost, completely lost.

'Pieter Szabo,' said a voice.

Pieter suddenly went rigid. And he immediately felt for the gun that wasn't there. Somebody had found him. Who had found him...and how?

He just sat there, not knowing what to expect. Maybe a gun's shot.

'Mr Pieter Szabo?' said the voice again. But this time it was different. This time it was a question.

Pieter slowly turned around. A large man was standing there behind him. And when Pieter looked up he immediately recognized the man. It was Arthur Morris.

For a moment, Pieter couldn't speak. Both men just stared at one another.

'I take it that you 'are' Pieter Szabo?' Arthur Morris asked.
Pieter stood up to face him.
"Yes I am,' said Pieter. 'How do you know me?'
Arthur Morris just looked at him.
'Mr Szabo, for the last few weeks I've walked past the waiting room, and you have always been there. And when we leave, you're still there. Sure, you may have changed seats a few times, I know that, but you are always still there.'
'And how do you know who I am?' Pieter asked him.
Arthur Morris stared at him.
'Because I've had to put up with your son for the last twenty years, and you both look alike. I knew I wasn't mistaken. I knew there was something, and that you were related somehow.'
'Why today,' Pieter asked. 'Why have you come to speak to me today? Does Leah know who I am?'
At the mention of Leah's name, Arthur Morris bristled, he stared at Pieter. There was a guarded anger there and Pieter saw it.
'No, it's nothing to do with Leah,' Arthur Morris replied sharply. 'That's why Leah wasn't with me yesterday,' and then he paused for a moment. 'Francine wanted to speak to me about something, but I knew what it was about. I've been waiting, day after day. I've known this was coming. And yesterday she finally told me everything.'
Arthur Morris was becoming slightly upset, but he continued. 'She thought you were dead, you see. We both did, it was all a lifetime ago. And now all this.'
And at that moment he visibly sagged and his voice began to tremble.
'She's got leukaemia and it's bad, but you know that. And there's the upset with Leah over her mother, and David's in prison. And now you've turned up from nowhere, and I know that it's all been a mistake. But that doesn't change the fact that she's in here and she's dying, and she's dying right in front of me and I don't know what to do. I feel as though my head's exploding and there's nothing I can do about it. '
Arthur Morris rubbed his eyes and then ran his hand over his head. 'I'm sorry, I'm really sorry, but my whole world's falling apart.'
Arthur Morris was in a state of utter despair, and Pieter suddenly realized something so obviously apparent, and something he'd never even

considered. Arthur Morris loved Francine just as much as he did. Here was a man who'd been married to Francine for over twenty years, and he'd taken care of her, and he'd taken care of her children. It had been a selfless act of love. And now they both shared the same anguish and upset.

Pieter had no other choice. He put his hands on Arthur Morris's shoulders to steady him.

'Mr Morris,' said Pieter, 'we need to talk. Come with me and let's go and have a cup of coffee.'

Arthur Morris just nodded, and he straightened himself, and Pieter led him out of the garden and took him to the hospital cafeteria which was also situated on the ground floor.

Mercifully for Pieter, it had always stayed open twenty four hours a day.

They sat in the corner and Pieter brought two cups of coffee over to their table.

Arthur Morris took a sip from his cup and thanked Pieter. He was back to his normal self.

Pieter suddenly felt that he had to start the conversation.

'I can understand that it's been a shock, Mr Morris, I really do.'

Arthur Morris looked at Pieter.

'I suppose at this point, you'd better start calling me Arthur, Mr Szabo. Or is it Pieter?'

And he held out his hand, and Pieter shook it.

Pieter gave him a wry smile. 'Pieter will do very well, Arthur, thank you.'

'We met in Cyprus, during the war.'

'I believe so,' said Pieter.

'We became friends. But for me it was more than that. The first time I met her, well, she just took my breath away.'

Arthur Morris stopped talking for a moment, and it took him a couple of seconds before he could continue. And Pieter just sat there, and he remembered all those years ago in Lodz, and how he'd first met Francine in the Library there.

'As I said, we became friends, Pieter. She told me everything, everything that had happened to you, and to the family. And she told me straight away that she was pregnant. I'd always known that from the very beginning. And when it came time for me to fly back to the States, I just couldn't leave her. I couldn't leave her there on her own and never see her again. So I smuggled her onto the plane and we flew back home and we got married straight away. While I was away on service she gave birth to the kids.'

Pieter listened. It was a life compacted into a couple of sentences, it was as simple as that.

Arthur Morris stopped, and he took a deep breath.

'I've always known that she loved you, Pieter. She never got over you, you see. And I knew that. I've always known that. But I've always loved her too, and we've had a friendship that mattered.'

He stopped for a moment. 'And now all this.'

Arthur Morris ran his hand over his head once more.

'The doctors have told us that she's only got a couple of months to live. I can't believe it, none of us can.'

'How's Leah handling everything?' Pieter asked.

'She's distraught, she's heartbroken. Leah and her mother are very close. We all are.'

And for a second, Pieter almost felt like an intruder. Prising his way into another man's life.

Arthur Morris continued, 'Francine wanted me to come on my own yesterday, she wanted to tell me about you. It's incredible, I suppose. Leah's in now, and Francine is going to tell her about you.'

He took another deep breath. 'We're going to have to do the right thing here, Pieter. For Francine's sake, and for Leah's sake too,' He paused for a minute. 'It's strange, but after all these years, we were never actually married. Francine was still married to you. We just didn't know it, none of us did,' and suddenly he began to weep.

It was as though Arthur Morris was giving her back to Pieter. As if he was letting go of a treasure that he'd never really owned. Pieter reached over and put his hand on his shoulder

'No Arthur. I don't see it like that, I really don't. You've looked after her for twenty years. You 'are' married to Francine. We both are. And we've both got to be bigger men over this. It doesn't matter anymore. It's how we're going to get through it that's important. For Francine and Leah's sake. And for David too, I suppose. '

At the mention of David's name, Arthur Morris shook his head.

'I believe you visited him in prison'.

'Yes I did, just over a week ago.'

'And how is he?' Arthur Morris asked.
'He's hard work,' Pieter replied gruffly.
'Tell me about it.' Arthur Morris replied.
'Francine tells me that he's always been a problem.'
Arthur Morris picked up his cup, and then he drank some of his coffee.
'David's been a thorn in my side since he was a kid. He was wild, and by the time he was thirteen or fourteen, he was uncontrollable. His mother made every excuse for him, but I could see what was coming and I could see where it was all heading. He's his own worst enemy. He's broken his mother's heart.'
'Yes,' said Pieter, 'well I didn't get much out of him either.'
'That doesn't surprise me, not one bit.' Arthur Morris drank the remains of his coffee.
'Well, there's not a lot we can do for David,' Pieter continued, 'but what about Leah?'
'I've been sort of thinking about that, Pieter. We'll see how she takes the news today. She's had a difficult time with all this, and I can understand that you'll want to meet her. But not today and not here, there's already too much upset here. I'd be obliged if you weren't around when we leave. Pieter, Leah needs time to think and we need to do this properly. She's already had enough upset in her life.' Arthur Morris then looked directly at Pieter. 'However, that said, you are her father, and you both do need to meet."
'I do understand, Arthur,' Pieter replied, 'and I know it's going to be a shock for her. David wouldn't believe me, he probably still doesn't. I'll leave everything to you and Francine, and we'll take it from there.'
'Give me your telephone number, and I'll phone you and we can arrange something.'
It was a moment of distraction, and Pieter gave Arthur Morris his home telephone number. And that was a mistake.
Arthur Morris took out a notepad and a pen and jotted it down.
'I'm going to go back to Francine, and then I'll take Leah home, Pieter. You can go and see her straight away.'
Pieter nodded, but Arthur Morris hadn't finished.
'I'd still like to keep our visits separate, Pieter, if that's alright with you. I don't want it to feel awkward. All of us together would be awkward for

Francine, and I don't want her to be upset. I realize that you two have things to talk about. And so do I, private things. And Leah and I are also very close, and we need to speak too, you understand?'

'Yes, of course I do. I do understand, Arthur. And I realize that this is all very difficult, for all of us'

Both men stood up, and then they shook hands.

'Thank you, Arthur, thank you for everything, and your patience,' said Pieter. And he meant it sincerely, it was the truth.

Arthur Morris gave a sympathetic smile. And then he turned and walked away.

When Pieter finally made his way back up to Room 219, Francine explained what had happened.

'He'd already spotted you, Pieter. Arthur's a clever man, he saw the family resemblance straightaway and he knew that you were somehow related. He just never expected it to be you. It's been a great shock for him, you do understand that?'

Pieter looked at her. 'He's a good man, Francine. We've spoken.'

Francine bit her lip.

'I need to tell you something, Pieter, something important. I don't want to hurt him. He's a good man and I couldn't bear to see him hurt or upset over this. I love him in my own way, Pieter, and he knows that. And Leah adores him, she loves her dad.'

She began to cry.

'Francine,' Pieter began, 'would it be better if I just disappeared for a while? If I just stepped back and let your family get on with things.'

She glanced up immediately.

'No...It would not. We can't step backwards, Pieter. Not now. Not after everything's that happened. The children need to know who their father is, and that you're still alive. And you deserve to know your children too. If not, what's all this been about? We've lost the rest of our family, your mother, your father, and your sisters. We deserve this, Pieter. All of us do.'

Pieter understood, and Francine was right.

He stayed late into the night until Francine became weary and eventually fell asleep. As he walked along the silent corridor and out of the hospital, Pieter thought about something that Francine had once said to him.

'Leah has always known something about your life, Pieter. At some point she'll need to need to know the rest of it.'

And that troubled Pieter. He couldn't tell anyone about his life.

However, fate and the future held different plans for Pieter Szabo.

When he got back to his apartment, the phone began to ring. He knew who it was, and he wouldn't answer it. He let it continue to ring as he went into his bedroom and lay back on the bed. It felt as though a thousand things were running through his mind. And still the phone continued to ring, and again he continued to ignore it. Yes, he knew who it would be.

And then...no! He suddenly sat upright on the bed. He'd given his phone number to Arthur Morris. And he immediately realized what he'd done. What on earth had he been thinking of, and why had he done it? It was a mistake, he'd been trying to be helpful. It had been an emotional moment and he'd quite readily handed over his phone number.

Pieter grimaced. And he lay back on the bed. It had been a mistake, he was a professional, he didn't make mistakes. And the phone continued to ring.

Pieter spent the next day in his apartment. He'd tried to read his newspaper, but his mind kept drifting elsewhere. And then at six o' clock, the phone rang. Pieter just stared at it, the phone usually rang late at night. So it could be Arthur Morris. Pieter walked across the room and snatched up the phone.

'Yes.' There was a moment's pause.

'Eagle. Is that you?' said a voice at the end of the line. It was Vernon Ballantyne.

Pieter's heart sank. He didn't speak.

'Eagle?'

'It's me, I'm here,' Pieter replied.

'Where in hell's name have you been? I've been ringing you for weeks.'

'I've been busy.'

'Busy?' Vernon Ballantyne was infuriated. 'What on earth with?'

'Family business.'

There was a short pause.

'You have no family.'

'I do now.' That was all Pieter was prepared to say on the matter.

There was another pause.

'Stiller wants you.' Vernon Ballantyne then gave Pieter a telephone number.

'I can't do anything for a couple of months,' Pieter tried to explain.

'You'd better tell that to Stiller,' said Ballantyne. And he slammed the phone down.

Half an hour passed, and then the phone rang again.

Pieter knew that it wouldn't be Vernon Ballantyne. He never rang back.

Pieter picked up the phone, and once again asked. 'Yes?'

It was Arthur Morris.

'Hello Pieter, it's me, Arthur. Arthur Morris.'

'Yes, Arthur?' Pieter replied, he was almost relieved. 'How did everything go?'

'Well, better than I expected. Leah and her mother have spoken. Francine's told her everything and she's explained what's happened. Leah was shocked, as you can imagine, and there were a few tears shed. But Leah understands, and she understands how her mother feels about you coming back into her life. She was overjoyed for her really. She's a sensible girl. And now there are no secrets. We've never had secrets, not after the problems we've had with David. We've always tried to be honest with one another, especially with the kids.'

'Okay,' Pieter replied, though deep down he realized the effect he must be having on this man's family, and once again he felt as though he was the intruder.

'What happens now, Arthur?'

'Leah wants to meet you,' Arthur Morris replied.

When does she want to meet me?'

'Well, now really. She wants to meet you tonight, here, if that's possible.'

Pieter was rather taken aback, He hadn't expected this so soon. But he had to see her.

'Give me your address. I'll be round there within the hour.'

Pieter showered and changed. Forty five minutes and a bus ride later, he found himself outside a block of nice apartments in New York's Soho District. Pieter was understandably nervous. He walked into the building through the main doors and took the lift up to the third floor. He walked along the hallway to apartment number 313. He felt hesitant, but then he knocked on the door.

The door opened, and there she was, the embodiment of her mother. At last, it was Leah.

Pieter looked at his daughter, and he had to stop himself from picking her up in his arms and hugging her. He just stood there.

'Hello, Leah,' was all he could manage to say.

She smiled at him, and Pieter looked at her, her mother's face, and the same beautiful eyes.

'Please, come in,' she said.

Pieter walked into the apartment and he followed Leah into the main living room. Arthur Morris was standing in the corner, looking slightly apprehensive, but he managed to smile.

Leah then turned around, and she smiled at Pieter as she held out her hand.

'Hello...and I'm Leah,' she said to him, 'and I believe you're my father?'

Pieter shook her hand. There were to be no hugs and no kisses. And Pieter suddenly realized that this young lady, his daughter, was guarded. He should have known really. He was the stranger here, and he was the man who had just barged into their lives. Unintentionally it may have been, but Pieter had arrived at an obviously difficult time.

He smiled back at her.

'Yes Leah. I am your father, apparently.' And straight away he wished he'd not used that last word. 'No. I mean, I am your father.' And he took a deep breath, and he felt that he needed to start again.

'I know that this has come as a shock to you, Leah. It's been a shock for us all, it really has.' And he glanced across at Arthur Morris. This was difficult for him too.

'Your mother and I, well, you know what happened to us. We thought we'd lost one another years ago. We didn't know that either of us was still alive. And we still wouldn't, if I hadn't been on the bus that day and seen you. But for that, I would have never, ever known that you existed.'

Leah suddenly looked at him sympathetically. She could see his emotion, and she could see that he was trying his best to explain everything to her. But she'd made a decision.

'I need to say something,' she said to him. 'I've thought about all this, and what's happening to us, and I need to say something straight away.'

Pieter watched her as she went across the room to Arthur Morris and took hold of his arm.

'Please, I don't want to offend you or upset you,' she continued, 'but there's something that we all need to know and understand. I realize that you are my father, my real father,' and then she looked up at Arthur, 'but this is my Dad, my real Dad.' And she kissed him.

Pieter stood there, and there was no jealousy and no malice. He understood everything.

'Leah, I wouldn't have it any other way,' he said, and he smiled at them both.

Suddenly, everyone in the room relaxed. It was done, and what had to be said, had been said.

And they began to talk, mainly about the seriousness of Francine's illness. But there were no answers, there never could be.

After twenty minutes or so, Arthur Morris made an announcement..

'I'm going to go out now. I'm going to leave you both to talk. I'll be about an hour, Leah.

Leah nodded at him. This had all been pre-arranged by them both, depending on the outcome of Leah's first meeting with her father, but things were good and everyone was relaxed.

As Arthur Morris left, Leah kissed him on the cheek. And once the door closed behind him it left the two of them on their own. Leah turned to Pieter and she raised an eyebrow, and she smiled at him.

'Well, this is different. I finally get to meet my real father. Who'd have ever guessed?'

Pieter looked at her.

'Leah, you're my daughter. Please, I never knew about you. You're so very beautiful, just like your mother.'

Leah stared at him for a moment. And then she went straight over to Pieter and threw her arms around him.

'Welcome back,' she said.

They sat and they talked. Leah made a pot of tea and they sat at the kitchen table and got to know one another. Pieter told her about his past, or the parts that she needed to know.

Finally, she turned to him.

'My mother told me everything,' and then she paused for a moment.

'My mother and I are very close, we don't have any secrets. I know that you're the love of her life, she's told me that. You always were. She's so very happy, she really is. You've made her life complete, Pieter Szabo,' and she smiled as she said the name. 'I'm going to call you Pieter. I'd wondered about that.'

Pieter grinned. His daughter had her mother's spark about her.

And then she stopped smiling. 'We both know that my mother's dying. I want the time that she has left to be happy for her. You are the greatest part of that happiness. She loves you so much.'

Pieter took hold of her hand. 'And I love your mother. There's never been another woman in my life, Leah. After your mother, there was no one.'

She smiled at him. He was telling her the truth, she knew he was.

'We're all going to have to work together, you know that?' said Leah.

'Yes, I know,' Pieter replied. 'But what about your brother? What about David?'

Leah looked at him and sighed.

'David. Well, I really don't know about David. I believe you went to see him?'

'Yes I did. And he's angry. I tried to explain to him that I was his father, but he didn't believe me.'

'No, he wouldn't. David doesn't trust anyone. To tell you the truth, that's always been his problem, I suppose. When we were kids, Mum and Dad sat us down and told us everything that had happened and about you being our real father. To me it made no difference, my dad will always be my dad. But David somehow didn't understand. He couldn't understand how the man who had always been his father, suddenly wasn't. He felt he'd been lied to, and that's when the problems started. He wouldn't listen to my dad anymore, and it was always the same, the childhood tantrums which always ended up with the same argument, 'You can't tell me what to do, you're not my dad...' My dad was heartbroken. He and my mother really tried with David. But there was nothing they could do with him, he resented the authority, and he ended up on the streets with the gangs. And from there it just spiralled out of control, and now he's in prison, and it's all very upsetting for my Mum.'

'I know it is, Leah. We've spoken about him, nobody knows what to do.'

She looked up at Pieter. 'You do know that David and I have always been very close?'

Pieter nodded.

Leah thought for a moment.

'I'm going to go and see him. I'll talk to him and try to explain what's happening. He needs to understand how ill my mother is. And I'll try to explain about you. There's the chance that he might listen to me.'

'I'll come with you,' said Pieter immediately.

'It's okay,' she replied, 'I'll need to speak to him on his own.'

'No, you misunderstand me. I'll take you there. Ask your dad if it's okay and we'll fly out to Chicago. We could be back the same day.'

Leah's eyes widened, and she nodded. 'Okay then, let's do it.'

When Arthur Morris came back to the apartment, they discussed their proposal with him, and he was in full agreement.

'There's nothing that I can do,' he added. 'David won't listen to me, he never has. For his mother's sake, I can only wish you good luck.'

Later that evening, Pieter went to the hospital to see Francine. She looked tired, it had been a long day for her. He sat on the side of her bed and told her everything that had happened and how he and Leah had met. For some reason he didn't mention David. It was enough for Francine to take in.

He left the hospital after midnight and this time he took a taxi home. The bus stops in New York City could be a dangerous place after midnight.

When he got back to his apartment he made some coffee. He sat there for a while, and then he went over to his desk. He opened a drawer and picked up a piece of paper with some numbers scribbled on it. It was Stiller's telephone number that Vernon Ballantyne had given him earlier. Pieter slipped on his jacket and once more left his apartment. He walked a short distance down the road to a payphone. He picked up the phone and dialled the number, and waited. The phone rang four times before it was finally answered.

'Eagle?'

'Yes,' said Pieter.

'I've been waiting for you.'

'Yes, I know. I've been busy.'

'I have a job for you.'

'I've already spoken to Ballantyne. I can't do anything for at least two months.'

There was a pause.

'That's okay,' said Stiller. 'This job will need a lot of planning, I don't have a problem with that. Two months. Okay then, ring me on this number when you're ready.'

And then the phone clicked off.

Conrad Stiller sat in his office in Washington. He unlocked the middle drawer of his desk and took out a green folder, it was something that he'd managed to acquire from the Secret Service Special Files. Inside the folder was President Kennedy's full itinerary for the next six months. Stiller checked the dates against his calendar, and then he took out his pen and drew a circle around a possible location.

He looked again and he smiled...'Dallas'. It would be perfect.

The next day, Pieter and Leah went to the hospital together. Arthur had offered to visit his wife later in the evening. He and Leah had spoken. It would be better that way.

And Francine was overjoyed. They sat on her bed, together, as a family. Almost a family.

They talked and laughed about the old days, and the present, and Francine told Leah how she and Pieter had first met all those years ago in the library in Lodz, and Francine was happy.

But finally, she once again became weary and tired, and so they had to leave her to sleep.

It was a step forward, or perhaps not.

Three days later, Pieter and Leah flew out to Chicago. Pieter once again rented a car and they drove to Joliet City, but this time they went straight to the Stateville Correctional Facility. Once they were admitted into the prison, Pieter stayed in the visitor's reception while Leah went to speak to her brother. Half an hour later, she returned. They left the prison and went straight back to the car and sat there for a while.

'How is he? Pieter asked her.

'Not good. He didn't realize how ill our mother is. It's come as a shock to him, and he can't see her, obviously. They won't let him out, they never do. I think he's feeling guilty and I think he's struggling with himself. He said something about 'looking in the mirror', like you told him to. He's recognized the resemblance. He really does look like you, Pieter. Anyway, he asked me if I believed you. I've told him everything, and how you found my mum and how you came to see me. Of course you're our father. But I think it's shaken him. He doesn't know how to take it all. In the end he said he would have to 'think it over'? That's typical of David. Anyway, now he knows. It's up to him I suppose, but he's locked in there. He can't do anything.'

And at that point, Leah became tearful.

'I don't think my mum is ever going to see David again, Pieter.'

Pieter put his arm around her. There were difficult times ahead, for them all.

It took a week, but then Leah received a letter from her brother. After reading it she couldn't wait. She picked up the phone and rang Pieter immediately.

'David's sent me a letter, Pieter,' she said at once. 'He wants to meet you again. He says that he needs to talk to you.'

'I didn't expect that,' Pieter replied. 'But I will go and see him, I'll make the arrangements.'

It took another two days before Pieter could return once more to Chicago and to the Stateville Correctional Facility in Joliet. And once again he sat in the same reception area until the guard came out and called out several names. Pieter was one of them and he was again led into the room full of individual booths. In the third booth to Pieter's left sat David.

Pieter went over to him and sat down. There was an uneasy silence, but it was David who spoke first.

'I...I'm glad you could make it.'

Pieter just nodded.

David continued, 'I've spoken to Leah. She's told me everything. I think I owe you an apology, I didn't know. I didn't know anything.'

Pieter looked at him. Finally, there was a chance.

Pieter leant forward.

'David, let me talk to you. You are my son. If I'd known that you and your sister existed, and if I'd known that your mother was still alive, we would have all lived a different life. Not for one moment would I have never come to find you, never. You're my family for god's sake. You're everything I thought I'd lost and never had.'

David stared at him. He'd just been told everything that he'd ever needed to hear. He had a real father, and suddenly his name wasn't David Morris. It was David Szabo.

'My mother, she's not well, is she?'

'No, she's not David. You've spoken to Leah, you know it's not good.'

David rubbed his eyes.

'I've not been the best of sons.'

'Yes, she told me. But she still loves you, David, always. She's your mother.'

David shook his head. 'I've had a lot of time to think while I've been in here. It makes you realize the mistakes that you've made, and all through your own stupidity. And then they lock you up and throw away the key. And then your life's over.'

'How long have you served?.' Pieter asked him.

'Just over twelve months, but I won't be coming out. I won't ever be coming out, not alive anyway.'

Pieter frowned. 'And why's that?'

David sighed and again he shook his head.

'I got involved with the wrong people. I've made enemies, I've upset the wrong people.'

'And who are 'they'?

'I was selling drugs, I got involved with the mob in Chicago. Once you work for those people you can never get away. I tried to, and that's why I'm in here.'

'I don't understand,' said Pieter.

David looked at his father.

'It's like this. We were living in Chicago. Me, my girlfriend Valerie and another guy, Tommy. We were dealing cocaine. Over a twelve month period we were selling more and more of it. Tommy and Valerie were brought up in Chicago and they knew people and we had access to the bars and clubs. The mob saw to that. Me, Valerie and Tommy, we were all living together in the same apartment. We had one of the bedrooms stacked high with cocaine, at any one time we must have had seven or eight thousand bucks worth stored in there. And there was the money too. We had a suitcase that we used. There was always around five thousand dollars in that suitcase. We used to go to one of the mob's warehouses in Tommy's van and deliver the money and pick up more cocaine. The mob has warehouses all over the city. The police know all about them, but they're on the payroll and it goes all the way to the top. Anyway, everything's going sort of okay, but then Tommy gets greedy, the stupid bastard. He used to talk all the time about setting up on his own somewhere and getting rich. The bloody fool, you can't just set up 'somewhere'. The mob runs everything, it's the Mafia for Christ's sake. Anyway, Tommy starts to cream it off from the top, he starts stealing the money, a bit here, a bit there. But, the mob has seen it all before. They have accountants for god's sake. They know exactly what their return should be. But he's stealing, and me and Valerie, we haven't got a clue, we think that everything's just fine and dandy. Then one night, me and Tommy go in his van to some warehouse somewhere and suddenly we're being threatened. This guy puts a gun to my head as Tommy hands over the case. They count the money as usual, but then they reckon that we're about twenty grand down on the amount of drugs we've handled over the last couple of months. Tommy then tells them that he's owed the money.

He tells them that he's got some new dealers on the streets that are working for him and he's waiting for the money to roll back to him. He explains that he's sort of expanding the business. It was all news to me. But he tells them that he'll get them the money, no problem. Anyway, they take the money but they won't give us any more drugs. They know we have plenty anyway, like I said, they have accountants. Tommy laughs and tells them not to worry, but I'm the one with a gun pointed at my head. They tell us that we've got a week to find the cash, and Tommy's like 'not to worry' and everything's okay. Eventually they let us go and we drive away, and I'm ready to kill him. But he's shaking his head and he's still laughing, and he tells me that there's no problem. When I asked him about these 'new dealers' he laughs and tells me that he's sick of doing all the clubs and bars himself and that it's easier and safer for us to let other people do all the footwork.

'I told you, I'm going to make us rich,' he said to me, 'and you're right David, we can't do it without the mob, we need them.'

When I asked him 'why' he hadn't told us what he was doing, he just shook his head.

'Because you're a worrier David, you always were. You're worried now, look at you. Look man, I'll have the money by next week, it's not a problem. We're going to be rich, David, and somebody else is going to do all the work for us, it's going to be easy money.'

'It was all bullshit, but I believed him. A week later I was in one of the clubs, it was late. Then one of the barmen who I know tells me that my girlfriends been ringing around, she was trying to get hold of me. I get to a payphone and ring her back and she's in a state of panic. She's come home and everything's gone, all the drugs, along with the suitcase full of the cash that we needed to pay the mob. I got in my car and I drove back home. Tommy's gone, all his stuff, the drugs, the cash, everything. So me and Valerie pack up and run. We find another apartment across town and stay low. We stayed there for a week and we'd decided that at some point we would have to come clean and tell the mob that it was Tommy who'd stolen everything. But that was a mistake, we should have ran and got out of the state. Maybe we should have got out of the country too and headed for Canada or somewhere south. Anyway, we never got the chance to speak to the mob. They found us first. I don't know how, but they found us. The mob spoke to the police. It was the middle of the afternoon, I'd been out, but when I came back to the apartment Valerie wasn't there. The next thing I know, the door's being smashed down and the police charge in. And then they suddenly 'find' a large stash of drugs in one of the other bedrooms and I'm arrested. It was all a setup, the mob owns and runs the police force in Chicago. Two days later they pull Valerie's body out of the Chicago River. She's full of drugs and the authorities put it down to either suicide or misadventure. A week later they found Tommy's body in a motel just outside Little Rock in Arkansas. Both of his hands had been cut off and he'd been shot several times. The Mafia always like to leave a message, it's a warning to others. Anyway, I get to live for the time being, and I go to court and get seven years with no reduction. But that doesn't matter, because I won't be getting out.'

Pieter looked at his son.

'You keep saying that, why?'

'Because the Mafia have people in here too, they may be locked up but they're still Mafia. Even the guards are on the payroll. Like I said, you never leave. I've already been given the word, it may take two years, it may take four years, but in the end they'll kill me. It's like death row. Only one day they find you strangled or stabbed, and that's it.'

Pieter started to say something, but suddenly a guard intervened.

'Okay buddy,' he said gruffly. 'Times up, it's time to go.'

David stood up immediately, it was over. But there was a reason for him standing up, he was buying a moment's time as the guard turned away.

'Tell my mum I love her, and tell her I'm sorry. I'm sorry for everything.'

Pieter was just about to say something.

'Hey you,' the guard suddenly shouted back. 'What did I say to you? It's over.'

Pieter stood up and apologized, but the guard just pointed his thumb towards the door.

Pieter turned as he left, to see his son just standing there, staring back at him.

When he got back to New York, Pieter went straight to St Vincent's Hospital to see Francine. He told her that he'd spoken to David and that they'd talked about the family, and she was pleased. But he couldn't tell her about the threat to David's life. She didn't need to know.

Several weeks passed by. Long, painful, heartbreaking weeks that rolled away like fading sunshine. The family sat there in turn and watched Francine slowly deteriorate and weaken.

In the end she was put on a mixture of morphine and drugs to kill the pain.

But Francine had made a decision, a last request.

It was on the fifth week. It was after midnight and Pieter was sitting by the side of her bed as Francine slept. He was looking at her, and then her eyelids began to flutter and she suddenly awoke. She looked around and then she immediately saw Pieter, and she smiled as he took hold of her hand.

'How are you?' he asked. It wasn't really a question.

She looked up at him.

'Hello husband,' she replied.

'Hello you,' he said in return.

It had become their own special way of greeting one another.

And then she looked at him.

'I need to talk to you about something, Pieter.' she said. 'It's something rather selfish, I'm afraid.'

He stared at her for a moment.

'I want you to do something for me, Pieter.'

'I'll do anything for you, you know that Francine.'

She stared back at him, and she bit her lip.

'You once told me that you'd always look after me, Pieter Szabo. And so I married you.'

Pieter nodded.

'Well, I still want you to look after me, Pieter.'

Pieter frowned, he didn't quite understand.

'Of course I'll look after you. You know that.'

She glanced up at him.

'Listen to me, Pieter,' she continued, 'I don't know what you do. But you're not a security consultant and you don't spend your nights doing 'loads of paperwork'. I know you, Pieter Szabo. You could never do that, it would drive you crazy, it always did.'

He looked at her and he sighed. It was time for him to tell her the truth.

'You know me too well, you always did,' he said to her. 'And you're right of course, that's not my job, Francine.' And then he took a deep breath. 'In truth, I suppose I live in a different sort of world from everyone else. After the war, I was recruited by a government agency. Over the years I've been employed to hunt down missing Nazis. I've killed a lot of bad people, and I still do, Francine. '

Her eyes widened, she finally understood.

'Good,' she replied. 'I'm proud of you. They were evil men who deserved to die, and I suppose there are others too, I can understand that,' and then she paused for a moment as she gasped for breath, she was becoming exhausted. And then she suddenly clung onto to his arm.

'I'm going to die, Pieter, I'm going to die soon. And I need to ask you something. You need to do something for me. I don't want to die in agony, Pieter. Please don't let me die in agony.'

And for a moment he still didn't understand.

'I want you to do something for me, Pieter. When the time comes, let me go. Take care of me. I don't want to suffer, Pieter.'

And suddenly, he understood.

'You mean..?'

She nodded.

'Promise me now, and let me have peace. When it's time, don't let me suffer. Promise me.'

Pieter was overwhelmed at what she wanted him to do, He'd found her, and now this. It was too much, too much for him to even contemplate. But he had to give her peace of mind.

'Yes Francine,' he said to her, 'Yes, I'll take care of you. Like I always promised I would.'

'Yes, like you always promised...I love you, Pieter.'

And with that, she closed her eyes.

Over the next two weeks, Francine's illness seized her.

She became uncontrollably weak and then began to slip in and out of consciousness. Arnold and Leah would sit by Francine's side during the days and Pieter would stay with her through the long nights.

And then her pain began to get worse, as the morphine and the painkiller drugs could no longer control her disease.

On the Friday evening, Pieter sat with her. Francine was unconscious, it was almost midnight and he'd been there for the last three hours, listening to her trying to breathe. Every few minutes she would groan as the pain inside her gripped her body. The nurse had been in twice to administer more morphine, but it didn't seem to help. And another hour passed, it was almost one o' clock and Francine seemed to be in almost constant agony.

Pieter was in a state of torment and anguish. She was suffering so badly now.

And at that moment, she moaned again as the pain wracked through her body. And she suddenly gasped as the shock of it made her regain consciousness. Pieter immediately leant over her and she just stared up at him. And then she groaned again as the pain returned with a vengeance. She stared at him and her lips trembled, and then she managed to utter the words.

'You promised me...'

Her words faded away. There was nothing more she could say, and she just looked up at him as a tear slowly ran down her cheek.

Pieter leant over, and he kissed her fully on her mouth. He remembered the first time he ever kissed her, all those years ago, in a cafe in Lodz, and now this would be their last kiss.

He slowly reached up and put his fingers on her nose and he pressed her nostrils together. And suddenly she couldn't breathe, and he felt her begin to strain, and he felt her trying to suck her last remaining breath out of his lungs, but he wouldn't let go, he couldn't. It was his promise to her. She strained in his arms, but he held on to her in a last embrace. And then suddenly, she stopped, she went still and almost seemed to relax. It was over. And he'd had to do the most terrible thing to the person he loved so much, all because of a promise he'd made. He let her go, and he looked down at her face, so beautiful. Her eyes were closed, she was at peace.

Pieter sat at the side of the bed and he wept. She was gone. It was over, another dream and another life together, never to be.

Finally, he kissed her once more and then he left to inform the nurse. After that, he went to find a payphone. He had to ring Leah and Arthur Morris. It was also a tragedy for them, as he told them both the sad news.

Francine was buried the following week at New York's iconic GreenWood cemetery. Arthur Morris's family were there as were friends and workmates. Arthur Morris was understandably distraught, as was Leah, who hung onto her dad's arm as they both openly wept and tried to console one another. Pieter attended, but stood back. He was from another lifetime, and he would forever shoulder the guilt of his wife's death. The last secret they shared together, the one that only they would ever know.

After the funeral, Pieter hugged Leah and he shook Arthur Morris's hand. But he turned down the offer to go back to their apartment with family and friends. It seemed out of place for him to be there, and Leah understood. She would need to look after her dad now.

Pieter went back to his apartment. On his way back there he stopped off at the liquor store and bought a bottle of vodka. Pieter very rarely drank, but that night he consumed the bottle.

Another week passed by. Pieter met up with Leah a couple of times for lunch and they talked about the family and about David. But life had to go on, as it does.

Eventually, Pieter had no other choice. He rang Conrad Stiller.

Pieter found a phone booth just across the road from Central Park. The phone rang three times before being picked up.

'Eagle?' Stiller asked.

'Yes, it's me,' Pieter replied. 'I'm ready.'

CHAPTER 15

Pieter Szabo stood in the phone booth opposite Central Park.

He was in conversation with Conrad Stiller. And what he'd just been asked to do was almost unbelievable, nevertheless, it had all been said with total conviction

Conrad Stiller had just informed Pieter that his next contract would be to assassinate President John F. Kennedy. Pieter Szabo was being asked to assassinate the President of the United States of America.

'Is this some kind of joke?' Pieter asked.

There was a pause on the end of the line.

'I never joke,' Stiller replied seriously, and then, 'and why are you asking? You've never asked before. Is there a problem, Eagle?'

There was a brief silence.

'I'll get back to you,' Pieter replied, and he hung up the phone.

Conrad Stiller sat in his office in Washington and he almost snarled with frustration. There was something wrong, something was going on. Codename Eagle had always taken on Stiller's work, always and straightaway and no questions asked, ever. And suddenly Stiller wondered why he'd not been able to contact 'Eagle' for so long. There was something different, and Conrad Stiller tapped his pen on the top of his desk as he thought things over. This was going to be Stiller's final job, and then he'd disappear for good. There would be no repercussions or reprisals, and then something crossed his mind. This could be the 'Eagles' last job too. Maybe it would have to be.

Pieter Szabo went straight back to his apartment. When he arrived there he didn't make any coffee or turn on the TV. He just sat there in silence.

He had to think. He had to plan. After this, nothing would ever be the same again.

Conrad Stiller had spent months planning everything. It was like a huge jigsaw puzzle. Every piece had its place. And a jigsaw with even one piece missing, was never completed.

Stiller had links with both the FBI and with the Chicago Mob, which was headed by the all powerful Mafia boss, Sam Giancana.

However, things went even deeper. And central to all of this was Cuba.

Sam Giancana had teamed up with Miami Mafia and they'd come to the decision that they wanted Cuba back. In the past they'd made vast profits there and the island's potential was huge, Yes, Cuba was an island, but it was also a country, and the Mafia wanted to run it, all of it.

To that end, at one time, Sam Giancana had actually been introduced to John F. Kennedy prior to Kennedy's 1960 Presidential Election. Giancana had taken Kennedy to one side and promised him a substantial amount of funding to help his election campaign, with the view that America would at some point reclaim Cuba and that it would be business as usual. Unfortunately, Kennedy reneged on the arrangement and put paid to that ideal. And what could have become the perfect moment to seize Cuba had once again been bungled by Kennedy's indecisiveness. And so the Mafia too, were not overly impressed with Kennedy's show of weakness, as they also realized that a much firmer hand was needed.

All of this placed Conrad Stiller very conveniently between the FBI and the mob. And he would use their extensive resources to his own end. Through FBI assistant director, Clyde Tolson, Stiller would have the use of certain trusted agents, the likes of Agents Sloan and Hughes. And Sam Giancana and the mob would supply him with the perfect stooge, the 'patsy', a man named Lee Harvey Oswald.

The next day, Pieter Szabo rang Conrad Stiller again.

'Eagle? Stiller asked.

'Yes,' it's me,' Pieter replied.

Stiller inwardly sighed with relief. If codename 'Eagle' hadn't rung back, Stiller's plans would have become unworkable. Finding someone else was not an option, not for this.

'I take it you're back on track.' said Stiller, but Pieter ignored the comment.

'Give me the details,' Pieter said coldly, and he took a notepad from his pocket.

Stiller told him everything, the whole plan, the days, the dates and the times. Pieter listened as he wrote down everything that was essential. It was all credible. And Pieter waited until Stiller had finished.

'We need to talk,' he then said.

Stiller paused for a moment.

'What about?' he asked.

'You need to listen to me,' said Pieter. 'This is different. This is different from anything we've done before and I need two things from you.'

'And they are?' Stiller interrupted.

'I want one hundred thousand dollars up front. I want that amount sending to Ballantyne in London, and it has to be transferred into my account before I do anything.'

Stiller did the calculations. He was going to charge the FBI the whole million bucks for his services, and they'd agreed to pay. So a hundred thousand for 'Eagle' and whatever Vernon Ballantyne required was hardly going to break the bank.

'Okay, no problem,' said Stiller, 'what else?'

'There's a young man called 'David Morris'. He's locked up in the Stateville Prison in Joliet. I want him released, straightaway.'

Stiller frowned. 'Who is he?'

'That doesn't matter. I want him released. And it's non-negotiable, I'll only move once I know he's out of there.'

'That could be difficult.'

'Not for you,' Pieter replied, 'pull a few strings.'

'I'll see what I can do.'

'You do that. When it happens, I'll get back to you.' And with that, Pieter hung up.

That left Conrad Stiller on the end of the line, wondering about the request. The money wasn't a problem, but who was 'David Morris'? He put down the phone and then he pressed the button on his office intercom which immediately connected him to one of his assistants.

'I want you to find out about somebody called 'David Morris', he's locked up in Joliet for 'God knows what'. I want to know everything about him, and I do mean 'everything'.'

The following day, Stiller's assistant walked into his office and dropped a folder in front of him. Typed on the front of the folder was the name 'David Morris'.

The assistant turned to Stiller, and he shrugged his shoulders.

'Just another loser selling drugs,' he informed Stiller. 'Not much family history. Lived in New York, went off the rails as a teenager and got locked up a couple of times. Then he goes off to Chicago and ends up selling drugs for the mob. He tries to get clever and apparently took off with the drugs and then he gets caught, that's according to the police reports anyway, but you never know. Anyway, he's locked up for seven years.'

'Okay, thanks for that,' said Stiller. His assistant then left him to read the report.

It was the mention of Chicago that caught Conrad Stiller's attention. Sam Giancana ran Chicago, all the drugs, the prostitution and the extortion, everything. Stiller quickly read the report in front of him. It told him very little about David Morris, other than the obvious. And he couldn't see anything that linked David Morris to an assassin named 'codename Eagle'.

With that in mind, he picked up the phone and dialled a number. A moment later it was picked up and a thickly accented voice replied.

'Yeah, what is it?'

'It's Stiller. I need to speak to Mr Giancana please.'

'Okay, right,' came the immediate reply.

There was a brief pause.

'Hey buddy boy, how are you?' On the end of the line was the rasping voice of Mafia boss, Sam Giancana.

'I'm fine Sam, just fine.'

'And how are our 'arrangements' going?'

'Fine Sam. It's all coming together. I've spoken to 'Oswald' in Dallas. I went to see him a couple of weeks ago. Yeah, he's in it up to his neck. He won't be a problem, and I offered him enough money to make his eyes spin. You were right about him, Sam. Just another 'commie' loving bastard with a cause. He's an idiot.'

Sam Giancan laughed down the end of phone. 'Nice one, Stiller.'

Actually Sam, I've rung you about something else, I need some information.'

'Go ahead, ask away,' replied Giancana, in his rasping tone.

'Do you know anything about a guy called 'David Morris'? He's in Joliet doing seven years for drugs. The Chicago police got hold of him, it's over a year ago now.'

Stiller stopped talking, as he heard Sam Giancana mutter something to someone in the room, there was a brief conversation. Then he came back on the phone.

'Yeah, I remember him. There was him and another guy, and a girl was involved too. They ran off with my money and a whole load of drugs, the smart bastards. We wacked one of them and we threw the girl in the river. I sent the cops around to grab Morris, they were supposed to let him try and run and then shoot the bastard. But somehow they messed up, the useless idiots. So anyway, this 'Morris' gets arrested and he's banged up in Joliet. But he won't do the seven and he knows it. We've got a marker on him. We'll give him a couple of years and let him suffer, and then he'll get wacked too. The cheap bastard, he thought he could steal from me and get away with it. What a prick.'

Conrad Stiller took a deep breath.

'I need him out, Sam. I need him to be released.'

There was a brief silence.

'You're kidding me, right?' Giancana replied.

'No Sam, its part of the deal I'm putting together with my shooter, my real shooter. He wants this, or he's not playing ball.'

There was another silence.

'But that bastard robbed me. How does it look if I start letting people walk away. It makes me look like I've gone soft.'

Conrad Stiller took a deep breath.

'I need this to happen Sam. I think we need to look at the bigger picture here.'

And suddenly, Conrad Stiller thought of something.

'Listen Sam, I've got an idea. Get David Morris released and I'll have him followed. When the jobs over I'll hand him back to you, or I'll have him shot. Whatever suits you?'

Stiller waited for a reply. And then suddenly there was a rasping laugh.

'Hey Stiller, you are a very clever man. Yeah, okay buddy, you do that, you shoot the bastard for me. Yeah, alright, leave everything with me and I'll sort out his release. And call me, let me know what's happening with Oswald.'

Conrad Stiller agreed, and then he put the phone down. And it was only then that he noticed the perspiration on his face.

The 'Patsy', Lee Harvey Oswald had lived in Dallas during his early years, with his somewhat disruptive mother. It was always considered by some, that she could have been the catalyst for his curious lifestyle. Oswald joined the US Marines but quickly became disillusioned with army life and was aptly discharged. He then took up the Communist cause and started to call himself a 'Marxist'. And it was at that point that Oswald's life took a stranger twist. In October, 1959, he decided to defect to Russia. Whilst there he married a nineteen year old pharmacology student and they later had a child, a daughter. After three years, Oswald also became disenchanted with Russia and with the miserable lifestyle that he was leading there.

In May, 1962, Oswald applied to the US Embassy in Moscow for papers that would allow him and his wife and child to immigrate back to the United States. By June they were repatriated and Oswald once more returned to Dallas

Oswald then decided to take up the 'Cuban' cause, fully supporting Fidel Castro with an almost hero worship. He regularly paraded the streets of Dallas, handing out pamphlets and pro-Castro propaganda to anyone who looked vaguely interested, and to the many who were not.

He became a nuisance, and in the end he managed to get himself noticed. Preaching any form of communism in 'sixties' America was a sure fire way of drawing attention to one's self.

And ultimately, he caught the attention of a Dallas bar and nightclub owner. The club was known as the 'Carousel', and the owner's name was Jack Ruby.

And Jack Ruby was connected.

His club was well frequented by all, and that included the Dallas police, and the usual 'suspect' city officials, all who were supplied with free booze as they conveniently turned a blind eye to the prostitution and the drugs that were readily available there for all.

Dallas was a big enough city, and could easily provide a procession of willing and able prostitutes. But the drugs had to be shipped in from Chicago, via Mr Sam Giancana.

Ruby and Giancana went back a long way. As younger men, they used to fly out to Cuba together and enjoy the delights that only that island could supply, back in those happier days.

And Jack Ruby still worked for Sam Giancana, indirectly. The drugs came in, and through the mob, Ruby bankrolled the police department. And it worked. Everybody knew everything that was going on, and everyone also knew how to keep their mouths firmly shut.

Word got to Ruby that Sam Giancana was looking for a stooge in Dallas. It was for something big. Jack Ruby rang Giancana and they talked, they were old friends of course. Ruby quickly realized that he had a possible 'stooge' right there on his doorstep, an irritating little guy who regularly passed by his club, handing out pamphlets. Lee Harvey Oswald was anti-government, pro-Cuban, and an exponent of Communism. He could be perfect for the job. From there, Ruby took Oswald under his wing. He invited Oswald into his club and supplied him with free drinks. Ruby always sat Oswald in a corner, well away from the regularly frequenting police and the other guests. When the club was quieter, Ruby would sit with Oswald and listen to his radical views. Ruby totally agreed with Oswald's cause and blamed Kennedy and the government for everything, in particular the constant threat to Cuba. Ruby wholeheartedly agreed with Oswald and commented on numerous occasions that Kennedy and America should leave Cuba alone. Over the next few weeks, everything became President Kennedy's fault. Jack Ruby told Oswald about the drugs and that he had to regularly bankroll the Dallas police, and that was the reason why the police were always in there. But Ruby then went on to explain that the drug money went all the way back to a higher office, and that Kennedy and the government were working hand in hand with the Mafia. He also told Oswald that it was a definite 'certainty' that in the end Cuba would be invaded, Kennedy wanted it that way and so did the Mafia. It was all about the money. And once his Presidency was over, Kennedy would receive millions of dollars in backhanders.

Oswald was incensed, Kennedy had to be stopped. Eventually, Ruby opened up to Oswald, and he told him about an organization in Dallas that he was involved with who wanted to do something about it, and something big. Oswald took the bait and asked if he could he be involved. Ruby said that he would contact someone and that a decision would then have to be made.

Oswald believed every word of it. And a few days later, Ruby gave him the 'okay'. Someone from the organization would contact him.

The following week, Lee Harvey Oswald met up with Conrad Stiller.

For Pieter Szabo, it had been a frustrating time.

He'd had to think long and hard about his future, and also the future of his son, David.

It was late morning when he left his apartment and made his way down the flights of stairs. He was heading for a payphone. And as he walked along the sidewalk, he wondered if Stiller had somehow managed to get a result. Would David be released from prison?

He finally found a phone booth and rang the designated number.

Stiller picked up, 'Eagle?'

'Yes, it's me.'

Stiller spoke before Pieter could say another word.

'It's sorted. David Morris will be released in the next couple of weeks. Your money has been forwarded to London and is being transferred. Ballantyne's okay with it, he's been paid too. I want you in Dallas in three weeks time, you know what you have to do. Everything's set up. So no more discussions, is that clear?'

Stiller was back to his usual 'no-nonsense' self.

'Clear,' said Pieter, and with that, Stiller hung up.

Three days later, Pieter once more flew out to Chicago where he made his way to the Stateville Prison in Joliet. He was booked in as a visitor and once again had to follow strict procedure before sitting down with his son.

David sat there facing him, he looked drawn.

'I didn't expect you,' he said. 'My mother, I know...' and then his voice trailed away.

But Pieter didn't have time for this. He had to tell David what was about to happen, and time was of the very essence.

'David, listen to me and listen good. I'm not here about your mother.

I'm sorry, but we can talk about your mother another time. What I'm going to tell you is important.'

David just stared at him, confused.

Pieter leant forward and spoke in a low voice.

'Listen to me. You're getting out of here.'

David just sat there, not seeming to understand what was being said.

'Listen to me, David, and damn well concentrate. Do you hear me?'

David's eyes widened in amazement, as he suddenly realized what Pieter was telling him. And then he started to say something, some irrelevant question.

'No,' said Pieter. 'Listen to me and concentrate. We haven't got time for small talk, you need to listen.'

David looked at him and nodded. And with that understood, Pieter continued.

'In roughly two week's time, you're going to be released. Do not discuss it with anyone, nobody in here must know about it, it's too dangerous. Once you're released, head for New York. I have an apartment on the Lower East Side.' Pieter then gave him the address. 'I'm going to be away for a while, but once you get there, stay there. Whatever you do, do not contact Leah, it's not safe and I don't want her involved. Nobody must know you're there. Don't use the phone, no matter what. Don't use it and don't answer it. I'll contact you.'

'I can't believe it,' said David. How have you managed to do this?'

Pieter looked at him.

'It doesn't matter, just keep your voice down and don't change your expression. These guards see everything.'

David went silent.

'Have you remembered my address?' Pieter asked him.

David nodded slowly. 'Yes.'

'Say it back to me then.'

David repeated the address he'd been given.

'Right,' said Pieter. 'In the lobby, there's a couple of large plant pots containing artificial trees. There'll be a key under the one on the left, okay?'

David nodded.

Pieter continued, 'There'll be some money in the kitchen drawer, use it.'

At that moment the guard began to make his way over to where they were sitting. Pieter stood up before the guard arrived. He nodded to the guard and then turned back casually to David.

'Okay buddy. I might see you again, or it could be somebody else from our office.'

Then he turned to the guard and shrugged.

'What a loser,' he said to the guard, and he shook his head as he walked away.

Conrad Stiller had made good his plans.

He'd contacted Clyde Tolson, assistant director of the FBI and he'd requested three 'good' agents.

'Send me Sloan and Hughes, and I need someone else that we can trust,' he'd said to Tolson over the phone.

'Yeah, I've got a good man,' Tolson replied. 'He's worked with Sloan before, a guy called Mallory. He'll do.'

An hour later, Conrad Stiller received a phone call from FBI agent Sloan. Stiller gave him his instructions.

'I need you to meet me in Dallas, we've got work to do. But first of all, get in touch with the Chicago police and find out the exact date that a 'David Morris' is being released from the Stateville prison. I want Hughes and Mallory in Joliet when Morris is released. I want him followed and I want to know his every move.'

It took nearly three weeks before David was released from the Stateville prison in Joliet. Apparently, the police had looked at the case once again and realized that it had all been a big mistake, 'a miscarriage of justice', as they called it. A friendly Judge was paid to 'look the other way' as he too completely agreed with the Chicago Police department's decision. David Morris was then proclaimed innocent of all charges. Papers were signed and rubber stamped and David Morris was then set free. He made his way to the nearest bus stop, he got on a bus and headed for downtown Joliet. From there he would take the Greyhound to New York.

As the bus pulled away, David failed to notice the blue Ford Sedan that was following it.

Pieter Szabo flew into Dallas on the 15th of November. It would give him a week to finalize his plans.

He booked himself into the 'Dallas Central Motel', a slightly worn and indistinguishable establishment about a mile and a half down from the bus station. Not the best of districts. From there he found a cheap car to rent, a five year old Chevrolet with about as many dents.

Pieter cruised around the city for a couple of days until he understood its layout and the roads. And then he found the whereabouts of the Dealey Plaza and with it the location of the iconic Texas School Book Depository.

The next day, Pieter made his way back to the Dealey Plaza on foot. He strolled around like an everyday tourist, taking in everything, but without drawing any attention to himself. He had a camera on a strap hanging around his neck, but he never used it.

He walked past the Texas School Book Depository a couple of times, it was a seven storey red brick building, and he glanced up at a window on the sixth floor. It was where Lee Harvey Oswald would be waiting, on the day.

Conrad Stiller had pulled a few strings and Oswald had been given a job at the Depository, working as an order filler. He'd also managed to become quite inconspicuous.

Pieter gazed around the Plaza, there were a few tall buildings, including one or two hotels. They would have been places that he could have normally used, but they were all facing the wrong direction. Not what Pieter wanted.

He crossed the road to an open grassed area and once again he looked back at the Book Depository. And then he saw it. To the left of the Depository was an open area. A raised grassy embankment, and at the top of it was a concrete wall, about five feet in height. There were no buildings behind it, just an open space with a couple of trees. Pieter strolled back across the road and then walked up the embankment. He looked over the wall to see what was there. It was a car park.

He walked back towards the Book Depository, and then made his way around to the rear and into the car park. Then he walked over to the concrete wall and again looked over it. In front of him was an open view of the main road where he'd just been stood.

From that wall on top of the grassy knoll, he would have plain sight of everything.

The next morning he drove his car, and this time he parked in the Book

Depository car park. He sat there and waited for a couple of hours. He watched the cars come and go, it wasn't particularly busy. Not on that day. He finally got out of the car and went to look at the wall again, it was about two feet wide and flat, and then he looked across the open road again. It was perfect. He then went to find a delicatessen where he could buy a sandwich. After that he walked back to his car and sat there for another hour. By then he knew what he had to do and exactly where he had to park his car. In another two days, he would return.

David arrived in New York City the following afternoon.

Agents Hughes and Mallory weren't really surprised, they'd already read Stiller's file on David Morris and they knew that he had family there. They were however, slightly surprised when he didn't make his way to the family home. Once David got off the bus at the Brooklyn Bus Station, Hughes and Mallory split up. Mallory followed David on foot, and Hughes stayed in the car and trailed them both from a distance, David finally made his way to the Lower East Side and to Pieter Szabo's apartment block. He went inside into the lobby, which was empty. And then as instructed, he went over to the artificial tree on the left and found the key. If he'd only looked around he would have seen Agent Mallory watching him through the glass doors to the entrance. David went over to the lift and stepped inside. As the lift doors closed Mallory walked into the lobby and he watched as the lift stopped at the third floor. He sprinted to the stairs and dashed up the first two flights, but then he slowed on the third set of steps and casually skipped up the rest. As he walked down the hallway, David had just come out of the lift and was walking towards him. David was checking the numbers on the doors and as they passed one another, Mallory nodded to him, just a good mannered gesture. David briefly nodded back and then continued to look for the right apartment. Finally, he found it. And as the key caught in the lock, the sound of it made Mallory quickly turn around, just in time to see the door slam shut.

CHAPTER 16

Texas, November 22nd 1963

It was eight o' clock in the morning and the Kennedy entourage were already in full swing.

The previous evening they had flown in Air Force One to Fort Worth in Texas. It had been a late arrival and the President and his wife had been driven by motorcade to the prestigious 'Hotel Texas', where they would stay the night.

Now it was morning, and it had started early in the Kennedy's hotel suite. Everyone had been up since six thirty and it was business as usual. The President was scheduled to make an open-air breakfast speech at Fort Worth's Central Square at eight forty five, and the White House publicity team were running like a well-oiled machine. Half an hour later he would be whisked back to the Hotel Texas where he would give a second speech in the hotel's Grand Ballroom.

John and Jackie Kennedy had an impromptu breakfast of coffee, toast and marmalade. And though they sat together at the table, they hardly spoke as the speech makers and advisors surrounded them. Everyone else however, seemed to be talking at the same time.

After breakfast, the hairdresser and the makeup artist arrived. Jackie went back into their bedroom where she was dressed and made up. The President stayed in the breakfast room where he changed into a clean suit and had his hair coiffed and combed. As he sat there he read his prepared speeches and discussed the various amendments with his writers. Eventually, it was almost time to leave and the White House staff began to gather everything together and leave. Jackie came out of the bedroom looking radiant and she smiled at her husband. He simply nodded his head. She'd hoped for more, but she wasn't surprised. Things were becoming a little difficult between them. The Presidency had put an obvious strain on their marriage and they hardly seemed to speak to one another anymore, except in public.

And of course, Mrs Kennedy had heard all the rumours about her husband, the countless women, along with that damn actress, Monroe. And yes, she'd watched the TV as the blonde trollop had sung 'Happy Birthday Mr President' to her husband.

But Jackie Kennedy had made an important decision. She was 'The First Lady' and she was going to act the part. She would be dignified, almost regal if need be. And she knew in her heart that the American people loved her. There was also the fact that she and John had children, children who adored their father. So she would accept what was happening and only hope that when her husband's presidency came to an end the following year, they could resume some sort of normal lifestyle. But at that moment, they were alone, and John Kennedy turned to the large mirror which hung over the elegant fireplace and he tried to straighten his tie. It was too tight. And so Jackie went over to him, and she smiled.

'You're hopeless, John. You could never get your tie right.'

Kennedy turned around and lifted his chin so that she could adjust the tie for him.

'We've got a busy day today,' Jackie continued, as she fiddled with his collar. 'You've got those two speeches, and then later on we're flying over to Dallas.'

As she continued to adjust his tie, she realized that he was completely ignoring her, and she quickly looked up. He was taking no notice of her at all, in fact, he was actually looking over her shoulder.

And at that moment, Jackie glanced in the mirror. Behind her, she saw her own personal Press Secretary, Pamela Turnure, as she walked past the open door. Pamela had suddenly paused and she looked over to Kennedy, and then she winked at him.

And that one action told Jackie Kennedy everything she needed to know. Her personal secretary and her husband, the President, were having an affair.

Truth be known, it had actually been carrying on for months.

Jackie looked up at him, but he just gave her a stupid grin. She spun around, but by then Miss Pamela Turnure had swiftly disappeared. Jackie went over to the open door and quickly closed it, and then she turned around to face her husband.

'Do you really expect me to put up with this, John?' she asked him angrily.

He just stared at her, and then he shook his head.

'I haven't got time for this, honey,' he said to her. 'We've got a very busy schedule.'

'Well you can damn well make time,' she demanded. 'Listen, I've heard all about your affairs with different women, and I've let it go. But now this? My damn secretary? Christ John, how much do you expect me to put up with?'

Once again, he grinned at her.

'Hey darlin', I'm surprised you've stayed around this long,' he replied casually. It was almost a joke.

Jackie stared back at him, she was absolutely shocked at what he'd just said to her, and also in the careless way he'd done it. And then suddenly she realized, he didn't care anymore, not one bit. She just looked at him, still not believing what she'd just heard.

'Listen to me honey,' he said to her. 'My Presidency ends next year. Once it's over we'll sit down and I'll sort everything out. You'll be okay. There's plenty of money.' And then he checked his watch. 'Look, I haven't got time for all this right now, we've got to go.'

And with that, Kennedy walked out of the room, he needed to speak to his advisors.

Jacqueline Kennedy just stood there and watched him go. She was speechless. After the Presidency he was going to divorce her, it was as simple as that. And at that moment she too made a decision. 'Screw him', if that's what he wanted. They would divorce. It was over.

She turned around and looked in the mirror, and then she ran her hand through her own dark hair. She was a beautiful woman, she knew she was. And she wouldn't be alone for long, she knew that too. There were other ships that she could sail.

Pieter Szabo returned to the car park behind the Texas Book Depository. He'd sat in his car and watched the other cars come and go until the right space became available. He needed to park his car right up to the concrete wall, and once the opportunity arose he reversed his car into the appropriate space. That done, he went around to the back of his car and sat on the trunk. From there he could easily rest on the top of the wall, it was as easy as sitting at a table.

He locked the car and left it there. The next day he returned, just to make sure that everything was okay. Then he went back to his motel to prepare.

Conrad Stiller rang Sam Giancana in Chicago.

'It's happening today Sam,' he told the mobster.

'What are you going to do about the stooge?' Giancana then asked.

'I'm here in Dallas with an FBI agent. We're going to shoot Oswald as he comes out of the Book Depository Building. The agent's FBI and I'm Secret Service, so nobody's ever going to ask any questions and it ties up all the ends. By the way, I've spoken to Jack Ruby too, he knows what happening. He's got that sucker Oswald eating out of his hand.'

'Good,' Sam Giancana replied. 'Give me a call later. Let's get this done.'

Just like the Kennedy's, Pieter Szabo had also risen early. Everything was prepared. At eight thirty he left the motel. He was dressed in a plain brown jacket and some casual slacks. It was going to be a warm and sunny day and to be wearing a long coat would have seemed slightly out of place, but a pair of sunglasses helped. He would walk to the Book Depository, on the way there he stopped off for a coffee and a bagel.

Along with his walking stick, he carried a canvas bag over his shoulder. In the bag was an old broken clock. He'd packed everything that morning, but today there was a slight addition. It was a handgun, a snub-nosed Smith and Wesson revolver.

It had been a last minute decision, but on the day he'd left for Dallas, Pieter had chosen to take his small but highly efficient little revolver with him.

In his apartment in New York, Pieter had always kept a small selection of handguns in a kitchen drawer. Self-protection had always been the name of the game, especially in New York City, where you could be robbed, burgled or mugged at any time of the day or night.

When he was on a contract, Pieter very rarely took a handgun with him. He considered himself a professional and he would always find the best possible vantage point and make sure that everything was undertaken with the utmost proficiently. But this contract was different. For a start, he was on ground level, and secondly, he was contained. And if there was any chance of him being seen or being caught, he would have to get away, and the use or the threat of a gun could make all the difference.

That morning, before he left the motel, he slid the short barrelled gun into his ankle holster. It was a precaution that might prove useful.

Pieter finally arrived at the car park and he went straight over to his parked car, everything was okay. The car park itself was fairly empty, it seemed that the good people of Dallas were more interested in seeing their President that day, rather than working. And along with that, many of the main downtown roads were closed to traffic in order to make way for the Presidential motorcade.

Pieter opened the car's trunk and placed the bag and the walking stick inside. Then he leant inside and took the clock out of the bag and quickly assembled his rifle. It was a tried and tested procedure, something that he'd done hundreds of times over the past twenty years. Once the rifle was assembled and loaded he closed the trunk and locked it.

At just after eleven thirty, John F. Kennedy, his wife Jacqueline, and the rest of the presidential entourage landed at Dallas's Love Field Airport aboard Air Force One. After a lot of handshaking, the Kennedys were finally loaded into the motorcade and then they set off for downtown Dallas.

The route was to take them through the centre of Dallas where they would turn onto Dealey Plaza and then head for the Dallas Business and Trade Mart where President Kennedy would give a prepared speech.

In the Texas School Book Depository, overlooking Dealey Plaza, Lee Harvey Oswald sat at an open window on the sixth floor. And in his sweating hands was a loaded rifle.

Less than a hundred yards away to Oswald's right, Pieter Szabo leant against the concrete wall overlooking the grassy knoll. He checked his watch, and he waited.

At 12-30 the motorcade turned onto Dealey Plaza and slowly proceeded on its way, passing by the Book Depository.

Up on the sixth floor, Oswald pointed his rifle out of the window as he watched the motorcade approach, he'd already picked out the presidential car, the President and his wife were sitting in the back, waving to the gathered crowds. Oswald's plan was to focus on the President's car as it came towards him and then take aim, it was a difficult moving target, but once the President had passed by he would take the easier shot.

Over on the grassy knoll, Pieter Szabo was sitting on the trunk of his car, leaning on the concrete wall with his rifle aimed. He already had Kennedy in his sights. All he had to do was wait. Wait for the sound of another rifle being fired.

As the Presidential car passed by, Oswald pulled the trigger, he fired off three shots.

The first bullet hit President Kennedy in the shoulder. The second shot hit Texas Governor John Connally, who was in the seat in front of Kennedy, Connally was also hit in the shoulder and the bullet passed through him and apparently chipped the nearby pavement. The third shot missed completely, the bullet buried itself deep into the ground several feet away from the motorcade and was never found.

Pieter Szabo heard the first shot and he fired, one second later. The President, who had already been hit in the shoulder, was turning to his wife when the bullet from Pieter Szabo's rifle blew the side of his head open.

Contrary to all that was written, the President died almost immediately.

President John F Kennedy, loved by millions, but detested by many, was dead.

Conrad Stiller and Agent Sloan had been standing across from the main entrance of the Texas School Book Depository. They were both were armed. They had watched the presidential motorcade coming towards them before it finally turned right onto Dealey Plaza. They had the main entrance to the Book Depository covered, and in the next few minutes, Lee Harvey Oswald would flee the building after attempting to assassinate the President of the United States. Even Stiller knew that Oswald was incapable, he'd read Lee Harvey Oswald's army records and it was well documented that Oswald couldn't hit the proverbial 'barn door'. But that didn't matter. Stiller had the 'Eagle'. The Eagle would take the shot.

Agent Sloan suddenly asked Stiller if he should check the rear exit and any of the fire exits at the back of the building. Agent Sloan had the front entrance covered. Shooting Oswald wasn't going to be a problem, but if he came out of another exit it could complicate things. Better to have everything covered. It made sense.

So Conrad Stiller ambled around to the back of the building. He was looking up at the fire exits to the different floors, they all led to the one metal staircase that ran down to the ground. If the building ever did set on fire, the people inside could make their escape down the stairs and onto the car park. And then for no particular reason, Stiller casually glanced behind him. And suddenly he stopped. And he looked again, and he froze.

To his right, not twenty yards away, a man was sitting on the trunk of a car, he was leaning on a concrete wall that overlooked the grassy embankment. The man was holding a rifle, and he was about to shoot the President of the United States.

After nearly twenty years, Conrad Stiller had finally managed to stumble into his assassin.

A hundred thoughts ran through Conrad Stiller's mind. And at that moment he couldn't do a damn thing about it. He needed Eagle to take the shot, but what then? He'd made a deal, he was supposed to take out Oswald, but he'd also made a deal with his longtime assassin. And up till now he'd stuck to that deal, he'd paid Eagle the money, and he'd got the man called David Morris released from prison. But Stiller had also made an arrangement with Sam Giancana, and once this was all over he had to kill David Morris to keep Sam Giancana happy. If he broke that promise to Giancana, their 'friendship' would be over. The Mafia would be set loose and a contract put out. And Conrad Stiller didn't want to spend the rest of his life running away and forever looking over his shoulder.

But there was a dilemma. Conrad Stiller didn't know who David Morris was, but he was obviously important to 'Eagle'. Maybe he was a friend, or maybe a relative? Stiller just didn't know. But if David Morris was killed, it all fell to Stiller. It was Stiller who had arranged everything and knew everything. Eagle would put two and two together and come to the obvious conclusion. That Conrad Stiller was involved.

And the result would be the same. Eagle was the most ruthless and proficient killer he had ever known. Over the years Stiller had been astounded at what the man was capable of. In the past he'd spoken to Vernon Ballantyne about him. Ballantyne had generally skirted the issue, but from time to time he'd hinted as to their assassin's past life.

Stiller had no doubt in his mind that Eagle would find him. Vernon Ballantyne would be the conduit. Eagle would find Ballantyne and somehow get the relevant information from him, one way or another. And then there would be no hiding place, ever.

So for Conrad Stiller, it was a simple choice. Once Kennedy had been shot, he would rid himself of the one single threat. He would kill his own assassin.

With that in mind, Stiller turned and quickly made his way back to agent Sloan.

'We've got a problem,' he said to Sloan, 'a change of plan.'

'What's wrong? Sloan asked.

'I've found our assassin. We've got to take him down.'

'What about Oswald?

'This is more important,' Stiller replied. And then he thought for a moment.

'You stay here,' he said to Sloan, 'but keep your eye on me. If Oswald comes out first, shoot him. But if I wave you over, forget Oswald, somebody else is going to have to kill him.'

Stiller made his way back to the rear of the Book Depository and he peered into the car park. Eagle was still there. There was suddenly a sharp crack from his rifle. The President of the United States of America was dead. Conrad Stiller just stood there, and for the briefest moment, he wondered about the enormity of it all. But then he watched as his assassin turned around and opened the trunk of his car.

It was time to move.

The moment Pieter Szabo's bullet hit Kennedy, he simply turned away. There was no joy or satisfaction. The only important concern for him was that his son was now free. He had a son, along with a daughter, and the memory of the wife who had been stolen from him. It was the sum total of his life.

Pieter opened car's trunk. He quickly disassembled his rifle and within a couple of minutes, all that remained there was a bag containing a clock and with it, an old walking stick. If for any reason he was stopped, nobody would give anything a second glance.

Pieter slammed the trunk shut and he looked up, and then he stopped. Standing by the front of the car was a man holding a pistol.

The man was looking directly at him, somewhat inquisitively.

'Stand exactly where you are and don't move,' he said.

Pieter stared at him.

A couple of seconds passed, and then the man glanced around as another man quickly approached, he too was carrying a gun.

'It's too late,' the second man said immediately, 'the police have just gone into the building.'

Both men then looked at Pieter Szabo.

'Get into the car,' the first man said to Pieter, 'Sloan, you drive, okay.'

Pieter continued to stare at him, and then suddenly he spoke.

'Stiller,' he said coldly.

They pushed Pieter Szabo into the back of the car and drove away. Pieter was jammed in behind agent Sloan, who was driving, and Stiller was in the back with his gun pointed at Pieter's chest.

'How did you know it was me?' Stiller finally asked.

Pieter looked across at him.

'You're voice,' he replied.

'Very clever,' said Stiller, 'but then again, you've always been a clever man, and useful.'

Pieter said nothing.

Agent Sloan continued to drive and he concentrated on the road ahead. Stiller almost smiled.

'What is your real name, Eagle? I've always wondered.'

'You'll never know,' said Pieter dryly.

Stiller just shrugged.

'No matter,' he said. 'But tell me something, who's your little friend, this 'David Morris', and what's he got to do with anything?'

Pieter said nothing, but his breathing changed slightly, and Conrad Stiller noticed it.

'What's all this about, Stiller? Pieter tried to change the subject.

'It's about tying up the loose ends, that's all. You see, you're a loose end, and Oswald's a loose end too, but now so is 'David Morris'.

Pieter looked around at him.

'What do you mean?'

Stiller smiled, he'd found a nerve.

'Oh come on now. Did you really think that he could just disappear?

He tried to cheat the mob for god's sake. He was never going to get away with that. And now he's hiding in some apartment in New York City, somewhere on the Lower East Side, I believe. I take it that's something to do with you too. Anyway, his tickets marked, we've had him followed from Joliet, all the way to New York. All we had to do was wait and let you do your job. And now that it's done, he's a dead man too.'

Pieter's stomach suddenly churned and he clenched his fists.

At that moment they turned onto the main highway. No one spoke, but Pieter could see Stiller looking at him, almost quizzically.

In the distance there was the sound of sirens, and within a couple of minutes several speeding police cars appeared, they were travelling in the opposite direction, lights flashing and sirens wailing, they were heading for downtown Dallas,

'Here comes the cavalry,' said Sloan. He glanced across at the array of oncoming cars.

Then Stiller looked at them too. And that was the moment.

Pieter immediately knocked Stiller's gun sideways and then he punched Stiller in the face. In a split second he reached down and grabbed the snub-nosed revolver out of his ankle holster, but the gun was in his right hand and he couldn't turn to get a clear shot. Stiller was fast recovering from the blow and he swung his arm back around, ready to shoot Pieter in the chest. Pieter launched himself at Stiller and grabbed hold of the barrel of Stiller's gun with his left hand. Then he turned and fired two shots into the back of the driver's seat, killing agent Sloan outright. He swung back to Stiller, and fired two more shots downwards and into Conrad Stiller's legs. Stiller screamed in agony as he dropped his own gun and fell forwards.

As the car slowly rolled off the road and came to a halt, Pieter grabbed hold of Stiller by the ear and pulled his head up, so he could face him. Stiller was still groaning in pain.

Pieter looked at him.

'After twenty years, and this is it?'

Stiller just looked up at him and gasped.

'You're like them all, Stiller' said Pieter, 'You're just a piece of shit.'

And with that, Pieter jammed the revolver into Stiller's mouth and then blew the back of his head off.

Pieter got out of the car and walked around to the front passenger door.

He opened it and leant in, and then dragged agent Sloan's body over onto the passenger seat. Then he walked back around the car and got in behind the steering wheel and drove away. At the first junction, he turned the car around and headed back to Dallas. A couple of miles down the road he found a quiet turning. He pulled in and parked the car. Pieter looked across at Sloan's body, and then rather bizarrely, he reached over and undid Sloan's tie. It was blue in colour, with an interwoven pattern.

He got out of the car and opened the trunk and took out his bag and his walking stick. Then he closed the trunk again. He opened the car's fuel cap and fed the end of agent Sloan's tie down and into the fuel tank, leaving about four or five inches exposed. He then lit the end of the tie and walked away. He headed back to Dallas.

Less than three minutes later the car exploded and burst into flames.

All hell was breaking loose. The country was in total shock at the loss of the President. However, at the FBI Offices in Washington, assistant director Clyde Tolson was becoming frantic. Lee Harvey Oswald had been caught alive. What the hell had happened? Oswald had been found hiding in a theatre and been arrested only an hour after Kennedy's assassination. And now he was in police custody. Tolson had spent the rest of that day trying to get hold of Stiller or Sloan, but nobody was answering and nobody was phoning him back. And then late in the afternoon, he'd been contacted by another FBI agent who had been working with the President's security team in Dallas. Two bodies had been found in a burned out car, both had been shot and the agent was looking to see if there could be any connection with the Kennedy assassination, maybe it could be something to do with the Mafia? Clyde Tolson almost had a fit. He wanted to scream down the phone for the agent to 'back off', but of course he couldn't. He made some excuse and slammed the phone down. Two men had been found in a burned out car, they'd both been shot. And Stiller was missing, and so was Sloan. It was all becoming frighteningly obvious.

Clyde Tolson paced up and down his office. Oswald was in custody. He would talk, of course he would talk, he would blab like a baby. There would be the mention of Jack Ruby and then the Mafia involvement, and then there would be a witch hunt that could lead all the way back to the FBI, and then all the way up the ladder to Tolson and to Hoover.

There was only one thing he left to do. Tolson pressed a button on his office intercom.

His assistant quickly replied.

'Yes, Sir?'

'Bring me the most up to date file we have on Sam Giancana...and straight away.'

Fifteen minutes later, the file landed on Tolson's desk. Tolson opened it immediately and ran through the pages, as he thumbed through the file he kept saying the same thing to himself over and over again...'phone number...phone number...'

And then he found it. He stared down at the number in front of him. And then he calmed himself. He had to speak to this man, and he had to seem to be in control. He took a deep breath, and then he dialled the telephone number.

The phone picked up. 'Yeah, who is it?'

'I want to speak to Mr Sam Giancana, please.'

'Yeah, and I said 'Who is it?' came the reply.

'Tell him that it's Clyde Tolson, the Assistant Director of the FBI.'

Words were said on the other end of the phone, there was a short silence, and then someone else spoke.

'Hello, Mr Tolson. This is Sam Giancana. We haven't met, but I've heard a lot about you. What can I do for you?'

Clyde Tolson listened to Giancana's rasping voice.

'Is this line safe, Mr Giancana?' he asked.

'It is, unless your boys are still listening in, Mr Tolson?' and Giancana laughed.

'Okay then,' said Tolson, ignoring the comment, 'we need to talk Mr Giancana, and I need to ask you something, something to which I need a straight answer.'

'What's your problem, Mr Tolson?'

'It's Stiller...Conrad Stiller.'

'What about him?'

'Did you have him killed?'

There was a brief silence.

'Stiller's dead?'

'Yes, I think so, along with one of my agents.'

'Oh shit,' Giancana replied slowly.

'Exactly,' said Tolson, 'and so I suggest we cut the crap, Mr Giancana. Because we're all up to our necks in trouble.'

'You may be right,' said Giancana slowly, 'And if Stiller's dead, that explains a lot of things.'

'Okay,' said Tolson. 'You and I know what's really happened in Dallas, and you and I worked it all through Stiller. So what can you tell me?'

'First of all Mr Tolson, I'm telling you that Stiller's death is nothing to do with us. Me and Stiller worked together, he's a good man, very useful. And to tell you the truth, I've been trying to get hold of him myself over the Oswald thing.'

'What do you know about Oswald?' Tolson asked.

'Well for a start, Oswald's still alive. Stiller was supposed to have wacked him straight away, you know, to tie up all the loose ends.'

'Yes, that was the plan,' said Tolson. 'But now Oswald's in police custody and if it all goes to trial, which it will, he's going to spill the beans and we're all going to get pulled in. This will go right to the top, for both of us. The lawyers will attack us with every inch of the law, they'll dig in deep and we're going to get ripped to bits. We're all going to end up in prison, Mr Giancana, or even worse.'

There was a moment's silence on the end of the phone.

'What do we have to do, Mr Tolson?'

Clyde Tolson sighed with relief. At last, he was getting somewhere.

'I need you to get to Oswald somehow, and I need you to kill him. I don't care how, but he has to be silenced. Have you any contacts in Dallas who can do the job?

Sam Giancana thought for a moment. 'Leave it with me,' he said, 'I may know someone.'

'Thank god for that,' said Tolson. 'If Oswald dies, we close the door.'

'Okay then,' said Giancana, 'but I need to ask 'you' something, Mr Tolson. Who do you think killed Stiller, because it wasn't us?'

I'm trying to think about that one,' said Tolson.

Giancana continued, 'You know he had some sort of special sniper, right? You know that it wasn't Oswald who did the job, he was just the stooge. It was the sniper who took out Kennedy.'

'Yes,' said Tolson, 'I know all about that.'

'Well, did you know that part of the deal was that someone called 'David Morris' had to be released from Joliet. And I know that the sniper wouldn't move until this 'Morris' was out.'

'I didn't know anything about that,' said Tolson. 'Who's David Morris?'

'He's some punk who tried to rip me off in the past. He was doing seven in Joliet but I was going to have him wacked before he came out.'

'And what's Morris got to do with the sniper?'

'I don't know. But Stiller had two of your agents tail him out of Joliet. They followed him all the way to New York, he's in some apartment there somewhere.'

Tolson almost slapped himself for his own stupidity.

'Oh my god, its Hughes and Mallory. They were working with Stiller. I'd never given them a thought.'

'Yeah, well,' said Giancana, 'the deal with Stiller was that when this was over, he was going to shoot Morris, as a favour to me. And now this Morris is a liability too, he's tied in with the whole plot somehow.'

Clyde Tolson thought about it for a moment.

'Okay then,' he said to Giancana, 'well here's the deal. You take care of Oswald, and I'll get rid of this David Morris for you.'

On the other end of the phone, Sam Giancana smiled to himself.

'Alright then Mr Tolson, we'll do that. And please keep in touch, it's been good to talk to you.'

And with that, Sam Giancana put down the phone.

Two minutes later, he rang Jack Ruby in Dallas.

Ruby picked up the phone.

'Jack, it's me,' said Giancana.

'Hi Sam, what's up?' Ruby replied.

'I need a favour Jack, a big favour. I need you to do something for me.'

Dallas was at a standstill. The planes weren't flying, all the trains were cancelled and the roads were blocked. Nobody was getting in and out. The only exception being the President's body, his now widow, and the immediate White House staff.

Also on the plane was the Vice President, the very soon to be President, Lyndon B. Johnson.

Pieter Szabo was stuck, but there was nothing he could do He needed to contact David and tell him to get out of there, and he had to tell him that he'd been followed and he was being watched. He needed to tell David to run, because those bastards were going to kill him. But he couldn't, he couldn't do a damn thing. He'd told David that under no circumstances must he pick up the phone, and now that decision had suddenly backfired. Pieter's only contact in New York was Leah, but there was no way that he could get her involved. It was far too dangerous. He'd lost too many of his family already, to risk the daughter he cherished, no matter what. So he went to the airport and he waited there along with the hundreds of other people who were also trying to leave Dallas.

That fateful place, a city that would forever be mentioned in the history books.

Two days later, Sunday the 24th of November.

In the morning, Jack Ruby drove into Dallas city centre and he parked his car at the back of his club. He then made his way towards the Dallas Police Headquarters on Main Street.

On that morning, it had been planned that Lee Harvey Oswald was to be transferred from Dallas police headquarters and taken to the Dallas County Jail, by way of an armoured car. Oswald was to be escorted by police detectives from the fourth-floor jail down to the basement where the armoured car was ready and waiting.

Ruby entered the police headquarters from an alleyway, and through a door that had been 'surprisingly' left unlocked. As Ruby made his way down the stairs to the basement, there were no security guards, in fact, there was no police presence at all. They'd been removed.

All and everything had been flawlessly planned.

The basement itself was crowded, mostly with officials and the press, and several policemen.

As the detectives escorted Oswald to the car, Jack Ruby stepped out of the crowd, and in full view of everyone, he pulled out a gun and shot Lee Harvey Oswald in the stomach.

The police immediately arrested Ruby.

The press heard one of the detectives say out loud... 'Jack, you son of a bitch.' It was reported as being an insult. But in fact, it was a verbal 'slap on the back' for a job well done.

Jack Ruby, with a little help, had managed to stop history in its tracks.

Sam Giancana had promised Ruby the world. Money would never again be a problem. Ruby would forever live under the protection and the wing of Sam Giancana. And when America finally won Cuba back from Castro, Jack Ruby could have the Casino of his choice.

It never happened. Cuba would never become the fifty first state. Jack Ruby was imprisoned and forgotten. Whilst he was awaiting trial, he was given a message. 'Keep your mouth shut.'

It took three days for Pieter Szabo to finally fly to New York. He took a yellow cab from the airport straight down to the Lower East Side. Pieter stopped the taxi a quarter of a mile away from his apartment block and he walked the rest of the way. As he approached, he slowed and then he finally stopped. He needed to see if there was anyone watching the apartment. Then he walked around the block several times, keeping his eyes open for parked or passing cars, anything that looked in any way suspicious. Pieter went into a coffee shop just across the road from his apartment block. First of all he checked out the customers, and then he sat at a table near the window and watched the comings and goings across the road. After two hours and several cups of coffee, he decided that he had to do something. He paid his bill and walked out of the coffee shop and then crossed over the road to his apartment block. He walked into the lobby, which was empty, and he checked under the large plant pot on the left. The key had been removed. As Pieter leant down he took the revolver from his ankle holster and put it in his pocket. Then he made his way to the stairs. When he reached the third floor the hallway was empty. He put his own key into the lock, but something was wrong, it was broken. Pieter then pushed the door, and with a bit of pressure it began to open and he realized that something was jamming it. He looked down to see that one of his old newspapers had been wedged under the door, presumably to keep it closed.

Pieter took the gun out of his pocket and he slowly walked inside.

'David?' he said to no one. He stood there for a moment, there was no reply.

'David?' he said again, but still there was no reply.

Pieter stood back, he was just about to go into the main living room when he saw the blood. The wall in his hallway was splattered with dried blood. Pieter just stared at it for a moment, and then he turned and walked straight into the living room, the gun in his outstretched arm. He didn't know what to expect, maybe he would find the dead body of his son.

There was nothing, the apartment was obviously empty. But there in the middle of the living room floor, there was a large pool of dried blood.

It took him less than ten minutes. Pieter gathered up the few essentials that he would ever need. He had to move, he had to get out of there. He came out of the apartment block and was just about to cross the road, when he saw him. A man, dressed in a dark grey suit, leaning against the wall and reading a newspaper. It was almost laughable. Nobody in New York ever leant against a wall and read a newspaper, no one.

Pieter walked away, knowing that he would be followed. He headed for the subway, and when he got there, the gods were finally smiling down at him. As he reached the crowded platform the doors on the subway train there were just closing. Pieter darted onto the train and he escaped, leaving behind an angry and very frustrated FBI agent.

Pieter travelled uptown and then he booked himself into the five star St Regis Hotel on 55th Street, just around the corner from Fifth Avenue. No one would ever think to look for him there.

He found a stationer's shop and bought a notepad and some envelopes. He couldn't use the hotel's own letter headed stationery, no way. Then he wrote to Leah. He gave her a time, a date and his telephone number at the hotel. She had to ring him from a pay phone only, and never from home. The calls from her home phone may be being traced. She was to tell no one, not even Arthur Morris. And she had to destroy the note immediately. He signed the letter 'Pieter'.

On the Friday afternoon at five thirty exactly, the phone in Pieter's hotel room rang.

He snatched it up immediately.

'Leah?'

'Yes, it's me.'

'Are you ringing from a pay phone?' he asked immediately.

'Yes. What's going on? And why all the secrecy and why would our phone be being tapped?'

'Did you rip up my note?'

'Yes, of course I did.'

"And have you spoken to anybody?'
'No, you told me not to. What's going on, Pieter?'
'Leah, I've got to ask you something. Have you heard from your brother?'
'No,' she replied. I've not had a letter off him since my mother died.'
'So you haven't spoken to him or seen him.'
'No Pieter, I've not been back to that prison, not since I went there with you.'
'Leah, he's not in prison. He's out.'
'He's what! Oh god no. Please don't tell me he's escaped.'
'No, he's been released. But I think he may be in some sort of trouble.'
'How did he manage to get out?' she asked.
'I don't really know?' Pieter lied.
'You're something to do with this, aren't you, Pieter?'
'I can't speak about it Leah, I really can't. But it's for your own safety.'
'So what do we do? Where do we go from here?'
Pieter stared at the phone.
'You mustn't say anything, and you don't do anything. But if you hear from him, or hear anything at all, phone me on this number, but only from a pay phone. We can't meet at the moment Leah, but if anything at all changes or if I hear anything from him, I'll write to you in the same way.'

Pieter said his goodbyes and he put the phone down. He couldn't tell her anything, and everything was a lie. He couldn't mention his past, and he couldn't mention the real reason why David had been released. And he couldn't mention that the apartment where David had been hiding was now covered in blood. Pieter sat on the edge of the bed. Was David still alive? Deep in his heart, he doubted it.

Three long and painful weeks passed by. Weeks where Pieter thought about his future and the things that had happened. Pieter had hardly left his room. Everything had changed again, and once again, the people who he loved were lost to him. All he had left was Leah, beautiful Leah. There were other things too. He would never shoot his rifle again, that part of his life was over. Never again would he work for any bureaucracy. His whole life had been devastated by bureaucracies. The only thing left in his world now was Leah, she was his only light. But again, there was nothing he could do. To be close to her was to endanger her life and the price for that was too much to even contemplate. So he'd made the decision. He would eventually return to his beloved Spain. He would live the rest of his cursed and fated life there, and dream of what could have been. And he cursed his god.

He could only hope that in the years to follow, things would change and he could possibly see his beloved daughter once more. He shook his head in despair.

On the Tuesday morning, an hour before midday, the phone rang. Pieter was in his room, as usual, he was reading the newspaper, it was an old habit. He looked across at the phone and sighed. It was probably room service or the laundry people. He put his paper down and walked across the room and he picked up the phone.

'Yes?'

'It's me. It's Leah. I've got a letter. It's from Canada. It's from David.'

Pieter Szabo just stood there and he gripped the phone in his hand. His son was alive. And he looked upwards and had to thank his god.

Pieter almost shouted down the phone.

'Where is he? Pieter's mind suddenly came alive.

'The letter says he's in Toronto. That's all. He's written down a phone number and he says to only ring from a payphone, not the house phone. He must figure the same as you, Pieter, that our phone calls may be being traced. He asks if I've seen you. I think he's scared. He says he can't come back.'

And at that moment, for Pieter Szabo, there was no other choice.

'I'm going to fly up to Toronto, Leah. I'll get on a plane straight away, with a bit of luck I'll be there later this afternoon, it's only a short flight. Please phone Pieter, tell him I'm on my way. Tell him I'll phone him once I've landed.'

She was silent for a moment.

'Pieter. You know I can't leave my dad, not now.'

'Yes, of course, I know. And your mother wouldn't want you to, Leah.'

He could hear her breathing down the phone.

'Thank you, Pieter.' she said.

'Okay, don't worry. I'll write and let you know what's happening. And also, destroy David's letter, and any other letters that we send you. Be careful, Leah. We're dealing with very bad people.'

Pieter walked out of St Regis Hotel, he was just about to hail a taxi cab when a thought struck him. He turned and he walked around to the rear of the hotel. There was an area there with a small loading bay, it was used for deliveries of meat and fruit and vegetables, along with the flowers and the laundry and everything that it took to run a five star hotel. Pieter looked around. In the corner were two skips. He went over to them. One of the skips was used for waste food, it stunk somewhat and the buzzing flies were ever present. The other skip was used for everything else, from waste paper to broken furniture. He opened the lid and he threw his walking stick and his bag into the skip. And then he walked away. If anyone opened the bag, all they would find was an old clock. It was broken, it didn't work.

It never did.

Pieter landed at Toronto International Airport at four o' clock in the afternoon. He found a pay phone and rang David straight away.

'I'm at the airport. Where are you?'

'I can't believe your here,' David replied nervously.

Pieter took a deep breath. Something needed to be said.

'Where else did you think I'd be? Where are you, David?'

'Go to Chinatown. Go to the corner of Dundas Street West and Spadina Avenue, I'll meet you there.'

Pieter grabbed a cab and headed for downtown Toronto. Very soon, the taxi was picking its way through the crowded streets of Toronto's Chinatown. It was so very busy. Pieter felt that he could have almost been in Hong Kong. The taxi cab finally stopped at a corner on Dundas Street and Pieter got out. He stood there for a moment, just taking in the mass of humanity as the taxi slowly trundled away.

'Hi', a voice said from behind him. And Pieter spun around. It was David.

It was the moment. He grabbed hold of his son and hugged him, and he felt the rising emotion.

'Are you okay, David?' Pieter asked him.

'Yes, I'm okay. I am now. I've spoken to Leah. She told me you were flying up here.'

David suddenly glanced around.

'You're sure you've not been followed?'

'I'm positive,' said Pieter. 'But I had to lose someone when I first arrived back in New York.'

David glanced at him.

'We need to talk,' he said, 'come on, let's go.' And he led Pieter down a side street that ran off Spadina Avenue. He took Pieter to a small restaurant, the yellow neon light above the door read 'The Little Dragon.' They went inside and took a corner table, it was still early and the restaurant was fairly quiet. The family who ran the restaurant seemed to know David, they were quite friendly, and David ordered the food.

'You've been here before,' said Pieter.

'All the time,' David replied, and then he smiled, 'I'm living upstairs, they're renting me a room.'

Pieter nodded, but now it was time for them to talk.

'What happened in New York, David, I thought you'd been killed?'

'I nearly was. It was a nightmare. When I arrived at your apartment, I found the key under the pot, just like you said. But I must have been followed or something because when I got to the third floor, there was a guy wandering down the corridor towards me, and I don't know why but he nodded at me, you know, it was like he had to. I just got a feeling that something wasn't right.'

'Yes, you were followed. You were followed from the moment you walked out of the prison at Joliet.'

'How do you know that?' David asked.

Pieter shook his head, 'I just know. They followed you all the way to New York and then to my apartment.'

'That guy though, he didn't look like the mob'

'He wasn't,' Pieter replied.

'Who was he then?'

'He was the FBI.'

David's eyes widened. 'Oh hell. If that's true, I'm in a lot of trouble.'

Suddenly the food arrived. Two waitresses filled their table with assorted dishes of meat and chicken, mixed with an array of vegetables, along with separate bowls of rice and noodles.

David thanked them nervously, and then the waitresses left them alone to enjoy their meal.

David wiped his face.

'I don't know whether I can eat,' he said, 'this is worse than I thought.'

'David,' said Pieter firmly, 'I need to know what actually happened.'

'Well, I never left the apartment for a start. I just waited for you to arrive. Then one afternoon I was sitting there watching the TV, it was the day of the Oswald shooting, and the next thing I know somebody's banging on the door. I didn't answer. But it didn't stop. Then someone tried to open the lock, but I'd bolted the door. The next thing, they were trying to kick the door down. I thought it was the mob, I thought they were there to kill me. So I ran into the kitchen. I knew you had those guns in the drawer, you told me that there was some money in one of the kitchen drawers, but I'd seen the guns too. So I grabbed one and ran back into the hallway and stood at the side of the doorway. Suddenly they broke in and the door swung back towards me. There were two of them. The guy who'd been in the corridor and another man, and they had guns too. I stepped out from behind the door and I fired at them before they could shoot me. But I thought they were the mob, I just ran, I grabbed the money and came to Canada.'

Pieter listened carefully to his son.

'Believe me, David,' he said, 'those men were there to kill you, not to arrest you. All of this is linked to the mob. I can't tell you what I know, I just can't. But you were a marked man from the moment you left prison. They were never going to let you walk free. When those two agents didn't report back, the FBI or whoever's involved must have known that something had gone wrong. They'd have sent someone up to the apartment and then found the bodies. It will all be covered up, they can't afford the publicity.'

'What am I going to do?' David asked.

'Eat your food for a start, it's very good.'

David looked down at the food, but his appetite was lost.

'No, seriously,' he asked, 'what am I going to do?'

Pieter continued to eat, and then he looked up at his son.

'You're going to change your life around, David. That's what you're going to do. And you're going to move, we both are. There's no going back to the States, not a chance.'

'What do you want to do,' David asked, 'do you want to stay here in Canada?'

Pieter wiped his mouth with a napkin. He'd already made the decision.

'No David, we're going to Spain.'

CHAPTER 17

Benicassim, Spain. 1978

The sun was just about to slowly descend into the sea. Like a huge orange ball, it spread the last of its rays across the peaceful Mediterranean waters before it went off to warm the other side of the planet.

For Pieter Szabo, it was the best part of the day. The blistering heat of the afternoon could become overwhelming, especially for a man who was born and raised in Poland. He'd grown up with icy winters and cold and chilly springs, and summers that were several short weeks of long-awaited, but much appreciated sunshine. The summers in Poland were there to be treasured.

But for Pieter Szabo, that was a past life, he'd lived in Spain for the last fifteen years and he never intended to live anywhere else.

Those fifteen years had added fifteen years to his life. And now those added fifteen years made him exactly sixty years old. And today was Pieter Szabo's birthday.

Sixty years old, and still fit and well, but his life had changed, and much for the better.

And now he sat on his veranda, surrounded by his family and closest friends.

It was Pieter's birthday party.

Two hours previously, his good friend Maximo Baroja had closed his restaurant and had loaded up his catering van with all the food and essentials that he would need, and then he and his family had driven up into the hills to Pieter's farmhouse and had set about the business of preparing the meal. The tables had been placed to make one long table, tablecloths had been laid and vast amounts of cutlery and crockery had been added, along with rows of wine glasses and opened bottles of wine.

Pieter sat there and looked down the table, friends and family were at either side of him.

Maximo and his family had cooked the most delicious food and had then sat down with everyone else to finally eat. Friends and family, and for Pieter, that was everything.

Fifteen years, fifteen precious years.

His son, David, had married into the Cercas family, the farmers who owned the adjoining farm. It was Arturo Cercas, who Pieter had bought his farmhouse from, in a deal that was advantageous to both of them. And now Arturo and his family were sitting at Pieter's table, in a celebration of Pieter's life, and of their family union.

It had been almost laughable really. Fifteen years before, Pieter and David had left Canada and flown to Spain. When they finally arrived at Pieter's farmhouse, David had been astonished. It was so beautiful, with views down to Benicassim and the sea beyond, it was simply stunning.

Pieter had then shown David around the house and then he'd taken him down to the extraordinarily well-tended gardens. David was amazed by the variety of flowering plants and had made some remark about possibly helping with the gardening.

'Ah well,' Pieter had said. 'I don't know about that, David. I already have a gardener, and she's pretty tenacious about anyone who goes anywhere near her precious plants.' And then he'd laughed. But David just frowned, he didn't understand.

A couple of days later, Teresa Cercas came over to the house to look after her garden. David had seen that somebody was down there tending to the plants, and he decided to walk down to the garden to introduce himself, with a view to asking if he could possibly help.

Teresa was at that moment, busily tending to the beautiful purple bougainvillea, and she was humming to herself as David approached.

He stood behind her for several seconds, and then he finally said out loud, 'Excuse me.'

Teresa spun around in shock and stared at the man who had crept up on her. And then she looked at his face, and she stopped. It was the same face, the face of the man that she had admired for years. She just looked at him and she almost trembled. And then, suddenly, she smiled.

David too had a similar reaction. As he'd walked up behind her, she'd been busily tending to some sort of beautiful purple plants and was humming to herself. She'd not seen him or heard him. And as she'd quickly turned around, he looked at her, and for an instant he was absolutely speechless.

Teresa Cercas was just twenty years old and stunningly beautiful. With deep brown Latin eyes and shoulder length dark hair, she stood there in front of him, barefooted and dressed in a loose white skirt and a matching short sleeved cotton blouse. She'd looked at him strangely, and then slowly, she smiled at him. And he smiled back. He was already smitten.

'So you're the gardener,' he said to her.

And so the chemistry began. When boy meets girl, and the girl sees the man in him.

The rest, as they say, was just history. Boy and girl fell in love and became man and wife.

Some saw it as strange, but when they married David took his wife's name and he became David Cercas. David Morris then disappeared forever. David had moved into the family farm where he worked with his in-laws. And it had been David's idea to plant olive trees, he'd seen the continuing success of olive oil in America, where people were trying to eat healthier and take on the flavour of foreign cuisine. The venture had been successful, very successful, it had been an ever-expanding market. Then they'd planted lemon trees and that market had flourished too. From there, the family had bought more land and were planning to grow vines, vines that would thrive in the never ending sunshine and hopefully produce more of Spain's good and glorious wine.

Pieter sat there, and he watched the Cercas family as they all talked and laughed at the same time in that typically Spanish way. David and Teresa had two children, two sons.

Pieter was a grandfather.

He looked down the table at David and he was proud of his son and what he'd achieved. He had managed to turn his life around.

Pieter stared at David for a moment, and then he looked further down to the bottom the table, and smiling back at him was the face that he loved more than life. It was Leah. She had flown over from America with her husband and their own two children. She'd always been a regular visitor to Benicassim, finally bringing with her the fiancé who would become her husband. There had only ever been one stipulation, that Leah flew to Canada first and then took a separate flight to Spain. It worked, and it still worked. They could never forget the possibilities of governments. Leah's husband, Richard was an accountant, and money was never going to be a problem, they were family and they were close.

Leah still looked after Arthur Morris, she would never let go of him. She couldn't.

Pieter looked down the table at his daughter, so much like her mother, and a thousand memories. And she looked back at him, knowing exactly what he was thinking. She picked up a random piece of bread and slowly stood up and made her way towards him, smiling. She then leant down and kissed him.

'Happy birthday, dad. I love you.'

And then she dipped her bread into his food and laughed cheekily as she made her way back down the table to her husband and her son and daughter, the daughter who was the image of her mother.

Pieter drank some of his wine, and he looked down the busy table. Everyone was happy and smiling and enjoying themselves.

And he realized something about his life. He thought about all the hurt and the pain that he'd had to endure, and the heartache that he'd suffered for the ones he'd lost. It had all been such a waste of life. But that had been his life, and there were good times and bad. And these were the good times.

He looked at his family, and he understood. He was finally content.

For Pieter Szabo, all was well. To him, they were all that mattered.

The end.

'EAGLES AND RED POPPIES'
... A BRIEF ADDITION

The Eagle is the National symbol for both Poland and America.

And at one time, it was also used as the symbol for Nazi Germany by the Third Reich, where it was known as the 'Reichsadler'. The people of Poland grudgingly renamed it, 'the Crow'.

The 'Red Poppy' is considered by many to be the National flower of Poland.

In central Italy in 1944 during the Second World War, the German army captured the Benedictine Monastery of Monte Cassino, and then made use of it as a strategically fortified stronghold. From there, the German forces had managed to stop the whole of the Allied advance which were heading towards Rome.

In early January, the battle for Monte Casino commenced. The Allied troops fought long and hard for over five months to try to take Monte Cassino, but they failed. It was utter carnage.

On May the 18th, the Polish troops were brought in. They charged up the hillside to Monte Casino through fields of red poppies, which were still in full bloom at the time

The brave Polish soldiers were shot to pieces, but they wouldn't retreat. They fought on, and against all odds they won the day, finally reaching the summit of Monte Cassino to raise the Polish flag.

The Battle for Monte Cassino cost the Allies 55,000 men, dead and wounded.

In Remembrance of those Polish Troops, a song was penned. Here are some of the words.

> 'Red Poppies on Monte Cassino
> Instead of dew, drank Polish Blood
> As the soldiers crushed them while falling,
> For anger was more potent than death.

*Years will pass and ages will roll,
But the traces of bygone days will stay,
And the Poppies on Monte Cassino,
Will be redder for drinking Polish Blood that day'*

My Father fought at Monte Cassino.

Adieu.